THE THRONE SEEKER

THE THRONE SEEKER

JAMIE JUNE

Book cover by Story Wrappers

First edition 2025

To the ones craving to get swept into a love
they don't believe exists...
This one's for you.

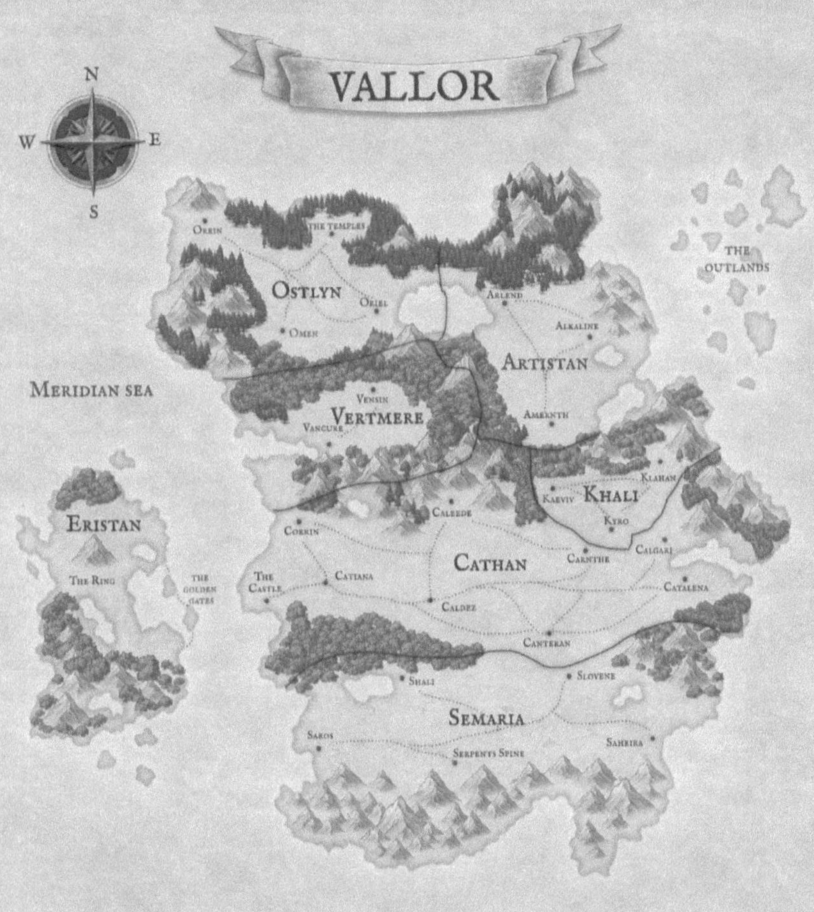
VALLOR
N
W
E
S
Orrin
The Temples
Ostlyn
Oriel
Omen
Arlend
Alkaline
Artistan
The Outlands
Meridian sea
Vensin
Vertmere
Vancure
Amernth
Klahan
Kaeviv
Khali
Kyro
Caleede
Eristan
Corrin
Cathan
Carnthe
Calgari
The Ring
The golden gates
The Castle
Catiana
Caldez
Catalena
Canteran
Shali
Slovene
Semaria
Saros
Serpents Spine
Sahrira

PART I
THE RETURN

CHAPTER 1

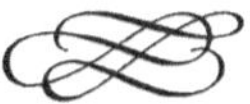

Rose gazed out the carriage window at a terrain as old and ancient as the dawn of the first sun. The land had been forged eons ago by the elements of fire, sand, and sea, maintained and preserved by a powerful family who once rode dragons like horses, coexisting amid a flourishing wealth of magic and creatures long since forgotten.

Little proof of the remnants of that world remained, and Rose wasn't sure if that was the truth. How could anyone be so sure of history, so often biased to the schemes and ambitions of men. But it was what the archives and books claimed—books that worshiped the sun. The very sun that now streamed upon her olive skin through pure crystal glass.

"Rosalie Versalles," her mother scolded across the carriage. "Please sit up. I don't want your dress soiled before we arrive." Leaning forward with a huff, her mother adjusted Rose's floor-length skirt to prevent it from grazing the speck of dirt on the carriage floor.

Rose straightened her back and shoulders, tearing her gaze from the window, unaware of her lack of posture. "Sorry, Mum." She fiddled with her fingers. "It's just hard to believe we're finally back… It's like a dream."

Her mother's mouth lifted into a plotting smile. "If we play our cards right, it may be our permanent home."

Home.

She peered back through the window, past the dirt road to the distant trees that stood centuries before human feet hit the soil—woods she'd played in as a child every summer since she was eight.

She'd always known her mother's aspirations for her life emphasized more of a material value than sentimental. Though her mother meant well, Rose wasn't blind. She was aware she'd plotted this arrangement since she was born, brought to the castle every summer to gain the favor of Henrik and, more importantly, one of his sons.

Her mother leaned back into her seat. "I do wish you'd take time for Xavier. You two used to be so close."

Xavier. That was a name she hadn't heard since…

She focused on familiar distant trees, her face void of emotion as she said, "I believe Xavier is fully content with himself for company these days."

Without warning, the carriage swayed, forcing them to brace themselves. The driver, bless his soul, earned a good scolding from her mother. She would've preferred arriving on horseback if her mother had allowed it.

Fat chance of that.

A brief silence settled between them as her mother observed her before continuing as if the conversation hadn't been interrupted. "Perhaps you're still more keen for Tristan?"

Rose's cheeks warmed, her eyes snapping to her mother.

Her mother gave her a knowing look. "We must be careful of our steps, Rose. Everything we've striven for comes to fruition tonight. This year, you'll need to either take a husband or find one elsewhere, Tristan or not."

Rose withheld a glare. She knew what was at stake. She could fall off her horse, hit her head, suffer a major concussion, and it would still be the first thing she thought of when she woke. Charged to bear the weight of her father's transgressions, she must put rumors to rest, and regain their family's good name.

She opted to stay silent, shadows running across her face. She'd need every personal reserve of energy she had for tonight. She'd learned long ago to choose her battles with her mother; this was not one of them.

"Ah! Finally, there it is! A year later, and this carriage ride still gives me a migraine," her mother added with a mumbled complaint.

Rose scooted to the window, ignoring her mother's scoldings. Her gaze lifted past the hills, over the outer wall, and landed on the towering structure rooted on the largest mound.

The enormous seaside castle had not gotten any less grand in their absence. Its fortified walls and bridges were made up of thousands upon thousands of splendid hand-carved stones. The high peaks held Cathan's gold and red banners that waved proudly in the breeze, surrounded by acres and acres of gorgeous, well-manicured grounds. The distant gardens were packed to the brim, bursting with color. To the west, the grounds sloped down gradually to meet the pearl granules framing the Meridian Sea. Nothing but a sapphire horizon lay beyond.

Rose raised her fingers to the warm window with reverence, her breath fogging the glass. The butterflies in her stomach multiplied as several imaginary scenarios surfaced, threatening to drag her into a hole that might not even exist.

Her anxious thoughts didn't have the chance to escalate as the carriage approached the outer wall, its lofty solid-iron gates built as the castle's first line of defense.

"His Majesty's friend, Lady Evelyn, and her daughter, Lady Rosalie," their driver announced from the coach to the guards above.

It took but a moment for the gate to unlock. A great many clicks followed as the door creaked open before their carriage continued down the dirt path to the front courtyard. The overflowing flower beds were scattered about, their green leaves and hedges all neatly trimmed and aligned—thriving, no doubt, from the queen's attention.

Just ahead, familiar doors of iron waited for them.

"Keep your head held high. I want you on your best behavior tonight," her mother reminded her.

As if she'd do anything else. She was half tempted to scream as soon as they got out of the carriage, just to see her mother's horrified face.

She nearly smiled at the thought.

The carriage reached its destination as the door swung open. "My lady," a servant greeted, holding out a hand to her mother.

Her mother acknowledged him with a curt nod, graciously taking his hand as she stepped out of the carriage, warm rays gleaming on her dirty-blonde hair.

She followed her mother's steps out of the carriage. The heat from the sun was a welcome blanket of warmth, but the cool coastal breeze swept in to claim it, leaving behind goose bumps on her arms. The weather was cooler here than in her home in Canteran, but soon, the full peak of summer would be upon them.

It wasn't a moment too soon when the head butler, Hugh, approached. "Ah! If it isn't two of the most beautiful women in Cathan." He bowed before his superiors.

Her mother glowed, brushing her hair back as she lifted her chin higher. "Oh, come now, Hugh, you spoil us!"

"We welcome you back to the castle, my ladies." Hugh caught sight of Rose. "My word, this cannot be our little Rose." His awed gaze flitted to her mother, then back to Rose. "You've grown even more in beauty and poise."

She gifted him a humble smile at the praise. "Thank you, Hugh. Your compliments are always appreciated."

His crinkled smile widened. "Please." He stepped aside, gesturing to the door. "You must be tired. Would you like to rest before you see His Highness?"

Her mother shook her head at once. "No. I dare say we've had enough of that in the carriage. We'd like to greet him first, if he's available."

Hugh bowed again. "Of course. I'll send your things to your rooms—goodness, is this all you brought? You usually have another carriage just for your wardrobe."

Rose glanced at the carriage. "Things" meant the mere two bags they'd brought—one for her mother, one for her. She cringed, shooting a nervous look at her mother.

Her mother didn't miss a beat, letting out a light laugh. "Oh, I restricted ourselves this go around. I like to travel light these days. Less likely for us to be targeted on the road." Her mother lied like a trained politician. Rose, on the other hand, had inherited no such trait. A shame.

It could be most helpful in times like this. "Please have them unpacked for us by the time we come up; thank you, Hugh."

Her mother led the way up the steps through the open iron doors into the front hall.

A wave of warmth greeted them from the fireplace crackling in the quiet foyer, relaxing her stiff frame; a year had changed nothing regarding the décor. The same tapestries and fine paintings lined the walls, though Cathan's flag was the main focal point. It hung front and center from the tall ceiling, crimson red in color, aside from Cathan's golden sun symbol in the middle, which presently reflected the light streaming in from the window.

It seemed fitting somehow, like a good omen for the future.

They continued in silence down the main corridor. Although the trek seemed like an eternity, it took mere minutes. Her body temperature rose alongside her heartbeat as they neared what she knew to be the king's hall.

Another smaller set of double doors appeared. They stopped, waiting for an invitation inside.

Her mother made the final adjustments to her appearance. "Blast that wind." She smoothed down Rose's thick brown hair that had barely moved, half braided on the crown of her head, while the other half lay curled past her shoulder blades. "Don't be nervous. Just be your charming self—and smile."

Rose nodded, not trusting herself to speak for fear she might be sick. In her short twenty-four years of living, she'd never been so shaky.

The doors opened and they stepped through to the massive room. Pacing her steps, she walked atop a long, rectangular red rug sewn with Cathan's golden sun, matching the flag they'd just passed. Monstrous pillars lined the room leading to the throne, holding up the high ceiling.

She dared to lift her eyes from the ground, landing on the king first, sitting rightfully on his gold throne. A sun was forged into the headrest with rays spiking into the air as sharp as swords, hovering just above his head. Behind his throne stood three giant cathedral windows, spreading the hazy sun's rays onto the golden chair, making it gleam. On his right sat his queen, and to his left, Xavier, Tristan, an empty chair where Roman usually sat, and their youngest, Harriet.

Out of respect, her attention went to the king first as she fought off the burning impulse to stare at Tristan beyond her cursory glance and see how he'd aged in the last year.

King Henrik was a broad man, particularly in the shoulders. He'd accrued more wrinkles, aging him some, and he'd let his beard grow out, now thick and full, matching his shoulder-length peppered hair. His blue eyes twinkled as they rested on her, exactly how she remembered. Her spirits lifted at the sight.

"Welcome, dear friends," King Henrik exclaimed with open arms, a full-width smile on his face. "It's so good to have you back." He descended the five shallow steps, awarding Evelyn a giant hug and ignoring formalities.

Her mother welcomed the warm gesture, beaming at her lifelong friend. "It's good to be back, Your Majesty."

"And my Rose! How you've grown!" the king said, sizing her up from head to toe.

"Your Majesty," she greeted with a warm voice. "It's wonderful to see you in good health."

She was caught in the king's embrace without a moment's hesitation. The warm scent of cinnamon filled her lungs as she returned the gesture, instilling a sense of ease within her.

The king's wife, Lenna, was not as keen to see them, remaining seated. Nonetheless, she gave them a most welcoming smile. "Welcome back. Forgive me for sitting. I'm afraid I'm under the weather this morning."

Her mother stiffened next to her. "Are you quite well, Your Highness?"

The queen waved her concern away. "Oh, quite well. Just a little cold, that's all."

A sharp pinch of pity nipped at her as she gazed at the queen. Gray hair, which had only been streaks last summer, had now taken over the majority of the brown. Her frame was frailer, too. It contradicted the ferocity of her facial structure, made of an angled jaw and piercing blue eyes—eyes keen to seek out any weakness and squash it.

It was an unspoken fact the queen suffered an inherited illness—an illness that, at times, was better than others. It would seem this visit wouldn't be one of those.

The king interrupted her thoughts, gesturing to the oldest of his offspring. "Xavier."

Rose's back straightened as she sucked in a discreet breath and held it.

Xavier came forward, though he made it a point to drag his feet, taking his sweet time to approach. Even as he stood just a few feet in front of her, he wouldn't meet her gaze. His once-short black hair was now overgrown, resting just above his shoulders. There was something... uncontrolled about him, something out of place. Rose couldn't pinpoint what it was.

Xavier greeted her mother first. "Evelyn," he acknowledged informally.

Her mother bowed. "I'm so glad you could be here to greet us. It's been too long."

Xavier gave her mother an expression she assumed was supposed to be a smile; it looked more like he'd strained a muscle. "Of course."

Her mother put her hand on her back, urging her forward. "And Rose is glad, too, of course."

Rose fought the urge to step hard on her mother's foot. Instead, she bowed with a small incline of her head, her heartbeats increasing.

His indifference cut straight through her core when his light, icy-blue eyes finally met hers, sweeping her from top to bottom, dissecting her like an insect under a magnifying glass—harsh enough for the icy air surrounding him to sink into her bones.

"Rose," Xavier acknowledged in a bored tone. He returned his attention to his father, releasing her from his scrutinizing gaze. "I'd love to stay, but I have obligations to attend to."

"You'll stay until you're excused, Xavier," the queen said, her voice as sharp as the edges of the swords spiking from the throne.

Xavier cast an apologetic glance at his mother, though his tone betrayed him. "I wish I could, but regrettably, I'm to oversee the hunt."

Before the queen could scold him, the king intervened quietly. "Let him go, Lenna."

With a brief bow to his parents, Xavier left, sidestepping Rose like a poisonous flower.

She couldn't help but stare after him. What in Vallor? It was true that they'd grown apart before she'd left, but she had still been expecting a warmer greeting than that.

The king didn't miss a beat, turning to his next oldest. However, Tristan made his introduction by addressing her mother first. "Hello, Evelyn; how wonderful it is to see you again. You look as radiant as ever."

Her mother blushed. "Oh, you flatter me. But look at you—you've grown! Just as Rose has."

Rose became carefully still as his blue eyes barreled straight through hers—hauntingly deep and as mesmerizing as the Meridian Sea. Sun exposure had highlighted his wavy blond hair, now shaggy and grown out, resting just above his brows. She liked it, she decided; it complemented his strong facial structure, resembling his mother's.

"Hello, Rose," he greeted, taking her hand in his and placing a feathered kiss on it.

A jolt of lightning traveled up her arm from the simple touch, warming her blood. She did her best to keep her feet steady, locking her knees before they failed—and was left wondering if he felt the same energy or if he'd hold their last encounter against her.

Her mouth split into a wide smile. "Hello, Tristan."

Before Tristan could utter another sentence, the last and youngest of the Montague family bounced towards her, forcing her older brother out of the way, unable to keep still any longer.

"Oh, Rose, how I've missed you!" Harriet exclaimed as the sixteen-year-old flung her arms around her.

She couldn't help but smile as her heart simultaneously twisted. Harriet had become a young woman in her absence, a tad shorter than Rose, though still growing. Her bright, icy-blue eyes and long black hair resembled those of her most favored brother.

The queen scolded Harriet from afar. "Harriet, have you learned nothing in our lessons?"

Harriet let go of her, pretending to be poised as she inclined her head. "My apologies. Hello to you, too, Evelyn," Harriet greeted with a sheepish grin. "It's so lovely to have you both back. I don't know why you insist on leaving at all. Surely, this is your true home by now."

Her mother smiled, patting her shoulder. "You make us feel right at home, but I'm afraid we cannot always burden you with our presence."

"Harriet makes a fair point, Evelyn," the king agreed. "Your husband wouldn't want you to be on your own."

The mention of her father made her shift in her stance. The king and her father had been close friends until his sudden death last year. Why the king had bothered to be friends with a man like her father was something Rose had asked herself many times. But then again, the king had never seen what she and her mother had.

"Yes, I know." Her mother didn't even deny it. "But we had other matters to attend to, as you well know... His passing has not been easy."

Rose's eyes fell to the floor as she pressed her lips together. And not out of respect for the dead.

"You'll have to forgive Roman's absence," the queen interjected, changing the subject before her husband could pester them further. "He's been away for quite some time as general."

Rose couldn't hide the shock wreaking havoc on her face.

Her mother recovered first. "Our little Roman? Off in the war against Vertmere?" She looked between the king and queen. "Goodness, I could swear he was just a boy the last time I saw him. Now he's off to fight wars? We are getting old."

Rose had to agree. Twenty-two seemed too young to be thrown into war. He was too fragile, too kind to carry such a burden. He'd always been the warmest of the brothers. To hear of him fighting a war as a general... It was nearly unfathomable. "Is it safe for him?"

A foolish question: war was dangerous for everyone.

The king and Tristan chuckled at her worry. "You haven't seen him for some time. Rest assured, Roman is *more* than capable of handling himself," the king informed her. "His leadership and tactical skills give us the upper hand in this war. Don't fret; he'll be back in time for the celebration tonight. He's negotiating a peace treaty with Vertmere on our behalf as we speak."

Before Rose could reply, they were interrupted by a servant. "Forgive me, your Highness, but the hunt is ready and waiting for your arrival."

The king gave a dismissive nod. "I'll be there momentarily." His twinkling blue eyes looked to Rose and her mother. "Would you two like to see the sport?"

"I'm afraid I've grown tired after our journey," her mother said in a regretful tone. Rose knew better. "But Rose may find it entertaining?"

The king glanced over to his son. "Tristan? Why don't you escort her?"

"I think I'll stay," Tristan said instead. "Go on a walk with Rose before the celebration. It's been a while; maybe it'll give us time to catch up." Tristan looked to her for confirmation.

Rose nodded, doing her best not to look too eager, even though her fingertips tingled with hope. "Yes, I'd like that."

The king accepted his answer as if he'd known all along that Tristan would prefer that instead. "Very well, then I'll excuse myself. I'll see you both tonight."

Before leaving, the king gave his queen a chaste kiss on the lips, whispering something into her ear. The queen's mouth raised into a poised smile as they rubbed their noses together.

Rose watched them with near envy, pleased to see the past year's hardships had not altered their devotion to one another. The older she became, the more she grasped how rare their love was. She'd never seen anything quite like it—her parents' relationship had been void of the affection she'd so regularly seen on display here. As a girl, she'd prayed that whoever she married would love her as devotedly as Henrik loved Lenna.

"Would you like to accompany Rose and me?" Tristan asked her mother.

Evelyn waved her hand. "Oh, no. I have so much to do before the celebration tonight, but you two go on ahead. But don't dally too long, Rose. We have to get you ready for your debut."

Harriet was about to speak up, but the look she received from the queen silenced her. Harriet let out a disappointed sigh. "I'll stay here with Mum."

CHAPTER 2

Not an hour later, Rose drank in every morsel of her second home as she and Tristan climbed one of the many mountainous staircases lined with a rich crimson runner.

"Did you miss it at all?" Tristan asked, observing her soft gaze. "Being here?"

She paused, daring to look back at his eager expression with a hint of sadness. "Every day," she confessed.

They roamed the corridors as she re-familiarized herself with the castle's splendor. Domed windows let in plenty of sunlight to light their way as they trudged through curved corridors like ants in an endless maze. Intricate ceilings rested high above them, adding detail through the countless arches. Cathan's sun symbol was engraved into each keystone they passed, brought over from the original castle structure that now lay overgrown in ruin. The floor under her feet was so clean she could see her reflection shining back at her.

Their footsteps echoed on the smooth stone in comfortable silence, passing a few court members on their walk as her muscle memory led her through the halls.

Tristan shot her nervous glances now and again as if he were double-checking that she was real and not just a figment of his imagination.

If she was honest, she fought hard not to do the same.

At last, they reached her favorite part of the castle—a place where she used to spend hours upon hours.

The library.

It was just as she remembered: antique cathedral windows lined the west wall, with Cathan's symbol hand-painted onto each panel. Books were neatly dusted and organized in alphabetical order. As usual, the library was empty around lunchtime.

The impressive collection of books covered a diverse range, including the history of Vallor, enchanted artifacts, herbology, and various magical creatures like dragons, sirens, and other beasts. No one knew exactly why Cathan had retained so little magic within its borders after Argarion Atticus split Vallor into seven provinces. Some speculated the land had lent its loyalties to those it favored, while others believed it was an equalization of power. Magic was a fickle thing, she'd discovered, almost an entity of its own.

Rose approached one of the wooden bookshelves, running her fingertips over the spines.

A small, delighted smile crept onto her lips.

"Do you still read?" Tristan asked from behind her.

She kept her gaze on the books. "Not as much as I used to. I haven't had the time or the luxury lately."

"You always were the smartest of us," he admitted. "Reciting phrases and quotes right out of a textbook. Our tutor favored you for it. I'd get so jealous that she let you leave before the rest of us."

"Well, I was easy to love," she teased, flipping her hair back over her shoulder with a small shrug. She froze, realizing what she'd said. She threw him an uneasy glance.

"Yes..." His longing eyes slid to catch hers. "Yes, you were."

She swallowed hard, averting her gaze.

She spotted her favorite bench nestled in front of a large, golden-framed window. The sun's rays filtered through the dust swirling in the air onto the dark-green cushions—the precise ones she used to read on. How she used to love looking out while she read, especially when it rained. She had always found the pattering splashes on the glass a soothing comfort.

"I remember that night we went into an absolute panic not being able to find you," Tristan recalled. "We searched high and low, worried you'd gotten lost or hurt somewhere in the woods. Until we realized we hadn't checked in here." Tristan's mouth slid up into a handsome smile. "And there you were, right on that cushion. Book and mouth wide open, planted on it fast asleep."

Her mouth mirrored his; she remembered all too well. "My mother was furious with me. I was forbidden from playing with you all for a week."

"Little did she know I'd sneak into your room to keep you company." His eyes lit with mischief.

"You even pillaged the kitchens to bring me food."

"It was worth every minute of the hour it took to get that damn shortcake from the kitchen to your room without being noticed." He gave a short laugh.

She raised her brows. "You brought me shortcake?" she asked, not recalling the small detail.

"It was your favorite, wasn't it?"

Her heart skipped a beat. Unable to find her voice, she felt lost at sea in his eyes. "Yes," she replied softly. "Still is."

She tucked her hair behind her ear, unable to hold his gaze any longer. She cleared her throat, disappearing between another set of bookshelves.

They weaved their way through the jungle of shelves, passing by the librarian, a short and stern woman who peered at them from behind spectacles as she wheeled a cart brimming with books to be sorted. Rose offered a brief hello and a small smile before continuing through the walnut aisles. Her fingers brushed against the spines again as if reconnecting with long-lost friends.

They had just paused before a tall cathedral window to admire the sea when Tristan spoke. "You look better," he stated in a less formal tone. "Why'd you wait so long to come back?"

She fixed her eyes on the infinite blue horizon. "After my father's death, my mother needed time away, and so did I."

Tristan's gaze bore into the side of her face. "I'm sorry. I don't know if I ever got to say that to you."

She strained to plaster a smile on her face. "Thank you. But you don't need to be. We're doing much better."

"If I'd known sooner that he'd passed, I would've come to you."

Her heart swelled at the sheer tenderness of his voice. "You were needed here. But I appreciate your thoughts all the same." She changed the subject, continuing through the shelves. She did *not* want to delve into that bag of worms today. "Your father must be so relieved about the peace treaty... I still can't believe Roman's a general."

"Not just a general. The general over *all* of Cathan's armies." His eyes glowed with pride. "The youngest Cathan has ever seen."

"I know it's been a long time, but I still feel so frightened for him." She kept picturing her younger best friend running toward her with a frog in hand and a bright smile.

Tristan's kind expression made her weak in the knees. She'd forgotten how small she felt to be pinned under his gaze. "You underestimate him. He's become one of the best fighters I've ever seen. I wish I could've joined him, but my father wanted me here."

"Xavier seems more distant. How is he?" she asked.

Tristan scowled at the sound of his name. "You'll find that, like Roman, Xavier has also changed, but not for the better."

Her eyes shifted to meet his in alarm. "Why? What's happened?"

Tristan's gaze lowered. "It's a story for another time." He dismissed the question as if shaking off a bad memory. "But Xavier's mistakes have cost Cathan dearly. Nowadays, he ignores his duties, drinks far too much, and disappears completely for days at a time. I'm starting to wonder what my father will do with him."

She stopped walking as they settled in a quiet, deserted aisle. "You don't mean they're thinking of stripping him of his succession?" she asked in disbelief.

Tristan shrugged, looking perfectly unsympathetic. "I can't be certain, but if my father challenges it, it'll be up to him and the council to decide."

"Would he do that?" She didn't want to believe the king had lost hope. "You know Xavier; he's always been so... grounded." Dare she say almost to a fault. He was a stickler when it came to obeying rules and orders. Always the voice of reason. Always the protector. Territory, she imagined, he'd gained by being two years older than Rose and Tristan.

"You've been gone longer than you think. If he continues like this... it'll be a disaster."

They couldn't be talking about the same Xavier. Not the one who'd spent all his time studying in this very library with her. Not the Xavier who had given countless hours of youth to his father preparing for his duties. Not the Xavier who had won his succession by nearly dying while climbing a treacherous mountainside.

"But who would be your father's successor?" Before he could answer, she pieced the puzzle together, her eyes widening. If Xavier were denounced, a new succession period would be forced open. "Does that mean you could be..."

"The next king of Cathan?" Tristan finished her sentence, neither looking happy nor sad about the fact. "Yes. But to be honest, it's a slim chance. Remember, there are many great Houses who could easily have a chance at the throne."

Her thoughts drifted as she looked through the sunny haze streaming from the window, shining on a volume of books. Never had she had a single reservation that Xavier would be the next king. The calmness he projected and the faith he instilled in others came as naturally to him as breathing. He'd always held himself to a higher standard because of it.

She came out of her daze, looking back at Tristan, his eyes already on her.

His face finally broke composure. "Hell, I've missed you." He lifted his hand to brush the hair out of her face.

Her pounding heart soared. "Nonsense." She tried to keep her voice light. "I'm sure you've been too busy to think of me."

"You can't be serious," he said in a sharp whisper. "Ever since you left, there hasn't been a day I haven't thought about you. When you didn't respond to my letters... I was afraid you'd moved on." He stepped forward, standing so close, his heavenly scent filled her lungs while his hand slid smoothly into hers.

She gazed at their entwined hands. How she could still feel so strongly for him was strange. After such a long time apart, she thought maybe her feelings would fizzle out. But they hadn't. It was like they'd lost no time at all—nothing had changed. An invisible thread pulled at her, bringing her closer to him.

Tristan lifted her chin so she had to look him in the eye. "I keep thinking about our last conversation before you left. I know you chose to leave because of the present circumstances, but we have to have it out, Rose. After all this time, you being here in front of me solidifies that I'm still in love with you. I never stopped loving you."

Her heart ached. The hope that he felt the same way had seemed slim to none. She'd told herself it would be foolish to believe he could still feel the same—that it was only wishful thinking. But here he was, standing before her as if none of that mattered.

It was enough to make the veins in her body burn to ash.

"I was afraid after I left… I wasn't sure if you hated me," she admitted softly.

"Are you mad?" He looked at her as if she were insane. "Did you not read *anything* I said in my letters? *Begging* you to come back?" His lips hovered close to hers, so close she was sure he would kiss her. Instead, the breath of his words brushed her skin. "You couldn't push me away even if you wanted to."

She looked back at him as longing poured out from her soul. She wasn't prepared for this—for the tug at her heart to be stronger than when she'd left, for the aching hole to be just as deep as before.

"Please." His hands slid up the back of her neck into her hair. "Promise me you won't leave again."

She wrapped her hand around his wrist. "I wish I could, but you know things still haven't changed."

"But don't you see? This could change *everything.*" Hope gleamed in his eye. "It won't matter if Xavier is married or not. And if I do become king, I will *need* to marry. My father will want it done quickly. He adores you. He'd approve the match, I'm sure of it. I could be the strongest leader this province has ever seen with you by my side."

"And if you don't become king?"

He hesitated, a small smile gracing his lips as he stepped into the sunlight, lightening his blond hair. "Then I'll marry you anyway, and I won't have to be away from you for a single moment."

Her lips cracked upward. Despite this "plan" he had for them, things could easily go awry. With all his endearing qualities, Tristan was also hasty, stubborn, and impulsive; she didn't want him blindsided by false pretenses. If either of them let their hearts take over, they'd both end up hurt.

Again.

Despite this, her body took over, closing the gap between them. Her arms interlocked around his neck, hugging him as she whispered into his ear, "I missed you, too."

Tristan quickly recovered from the sudden gesture, wrapping his strong arms around her, pressing her firmly into his chest, and cradling her like she meant the world to him.

The distant sound of someone calling out interrupted them.

"Tristan? Rose? Where are you?" Harriet's voice carried through the library, growing closer.

Rose let go of Tristan, smoothing her dress as she peeked through the books. If Harriet caught them embracing, the news would be all over the castle before you could say the word *gossip*.

Tristan looked at her intently. "I want to spend as much time as possible with you this season," he whispered.

"Won't your father be concerned we're getting too attached?" With Xavier still unwed, she didn't know if he'd frown upon it.

"Do you honestly think I care?" Tristan dismissed with a raised eyebrow.

Her lips curled into a radiant smile.

"There you are," Harriet huffed, her petite frame coming into view at the end of the aisle. "Didn't you hear me calling you?" Her eyes narrowed at the two.

"No," Tristan said quickly. "Sorry, Harriet. We've been catching up."

Harriet's face grew into a smile as if she'd just discovered something that pleased her. "Mother sent me to fetch you." Before Tristan could retort, she added, "Oh, don't give me that look. You'll have plenty of time with her later."

Tristan let out an irritated huff. "I'll see you at dinner?" he said to Rose.

"See you at dinner," she reassured him.

Tristan hesitated, as if he were worried that if he left, she'd vanish again. He gave her one last look before he was finally forced to follow Harriet down the aisle and toward the door.

She ventured deeper into the shelves in the opposite direction, absent-mindedly twirling her hair with her fingers while getting blissfully lost. She bit down on her lower lip—a sheepish smile on her lips.

And she wouldn't be rid of it for a long while.

CHAPTER 3

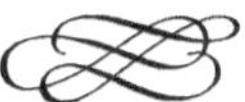

Dinner that evening took place in the grand hall, though "grand" seemed an insufficient word to describe it. Twelve large wooden tables sat upon the smooth, grouted stone floor, carved from the great forests of Vertmere's sacred woods decades earlier. Their fine grains took up most of the room, along with matching benches—each capable of seating over fifty people.

Above, a large, round chandelier made of steel and lit with candles gracefully hung at the center, suspended by irons forged by ancient dragons during King Segain's reign several hundred years ago. Torches lined the walls, giving more light and warmth during the chilly months, while an oversized stone fireplace rested directly behind the head table, where the royal family sat.

The king's chair was empty, alongside Roman's, who usually sat three seats down. Xavier was also absent, but his seat next to his father's was currently taken by Tristan.

Rose hid her surprise as she finally picked up on a strung tension in the room. No one was to sit nearer to the king than Xavier. Why was Tristan sitting in Xavier's seat?

Tristan spotted Rose as soon as she walked in, seeming unfazed by the odd seating arrangement. His subtle smile plunged her heart into a daydream—a daydream she dreaded waking from, worried she'd find herself back home in Canteran.

Just as she and her mother were about to sit down at a table on the far side of the room, a piercing voice rang out over the crowd.

"Ah, Rose, Evelyn!" Queen Lenna rose to her feet. "My husband would like you to join us this evening for your welcome back. Rose, you'll sit here." The queen gestured to the vacant seat right beside Tristan where he usually sat. "And Evelyn, you will sit beside me and Harriet."

"Certainly, Your Highness," her mother accepted with a tight smile.

Rose went to take her seat, but not before exchanging a subtle glance with her mother. A sense of unease coiled within her as she ignored the watchful eyes of the court. Now, both she and Tristan would be sitting closer to the king than Xavier.

Once she sat down, the crowd gradually lost interest and returned to their own conversations. Her relief was fleeting, however, as Xavier soon appeared through the double doors.

Xavier kept his face carefully blank when he saw Tristan and Rose. However, she swore a slight shadow crossed his face.

Without a word, he took the empty seat beside her.

"Xavier," she dared to acknowledge him. "Did the hunt go well?"

Xavier gulped his wine. He took so long that she wondered if he would reply at all. Without looking at her, he simply stated, "It did."

She took the hint he didn't want to talk. As she took her napkin, her gaze shifted to Tristan to see if he saw the color burning her cheeks. His expression softened, worried that Xavier had upset her. She offered him a gentle, reassuring smile.

But of course, Tristan wouldn't have it. "You must have fallen from your horse during the hunt and banged that large head of yours, Xavier. Surely, you should know how to speak to a lady."

Xavier's dead eyes slid to Tristan, disregarding the fact she was sitting between them. "I don't care to waste my breath." He took another drink.

Her eyes fell to her plate. What in Vallor was wrong with him? She couldn't think of anything she'd done to warrant such hostility from him.

Tristan narrowed his eyes at his brother. She shook her head, silently urging him to let it go, but he was already agitated.

"Interesting seating arrangement Father chose, isn't it?" Tristan remarked nonchalantly, sipping on his drink.

Rose nearly choked on her water.

Xavier's hand on the table tightened into a fist, but he remained calm, ignoring Tristan's bait. In any case, he didn't have time to respond as the grand hall doors opened to reveal their father.

Everyone stood in unison in respect for their king. Out of the corner of her eye, Rose noticed Xavier was still seated. She worried he wouldn't get up at all. However, slowly but surely, he stood with the same unreadable expression.

The king cast Xavier a long, measured stare as he strutted past them toward his chair. With a simple wave of his hand, he signaled for everyone to sit.

Xavier took another swig from his drink before pounding his glass down with a loud thud. He swiped the bottle from the table, rising so quickly he almost toppled his chair. The screech against the stone was so loud it made her jump. He stalked away, not caring if he made a scene.

After a brief glance at his son, the king turned to address the court, unfazed by his abrupt exit.

Perhaps that had been his plan all along.

He extended a warm welcome to Rose and her mother and praised the successful hunt the party had earlier that day. The servants brought out the hefty pig they'd slaughtered to be butchered and divided, along with a medley of vegetables, berries, and wild herbs. It was hard to recall the last time she'd enjoyed a feast like this. Since her father's death, they had no longer been able to afford such luxuries.

The moment her plate was full, Rose dug in, but as dinner continued, she occasionally glanced at Xavier's empty chair. She couldn't help but feel partially responsible for him leaving, like somehow her simple presence had added more strain to the situation.

Tristan must have noticed her downcast glances because he said, "Don't worry about him. I stopped a long time ago."

She set down her fork, shock forming on her face. "How can you say that? He's your brother."

Tristan's eyes turned molten. "Blood doesn't make a brother."

She was stunned by the bitterness in his voice. Sure, their relationship had always been rocky, but she hadn't realized it had become near nonexistent.

He sensed her apprehension. "There are things you don't know."

"Tell me."

Tristan hesitated, considering whether to confide in her. He peered over his shoulder to see if anyone was listening. Satisfied, he lowered his voice as he said, "Soon after you left the castle last summer, we were dispatched to train troops in Corrin. My father appointed Xavier to lead the expedition and sent Roman and me along with him…

"A few weeks into training, we traveled just outside the city to practice a few formations. But when we returned, we found the city burned to nothing but ash. Homes were destroyed, property stolen, bodies mauled and left scattered. It was enough to shower ourselves in their blood a thousand times over." He paused, attempting to shove the memories aside. "There were no survivors. However, a few people living outside the city reported a group of masked men with no symbol but who wore a strange mark on their arms. We soon discovered the men were not soldiers from Vertmere's army at all."

She absorbed the information, but it still didn't make sense. "If they weren't Vertmerian soldiers, then who were they? What motive could they have for attacking an innocent city?"

Tristan shrugged. "We can't be sure. However, Corrin sits close to the Vertmere border, and rumors circulated that there was illegal trade between them. According to the survivors, Corrin's controller had made enemies with a rebel group just beyond the border. We suspect this band of rebels was responsible for attacking the city…" He paused as a servant refilled his glass, then took a sip, waiting for him to leave before continuing. "We informed the king of Vertmere of the rebel group in his territory. He insisted that he knew nothing of the quarrel."

"I don't understand. What's this got to do with Xavier?" she asked.

"After we discovered the city had been burned, something in Xavier… *snapped*. We were welcomed into Vertmere's province a few weeks later. The Vertmerian king presented us with gifts, food, and even gold," Tristan recounted. "It was evident he had no involvement in the attack nor a desire for war. He understood Vertmere would likely lose in a conflict with Cathan. It made no sense for him to send men to attack us. We believed it was only an isolated group of insurgents—except for Xavier. Just as we were about to leave, Xavier unexpectedly attempted to assassinate the Vertmerian king."

"What?" She gawked at him. "Why would he do that?"

Tristan's eyes cooled a few degrees. "Because that is who Xavier is now. He doesn't think with his head anymore. He lets emotion rule him like a fool. He had no care for what the actions of that day would lead to—war."

"But he must have had a reason."

His expression was unforgiving. "None that could justify what he did."

She struggled to believe it. Xavier must have known the consequences of such a violent action would lead to war. So it raised a critical question: what could have been so vital that he would risk it all?

She had been so engrossed in their conversation that she didn't realize the others had nearly finished their meals.

Tristan stood. "I need to take care of a few things before we move to the ballroom. Will you save me a dance?"

It was a good thing she was sitting, or his dazzling smile might have made her stumble. It was nearly enough to make her forget their earlier conversation.

She arched an eyebrow. "You're going to dance with me? Willingly?"

Tristan rolled his eyes, leaning in to whisper, "Only so I can be close to you."

CHAPTER 4

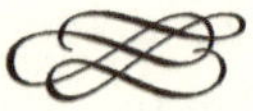

Following dinner, Rose headed to her room to get ready for the celebration.

Her room was in the east wing, close to her mother's. Not a thing had changed. The huge canopy bed stood against the left wall, draped with her favorite creamy-white sheets, matching the flowing curtains next to the wide-open balcony doors, revealing a wide view of the gardens and sea. To her right sat a washtub, dresser, and vanity, along with the floor-length brass-framed mirror she was currently facing.

She stared at the stranger looking back at her. She was a bit unnerved to be in such a sophisticated gown, having grown used to wearing the same ten or so dresses over the past year. Being surrounded by those whose sole purpose was to attend to her every need was equally unnerving. They fussed over her hair and makeup like she was someone important. It wasn't something she was particularly accustomed to and probably never would be. Part of her wished they would leave her alone, yet she was eternally grateful when they finished because she knew she couldn't have achieved what they did in an hour, not even if she had a week to prepare.

She was swimming in a sea of blue and gold. Her long, ashy-brown hair was partially braided, while the rest cascaded into a waterfall of curls past her shoulder blades, sparkling with a soft dust of gold. It went perfectly with the golden flecks they sprinkled on her collarbone and cheeks. The steel-blue dress fell effortlessly to the floor, smooth as butter against her skin. She was used to the flowy, loose fit, designed to conceal the growing lean muscle she had recently gained.

The modest fit was aimed to portray an illusion of weakness. "Appear weak and delicate, and no one will suspect you're a threat," her mother had once said.

In truth, Rose and her mother hadn't simply been absent from court for an extended grieving period like they had led everyone to believe. After her father's passing left them vulnerable and without family support, her mother had enlisted the help of Warren, a retired soldier, who'd agreed to teach them self-defense. During this training, Warren also had Rose volunteer to assist the healers when the troops passed through Canteran. Initially, helping the healers had just been part of her training, but she'd soon discovered she liked being useful and she was quite good at it. As those grueling, character-building months went by, she had become accustomed to dirt under her nails and sweat trickling down her brow. Now, to be standing in such a lovely gown…

Her appearance exuded royalty. But inside, she felt like a fraud.

Naturally, her mother was completely in her element—overseeing and directing the final touches to her dress and makeup. It reminded her of how her mother had been raised in one of Catalena's wealthiest Houses, born into a life of luxury and prestige. The loss of that lifestyle had been distressing for her mother, to say the least. If Rose sparkled like a diamond tonight, she'd have her mother to thank.

Once her mother was satisfied, she thanked the servants and dismissed them.

"Oh, Rose, you look beautiful." Her mother admired her in all her glory.

She beamed at the praise. "I must get it from my mum."

Her mother wore a slimming plum dress that brought out her hazel eyes and long, sandy-blonde hair, which was elegantly styled in a neat updo, pinned and tucked into soft, graceful waves.

"Well, of course." Her mother winked with glittering eyes. "No one will be able to keep their eyes off you. Mark my words. You'll be the talk of the entire province by the time the night is over. Tristan will have his hands full trying to keep suitors away from you tonight."

Rose faced the mirror again. Before she could gather her thoughts, an overwhelming grief nearly flattened her, bringing her father's face to the forefront of her mind.

What would he have done if he were here? Would any part of him regret what he did?

Her grief transformed into molten steel, simmering the anger that bubbled just under her skin. She clung to that rage, holding on to it for dear life because, by the gods, it was all she had left.

She scolded herself for even giving a damn.

Her mother's face fell. "Rose? What is it?"

She hesitated, wondering if she should even honor his memory by speaking of him. "Is it odd to wonder what he'd do if he were here?" Her tired eyes met her mother's in the mirror's reflection.

Her mother stared back at her, knowing who she spoke of. Surely surprised that he was on Rose's mind at all, especially since she insisted they never mention him. "No... no, it's not, sweetheart."

Her mother's reply didn't make her feel any better. "It's just as well." She glared into the mirror. "He'd have only auctioned me off to the highest bidder."

Her mother took a step toward her, determination radiating in her eyes. "He was a fool. A fool who couldn't see the things he had, only the things he didn't."

"Why was I never enough for him?" She allowed her pent-up anger to surface.

Her mother gazed at her with a strength she was sure she'd never possess. "What he did can never be forgiven by mere mortals. It's natural to hold onto hate. But you'll discover that the greatest revenge you can ever hope to have is to be happy. There are two roads you can take. You can either go down the road that keeps you crippled and let him destroy every happy day for the rest of your life, never to escape him... or you can free yourself from the poison and decide to be happy—*genuinely* happy—and give yourself the life you deserve."

Rose paused, allowing the words to sink in. Clinging to her hatred was only crippling her. Not her father—*her*. It was a poison she kept choosing to drink. And only she had the power to set down the glass.

She offered her mother a tender smile, forever grateful for the strength she instilled in her each day. "Thank you," she murmured, allowing a tear to escape.

Her mother gasped. "Rose, your makeup!" She rushed to catch the tear with a handkerchief.

And just like that, the moment was gone.

"There." Her mother carefully extracted her hand. "No harm done." Stepping back, her mother scanned her one last time. "You're ready. Now let's go show you off—Blast, where did that fan go?" She searched around, retracing her steps.

Rose gathered her skirt to take a look with her until a distant noise came from the balcony door. She strained her ears. It sounded like... carriages—a great deal of carriages. Intrigued, she forgot about her mother's missing fan and went to the balcony, ignoring the crisp evening chill threatening to seep through her dress.

She peered through the faint glow of the twin moons as their light filtered down to the grounds. It didn't take long to find the source of the commotion.

A multitude of men swarmed the long road to the castle. Some walked, while others rode on horseback. Their red and gold uniforms gave them away immediately—the soldiers.

A wave of warmth washed over her at the sight of so many returning home. Although she knew she shouldn't linger, her feet were rooted to where she stood. She watched as they approached the castle doors, eager to enter. They all appeared to be in high spirits, undoubtedly pleased to have a good meal and a warm bed to sleep in tonight.

One soldier in particular stood out to her above the rest. He wore a different uniform than the others, and though it was hard to see through the darkness, she gathered he was a broad man, with dark, wavy hair that reached just below his ears. He spoke with two castle guards while pointing and directing them. He didn't seem as eager to enter the castle as his fellow comrades.

Her eyes shifted away from him, searching the crowd for any trace of Roman, but it was futile. The night's darkness obscured any recognizable faces. She returned her gaze to the soldier, who, this time, met her stare.

She inhaled sharply as her limbs stiffened, unnerved by the unexpected connection.

In that instant, something dormant inside her stirred as if a long-lost part of herself had been jolted awake. The unfamiliar feeling swelled within her, struggling to seize control of her limbs. She pinned her arms to her side, trying to take steady breaths.

The soldier gradually removed his hat, maintaining eye contact as he let the faint moonlight shine on half of his face. Although his hair resembled Roman's, he was far too muscular to be him. Roman was merely a boy; this was clearly a man. They stayed trapped in each other's eyes until another soldier drew his attention away.

Set free from the daze, Rose regained control of her limbs and quickly backed away from the balcony.

She returned to the room's warmth, swiftly closing and locking the door behind her. Her heart raced as she pressed her back against it.

"Rose?" her mother said, reminding her that she was still waiting. "What were you doing out there?"

"Nothing," she replied at once.

Her mother shot her a strange look but dismissed it. "Well, come on then, or we'll be late!"

She followed her mother, hesitating at the door. She glanced at the balcony one last time, shaking off the lingering strange feeling, before shutting it behind her.

CHAPTER 5

Rose surveyed the crowd from the balcony above the ballroom, taking in the colorful array of gowns and tunics below. The turnout was far better than she had expected. Men and women from every corner of Cathan had come to celebrate, with some traveling from as far as the eastern cities. A few familiar faces belonged to the king's relatives, but most attendees were soldiers, proudly wearing their red uniforms embroidered with gold accents and the sun emblem.

Every inch of the ballroom was bursting with extravagance, decorated with large, lavish flower bouquets and tables filled with an array of fruits, vegetables, and cheeses. Another table was dedicated solely to drinks, desserts, and pastries. She hadn't seen the castle in such a splendid state since the last succession.

Her eyes darted to the colossal golden clock hung on the wall atop the grand staircase.

The familiar nervous butterflies in her stomach morphed into a chaotic swarm of raging moths, rising up into her throat and threatening to escape. The air suddenly grew warm and thick, making it hard to breathe.

"Deep breaths," she murmured to herself.

She was so engrossed in her thoughts she barely noticed her mother approaching from behind. "Isn't it glorious?" Her mother smiled at the crowd. "At last, you'll find a husband, and we can leave last year behind us."

"You know this would be a lot more enjoyable if we were *both* hunting for a husband," Rose said, knowing full well she was poking a bear. "Lord Barron has never taken a wife, and we both know he's the best-looking high council member, hands down."

Her mother rolled her eyes. "You think I want to do that again after a marriage like mine? No. I think my efforts are better invested in you—Ah!" She pointed down to the crowd. "There's Tristan."

Rose's gaze dropped to find Tristan already dancing. The young ladies of the court had always favored him. During past visits, she'd attempted to befriend many of them, but for some reason or another, she'd had no such luck. Beth was the only true friend she'd acquired—aside from the royal family—but she seldom visited except during holidays or special occasions. She suspected their prejudice stemmed from her humble status, which made it difficult for the court women to accept her. Her mother insisted it was jealousy.

"Come on." Her mother interlocked her arm with hers. "Can't dance with him from up here." She winked, bumping her hip against Rose's. Rose smiled, bumping hers back.

Her mother led her down the grand staircase to the dance floor. They had barely taken two steps into the crowd when the music came to a halt.

All eyes turned towards the staircase. For a brief moment, she thought they were looking at her. Out of instinct, she straightened her posture and glanced over her shoulder—discovering what really caught their attention.

The king was elevated above the crowd, standing on the wide marble staircase with veins of real gold interwoven in the grain, creating a glittering river beneath his feet.

"Ladies and gentlemen, I ask for your attention. As we begin this wonderful evening, I want to express my deep honor in being here with you. This is truly a night for celebration. To those in uniform, we are profoundly thankful for your return. This evening, we honor both you and the heroes we have lost." He paused, and the sparkle in his eyes dimmed. "I am particularly grateful for my son's safe return. His tactical skills and bravery have shown leadership beyond his years. He has proposed a peace treaty with Vertmere to unite our provinces, marking the first step to reuniting Vallor!"

The crowd broke out in applause.

The king raised his voice over the claps. "Please join me in expressing our gratitude for my son, Prince Roman Montague!"

Thunderous cheers erupted from all directions. The soldiers' cries were so loud they nearly made her go deaf. Many chanted a name she had never heard before. "Drengr! Drengr! Drengr!" they called.

Roman separated himself from the crowd and climbed the staircase to his father. The king immediately took Roman's hand and thrust it into the air, amplifying the cheers. Roman turned to receive their praise, but his mouth remained in a thin line, offering only a rigid nod.

But she barely noticed his manners. Instead, she was captivated by the man who now stood next to his father.

Awe consumed her, leaving her convinced she wasn't looking at her childhood friend but a stranger. Gone was the little boy she once knew, replaced by a tall, broad man. His new muscular build was living proof of his commitment to training and fighting in the war. What was once a youthful, innocent face had grown into a square, powerfully sharp, clean-shaven jaw. He was vaguely familiar but entirely foreign at the same time.

But more shockingly, it was him—the man she'd seen from the balcony.

Roman was oblivious to her stare until his wandering eyes locked on hers. She managed a small, inviting smile, tilting her head slightly. He, however, did not return the gesture.

Their eye contact was severed when the king firmly placed his hand on Roman's shoulder. He leaned in closer, whispering something into Roman's ear with a proud smile before dismissing him. Without a word, Roman descended the staircase and submerged himself back into the crowd.

She thought the speech had ended, yet the king remained on the stairs. His all-powerful gaze scanned the room before fixing on her. A spark of admiration glittered in his twinkling eyes. Her heartbeat became steadily audible; she knew that look by heart. It was the same look she had treasured in her childhood—the one that made her feel like she was a part of this rich world.

"I couldn't let the night pass without expressing a few words for someone else we're celebrating tonight—someone I've sorely missed." The king's commanding gaze fell upon her once more. "Rose, will you come join me?"

She felt as if the air had been sucked from her lungs. At first, she thought that his words were just her imagination, but as every gaze turned to her, it became clear that it was indeed real. She had thought that he might offer a toast to congratulate her, but standing beside him? Elevated above everyone else?

She must have hesitated for too long because her mother pressed a hand on her lower back, encouraging her forward. "Go on, dear," her mother whispered in her ear, smiling to save face for the crowd.

No getting out of it now.

With careful steps, she gathered her dress to conceal her shaking hands; the stillness of the room made her light footsteps echo through the hall.

The king's reassuring smile was her sole comfort as she stopped one step below him.

He placed his gentle hand on her shoulder as she faced the crowd with him. "Many of you know that Rose has visited us every summer since childhood. The moment I first met her, I knew she was exceptional. Throughout her time here, I have grown fond of the intelligent young woman she has become. Now that she has been absent from our lives for the past year, I've come to understand just how much of a treasure she is to us... to me." His large hand gave her shoulder a reaffirming squeeze. "As you can see, my little Rose has fully blossomed and will make her debut into society tonight. Many of you are aware that Rose lost her father under tragic circumstances. If he were here, I am certain my friend would be giving the toast this evening. While I know I can't truly replace a father, I hope she grows to view me as a present substitute." He gifted her a hearty smile when she looked over her shoulder at him. "I give her my full trust and support as she embarks on this exciting new chapter in her life. Rose, I hope you realize how cherished you are. Congratulations!"

Her eyes burned as she blinked rapidly to hold back the tears, moved beyond words. Though he never knew of her father's true nature, his words still filled a void in her damaged heart.

The king called for a toast as a servant approached them, carrying a golden tray with two wine glasses. "Let us raise our glasses to Rose," the king bellowed. "And to a bright future for Cathan!"

"For Cathan!" they chanted back.

The room filled with applause as she peered out at the sea of faces, keeping her gaze just above their heads, afraid that making direct eye contact would reveal her façade. She strained to shape her lips into a practiced smile, drawing upon years of training and lessons.

King Henrik's hand remained on her shoulder as her eyes finally landed on the royal family. The instant she saw the queen's icy stare, she felt a chill emanate from her like a bitter storm, making Rose confident that a single touch would result in frostbite.

Unable to hold her gaze, she shifted her eyes to Harriet, who stood next to Roman, both of whom offered no warmth either. Lowering her chin, she compelled herself to look away.

Perhaps coming back here was more than she'd bargained for.

CHAPTER 6

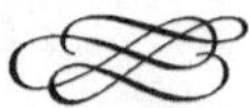

"Did you see Roman?" her mother asked, eyeing him across the ballroom while Rose rummaged through the dessert table. "An astounding transformation if I've ever seen one. I barely recognized him! Why don't you say hello? I'm sure he'd be happy to see you."

Rose feigned indifference, concentrating on the cake before her, watching the blue flames that danced on charred peaks of the meringue. "I'm sure he's been bombarded with people wanting to see him, Mum. I'll let him catch his breath." Still, she peeked through the desserts when her mother wasn't looking, finding him speaking with a handful of soldiers.

"Rose?" a delicate voice said from behind.

She spun around. A bright-eyed blonde girl stood smiling at her. She looked gorgeous, of course, just as she always did. The magenta dress she'd chosen suited her fair skin perfectly. Really, she could wear any color and it would suit her. But that's just how she was—effortlessly herself.

"Beth?" Her voice rose in pleasant surprise as she smiled back. "I thought it was just your brother and father coming."

Beth wrapped her in a tight hug. "My mother begged me not to, but I couldn't miss out on all the fun." She stepped back and nodded to Rose's mother. "It's good to see you, too, Lady Versalles."

Her mother's face brightened as she plucked a chocolate-covered wildberry off the table. "Oh please, Beth, you know how old that makes me feel," she said with a wink. "It's wonderful to see you, too, my dear."

"Well, I won't keep you. I just wanted to say hello. You must have a line of suitors waiting to meet you tonight." Beth squeezed her hand. "I remember how nervous I was when I came out."

"Any tips?" Rose asked, wiggling her eyebrows.

"Oh, it's quite simple. Don't talk too much about yourself, don't step on their feet, and if they can't find something more interesting to talk about than the weather—run," Beth advised with a playful smile.

She laughed. "Simple. I like it."

"Right, well, I'll see you later then. Don't forget to have fun!" Beth said, rejoining the sea of gowns and uniforms.

Her mother watched Beth until she was out of earshot. "She has grown to be much more amiable than I thought. You better watch out, Rose; she's sure to catch some eyes."

Rose looked to see if Tristan had noticed Beth, but to her pleasant surprise, his deep blue eyes were already on her as he stood next to his mother across the dance floor. Reassurance dissipated her fleeting worry.

Despite herself, she flashed a coy smile.

"I wasn't worried about Tristan." Her mother rolled her eyes. "It's Roman she has her sights on. She's barely left his side all night."

She watched Beth's distant figure to see what direction she'd go. Sure enough, she headed straight for Roman, who was still talking to the same group of soldiers.

Discomfort squirmed inside her as she pressed her lips together, judging the pair. "Isn't she much older than him?"

Her mother took a sip of the frosted-rimmed red drink in her hand, infused with floating cranberries and a rosemary sprig, before answering. "Heaven knows why her family has waited so long to put her out into society. But I suspect they thought their efforts would be better rewarded if they waited until the war was nearly over."

"I think they'd be a good match," Rose concluded after assessing them, her eyes going back and forth between the pair. But even as she said the words, her gut twisted with something ugly that she couldn't quite explain.

Her mother dismissed it with a wave of her hand. "She can try. But I have a feeling Roman will be quite the popular item."

Rose refocused on Tristan, who was engaged in conversation with his mother, wearing a determined expression. She knew that look, having seen it many times during their childhood games. It was the face that declared he would stop at nothing to win. But Tristan had met his match against his mother, her face stern and sharp as she lectured him. As they argued, she noticed how Queen Lenna's ghostly complexion was paler than usual.

"I hope this war wasn't too much for her," she said, still studying the queen. "Do you think her illness has taken a turn for the worst?"

Her mother put a hand on her arm. "Keep your voice down," she whispered, looking over her shoulder. "Her condition is still not widely known. But yes… I was hopeful that the tinctures were helping, but I'm afraid they haven't been as successful as the healers had predicted."

Rose played with her gold necklace, watching the pair argue. "I hope we weren't too hasty to return. Having the ball tonight must have taken a lot out of her."

Her mother scoffed. "It was she who requested it be moved up, said it would make sense with the soldiers' return. She was most insistent upon it."

Rose blinked, perplexed. Why would the queen care to rush the ball? Unless… unless the queen intended to get Rose married off before she stood a chance with Tristan. "Do you think the queen is opposed to me marrying Tristan?"

Her mother hesitated with empathetic eyes. "Honestly, sweetheart, I don't think she's too keen on the idea right now."

Rose's heart plummeted as she dropped her necklace. "Why not? Does she not approve of me?"

"No, it's not quite that. I think it's… something else," her mother said.

Rose's brows drew together in confusion.

Her mother gave an exasperated huff, moving closer. "You must have noticed their family's fragile state," she whispered. "She's afraid one small tear might leave them all in ribbons."

Rose had never shared a close bond with the queen, like she did with King Henrik, but she had thought they got on well enough. The queen had always enjoyed listening to her sing and frequently requested performances when Rose was a girl. She had often assisted in planning Rose's birthdays, arranging for special desserts, and allowing Rose to select flowers from the garden. It puzzled her to imagine what had changed.

She fought hard to conceal her disappointment, recognizing that her potential mother-in-law might not want her as a daughter after all.

She glanced back at Tristan and his mother, only to catch both of them staring at her.

Embarrassed for prying, she quickly looked away. But, from the corner of her eye, she saw Tristan's expression harden, snapping at his mother with a short remark before stomping away.

And to her surprise, he was headed straight for her.

She tracked him through the crowd until he was standing before her like a gallant knight. His self-assured presence calmed her worries as the rest of the room faded into the background. For that moment, she focused solely on him.

On the only thing that mattered.

He reached his hand out for hers. "May I have your first dance?"

She responded by gripping his hand. He held it firm as he guided her to the dance floor. The crowd parted for them as they glided to the heart of the room. She did her best to keep from falling over as they bowed to each other.

He closed the space between them, his free hand sliding around her upper back, supporting her arm on his. The mere contact made her very bones tremble. Her face burned as blood rushed to her cheeks, leaving her unexpectedly thankful for the thick layers of makeup. "Tristan, what—"

"Do me a favor?" he interjected. "Don't overthink this… Just dance with me. Dance with me and pretend the rest of the world isn't watching."

His tone was so sincere, she allowed her fortified walls to crumble.

A new song floated through the hall, reaching her ears in a soft, comforting quartet as the cello's deep notes resonated through the floor.

The rehearsed movements coursed through her trained body. Dancing with him felt as effortless as water flowing downstream—serene, yielding, and graceful.

Other couples gradually joined in, relieving her nerves as the focus shifted away from them.

"You look incredible tonight," Tristan whispered at last.

She smiled, looking through her darkened lashes. "Thank you. It only took a few hours."

Tristan's face broke into a handsome smile. "Then I suppose at least one good thing came from all this… Though I still don't know why you wanted this ball at all. Why did you request it be moved forward?" He twirled her, bringing her back into his arms with ease.

"What do you mean *I* requested?" she asked, confused.

His brow quirked. "You didn't?"

"No. My mother said your mother requested it be moved to today. She said she practically insisted."

Tristan clenched his jaw and squeezed the hand holding hers. "Of course you didn't. I should've known."

It only took one guess as to whom might have told him that lie—his mother. Yet another confirmation of her suspicion that the queen disapproved of their relationship.

"I know your mother cares for me… but I'm beginning to think she isn't fond of us together," she said.

He shook is head in denial. "That's not true. She adores you."

She pushed down the rising doubt. "Perhaps in a way." She stepped away as their hands rose above their heads with the choreography. "But in another way, maybe it's more complicated."

He spun her around and pulled her closer to his chest. "Even if that were true—which it's not—it doesn't matter. I'll marry you whether they like it or not."

She nearly flinched at the words. "Don't say that."

"No one will tell me who to marry. What they think doesn't matter."

"Don't be daft. It means everything."

"I'm serious." Tristan's grip on her waist tightened, redirecting her gaze back to his so she could see the ache harbored there. "For a year, I had nothing to hold on to. At times, you felt like a distant dream instead of a memory. Time paused and didn't start again until the moment you walked back through those doors. Life is too short, and I've already lost enough of it. I'll tell you exactly what I told my mother—I won't agree to stay away from you. Even if the world were on fire, I'd cling to you… with every ounce of strength, I'd cling to you."

He'd always had the ability to express himself without fear of what was to come after. She couldn't help but admire him for it. It was a wonder another girl hadn't caught his eye.

"After all this time… there must have been someone else?" she asked hesitantly.

Tristan grimaced. "No. I'll admit, I tried—more than once. But there is no one I've wanted more. I keep telling you, Rose, I want *you*. So much, I'm sure it can't be healthy."

Her heart skipped as her breaths grew shallow. "Can I ask what motivates you to be so loyal to me?"

The corner of Tristan's mouth lifted into a smile, pulling her closer. "Because you're one of the few people who wants me, not what I can give you. You want *me*, Tristan. Not the prince of Cathan. What's more, is you… You're the only one I ache for, the only one who gets under my skin." His eyes lowered to her lips, then returned to hers. "It scares the hell out of me how you can control me with a mere glance." He dipped her backward, her blue dress skimming the floor. When he lifted her, he asked, "Was there someone else for you?"

She almost laughed. "So many," she teased. Her smile was meant to ease his worry, but something hidden in his eyes made her uncertain.

"I'd believe it."

She shook her head. "There's been no one. My mother's tried to persuade me, but… no one is you."

Tristan pulled her closer in response, so close she could feel his breath on her face.

All too soon, the song ended, and the couples dancing separated. The crowd clapped, their applause spreading through the dance floor.

She didn't want him to let go. She didn't need to dance with anyone else. She'd found him—the person she wanted to marry was right here in front of her. Entertaining anyone else would be a waste of time.

He must have been thinking along the same lines because he whispered, "Meet me tonight at our spot after the celebration."

His words played with fire. It had been different when they were children. Back then, no one batted an eye at kids playing on the beach. But now that she was of age…

"We have the whole summer, Tristan," she pointed out.

"And I plan to take full advantage of every night," he declared with a cocky grin.

Still keenly aware of the spectators on the sidelines, she caved with a content smile. "Alright." Without waiting for a reply, she turned away, biting her lip to disguise her joy as she left.

She had taken all but ten steps before her mother joined her. "Rose! I want you to meet someone." She tugged at her arm, her determined strides hinting at a secret agenda. The next thing she knew, Rose stood in front of a short, heavyset man with a scruffy black beard. "Rose, do you remember the Grand Duke of Sansburry?"

The duke peered through his bushy eyebrows as a smile creased his cheeks. His famous dimples were still noteworthy but accompanied by more wrinkles. If she recalled correctly, he was one of the major gold traders in Cathan—and the richest man aside from the royal family.

Rose lowered her head, throwing on her society smile. "How could I forget the man who owns my favorite vineyard in Cathan? I remember my visit quite well."

He beamed as proud as a peacock, resting his hands on his protruding belly. "I'm impressed! You were no more than knee-high when you came to my humble home. Not too much younger than my son, if I remember correctly. You remember Dawnton. Dawnton!" he called over his shoulder.

A younger man appeared, the spitting image of the duke, though slimmer in the middle and barely her height. He held his chin high as if he owned the air around him, swirling a glass of red wine with utter boredom.

"Dawnton, you remember Rose, don't you?" the duke said, gesturing to Rose.

Dawnton greedily assessed her from head to toe. "Of course." He took her hand and kissed it. She fought against the impulse to yank it back when he held it for too long. "It's a pleasure to be here to celebrate with you."

"Why don't you two dance?" her mother urged. "You may not get another opportunity, Dawnton. She's quite popular."

"I'd be honored," Dawnton answered at once, coming forward and extending his arm.

She took it, ensuring she sent her mother a "thankful" look.

And so, the night continued. Suitor after suitor appeared, each making their introductions. She lost track of time—were they minutes or hours? All she knew was she'd met more than a dozen men and danced with every single one of them.

Throughout the night, she made it a point to find Tristan. Like her, he danced with a different partner for every song that played. She found it odd he'd be adamant about dancing with so many partners, but everything became clear when she noticed the queen observing him like a hawk. No doubt to see if another girl could catch his eye.

Rose said good night to her dance partner and tiptoed to the edge of the ballroom to find her mother. Unsurprisingly, her mother had prepared a new victim as she stepped aside to reveal a tall, broad, beefy blond. "Rose, you remember Grant Montague," her mother said, hanging on his arm.

Rose looked him over; she did indeed, though she'd only encountered him a handful of times. He used to be a heavier-set boy, brimming with snide remarks and mischief. His cousins, Tristan and his brothers, had always loathed him, grumbling complaints whenever Grant's family visited. Grant all but reciprocated the ill feelings, making their lives miserable when he came. She had gotten in trouble countless times because of him—and his strict father, Neith.

There were even rumors that Neith himself had hired the raiders who attacked one of Cathan's ships a few years ago, resulting in the death of his own brother—who just so happened to be the successor should King

Henrik die. However, no concrete evidence had ever been found against Neith.

Rose doubted the rumors herself. There were plenty of powerful family Houses who would gladly see the succession reopen. Regardless, the "accident" had allowed Grant's older brother to compete to be the heir to the throne, which Xavier had ultimately claimed instead. So, if Neith had gone to all that trouble, it was all in vain.

Grant flashed a giant smile the instant their eyes met.

She lowered her head, working hard to mask the repulsion she felt. "I've heard your name mentioned once or twice," she teased with a tense smile. "You're the one who let out all the horses the morning before the hunt... and destroyed the courtyard... and nearly got Xavier killed on the cliffs."

Grant's smile broadened. "I am ashamed to admit it's all true. But luckily, you'll find I've matured over the years, and so have you. Then again, you were always the pretty one."

Her mother's eyes sparkled at the compliment, while Rose fought not to roll her eyes. Her mother didn't hide her enthusiasm as she said, "Grant has been most gracious in keeping me company while waiting to dance with you."

Before Rose could refuse a dance, Grant intercepted. "I promise not to bite," he said, holding out his arm.

She took a deep mental breath before forcing a polite smile. "Of course."

Her mother put a hand on her lower back, gently pushing her towards him, whispering in her ear, "Stand up straight and try not to step on his feet. He'd be quite a catch."

She pretended not to hear as Grant led her to the dance floor. He spun her around and drew her close—too close.

"You've been a popular topic among the men tonight."

She smiled, but it was a feeble attempt. "All good things, I hope." *More like wishful thinking.*

"Don't bother yourself so much about what people say," Grant said as if it were simple. "If everyone believed gossip, I wouldn't be standing here today."

He sparked her curiosity. "What do you mean?"

He looked around, lowering his voice. "It was once said I was to blame for the 'toad in the punch scandal' at Tristan's tenth birthday party. I can most assuredly testify it was *not* me."

She scolded herself for thinking he might actually be serious for once. "And just how exactly is that life-altering gossip that could have resulted in your not being here today?" she asked with a raised eyebrow.

"If my mother believed it, I would've been killed on the spot," he said with a lazy smirk.

It was a stupid joke, but she was having a terribly serious night. A smile slipped through her defenses.

He looked all too proud of himself. "Ah, so she does have a genuine smile," Grant remarked as he dipped her, effortlessly supporting her weight. Rose tilted her head back, her hair almost grazing the floor. In one fluid motion, he lifted her back into his arms.

Grant's gaze shifted, focusing on something across the ballroom; his smirk turned wicked. She followed it to see an angry face dancing with a different partner. Tristan.

Her mask slipped as she shot a glare at Grant, knowing exactly what he was up to. It was the same antics he'd resorted to when they were young—getting a rise out of Tristan for entertainment.

She bit the inside of her cheek to keep herself from saying something she'd regret.

Grant turned his attention back to her. "Listen, Rose, I know you don't know me well." Grant's green eyes held hers with confidence. "But you do know my family is well respected, wealthy, and holds a powerfully close line to the throne... If I asked to court you, would you agree?"

Her shoulders tensed, surprised that he'd be so bold. Not when she'd only been out in society all but a few hours. Grant knew Tristan had feelings for Rose. But, of course, the fact didn't bother Grant. In fact, he reveled in it, which was precisely the problem.

Her mother watched them eagerly from the sidelines, giving her an encouraging nod.

Defiance reared, knowing her mother would scold her for what she was about to say next.

"I'm flattered. But I'm afraid I'd have to say no."

Grant wasn't fazed in the slightest, almost like he'd anticipated her resistance. "Perhaps you'd like to take some time to consider?"

She suddenly pretended to be interested in the white orchids on the far tables. "I don't think I need to drag it out."

"Can I ask why you'd offer me so little consideration?"

"Because I know what I am to you."

"And what is that, pray tell?"

"A chess piece," she clapped back. "You're only interested in me because Tristan is. I'm not a pawn for your amusement."

To her dismay, her rejection only added to his fire. His lips grew into a dangerous smile, clearly not used to being told no. "I danced with you to get underneath Tristan's skin. That is true." He didn't deny his shallowness. "But now, well, I'm curious about you. Not only are you beautiful, but now I've discovered you might even have something of substance under that perfect skin. Perhaps you and I are more alike than you realize."

Her eyes grazed her mother's, who watched from the sidelines, distressed by being unable to control their conversation.

"I'm sorry." She refused to be persuaded. "But my answer is still the same."

Grant's face, however, didn't falter. "I expected as much. I admire your loyalty. But I don't think it'll take long for your mother to convince you otherwise. She and I have become quite close, you see."

She cocked her head. "Is that so? How are you so sure?"

Another deadly smile. "Because I've already spoken to her and received permission to pursue you."

Her eyes widened, racing to her mother for confirmation, but she was busy conversing with a small group of men—including Grant's father.

Grant looked as smug as a feline. "See? They're thrilled about the prospect already."

"Well, unfortunately for you, *I'm* the one who decides who I'll court." She glared at him as she sidestepped with the music.

"We both know people like us don't get to choose our marriages." The statement was true enough. "But I'll be here a while; it may just be enough time for you to change your mind."

The song couldn't have ended at a more perfect time. She released his hand and stepped back, offering him a rebellious smile. "I wish you all the luck in the world."

His smirk spanned the entire width of Cathan, her resistance raising the stakes of his little game. He took her hand and kissed it. "Thank you for the dance, Rosalie Versalles."

Without missing a beat, she marched over to her mother. Just as her mother was about to speak, she caught sight of Rose's expression and nearly rolled her eyes, asking, "What is it now?"

"Did you give Grant permission to court me?"

Her mother laughed briskly. "He sure gets to the point, doesn't he?"

Her eyes bulged. "You did!"

"Oh, you're so dramatic." Her mother took her elbow and drew her closer, lowering her voice. "I've already told you we need to keep your options open, and if Tristan doesn't work out, Grant may be the next best thing for you. He's young, handsome, and incredibly rich, with royal blood. His family owns the largest trading company in Cathan. What's not to like?"

There were so many things, she could scarcely name them all. She let out a puff of air, too tired to argue.

What in Vallor had she gotten herself into?

CHAPTER 7

As the night went on, Rose danced with more men than she could count, with new partners continually emerging. Her mother dedicated herself to ensuring Rose stayed occupied, introducing her to a fresh dance partner with each song. It wasn't until a gray-haired man asked her mother to dance that Rose finally managed to slip away.

With a sigh of relief, her feet led her to the beverage table. Her throat was dry as bones. She picked up a rose-shaped glass filled with a bubbly concoction, savoring the flavors of pear and mint on her tongue.

She'd barely taken her third sip when a male voice came from behind her.

"Would you care to dance?"

She groaned internally. So much for a break.

Setting her glass back down on the table, she braced for another round as she turned to look at who she'd be dancing with this time.

She almost stepped back when she discovered Roman towering over her, now close enough that she could take in his transformation properly.

Despite being two years younger than her, he towered a whole head taller. His training had doubled his body mass, and his pristine gold general's uniform accentuated the muscle he'd accrued, bringing out the warm hues of his tanned skin and the gold flecks in his amber eyes.

He was still waiting for an answer when she finally found her voice. "Of course," she said, even managing a bright smile for her close childhood friend.

His mouth didn't curve upward with hers as he extended a rigid arm.

She peered at it hesitantly. The gesture felt so… formal. Still, she accepted it, her gaze locked on him as he guided her to the dance floor. It was hard to believe she wasn't dancing with a stranger. In a way, she supposed she was.

With a single step, he bridged the gap between them. His rough, calloused hand gently grasped hers, their fingers intertwining, while his other hand splayed on her upper back, drawing her close.

She fought the hitch in her breath. There it was again—the unfamiliar energy, just like on the balcony, heightened by his touch.

They fell into rhythm with the music as Roman took the lead. She tried to read his expression, but he kept his face carefully devoid of emotion.

It was silent for the first few bars until she spoke. "We're all so glad to have you back," she said, trying to engage in conversation as they navigated through the dancing couples. "I know your mother must be thrilled. I'm surprised you aren't in her grasp right now. How did you manage to escape?"

He glanced over the shoulder of his padded uniform as if he could see her from there. "It seems she's occupied with Tristan tonight." Even his voice was deeper than she remembered. "I'm sure Xavier is relieved to have the attention off him for a night."

Xavier. Where had he gone? She scanned the room, but there was no sign of him. Now that she thought about it, she hadn't seen him since dinner. But then again, she should have expected it. Xavier had always detested dancing more than both of his brothers combined.

Roman drew her attention back to him as he spun her. She moved with trained elegance, her blue dress trailing behind her.

"You handled the spotlight well tonight," Roman said.

"I'm glad it looks that way, but I must admit it doesn't come easily to me."

"Oh, I wouldn't be so modest; you've always handled it well." A tight, distant smile formed on his face, but it didn't reach his eyes. "You're all my father and Tristan can talk about since I arrived. I was surprised to hear you came back... I didn't think you would."

His tone was too cold for liking. A lump lodged in her throat. Something wasn't right. This wasn't like him. "Why wouldn't I? I always have."

Before answering, he grabbed her by the waist, lifted her into the air, and gently lowered her back into his embrace. "Why didn't you come back last summer then?"

She had expected that question, even prepared for it. She wished she could tell him how she'd spent the last year fighting her own battles while he was off fighting his. But that wasn't the answer she and her mother had agreed upon.

"There were things we needed to take care of at home. After my father died, we needed space... *I* needed space." She relayed the same excuse she'd given everyone.

His shoulders tensed beneath her hands. "That's it? You needed space? That's all I get?"

"We just needed time to cope with everything. You might think it was selfish, but it was necessary." Gods, she wished she was a better liar.

Roman's jaw ticked as his eyes blazed into hers. "You know, after you left... everything fell apart. Xavier spiraled out of control, Tristan was heartbroken, my mother's condition worsened, and I was sent to hell. But do you care? Do you even take the time to write? No, you just disappear. I made excuses for you for a time after your father passed until I realized that you only lost interest in our family *after* Xavier rejected you. That day, I understood—we were merely a means to an end for you. I was wrong to idolize you as I did."

He could have just as easily plunged a rusty knife into her heart. "That's not true. You know that."

Roman crushed her with a stinging glare. "You can keep your excuses, lies, or whatever you want to call them. But if you think you can return out of the blue and expect things to go back to how they were, you're even more naïve than I was."

She parted her lips to respond, but no sound left her mouth. He was right, of course. She had been a fool to think everything would be the same, leaving without so much as a quick goodbye, then never answering their letters. But it was also unfair of him to assume she didn't have her own demons to face.

She'd been so absorbed in the moment, she hadn't noticed the music had stopped until Roman dropped his hands.

"Thank you for the dance," he said, as though they were barely acquaintances.

Her body reacted for her, giving him a slight bow, then leaving before he could see the moisture threatening to fill her eyes.

She had only taken a few steps when Roman called out, "And Rose?"

She looked back over her shoulder.

"I hope you know I won't let you hurt them again." He gave her a hard stare.

Her eyes fell. Knowing she had caused them pain, even unintentionally, gutted her to her core.

Before she could respond, the crowd swallowed him.

She took the chance at freedom by retreating to a far corner. She scanned the room for Tristan. At last, she found his messy blond hair still on the dance floor. To her dismay, he was dancing with Kristiana—a pretty dark-haired girl who was unquestionably seeking his attention, throwing him flirtatious smiles.

She had enough of dancing.

She weaved in and out through the sea of people as stealthily as possible and slipped away into the night.

CHAPTER 8

Relief came with the chilly breeze nipping her skin as Rose exited the castle—a welcome contrast to the stuffy, hot ballroom. She drank it in, calming her rapid heartbeat.

Continuing along the stone patio, she made her way to the beach where she and Tristan had agreed to meet.

She descended the stoned steps as her shadow trailed behind. The stars and twin moons cast their bright, cool rays, lighting her way through the tall sea grass swaying in the wind.

The moment she reached the sandy shore, she took a deep, medicinal breath, casting her gaze on the sea. She hadn't entered its depths since she was a child, not daring to go more than ankle-deep.

Without thinking, her hands went to her hair, unbraiding it to let it fall freely. Relief came to her scalp as she shook it loose. She slipped off her shoes next, kicking them away to feel the cool, soft sand under her feet.

"Lovely night, isn't it?" a male voice said, shattering her solitude.

She swiveled, expecting Tristan. Instead, she spotted a dark-haired, very red-eyed Xavier sitting in the sand.

She instinctively stepped back. "Xavier." Her cheeks burned. "Sorry. I thought—"

"I was your lover, Tristan?" Xavier finished, his words slurring into a smirk. The same bottle from dinner rested in the sand between his ankles where he leaned against a large rock. Her face must have given her away because he let out a faint scoff. "Don't look so surprised. I've known you practically my whole life. You've had my brother wrapped around your pretty little finger for years."

She shot him a glare, wrapping her arms around herself to ward off the cold, ignoring his dig. "What are you doing out here?"

A sharp smile spread while he raised the bottle in a mock toast. "I was just out for a lovely evening stroll, of course. I don't care much for dancing. But the real question is, what are *you* doing here? Isn't that your ball going on inside?"

She hesitated, not sure how much she should disclose, but she didn't want to lie. "I'm waiting for him."

Xavier gave a bitter laugh. "Of course you are... Doesn't everyone just *love* Tristan?" He took another gulp of his drink, wiping his mouth sloppily as he stood up.

Her insides squirmed at his drunken gaze. "He seems to be the only one of you two with his wits about him."

Xavier's grin widened. "You *have* grown up." He took a menacing step towards her.

She was tempted to retreat, but she wouldn't give him the satisfaction. So she stood her ground, steadying her feet in the sand.

"Look at you with your hair down and shoes off," he appraised her. "You're so much more attractive, wild, like this."

He was taunting her now. "Excuse me, I think I'm going to go back inside." She tried to sidestep around him.

He blocked her path with one step. "So feisty. I like this Rose."

Now she *knew* he was just trying to get on her nerves. "Stop it."

"I'm just pointing out the obvious. I see why Tristan's so smitten with you."

The look in his eye unsettled her. It was as if a stranger stood there—different from the change with Roman. "What's gotten into you?"

"This is how I am now. Haven't you heard? Surely *someone* has told you what a disappointment I've turned out to be." He took another swig of his drink.

She sent a hostile look at the bottle, wishing she could rip it from his hands. "Don't do that; don't pretend you don't care. You may have everyone else here fooled, but you'll have to try harder with me."

"That's just it, *Rosy.*" He used her old nickname to antagonize her. "I *don't* care. Not anymore."

"Tristan told me what happened in Corrin. Is that supposed to be you not caring?"

Xavier grew deathly still, proving she'd struck a chord. He leaned in closer, the stench of alcohol reeking on his breath. "What did he tell you?"

She lifted her chin. "Enough."

"Oh, I doubt that."

Her brows knitted together. She had just opened her mouth to speak when she caught him staring at her lips, then back up to her eyes. The gesture reminded her eerily of Tristan.

"Don't." She knew what he was thinking. She stepped back. "Don't do that."

"Do what? You'll have to be more specific," he coaxed, stepping forward.

She refused to play into his distraction. "Don't let them take the crown from you."

Xavier's gaze ripped from her lips back to her eyes.

No more coddling. She was going to drag him up from whatever hole he'd dug for himself. A year ago, he would've done the same for her.

"That's exactly what they're going to do. But you already know that, don't you? They're on the verge of excluding you from your succession. I don't know what happened, but the boy I knew wanted nothing but to be king. Don't give them an excuse to take that from you."

Xavier remained deadly still, pinning her under his icy eyes as the wind blew her hair across her brow. "You know, you're the first one to say it. Everyone walks on eggshells, and you've been here all but twelve hours, and you just… come out and say it." He paused as if deep in thought. "But you should know I've already lost."

"That's not true. You have the crown, your family, this home. Talk to your father. Let him see—"

"You don't understand!" He slammed the empty bottle against the large rock next to him, breaking the bottom half as she recoiled. "I don't want to see burned corpses. I don't want to find ships full of good men at the bottom of the sea. I don't want to look down and be covered in the blood of my best friend. And what's more, I have no desire to be a part of this family." He came closer.

She rooted her feet to the sand, fully aware he'd had more than enough to drink, the scenario too reminiscent of her past. A stronger breeze blew over her, enough to sweep her hair back over her shoulder.

"I hate my brother, I hate my father, and I wish nothing but misery for both of them," Xavier fumed, the broken bottle still dangling in his hand by his side. He lowered his voice. "If you'd stayed away, perhaps Tristan would finally know what it's like to lose something."

She sucked in a nervous breath, looking at the bottle, then back to him. "You don't mean that."

His eyes grew hooded as he leaned in, drawing his lips closer. A long-forgotten ache surfaced—something her teenage heart had once dreamed of. He knew that. And now he played with that knowledge to get back at Tristan. A fire grew in her belly and spread through her limbs.

Before his lips could meet hers, her palm struck his cheek. Hard enough that his head whipped to the side from the force.

At an excruciatingly slow pace, his head turned back to her, his icy eyes flaring.

"That was low, even for you." She sidestepped him, but Xavier's arm shot out, yanking her back. "Let go." She struggled to escape, but his grip didn't falter as he attempted to pull her back. "I said let go!" She swung to hit him again.

He was faster. He captured her wrist, forcing her closer once more. In one swift motion, the hand gripping the shattered bottle swung at her, coming at a perilous speed. She didn't have time to dodge as the jagged edge sliced her neck.

She stumbled backward, tripping over the hem of her dress and falling onto the sand. She scooted back, putting a hand over her neck to discover blood leaking from it. Her horrified eyes lifted to his. She didn't dare breathe, too afraid to speak. Too shocked to move.

He loomed over her as his electrifying eyes shocked her. After a few moments, his gaze softened. For the first time since she'd been back, she glimpsed through them, like a transparent window into his soul, betraying an internal war raging inside. She swore she saw a flash of regret, but it was gone as quickly as it came.

He dropped the blood-streaked bottle. "For your own sake, Rose, stay away from me." Without another word, his drunken figure walked away down the beach until he disappeared into the night.

She remained still until he was out of sight, finally releasing the breath she'd been holding. She removed her hand from her neck, her fingers covered in crimson red. She clutched her neck again, alarmed. She couldn't let anyone see her like this.

Her eyes lifted to the sea. She willed herself to stand, stumbling toward the water. Her head spun—dizzy from rising too quickly. She didn't know how deep the cut was, but with each passing moment, her pain only grew.

Once she reached the damp sand, she tore the hem of her dress, sank to her knees, and submerged it in the water. She pressed the cloth to the side of her neck to staunch the bleeding, but as soon as it made contact with her skin, the salty water stung her. She cried out, jolting the cloth away. Biting her lip, she steeled herself for the sting as, with a trembling hand, she returned the fabric to her neck, shock coursing through her body.

With every wave the ocean sent, her knees sank deeper into the sand, ignoring the cold it brought. Tears hovered in her eyes, but she shoved them back, refusing to expend the energy.

In the distance, a happy voice beckoned. "I didn't realize when I said to meet at the beach that we'd be night swimming."

She closed her eyes, cursing to herself. How in Vallor could she have forgotten why she was out here in the first place?

When she didn't respond, his footsteps quickened. "Rose?.... Rose!" he exclaimed in horror, dropping to his knees by her side. "What happened?"

She didn't fully comprehend why her first instinct was to lie. Perhaps it was because she partly felt responsible for the whole situation. And Xavier was already walking on thin ice. If his father or Tristan found out what he had done... It could be the final crack to break them all. "I tripped... fell onto the rocks."

He gently lifted her hand away from her wound. His eyes widened with concern. "That looks deep." He scooped her up in his arms, cradling her against his chest. "You need help."

She tried to speak, but her vision started to blur. He stood and began rushing her back to the castle.

"You stay with me, you hear me?" he commanded. "Dammit, stay with me. I've got you. Stay with me."

The desperation in his voice... it sounded like he was trying to will her to live, but still, her eyes fluttered, threatening to close.

His grip on her tightened, crushing her into his muscular frame. "No. Hey, no, stay with me. Please… to the everlasting gods, *please*."

She held on to consciousness as long as she could, but within moments, her mind faded into darkness.

CHAPTER 9

The next thing Rose knew, she was in her room, safe in bed. She blinked several times to confirm she wasn't dreaming, unaware of what had happened until pain stemmed from her neck.

Her hand went to the wound, finding a thick bandage covering it. The blood that once stained her hair had been washed away, and her dress had been swapped for a fresh clean nightgown.

Her mother sat by her bedside, her creased forehead relaxing into relief. "Oh, honey." She took Rose's hand, still in her purple ballgown. "Are you alright? How are you feeling?"

"Mum?" She lifted her head off the pillow, still a bit disoriented. "What happened?"

"Tristan found you down at the beach. What in the world were you doing down there so late?"

Memories of Xavier flooded back. She reclined back onto the pillow. How she wished it was all a fleeting nightmare.

"I just needed fresh air… I was hot from dancing," she lied.

As her senses sharpened, muted voices drifted from across the room. The healer, the guard captain, and Queen Lenna were gathered in the far corner, their heads huddled together, speaking in hushed voices.

"She's awake!" her mother called to the healer.

Their conversation halted, and the healer immediately came over, placing his cold, clammy hands on her forehead. "How are you, my dear?"

"I'm fine." It was true enough.

The healer nodded, satisfied. "That's quite the cut you've got. But fortunately, it looks worse than it is. It's a clean slice, and it missed your artery by a few good inches, so there wasn't too much blood lost. I took the liberty of sterilizing and bandaging it. You have a few stitches, so I've instructed your maid to change your bandage twice daily until it heals. With the healing oil I've provided, you should recover quickly."

Rose gave a small, relieved nod, careful not to rip her stitches. "Thank you."

"Here." He took a glass of tea off her night table. "Drink this."

The queen glided across the room, stopping at the foot of the bed to inspect Rose for herself. Her worried eyes roved over her as she gripped the footboard with white knuckles. "What happened, Rose? Tristan said you fell onto the rocks?"

Rose took a sip of her tea, giving her time to scramble for a response. "Yes. I'm so clumsy. I must've tripped on my dress and fallen."

The queen nodded, glancing at her mother and sharing a skeptical glance, but the queen didn't pursue the matter further. "Well, my dear, now I know you are well. I must attend to the watch and give them instructions."

"Thank you, Your Majesty."

Queen Lenna gave a tight smile and exited the room, looking to be on a mission.

"Thank you so much for your efforts," her mother said to the healer, "but now I think my daughter requires rest."

The healer understood. "Of course, quite right. Please let me know if you need anything else." Without another word, he picked up his bag and left, closing the door behind him.

"Where's Tristan?" Rose asked, extending the teacup to her mother.

Her mother placed it back on the nightstand. "He was insistent about not leaving you. The guards practically had to force him out." Her face must've fallen because her mother added, "Oh, don't look so worried. I'm sure he's just outside the door waiting to see you."

Just then, a knock sounded, and Tristan poked his head around the door. His eyes went straight to Rose. "I'm sorry, but they said you were awake, and I had to see you myself."

Her mother threw her a knowing look before turning to Tristan. "Yes, of course." She stood, smoothing her dress. "I was just about to have a word with the guards. Would you stay with Rose for a moment?"

"Of course," he agreed, entering the room. He waited until her mother closed the door before he slouched into the chair next to her bed. "Are you alright?" He put a soft hand on her cheek.

"I'm fine, Tristan, really." She wrapped her fingers around his wrist to hold it there.

His thumb glided over her skin. "I'm so sorry I took so long. I should've left as soon as I saw you leave."

She didn't want him blaming himself. "It's not your fault I'm clumsy."

He withdrew his hand. "You know I don't buy your story. My mother told me the guards scoured the beach and found a broken bottle covered in blood. The healer said the gash was too clean to come from a rock. He says it had to be from something sharp… like glass."

She lowered her eyes for a split second, fear striking as Xavier's drunken face came into her mind. "Yes, um, I was drinking," she said, struggling to get around it. "I must've tripped and broken the bottle when I fell."

He folded his arms, leaning back into his seat. "I've never seen you drink a drop of alcohol in your life, let alone a bottle. Did someone hurt you? Did you see who it was?"

"No." She shifted her gaze downward, attempting to hide her lie. "No one did anything."

"Rosalie Versalles, look at me." His fierce eyes burned into hers. "Don't you dare lie to me again."

She avoided his gaze, playing with the hem of her sheets, still wishing she was a better liar.

Tristan's face grew stern as he leaned forward, resting his arms on his knees. "Answer me."

She let go of the fabric, knowing she couldn't lie again if she wished to keep his trust. "There was someone…"

His body stiffened. "Who?"

She closed her eyes, mustering the courage to say his name before she opened them again. "Xavier."

Tristan's arms dropped to his sides as the realization sunk in. His gaze slipped away from hers, his eyes darting back and forth like he was piecing a puzzle together.

"I don't think he was in his right mind," she explained, filling the silence. "He was drunk and upset by your father's public display of rejection. I spoke foolishly; I provoked him."

Excuses didn't matter. Tristan stood so quickly that he toppled the chair. She jumped at the noise as he strode toward the door. When she realized that he was going to take matters into his own hands, she tossed the sheets aside, standing up to follow. But she must've stood up too fast because black spots threatened to blur her vision, and she grabbed the bed frame for balance.

"Tristan, wait."

He didn't even turn around. "Get back into bed," he commanded, chiding her failed attempt.

Her body demanded she sit back on the bed, but she called after him, "Tristan, please don't. He wouldn't have done it if I hadn't provoked him."

He whirled back around. "That's your defense for him? What do you think would've happened if I hadn't come? For all I know, you would've passed out and drowned. I'm not protecting him anymore. He's crossed the line this time."

Tristan flung the door open and marched through, shouting for the guards. He spoke to the two men in uniform, pointing down the corridor. They both bowed and departed at once.

He came straight back in, wearing a treacherous scowl. "He knew. He knew you'd be down at the beach. Why else would he be at our spot?"

"I don't think he intended to hurt me."

"Of course he did."

She didn't let herself consider the possibility of it being premeditated. But she'd also witnessed the look in his eyes. It had been so estranged, so wild, so… unlike him.

Tristan's face softened at her fallen expression. He sat on the bed with her this time, his weight sinking into the duvet as he reached for her hand. In a firm motion, he drew her into his chest. She molded into him, his touch relieving the pain more than any medicine could.

"I just got you back. I don't know what I'd do if I lost you," he whispered into her hair as he gripped it. "I thought when you passed out…"

She squashed those thoughts before they could spiral. "I'm fine."

"I kept trying to come back to you during the ball. I'm sorry I didn't."

"You were busy." It took everything in her to pretend she didn't have to fight the urge to pry him from every dance partner.

He reached out through the moonlight streaming in from the window, cupping her cheek. "It nearly ripped me to shreds to see you dance with Grant."

She gifted him a subtle smile, secretly reveling in his jealousy. "Don't be mad. My mother insisted."

"I'm not mad at you." He slipped his hand to the back of her neck, bringing her close so she could feel his breath on her lips. "I'm angry I can't just marry you."

Her mouth grew into a smile. "After all this time, you'd marry me just like that, huh?"

"Just like that," he said in a heartbeat.

Her heart raced, nervously tucking her hair behind her ear. "I was so scared you'd hate me," she confessed, peering back up into his eyes.

Tristan knew what she meant. "I could *never* hate you. I'll admit, I tried hard to after you left. But as soon as I saw you walk back through those doors, hate was the furthest thing from how I felt." His lips went to her ear, his cheek brushing hers as he did. "I don't care how many come and try to steal you from me… I *will* have you, Rosalie Versalles."

Her thoughts became increasingly irresponsible as she leaned instinctually closer to his lips. But before they could meet, her mother reentered, saving her from herself.

Her mother stopped abruptly, taking in the scene and raising a discreet eyebrow at Rose. "Forgive me, Tristan, but I think it's time for Rose to get some rest."

"Of course." He stood from the bed as he reluctantly released Rose from his embrace. "I'll make sure two guards are at your door tonight.

Don't hesitate to ask them for anything." He bent down, lowering his voice so only she could hear. "If you want me to come back, just snap your fingers and I'll be here." He kissed her forehead before saying his goodbyes to her mother.

The door had barely clicked shut when her mother's astounded eyes shifted to her. Still, a glint of triumph rested in them. "I highly underestimated his attachment to you." After a moment of silence, her mother's tone grew serious. "I heard what Tristan told the guards… Was it truly Xavier?"

Rose stared at the dying fire, wishing she could say it wasn't true, but —"It was."

Her mother's face fell with pity as she gazed into the air. "Goodness, how the mighty have fallen."

"What will happen to him?"

"I'm sure they'll figure that out tomorrow." Her mother came and helped her back into bed before covering her up with the sheets. "But let's not worry about that tonight. Right now, you need to rest."

She wanted to protest, but she could already feel her eyes drooping. She laid back down as her mother tucked her in, planting a kiss on her head as she played with her hair.

Within a matter of minutes, her exhaustion after the events of the last twelve hours and the chamomile tea lulled her into a dreamless sleep.

CHAPTER 10

Rose woke to find another steaming cup of tea and honey beside her bed. Her maid, Thea, was already present and ready to tend to her. Together, they changed her bandage, and the wound already looked far better than it had the night before. Thea tried to adhere to the healer's orders by urging her to return to bed, but Rose insisted Thea help her into the sage-green dress she'd chosen.

As Thea helped her dress, Rose finally noticed the three large bouquets waiting for her on the table. "When did these come?"

The timid blonde gave a sly smile. "Last night before the ball. I'm surprised you didn't see them… I heard Prince Tristan came back *three* times to check on you."

A smile broke through as Rose bit her lower lip. Redirecting her focus to the flowers, she approached the beautiful arrangements to read the notes attached. Thea followed behind, still tying up the back of her dress.

Rose went to the blue hydrangeas first. Her favorite.

Good luck tonight. I can't wait to dance with you.
- Tristan

She lowered the note, replaying the scene of them dancing the night before, thrown back into his sea-blue eyes, knowing she'd gladly drown in them.

She cast her feelings aside like she did every minute of every day and moved to the next flower arrangement—a lavish, colorful arrangement of lilies.

No flower can compare to your beauty, but these will have to do.
- Grant

She almost snorted. She was somewhat surprised, but she supposed she shouldn't have been. Grant was used to getting his way. He wouldn't give up, especially with her mother's encouragement. She didn't stand a chance of refusing if they were on the same side.

She put the card on the table before moving on to the last bouquet.

Her heart stopped midbeat.

An arrangement of beautiful black roses rested elegantly in a gold vase that looked like it had been melted into its beautiful shape. She peered into the bouquet, but she didn't see a note. She lifted the vase—nothing. When Rose asked Thea about it, she said it hadn't come with one.

She stared at the roses in wonder. They weren't pure black, but rather a deep, rich shade of red—surprisingly beautiful for such a somber color. Who would select such a bloom?

The question brought a memory to the forefront of her mind.

"I'm so sorry for your loss," a compassionate stranger said to her, repeating the same phrase for what felt like the hundredth time.

She plastered a smile on her face. "Thank you," she said, accepting the flower arrangement.

The elderly woman patted her hand before joining the others gathered around the grave.

She was left alone while the others readied for the burial. Numb to the cold, biting wind swirling around her, she stared at the pile of freshly dug dirt, shadowed by the gray sky above.

"Rose," her mother called, awakening her from her daze. "Will you please put these with the others?" she asked, handing her another flower arrangement. "I don't know who they're from. The tag must've gotten lost with the rest of them."

She took the vase. "You know you don't need to make such a fuss over this," she whispered. "He wasn't worth—"

Her mother cut her off with a cross look. "We will not talk like this—not now, not here. Not today. Do you understand me?"

She bit her tongue. "Yes, Mum."

Her mother nodded sharply. "Now please do as I've asked, then come help with the food."

Rose took a deep breath, looking down at the flowers—an arrangement of black roses in a beautiful gold vase. What a terrible color to choose, so depressing and melancholic. Who would select such a bloom?

But the longer she looked at them, the more she knew they were exactly what she needed. They symbolized that a part of her was dying, saying farewell to a chapter she was eager to forget.

They were a pool of beautiful darkness.

Just like her.

Thea was still tying her laces when Rose's mother appeared, pulling Rose out of the memory.

"Oh good, you're up," her mother said, relieved, hastily shutting the door.

Rose glanced at her, then did a double take. Her mother looked… disheveled. Her mother was *never* disheveled.

"What is it?" she asked, worried someone had died.

"The king and the high council have called for a tribunal for Xavier." Her mother came straight over to assist Thea with her dress laces, her fingers working overtime. "They've requested that you attend."

Her eyes widened in disbelief. A tribunal? For last night? She'd assumed Xavier would face consequences for assaulting a court member, but a tribunal? Such gatherings were mainly for individuals guilty of serious offenses against Cathan, typically foreigners. Holding one for the successor was unheard of.

It could only mean one thing—they were considering throwing the succession.

"Why do they want me there?" Rose asked.

"I don't know. I can only assume they will ask you to testify." Her mother cinched the last lace and gripped her shoulders, forcing her to look at her head-on. "Listen to me, Rose. The high council insists on your attendance, but I told them that you are still recovering. You don't have to go if you don't want to."

She weighed her options. If she didn't attend the tribunal, the king and the high council would be left to their own assumptions to decipher Xavier's fate. And if Xavier was indeed denounced, how could she bear to live with herself, knowing she could have altered the result? What Xavier did was terrible, but he didn't deserve to be stripped of his succession because of it.

"I want to go."

"You understand you owe that boy *nothing*," her mother emphasized. "Are you sure?"

Rose thought for another moment and nodded. "Yes… Yes, I'm sure."

Her mother accepted her wishes without a fight. "Okay." She pivoted Rose's shoulders to face the floor-length mirror. "Then let's finish getting you ready. You're going to need all the confidence we can get."

CHAPTER 11

Rose had never set foot inside the high council chambers, nor had most in court. It was a room used solely by King Henrik and his high council for private meetings and affairs. It was made up of three rows of tiered benches along the walls. At the front, a long rectangular wooden table stood on thick, stubby, hand-carved legs with sun markings, providing seats meant for the king and his twelve council members. Three narrow windows behind them let in the morning sun's rays, warming the stuffy room.

She was startled by the number of bodies that greeted her. She had expected only the king and the council members, but the rows lining the room were packed. Despite the crowd, an unsettling silence lingered. She and her mother settled into the front row nearest to the king's high table.

She was painfully aware of the stares and whispers directed at the bandage that covered her neck. She wished she could have left her hair down, if only to shield it from their prying eyes. Nonetheless, she sat up straight, refusing to show any sign of weakness.

King Henrik sat slumped with an invisible weight on his shoulders. She would wager her last gold coin that he'd not slept a wink last night, the bags under his eyes a solid testament. Harriet, Roman, and Queen Lenna were seated directly across from them, with an empty seat beside

Roman that she presumed was intended for Tristan, who had not yet arrived. The queen's face betrayed no emotion, but her fragile form appeared even more delicate than the night before. Harriet was an open book, her eyes flickering about the room nervously as she bit her lower lip and twisted the ends of her dark hair.

Roman was among those who openly stared.

She braced herself to confront his gaze.

His amber eyes blasted straight through her defenses, holding her accountable. A pit settled in her stomach, tangling it into knots as his face morphed into a scowl. She reminded herself she wasn't the one on trial. She didn't want this any more than the rest of them did.

Only when Tristan took her hand did she notice that he had sat beside her. His grip was like a tether, grounding her.

"How are you?" he asked, his eyes flickering down to her bandage.

"Better." Her throat was dry as she said it. "Shouldn't you be sitting with your family?" She didn't bother looking to see the sneers directed her way.

"I'm right where I'm supposed to be."

She gave him a faint smile, squeezing his hand while she fought the impulse to rest her head on his shoulder.

The massive wooden doors swung open to reveal two guards escorting Xavier in, his wrists and feet chained together. The metal clinked with each step, sending an echo throughout the quiet room. His usual well-kempt dark hair was matted, and he was still in his clothes from the previous night. A black eye and various scratches marred his handsome face, his knuckles bloodied and bruised like he'd been punching something or someone. He kept a neutral expression, his eyes locked straight ahead.

Seeing him in such a pitiful state stabbed her all over again.

Xavier walked up to the high table and halted in front of his father and the high council, a mere few feet from where she sat. His foul odor was a mixture of alcohol and vomit.

The king frowned as he stood, the unspoken agitation simmering beneath his gaze more potent than the hot morning rays spreading across her lap. "Xavier Montague, you are accused of assault by one of the members of this court. The offense occurred last night on Cathan's shoreline near the hour of midnight, making the crime fall under the jurisdiction of this court." He paused as the spectacled scribe behind him hunched over a small desk, scribbling furiously with a quill. "How do you plead?"

Xavier didn't miss a beat. "Guilty."

A wave of whispers flooded the room.

King Henrik's frown shadowed into something darker. "Do you have any defense for yourself?"

"None," Xavier drawled.

She gaped at Xavier, confounded. He wasn't even going to contest it. She didn't know what she'd expected, but she'd hoped he might explain *why*. So that she could discover if he felt even a hint of regret or remorse. But he just stood there with his hands at his sides, with that stupid blank stare that made her want to stride up and rattle him awake.

One of the men in the council rose to speak. She recognized him as Lord Martin, a short man with beady eyes who valued his status more than anyone else in the room combined. He had a short, thick beard, while his hair was thinning, forming a ring around his shiny scalp. Although she didn't know him well, she found herself irritated by his tendency to insert unsolicited opinions whenever he felt like it. In past social gatherings, she had deliberately kept her distance whenever possible. "Your Majesty, may we ask a few questions to the accuser?"

The king's eyes shifted from Lord Martin to her. "Rose?"

The pack of wolves honed their attention on her, but her gaze went to Xavier, who still kept his eyes locked forward.

She stood, keeping herself steady. For once, she was thankful for her loose-fitting dress, hiding her shaking frame.

Lord Martin began, "Miss Versalles, the council, and no doubt many of the court members, are trying to understand what would motivate the next heir to the throne to jeopardize his succession by harming someone… such as yourself." He gave a tight, lifeless smile as his gaze ran over her with scrutiny. "It makes one wonder what was said… or done."

She met his dissecting gaze with forced confidence. "If you're insinuating I instigated or wished for this, you are sorely misguided."

Lord Martin inclined his chin. "Of course not, my lady, of course not.

Forgive me; I hope I didn't cause offense. Only… the council does not believe it is in Xavier's nature to be violent."

Tristan sprang up. He composed himself enough to keep his tone neutral. "Lord Martin, you are aware that Xavier's violent actions caused a war."

Lord Martin was unfazed by the sudden outburst. In fact, the gleam in his eyes could almost be described as conspiratorial. "Quite right, Prince Tristan, quite right. However, in that instance, there was a fairly defensible motive, don't you agree?"

"If you think killing on impulse with no forethought of the consequences is a defensible motive to start a war." Tristan gave a tight smile before dropping it entirely.

Lord Martin's face broke out into a nasty grin as he faced Tristan head-on. "It appears you and Miss Versalles have grown close in her short time back," he observed all too casually. "I'm told it was you who found her on the beach. Quite lucky you were there. Do you often go strolling on the beach at midnight?"

She stole a glance at Tristan. Lord Martin's words dug into something she hadn't considered until now. If the council became aware of their attachment—which clearly they were—they'd see that Xavier was the only obstacle preventing Tristan from pursuing the throne. It had happened many times in history. Previous heirs had often been targeted and murdered, leading to new succession periods and turmoil in the province. She recalled one history lesson in particular when Queen Lucidia allegedly killed her brother in a tragic hunting incident. Rose wouldn't be the first to be accused of concocting a plan to seize an opportunity, and she wouldn't be the last.

She clasped her hands, locking her knees to keep herself upright. So this was what they all thought of her? Of Tristan? They truly thought they'd consider ruining Xavier to make room for Tristan's reign? Which, in turn, would make Rose the next queen of Cathan? Did they truly believe they'd just committed treason?

Her initial reaction was denial, refusing to accept that they believed her capable of such deceit. Yet another emotion overshadowed everything else.

Fear.

More specifically, fear that Lord Martin's implications and falsehoods might not seem so far-fetched to others. She could understand how it might make sense to an outsider. But if they believed she would do something that evil… she was standing on quicksand.

"Enough!" King Henrik thundered, directing a berating glare at Lord Martin. "This tribunal is for Xavier. It appears *I* will have to ask the important questions."

Lord Martin bowed, silenced to submission, perching back on his chair—more like a snake coiling back into its hiding spot.

The king faced her directly. "Was Xavier on the beach with you last night?"

She glanced at Xavier again, who, like a stubborn mule, refused to meet her gaze. She considered fibbing, but she knew how bad she was at that. It would only make things worse for Xavier if she couldn't execute it perfectly, so she simply answered, "Yes."

"Did you threaten him?"

"No."

"Did you intend to do him harm?"

"No."

"Did you have any weapons?"

"No."

"Did he strike you?"

"Yes."

That was enough for the king. "Sit," he commanded. He was addressing her but gave Tristan a look that clearly instructed him to do the same. He focused again on Xavier as his silent rage erupted. "Whether or not you were antagonized, it does not matter. A successor does not yield to *whim*!" He roared the word as he pointed a finger at Xavier. "You let emotion rule you like an animal. I expected you to learn from your catastrophic lessons, but you have proved me a fool one too many times. Do you have anything to add to your defense before your sentence is passed?"

Xavier's blank expression did not falter. "No."

A savage scowl unfurled on the king's face. He leaned forward, placing his hands on the table. "This is merely the tip of the iceberg on the long list of your offenses. The assassination attempt on the king of Vertmere, the battle at Fort Merth, the unauthorized invasion into Khali, and the numerous fleets sunk in the Meridian Sea—all of these, along with the countless dead bodies, now rest on your weak, pathetic shoulders. Your pride, arrogance, and stupidity are just a few reasons the council and I can no longer support you. Not anymore. We have reached a decision." The king's eyes flickered to the queen for a minuscule moment, a flash of sorrow for her sake, and then it was gone. "Xavier Montague is hereby stripped of his succession and banished from these lands."

The room erupted with astonished gasps, followed by murmurs and cries of rebellion. The queen's eyes glistened as she hung her head.

The ringing in Rose's ears dulled the voices into muffles.

This couldn't be real. Not because of last night. Not by what she had ignited. What had she been thinking, poking him like that when it was evident he was struggling? How had she believed things could return to how they once were? To simply have a heart to heart, then expect him to listen to her?

Roman had been right. She'd been a fool.

Xavier accepted his fate without resistance as the guards grabbed his arms and began hauling him off to the dungeons.

Before she knew what she was doing, she stood. "Wait!" she shouted above the rest.

The room fell silent, all eyes turning to her. Even Xavier, who had avoided eye contact, looked at her, surprise evident beneath his indifferent façade.

"Rose? What is it?" the king asked.

She took a step toward him, knowing full well it wasn't permitted for someone of her rank to address him in such a way. "Don't banish him."

The court's confounded gazes moved to the king, waiting for his reaction.

"Rose, don't," Tristan whispered from behind her.

Her eyes remained fixed on King Henrik, bracing herself for the sting of his sharp tongue for daring to interrupt. But it appeared that his fondness for her allowed for it. He waited for her to continue.

"You and the council have denounced him from the throne. I know that cannot change. But don't banish him. I..." She looked back at Xavier, whose unreadable gaze rested on her. "He and I... we used to be close. I don't want to be the reason he is banished from his homeland... Please."

The king's stare pressed into hers like a lion eyeing its prey, but she refused to cower. She wouldn't allow herself to.

The room was so quiet, only the sound of distant waves from the open window filled it. His silence lasted so long that she was sure she'd face harsh punishment. She braced for his wrath.

"You wish for me to retract my sentence?" the king clarified at last in a low voice.

"Yes." She couldn't take back her words now.

He scanned her as if seeking something hidden. "Do you sincerely wish it?"

"I do."

At last, his face softened. "You never cease to amaze me with your generosity," he said with glowing admiration. "But I'm afraid that I cannot change my sentence. There is an important lesson to be learned. Xavier's banishment remains. As of today, the succession is reopened."

Her heart plummeted, but she bowed, accepting his answer this time.

She turned to Xavier, and for the first time since she returned, she recognized him. There was her best friend—the boy she would have once given a left lung for. But before anything else could be done, the two guards pulled him away. She watched him until he was out of sight.

Soft hands gripped her shoulders. "Come on, honey," her mother said, looking over her shoulder at the vultures circling. "We should go."

Tristan took her hand in his, forcing her to look at him. "Go back to your room. Don't do anything until I come for you."

She nodded numbly, following her mother out in a daze.

Good gods, what had she done?

CHAPTER 12

Later that evening Rose sunk into her vanity chair, still absorbing the news. Her mother had gone downstairs on an errand and hadn't returned, likely managing damage control. She'd attempted to fill the time by reading one of her favorite novels, but even that had failed to capture her attention today. Thea had kept her company until she was summoned back to her duties. Hours had passed, and she still hadn't heard anything.

As the sun dipped closer to the horizon, she let out a deep sigh, placing the makeup brush she had been playing with back on the vanity. Rising from her seat, she made her way through the adjacent doors to the balcony, leaning on the railing.

The once-sparse clouds had disappeared as the sun fell, painting the blue sky with gentle strokes of orange, purple, and pink. The soft colors floated on the waves below, flooding the horizon. Sunsets in Cathan were always like this: unmatched to all others.

A sight Xavier would never see again.

She still didn't understand. Why hadn't he defended himself? Why did he care so little about his future? Or his family? Did he despise them all so much he'd rather spend the rest of his life in exile? Countless questions swirled, and she feared she'd never get answers… or maybe she could.

An idea popped into her head. It was a terrible one, and it would probably get her into trouble if she was found out, but she had to try.

She didn't stew on it long, acting before she could come to her senses.

~

She reached the southeast wing in record time, the halls oddly barren for this hour. She assumed everyone was gathered in the grand hall, chatting and wagering on the next successor. It wouldn't surprise her if they were already putting forth nominees. It disgusted her to think of how many had prayed for this opportunity.

And she'd just given it to them on a silver platter.

She navigated the winding staircase and continued down the stone corridor, turning right towards the dungeons.

When she arrived at the iron-gated door, she found two guards stationed at the entrance.

"Open the gate," she commanded.

The taller one put his hand up in protest. "My lady, I don't know if—"

"Please," she pleaded, her voice strung with desperation. "I'll only be a moment."

The guard hesitated, contemplating her request. To her surprise, he agreed. "Stay six feet from the cell door," he cautioned, letting her through.

"I will, thank you."

She stepped over the threshold and walked down the dark, wide stone corridor. The air felt different here, like a damp swamp on a hot, humid day. She resisted the urge to cover her nose as she glanced into each dim cell. All empty. It wasn't until she reached the final cell that she spotted him.

He was sitting on a flimsy straw-stuffed bed, hunched over as he rested his elbows on his knees. His hands were interlocked on the back of his neck, his head hung down, staring at his feet, dark hair concealing his face. The sparse torches left him shadowed as she studied his pitiful frame.

"I thought I told you to stay away from me." Xavier's rough voice ground out without moving from his hunched-over position.

She took a few small steps closer to his cell, doing her best to quell her nerves. The longer she stood there, the more she regretted not thinking this through. "I came to ask, why? Why did you do it?"

He ignored her, offering nothing.

She tried a different approach.

She lifted her gaze to the dancing flames of a nearby torch. "You know, when I watched you go through your succession trials, I remember being so worried for you. You were only eighteen, going up against three fully grown men, and I thought there was no way you could manage it... But against all odds, you won." Her gaze returned to him. She crept closer to his cell, her voice growing stronger. "You *won*, and not just by the skin of your teeth. Every obstacle thrown at you, you not only beat but excelled at. Your men followed you into the heart of the bog without question. You outsmarted a Sphinx. You climbed to the top of a mountain with bloodied hands and three arrows embedded in your back. I remember scolding myself for ever underestimating you. I promised myself I would never do it again... but now, I don't see that man anymore."

She waited.

No response.

She dug deeper. "Do you remember when you saved my life at the river? When you sprinted for miles, carrying me?"

No response. Not a sigh, a scoff, a glare. Nothing.

She ground her teeth in frustration. Her questions became rhetorical. "After all that... I suppose I'm just wondering. What happened? What did *I* do? I don't understand what I could have possibly done to make you hate me so much."

She stood there for what seemed like ages, hoping he'd say something, anything. After a long moment, she realized she was misguided in expecting any answers. She was wasting her time.

She went to leave.

"I hurt you," he uttered at last, his voice so low it was almost unrecognizable.

She turned back. He was not only speaking but standing, moving across the cell, clutching the bars of the door with his bruised knuckles as he finally looked at her. "I *hurt* you," he repeated. "Do you even get that? Are you really that stupid?"

A flash of anger flared within her. "I was there. I know what you did." She lifted her chin and exposed her bandage. His eyes flickered to it as they hardened. "But it doesn't help the guilt of knowing I sparked this."

He hit the bars, and she jumped as the reverberation echoed. "Dammit, Rose!"

The sudden commotion alerted the guards down the hallway, but she raised her hand to signal it was all right.

Xavier gripped the bars tighter, his voice unforgiving as he said, "You don't get to feel guilty for my decisions. *I* own them." He glared at her with disgust—with her or himself, she didn't know.

Their eye contact was severed when an angry voice echoed through the dungeons.

"Open the door!" Tristan's voice echoed.

She swerved towards the iron doors while Xavier muttered a curse under his breath.

Within moments, Tristan was at her side.

"What the hell are you doing down here?" Without waiting for an answer, he took her arm, trying to drag her from the cell.

"Tristan, stop." She tried to yank her arm away from him, but he didn't move. Not an inch.

"Yes, please," Xavier drawled. "Keep going, and you'll end up in a cell just like me."

In a flash, Tristan's fists pounded on the barred door, while his other hand shot through the bars, gripping Xavier by the neck.

"Tristan!" she yelled.

"You are dead to me," Tristan spat with a vile sneer. "If I ever see you anywhere near her again, I swear, brother or not, I will break you." He released him, shoving Xavier backward.

She didn't get another word in before Tristan grabbed her hand, forcing her away. She didn't resist this time.

They didn't speak as he led her through the corridors. He didn't let go of her hand until they were outside on the main patio. She would've stopped to admire the geraniums lining the railings if she wasn't so preoccupied.

She readied herself for his disapproval. "Tristan—"

"You asked for him to be *pardoned*?" He rounded on her, his boiling anger steaming out of his ears. He ran his hands through his hair, tugging at it. "What the hell, Rose? What part of *he hurt you* do you not understand?! What *possible* reason could you give me that makes sense!"

"Tristan, that's not who I grew up with." She pointed back toward the door. "What the hell happened to him?"

Tristan let out a harsh sound, something between a laugh and a scoff. "Rose. Things. Have. Changed. *People* change. He hurt you, and you're asking what's wrong with *him?* In what world do you think he deserves even another *second* of your attention?"

She folded her arms. He was right. She kept expecting things to be the same, but they weren't. It was a fool's wish. Xavier had gone through so much in the past year—things she couldn't imagine.

"What if I told you you were right? I shouldn't have gone to see him."

"So why did you?"

"I thought I saw something," she snapped. She took a deep breath as she started again, this time calmer. "When I was away last year, I helped in the medic tents when troops came through Canteran. I saw what war did to the men who survived. I can't describe it, but it was like they were bleeding internally. I did everything I could to help them physically, but they still couldn't recover. To everyone else, they seemed fine, but when I looked into their eyes... they were drowning." She looked off at the distant shore. "Last night on the beach, I thought I saw the same thing in Xavier. I thought he just needed someone to see if he was bleeding. But I was wrong... It was naïve of me."

His expression eased with understanding. "I know you feel like this is your fault, but this has *nothing* to do with you. He wanted to hurt you because he was angry at me. If this is anyone's fault, it's mine. I provoked him at dinner."

"Then why do I feel horrible?" she said quietly.

Tristan's anger disintegrated into nothing, his voice softening. "Because you're an amazing person who only wants to see the good in people, no matter how undeserving they may be." His hand slipped into her fragile one. "He's only been banished, Rose, not hung."

A pause fell over them as she peered at their intertwined hands. "So what happens now? When will they have the open ceremony?"

"Tonight."

Her eyes bolted upward. "So soon?"

"They are eager to have a successor. 'There must always be an heir,' remember?"

She looked out again, biting her lip. That meant tonight, the council and the king's kin would all rally together to nominate and announce their four chosen candidates for the throne. After that, the candidates would have to participate in three challenges, just like Xavier had eight years ago.

"You know what this means, don't you?" Tristan said.

Her eyes grew with understanding. Tristan could become the next king of Cathan. With nominations and backing from both the council and his father, Tristan would have a high probability of winning. Of course, there would be others to challenge him, but he'd have a strong advantage.

"After this is over, I'll finally be able to marry you," he said, leaning his forehead to hers.

A tingling sensation coursed through her limbs as the blood surged from her heart. Countless times, she had wished for the moment when they could finally be together, but she hadn't allowed herself to believe it was possible. But here it was, close enough to touch.

A smile crept onto her lips. "I thought you were talking about being king."

Tristan returned the smile and shook his head. His hand gently grazed her cheek while the other slipped around her waist, pressing her into his chest. "No... No, I don't give a damn about that."

Her eyes closed, savoring the words as his breath brushed her face.

When she opened her eyes, his gaze had dropped to her bandage. His smile faded the longer he looked at it. "Does it still hurt?"

"I'm fine, really."

"That's not what I asked."

Yes. Yes, it did hurt. As a matter of fact, it throbbed with every heartbeat.

"A little."

He cringed, then his eyes hardened. "I need you to promise you won't see him again."

An image of Xavier's pitiful figure in the dungeons flashed in her mind. There would be no reason to, so she saw no harm in saying, "I promise."

Tristan gave a relieved nod. "Come on." He slid his hand into hers. "Your mother will be wondering where you are."

CHAPTER 13

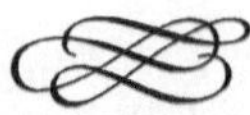

That night, Rose found it hard to believe whether she had entered the grand hall or a foreign province. Unfamiliar faces loomed in every direction—voices and the clanking of forks and knives filling the air. The temperature was at least twenty degrees warmer than the halls, even without the normally lit fireplace, leaving only the torches lit out of necessity.

She and her mother were about to sit at a table when a hand grasped her arm, startling her. The unexpected touch propelled her straight into a hard chest.

"I'm sorry," she apologized, until she saw it was Grant. "Oh, good. Just you."

Grant flashed her a wide grin. "You've hurt my feelings." He leaned in to whisper, "Though next time, I'll be sure to stand closer." He straightened, his attention transferring to her mother. "Would you care to join me?" He gestured to a few open seats.

Her mother accepted without a second thought. "Of course! We'd be delighted."

Grant glanced at Rose, to see if she'd accept as graciously as her mother.

She forced a smile. "Of course," she repeated her mother's words, reluctantly taking his hand as they sat, Rose sitting between Grant and her mother. She threw a fleeting glance at Tristan who was already sitting at the head table, cursing her luck to be stuck next to Grant instead.

"It's such a lovely time of year, isn't it?" her mother remarked while pouring herself a drink. "The garden is just absolutely gorgeous, don't you agree, Grant?"

"To be honest, I haven't had the pleasure," Grant said, gathering food onto his plate. He offered the dish of ham to Rose, but she shook her head.

Her mother gasped, appalled. "Oh, you must! It's gorgeous. I'm sure Rose would be more than happy to give you a tour. She's there so often when we're here, I swear only the caretakers and the queen know it better."

A hint of a smirk played on his lips. "That sounds like an excellent idea. What do you say, Rose?"

"Only if it's something you wish to see," she prefaced with a polite smile, making a mental note to reprimand her mother later.

"Of course it is. Your mother makes it sound irresistible," Grant said, sipping from his goblet.

"How about tomorrow night after the feast is over?" her mother suggested, ignoring the death stare from Rose. "After all, the garden will be well lit for the festivities."

"It's settled, then," Grant said.

Rose darted her eyes between them—they were both far too pleased with themselves. Gritting her teeth, she cut into her steak a little too thoroughly, scratching the plate.

Before she could even take a bite, the side entrance doors flew open to reveal the king. Instantly, everyone rose and bowed as he strode swiftly past the tables. Once he reached his chair, he signaled for them to take a seat.

"First and foremost, I want to extend a warm welcome to everyone," King Henrik began. "This evening, we come together to honor our ancestors' legacy and mark the start of a new succession period. It was just a few years ago when we convened in this hall for this very reason. Although it was a challenging decision to announce another succession, I am proud to introduce the first candidate nominated by the high council."

He placed his hand firmly on Tristan's shoulder. "Prince Tristan from the House of Montague!"

The room filled with loud cheers, but Grant didn't so much as look up, lazily taking a drink.

The king continued, "And we have three other kinsmen nominated to enter the succession as well. From the north, my nephew, Grant, also from the House of Montague!"

More claps and cheers filled the room as Grant stood beside her, his handsome grin splayed across his face as he raised his hand. His nomination came as no surprise. Grant's parents, sitting at the far end of the table, shined with pride as they clapped loudly.

"Representing the east… Dawnton, from the House of Sansburry!" the king announced, prompting Dawnton to stand up with pride. The man she'd danced with the previous night lifted his dimpled chin as cheers grew louder. Of course he'd be nominated. The sheer wealth he could offer the crown was enough to earn anyone's backing. In fact, she wouldn't be surprised if that was the very thing the Sansburrys had used to secure the nomination.

Finally, the king announced the fourth candidate. "And representing the south… Emmett, from the House of Alterridge!"

Beth's older brother rose, puffing out his chest in an attempt to make himself look more intimidating. He was nearly a mirror image of his sister in male form—tall, slim, and easy on the eyes. Their family had historically been rivals for the throne; however, it had been nearly fifty years since anyone from their bloodline had claimed a succession.

"A lively chap, that one," Grant whispered to her over the cheers. "I don't think I've ever seen him smile. Once."

It pained her to admit but she agreed. Emmett was many things, but a charmer wasn't one of them. "Are you worried about your competition?"

Grant shook his head. "Not in the least. The only one I really have to worry about is your lover," he drawled with a smirk.

She rolled her eyes, about to retort, but the voices and claps quieted again.

The king stayed silent as he looked over the crowd like he was…

contemplating something. The crowd waited in silence. "I wish to make a fifth nomination."

A loud rumble of surprise spread like fire throughout the grand hall. A fifth nomination? That hadn't happened in over a decade, long before the Montague line had obtained the throne.

"Last but not least... Rosalie, from the House of Versalles!"

Shock rippled through the high council, gaping at their king, who had clearly gone rogue. The royal family looked just as baffled as everyone else. From the utter alarm on Tristan's face, she doubted he had any knowledge of his father's intentions either.

Rose barely registered any of it as each heartbeat thundered in her ears. It didn't make sense. She couldn't be in the succession. She was no one. Sure, anyone within the court could theoretically be nominated, but never had anyone outside the strong bloodlines been chosen.

The court looked at her expectantly, waiting for her to stand.

Summoning her courage, she pushed herself up, clenching her hands to quell their shaking. The tension was so thick, every movement she made felt like it faced resistance. She avoided eye contact—she didn't need eyes to see their objections. She didn't need ears to hear their whispers, or lips to taste their judgment, or even hands to feel their disapproval.

In the midst of the quiet, the king clapped. The sound echoed, encouraging a weak wave of claps to follow. She couldn't force a smile or a wave. Instead, she offered a slight bow, and took her seat as soon as it was appropriate.

She leaned toward her mother. "Did you know anything about this?" she whispered.

"Not a damn thing," her mother replied, taking a long, self-medicating sip of her wine.

"What do I do?" She tried to swallow, but a lump got stuck in her throat.

Her mother plastered a smile onto her face to maintain appearances as the court continued to stare at them, whispering behind their hands. "I don't know, but smile. People are watching."

The king reclaimed the floor with his booming voice. "This year's succession challenges will test our candidates in every way. For the first challenge, each candidate will lead their company and attempt to retrieve a golden sun amulet. To do this, we will hold a rally in which they will have a chance to sway a hundred men to join their company. Once the companies are decided, the real challenge will begin.

"One of the most important things a leader can learn is how to earn the respect and support of the men who serve them. To know when to stop and think, or when to surrender… or to break every last bone!" the king said louder. "In two weeks, we will begin with the rally to see who has what it takes to lead the people of Cathan."

With a triumphant smile on his face, the king raised his glass. "*To succession!*"

"*To succession!*" the court shouted back, raising their chalices. Rose lifted hers with them, taking a long, *long* drink.

Beside her, Grant placed his empty goblet on the table, smirking as he leaned closer to whisper, "Perhaps I have another opponent to worry about after all."

CHAPTER 14

Two hours after the opening ceremony concluded, the king, Tristan, Rose, and her mother met in the king's study. Although her neck throbbed with every pulse, the pain was nothing compared to the more pressing matters.

Like why the king had chosen to put her in the succession.

The study felt smaller than she remembered. It had high ceilings, but every nook and cranny was stuffed with books, parchments, and maps, except for the large window looking over the sea. The dark, relentless rain from the storm left crooked streaks on the glass, allowing the burning flames from the fireplace to cast shadows throughout the room.

The king settled in his chair across from Rose and her mother, sliding an old mug aside to clear the parchment-laden desk, and leaving Tristan to brood by the fire.

"What in Vallor were you thinking, Henrik?" her mother said, so cross she risked addressing him informally. "How could you do such a thing without consulting us first?"

The king interlocked his hands on the desk. "I know you're upset—"

"*Upset*?" her mother scoffed. "You *know* how dangerous these successions are."

"I agree with Evelyn," Tristan said, doing a masterful job of keeping his tone even. "The nomination alone puts a target on her back."

"I will assign a skilled personal guard to stay with her at all times," King Henrik reassured.

This did not appease her mother in the slightest. "How is that supposed to help? There's no protection during the challenges!"

"She is every bit as prepared as the other candidates," the king quipped, unyielding. "Her intelligence is enough to rival that of any successor this castle has seen in decades. She has the heart of a natural leader, and I know she is more than capable of the task."

Her mother glared so fiercely, she was amazed the king didn't have a hole burned through his head. "You ask too much this time."

King Henrik didn't reply as he exhaled, looking to Rose instead. "Rose? What do you think?"

She absentmindedly lifted her eyes from her lap, refocusing on him. As much as she'd like to own up to all the wonderful things he claimed, it was madness. Absolute madness. How could someone like her, with no political influence, power, or wealth, possibly be suited to be in the succession? Her goal was to marry and secure a future for herself and her mother. That was it. She had no desire to be involved in the challenges.

She found her voice. "Though I am flattered by Your Majesty, I believe you're overestimating my hand; I don't possess the qualities to tempt anyone—let alone the council—to support me in the succession."

"You see?" her mother pipped in. "She doesn't want it."

The king gave her mother a rare impatient look, clenching his jaw as he looked from her mother to Tristan. "Could you both please leave us? I need a moment to talk to Rose—alone."

"But—" her mother protested.

"Evelyn," the king warned with a dominant stare. "This *must* be Rose's decision."

Her mother's expression withered, admitting defeat. "Fine." She stood, putting a hand on Rose's shoulder, whispering, "I'll be just outside if you need me."

Rose gave her mother's hand a light squeeze before she left.

Tristan's stubborn eyes challenged his father, but he kept his voice even and controlled as he said, "Xavier nearly died in his succession. *Twice*. Are you prepared to make Rose suffer the same fate?"

The king's commanding eyes drilled into his son's. "I believe you heard me when I said the decision is up to Rose."

Tristan's eyes hardened, flickering to her for confirmation. She gave him a nod, wanting to hear what the king had to say. His mouth tightened into a straight line, but he respected her wishes and followed her mother out.

Finally, she and King Henrik were left alone, alongside the crackling fire. Silence invaded as shadows roamed the stone walls.

"It's been a long time since just the two of us talked. It must seem like I haven't cared much about your hardships, but I care a great deal." He rubbed his face, letting out a deep breath. "Forgive me for being straightforward, but I'm tired, and it's been a long day. You must understand. However the events played out, I sincerely mourn that Xavier will not be my heir." He peered down into the contents of his mug. "He was everything I could have wished him to be. Without asking, he stepped up and fulfilled every unspoken expectation placed on him. To see him lose his succession is disheartening... but the true pity is to see him lose himself."

She reached out to take his rough hand, trying to absorb some of his pain. "It didn't need to be done for my sake."

A twinkle of a smile appeared on his face as he patted her hand. "Yes, well, we aren't here to talk about Xavier. You and your mother are dear to my heart. I'm not blind to my family's attachment to you over the years—each of them, despite what recent events must look like." He spoke with a new tenderness now. "I have come to admire you, Rose. I have watched you over these past years, and despite your trials and misfortunes, you've still grown into the beautiful young woman I've always hoped you'd be. I dearly missed you during your absence... Your mother has told me about your present situation."

She let go of his hand, sliding it back to her lap as her gaze fell. "How much did she tell you?"

"Everything," he said with an all-knowing stare. "Even about the night at the tavern."

Her eyes snapped up as ice crept in. Her fingers clenched around the armrests of the upholstered chair. Without warning, tears pricked at the backs of her eyes, but she shoved them back, desperate to forget.

He grieved with her as he studied her bandage. "I'm only sorry it was one of my own who added another scar for you to carry... I hope the healer was satisfactory?"

She nodded, eager for the change of subject. "Yes. Perfect, actually."

"I remember you were quite the student yourself." He grinned as he reminisced. "I'm sure you could have healed yourself if you hadn't lost so much blood. Your tutor was always impressed with your consistent marks. Let's see, I think she once referred to you as a 'walking sponge,' if I remember correctly. She told me, 'This girl has beauty *and* brains. She'll steal many a man's heart one day.'"

A smile appeared on her lips despite herself. "She didn't favor me for my beauty or brains. She favored me because I snuck her my pastries during our lessons."

The king bellowed a hearty laugh as the twinkle in his eyes shone brighter. "I wondered why she always had a hard time getting up on that damn horse of hers." His smile slipped away slowly. "But I've thought about that conversation often over the years and realized that she was speaking in more than just romantic terms. You reminded me of that today when you tried to pardon Xavier despite what he did to you... despite what I or the court thought. You were able to see past the action and find empathy. It is a highly underestimated characteristic."

He looked at her like he saw more than the girl sitting before him, as if he saw potential—what she could achieve if given the opportunity. She couldn't help but feel grateful for the belief she could be a part of something greater. To think she'd be brave enough to try. Somehow, his faith stoked her own.

"I'm starting to realize just *how* attached Tristan, in particular, is to you. He tells me you two have a mutual attachment for each other. Is this true?" He carefully watched for her reaction.

She tensed, her gaze dropping to her hands. She couldn't get her mouth to open, so she merely nodded.

Despite her worry, he didn't lose his warmth. "I couldn't be happier to have you as a part of my family," he said in such a way she knew he meant it.

She let out a breath—but her relief was short-lived.

"But the gravity of the situation is more heavy than a union..." His frown became grave. "There is a dark storm headed our way, Rose. Unrest brews on the horizon. More catastrophic than you can imagine. The bloody storm you've witnessed with Vertmere is no more than a light rain. We will be bathed in it when the hurricane comes. And we must fortify if we are to survive." His gaze turned distant. "I have a dream to reunite the seven provinces to reinforce against that mighty storm. This alliance with Vertmere, along with you and Tristan, may just be our best chance to brace for it."

She stared at him. This was no bluff. There was no foul play in his eyes. This faceless enemy was real, and King Henrik was not shying from it. It pressed a hefty weight on her shoulders.

"I'm speaking to you first because I know you'll heed my words better than my son. There will be a time for you two to sort whatever is between you, but right now, you must focus on the succession if either of you wants the slightest chance of winning. Lord Martin's words today have sparked rumors that you two planned this scheme."

Fear bloomed in her chest. "You can't believe—"

"No," he cut her off, but his eyes didn't retreat. "But it doesn't matter. It is how they see it, and the council will look for any reason to dismiss you both from the succession. That includes treason against Xavier. But you see, if your attachment is true, there is an advantage to having you both in the succession."

Her gaze drifted to the rain still pattering on the window. If she and Tristan entered, they wouldn't be competitors but allies. If one were to win, they *both* would. It would solve her financial worries, and she and her mother could move into the castle permanently. The rumors would be put to rest, and no one would question her place in court again. If she or Tristan happened to win—by some outlandish miracle—they would be married, and they would both have the crown anyway. It would double their chances of keeping the throne in safe hands.

"I would never force you to enter the succession, and I'm not saying there isn't great risk, but please, for the sake of all Vallor... say you'll think about it. You may give us your answer at the rally."

She paused. Nothing but the sound of raindrops on the window and the crack of embers filled the room as she weighed the balance she was about to tip. "I'll think about it."

His shoulders relaxed and he nodded, seeming to accept her answer. "That's all I ask. You must be exhausted. You may go."

She took her dismissal and stood, giving him a bow before moving toward the door. She'd barely put her hand on the handle when he spoke again.

"And Rose?"

She turned back.

"You must know I thank the lost city above you're safe," he confessed. She swore his eyes became glossy, but it could have been a trick of the light. "Truly. I am glad you and your mother are back with us. I hope you choose to stay this time."

A warmth spread through her chest, taken aback by his sentiment.

She gave her only real father figure a sweet smile, bowing again and leaving before her emotions could get the best of her.

Because, by the gods above and below, she had a great deal to think about.

CHAPTER 15

The longest day of Rose's life came to a close as she made her way back to her room. Her mother offered to join her, but she persuaded her that the two guards stationed down the hall would be enough to safely return her to her chambers.

She yawned as she closed the door to her room. It was dimly lit by flickering candles, left clean and tidy; Thea must have already made her rounds.

She removed her shoes, unfastened her dress, and tossed it aside. She reached for her nightgown, hanging neatly on the chair by her vanity. After that, she lifted her hands to her hair, carefully taking out the pins from her updo.

On her way to bed, a cool draft floated over her. She turned to find the balcony doors slightly cracked open.

Strange. I wonder if Thea forgot to shut them.

She closed the double doors, pain throbbing in her neck from the motion. She massaged it, realizing she hadn't changed her bandage.

She retraced her steps to her vanity, removing the old bandage and cleaning her wound with a wet cloth before reapplying the healing oil. She looked back into the mirror—this time, her reflection wasn't the only one she saw.

She spun to confront the intruder, but before a scream could escape her lips, a rough hand smothered the sound.

This was it. This was how she would meet her end—a stranger taking her life out of resentment for being nominated for the succession.

The icy-blue eyes were a dead giveaway.

Xavier.

Her eyes widened. What was he doing here? How did he get inside? Was he here to seek revenge on the girl who took the throne from him?

She fought to break free, but he held her firm. "Don't scream," he said. "I promise I won't hurt you."

She held still, considering running, but she'd never make it. She could go for the hidden sword she kept stowed away under her bed, but she'd never reach it in time.

Slowly, he removed his hand from her mouth. She didn't scream, even though every bone inside her wanted to.

Xavier was cleaned up now, dressed in a black cloak that covered him from head to toe, with warm furs lining the thick fabric. Though his eyes were tired, he seemed sober and restored to his former self.

After the shock wore off, she wrapped her arms around herself, the air still chilly from the draft. "How'd you get in?"

Xavier eyed the double doors leading to the balcony. "I thought it was obvious."

She followed his gaze. Of course—she should have known. He'd often scaled the walls up to her room when they were children, a habit that earned him frequent scoldings from his mother.

"What do you want?" she asked, mustering a glare.

"I need to know why you requested me to be pardoned."

She blinked. That was it? He had gone through all that effort to scale the castle walls to ask her a silly question? Among all the scenarios she had anticipated, she wasn't prepared for that.

"What?" She raised her brows.

"I don't have much time. The guards will notice I'm gone soon." He inched forward, distracting her as his citrus scent filled her nose, thrusting her back to that day by the river—when she'd been cradled in his arms with the warmth of his body against her mangled one. His hands clenched so vigorously on the fabric of her dress that he nearly tore the garment in half.

"Why?" he demanded again, pulling her out of the memory.

"Because I still care about you," she snapped.

Xavier's body became still, staring at her like she'd just said something obscene.

"Is that all you came here for?"

He studied her for a long moment before softly saying, "You really are a fool, Rose."

Her eyes narrowed—*the nerve of him.*

"Well, if that's all you came to say, you can leave. Unless you came here to finish what you started on the beach." The glow of the candles flickered across her face. "You'll never get a better opportunity. If you want to kill me, you should do it now."

"I wouldn't," Xavier bit back, at last a hint of humanity shining through. "I could never in a million years truly hurt you. I only did it because I knew my father wouldn't throw the succession if it were anyone else. I made sure that scratch was shallow and nowhere near any place that would permanently harm you." His gaze flickered down the exposed wound.

His sincere response made her pause. Xavier was excellent with daggers and arrows. He never missed his target. If he wanted to inflict permanent damage, he could have. But she still didn't understand one thing.

"Why would you want out of the succession?"

Xavier's eyes built an invisible barrier to protect themselves. "Because… being here is just a painful reminder that I don't deserve to be here at all." His tormented gaze lowered to his leather gloves. "My father is right. I shouldn't be king. I don't deserve to be… Not anymore."

Her heart softened. She couldn't judge anyone who'd dealt with war—only left to imagine the horrors that would plague his mind and peace forever.

But it still didn't change the fact that he'd used her.

"So cutting me open and running from your problems was your solution? To leave everything and everyone behind?"

He prowled to her, stopping only a breath away from her face as his savage eyes locked down on to hers. "Like *you* stayed a year ago? When we all had to stay and bear it while you left? What makes you exempt from the same fate?"

There it was. Just like Roman, Xavier was angry at her for not returning.

"It wasn't my choice." A half truth. "And besides, you made it clear you didn't care if I stayed or left."

"Of course I cared," he hissed. He opened his mouth to continue, but he closed it again, shaking his head and dismissing it. "You know what? It doesn't matter. I'm leaving. This is the last time you'll see me. I don't expect you to forgive me... but I couldn't leave without you knowing I would never *truly* hurt you."

Before she could even form a thought, he headed for the door.

She stared at the void he'd created, figuring out what to feel. But he was leaving in the next few seconds, and she didn't want to have regrets. She cursed, knowing she couldn't let them part like this. Not after all that they'd been through.

She finally jumped off the vanity chair to follow him. "Xavier, wait."

He had barely grasped the latch when she placed her hand on top of his.

Xavier stiffened under her touch as he peered down at her hand over his. His eyes radiated pain—as though her touch hurt him. He turned slowly to face her, his hot breaths hitting her face.

With a look as strong as armor, she barreled past his invisible wall. "Everyone makes mistakes, Xavier. And I'm sorry to break it to you, but everyone in this world will go on making them. But that's *life*; if we don't make mistakes and take risks, we're not living. Don't punish yourself so harshly for past mistakes that you won't live to make new ones... I know I won't."

The mask he wore slipped away, letting her catch a glimpse of his soul.

There was the man who'd spent late nights reading with her, quizzing her endlessly to prove who was smarter. The man who'd looked up at the sky, found a constellation shaped like a rose, and proclaimed it hers. It was as refreshing as plunging into icy water on a scorching day—shocking every pore, but also made her feel entirely alive.

His crisp breath brushed against her skin, slowly tucking her hair behind her ear. Her breaths became shallow as he tilted his head and whispered, "It's good I'm leaving, because there is no way in hell I could stay and watch that bastard have you… Tristan better take damn good care of you."

Her eyes fluttered shut. He said it like… like she meant something to him. He'd never seen her as anything but a little sister—he'd said so himself. But as she opened her eyes again to meet his, she couldn't help but wonder if he had ever felt something… more. Or if it was her teenage heart still grasping at straws.

Xavier leaned in, his lips nearly brushing hers as he spoke. "Goodbye, smart-ass," he whispered.

Her heart halted at the sound of her old nickname on his lips.

It caught her so off guard, she couldn't even form a sentence before he opened the door and left.

She stared at the door, silence ensuing. She should feel comforted by the fact that he'd come to see her, but all it had done was fill her with more questions.

Xavier had been angry at Tristan *before* he'd lost the crown. So what was it exactly that he was so angry about? What could be so grave as to merit all of this hate?

The more she thought about it, all roads led to Tristan—Xavier's resentment, anger, and even his outbursts toward her seemed to be solely directed at his brother. But Tristan claimed to have no idea why… or did he? If so, what horrible act could Tristan have done to make Xavier willing to lose everything he'd once had?

She didn't know. But what was more unnerving was the thought that perhaps she didn't know Tristan as well as she'd thought she did.

"Goodbye, Xavier," she whispered into the empty void.

CHAPTER 16

In the coming days, the servants dedicated hours to preparing the castle—setting up additional rooms, stocking pantry supplies, and rearranging the grand hall for all the supporters coming for the succession. The groundskeeper had outdone himself, trimming the boxwood bushes on the patio into a perfect replica of Cathan's sun symbol. They even added extra torches to light the gardens at night, showing off Rose's favorite bed of summer carnations.

She knew Xavier's departure would cast a gloom over the castle, but she didn't realize how ominous that cloud would be. Stares and whispers trailed her wherever she went, some out of harmless curiosity, others with harsh judgment. She would be thankful when the visitors arrived, if only for the sliver of distraction they'd bring.

As promised, she had acquired a personal guard, Zareb. He was a formidable man, his wide, muscular frame living proof of his prowess. His deep brown eyes were set in rich beautiful brown skin and framed by buzzed black hair. He was ten years older than her and rumored to be an exceptional fighter, hand-picked by the king himself. He'd just returned from the war and hailed from the Semaria province, a fact that explained his refined combat skills. Despite his intimidating appearance, she soon discovered he was a man of few words, which she found oddly refreshing.

Since her debut, she waited for suitors to call on her, but none did. Not a single one. While she felt a twinge of relief—and a slightly bruised ego—a growing concern gnawed at her. Was she not the catch she and her mother had thought? Were the rumors surrounding them worse than she had feared? Perhaps they deemed her too low in rank?

Rose thought she might be imagining things until the morning she had tea with her mother on her bedroom balcony. A gentle breeze came from the west, brushing the tablecloth against the stones at their feet while the distant waves crashed onto the shore.

"Rose, I'm worried," her mother confessed after setting down her teacup on the rounded glass table.

"Why? What's happened?" she asked, putting her cup down beside her mother's.

"Nothing, that's what," her mother snipped, whipping out her fan and fanning her face in tiny flutters to keep the heat at bay. "So far, no one besides Tristan and Grant have shown the slightest interest in courting you."

She had a hard time being upset by the fact. "Maybe it's for the best… I'd only disappoint them."

Her mother stopped fanning herself. "You most certainly would not. I was there. I saw how they all looked at you. They couldn't keep their eyes off you! After the succession nomination, men should be lined up at the door. It just doesn't make sense." She leaned in, lowering her voice. "You haven't told anyone of our circumstances?"

Rose glared at her, appalled. "Of course not."

Her mother leaned back, flapping her fan once again. "Then what in Vallor are they waiting for?"

"Perhaps they don't like me as much as you had presumed," she said, playing devil's advocate.

"No, I have a keen intuition when it comes to these things. I'm never wrong… But I suppose there's still time. Tristan will surely be glad to hear —" Her mother stopped, her eyes widening. "Tristan."

"What about him?"

"*He's* the reason you don't have suitors!" her mother exclaimed, like she'd just solved a mystery.

Rose gaped in disbelief. "Mum, don't be ridiculous."

"I bet he's made it his mission. It's certainly something he'd do."

"What of Grant? He asked to court me."

"Oh, that's because Grant is the only one who isn't afraid of Tristan. He still can't officially court you until the king permits him to do so, and Henrik has already made it clear he won't allow for it until the succession period is over." Her mother paused, her eyes searching the air. "The next time you see Grant, I want you to welcome his advances."

Rose recoiled at the thought. "Why should I when I have Tristan?"

"That's just it. You *don't* have Tristan. He's no one's to have. At least not yet."

Rose pressed her lips together. Her mother was right, of course. Tristan was as much hers as he was the next girl's. She had to keep the council thinking she and Tristan were innocent in all of this, and the best way to do that would be to court someone else.

Unless… unless she joined the succession. If she did, it wouldn't matter if she had any suitors. She wouldn't have to deceive anyone into marrying her. And if Tristan won, she'd still be queen. If they helped each other, they'd have a good chance at winning back the throne.

She smoothed out the white napkin over her lap. "There is another way," she said quietly, looking up at her mother.

Her mother knew precisely what she hinted at. "No."

Rose scooted her chair closer. "Think about it. If I join the succession, it could help our chances at securing a place here."

"No. I won't let you risk it." She shook her head.

She grasped her mother's soft hand, looking straight into her eyes. "Isn't this what I've been training the last year for? Why I've had to hide under all this fabric?" She gripped at her dress.

"We trained to *protect* ourselves, not to throw ourselves into life-threatening situations, least of all the succession. I thought you didn't care to be queen."

"I don't. But if Tristan wins the succession, I'll be queen then, too. Either way, I'm destined for it."

"And if either of you don't win?"

She shrugged. "Then we'll be no worse off than we were before."

Her mother sighed, looking out to the horizon, giving her hope she was at least considering it. She stayed silent, letting her mother think.

Finally, her mother looked back at her, but didn't say a word.

"I could do it," Rose said, trying to convince herself as much as her mother. "You know I could."

At last, her mother's resolve broke. "Alright. I'll make you a deal. I don't want you to decide now, but *if* you decide to join the succession, I'll only support your decision if you promise to keep *all* avenues open until we are sure of our position, and that includes courting Grant and any other suitable matches. Agreed?"

"Agreed." After all, Rose was sure it wouldn't come to that.

Her mother gave a sharp nod. "And if you're going to contemplate doing this, you'll need a firm polish on your combat skills. We'll need someone more skilled than your last trainer. Someone discreet, who will keep the knowledge hidden to give you the element of surprise..."

Rose glanced at her bedroom door, aware of who stood guard just beyond the wooden frame. "I think I know just the person."

Rose flew through the dense woods on horseback, Zareb trailing behind. The clear sky easily allowed the sunlight to stream through the gaps of the leafy branches, casting dancing shadows across the forest floor, offering just the right conditions for the wild plants to thrive. The smell of damp soil filled her nostrils, still wet from the light rain last night. It was a welcome change of scenery from the castle's hustle and bustle.

It had been months since she last rode bareback, which was a shame, because she couldn't keep the smile off her lips as she urged her steed to its limits. Her brown hair flew wildly in the wind, relishing the simple joy of a silly race. Zareb was at her heels, quickly closing the distance.

He surged ahead right before arriving at their destination, claiming victory.

As they neared the small stream, they both slowed down to a stop, letting the horses drink.

"You ride well," Zareb praised, catching her off guard by taking the initiative to speak first. "But I still won, so not that well, I'm afraid," he poked with a dry tone, still straight-faced.

She raised an eyebrow. It was the first sentence he'd strung together that consisted of more than three words, and teasing no less. "Well, you're the soldier. I would hope you'd be."

They climbed off their horses and tied them to a stumpy tree trunk. She gave her horse a thankful pat before walking into a small clearing. Zareb followed suit, not far behind.

"What are we doing out here?" He seemed more at ease now that they'd gained distance from the castle. Maybe he was just as glad for the scenery change as she was.

She shrugged. "I just needed to get out for a while."

"Is that why you kept looking over your shoulder to make sure no one was following?"

She stopped, his dark eyes fixed on her. He was too perceptive for his own good. Even knowing it was probably a fool's errand, she decided to put aside casualties and get straight to the point.

She faced him head on. "I need to tell you something, and I need you to promise to keep it between us."

A hint of curiosity shone in his eyes. "I promise."

Zareb's expression appeared too sincere to be dishonest. Over the past few days, she had grown used to having Zareb by her side, even a bit fond of him. And maybe it was because the king had trusted Zareb first, but she'd come to trust him, too.

For the first time, aside from the royal family and Beth, she thought maybe she could have a real friend.

So she opened up to him. "I've been training in combat for the past year. I'm a decent fighter, but my last trainer doesn't hold a candle to your physical skills… I know this is improper of me to ask, but I was wondering—I mean, I was hoping—if you'd be willing to continue my training? I'm afraid I can't pay you, but—"

"No," he said, saving her from her ramblings.

Her hope sank, his hasty answer making her falter. "I know it's a small risk—"

"A *small risk*?" Zareb exclaimed in an mock-whisper, looking over his shoulder at the empty forest. "You have more enemies here than you think. The council does not want you on that throne. If they find I'm aiding your chances in the succession, and if you don't win, I could lose my position and title here. Not to mention, it's not customary to train a lady of the court."

She understood his hesitation. To rise to Zareb's title and rank within Cathan's guard was no small feat, especially coming from an outside province. If he went against the council's wishes and they saw it as disobedience, he could lose the home he'd worked a lifetime to earn. He had to keep the favor of the council if he wished to remain in Cathan.

"I'm the first woman of the court to be nominated for the succession in nearly fifty years," she said, challenging his rebuttal. "I would say customs and traditions are damned at this point, wouldn't you? If I join the succession, how will I stand a chance at the throne without proper training?"

"Then ask the king to get you a proper teacher. I'm not the one you need." He tried to sidestep her, but she blocked him.

"You're the only one people won't be suspicious of if we spend time alone together. Please, Zareb… You're the only one I trust."

He paused, searching her eyes that were sure to be reeking with desperation.

"I promise I won't be wasting your time," she added, just on the off chance that it was one of his reservations.

Zareb's stern brow grew together like she'd offended him. "I'm not worried about time or money." Another long silence followed as Rose patiently waited for him to think. But to her utter dismay, he shook his head. "I'm sorry, Rose, but I have my own reasons. You'll have to find a different teacher."

She tucked in her chin, trying to hide her crestfallen face. She had no choice but to accept his answer this time. "Of course. It was too much to ask in the first place."

Zareb studied her a moment longer, looking like he was about to say something, then thought better of it. He cleared his throat, gesturing to the horses. "Come on… We should get you back."

CHAPTER 17

At dinner, Rose looked for Tristan, but with a multitude of unfamiliar faces swarming the grand hall, he was nowhere to be seen. She, her mother, and Zareb were confined to a cramped corner, far from where they normally sat.

Rose managed to steer clear of any social interaction by indulging in wild turkey and roasted asparagus, making sure to save room for the raspberry tart she'd been eyeing—so delectable that her taste buds demanded a second helping.

She was just about to retreat to her room when Grant appeared out of thin air.

"Rose." His infamous handsome grin was plastered on his face. Didn't he ever get sick of smiling all the time? "I'm glad I caught you. I saw that the gardens are lit tonight. What do you say about that tour?"

She wanted, with every fiber of her being, to say no, but before she could answer, her mother put a hand on her forearm, digging her fingers in to keep her from denying him. "Oh, I'm sure she would love that! She was just telling me how she needed to stretch her legs."

Rose forced a smile. "Why not?"

She let Grant lead the way, weaving them through the crowd and out through the double doors.

The trees in the garden swayed in the soft breeze, rustling the leaves above. The summer hydrangeas were now in full bloom, with freshwater trickling beneath them through small trenches. The additional torches lit their path perfectly in the darkness, adding their light to the two moons. Zareb and Grant's guard followed quietly behind them in the shadows, giving the two space.

"You've made it a point to keep yourself scarce around the castle," Grant noted as they strolled down the path. "I hope that it hasn't been my doing."

She wrapped her arms around herself, warding off the chill. "No. Of course not. I've just been keeping myself busy."

"Busy from what, I wonder." He tilted his head.

"More than you imagine," she said, tucking her hair behind her ear. "I'm not the most popular guest in the castle at the moment."

"It is strange that I don't have more suitors to compete with," he agreed.

"I suppose both you and my mother gave me more credit than I deserve."

He smiled like a sly fox who knew something. "I suppose."

She quirked an eyebrow. "You don't agree?"

"Oh, come on, Rose. You must know."

She stared at him, bewildered.

"Tristan has made sure no one else pursues you," Grant said, confirming her mother's theory. He plucked a leaf from a bush along the pathway. "He's gone as far as threatening each and every suitor who has expressed interest in you."

Rose immediately shook her head in denial. "You're wrong. He wouldn't do that."

He inspected the leaf in his hands, twirling it with his fingers. "Go ask any of the men you danced with at the ball. I'm sure they'll tell you the same."

She fixed her eyes on the pathway ahead as something ugly twisted in her gut.

They stopped when they reached the central fountain. It towered over both of them, fanning water high out into the air, only for it to cascade down to the lower tiers and eventually gather at the base.

"I have to ask," Grant said, lifting his clover eyes. "You've made it clear you have no interest in me, but I can't help but think you and your mother must have some reason to believe a marriage with Tristan is unobtainable. Or your mother wouldn't go to the trouble of pushing me onto you. If I'm right, Tristan must think this so-called 'reason' is irrelevant because he has made it clear he'll marry you anyway. Or..." He dropped the leaf, watching it flutter down into the water and drift away.

"Or?" she prodded, curious to hear his other theory.

Grant snuck a side glance. "Or perhaps Tristan is much more attached to you than you are to him."

Her eyes returned to the fountain. "That's not true. The situation is... complicated."

He flashed a smile. "Is that why you choose to tolerate me?"

Her eyes narrowed, not liking how he presumed to know so much. "Would you rather I didn't?"

For the first time, Grant's face turned somber, gazing at her sincerely. He edged closer, his tall frame towering over hers. "I'd rather you choose to do so because *you* want to, not because it's what your mother or anyone else wants. Look, I'm not asking you to marry me... I'm just asking for some time."

Her throat tightened as she slowly lifted her eyes to meet his. Her first instinct was to say no, but she'd promised her mother she'd keep all avenues open, even if she thought them unnecessary.

So she gave him hope.

"I think I can do that."

His large, handsome grin returned. "I can ask for no more."

They made their way around the fountain, choosing the southern path this time. They passed a group of spectators who became silent as they passed, then began whispering amongst themselves as soon as they were out of earshot, showing no effort to hide their gossiping.

"It seems as though I'm the envy of the castle," Grant observed.

She put a hand to her chest dramatically. "I'm sorry about that. I know how much you hate the attention," she replied with sarcasm.

Grant smirked, his sparkly white teeth practically glowing in the dim light. "You know, you aren't what I thought you'd be."

She kept her eyes on the blooms, running her fingers over the velvety petals. "What do you mean?"

"I thought I'd have trouble liking a girl like you."

Her eyebrows rose. "A girl like me?"

"Gorgeous girls with money, genes, and status like you are usually a bit more… pretentious. I admit that this is what I believed you to be from the first time I saw you. But you possess quite a charm about you. So much so that you've won over not only the king's favor, but, dare I say, his affection as well. That speech at the ball had everyone reeling. You have all the cards laid out in your favor, and you still have a humble aura. It's quite the breath of fresh air. It's as if you…" He drifted off.

She cocked her head, curious. "If I what?"

His eyes hung onto hers. "It's as if you're too good to be true."

She shifted, letting the shadows hide her face before he could see the flicker of shame. If only he knew she didn't have two gold coins to rub together. He wouldn't be so keen on her then.

Still, his flattering words chipped away at her defenses.

"You make me sound like a rare gem," she teased, flipping her hair with a coy smile. "So tell me, do you think I'm a master manipulator like the rest of them?"

"No, though you *have* done extremely well for someone like yourself. Worming your way into the affection of the king was brilliant. But knowing your mother, I think the effort was more on her part than yours. Just look at you, an upper-middle-class House being nominated for the throne. So tell me, are you going to accept the nomination?"

She fiddled with her fingers. "I haven't decided."

Grant sidestepped, cutting her off mid-stride. She looked up to find a fire burning in his eyes. "If you are, I suggest you weigh your options before putting all your eggs in one basket. Tristan isn't the only player in this game, and personally, I'd rather see you and I as allies than enemies. I want you to wear the same colors as me at the rally."

His bold request took her by surprise. If she did what he asked, it would mean she'd be wearing the same colored dress as his tunic, implying an alliance, not only for the rally but for the entire succession. Alliances in past successions weren't common, but they had proven to be effective when made carefully.

The longer she searched his eyes, the more she began to piece together his true intentions. Grant knew that if she chose to enter, she and Tristan would become a force to be reckoned with, and he was looking for a way to stop it.

And getting under Tristan's skin would be an added bonus.

She bit her lip to refrain from saying something she'd regret. "You know I can't do that."

He tilted his head, trying to catch her eye. "Why, pray tell?"

Her eyes sharpened in defiance. "I'm not going to be used as a pawn in this game by you or anyone else. If you want to win the succession, you'll have to find another way."

A dangerous smile crossed his lips. "I see. Well, it was worth a shot. Like I said, I can't be mad at your loyalty. But soon, I think you might find yourself switching teams, especially when Tristan starts to crumble. It will happen sooner or later during this succession, I promise you."

A molten fire grew inside her, but her etiquette kicked in as she managed to keep her mask on. *All avenues open*, her mother's words rang in her mind. "I think you're underestimating him."

He didn't look the least bit bothered. "Perhaps, but I've known Tristan his entire life. He's not level-headed like Xavier—well, the old Xavier. He has more to lose, which means he has more weaknesses. *And* he has one the whole province can see, and I'm staring at it right now… He'd better tread carefully, or the throne won't be the only thing he'll lose."

She wanted to lash back and deny the claim, but she held her tongue, choosing not to take his bait.

Instead, she changed the subject, directing her attention to a large, closed bud. "Are you familiar with the lunar flower?"

The evasion didn't faze Grant as he approached the flower with her. "No. Should I be?"

She shrugged. "You might want to be. It does have quite useful healing properties. It's a moonflower."

Grant lifted an eyebrow in question.

"It means it only blooms in darkness," she explained, using the torch snuffer on the side of the path to extinguish the nearest torches. After a brief moment, as complete darkness crept upon the petals, the fist-sized bud opened, exposing its midnight-blue and purple petals.

She pointed to the whitish-yellow pistil at the center. "If you boil these with water and drink it, it will help reduce swelling around a wound and ease the pain. I used it a lot when I helped in the medical tents last summer." She glanced up to find Grant wasn't looking at the flower.

His eyes flickered with surprise. "You helped in the medical tents?"

"Yes. My mother was insistent last year that I learn more about the benefits of healing," she lied.

In reality, it was her previous trainer, Warren, who had insisted that she learn. He'd said that if he was going to teach her how to kill and destroy, she would have to learn how to heal and save as well. He'd said life was a delicate balance, and she wouldn't be able to understand one without the other. Without that understanding, one would be led into darkness. Though he had been too old physically to spar aggressively, he gave her a unique spiritual outlook that made a lasting impression on her. She mourned deeply after his passing just a month ago.

"I had a nurse last year," Grant said. She'd nearly forgotten, from all his lightheartedness, that he, too, had just returned from war. "Though she wasn't nearly as pretty as you. I'm quite jealous."

Her brow quirked. "Of what?"

"Of the men you helped." He took a subtle step towards her in the darkness, all trace of humor gone. "To have you touch my bare skin is something I've only dreamed of, and they got to experience it."

Her cheeks burned. She opened her mouth to respond, but no sound came out.

Grant's cocky grin returned. "Where's that cheekiness now, Rosalie Versalles?"

She clapped her mouth shut. A cold smile grew on her face. "I'd have to find you bleeding out on the floor before I touched your bare skin."

Grant simply laughed into the cool air.

They explored the garden until she'd led him down each path.

Throughout their walk, Grant tested her knowledge on the various flowers and herbs, making small talk.

After finishing the tour, Grant escorted her to the castle and wished her good night.

And to her utter surprise, she no longer found Grant as repulsive as before.

CHAPTER 18

Rose tucked a stray hair behind her ear and peered down the dark, empty corridor. It was nearly midnight when she returned from her walk with Zareb, who followed her dutifully through the drafty halls. Judging from the lack of people, most of the court had already retired for the night.

She covered her mouth as she yawned, ready for sleep, and she planned on doing just that until the echoes of voices reached her ears.

She didn't think much of them until she heard her name being spoken. She recognized those voices.

She halted. Raising a hand, she signaled for Zareb to do the same and pressed her finger to her lips.

Cautiously, she peeked around the corner, Zareb doing the same. Five high council members, including Lord Martin, stood together in a circle in the middle of the next corridor, their backs to her.

"It just doesn't make sense." Lord Orrin's voice carried through the hall. "To throw the poor girl in the succession is borderline cruel. She has no chance of winning; to place her in danger and under this scrutiny just to prove a point is downright imprudent."

A rumble of agreement echoed from them in disapproval.

"And why nominate someone who lacks the basic core skills to lead a province?" Lord Stoddard joined in—a large, fat man with a thick amount of blond hair. "We all know of the looming dangers that approach—raids happening every other day, cities being ravaged, and goods stolen. Why, just days ago, another city was reduced to ashes. If we are to retaliate, we'll need a formidable leader. Not some middle-class girl from Canteran."

She frowned, thinking back to her conversation with the king. Was this the same unforeseen threat he had spoken of? He hadn't mentioned the continued raids. Weren't they working for a peace treaty? Who would be doing this, if not Vertmere? She didn't know, but the thought of another city burning made her insides threaten to exit.

Lord Rensin interrupted her thoughts. "I quite agree. We'd be a laughingstock to Vallor. And rumor has it that her father was a *hefty* gambler—my friend's son swore he saw him enter a slave auction one night."

Her heart dropped, her limbs locking into place to keep her upright.

"And how are we to trust her after her involvement with Xavier's denouncing?" Lord Martin chimed in, his gaze shifting cryptically. "How are we sure she didn't plot this situation for her own benefit? Do we want a leader capable of such evil? We all know what happened to King Sorthen—why he was found cut to bits a few months into his reign, only to discover his son had done it to reopen the succession! How are we so sure she isn't another throne seeker?"

The others mumbled their agreement.

Lord Beckett rubbed his forehead as he sighed. "Just let us pray she has enough common sense not to enter."

Her hands clenched, their words only adding to her self-doubt. It pained her to admit that their concerns were valid. She was raised to be a lady, not a leader. She didn't know the first thing about managing a court, let alone an entire province. Just look at this lot. If she did become queen, managing the high council would be the bane of her existence.

"It sounds like this topic should be brought to the king's attention," another voice added.

She recognized that voice all too well. Peeping around the corner once more for confirmation, she spotted Lord Barron—a tall, handsome man with dark hair with matching scruff, and striking dark-blue eyes that demanded attention. Known as a lone wolf, he had neither a wife nor family. Despite being in his late forties, she had often witnessed his brilliant combat skills during training sessions. She even recalled once that he'd gifted Rose her favorite flower from Ostlyn, having gone to the trouble of bringing it all the way home. That small act of kindness had remained close to her heart for years. If Rose had to choose a favorite high councilman, it would be him.

The huddled group of men disbanded from their circle at once.

"Is there a reason you are all gathered?" Lord Barron said. "A meeting that I wasn't aware of?"

Lord Martin recovered first, putting on a fake smile. "No, of course not, Lord Barron. We were just discussing our concerns. We are allowed to have our opinions, are we not?"

"Yes, but questions regarding the king's decisions should be addressed with him directly. If not, that could be considered a form of treason, if you think about it." Lord Barron gave a tight, threatening smile—dark enough that goose bumps rose on her skin. "The very thing you are accusing an innocent girl of."

Lord Martin's lips grew into a thin line at Lord Barron's insinuation, but he conceded. "Of course, Lord Barron. You're right."

Lord Barron's gaze pierced each of them. "Perhaps we should all disperse and reconvene at a more appropriate time before someone overhears this treasonous conversation and tells the king."

The five councilmen exchanged nervous glances, clearing their throats. Without another word, they disbanded.

She didn't move an inch, not wanting to give away her position as their faint footsteps echoed off the stone walls until they faded away completely.

She let out a large breath, closing her eyes, running her hands through her hair.

"You can come out now, Lady Versalles."

She jumped at the sound of Lord Barron's voice carrying through the corridor.

After her heart recovered, she abandoned her hiding spot and rounded the corner to find Lord Barron waiting for her in the middle of the corridor.

"Lord Barron," she acknowledged with a sharp nod as Zareb followed, staying a few feet behind her.

The light draft wafted Lord Barron's familiar, pleasantly sweet, woodsy scent in her direction. "It's been a long time since I've seen that pretty face. I apologize for not coming to say hello to you sooner. As the king's right hand, I've been delegating the conditions of Vertmere's surrender alongside the general. I won't bore you with details, but let's just say it hasn't been the easiest of negotiations."

That was news. "It's still ongoing?"

"Oh yes," he said with an exhausted tone. "Still a few details to sort out, I'm afraid. I feel it will be dragged out as long as possible, especially now with the succession reopened. The king of Vertmere is not the easiest to be persuaded. He's holding a grudge for an assassination attempt. You know, politics."

Her eyes fell as she considered his words. "Indeed I do."

"Do you?" he asked.

She lifted her gaze back up in question.

"I only hear rumors." He peered over his shoulder—referring to the conversation she'd just overheard.

She pressed her lips together. "You know what they say about rumors." Her voice came out a little sharper than intended.

The corners of his eyes crinkled with his smile. "Luckily for you, I'm not easily persuaded by them. I like to use my own judgment. I find it to be much more reliable." He paused, thinking carefully about what he was going to say next. "I have a question for you. One simple question, and it's imperative, Lady Versalles, that you answer honestly… Do you *want* to be queen?"

The sudden question surprised her. "I'm sorry?"

"Do you *want* to be the queen of Cathan?"

It was a harmless question, but for some reason, it held a weight over her that she wasn't expecting. For the sake of all those involved, she would gladly bear the burden of the crown. But that wasn't what he'd asked. He wanted to know if she *desired* to be queen, and to that… she didn't have an answer.

Her hesitation seemed to be enough for him. "You know, I've been in this court a long time. I became a high councilman right around the time you were born." His eyes diverted from hers, trailing after the ghostly presence of his colleagues. "Most of the council is convinced you committed treason, that you're a beautiful seductress sent to rule over Cathan."

"You all give me far too much credit." Her jaw tightened in annoyance.

"Perhaps," Lord Barron agreed with a nod, contemplating the idea. "Or perhaps you are simply a girl caught in the line of fire. I believe the latter."

Her heart lifted despite herself. "You do?"

"Yes. But it's not so much a matter of believing you as it is you not being able to answer my question." He inched closer, his scent overwhelming her, fogging her mind. "If you want to be queen and live here for the rest of your life, then carry on and don't mind what others say. But if you have the slightest doubt, I'd tread carefully. This court life isn't for the faint of heart. They'll tear you apart, given the chance. If you aren't willing to live or even breathe it, then I'm afraid you'll find yourself being persecuted for a life you didn't even wish for."

The air around her swirled with a new rich, thick coating, making it difficult to breathe.

"Why are you telling me this?"

His face relaxed a bit. "Because I'm afraid for you. And despite my distance, I care for you and your mother. My best advice to you, Lady Versalles, is to find out the answer soon. Not just for yourself, but for all of Vallor." He bowed to her, entirely unnecessary given their positions in court, but for some reason, he had always done it for her. "I should go. It's getting late."

And with that, Lord Barron dismissed himself, turning around and heading back the way he'd come. She wanted to thank him, but the words failed to form before he vanished around the corner.

She retreated to the opposite corridor, retracing her steps to her room as she stewed over the high council's conversation.

While they might be correct about her inexperience, that was where the truth ended. Their doubt stoked a fire within her that she hadn't known was smoldering, filling her with a renewed determination to show them how mistaken they were.

It was clear now. She had to prove she wasn't merely a foolish girl from Canteran, that she was capable of far more than their narrow, trivial minds could imagine. That if she desired, she could become the most formidable queen that Cathan had ever seen.

She'd almost forgotten Zareb was walking alongside her when he said, "We start your training tomorrow."

CHAPTER 19

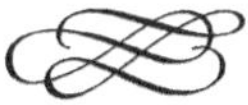

Somehow, in nothing short of a miracle, Zareb kept his promise to train Rose. The night's cold front had left a delicate frost on the ground and trees, but as the sun crested the hills, it warmed the ground, creating a light fog. The servants were barely putting out the torches when Rose and Zareb entered the stables to ready their horses.

"We're going to train in the forest. It is a bit of a ride, but under present circumstances, I think the distance is best if you want to keep the element of surprise," Zareb stated, scanning their surroundings for any onlookers. "Did you bring a change of clothing like I told you?"

"Yes," she confirmed, gesturing to her shoulder bag. She swung her leg up and over, mounting her horse.

"Good." Zareb checked her saddle straps to confirm they were secure. "Those dresses will only hinder you in a fight." He eyed the green fabric draped over her horse.

They traveled along the main road until Zareb veered into the dense trees. Eventually, they came upon a small, open meadow with a narrow creek on the far side. They guided their horses to the water, allowing them to drink first.

"Change here," Zareb instructed. "I'll wait for you in the clearing."

She made quick work of the swap, replacing her dress with a fitted tunic and pants, the same ones she wore while training with her former mentor, Warren. The black fabric hugged the lean muscle she'd built while she was away. Not that her muscles were large by any means, but the modest dresses she wore dissuaded questions they'd rather not answer. In a way, her sparring clothes were liberating. They gave her permission to be someone different. Someone bolder.

She threw her hair into a ponytail and rejoined Zareb in the middle of the meadow.

Zareb turned to offer her a sword but paused mid-motion as soon as he caught sight of her. She couldn't tell if he was judging her or if he was simply surprised. A flush crept onto her cheeks.

He cleared his throat. "We'll start with the basics and go from there," he said, handing her the sword. "I want to see how skilled you are."

She grasped the hilt, becoming accustomed to its weight, relieved to find it similar to the one she'd used sparring with Warren. It'd make it easier to get used to.

"You advance first," Zareb said, taking a few steps backward. "We'll keep going back and forth until it flows naturally."

Warren's encouraging voice filled her thoughts as she paused to take in her surroundings. *The first thing I always want you to do, no matter what you are doing or where you are going, is observe your environment. Awareness of where you are will always be vital in protecting yourself and others. There can be advantages and disadvantages; if you're aware of them, you can maneuver yourself to deflect or attack better.*

She looked to the sky; she could use the sunlight as a blinder, making it harder for Zareb to see her. Her gaze shifted back to the tree line. It could serve as a shielding barrier if necessary. But natural obstacles could also pose a terrible risk, potentially blocking off escape routes and restricting her mobility—cliffs and water especially.

She refocused on Zareb, observing him as an opponent. She couldn't compete with his strength, so she'd have to play to her own advantage. Throughout her training, she'd learned the importance of speed and precision, which she'd honed lethally—at least according to Warren. He had ingrained it into her with countless drills and footwork exercises.

Being smaller had its benefits: less mass to target, a lower center of gravity.

She searched for a weakness, but she doubted Zareb had many, if any. Her one advantage lay in the element of surprise, which she had learned to exploit to the fullest.

She widened her stance and rotated her hips toward him. Firmly grasping her sword, she bent her elbows, keeping them tight against her sides. In a flash, she lunged forward, keeping her arms tucked inward to prevent overextending. She aimed for his exposed left side.

Just in time, he blocked her strike, the clash of steel resonating through the trees.

Undeterred, she tried again, now more confident, swinging her sword toward his other flank. Zareb countered her blow, pushing her attack back. She jabbed at him again.

Almost immediately, she realized her mistake.

Zareb sidestepped, jamming his sword's hilt into her side.

She winced, stumbling from him. Although her pride was the only thing truly wounded, knowing it wasn't even close to a hard blow for him.

"Avoid jabbing like that," he instructed, mimicking her movement. "Jabbing too soon leaves your upper body and side exposed. Only use it when your opponent is extremely vulnerable. Just as raising your hands above your head would be."

She nodded, still rubbing her side—a stupid mistake.

"Remember, your sword is simply an extension of yourself." He held out his arm and blade. "Your body is the weapon. Now, I'll attack first."

He waited until she was ready. When she gave the go-ahead, he lunged.

She sidestepped, raising her sword quickly to meet his. Her instincts took over, and rather than blocking the strike altogether, she angled her sword downwards while advancing, redirecting his blade away, using her back leg to deliver a powerful kick to his chest.

The move caught Zareb so off guard that he lost his balance and fell. She quickly kicked his sword out of his reach and pointed hers straight at his chest.

She gazed at her own arm like a foreign object.

Zareb looked up in sheer astonishment, his eyes glinting in admiration. "Now, *that* was worthy of a soldier."

Her mouth curved into a triumphant smile, reaching down to help him stand.

He dusted himself off. "Again."

He never let her get the upper hand after that.

They spent the following hours sparring, the movements becoming more natural to her. She was grateful for his unwavering patience as he offered tips and suggestions. He praised her small victories and pushed her to her limits. For the first time, she could use her full strength.

When their time was almost up, Zareb had them do foot drills, performing each one alongside her. At last, when he was finally satisfied with the work she'd put in, Zareb relented.

"That's enough for today," he said, panting as beads of sweat ran down his temples. She was glad to see he was just as out of breath as she was. "You did well," he praised, handing her a canteen.

"Thank you." She gave him a breathless smile, taking it.

"No, really," he continued. "I don't know anyone who could fight like that with only a year of experience. You were trained well. You're ready for the succession if you choose to join."

Her heart warmed at the praise. She raised the canteen to her lips. "Do you think I could use these tactics to fight off some of my suitors?"

Zareb let out a harsh scoff. "I'm afraid you'd have to get past your most skillful foe first." He paused, amusement dancing in his eyes. "Your mother."

A light, airy laugh escaped her as she handed him back the canteen. "A worthy opponent indeed."

"I'll give you some minerals for your bathwater," Zareb said. "You'll want to stretch, too."

"It's not all that bad." She craned her neck. It wasn't like this was her first training session.

Zareb gave her a knowing look. "By morning, you'll be saying different."

CHAPTER 20

Zareb hadn't been exaggerating.

In the days that followed, Rose could hardly move, despite consistently using the minerals Zareb had provided to ease the soreness.

Each morning, he woke her at dawn. Sometimes, they practiced sparring, focused on footwork, or simply ran for miles. She was run so ragged, she nearly regretted asking for his help at all. However, after their sessions, she felt free in a way. Stronger. In just a few days, she found herself looking forward to them.

After the initial wake up, that is.

Each day, she desperately wanted to go and find Tristan, but then she remembered the king's request to keep her distance until the succession began. She refused to give anyone a reason to dismiss their nominations. So even though it crippled her, she stayed away.

At last, the morning of the rally arrived—the day she would formally announce her decision to accept the succession nomination. Over the past week, she had attempted to compose her speech dozens of times, but all she'd done was gaze at an empty piece of parchment. Nothing profound came to mind, resulting in her throwing down her quill in frustration. Public speaking had never been her forte, and it never would be. A pit of unease formed in her stomach, realizing that if she did become queen, that would have to change.

When it came time to head to the grand hall for breakfast, she and Zareb managed to shuffle through the packed room, claiming the seats her mother had saved.

Glancing across the tables, she spotted Tristan, who looked as anxious as she felt. His tousled, loose curls framed his face as he focused on his plate. Somehow, it was reassuring to see that even Tristan, who was a natural at public speaking, seemed nervous.

Her mother eyed her blue dress with disappointment. "I wish you'd worn the pink dress for once. It looks so elegant on you. Oh, and I got you fruit." She slid the plate toward Rose. "I kept it light in case you begin to feel woozy like you do when you get anxious."

"If anything is going to give me anxiety, it's you," Rose snapped, pouring herself a glass of juice. She immediately felt guilty for her tone, blaming her nerves for being on edge.

Her mother ignored her snide remark, looking out over the crowd. "You better be careful, Rose; I saw Grant eyeing you on your way in."

"I'll try to keep my wits about me," she drawled, sipping her drink as she eyed Zareb's plate of eggs and bacon with jealousy.

She scanned faces of the court members around her, until something made her eyes stop in their tracks.

Beth and Roman sat side by side, engaged in conversation. About what, it didn't matter. What mattered was the smile that grew on his face as Beth leaned over and whispered something into his ear. *A smile.*

An invisible hand clenched at her gut.

She forced her gaze away to the head table—where something even more pressing caught her attention.

Two unfamiliar women had joined the front table. The first was an older, pale woman with short brown hair, hollow cheeks, and thin, pursed lips. Her sharp eyes surveyed the crowd, reflecting a look of disgust. Unlike the typical attire of Cathan, she wore a green and brown dress woven with small leaves.

Beside the stern-looking woman sat a younger girl in a similar outfit, likely just a few years younger than Rose. She was a tad plain-looking, with long, light-brown hair and matching brown eyes. A splash of pink rested on her high, rosy cheekbones. Her green dress almost swallowed her, draping elegantly around her petite figure.

It was obvious they were from Vertmere by their forest-green attire, but what were they doing here? Moreover, why were they at the head table? There must have been a dozen guards in green uniforms standing behind them.

As the older woman turned, a small, gold crown made of vines gleamed from atop her head. They both wore one.

A sinking sensation twisted in her stomach. "Who are they?"

Her mother followed her eyeline, her face shifting into an expression Rose couldn't decipher. "That is Queen Isleen and Princess Satin of Vertmere," she informed dryly.

Rose's face contorted as her mother confirmed her suspicions. "Why are they here?" she whispered.

"They are here to finalize post-war negotiations—or so I've heard. They'll be here for the remainder of the succession."

Rose frowned, popping a sour grape into her mouth. Why did they need to come in person? And why were only the queen and princess present? The rest of the court seemed to share the same questions, all eyes fixated on the foreigners. But then it dawned on her that if they sought to ensure this peace treaty would last, the next ruler would need to align with the terms—no use making a peace treaty only for it to be unraveled in the next generation.

Without forewarning, a servant presented a large bouquet before her, drawing her gaze back to the table.

To her surprise, they were the lunar flowers she had shown Grant during their garden tour, elegantly arranged in a milky-white vase, untouched in their expansive pods.

Her mother's eyes lit up at the bouquet, scooting toward it. "Oh, those are stunning. Who are they from?"

Her mother made a grab for the note, but Rose swiped it from the bouquet first, throwing her mother a reprimanding look as she opened the card discreetly. But it didn't stop her mother from poking her nose over her shoulder.

For the woman who opened up in darkness the same way these did.
Good luck at the rally tonight.
- Grant
PS I hope you think about touching my bare skin when these bloom.

She couldn't help the small laugh that escaped her. He was persistent. She'd give him that.

She looked up to find Grant just a few tables down from hers. His bright green eyes were already hooked on her, a hint of a smirk playing on his lips, looking satisfied by her reaction.

Her mother nudged her in the ribs. "Careful, Rose, you might look like you're enjoying Grant's advances."

She wiped the smile from her face and nudged her mother back.

"Ah! It's Penelope Lownton. I must say hello," her mother said, standing in haste. "Remember to meet back in your room at five. Don't be late."

She nodded, letting her mother scurry off to her old friend—no doubt to gather gossip on everyone that had arrived. Rose was certain that before nightfall, her mother would learn everything she needed to know for the rally tonight.

She went back to her plate, surprised to find that eggs and bacon had replaced her fruit.

Her eyebrows grew together, looking up at Zareb.

"You need to eat protein if we continue to train," he said, gesturing to the food.

She gave him a thankful smile.

After just a few bites, she heard footsteps nearing their table. She half expected it to be Grant, but it was Roman—wearing his familiar scowl as his eyes darted to the flowers on the table. She was tempted to turn the other way, if only to avoid more scrutiny. The moment he sat down in her mother's empty seat beside her, her muscles stiffened.

"What do you want, Roman?" she asked, knowing full well this wasn't a friendly visit.

Unfortunately, her tone didn't deter him. "I'm not here for you. I came so Tristan wouldn't." His voice was just as irritated as hers.

She raised her gaze to meet his. He was much closer than she'd expected. Leaning back slightly, she asked, "What do you mean?"

His golden eyes cut to the flowers. "If you're going to play with your toys, could you at least not bait them in front of my brother?"

She cursed under her breath—the flowers. Tristan must have witnessed everything. She couldn't bring herself to check if he was watching. "I'm not *trying* to hurt him," she said lamely.

"And how is that? Keeping your options open to all of the succession contestants? Tell me, should I get Sansburry next? So you can tell Tristan it's all in the name of love."

She set her fork down. "What would you have me do? Your brother has kept all other suitors from me."

His fortified expression faltered. After a brief pause, his eyes sharpened once more. "I don't believe you."

"Have you asked him?"

"Have *you*?"

"Grant told me so."

"And you trust that weasel?"

"I think so." She shrugged, nonchalantly clutching her glass. "You've known Grant longer than I. He may have a spotty track record, but I doubt he's lying about this one." She sipped her orange juice, the tang bursting in her mouth.

Roman paused again, clearly contemplating the accusation.

Thinking he was done, she set down her glass, about to leave, when Roman spoke again. "What happened that night? With Xavier. What happened on the beach?"

She didn't know why he needed an answer. He had been at the tribunal.

She stalled by slowly shifting her body to face him again. "You know what happened."

"I want to hear you say it." He squared his shoulders, like he needed *that* to look more intimidating. "My father and Tristan assure me you're quite blameless in the situation."

"But you don't agree," she said, already having anticipated his response.

"Let's just say I'm not as easily persuaded when it comes to you. Unlike my father and Tristan, I don't hold a strong attachment." He offered a tight smile that disappeared quickly. "I don't believe Xavier would give up his crown just to hurt someone, especially you."

If he wanted to get under her skin, it was working. His golden eyes scorched hers, reminding her that interrogation had been a part of his job for the past year. He was just like everyone else—the council, the court, all of them.

"You think I *wanted* this?" she asked, exasperated.

"Do you honestly think my father would have denounced Xavier if it had been *anyone* but you?" Roman spat, his tone full of resentment. "You knew about my father's attachment for you and how Tristan feels about you… It's a shame you could never make Xavier feel the same. Maybe you never let that grudge go."

His words struck a nerve. She dug her nails into her palms. "Look at me, Roman." She gestured to herself. "Do you honestly believe *I* could've forced *Xavier* to do anything he didn't want to do?"

Roman leaned in closer, a breath away now. Out of the corner of her eye, she caught Zareb about to rise, but she signaled it was alright, keeping her focus on Roman.

"If I'm correct," he said, "your *first* story was that you 'slipped and fell,' but then your story ever so conveniently changed to Xavier being responsible. Maybe you saw your opportunity and took it. A small price to be queen. By the looks of it, your wound is already healing quite nicely." He tilted his head, assessing her neck, now unbandaged.

Her eyes narrowed. "It's amazing what healing oil and a few Alofa leaves can do."

A tense silence settled between them as they glared at each other.

She didn't back down. "I didn't plan any of this. And the fact that I have to say it means you don't know me at all."

"And that's where we agree," Roman said. "If you don't care for the crown, don't enter the succession. Do us all a favor and stay out of it. Better yet, leave; that's what you're good at."

His words stung more than she cared to admit. She was done playing nice.

Speaking in a steady voice, she said, "Tell me, Roman. What would

Tristan do if he found out I was leaving? Do you think he'd just let me walk out of these halls? Even if I managed to escape without his knowledge, are you willing to risk that he might throw the succession and leave to come find me?"

His fists clenched. "That's just the way you want it, isn't it? You have your claws in him so deep, you'd let him destroy his own life for you."

His words struck a painful chord. "If I wanted to destroy him, I'd be playing my cards very differently."

"So you admit it's a game?"

She stood her ground, locking her eyes onto his. "Of course it's a game. That's all this place is—*games*... What choice do I have but to play them?"

Whether it was her response or the shift in tone, his eyes softened, if only minutely. If she hadn't been less than an inch from him, she might have missed it entirely. Suspicion clouded his expression once more.

"Well, Rose, we'll see who wins this game. But I'd be very careful which hand you play next, or you'll lose. And I can promise, you'll lose more than you bargained for." Without waiting for a reply, he stood and stalked away.

She waited until he was out of sight before daring to exhale. She rested her elbows on the table, lowering her forehead into her palms. Even Roman didn't believe her. Fantastic.

What was worse was the fact it mattered to her.

After taking a moment, she regained her composure and straightened.

Rising, she left the grand hall, striding through the towering arched ceilings. Despite her quick steps, Zareb kept pace beside her, passing another group of court members.

"Are you alright?" Zareb asked once they were alone, the voices echoing down the corridor fading.

Rose nodded too swiftly, giving him a strained smile. "Yes. Why? Oh, that? I'm fine, I'm great."

Zareb's face twitched, knowing better. "You don't have to do that with me, you know."

"Do what?"

"Pretend."

She stopped, finally looking him in the eye.

"Did he threaten to hurt you?" Zareb asked.

Rose shook her head, wrapping her arms around herself. "No, of course not… But rest assured, his words worked just as effectively as a sword."

"Tell me, what sort of gentleman says such things to make a lady cower like that?"

She attempted to look past Roman's anger to understand. "I suppose one who thinks she's destroying the thing he loves most. Even with our history, I'm afraid he simply sees me as many others do."

"And how is that?" Zareb asked.

She bit her cheek. "A power-hungry woman who'd do anything, use anyone, to get what she wants… A throne seeker."

Another group of courtiers made their way down the corridor, their laughter ringing out, stirring envy in her, catching sight of their carefree smiles.

"What is it you want, then?" Zareb asked once they'd passed.

She'd asked herself that question often. "I simply want to see my mother settled, happy, and cared for. And if it's not too much to ask, I'd also like to marry the man I love and have my own family."

Zareb nodded slowly. "So why have you been training? What is it you hope to gain?"

She recalled a promise made long ago. "I suppose I just want to be able to take care of myself, too."

Silence settled over them as Zareb considered her words. After a moment, he nodded, coming to an understanding. "I can see why they are frightened of you."

Her face contorted. "Frightened? Who?"

"The council, the court, the queen. Everyone," Zareb listed.

She gaped at him like he had grown two heads. "Why should anyone in this castle be afraid of *me*?"

Zareb looked her dead in the eye and said something she wouldn't soon forget. "Because I happen to know the most dangerous woman is one who refuses to rely on anyone's sword because she wields her own. You underestimate yourself, Rose. You're a great deal more powerful than you realize."

CHAPTER 21

That night, Rose found herself immersed in a sea of red and gold. The grand hall's tables were stuffed to capacity—the sheer numbers forcing everyone into a tight proximity. Five rows of soldiers stood in the back of the room, waiting for the rally to begin.

Zareb was rigid, keeping closer to her than usual, scanning the room while leaving a hand on his sword's hilt. It would seem he didn't care for large crowds. They had that in common. Across from them sat her mother, tapping her nails nervously on the table.

Rose had worn a blue dress with bell sleeves, representing the House of Versalles colors, signifying that her loyalties would remain to herself. She was glad, for once, for extra fabric to hide her trembling hands.

Biting her lip, she bounced her foot as she waved a napkin to fan herself, wishing she could have sat by one of the open windows. The lack of circulation only added to her nausea. Her eyes fell to the scroll she held. There was no worse form of torture than public speaking.

Zareb glanced at the scroll. "Do you know what you'll say?"

She strained to give him a tiny smile. "I have things written down, but I don't know if any of it is noteworthy."

Zareb leaned forward. "We have a phrase in Semaria—*hearts before arms*. Do you understand what that means?"

She thought back to her studies of the southern province. "It means you must capture men's hearts before you gain their loyalty," she interpreted. "If you do that, you'll not only gain bodies for an army, but obtain spirits, which fight stronger, far more powerful than any sword." Before Zareb could reply, she continued, "And for that matter… it means men do not fight because they believe in you or I, but because we are the representation of what they believe. What better for a leader than to embody those beliefs and encourage them to do the same?"

Zareb's face morphed into a rare soft expression. "You'd do well in Semaria, Rose."

Before she could reply, the king and his advisors arrived to relieve her suffering.

The crowd rose together as they took their seats at the front table. Following them were the foreign queen and princess, accompanied by guards in green uniforms.

King Henrik stood tall and spoke with clarity. "It is an honor to have you all present tonight. I thank everyone who has traveled far and wide to support this new succession." He gestured to the Vertmerian women at the head table. "As you may have noticed, we have Queen Isleen and Princess Satin from the Vertmere province here to witness the challenges and finalize post-war affairs." Next, the king turned to the soldiers in red and gold uniforms. "To the soldiers who have just returned home from the war, we thank you for your willingness to come and support our succession."

The room erupted in applause.

"Tonight, we will hear from the nominees to aid the soldiers in deciding who to fight for. If the candidates accept their nomination, they will enter the first challenge and be included in the vote." The king scanned the crowd, his gaze briefly meeting Rose's. "Let us begin."

Tristan, Grant, Dawnton, and Emmett rose from their scattered seats in the crowd and approached the front.

Just as she prepared to join them, her mother grasped her hand.

"Remember, I'll support you no matter what you decide. Just… make sure it's for yourself, not me or anyone else." She squeezed her hand tightly before letting go.

Rose returned the squeeze before joining the others at the front. She kept her head up and eyes determined, disciplining her feet to maintain a steady pace.

The five candidates had formed a line at the front, each of them also in their respective House colors. Tristan moved to stand beside her, offering a small smile. His knuckles discreetly brushed against hers—a simple touch, but it gave her the reassurance she needed.

The king announced the order. "First, we will hear from Dawnton Sansburry, next Emmett Alterridge, then Grant Montague, followed by Tristan Montague, and lastly, Rosalie Versalles."

Applause filled the room as Dawnton stepped onto the small pulpit centered in front of the head table. He raised his dimpled chin and broadened his shoulders, having cut his black hair since their dance at the ball. His cheeks were flushed, likely from the heat in the room, or perhaps nerves.

Dawnton recounted his role in helping his father build their fortune and boasted about his contributions to improving the city of Caldiz. He proved to be an engaging speaker, and although he had a somewhat off-putting presence, she could see why others might be drawn to his directness.

He was much too slimy for her taste.

Next came Emmett. He delivered a remarkable speech on the origins of Cathan and its traditions. While he was quieter and more reserved than the others, he recounted a heroic story of how he'd assisted in preventing a large group of Semarian slaves from being transported to Khali, earning him enthusiastic applause and tearful reactions. She couldn't help but admire him for it.

Grant established a strong rapport with the soldiers by sharing war stories, particularly one where he saved his men from being burned on a ship at sea after having fought alongside them. Unsurprisingly, the crowd took him as charismatic and charming. Although he was somewhat pompous, at least he wasn't a brute like his elder brother, Mateo, who had competed in the previous succession. Beneath his exterior, she discovered a layer of self-awareness and the capacity to see beyond himself when necessary. If she or Tristan didn't win, she'd much rather he take the crown than Dawnton.

To no surprise, all three of them had accepted their nominations.

Her nerves escalated as she squeezed the scroll in her hands, keenly aware that none of them had needed to prepare written speeches. The sound of her racing heart drowned out everything else, quickening with each passing minute as it came closer to her turn.

She hardly noticed that Tristan was next. From the moment he opened his mouth, he captivated everyone. He shared a great deal about his heritage and how influential his father had been in his upbringing. What truly touched her was his recount of when he'd discovered the city of Corrin had been burned, and how it had given him the motivation to help the people of Cathan. He received the most thunderous applause of the evening as he accepted his nomination.

Before she knew it, it was her turn.

All eyes fell on her as she stepped up to the pulpit. Fighting to steady her shaky hands, she opened the scroll. Her body tensed as she glanced at the hasty scribbles. She bit the inside of her cheek until it bled, leaking the metallic taste of rust and salt into her mouth.

She glanced at the crowd, determined to keep her eyes above their heads, but they inadvertently landed on the high councilmen—specifically Lord Martin, whose twisted, beady eyes gleamed pleased by her fear.

A roar of rebellion took over her body.

She closed the scroll and kept her tone even as she began. "It's no secret that, in many ways, I am ill-fit for the crown. I am a woman with no land or power. I am neither a politician, nor high in rank. I was not there on the battlefields—" her gaze fell on the soldiers, "—but I did help those injured in the medical tents. I was forced to witness many good men die with their blood-soaked on my hands." A lump formed in her throat as she recalled a handful of soldiers she couldn't save. "I saw the cost of war, and I will never forget that blood payment—*your* payment. I stand here before you not as someone above you, but *because* of you. You've carried the weight of the sword, and if I lead, I will help carry it again if it comes down to it. Because although this war has been won, the storm coming for

Cathan is far from over. If we are to stand a chance against it, we're going to need to stand together."

Her gaze pierced down at the five council members who had criticized her. "You may think I have no chance of winning the succession. You may think that me standing here before you is a joke, and you may even be right," she admitted. "But I do not wish for your approval, nor do I need it... However, I do hope that rather than fighting, we can set aside our differences so Cathan can become as strong as it can be. Let us face the storm as we always have... *Together.*"

Taking a deep breath, she concluded her speech with one final statement. "I accept the nomination."

The room went deathly silent.

That was until a single set of claps sounded.

She turned to find Tristan, his handsome face lit up with a gloriously proud smile. Soon, the king, her mother, Lord Barron, and Zareb added to his applause.

Slowly, more people joined in, and before long, the entire room was clapping together.

She glanced at the lone councilman who was not applauding. Lord Martin's expression grew into a scowl.

She met his gaze with challenging eyes.

After all, if she was going to be called a throne seeker, she might as well live up to the name.

CHAPTER 22

An hour later, the results were in.

Out of the one hundred votes cast, Tristan gained the highest support from the soldiers with thirty-two votes, followed by Grant with twenty-four, Emmett with eighteen, Rose with fourteen, and Dawnton with twelve. She joined in the applause as the candidates received their congratulations. Although she felt let down by her low number, she held her head high. Dawnton, on the other hand, did not accept his results with as much grace, furiously whispering into his father's ear, glaring daggers at her when he caught her staring.

She wanted to congratulate Tristan, but the thick crowd made it impossible to move anywhere.

She'd only managed to make it a few feet when a voice stopped her.

"You're looking as lovely as always," Grant remarked above the clamor. "Congratulations on your number." She almost took it as sarcasm, but then he added, "If it's any consolation, I would have added another vote to your roster if I weren't in the running."

A weary smile spread on her lips. "Thank you. I'd say congratulations are in order for you, too. I wasn't sure you'd get five men to join your cause."

Grant's emerald eyes shone brighter at her taunt. "I may not have recruited as many men as your lover, but it's all I need to win tomorrow. I go for quality over quantity."

"Of course you do." She rolled her eyes.

Grant slid closer, bridging the distance between them as his lips hovered near her ear. "If I get you, that'll be the true prize, won't it?" he whispered in a voice she was sure let him get whatever and whomever he wanted.

She raised her chin so she was only inches from his face. "I wish you all the luck in the world," she said with a smirk, repeating her words from the ball.

A large, dazzling smile broke out on his face, lighting up his eyes. He boldly stroked her cheek. "You may just be worth all the work, Rosalie Versalles." He broke eye contact, his gaze straying behind her.

She followed his gaze to find Tristan looking murderously at the pair.

Of course.

Taking a quick step back, she said, "Excuse me." She meant to leave, but the sea of people blocked her quick escape.

Grant caught her arm with little effort.

"I didn't mean to taunt him." His face was filled with rare remorse.

She tried to pull her arm away, but he held it firm. "It's *exactly* what you meant to do."

He pulled her closer, forcing her to face him. "Why can't I show you off? Why can't I flaunt you? If I marry you, I'll make sure every man in the room is jealous of me."

"You don't want *me*; you just want a gem on your arm."

"I'll prove to you it's not true."

"I suppose you'll have to," she bit back, finally freeing her arm. "I'm afraid I'm tired. Please excuse me."

"Let me walk you back to your room."

"No. Good night, Grant." She exited the grand hall, feeling the stares of both Grant and Tristan piercing her back. She didn't look back, not even to see if Zareb was behind her.

As soon as she got to her room, she sent Thea out and began undressing herself, changing into her nightgown.

She was just pulling back the sheets when a gentle knock came.

She froze, straining her ears, wondering if she'd imagined it.

Tap... tap tap... tap.

She recognized the pattern at once.

She cracked the door open only a sliver to see Tristan.

Without thinking, she let him in.

Just as she closed the door, the last shred of her self-control was stripped away. She knew she should have shoved him right back out, but instead, she flung her arms around his neck, crushing him into her body.

He froze, caught off guard by the sudden gesture, but he welcomed her, crushing her against his chest. "I wanted to come scold you," he whispered. "Damn you, I just forgot all the snarky remarks I prepared."

She lifted her head from his shoulder. "I'm sure I deserve it."

"No, you don't. You don't deserve any of it." He brushed a stray strand of her hair away. "You were incredible tonight, Rose. I've never seen anyone stand up to the council like that."

A smile cracked onto her lips. "So were you. Truly."

Tristan lifted her jaw so she peered straight into his bottomless eyes. "I don't care what my father says. Now that we're both in this succession, I want to face it together—just like you said, not as two separate candidates, but as one. I promise to support you in every way possible. My men are just as much yours as they are mine."

Her gaze softened, touched at his unwavering loyalty. He wanted to be a team, to win not just for his sake, but for hers, too. A wave of gratitude flooded her heart, melting her defenses away.

"You'd do that?" she whispered.

His eyes roamed her face, becoming hazy. "Rose, everything I own already belongs to you. We can just consider this a… rigorous relationship exercise." His mouth turned upward into a smile.

She smiled back, her heart beating faster.

He held up his pinky. "You and me?"

It was something they used to do when they were younger. She intertwined her finger with his. "You and me," she repeated.

The moment her finger latched on to his, he leveraged it and pulled her into him. "We'll be the fiercest king and queen this province has ever seen." He stroked his thumb across her cheek. "I'm sorry about earlier… I just can't stand how Grant looks at you and how I thought you were looking at him."

She pulled away. "Listen, Tristan, I need you to be honest about something… Have you been dissuading suitors from seeing me?"

He massaged the back of his neck as his eyes lowered. "Would you be angry if I said yes?" He braved her gaze again.

She let out a sigh and rested her forehead against his before responding honestly. "No. I suppose I ought to be, but you'll have hell to pay if my mother confirms it."

"I know I shouldn't have," he apologized at once, "but I can't stand the thought of you with someone else."

The mere thought crippled her heart. "Come sit." She tugged his hand, her pinky still linked with his.

He sat down on the bed first, leaning against the headboard. She joined him, resting her back against his chest.

His strong arms snaked around her waist as he closed his eyes, taking a deep breath.

After a brief content silence, he spoke. "Can you imagine falling asleep like this?"

"It'd be the best night's sleep I'd ever had." Her body ached for it as she said the words.

"Or the worst," he murmured huskily into her ear. "When we get married, I'm certain I'll barely let you escape to eat."

She tilted her head to meet his gaze, her mouth splitting into a grin before his followed suit.

He placed a feathered kiss on her forehead. "I like seeing you like this," he whispered against her skin.

"Like what?"

"Relaxed. Happy… I haven't seen you like this since you've been back," he said as he played with her hair lazily.

"It was simpler then. No one cared what we did." She hesitated, contemplating what was ahead of them. "What will we do if we don't win the succession?"

"What do you mean?"

"If neither of us wins, what would we do? Where would we go? What happens to your family?"

"You doubt us?" He raised his eyebrows at her with a small smile playing on his lips.

She shook her head. "I just wondered if you'd thought about it."

"Well, if we lose by some terrible circumstance, my father is still the king. So until he dies, this will be our home. My mother will not outlive him, I'm afraid. Even if she did, she'd move back with us to our home in the mountains."

"Highland Haven," she recalled. She had never been to the manor, but the name lived well in her memory. Tristan and his family spent a few weeks there every summer for their family retreat. She longed to see what it was like, but she and her mother had never been invited. It remained a special place meant only for their family.

"But what about you?" she asked. "Would you be happy there?"

"As long as I had you." He kissed her temple. "I never thought I'd be king. I knew there was a slight chance if something happened to Xavier, but I never planned this. I'd be disappointed if I didn't become king, but I'd live... I just can't stomach Grant being the next king of Cathan. The thought alone gives me the determination to win." He gave a harsh laugh as a pause fell. "Are you worried?"

She sat up to face him. "I just don't want whatever happens to change... this." She cupped his cheek.

He wrapped his hand around her wrist, pressing her hand firmer against his face. "How do I get it through to you? Each and every bone in my body belongs to you. Every drop of blood, every daydream, every simple breath—hell, even every inappropriate thought belongs to you. I think of you every chance I get because seeing you isn't enough. It'll never be enough. And in case you ever foolishly forget, I'm never *not* thinking of you."

Her eyes fluttered as tears pricked; never had a man spoken to her like that. The absence of affection with her father had never let her believe that love could exist. She didn't know what to say. How to tell him how much those words meant to her.

Her mouth became dry. "I love you, Tristan," she whispered.

It was the first time she'd uttered those words to him.

His body stiffened beneath hers. He gazed at her like he was questioning if he'd imagined it. Once they sank in, his steady eyes wavered. "And I'm the luckiest man alive because of it." He drew her in, kissing her temple again.

This time, he lingered close, his gaze shifting to her lips then back to her eyes.

The last of her willpower failed. She settled herself onto his lap. "Kiss me," she coaxed in the softest, most persuasive voice possible.

His jaw clenched, resisting the command. "I can't."

"Why not?" Her eyes grew together, hurt.

"Because if I start… it'll be the end of me," he whispered, as if he knew that once he got a taste, there would be no going back.

"No… it'll be the *start*." Her hands grazed his soft, blond hair, sliding her fingers through the smooth curls.

Unable to hold back any longer, she closed the gap and pressed her lips against his, moving slowly and gently as she molded them together.

For a moment, he was unresponsive. Terror surged through her veins, wondering if she'd made a grave mistake.

She was about to crawl into a hole from embarrassment when his lips came alive, responding to hers.

He drank from her like she was a bottomless well, as though he'd been roaming the seas with no fresh water, and she was the first drop he'd come upon in weeks. He quenched his thirst greedily for fear he'd be dragged back to sea.

It wasn't like their first kiss. No, that kiss, initiated by Tristan over a year ago, was quick, nervous, and impulsive. This kiss was intentional. Purposeful. Deliberate. Grown.

He combed his fingers through her hair, settling at the nape of her neck. She suppressed a contented sigh.

Within moments, their breaths became heavy.

His hands roamed over her back, moving down to her hips, drawing her closer.

She encircled his neck with her arms, pressing herself as close as she physically could. It was better than she'd ever imagined. To finally feel him like this—to know what he tasted like beyond those lips was all she'd dreamed of.

In one fluid motion, Tristan guided her onto her back, his form hovering above hers.

His lips left hers to graze her neck, caressing it with the utmost grace.

Without warning, he ground his hips into hers.

A soft, grateful moan slipped from her lips.

He grappled a fistful of sheets at the mere sound.

The next moment, he was gone, shooting upward off the bed.

His wild hands tangled in his hair, pulling at it as he gasped for breath. "Damn you, Rose," he growled, pacing on the rug.

"I'm sorr—"

"Don't." He pivoted to face her. "Don't *ever* apologize for that. You'll make me think you regret it… and I couldn't live with the thought."

Her cheeks heated, her chest rising and falling hard as her lungs fought for air.

She forced herself to stand, maintaining a safe distance.

He came straight to her, cupping her face. "You are everything to me. *Everything,*" he whispered, gazing at her in a way he never had. "If I carry on like that, I won't be able to stop… Gods, I'd never stop."

A flutter flew in her stomach, trying to control the impulse to kiss him again as he continued.

"I want to do this the right way. As the goddess you are, you deserve nothing less. I will have you, Rosalie Versalles. As the gods as my witness, nothing in this world can keep you from me… me and you," he whispered.

She leaned her forehead against his, reassured by the childhood sentiment. "Me and you."

He took a deep breath as he regained his composure. "I hate to say it, but I should go. My family will be furious with me if they find me here. Roman's bound to be looking for me to discuss tactics for tomorrow."

"Right. Of course." They'd need their full strength for tomorrow's challenge—they'd be up at the crack of dawn before long.

Still, he leaned back into her, his mouth so close his lips brushed against hers as he said, "I'll miss you." The way he said the words… they had a whole new depth than before.

"I'll miss you, too," she whispered back.

He pressed another soft, feather-light kiss onto her lips, reigniting her simmering heart. "Good night, Rosalie," he mumbled, looking ready to pick her up and lay her right back down on the bed and take her anyway.

Instead, he gave her hand a final squeeze and departed as swiftly as he'd arrived.

Her heart continued to race long after he'd left.

They would win this, and they'd win it together.

She'd burn all of Vallor if she had to.

PART II
THE SUCCESSION

CHAPTER 23

Zareb promptly met Rose outside her room early the next morning. The sun was barely rising over the hills, splashing magenta across the light blue horizon, while the two moons remained visible in the distance. She was instructed to wear her House colors, uncertain of what exactly the challenge would entail, but she knew it would probably involve teamwork, similar to Xavier's experience in the bog. Just the memory of him covered in foul slime made her skin crawl.

Despite the early hour, the castle's corridors buzzed with excitement as everyone prepared for the first challenge.

"You ready?" Zareb asked, navigating through the bustling hall beside her.

"Yes," she declared, burying her building nerves. She finally took note of what he was wearing. "Is that your uniform?" she asked. His red and gold tunic had been swapped for a blue one with a small golden dragon on the chest.

"It is," Zareb said, squinting out through the bright window toward the grounds, pointing at the clusters of men already active in the courtyard. "Each team is wearing their respective House colors and symbol: the griffin, the dragon, the wolf, and the serpent. Grant's men are wearing brown, and Tristan's are wearing red to avoid confusion. The yellow flags attached to our belts will act as our lifeline. If they get cut off, you'll be considered eliminated from the challenge."

She tracked his gaze. Although it was strictly forbidden to kill the other candidates during the succession, it didn't mean "mistakes" couldn't happen. It was an "accident" when Mateo drove *three* arrows into Xavier's back while climbing the mountainside that nearly killed him. At one point in history, it was even encouraged to eliminate the competition. However, after decades of bloody successions, the council deemed it too barbaric, recognizing it didn't necessarily call upon the most qualified candidate—just the most brutal.

Her gaze returned to Zareb as the corners of her mouth tugged upward. "You're one of my men?" she asked, eyeing his blue uniform.

"Of course," he said, as if it were obvious. "I can't have you getting killed. I was just starting to like you." He jerked his head, urging her to follow, ignoring her wide grin. "Come on, we'd better join them. It'll be starting soon."

Bright sunlight warmed the frost-covered ground, dampening the hem of the tents. Soldiers scurried about, collecting weapons and armor, while some sparred to warm up. The whole ordeal felt ominous somehow. Despite knowing it was a "staged" fight, it felt all too... *real*, like they were gearing up for an actual battle.

"Where is this being held?" she asked Zareb, feeling foolish she hadn't thought of the question beforehand.

"It starts at the river," he replied, pointing toward the trees. "Then we row upstream to the firewall—"

"The firewall?"

"A barricade of sorts—a high stone wall manned by soldiers with flaming arrows. We'll need to make our way up and over it. You could try to go around, but that would take too long. Fighting your way over the wall is your best bet. Once we're past it, we'll reach the old ruins, where our main objective is to locate the sun relic."

She peered into the distant woods. The river. Naturally, it would have to start with the river. The very same one she'd almost drowned in as a child—she still had the hidden scar on her scalp to prove it. She stowed away her fear—no time to be scared now.

Something was off as they drew nearer to the tent. There were only eight men in blue uniforms, including Zareb. Perhaps the others were still on their way? She scanned the area, but no one else wore her House colors.

Determined, she entered the tent, addressing her men. "Where are the others?"

The men exchanged hesitant glances. A large redheaded man to her left was the first to answer. "There's been no one but us."

Zareb nudged her shoulder. "How many men were you supposed to have?"

"Fourteen," she answered.

"And how many did Dawnton have?"

"Twelve. Why?"

Zareb's expression hardened as he motioned to the green tent a short distance away. "See for yourself."

Her eyes clapped to the green tent, the forest green serpent flags fluttering in the breeze. Dawnton's tent was more crowded than it should have been—no, that couldn't be. One... two... She counted eighteen. Somehow overnight, Dawnton had accrued six more men—the exact amount she was short.

"He came to us and offered a bribe to switch over to his team," the bearded redhead said, glaring at the serpent tent with them. "It was no small amount."

She swore under her breath, reprimanding herself for not having thought of the possibility before. Of course Dawnton would aim to target her—the one he deemed his easiest prey. The serpent symbol suited him and his House perfectly.

Dawnton, as if aware of her stare, locked eyes with her and flashed a smug smirk.

She resisted the temptation to lift her middle finger—the slimy git. The limited number of men posed a significant drawback, especially if they had to row upstream.

She sized up the men in front of her, thanking her lucky stars they all appeared strong and capable.

"Your loyalty is greatly appreciated," she said, wishing she could offer a reward for their fealty. "I promise I won't forget."

A burly man with dark-brown hair and tattoos stepped forward. "If you become queen, a large number would support you. Many of us here have witnessed your miracle work in the healing tents." The others behind him nodded in agreement.

Familiarity tugged at her the longer she looked at him. "Have we met before?"

"You helped tend to me when my arm was nearly severed." He rolled up his sleeve, revealing his scarred arm as proof.

She recognized the wound at once. "Khan?"

"You remember?" Khan's mouth split upward.

"Of course." She scanned the healed handiwork with a critical eye. He had been among the first patients she'd assisted during her initial week in the healing tents. He'd arrived with a severely bleeding arm, nearly hacked clean off. It had taken her and another nurse half the day, but they managed to save it. Twice, she'd thought him gone. It was nothing short of a miracle they were able to save it—and him. "I'm glad to see you've managed to keep it attached."

He gave a hearty laugh. "Just as I promised." He gestured to the men behind him. "These are my friends. We are all with you."

She gave them a grateful nod. "Thank you for your faith in me."

Not a moment too soon, Tristan appeared by her side in his red uniform with the golden griffin on it. His grave face told her he had already been made aware of her predicament. "What happened?"

"The men say they were bribed," she conveyed with a sour tone. "Is there anything to be done?"

He shot a scowl in Dawnton's direction. "Maybe under different circumstances, but it seems the high council has made an exception this time since there is a fifth contestant. My father fought it, but he was outvoted."

Wasn't that just convenient?

After a still moment, she nodded in acceptance. "If a full purse could persuade them to abandon me, then they were never true supporters… I'll just have to make the best of it."

Tristan wasn't so easily beaten. "Take some of my men."

She shook her head. "I won't let you do that."

"Yes, you will." His voice was as set as stone. "If *they* get to use loopholes to gain the upper hand, then so do we." He held up his pinky. "Me and you, remember?"

She gazed into his eyes, to the tranquil blue sea that grounded her. Linking her pinky with his, she repeated, "Me and you."

He raised her hand to his lips, kissing her knuckles where they intertwined with his. "I'll go send my men over now. We'll meet you at the river."

She attempted to keep her expression neutral as he mentioned the river, but Tristan noticed the shift in her. This time, he whispered. "You're still afraid of the water?"

Her fallen gaze gave him all the answers he needed.

"Keep your eyes off the river and stay in the boat. You won't have to swim; just keep as far away from the other boats as possible and watch for the rocks. It'll be over before you know it." With that, he kissed the back of her hand one last time, heading to his own crimson tent.

Soon after Tristan departed, she and her men collected their weapons and strategized. They were each allowed swords, one set of bows and arrows, and a handful of daggers. It wasn't a lot, but the restrictions would apply to others, too.

She had barely strapped a dagger to her thigh when Khan called out with a grin, "Drengr!"

Her hands froze. *For the love of the gods, please no.*

She spun around. Roman and nine others in red uniforms entered her tent. As promised, Tristan had provided a handful of men. But she'd had no idea that would include his brother.

Roman greeted Khan like they were old acquaintances, clasping hands and embracing with a firm pat. A flash of annoyance seized her, irritated by how his rare smile was so freely given to others—another form of punishment.

The rest of the soldiers joined in for the reunion. She held back an eye roll, yanking her sword off the table and securing it to her back. *Oh good, all of them are friends.*

Roman's golden eyes blazed in her direction, scrutinizing her from head to toe.

She folded her arms, popping out her hip. "What are you doing here?"

His mouth tightened, slinking closer. "A simple thank you for the help would suffice."

Help indeed. She had enough on her plate without worrying about internal resistance.

"You didn't have to come."

"It wasn't my choice," he replied with a sharpness that matched hers. "Trust me, I like the arrangement as much as you do." He paused as he looked over to the green tent. "But if Dawnton wants to embody his symbol, we'll do the same."

She eyed him; she could almost mistake his expression for protectiveness. She gathered her courage to ask a question that had been gnawing at her. "They call you Drengr?"

His jaw feathered, pausing before he answered. "Yes."

"What does it mean?"

"If you want to be on time, I suggest we get going." He turned on his heel, stalking off for the horses.

It took a moment for her to realize he wanted her to follow. So, with her arms still crossed, she followed him to his horse, annoyed that he hadn't answered her question.

He motioned for her to mount.

She met his gaze with resistance. "I can ride my own horse."

"We are short on horses. We'll all have to pair up."

She didn't move.

He let out an irritated sigh. "Look, I made a promise to Tristan that I'd look after you, so that's what I'm doing."

She'd rather walk the miles barefoot just to avoid sharing a saddle with him. But Tristan had offered his aid, and she was in no position to deny that. Plus, she didn't want to give Roman the satisfaction of thinking she was intimidated by him.

So her pride got her up onto the horse, ignoring his helping hand. She mounted it like second nature.

Roman climbed on behind her. His chest pressed against her back as his powerful forearms extended around her to grasp the reins, as though he was demonstrating how effortlessly he could overpower her. His warm breath brushed against her cheek as she was engulfed by a blend of musk and cedar—a scent she'd never bothered to acknowledge before now.

"On your order," he drawled next to her ear.

She shot him a vexing glance over her shoulder. Nonetheless, she looked past him at the men. "Mount your horses."

And may the sea and sky gods help her get through this alive.

CHAPTER 24

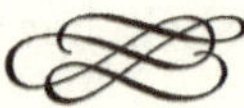

Rose braced herself at the sight of the roaring water. It was unusually high for this time of year, remnants of the harsh winter reinforcing its depths. The rapid current crashed against the massive boulders, sending echoes through the tall, slender trees.

In the midst of this raw power, a smooth body of water lay at the edge of the river, cradling five large boats. Each of them bore the designated House flags. In addition to Tristan's red griffin, Dawnton's green serpent, and Rose's blue dragon, she spotted Grant's brown griffin and Emmett's purple wolf, waving proudly in the wind.

Roman dismounted first, not bothering to extend a hand to assist her down. She didn't need it, gracefully dismounting the horse on her own.

She didn't waste a moment before she strode to join the others waiting by the riverbank, trying to leave him in the dust.

Roman's voice cut through the silence, his powerful strides easily keeping up with her pace. "Just so you know, most women in Cathan don't know how to ride a horse like that… or feel like that." His words hung in the air, thick with suspicion.

Her stomach sank, but she kept walking with quick strides. "And how is that?" Rose played it off, putting on her gloves.

"Like a soldier."

Her cheeks flushed at how closely he'd been paying attention. "My mother's always complained that I'm a tomboy." It wasn't entirely untrue. Thankfully, he didn't have time to pursue it as they reached the crowd.

After regrouping, she and the other participants clambered into the rowboats. She squashed the growing fear that threatened to take over as she took her place at the front. She spotted her mother among the spectators on the riverbank, including the royal family and the queen and princess of Vertmere. Behind them, the rest of the court eagerly waited for the challenge to begin.

Her mother frowned at the sight of several of Tristan's men in her boat. Rose managed to give her the brightest smile possible, trying to soothe her mother's worries along with her own.

The king and all twelve council members were the last to arrive, making their way to the shore. Lord Martin looked especially smug until he spotted Tristan's men in her boat. A blink later, he stomped over to the king, jabbing a grubby finger in her direction. Although she couldn't overhear their discussion over the river, it was clear that Lord Martin's argument held no weight. The king did nothing about it. Lord Martin's expression curdled like sour milk.

The king treaded for the docks, yelling over the rushing river. "Today's challenge is simple." He held up a golden replica of the sun relic of Cathan. "Retrieve this first, and you win the challenge. You must row upstream, cross the firewall, and locate the sun relic hidden in the ancient ruins. A true leader never abandons his men. Therefore, all of your men must be present at the ruins when you capture the relic, or you will lose points. No killing is allowed under any circumstances. Any who commit the crime will also meet the same fate." The king's threatening gaze ran over all of them. "We'll begin at the sound of the cannon. Good luck to you all." He raised the flag in his hand. "*To succession!*"

"*To succession!*" they roared back.

She glanced fleetingly at Tristan, his boat anchored beside hers. He gave her an encouraging nod, though his white knuckles clutching his oar gave him away.

On the opposite side sat Grant, who winked at her. Emmett and

Dawnton, further down, wore only scowls, their enraged eyes fixed on Tristan's men in her boat.

"On your mark," King Henrik called, holding the white flag higher.

The moment the king lowered the flag, a thunderous cannon blast erupted through the forest, startling a flock of geese into flight. The contestants sprang into action as she plunged her oar into the water and rowed as if her life depended on it.

She and Tristan were the first out of the docks, but only by a fraction. She would deny it until her last breath if anyone asked, but in those first crucial moments, she was glad to have Roman's lethal arm strength on her side as they surged upriver.

She risked a quick glance back. Grant was tailing her closely, while Dawnton and Emmett lagged behind, with Dawnton edging slightly ahead, taking longer to enter the current.

She pushed her arms to go faster, clutching her oar with a death grip, throwing her upper body into it.

They had only made it a few yards down the river when she heard shouting.

Her head whipped back. Dawnton's boat had slowed to a sluggish pace, taking on water as he bellowed orders at his men. She hadn't the faintest idea how that could have happened so quickly until she saw Grant parading a smirk. The accumulating water in his boat forced Dawnton to devote half his men to bailing it out with buckets, allowing Emmett to advance.

She did her best not to gloat about it.

Halfway down the river, Grant's boat pulled ahead of hers, a broad smile appearing on his face as he passed.

Gritting her teeth, she rowed faster. Despite her fear threatening to lock her joints, she managed to keep her eyes off the raging water.

Her arms screamed with exhaustion by the time she saw the dock. Tristan's men reached land first, with Grant at his heels. She and her men docked next. She didn't spare a glance to see how far back Emmett was as they scrambled out of the boat.

She didn't need to tell them to run. The moment their feet touched dry land, they were off in a sprint.

She found a steady rhythm, mindfully managing her breathing, pushing her legs to move faster, suddenly grateful for the miles Zareb forced her to run during their early-morning sessions. She had always been a decent runner, but today—today, she soared faster than the wind. Her feet barely scraped the ground, attributing her speed to the adrenaline pumping in her veins.

When they cleared the tree line, they were met by a high stone wall at the edge of the forest—the remnants of the first castle of Cathan. It meant the ruins weren't far past this point.

Five ropes hung off the wall, along with their House flags, equally spread apart from each other. Guarding the battlement wall was a group of soldiers who bore no colors. They were firing fire arrows at Grant's and Tristan's men, already clambering up the ropes.

"Raise your shields!" she shouted, raising her own high as they plowed for the thick rope hovering atop her flag. One by one, they climbed, scaling it while swerving to dodge the fire arrows.

She remained on the ground, letting her men go first to confirm they all made it over. The relentless fire arrows continued to rain down, making it difficult for them to scale quickly. She had to do something.

"We need to take out the arrows," Roman advised popping up next to her, sidestepping one just in time.

"Thank you, I'm well aware," she snapped, already thinking of a plan. "You stay here and make sure everyone gets over. I'll bring Zareb and take out the fire arrows."

Together, she and Zareb climbed. Halfway up, her arms started to tremble, still weary from the river. She pushed on, shifting the brunt of her weight to her legs, dodging an arrow aimed for her shoulder. She twisted to the side, with Zareb mimicking her below.

She peeked over her shoulder to see how Grant was faring. He was already atop the wall, taking out the fire arrows for his side. Meanwhile, Tristan's forces were nearly all over the wall. She needed to act quickly if they were to combine forces at the ruins as planned.

When they reached the summit, she and Zareb unsheathed their swords and disarmed the three men with fire arrows. Another soldier rushed her, but within a few moments, she sent his sword flying from his hands, slicing off his yellow life flag, forcing him to surrender. Meanwhile, Zareb fought the other two, bringing them to their knees.

She still had five men below, including Roman, but to her dismay, Dawnton's and Emmett's men had now joined them at the wall—Emmett's men brawling with Grant's on the ground. Unlike the others, Dawnton's men weren't all climbing. Instead, he split his group into two, sending some upward while he led a handful in another direction toward... Roman.

"Look out!" she shouted over the battlement wall.

Roman spun in the nick of time to deflect Dawnton's blow, fighting him and four others off while allowing the tail end of their party to climb. Dawnton seemed determined to push past Roman, but why? Why fight them instead of focusing on getting over the wall himself? Then it hit her—Dawnton was trying to sever her rope.

She quickly handed over the bow and arrows to Zareb. "Try to shoot them down. I'll be back."

Without another thought, she raced down the stony ramparts, passing through Tristan and Grant's turrets. Dodging their men as fast as she could, aiming straight for Dawnton's turret.

Dawnton spotted her, shouting a warning to his men climbing, but it was too late. She reached his turret just in time to sever the rope before his first man could reach the top. It sent all four of them back to the ground with a loud thud. She struck down his flag along with it, tossing it onto a torch for good measure.

Her defiant stare bore into Dawnton's. He glared back with vicious eyes, letting out a frustrated roar.

A smirk sadistic enough to rival Grant's claimed her lips.

Dawnton ripped into his bow and arrow, yanking it back as he aimed. She dashed away, evading the arrows as she fled.

She returned to her turret, finding her men had not only ascended the wall but were already down the other side, waiting for her. She maneuvered herself over the parapet wall, letting the rope glide between her fingers, the friction warming her palms.

She braced for impact, but strong arms caught her before her feet touched the ground.

She looked up, only to be thrown into a bottomless sea, plunging straight into Tristan's eyes. And for once, she wasn't afraid of the tranquility of the water. She wished to linger in its depths, to dive deeper and be so consumed by the vastness that she had no desire to escape.

She was ripped to the surface for air as Tristan's mouth lifted into a glorious smile. "Come on, warrior princess. Emmett's men are holding off Grant, but not for long. We have a clear shot." He set her down, sliding his hand into hers.

She gripped it back with all the strength she possessed, and together, they ran like hell's fury for the ruins.

CHAPTER 25

They charged up the steps leading to the crumbling rubble, its charred stones entwined with thick vines and overgrown moss. Gaps gaped in the towering walls, letting a few hazy streaks of sunlight sneak through the pillars. A damp mist hovered in the cool air, clinging to her clothing. They needed to search the deserted castle quickly; they might have had a lead, but Grant and his men would undoubtedly be close behind.

"We'll split up." Tristan faced Roman and Zareb. "You both stay here with the men and guard the main entrance to buy us time. Rose and I will look for the relic."

Roman and Zareb didn't argue, giving an obedient nod before they split up.

Together, she and Tristan navigated through the ruins, clambering up the deteriorating stairs.

Sacred—that's what this place had always been. These walls, which had once symbolized strength and unity, now only served as a painful history lesson—burned centuries ago when the dragons of old unleashed their wrath on Cathan. She'd often stare at it during her adventures with Xavier and Tristan, though she had never once dared enter. Rightfully so.

The dead deserved peace, too. Legend said the ghosts of the burned souls still lingered within their walls.

She believed it.

Only the echoes of their footsteps reached her ears as they searched the dreary halls, inspecting every room and surface they could find.

The sudden clash of swords drifted from outside.

Grant. Urgency drove her to move faster, frantically examining every crevice and hidden nook.

They were climbing the final staircase when a deep groan moaned from below, shifting the stone beneath her feet.

With little time to react, she sprinted up the remaining steps, with Tristan at her heels.

One second he was following her, and the next he wasn't.

Tristan's leg disappeared through the floor, alongside a large chunk of the staircase. He immediately grappled for a hold on the stairs, dangling from the gaping hole. He tried to lift himself, but the stone had swallowed his leg, pinning him and leaving a large gash on his upper thigh.

"Tristan!" She didn't think twice before returning to retrieve him.

"No! Go," he said through a sharp breath. "Go and find the relic before Grant does."

Like hell. "Not without you."

She tiptoed back down the steps, pausing when the rock groaned underneath her weight.

"Don't," he pleaded, trying to mask his pain. "Just go."

"No," she refused. She crouched down, cautiously distributing her weight as she extended her hand. "Me and you, remember?"

His blue eyes shone up at her like she was the sun relic itself. "Me and you," he murmured. He grasped her hand with his, and she braced, about to pull him up—

Grant materialized at the bottom of the stairs. A slithering smirk played on his lips. "Well, well, look what we have here." He widened his eyes dramatically at the two. "Oh, don't let me interrupt—I just need to get by, and then you two can continue to profess your love." He took a few steps up the stairs.

"Stop!" she warned. "You'll make the whole thing collapse."

Grant ignored the warning, continuing. The stone groaned again.

Acting quickly, she hauled Tristan upward, heaving with every ounce of strength she had as his leg finally came free, but in the process, a fresh, deep cut tore open his lower leg. Tristan hissed.

She draped his arm over her shoulders, helping him stand as they hobbled up the stairs, mindful to hug the wall as they did. Grant's footsteps were gaining on them.

Just as she and Tristan reached the top, the stones groaned again and the ground shook. She checked back just in time to see Grant disappear with a cry.

They had no choice but to continue, inching their way down a dark, lengthy hallway. Rose bore what weight she could as Tristan limped beside her, a trail of blood running down his leg.

When she was sure they were safe, she let Tristan slump against the wall. "Are you okay? Let me see." She went to crouch down to get a better look at his gash.

Tristan stopped her, shaking his head as he breathed heavily. "No. I'll be fine, let's keep going. I don't want any more surprises."

She didn't argue as she draped his arm back over her shoulders, shuffling their way down the rest of the dark hallway.

Finally, they came upon what she could only assume was the old throne room. The ceiling had all but collapsed, letting the sun pour its light onto the timeworn stone throne at the heart of the room. A lone, rusted, cobweb-covered, full-length mirror sat in the corner, shrouded in a thick layer of dust.

This place felt… familiar somehow, like a remnant of a long-lost memory. She gazed upon the throne, feeling a ghostly breeze in the air as something stirred inside her. It tugged at her like an invisible string, like… like it was supposed to be hers.

The sun relic was nowhere in sight.

She left Tristan near the entrance and quickly began searching the room, examining each pillar, searching under every stone, scanning the scorched remnants of the throne. Nothing. Her throat bobbed.

"It's not here," she whispered, letting her hand slide off the dusty throne.

"That's impossible," Tristan said, limping over to help her look. "It has to be here."

She glanced back at the crumbled staircase entrance. Grant hadn't discovered it either. Or maybe he just assumed it wasn't there because they had yet to find it. But soon enough, Emmett and Dawnton would arrive to add to the chaos, and they'd have a brawl on their hands.

She muttered a curse under her breath. Perhaps they had looked too hastily. Perhaps she had—

A subtle multicolored glow caught her eye, like an invisible bubble or force field hovering above the throne. *A glamour.* She remembered them from her studies on magical artifacts. A form of old magic wielded long before she was born. They must have discovered something to create the glamour, but what? She swept her eyes over her surroundings again, seeing if—

Of course!

She marched straight up to the aged mirror. Using her sleeve, she wiped away the dust to unveil a bright reflection. Her eyes combed the image, examining it. She spotted a tiny sparkle. There, hanging off the half-charred stone throne, was the relic.

Her mouth broke into a triumphant smile. "Tristan!"

She helped drag him over to see for himself. His eyes filled with awe, looking back and forth between the reflection and the stone throne. "How in Vallor did you know?"

"I saw the glamour, and I remembered our lessons about enchanted objects."

Tristan's lips grazed the top of her head. "You are *brilliant,* Rose. Brilliant."

She didn't disagree, shrugging with a proud grin.

The pair didn't waste a moment as she supported Tristan over to the weathered throne.

"Together?" Tristan said with a conquering smile.

"Together," she agreed.

At the same time, they stretched out their hands, grasping the relic as it materialized.

CHAPTER 26

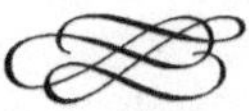

White tents sat pitched in the open fields, nestled between the woods and the ruins, caring for the injured participants. Campfires blazed as servants flitted back and forth, readying the celebration following the challenge. Rose wanted to be the one to attend to Tristan's leg, but another healer insisted she be brought to a separate tent for her own examination despite her reassurance that she was perfectly fine.

Once the healer and her mother had finished fussing, she checked on Tristan. His family and a few others had already swarmed his tent. So she made herself useful by helping those suffering from burns from the fire arrows.

She'd just gotten done tending to a third-degree burn when a healer stepped out of a far tent. "Rose! This one is asking for you!"

Curious, she wiped her hands on her apron and entered the tent. She peered down at the man on the cot; despite the thick layer of dust covering him, the emerald-green eyes stood out at once. *Grant*. A large gash had sliced his chest and cheekbone from the fall. Both of which were bleeding out onto the cot.

"Hello, Rose." His signature smile was still fixed in place despite looking like he had just emerged from a grave. "I was just wondering if you might be kind enough to sew me up."

She hesitated in the doorway but dragged her feet to the cot. A small sliver of guilt formed for not stopping to check if he was alright after he fell through the staircase.

As if he knew, he said, "You're not going to even fight me on it?" His smile widened. "The guilt must be eating you alive."

With narrowed eyes, she grabbed a fresh apron, threw it on, and washed her hands. "In all fairness, I *did* warn you." She swiped the clean rag by his bed and dipped it in a bowl of water so hot it made her hands throb.

"That's true, but how was I... supposed to know you were... telling the truth?" he managed through graveled coughs.

"Try to hold still." She focused on his chest first, dabbing it clean. Out of the corner of her eye, she caught him staring. "What?"

"You're touching my bare skin," he said with a crafty grin.

She stopped mid-movement. "Did you plan this?"

He attempted to laugh, but another cough consumed the sound. "How could I plan to fall through those stairs? No, this is just a lucky turn of events for me. It's the least you could do since you and your lover teamed up against me. I should feel flattered that you had to go to such great lengths to beat me; it feels quite unfair, really. Though I suppose Dawnton being allowed to bribe your men wasn't quite fair either."

She peered up from the wound. He was staring at the tent ceiling, uncharacteristically sober. "It was you who sabotaged his boat, wasn't it?" she said quietly.

"I don't know what you're talking about." But the gratification in his eyes said otherwise. He cleared his throat, coughing again. "So, are you going to help me?" He looked at his wound, then at her, reinstating his famous grin. "You did say you would if I were ever bleeding out."

He was pushing his luck, but an unsolicited warmth spread in her chest as she dipped a separate rag in alcohol. He winced as she brought it to the edge of his gash.

"Not the kind of touch you were hoping for, is it? Wait 'til I get the thread and needle."

~

An hour later, the court gathered beneath three large tents sandwiched together for the placement announcements. The sun had dropped, diving for the tree line, blocking the view of the sea just beyond. Thankfully, the warm air had turned crisp as the wind picked up, sending a fresh breeze over the camp.

A small wooden platform was positioned at the center of the tent, where the council, the king, and the contestants stood. Tristan's and Rose's men remained just behind them on the wooden platform, still wearing their respective uniforms. After all, this victory was as much theirs as it was hers and Tristan's.

Rose's mother, the queen, and Harriet sat in the front row. Harriet's smile beamed brighter than it had in days, and even the queen seemed cheery. Meanwhile, the Vertmerian queen and princess remained present, their usual guards, dressed in green uniforms, surrounding them. She was still perplexed as to why they were entertaining the succession at all; perhaps the peace treaty negotiations were faltering, as Lord Barron had suggested. She didn't have long to dwell on the thought as the king began to speak.

"The first succession challenge is concluded!" King Henrik proclaimed from the elevated wooden platform. "This is a challenge that will be remembered for generations. We take pride in the valor displayed by each contestant today. In fourth place, we have Emmett with thirty-eight points!"

The audience broke out in applause.

"In third place, with forty-six points, is Dawnton! In second place, with fifty-eight points, is Grant! And in first place, with sixty-two points each, are Tristan and Rose!"

Tristan grasped her hand and raised it high in victory. After which, they encouraged their men to bow as a fresh wave of applause erupted. Roman squeezed his way through to stand next to Tristan, clapping him on the shoulder, exchanging broad smiles.

The applause echoed in the fields until the king resumed speaking. "In closing, I want to leave off with a treat. I've witnessed a creature like this only once in my life as a young boy." He signaled for the servants to bring forth the surprise.

She almost didn't believe what she saw.

Two men carried a phoenix to the wooden podium. Gasps of awe spread at the sight of the magical creature. Its yellow, orange, and red feathers shone so vibrant they seemed to emit their own light, shimmering brightly in the warm rays of the setting sun.

"I can still recall the song it sang, and how it inspired me to face my own succession challenges. Tonight, we all have the rare honor of listening to it sing." The king stepped back, and everyone applauded as the servants held it high.

Everyone's attention remained fixed on the phoenix when a bad feeling twisted in her gut, creeping into Rose's senses, like a premonition. She scoured the crowd, seeing nothing out of the ordinary. She brushed the feeling aside.

A hush fell over the tents as the phoenix unfurled its majestic wings, displaying its proud feathers. It opened its beak and began singing a melody so pure and clear she swore the tune captivated every creature close enough to hear.

Another wave of foreboding coursed through her, more urgent this time. She scanned the audience again. Still nothing. Maybe it was just the remaining adrenaline from the first challenge that kept her on edge.

She almost dismissed the feeling again until yet another wave consumed her, more powerful this time, like a pulse of energy that she could follow, guiding her gaze along the tree line.

She froze at what she saw.

At the heart of the aura, a hooded figure crouched on a branch concealed by the foliage. He was so well camouflaged, she would have missed him entirely if she hadn't sensed the energy. Although he was too distant to make out his face, icy-blue eyes flashed from beneath his dark hood. She could have sworn he resembled—no, it couldn't be.

Xavier?

The unknown figure swiftly readied a bow and arrow, directing his aim at Tristan as the phoenix's song faded into its final notes.

She spun to warn Tristan, but Roman stood between them, blocking her way. She wouldn't have time to reach him.

"Roman, the trees!"

Whether it was the way her nails dug into his forearm or the sheer panic in her voice, Roman acted without hesitation, springing into action just as the phoenix's last note dissipated into the air.

If she had blinked, she would've missed what happened next entirely.

Roman pushed Rose behind him before propelling himself in front of Tristan, shoving him down, raising his shield. The black-tipped arrow flew with such speed that it blasted right through Roman's shield, leaving a deep scratch on his forearm before it stopped, narrowly missing his face.

A scream pierced the air, alerting the crowd. Chaos ensued as everyone scattered, seeking shelter from the anonymous attacker.

Tristan jumped to his feet, eyes widening. Roman had saved his life.

"Stay low," Roman instructed, yanking out the arrow that had pierced his shield. "There may be more."

Her eyes raced back to the trees, but there was nothing but branches swaying in the wind.

A hand landed on her arm, making her jump. "Zareb!" she gasped in relief.

"Get her out of here," Tristan ordered, whipping out his sword and shield.

Zareb didn't need to be told twice. He dragged her away from the platform and charged for the castle.

"Zareb, my mother," she said as she ran with him.

"She's waiting for us," Zareb assured. He led her to the camp's perimeter, where her mother and two horses waited for them.

"Rose! Thank the gods!" her mother cried, hugging her.

"Come on," Zareb urged, grabbing Rose's waist without permission and hoisting her up on the horse.

"I'll ride with your mother," Zareb said. "Stay close and avoid riding in a straight line in case there are more." He sent her steed off with a smack.

CHAPTER 27

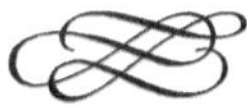

Rose, her mother, and Zareb were directed to their rooms, just as the rest of the court had been. They remained together in her room, waiting for the all-clear. Even as the night progressed without a word, they waited. It must have been near midnight when her mother began to crack.

"How did this happen?!" her mother exclaimed to no one in particular. "There were guards all over those woods."

"The woods were secure. We made sure of it," Zareb said with confidence.

Her mother was not reassured. "Well, thank our lucky stars that Roman was there, or else Tristan would have gotten that arrow for certain." She snatched a fan off Rose's vanity and fanned herself in quick flutters.

"It was lucky," Zareb agreed, throwing a glance at Rose. "Incredibly lucky."

She averted her gaze. She still hadn't figured out how she'd managed to spot him. Maybe it was a strange intuition—a sort of sixth sense. All she knew was that if she hadn't warned Roman, and he hadn't acted as quickly as he did, the arrow would've struck Tristan. A direct hit like that—she shivered to think of it.

"Perhaps we should leave? Go find shelter somewhere else?" Her mother threw the idea to Zareb.

"We wait," he said.

Her mother let out an irritated sigh. "I hate waiting. We should've heard something by now. What if something bad has happened, and we're just sitting here like ducks?"

In perfect timing, a familiar sequenced knock at the door.

Zareb's eyes met hers.

"Open it. It's Tristan," she said.

Warily, Zareb opened the door with one hand on the hilt of his sword, though the precaution was unnecessary. Tristan's exhausted, dirty figure stepped through the door.

"I'm sorry I didn't come sooner," he apologized, his expression grim.

Her body came to attention at once. "What's the matter? What's happened?" she asked.

His grave eyes made her heart pound. "It's Roman. I don't have much time, but something's wrong. He's got a fever, and he keeps throwing up. He can scarcely breathe. The healers think the arrow must have been laced with some sort of poison."

Her mouth parted in disbelief. Roman had been the epitome of health just a few hours ago—not even a scratch or a burn to indicate an infection, and even that wouldn't have come on that fast.

"Can anything be done?" she asked.

"The healers are doing everything they can, but I'm afraid none of them are familiar with the poison. We need someone well-versed in herbology…" He swallowed, giving her a desperate look.

She knew what he was asking. "I don't know if I'll be better help than the healers, but I'll see what I can do."

"Please be careful," her mother warned, surprising her by not forcing her to stay.

"She'll return safe," Tristan promised.

"Stay with my mother," Rose said to Zareb. "I'll be back as soon as I can."

~

Roman's large room was crowded and cramped. Three healers stood clustered by his canopy bed, alongside his parents and Harriet. To her surprise, Beth was there, too, sitting beside Roman, holding his hand. The queen looked beside herself, with tears flowing down her face. Roman's deep groans filled the room above the voices.

Rose went straight to Roman. His body was a sweaty mess.

"He's gotten worse just in the time I went to get you," Tristan whispered bitterly.

The others finally looked up, surprise plastered on their faces as Tristan and Rose edged up next to the bed.

"What are you doing here?" the queen asked sharply.

Rose pulled her gaze away from Roman to the queen, pained by the underlying hostility in her voice.

"I asked her to come," Tristan retorted with a voice as strong as iron. "And you will let her help—that is, unless you want Roman's death on your conscience."

The queen's piercing eyes didn't falter but she said nothing in rebuttal, knowing she couldn't refuse help.

Roman's weakened gaze connected with hers. She could have sworn his eyes softened the moment he saw her, almost making her believe he was relieved she was there. That was before he gasped for air, rolling over onto his side to empty the contents of his stomach into a nearby bucket. To her credit, Beth quickly positioned herself beside him, holding the bucket steady.

"Do you have the arrow?" she asked Tristan.

The healer with a snooty expression came forward, holding the arrow wrapped in white cloth. "It's obviously a nightshade poison," the healer snipped.

Rose took it, examining the arrowhead, careful not to touch it with her bare hands.

"I don't know why she's here, Your Majesty. We are more than capable—"

Tristan cut the healer off. "You and the other healers can step outside for the time being. I'll summon you back when you are needed."

"Tristan, they're trying to help," the queen scolded.

The king agreed with Tristan, interrupting their spat. "Leave us," he ordered.

The healer bowed, her wounded pride accompanying her as she strode out with the other two healers.

Rose's attention went back to the arrowhead, filthy and covered in dark soot. At first glance, it did resemble nightshade. However, upon deeper inspection, there were traces of a blood-red color...

No.

Oh, please, gods, no.

She hurried to the candles beside Roman's bed, holding the arrow toward the light. As she suspected, the red streaks shimmered in the flicker of the flames. This wasn't nightshade.

"What is it?" Tristan asked, stepping beside her, his eyes on the arrow.

"Dragonshade," she whispered, so low only Tristan could hear, not wanting to alarm the others.

Tristan's mouth fell open. "What? How is that even possible? Are you sure?"

"I'm certain," she said, and she was. His body's inability to cool itself, the way he couldn't keep any liquids down, his dilated pupils. "Don't you see the traces of red?"

Tristan shook his head, inspecting it himself. "I don't see anything."

Her brows pinched, wondering why he couldn't see what was so clearly right in front of him, but it didn't matter.

"Please tell me there's something that'll save him," Tristan whispered.

"There's an antidote, but it grows far to the north—too far. Past the borders and into the lands of Ostlyn. I'm afraid he doesn't have nearly that much time... He'll be lucky if he lasts the night."

Tristan's expression hardened into determination. "There must be something else."

She searched her memory. Dragonshade was a poison cultivated from finely crushed scales of dragons. And like all magical elements, they held unique attributes... She had an idea.

"When it comes to things with magical properties, often its opposite is what can bring balance," she recounted, remembering a quote from a book she'd read.

"I don't understand," Tristan replied. "What's the opposite of Dragonshade?"

"Not the poison itself—the opposite of the dragon's power source."

"What does that mean?"

"It means we need something powerful enough to match the Dragonshade's properties," she explained simply.

"What could match one of the most powerful species of our realm?" Tristan asked, shifting his distressed gaze to Roman.

She didn't know. The dragons of old had not been sighted for centuries. The only thing that could come close was another magical creat—

"The phoenix." Her head snapped up, wondering why she hadn't thought of it sooner. "Its tears might be enough to match its properties with its healing powers. It's the only thing that might be able to help him."

Tristan turned to his parents, who were eagerly watching them. "We need the phoenix. Where is it?"

His mother took two timid steps closer, concern brimming in her wet eyes as she looked to her husband for an answer.

Understanding flooded the king's gaze. "It's being returned to its home as we speak. As soon as the ceremony ended, its caretaker took off with it."

"We have to stop them," Rose said. It was Roman's only chance. "I'll get a horse and see if I can catch them on the road."

Tristan's hand shot out, locking on her arm, looking at her like she was mental. "No. I'll go. I don't want you putting yourself in danger."

"You'll both go," King Henrik said, ending the debate for them. "We'll stay and look after Roman. Go… and hurry."

The queen muffled a sob.

"We will," Rose promised.

There was no time to lose.

CHAPTER 28

The two made it to the stables in record time, Tristan mounting his horse first. Rose slipped past her steed to uncover the sword she had hidden in the hay for her training, securing it to her back before climbing up onto her horse.

His eyes widened as he watched her. "Since when did you get a sword? And how did you know it was there?"

"I put it there because I've been training with it. Come on. We need to reach them before they get to the boats."

Tristan still paused, eyeing her like he didn't know who he was looking at. But he dismissed it; there were more pressing matters at hand.

Rain battered the night sky as they raced toward the front gate, already drenched from the heavy droplets. Though the weather would slow them down, she prayed it would do the same for the phoenix.

Just as they were about to pass through the gates, a servant rushed to Tristan, startling his horse into an abrupt halt.

"I nearly ran you over," Tristan hissed. "Move!"

"Sir, there is a woman here; she says it's urgent," the servant explained.

"I have no time."

The servant didn't budge. "But sir, it's the caretaker of the phoenix."

Rose's eyes widened as she and Tristan exchanged awestruck glances.

It was a miracle.

She dismounted her horse at once.

"Take us to her," Tristan ordered, following suit.

They entered the grand hall just minutes later, rainwater dripping a trail from their cloaks. Rose let out a breath in relief when she saw the phoenix perched at the head table with its caretaker beside it.

The woman had wild, curly black hair, save for the one white streak framing her face, the length of it almost reaching her hips. Her skin was so pale and smooth that it resembled porcelain. Her bright blue eyes seemed to hold the knowledge they would come in haste, unalarmed at their abrupt entry.

"Your Highness," the woman greeted Tristan first with a respectful bow. "I am Ingrid, caretaker of the phoenix."

"How did you know we'd need you?" Tristan asked.

"I didn't." Ingrid's light, airy eyes glided to the phoenix. "He did. He wouldn't let me leave. He sensed that after tonight's events, he would be needed."

Rose studied the creature with wonder. They were brilliant, majestic creatures, to be sure, said to roam the skies centuries ago. They possessed incredible healing and regrowth properties alongside their ability to cut or destroy practically anything. And, of course, they were best known for being capable of rising from their own ashes, born new again. The phoenix's intense, vivid-yellow eyes stared back at her.

"He's been waiting for you," Ingrid said to her.

"We need help," Rose explained, looking between phoenix and Ingrid, unsure who to address. "Tristan's brother saved him from an arrow dipped in Dragonshade, but it scratched his arm. He's growing weaker and weaker by the moment. I fear he'll not last until morning."

The caretaker knew what they desired. "And you want the phoenix to heal him?"

"Yes," Tristan said. "Whatever your price, we'll pay it."

Ingrid raised an eyebrow. "I cannot speak for the phoenix, as he chooses to do as he wishes. But I can tell you he'll require something in return. And only he will decide how that debt is paid."

Rose studied the phoenix with hesitancy. "Does it speak?"

Ingrid nodded once, her mystical eyes glowing. "In his own way."

Tristan addressed the phoenix now. "Will you help us?"

A heavy silence filled the room, holding their breath. Finally, the phoenix nodded, its brilliant, smooth feathers ruffling gracefully. Its curved orange beak sharpened to a lethal point.

"What is it you want in return?" Rose asked, knowing something so valuable as a phoenix tear would not come without a price.

The phoenix's eyes rested on her, its essence brushing against her mind. She stepped back involuntarily at the contact.

The phoenix's smooth, silken voice resonated deep within her mind. *I know who you are, Rosalie Versalles,* the phoenix said, *even if you do not. I can see into your past, present, and future; your path is not easy, but vital for our realm. You and you alone will have to face an ancient enemy to safeguard the future of Vallor. You are a kindred spirit, Rosalie. For this reason, I require a simple favor. I grow near the end of my life cycle, and I need you to help me as I am reborn.*

Her breath caught. To be a part of phoenix's rebirth was a privilege only given to individuals like Ingrid, who were sworn to protect them.

She spoke back with her thoughts. *I don't understand. How can I do that?*

You see, during my last rebirth, I was caught in a trap and injured during the transformation. Ingrid saved me, but my wing has never fully recovered. He lifted his wing to reveal a crooked bone that had healed incorrectly. *I've been unable to fly ever since. We are incredibly vulnerable during the rebirth, and if I am to emerge healed and stronger, I will need more than Ingrid's help. I would ask you to sing as I am reborn.*

Rose's joints locked. She stared into the phoenix's yellow eyes as if sensing he knew what he asked of her. She hadn't sung a note since… since her father died. She had promised she'd never do it again. Her voice felt tainted and ugly. Misused and evil.

You want me to sing? How would that help mend your wing? I don't possess the power you seek.

Sing and find out, was all the phoenix said.

She lowered her gaze. She didn't know how her voice could make a difference, but it was a simple request, and if singing alone could save Roman, how could she refuse?

The creature awaited her answer with bright eyes. She simply replied, *Okay.*

Then it is agreed. Tears for a song, the phoenix said.

"He's agreed, but he's asked for something in return," Rose said, summarizing the conversation to Tristan.

Tristan's face contorted, glancing at the phoenix and then back to her. "What does he want?"

"He wants me to sing," she replied simply.

The phoenix turned to Ingrid, lowered its head, and blinked. Ingrid nodded, going to a large oak chest sitting on one of the tables. She pulled out what appeared to be a nest made of various twigs and materials. Ingrid placed the nest gently on the table and then took a small jar containing what she assumed were ashes. Ingrid opened the jar and sprin kled the dust over the nest.

Come, the phoenix commanded.

With steady steps, she left Tristan's side and approached the bird. He gazed at her, prompting her to extend her right arm. Slowly, the phoenix perched upon it, its talons gripping gently but with a strength that she knew could rip off her arm if he wanted to. It took the whole strength of her arm to bear his weight, but she held firm. His vivid-yellow eyes watched her closely as he blinked expectantly.

What should I sing? she asked.

Something from your heart.

She stopped wracking her brain and took a deep mental breath, closing her eyes to search in her heart instead. The phoenix raised his wings up, revealing his beautiful ombré plumage, while he closed his eyes.

And then she sang a poem she'd read years ago.

In the depths of night,
darkness reigns supreme,
lost in the shadows of a
long-forgotten dream.

But within the quiet whispers of the night,
an ember starts to glow,
from the ashes of the past,
a new life begins to grow.

A radiant glow surrounded the phoenix, becoming brighter with every word she sang.

Rise from the ashes,
phoenix in the sky.
With wings of flame and courage
we'll watch you soar and fly,
from the embers of your heart,
a new dawn will rise.
Rise from the ashes,
phoenix in the sky,
and reach beyond the clouds.
With every breath, comes a promise
of strength that never dies.
Rise from the ashes,
phoenix, rise.

The glow transformed into a searing flame, so hot it was as if the sun itself had spilled onto her arm, so blinding she had to shut her eyes. Her arm shook under the weight, but she refused to let it fall. The phoenix's flame moved up her arm, engulfing her entire body, its power making its way through her veins—so encompassing, she feared she might burn to ash with it.

But as soon as the blinding light ceased, so did the burning in her veins. Rose slowly opened one eye to find her arm still in the air, but the phoenix was gone. She peered down at the large pile of ash that now sat in the nest. A suspenseful silence settled as she stared at the pile of ash in hope.

The ash stirred as a small head appeared, revealing gold feathers and large amber eyes. The phoenix was just a baby, but every bit as majestic and grand as he was before. He shook off the remnants of the ashes, leaving the brilliant bird gleaming gold, shiny, and pure. The phoenix examined his wings as he spread them wide, revealing the damaged wing had healed.

She'd done it.

The phoenix let out a triumphant cry as he flapped his wings, launching himself into the air, soaring as a puff of ashes trailed behind. A broad smile filled Rose's face, and she felt lighter than she had in ages. Free, even. Like she could spread her arms and fly herself. Perhaps it was the lingering magic of the phoenix in her body, but deep down, she sensed it was something more profound.

The phoenix returned, settling once more on her arm. *Just as you have healed me, you have healed yourself. Your gifts are not evil; they can be used for great good. Even in the darkest of times, you must remember that the small choices we make every day reveal who we truly are, not what we are foretold to be. We become only what we believe we are.*

She hadn't even realized she was crying until she felt a warm tear trickle down her cheek.

Your friend needs you, the phoenix said.

With the phoenix still perched on her arm, she turned to Tristan. "We'll need something to hold the tears."

Ingrid was the one to step in. "I have something." She reached into the oak chest and, a moment later, handed a small vial to Tristan.

Despite appearing as if he'd encountered a ghost, Tristan stepped forward, emerging from his daze. He retrieved the vial from Ingrid and carefully presented it to the small phoenix. The creature leaned in, allowing a graceful, glistening silver tear to roll down his cheek. One... two... three tears.

Mix them with water and make sure he drinks all of it, the phoenix instructed.

"Thank you," she replied.

And thank you. You should go, the phoenix said in parting. *Dragonshade moves quickly.*

Tristan bowed before the phoenix. "Thank you—both of you. The crown will never forget this."

"I would thank your friend." Ingrid's mystical eyes landed on Rose. "A phoenix's tears come at no small price."

With the flask in hand, Tristan made for the door.

Ingrid's voice stopped her from following. "Whatever the phoenix told you, you would do well to remember it. Advice from magical creatures like a phoenix will bless you if you do."

"I'll never forget," Rose reassured her. She couldn't even if she wanted to.

Ingrid gave a gentle smile in farewell. "I hope you do; good luck, fair one."

CHAPTER 29

With the phoenix's tears in hand, Rose and Tristan rushed back to Roman's room, their figures sure to be a blur in the vacant corridors as their hurried footsteps echoed off the cold stone floor.

When they entered the room, there was a stillness—a clear indication that Roman's condition had worsened. The king and queen remained by his bedside, his mother's eyes swollen and red. Beth and Harriet were still present, their faces reflecting the queen's distress.

Roman lay drenched in sweat, his body unnervingly still. A weak wheeze accompanied each breath, eyelids squeezed shut, letting her know even though he was exhausted he was in too much pain to sleep.

"You're back already? Did you find them? Was it too late?" the king asked, preparing for the worst.

"We got it," Tristan answered, holding up the vial. "I'll explain everything later, but we need to give him this. Now."

The queen, Harriet, and Beth all let out a sob of relief.

Tristan made his way over to Roman. "Move," he barked at the lot of them. He handed Rose the vial.

With precision, she added the drops to a glass of water on the table beside the bed as Tristan and the king propped Roman's large body upright.

"Roman, can you hear me?" She searched his dull amber eyes for his focus. "You need to take this. It's important you drink all of it, so I need you to try to keep this down, okay?"

She could barely make out the slight nod of his head as she cradled his jaw in her hand, tilting his face upward. His groggy eyes fluttered open, revealing a rare glimpse of vulnerability she had seldom seen. She brought the cup to his cracked lips, gradually tilting it. With each gulp, his chest heaved as his hands clenched the sheets, but he swallowed every last drop.

The moment she withdrew the cup, Roman collapsed backward. Tristan and the king caught him and lowered him back onto the bed as he struggled to regain his breath.

"There, that should make you feel all better," Beth comforted as she returned to the bedside, almost as if she hoped her words could turn into reality.

Something in Rose's gut twisted at the sight.

"How long before we know it worked?" Harriet asked, speaking up for the first time, her voice weak and fragile.

"I don't know," Tristan confessed, looking disheartened that Roman's suffering hadn't immediately ceased.

"Give him time," Rose advised. "Dragonshade isn't something most live through." She hadn't grasped the gravity of her words until they'd escaped her lips, her gaze slipping from their horrified eyes.

"What do we do now?" Beth asked, holding Roman's hand.

"Let him rest," Rose instructed. "And let the healers back in. Keep him comfortable until he pulls through."

"Thank you, Rose." The queen stepped in front of her, blocking her from Roman. "We'll take it from here."

She was so shocked that she nearly convinced herself she had imagined it. Tristan fumed, outraged at his mother's impertinence, while Harriet mirrored his expression. Beth's, however, was quite the opposite—a confident sliver of smugness creeping in.

Tristan readied himself for a fight. "Don't you realize what Rose has just done—"

Rose grabbed his arm to silence him. "Of course," she interjected over Tristan. "I'll get out of your way." Her tone was gentle, skillfully concealing her pain. She pulled Tristan toward the door, leaning closer as she whispered, “Let me know when he's okay.”

He shook his head, still livid at his mother's behavior. “Stay. You have every right to be here—I don't trust the other healers as much as I do you.”

She offered him the warmest smile she could muster. “He'll be fine.” She wouldn't let herself think otherwise.

She let go of his arm and moved to leave, but the king stopped her in her tracks. His sparkling eyes were fixed on her, exuding deep gratitude.

“Rose, my dear, beautiful, clever girl.” He cupped her face with his large hands. “Once again, I'm in your debt.” He pulled her in for a tight hug. “I don't know how I can ever thank you.”

His embrace was so powerful, she could almost feel the love and gratitude pouring into her. Once she collected herself, she hugged him in return. “Of course,” she softly replied.

She could have cut the tension in the air with a dull knife, without even having to look to know that the queen and Beth were throwing daggers her way at the public display of affection.

Tristan opened the door for her. “Let me walk you.”

Rose shook her head. “No. He'll want to see you when he wakes.”

Tristan's face grew stubborn. “He'll want to see you, too. Don't be afraid of my mother. *Stay*.”

“I won't stay where I'm not wanted,” she said, despising the rejection.

“I want you here.”

“I know. But she's right. There's nothing more I can do. I'll only be in the way.”

Tristan's jaw clenched before finally conceding. “I'll come find you as soon as I can.” He grabbed her hand and drew her into his chest, pressing his lips against hers.

She froze under his touch, shocked that he'd dare with his family just ten feet away, knowing he'd have to face his mother's wrath later for it. Despite all this, she welcomed it, kissing him back with a longing she didn't know she had within her.

All too soon, he pulled away, subjecting her lips back to the cold air. “I love you, Rosalie Versalles.”

"And I'm the luckiest woman in the world because of it," she professed, squeezing his hand before slipping out the door.

Walking down the corridor, she rested a hand on her sword, her thoughts wandering back to the phoenix's words. He had warned that her journey would be crucial for their realm, that she would need to confront an enemy to protect Vallor's future. What could that possibly mean? What enemy? How was she to fight against an enemy who she didn't know?

Rose returned to the grand hall, hoping to find Ingrid and the phoenix, but to her disappointment, they were already gone. She was on her own to decipher the meaning behind the phoenix's words.

And she had a horrifying feeling that the answers may just alter her life forever.

CHAPTER 30

Rose felt like she'd just fallen asleep when warm yellow rays flooded through the window. She sat up slowly, wondering whether the knock she'd heard was real or just a figment of her imagination.

Another knock came.

"One moment," she called sleepily.

She snatched a dress, threw it on, and went to unlock the door. As soon as she opened it, Tristan embraced her.

"He pulled through," he said as his face buried into her hair. "We did it. He's alive."

She sighed in relief as she gripped him. "Thank the gods. I was so worried."

"He wants to see you. He's been asking ever since he woke… But first, how are you?" Tristan asked, his hands cupping her face as he searched her eyes.

"I'm fine," she said, sliding her hand onto his wrist.

His thumb stroked her cheek tenderly. "I don't believe you."

Her gaze fell away from his. How was she supposed to explain how she'd sensed the danger at the ceremony? It had all happened so fast. She'd barely caught a glimpse of the man's face before the arrow flew. Her eyes were sure it was Xavier, but her mind argued that it was impossible. He had been so far away, so how could she be sure? He had been banished and would be killed on sight if caught in Cathan. It couldn't have been him… or could it? The question created a whole new dread in her heart.

"What's wrong?" Tristan asked, his brow pinching together at her hesitation.

"Nothing. Really. I'm just… trying to wrap my head around what happened yesterday." She observed his sunken eyes. "How are you?" She reversed the question, placing her hand in his as he dropped them from her face.

Tristan relaxed at the touch. "Well, I'm alive, thanks to you and Roman. I still have no idea how you managed to see it. It was a miracle."

"I'm just glad you're okay," she said, looking down at his leg. "I should've said that already."

"There's been a lot going on." He tucked her messy hair behind her ear, his voice becoming more raw. "You scared me yesterday with the phoenix; I thought it was burning you alive. I went to you, but Ingrid assured me you were okay."

"She was right. I think it… it bonded us in a way." Her eyes met his. "Have you told anyone?"

"No one except my father and Roman."

Rose nodded, relieved. She was still trying to understand what had happened. She wanted to avoid raising suspicion, particularly with the high council. "Don't tell anyone else, please. I don't want anyone to worry more than they have to."

Tristan's gaze shifted to the sword resting beside her bed. "You… you've changed over the past year," Tristan said, his eyes roaming over her. "How long have you been learning to fight?"

Her heart dropped. She'd forgotten he knew about her training. She hesitated to respond, not sure if he'd understand if she told him. But maybe… maybe she should give him the benefit of the doubt. "When I was gone, my mother and I… we wanted to learn how to defend ourselves."

His eyebrows raised. "That's what you were doing while you were away? Why didn't you say anything?"

"Because there were more important things going on." Which was more or less true.

"And are you still training?"

"No," she said. She hated lying to him, but she didn't want him finding out that Zareb was involved.

Tristan folded his arms—his infamous stubbornness rearing its head. "Don't play me for a fool. I've been around my fair share of soldiers, and you handled that sword like you had done it a million times. Who's been teaching you?"

For some reason his tone made her walls go up. "I had a trainer before I came to the castle. But since then, I've been teaching myself. I go out in the woods and practice motions, that's all."

He nearly scoffed. "Don't insult me. I'm not stupid. You've been lying to me, and you still are. What else aren't you telling me?"

It was happening—the judgment, the misunderstanding. The very reason she hadn't told him in the first place.

"Why is it so bad that I don't want to always rely on others for help?" she asked, her voice matching his in defensiveness. "Why can't I learn? Tell me, what is so wrong with that?"

Tristan pressed his lips into a fine line. "Nothing—the problem is you *lied* to me about it. You told me you were mourning your father, that you were broken beyond repair, and now I find out you were just playing fake soldier for an entire year?"

"I'm sorry, but don't tell me you can't see the benefit of me knowing how to defend myself." Her spine straightened, not backing down. "Look how handy it came in the trial yesterday. How could I have done that if I hadn't had the training?"

"What happens when a real enemy is on the other end of that blade?" Tristan asked, his hard gaze never leaving hers. "You might think you're capable, but what happens when you take on more than you can handle? You'll only be putting yourself in danger. You could get yourself hurt or even killed."

"Right. So to you, I'm just looking for trouble," she summarized.

The wheels in Tristan's eyes turned as they narrowed. "Who's been teaching you now? Is it someone here?"

She panicked. If the council discovered the truth, they might take their rage out on Zareb—strip him of his title or, heaven forbid, banish him like

Xavier. She may have the protection of the king and her name, but Zareb did not. He had already been reluctant to train her. If he was punished for helping her—she didn't want to think of it.

Tristan's face darkened at her hesitancy. "It's Grant, isn't it?"

Without thinking, she blurted out, "Maybe."

Tristan's warmth deviated into a cold stare. "I'll find out soon enough for myself."

She stilled. "You can't be serious."

"I am. In fact—" he grabbed the sword, "—I'm taking this, since you won't be needing it."

She balled her hands into fists, her anger fully inflamed. "You know I can just get another one."

"I don't care. You'll thank me later."

She'd had enough. "I'm going to see Roman. Don't follow me."

"Rose—" Tristan called out.

But she had already slammed the door behind her.

The morning sun streamed through Roman's balcony doors and onto his bed, giving the room a warmth that seemed fitting for his recovery. It was gratefully empty except for Roman, of course, still lying in bed, now propped up by a mound of pillows stacked behind his back. His brown hair was clean and free of sweat, and his skin had returned to its usual golden tone.

She couldn't tell if he was pleased to see her as she walked in. His eyes locked on her with a different gaze than before—softer, less threatening. Even the way he shifted his body towards her was different, but she couldn't pinpoint exactly what it was.

"Rose," he greeted hoarsely, attempting to sit up straighter.

"Hello," she said with a faint smile, making an effort not to let her argument with Tristan affect her mood. "I'm surprised to find you here alone." She stopped at the foot of his bed. "Where are the healers?"

"I sent them away," he replied, with an irritated glare at the door. "I wanted to be alone."

"Oh." She gestured back to the door. "Should I come back later?"

"No," he answered at once.

She raised an eyebrow. The corner of her mouth threatened to rise.

Roman's eyes shifted as he realized his hastiness. "I mean, no, it's fine." He motioned to the chair beside him.

She settled into the upholstered seat. "How are you feeling?"

"Better." He reclined back onto the pillows. "My father tells me I have you to thank for that. He said you spoke with the phoenix somehow and made a deal to save me." His golden eyes carefully locked onto hers.

She couldn't hold his gaze. "Yes, well, Tristan helped."

An awkward silence fell before Roman said, "Where is he? I'm surprised he didn't come with you."

"I told him I wanted to come alone."

He studied her as though he were searching for a hidden truth. "How are you always at the center of all of this?" he asked at last, not in his usual cold voice, but with a tone of genuine curiosity.

She inspected her intertwined hands, swallowing hard. "I've been asking myself the same question lately."

"Why'd you do it?"

"Do what?"

He swallowed hard before his voice broke. "Save me."

Her eyes finally raised to meet his, catching her off guard with the sincerity held there. "Because despite what you think of me, I would *never* let you die, especially after you had just risked your life to save Tristan… And despite recent events, I still honor the friendship we used to share."

Her answer seemed to throw him. He resituated himself on the goose-feather pillows, looking away, as if he couldn't handle the contact. "The man in the trees… How in Vallor did you see him?"

She did her best to keep her unease under wraps. "I don't know. I was just looking out at the crowd when I saw him. You were the first person I could reach to warn."

"And the man, did you see *him*?"

Xavier's face flashed in her mind. She considered telling Roman the truth, but if she accused Xavier and she was wrong, she'd be put under more scrutiny by the council. And if it was Xavier, he could be imprisoned or hanged. She had to be sure it was him, and right now, she couldn't be certain.

"I didn't get a good look at him." It wasn't totally a lie.

He accepted her answer with a nod. His attention shifted to the nightstand, his hands shaking as he tried to reach for a cup. Witnessing his struggle for control over his limbs was downright painful. "I don't know why I'm still shaking so much," he said bitterly.

"Here, let me," she said, moving to sit on the edge of the bed. "May I?" She gestured to the cup.

He looked at her, hesitant, then gave a reluctant nod.

She poured hot water and added the herbs, well aware of Roman's studious gaze watching her as if he were expecting to be poisoned again.

She let the tea steep. Once it had, she took his rough, calloused hand in hers, guiding it to the cup. She kept her hand over his until she was confident he had a secure hold of it.

Roman's free hand caught her arm. "Thank you." The warmth in his voice sent a shiver up her spine. It was the voice she remembered as a small girl—the caring, friendly, charismatic one that reminded her of her best friend.

Her body was still frozen from the foreign softness as she said, "You're welcome."

Roman swallowed hard. "Not just for the tea… Thank you for saving me. I know after some of the things I said to you… you could have very well been tempted to let me die."

She nearly laughed at the idea, though the thought hadn't once crossed her mind. "There was a fleeting moment when I thought it could be to my advantage," she replied with a coy smile, taking the risk of teasing him.

Roman's amber eyes sparked with a hint of warmth, and for a moment, she thought he might smile. But that was the most she got out of him. She could read from his uncertain expression that he hadn't gained enough confidence to trust her fully.

But perhaps it was a start.

She leaned back. "Thank you for believing me," she whispered, holding his gaze head-on. "I can't imagine what would've happened if you hadn't."

Roman's face twitched, as if accepting the realization that he had, in fact, trusted her in a way. The expression instilled hope that she may yet have a redeeming quality in his eyes after all. "I have a hard time trusting things I don't understand." He swallowed hard again. "And you… you're a glorified maze to me."

Her heart softened, her mouth parting to give him a map until—

"Roman!" Beth called, swinging the door open.

Her head snapped away at the same time that Roman's did, both of them watching as Beth's long, yellow dress swayed behind her.

Rose stood from the edge of the bed, offering Beth a warm smile. But to her dismay, Beth's eyes glazed right over her, fixating on only Roman.

A sinking sensation settled in her heart. It appeared as though her friendship with Beth had come to an abrupt end. Ever since she'd entered the succession, her friend had barely looked in her direction.

It shouldn't have come as a surprise. She'd never excelled in the art of making friends—well, friends among the girls in court. In her younger years, she'd tried hard to get them to like her. Countless times, she'd tried to reach out and befriend them. Each time, it was fruitless, and it usually resulted in tears. She'd hoped that maybe—just maybe—Beth was the exception. But it seemed that, too, was a foolish notion.

"I'm so glad you're finally looking better," Beth said, perching on the edge of the bed as she slid her hand into Roman's, coming in close.

Rose glanced between the two. The clear display of ownership all too obvious. She wanted to laugh. If only Beth knew how much Roman loathed her.

Roman, however, pulled his hand away from Beth's. The withdrawal made Beth recoil with hurt eyes, but she regained her composure in a flash, sitting up straight and smoothing out her dress.

"Rose was just checking on me," he said in a cool tone. "She saved my life."

"Of course." Beth recovered with a smile that didn't reach her eyes as she acknowledged Rose's presence for the first time. "It's so lucky you happened to know the cure to such a rare poison."

Rose recognized the suspicion in Beth's tone. She looked her squarely in the eye. "Isn't it?" she replied with a smile of her own. Dismissing her friend, she said to Roman, "Well, I can see you are in good hands; I'll let you get some rest."

He gave her a curt nod, still looking like he had more to say, but the medications had him still slightly disoriented, pinning him to his bed.

"Zareb is just outside waiting for you," Beth called with a strained smile.

Rose left and closed the door behind her, pretending not to hear them bickering as she left. It seemed that she and Tristan weren't the only ones to have troubles in paradise today.

When Rose saw Zareb, she knew exactly what she wanted to do.

CHAPTER 31

Initially, Zareb resisted Rose's request to spar, knowing she was exhausted and insisting she'd been through enough in the past twenty-four hours. But with just one look from her, Zareb conceded, accepting he wouldn't win the fight. She knew Zareb craved their sparring time just as much as she did. It was how they both released stress and frustration. In many ways, the two were much alike.

Relentless heat beat down from the sun that day, setting her shoulders on fire. The only saving grace was the west breeze blowing over the field, tasting like the salty sea itself. Above, the aspens' leaves trickled like a gentle stream, catching the sun's light like sparkles on the water.

"Where's your sword?" Zareb asked when they reached the fields.

She focused on anything but his eyes. "It was taken."

His head snapped to her, alarmed. "By who?"

"Tristan." Her voice dripped with guilt. "When we were about to go retrieve the phoenix, I took my sword in case we had any trouble on the road, and he asked about it."

Zareb's body went rigid. "Does he know—"

"No," she replied, knowing what he would ask. "He doesn't know it's you, not yet anyway. But I'm afraid he won't stop until he finds out."

Zareb glanced back to the path they'd just left, scouring the forest's edge, almost as if he expected someone to appear. After a brief pause, he nodded in acceptance, easing his tension somewhat. "We'll have to be more careful. It won't end well for either of us if anyone finds out."

She gaped at him in surprise. "You mean you're not going to tell me we should stop?"

Zareb's eyes fell to the sword in his hands. "We *should* stop. That much is certain." His hands traced over the detailed brass scabbard. "I admit, when we first started, I had many of the same thoughts Tristan must have —how dangerous this could be for you, if it was something you really needed. I almost told you I wanted to stop the training altogether." His eyes met back with hers. "But then I saw something change in you."

Her eyes held his, wading in his dark pools as she waited for him to explain.

Zareb stepped closer, his dark, rich skin glistening in the sunlight. "A light in your eyes I'd never seen shone through. Each day, it grows brighter as you become stronger. Your training has not only helped you fight physically, but it's also helped you fight here—" he pointed to her head, "—and here." He shifted his finger to point at her heart. "That's when I knew I was wrong to doubt you. I promised myself I'd never tell you what you could or couldn't do. You are the only one who should decide that."

Her heart swelled uncontrollably in her chest, comforted by knowing someone else believed in her, that someone had taken the time to understand and to realize she needed this. That this was becoming a part of who she was. "You know, sometimes it feels like you are the only one who truly sees me."

Zareb lifted an eyebrow. "You feel like Tristan doesn't?"

She paused, contemplating the question as her eyes faltered. "I don't know... I know he loves me."

Zareb's eyes roamed over her, like he could see her internal struggle. "May I say something without overstepping my place?"

She nodded, welcoming his thoughts.

He gazed deeply into her eyes, softly, gently, as if cradling her with his own. "When a man is able to listen to a woman's feelings without drawing a negative response, he offers her the most precious thing he can give,"

Zareb explained. "It makes her feel safe. Safe enough for her to share her needs and concerns. Safe enough to know that no matter what she says, he'll listen in earnest. Even if it's something he doesn't want to hear, he won't use a belittling tone or shrink her thoughts or opinions. It doesn't mean he can't disagree, but he'll never discount them. If he's successful in that, a woman will willingly give him her trust, her respect, her admiration… and perhaps, if he is so lucky, even her heart."

She clung to each word as she absorbed them, letting it settle deep into her bones.

"So let me ask you this instead… is Tristan that man to you?" Zareb asked.

A lump formed in her throat as she struggled to give him an answer. But she was afraid to let herself doubt, even if only for a moment. Because if she did, the glass holding her together might shatter.

Zareb took her silence as answer enough. "You don't have to answer me, Rose. But you deserve to answer it for yourself."

Rose stared at Zareb in awe. For the first time, she wondered how he had so much wisdom for someone only in their thirties. She was ashamed she'd not bothered to ask him more questions, to ask about his past—how he stayed so calm and collected, and what exactly was a warrior like himself doing here? How had he been assigned to protect a small city girl who held no great importance when he should be in charge of a group of his own men?

"Where did you get all the strength and wisdom you carry?" she asked, speaking one of her questions out loud.

"I had a strong mother," Zareb responded with pride. "Much like yours."

"Had?" she questioned softly.

Zareb nodded solemnly. "Had. She died when I was young."

"Is that why you never smile?"

Zareb's eyes drifted to the horizon, telling her he wasn't gazing at the landscape in Cathan but at a far-off place. "Partly, yes."

"Will you tell me about her someday?"

Zareb's eyes graced hers again with appreciation. "For you, Rosalie Versalles, perhaps I will… Someday."

She gained a new curiosity about him. "Well, Zareb, you've given me something to look forward to."

"What would that be?"

"The day I make you smile," she answered with a broad smile of her own.

His eyes brightened at her words. "I look forward to that day." Zareb peered down at the sword in his hands, gripping it tighter. "Uh." He cleared his throat. A bead of sweat formed on his forehead—not from the heat. "I suppose it's a good thing I got you this." He extended the sword to her.

She was rendered speechless. She looked at him, then back to the sword, receiving it with reverent hands. It was the most exquisite sword she had ever encountered, engraved with intricate swirls that glistened on the bronze hilt, along with a rose etched on each side. The slender blade was honed to lethal perfection and was, to her pleasant surprise, lighter than the one she'd been training with before.

"It's made of the finest steel Vallor can offer, straight from the Spine mountains of Semaria," Zareb stated, his gaze fixed on the blade. "It's lighter than most, but it keeps its integrity even still."

"It's perfect," she breathed. She slid the sword back into its sheath, and without warning, she stepped into him, throwing her arms around his neck and closing the gap between them. "Thank you," she whispered into his ear.

He was rigid, of course, every one of his overly large muscles tense from the sudden display of affection. She was sure he'd only stand there awkwardly, but after a long moment, he slowly lifted his arms around her upper back, returning the gesture and squeezing her tightly into him. "You're welcome," he whispered back.

She let go, looking back down to the sword. "People will wonder where it came from," she thought out loud, already thinking of multiple hiding places.

"I'll keep it safe for you until the time is right and bring it for you to use during our training." He strode over to his horse and drew his own sword. "Now let's begin, or else we'll be late for dinner, and your mother will have my head."

CHAPTER 32

Zareb and Rose stayed in the fields until dusk, the sky splashed with a lovely blend of blue, pink, and orange that spanned the horizon. It was the kind of evening she'd loved as a child—the perfect time to catch fireflies while crickets chirped gently in the background. By the time they reached the castle, darkness had nearly settled in.

They had just entered the darkened halls when her mother appeared. "Rose! There you are. Where have you been?" she huffed, peering over Rose's shoulder to glare at Zareb.

"We went for a... *ride*," she explained, emphasizing what they had *actually* been doing. "What's going on?"

Her mother pulled her arm, bringing her closer, peeking over her shoulder as if someone in the empty corridor could hear them. "The king and council have just called for a meeting for all the candidates. They've been waiting for you in the high council chambers."

She began walking at once. "How long have they been waiting?"

"About an hour. I managed to buy you some time."

"What's the meeting for?"

"How should I know? No one bloody tells me what's going on," her mother said as they strode through the shadows of the torches. "I'm worried we are biting off more than we can chew. Are you sure you want to continue with the succession? You can always drop—"

"Drop out and be tyrannized by a bunch of old men? No, I'm not going to give them the satisfaction."

Perhaps that's what the council wanted. Her triumph in the first challenge must have unsettled them. It got her thinking... What if the arrow had been intended for her instead? What if it hadn't been Xavier in the trees, but an assassin hired to murder her? These were all questions she feared she'd not soon gain an answer to. Not without paying a steep price.

They reached the council chambers just as Grant appeared, coming from the opposite direction. He held the door open for her, allowing her to enter first, giving her a playful wink as she passed—ever the optimist. She refrained from an eye roll. Her mother and Zareb waited just outside as Grant shut the door behind him.

King Henrik, his council, and the contestants had gathered on the large red rug in the center of the room, creating a close-knit circle. The open windows let in the sea breeze behind them, forcing the torches to work overtime to avoid being snuffed out.

"Ah, here they are now," the king said, nodding at her and Grant.

All heads turned to the pair, including Tristan's, whose eyes skewered Grant as he remained beside her.

The king started by saying, "I know you're all wondering if we have caught who was responsible for the attack. We scoured the entire forest, questioned everyone in attendance, and looked for any possible escape routes on the roads. But unfortunately, whoever was responsible escaped."

Tension rippled in the air. The more she thought of it, the more the question begged how the man had even gained access to a black market commodity like Dragonshade. Given that dragons had been extinct for centuries, it shouldn't even exist. It would have had to come from somewhere long forgotten to the north. But who would know where something like that was hidden?

"The good news is that Roman should make a swift recovery," the king continued. His eyes flickered to her, still filled with gratitude. "But due to this unfortunate event, we have decided to move the second challenge to tomorrow."

Their eyes grew wide. The next challenge? So soon? It was customary to have at least a week or so between. Tristan and Grant hadn't even recovered from their wounds.

Lord Wellington stepped forward. "This next challenge will be a psychological challenge of sorts. Each of you will be questioned under the influence of the salvia lotus, to see if you are equipped to handle the mental strain that comes with the challenge of ruling."

Rose fought a shiver—the salvia lotus, another black market item. The council must've paid a pretty penny to get their hands on a substance like that in Cathan. It was prohibited under any normal circumstance. Its effects were often considered unpredictable, which was exactly why they couldn't use it for Xavier's tribunal, or anyone else's for that matter.

Xavier—he had likely ignited this challenge. They must be aiming to test whether the contestants would falter under pressure and if they could be manipulated, controlled. If she partook of the lotus, she'd be opening the floodgates of her mind to the high council.

Fear encroached upon her like a snake slithering up her leg. They would find out everything she'd worked so hard to keep hidden—about her financial situation, about that night with her father, about everything.

She glanced at Lord Martin, whose beady eyes attempted to flush her weakness out. His smug face leered, glad to see fear planted on her own. No doubt it was him who had suggested this challenge in the first place.

It hit her then. They weren't just doing this because of Xavier. No, they wanted the opportunity to look into *her* head specifically. To find a way to weed her out of the succession—and they'd just found a means to do it.

Tristan and the others were equally stunned—even Grant was lacking his usual permanent smile.

"This is outrageous," Dawnton said. "It is a highly potent, unreliable substance. It is not within your right to force us to partake of an illegal drug."

Emmett chimed in. "I don't see how it could give an accurate depiction of us as candidates. If it cannot be held in court, it cannot be used for succession."

"It is only unreliable and unsuitable in court because of how it responds to each subject," Lord Martin interjected. "The drug works like any medication or food—effects can vary for each individual. The same goes for the lotus. This is not to find truth, like in a courtroom, but to see into the workings of a mind. Which is exactly what this drug can achieve... Anyway, as long as you have nothing to hide, you have nothing to fear." His gaze landed on Rose.

"So you've all taken of this lotus, have you?" Tristan said with a polar glare at the greasy lord.

Lord Martin didn't falter as he replied, "No... but neither have we aspired for the throne."

Lord Barron stepped in. "Your concerns about the lotus are heard, but the king and the council have agreed only because the questions distributed will be solely targeted to your capabilities of being a leader and no others. Lord Martin is right—if you have nothing to hide, you have nothing to fear."

Knowing the questions would be censored didn't make her feel any better. She had been expecting physical challenges like the first trial, but this... this wasn't something she'd ever anticipated.

"The choice is yours," King Henrik said, breaking the tangible silence. "Partake of the lotus or drop out of the succession. Those are your options." His words were as sharp as blades.

Everyone understood the beaten horse was dead. The contestants' eyes raged, but arguing was futile.

King Henrik took the silence as submission. "We will gather in the great hall tomorrow morning. And fortify your minds... this challenge isn't for the weak-hearted."

CHAPTER 33

After the meeting ended, Rose left the council chambers with her mother and Zareb, walking down the darkened corridors back to their rooms. She didn't notice her mother's drained, pale face until they were on the winding staircase down to the second floor.

"Rose, I wish you would reconsider," her mother whispered, so low that her voice couldn't carry in the echo of their footsteps. "The council could find out everything if they ask the right questions."

She had been considering that since the challenge was announced. She might have been willing to risk her own secrets, but what of her mother's? Zareb's? Was it fair to risk their livelihoods?

"The lotus plant isn't as bad as it sounds," Zareb said from behind, making them jump, not used to him speaking up.

Rose stopped mid-step on the stairwell, looking up at him. "You've taken it?"

Zareb nodded. "More than once. It's common where I'm from. It's often used in Semaria for spiritual cleansing to determine what ails the mind. If untrained, you'll easily spill out the first words that come into your head, but if I help you prepare and recognize what's happening, you can fortify your mind and slow your words, answer questions with part truths."

His words offered her hope. After all, the king was aware of her situation, and he'd make sure the council didn't stray from the questions regarding her capability as a ruler. She had to believe King Henrik wouldn't have put her up for the challenge if he'd thought it would endanger her.

"I can help you," Zareb reassured her. "Don't let them scare you. Training your mind is similar to training your body. You just need practice."

Her eyes settled on her mother, wondering if it offered her any reassurance. Her mother's eyes pierced into Zareb's. "Are you absolutely sure you can help her?"

"Yes," Zareb said confidently.

Her mother conceded, the look of death still upon her face, even as she gave a slight nod. "Alright."

And it was settled.

They exited the stairwell, and their conversation fell into a thoughtful silence. She had just rounded the corner when she spotted Grant sauntering alone down the hall ahead of them, going back to his room.

An idea popped into her mind—an idea that might just save Zareb from Tristan and the high council if things went awry tomorrow.

"I need to speak to Grant," she said out of the blue.

Her mother's eyes widened in surprise. "What now? Whatever for?"

Without answering, Rose turned to Zareb. "I promise I won't be long. I'll meet you back at the room." Without waiting for a response, she padded after Grant, practically having to run to catch up with his large strides.

Grant must have heard her light footsteps because he glanced over his shoulder. His face brightened as soon as he spied her. "Fancy seeing you here. You know, you scared me when I couldn't find you after yesterday's ordeal."

"Glad to know you still care."

Grant's smile morphed into a sly one. "Only for you."

She was counting on it. "Can we talk in private?"

His brow quirked. "Of course."

Neither spoke as she brought him to the edge of the large terrace facing the western sea. The midnight sky was netted with stars and two moons, shining their cool light. Grant observed her as they leaned against the railing, as if trying to figure out what in Vallor was going through her mind.

"Look, I'm sorry to bother you when the second challenge is less than twelve hours away." She nervously threw the skirt of her dress behind her.

Grant slid closer. "Are you going to tell me why you look so worried? I assume it's not because you're ready to declare your secret undying love for me." A ghost of a smirk crossed his lips.

She wasn't in the mood for teasing. "I need to ask you a favor. And I need you to give me your word you won't tell a soul."

His bright green eyes flickered with curiosity. "You have it."

She took a mental breath, hoping she wouldn't regret this later. "I've been learning how to wield a sword," she admitted as quickly as ripping off a bandage. It was too late to go back now.

Grant's brow peaked in surprise, keeping his eyes fixated on her, waiting for her to continue.

"Tristan found out this morning, and he thinks it's you who's been teaching me. It's a long story, but I may have alluded to it. If he comes to you, I need you to tell him it's true."

Grant cocked his head slightly, his expression serious for once. "You want me to admit I've been training you? To fight?"

She nodded, slipping her hand into his, knowing full well what she was doing—and so did he. Nonetheless, he gripped her hand back tightly.

"Yes," she whispered into the cool air.

Grant's green eyes shifted out into the night, considering her offer as new clouds on the horizon crept across the sea to the shore. His silence lasted so long that she questioned if she'd made a mistake.

Finally, his dangerous green eyes flashed back to hers. "I assumed as much in the first challenge… You continue to be more than meets the eye, Rosalie Versalles," he said as he finally came to a conclusion. "Okay."

Now, it was her turn to be surprised. "Okay?"

"Okay," he repeated.

She was amazed that he would trust her without question. At that moment, she let herself wonder if she had to marry Grant, would it be as bad as she'd made herself believe?

"That's it? You're not going to ask more questions?"

"I don't need to, but you do have to promise me something in return."

She reinforced her walls; she should've expected as much. "And what's that?"

"When the time comes, you won't stop me when I try to kiss you." He eased closer, his lips millimeters from hers. "You'll give me a fair shot and remember how willing I was to help when you needed it."

Her eyes held steady despite being surprised by his request, trying to discourage any second thoughts about his promise.

"And I get to pick the time and place for this kiss." He tucked her hair behind her ear.

She cursed herself for how much power she'd just given him, wholeheartedly counting on his feelings for her to keep it a secret. And he knew it. "Agreed."

A large, flirtatious smile filled his face as he tilted up her chin. "Don't look so worried, love... I promise it won't be as painful as it sounds."

"Rose?" Tristan's voice called.

She withdrew from Grant, dropping his hand and whipping around to find Tristan.

"Am I interrupting something?" he asked, his voice painfully cold. So unlike him.

Grant's grin resembled that of a Sphinx. "Actually, yes. I was just telling Rose how talented she is. She has so many talents, wouldn't you say? Talents most women don't acquire..." He placed his hand strategically on the hilt of his sword.

Tristan's agitated gaze darkened—if it was even possible. "It's you," he seethed, his eyes narrowing with pure hatred. "Of course it's you."

"I don't know what you mean," Grant said, knowing Tristan had no proof of what he insinuated.

Tristan went to pull out his blade.

"Tristan, don't." Rose took five quick steps, swiftly putting her hand on his to keep his sword in its scabbard. "You'll be thrown out of the succession."

"I don't care," Tristan spat.

"Tristan." Rose snatched his chin, forcing him to look at her. "*Don't.*"

At last, Tristan looked at her. His eyes softened—but only minutely.

She let go of his face but kept her hand on his as she faced Grant. "You can go, Grant."

"Are you sure?" Grant asked, his eyes darting back and forth between the pair.

"She's sure." Tristan's hand tightened on his hilt.

Grant's gloating arrogance reappeared. "Well, I'm not so sure. Not to be rude, cousin, but you don't look well. I'm not sure you're in the right… *mindset* for this next challenge." His smile came and left, falling into an uncharacteristic line. "But I guess that's good news for me."

Tristan went to draw his sword again, but she held his hand down firm.

"I'll be fine. Please leave," she said, glaring a final warning at Grant.

To her relief, Grant threw up his hands, retreating. "Alright… I'll be in the grand hall for an hour if you need anything," he said pointedly to her.

With that, he strutted back inside.

She didn't let her hand off the hilt of Tristan's sword until Grant was well out of sight.

Tristan didn't waste a moment, rounding on her. "Where have you been all day?" His tone didn't waver an inch in Grant's absence.

"I went riding with Zareb," she said, her words clipped. "I didn't think you wanted to see me after what happened this morning."

Tristan's fingers combed through his hair. "You think after telling me something like that, I wouldn't wonder where you'd gone? Is that why you were both late? Were you with Grant?" His anxiety was near tangible. She could almost feel it creeping out of him.

She attempted to move closer, but he skirted around her like a whip, going to the edge of the balcony.

He ran his hand through his hair again. "I need you to stop seeing him."

She prepared herself for another fight. "You know I can't do that."

"Why? Have you gotten attached?"

The jealous territorial git. "Stop it. Everything I've done, I've done for *you.*"

"Bullshit. You courting Grant is for me? Alright, well, let me relinquish that notion right here, right now. I don't want you seeing him, touching him, or even being near him. I don't want you seeing anyone. I. Want. You. I don't give a damn what my father says, what my mother says, what the high council says—"

"Shhh!" She shushed him before someone heard. "You can't think like this! Not now. Not with this challenge tomorrow."

"Let them invade my mind. Let them see just how strong I am and what I can do. I'm not afraid."

"Tristan, we're so close. A few more days—just a few more days, and this will all be over."

"Do you have feelings for him?"

Her expression hardened. "No, and I'm getting tired of reassuring you I don't."

"Then maybe you shouldn't give me reasons to believe otherwise."

She scoffed, shaking her head. "I'm not doing this." She whirled to leave, but his hand shot out and grabbed her arm.

"Imagine if you'd just walked in on me that close to another woman." His voice broke. "How would you react?"

She clenched her jaw. She wouldn't handle it well. That she knew.

"I know how it would feel. It would hurt. But I'd also trust you when you said you love me."

She tried to leave again, but his grip was firm. Finally, she confronted his gaze on the imaginary battlefield.

"I'm sorry," he said, defeated. He looked down at his hand on her arm, his eyes softening. "I'm sorry," he repeated, quickly letting go of her arm as he paced.

If it had been any other day, she would have stormed out. Yelled at him. But he'd be in no state to go into the second trial. And Zareb was still waiting for her. So, instead, she resigned.

"I'm not going to hold this against you because I know what tomorrow means," she said, her words coming out as sharp as carefully poised icicles. "I'm going to go to bed. I'll see you at the challenge."

Tristan parted his lips to speak, but she silenced him with, "Good night."

She left him alone on the balcony without a backward glance.

Tomorrow's challenge might be the most dangerous task she'd faced yet.

And she would be her own undoing.

CHAPTER 34

It felt like no time at all before Thea came to wake Rose the next morning. Zareb had spent the late hours of the night coaching her on what to expect, leaving her eyelids heavy. Thea had laid out a pink dress today—the very same her mother had been begging her to wear. And although Rose had been reluctant to wear it, the dress did have its perks—the dusted-pink color beautifully suited her olive skin, fitting perfectly without being too tight. The beading started at the chest, cascading down to her waist and flowing elegantly with the fabric to the floor. Her mother would claim all the credit, she was sure.

The energy in the grand hall was nothing like it'd been for the previous challenge, the court's numbers dwindling by half. Due to recent events, she could only assume many had chosen to return home for their own safety. For whatever reason, the Vertmerian queen and princess remained on enemy territory—though the number of forest-green uniforms had doubled. On the bright side, it left more than enough seats to house everyone.

Rose was surprised to see Roman already out of bed with Beth sitting beside him—their hands interlocked, suggesting that they worked through their fight. Tristan sat on the other side of Roman, catching her eye as soon as she entered.

His gaze devoured her from head to toe, clearly admiring the dress as much as her mother. He looked just as dashing, the color of his tunic matching his blue eyes, bringing out the highlights in his soft blond curls. The warmth of the room had flushed his strong cheekbones with an undertone of pink. Although still upset, she still mustered a faint smile. He returned it, but it lacked its usual warmth.

She had barely sat down when her mother practically bounced in her seat, looking positively ecstatic. "You wore the dress!" her mother exclaimed in victory.

Rose brushed her hair back, exaggerating her movements for dramatic effect, pretending that the dress was all she needed.

The room quieted when the king arrived a few short minutes later with his queen, holding hands as they claimed their seats. Queen Lenna's pale complexion looked a little more drained than usual. Behind them, the high council entered in a steady stream, the silence emphasizing every footstep, echoing off the vaulted ceiling.

King Henrik gestured for everyone to sit. "Today may arguably be the most paramount succession challenge we've conducted. As we all understand, it takes a great deal more than brute strength to be a strong leader. So today, each of the contestants will undergo an intense psychiatric examination meant to appraise their capabilities of handling not only the battles of Cathan, but the battle which rages within themselves."

All of the contestants paled, except Grant, of course, who only smirked.

"Before we begin, I find it fitting we remember Cathan's oath." The king raised his chalice.

Everyone stood.

King Henrik led the chant Rose had heard a thousand times over—a chant that every child in Vallor knew by heart.

"*In strength*!" the king projected.

"We can endure!" the room chanted back in unison.

"*In truth*!"

"We find purpose!"

"*With loyalty*!" he shouted louder.

"We serve!" the crowd said, some pounding their fists on the tables.

"In honor," the king cried.

"We live, fight, and die!" the court roared.

"For Vallor!" the king finished, raising his fist.

"For Vallor!" they all cheered back.

The energy in the room was revived, the chant fulfilling its purpose. The king's bearded smile grew as he gazed out at the spirit he'd just instilled.

He waited for the room to quiet down. "The second challenge will be held in a sweat lodge on the sea cliffs. Regrettably, due to recent events, only the contestants' close friends and family will be permitted to attend. The rest of you will remain here at the castle. For those invited, follow me."

CHAPTER 35

The sky hung low with a thick layer of gray clouds as the party trekked their way to the sea cliffs. Rose had only been there a handful of times—warned by her mother that more than one innocent soul had met their death along its edges. But every time she saw the elevated view, she stopped to stare. From here, she could see the Meridian Sea spread for miles, its waves dancing like silk in the wind or rippling sand across the desert. The sheer vastness terrified her while simultaneously reminding her of home. This home. The home she had built here. And she intended to keep it.

An excessive number of guards guided the small group, taking no chances. The king and queen led the way with the high council, followed closely by the five contestants. Tristan was solemn and withdrawn, while Dawnton and Emmet each wore a brave poker face, though their stiff frames exposed their hands. Grant, on the other hand, whistled without a care in the world, giving her a playful wink when he caught her eye.

A small cluster of emerald-green uniforms stuck out like a sore thumb amongst the red and gold. The foreign queen strutted at the center with a grotesque look on her face, while her daughter's curious gaze seemed quite intrigued by the whole ordeal.

Zareb and her mother walked alongside her as the wind whipped at their skirts, regretting her decision to wear the pink dress. Rose had to pin her arms to her thighs to keep it from flying up.

"I hope it doesn't rain," her mother complained, taming her own dress and glowering at the gray sky. "Why did they have to pick the cliffs?"

"I don't think they wanted another incident like the woods," Zareb said. "This is open land. Not nearly as many hiding spots for an attack, and we have the high ground."

"Unless someone wants to push us off the edge," Rose pointed out.

Her mother shot her a terrifying glare. "Of course you'd put *that* into my mind."

"You don't need to worry," Zareb said. "We'll be a safe distance from the edge."

An octagon-shaped hut waited for them. A plume of smoke escaped the narrow chimney, which the wind immediately swept to claim. The door was closed, leaving it a mystery as to what lay inside. A fair distance away sat a large white tent for them to wait for the duration of the challenge.

Once they had all gathered around the hut, the king addressed the small company. "This is where the contestants will perform the challenge. Unless you are invited to enter, we ask you to wait in the tent until the challenge is completed. We'll begin with the contestant who finished last in the first trial. This puts the order as Emmett first, then Dawnton, followed by Grant, then Tristan, and lastly Rose. Let us begin… Emmett."

Emmett held his chin high, striding through the threshold of the hut with Beth and his parents. The king and the high council followed, filing in one by one after them.

"Now we wait." Her mother sighed, already bored, heading towards the white tent for warmth. "Are you coming?"

"In a moment," Rose replied, wanting a better look at the view.

Zareb watched her mother march away with concern.

"She's terrified of heights," Rose said, explaining her mother's foul mood. "I'll join you in a minute."

He nodded. "Stay where I can see you."

She strolled toward the gray horizon, approaching the edge as close as she dared. She took a deep, medicinal breath, closing her eyes and letting the cool wind brush over her skin as the hem of her pink dress swept around her feet.

She had never traveled outside of Cathan, nor explored much of her home province, for that matter. Every time she'd expressed the desire to see more, her mother had quickly squashed the idea, insisting it wasn't safe or proper for two women to travel alone. It was an excuse; her mother had never been fond of traveling and grew near frantic at the mere mention of the idea, so Rose had stopped mentioning it. Looking back, she supposed the real reason might have been their financial situation.

For the first time, she gazed out into the depths of the sea without fear. Instead, she felt something... calling to her. Like a mysterious being was summoning her from the void, liberating her, as if she could travel wherever she pleased. She envisioned crossing the seas to Eristan, visiting the tribes of Semaria, or meditating in the tranquility of the Ostlyn temples under the beautiful cherry blossom trees she had only read about in books.

"It's beautiful, isn't it?" Grant praised from behind.

She didn't turn to look at him as she replied, "I like it." She tamed her windblown hair behind her ear. "It makes the day feel less ominous."

"Quite." He stepped beside her, his eyes fixed on the horizon, shifting his broad shoulders, nearly large enough to compete with Zareb's or Roman's.

She felt a pair of eyes searing into her back. She peeked over her shoulder to see who it was. She wished she hadn't. Tristan and Roman stood side by side near the opening of the tent, Tristan glowering at the pair with envy, while Roman glared, irritated by the distraction.

"It's good for the council to see you with someone else right now," Grant said. "Now more than ever. Our minds are about to be dissected under a microscope. Perhaps they won't ask about you if you're no longer a weakness for him."

"Am I not a weakness for you?" she asked, cocking an eye brow, taunting him.

A seriousness crept into his eyes as he frowned. "I told you once I only pursued you to get underneath Tristan's skin, but... I have, in fact, started to grow wildly attracted to you and your fire. When you confided in me last night, it had me foolishly hoping it was a sign you wouldn't be so unhappy if you ended up with me after all. So to answer your question, no. You're not a weakness to me, not yet. Although you very well could be."

Grant spoke in a way that would've made any other young maiden swoon, but it only made her shift her gaze, catching a glimpse of Grant's parents as they lingered near the tent. They, like Grant, regarded everyone with an air of superiority, convinced that they were destined to become the next royal family. They must think she was at least somewhat of a good match to let him continue pursuing her. She didn't doubt her potential chance at the throne, and the fortune they assumed she had played a significant role in their approval.

How little they knew.

"I like how open we are," Grant admitted, twisting her guilt further. "I feel like we understand one another. So I will be truthful with you like you were with me. The high council, Lord Martin in particular, came to me and told me if I do become king, it'd be in my best interest *not* to marry you."

Her eyes bounded to his, wondering if she'd heard him right. "They what?"

"You scare them for some reason." He scanned her up and down as if asking himself what they could be afraid of. "But they aren't being coy about it anymore. It's not just Tristan they don't want you with. They don't want you to become queen. Period."

She gazed back out at the stormy horizon. "I see."

"Which, of course, makes me want you all the more." He smirked, creeping closer, brushing her windblown hair back.

Her head tipped skeptically. "I know you, Grant. If I was in the way of you becoming king, you'd gladly trample me under your feet."

Grant put a hand over his heart. "I'm offended you think so little of me."

"Why? You and I both know you wouldn't pass up the crown for the world."

He gazed at her as though he possessed all the confidence in the world.

She envied that confidence. "I'd be *king*. I wouldn't let them tell me who I can and cannot marry. And I sure as hell wouldn't let them bully me like Tristan."

She paused, stunned at his declaration.

He took advantage of her silence, slowly shifting to tower over her. He spread a hand on the small of her back, drawing her closer. Her breath caught. He was close—too close. His lips parted over hers.

She knew what he was about to do. She went to pull back, but Grant's hand trapped her, blocking her escape.

Zareb broke like a statue coming alive, taking a quick step toward the pair. Tristan also lunged, but Roman stuck an arm out, ripping him back, furiously whispering something into his ear.

"Call Zareb off. We had a deal." Grant leaned in, smelling her hair as the bridge of his nose grazed her neck.

She swallowed hard. Damn him. Her eyes flickered to Zareb, shaking her head. Zareb stopped in his tracks.

"I'm not going to hurt you," Grant whispered into her ear. "You might even like it."

Before she could think about what was happening, Grant captured her lips.

His warm mouth molded against hers with ease, both arms snaking around her waist. It was a possessive, slow kiss. If she was being honest, it wasn't half bad. In fact, it was quite good. If Rose had any real feelings for Grant, she might have savored it. But he wasn't Tristan. There were no sparks, no butterflies, no fire surging through her veins.

Grant came up for air. His eyes changed—hooded. "Bloody hell," he murmured, as if something had just clicked within his mind. "I get it now."

The wind stole her heavy breaths as she stared at him, still trying to process what had just happened until she remembered where she was—and who was watching.

Her eyes sprang to Tristan, who was nowhere to be found. To make matters worse, the queen and Harriet had seen the kiss, too. Harriet's eyes widened, hurt and betrayed, while the queen's narrowed. Roman's expression went straight back to malice the longer he stared. Whatever faith she'd gained had just been lost.

She swiveled back to Grant, pushing him, but the shove barely made his shoulder move. "You snake. You manipulated this whole thing to mess with him."

Grant wasn't the least bit sorry. "I haven't done anything to hinder his chances. His own mind will do that."

She opened her mouth, ready to round on him—

With a creak, the hut's doors swung open, and Emmett stumbled out, his face ghostly pale with sweat streaming down his cheeks. He had been sick to his stomach, the evidence of it clinging to his cloak. The confidence he'd had all but vanished, dissipating along with the smoke from the chimney. His mother and Beth supported his arms as he wobbled. His father trailed after them, his frown creased into harsh lines.

That had been fast.

Too fast.

The king exited the hut, his expression blank as he called for the next candidate. "Dawnton!"

Dawnton was present in a flash, though his usual pompous demeanor was nowhere in sight. His legs trembled like a newborn calf as the dark hut swallowed him. Following him were his two younger brothers and their parents, all hesitant to step into the lion's den. With that, the door closed again.

Rose spun on her heels, intending to go find Tristan.

Grant tried to tame her fire. "Rose—"

"Don't."

At her viperous glare, Grant surrendered, letting her go.

Zareb read her fury, leaving her alone. But he'd make sure he could see her still, even if she wasn't aware of where he was.

In the distance, she spotted Tristan's figure near the cliff's edge. Though he saw her coming, he didn't bother to acknowledge her, keeping his eyes on the horizon.

She stopped within a few feet of him. "I didn't know he was going to do that," she said lamely.

"I did," Tristan replied in a voice so soft it was almost a whisper.

She would've preferred for him to yell at her.

He was angry, that was certain, but more than that, he looked broken. And she'd just added another large crack to his fragile frame.

"I thought we were in this together," Tristan said, still in a soft whisper.

She bit the inside of her cheek in regret. "We are."

"Today, of all days."

"I know."

"Why are you torturing me?" he asked. "Last night and now this? Is it because I took your sword? Are you still so angry with me?"

"No—yes—but I didn't mean for it to happen."

He lifted an eyebrow. "You didn't stop it either."

"If you only knew—"

"Isn't that the phrase of the century—if only I knew." He paused, scoffing. "But how could I, when you tell me *nothing?* I am not a simpleton, Rose. You forget I've known you practically your whole life."

"I *want* to tell you everything."

"Then tell me!"

She opened her mouth to answer, then faltered. How was she supposed to explain why she had to entertain Grant without telling him the rest of it? About her fortune, how they'd lost it, about the true nature of her father, why it had led to her training, all of it. And heaven help her, she didn't know if she was ready for him to see that side of her.

She'd bolted it up so tight with a lock and key, she feared if she opened it, it would all come spilling out. And if the council found out Tristan knew of her fake fortune and soiled reputation, they might find a way to use it against them both in the succession. She couldn't risk it. At least not until today was over. It was better he didn't know. For now.

"It's not that simple."

He barked a harsh lifeless laugh, the wind blowing through his tousled curls. "It never is with you, is it?"

Her fingernails dug into her palm. "You don't exactly make it easy. You've been under so much pressure—I didn't want to add more to your plate."

He shook his head sharply. "Don't throw that at me. Don't tell me what I can and cannot handle."

"You realize that's exactly what I asked of you the morning you took my sword," she said, throwing it right back.

The point made him pause, letting her know she'd struck a chord. His expression relaxed as the realization set in.

She came closer, wanting to reach out, but she refrained, fearing he wouldn't want it. "Please don't hold it against me. I'm so sorry."

He clenched his jaw, looking like he was debating whether to throw her off the cliff or kiss her madly.

"Tristan!" Roman's voice called, a scowl engraved on his face. "You're next. You should stay close."

Tristan gazed at her with an empty expression, sending a dull pain through her heart. He didn't move, his face growing into something fierce. "I refuse to let Grant come between us. He wants this to happen because he knows he doesn't stand a chance against us together. I'm not going to be so easily goaded by him." He slid his hand down into hers, intertwining their fingers.

A wave of relief rushed through her. She gripped his hand back. Without warning, Tristan pulled her into his chest. His lips dipped to meet hers, parting her mouth with little effort.

She didn't resist in the slightest, welcoming the kiss. They shouldn't be so careless, but she couldn't think straight. Not when he held her like this. Not when he kissed her like she was life itself. With lips so hungry, she was sure he was trying to consume her whole.

Regretfully, he pulled away. "Walk with me." He didn't wait for an answer as he tugged her along.

Roman sneered in disgust as they passed, his blazing golden eyes fixated on Tristan. Despite his brother's fury, Tristan clung to her hand.

Everyone was still waiting in the tent when they rejoined the group. Grant was gone. It must have been his turn. Her mother raised an eyebrow at her, giving Rose a look that seemed to say, *I hope you know what you're doing.* All the while, Tristan held firm to her hand. Even when his mother discreetly shook her head at him, he pulled Rose closer. She did her best to block them all out, trying to focus on the task at hand.

The minutes dragged on, but eventually, Grant emerged with his parents. Unlike Emmett, Grant returned with his dignity intact. His face was grim, but not sickly like Emmett's. As he exited, his eyes sought out Rose and Tristan, hardening at the sight of the pair holding hands. Tristan moved in front of Rose, conveying a clear message.

The king exited the hut with Lord Martin. "Tristan," the king called next.

"Good luck," Rose whispered, giving his hand one more squeeze of encouragement before she let go.

The queen, Harriet, and Roman were there in a blink, ready to follow Tristan into the hut. But to her utter surprise, the king spoke to her. "You too, Rose," he instructed, gesturing for her to enter.

Her heart dropped onto the mossy ground beneath her. Her eyes flitted back and forth between Tristan and the king. "Me?" She pointed to her chest.

Lord Martin looked all too pleased. "Yes. The council has decided that since you worked on the first challenge together, you shouldn't have problem combining this challenge as well."

The king's face grew beet red, but he said nothing in rebuttal. Clearly, he had been overruled.

Queen Lenna's eyes almost bulged out of their sockets. "But this isn't—"

"The council demands it," King Henrik stated, silencing her.

The queen said nothing more—she couldn't. Not when he spoke like that, not when the king commanded his queen. Rose had never seen Lenna give her husband such a haughty gaze as she strutted past him, followed by her children. Roman made it a point to sidestep as far away from her as possible, disgust still burnt on his face.

The council had a venomous snake hidden up their sleeve. There was an ulterior motive for wanting Rose and Tristan in that hut, and it wasn't good. This was revenge for having been made fools during the first challenge.

Dread coursed through her like cold winter snow. She could only hope that Zareb's quick lesson on mind fortification last night would be enough to save them.

She turned to find her mother and Zareb, but they were already behind her. Her mother's face was drained of color, but there was nothing she could do to shield her this time.

Her mother had been right. Rose had put too much faith in herself for this succession. If she couldn't keep their secrets hidden… she'd lose a great deal more than a crown.

Tristan leaned closer to his father. "What do they want?" he whispered.

King Henrik's defeated eyes faltered. "I don't know, but I'm afraid I cannot deny their request. But don't worry, it will be alright."

Rose and Tristan shared an anxious glance.

"Me and you?" Tristan said, holding up his pinky.

The cold winter snow encasing her melted as she wrapped her finger around his. "Me and you."

There was no backing out now. She could do this. *They* could do this. Together.

With a deep breath, she squared her shoulders and entered the hut.

CHAPTER 36

A surge of heat and humidity hit Rose like a brick wall—so intense she wanted to rip her shawl right off first thing. The hut was pitch black, save for the well-stoked fire at its heart—the source of the beating heat. She paused in her steps, allowing her eyes to adjust. The aroma of burning sage wafted through the air, providing a touch of relaxation to her nerves. Other than the crackling of the fire, silence filled the air.

The high council sat on benches bordering the rounded hut, all watching her and Tristan with blank expressions, except Lord Barron, who offered a fleeting smile in acknowledgment. The others, including Tristan's family, her mother, and Zareb, filled the vacant chairs to their left. Rose locked eyes with Harriet, but the usual warmth in Harriet's gaze was gone.

She almost overlooked the stranger sitting on a pillow beside the crackling fire. Rune markings covered her forehead and body. Rose's eyes widened in recognition—a seer. The woman was old and frail, with soft, leathery pale skin, wispy white hair, and piercing iceberg-blue eyes that seemed to peer right into her soul.

The seer paid her no mind as she entered, remaining cross-legged and focused on the mixture of herbs and oil in the mortar and pestle she was holding—surely preparing the lotus.

Lord Palmish stood to address them. "Welcome to your second challenge. Today, we will evaluate your ability to rule Cathan. Seers can uncover what is hidden from others, understand troubled thoughts, and even foresee potential futures. We will base our judgment on her insights and your responses. Through this, we will determine your readiness to lead Cathan."

A deep dread rooted itself inside Rose. This was the first time anyone had mentioned that a seer would perform the evaluation. How in Vallor was she supposed to deceive *a seer*? Zareb hadn't prepared her for this.

She glanced at her mother, who looked worried enough for the both of them, fanning herself quickly as she whispered furiously to Zareb. When Zareb caught her gaze, he gave her an encouraging nod as if to say she would be fine.

"Before we begin, you'll need to remove your clothes and sit by the fire across from the seer," Lord Palmish said as he settled back with the council.

Of course. She curled her fingers into fists as she peered down at her pink dress. She wanted nothing more than to refuse, but sweat was already dripping from every pore. If she kept this dress on and sat next to the fire, she'd faint—so much for keeping her training a secret.

Tristan removed his clothes, exposing his bare skin to the firelight. His muscular body moved effortlessly through the shadows. She'd already been uncomfortable from the heat, but seeing Tristan so vulnerable made beads of sweat form at her temples.

Accepting her fate, she removed her dress, slipping out of it until she only wore her thin slip, and gave the pink dress to her mother to hold. She felt exposed, out of place, but above all humiliated. All she wanted to do was crawl into a hole and never come back out.

Rose didn't have to look to see the council's shock. She wrapped her arms around her waist, trying to cover herself, not daring to look at anyone but Tristan. His eyes explored her, glued like a moth to a flame, worshiping her from head to toe. Another bead of sweat dripped down her temple.

Tristan held his hand out to her. She took it, finding courage in their interlocked hands.

The seer grasped a bowl filled with a substance resembling brown paint. She approached Tristan first, examining him for a long moment before immersing her fingers in the blend and drawing a mark on his chest. "This rune," the seer began, her voice as light and airy as the wind, sounding much younger than she looked, "is the emblem that emanates energy to combat unnecessary doubt and insecurity, freeing one from vanity and ambition. It facilitates easy connections with others and helps in achieving one's goals. It represents a person who bestows blessings upon others through inner strength."

Next, the seer stood in front of Rose, examining her. Her nervous heartbeats quickened.

After a brief search, the seer plunged her fingers into the herb blend, bringing it to her chest, the sticky, cool liquid contrasting against her warm collarbone. She caught a whiff of the mixture, a sweet aroma that smelled like Tulsi. "This is a bindrune," the seer said. "Do you know what that is, child?"

Rose nodded, visualizing the thick books about runes she'd read in the library, though it felt like ages ago. A bindrune fused two or more runes, amplifying their meaning and power. Legends claimed they had held a powerful form of magic crafted long ago by ancient kings and queens. But much of the knowledge had been lost or was destroyed to prevent it from falling into the wrong hands. Although some still believed in their power, she had never witnessed anything magical come from them.

Rose held still as the seer continued to paint. "You carry many symbols within you, some of which you have yet to discover. One of them signifies dawn, an awakening, or a journey you must undertake."

The seer paused, stepping aside so Rose and Tristan could peer into the water basin on the pedestal.

In contrast to the straightforward design of Tristan's symbol, which at least looked familiar, her bindrune was completely foreign to her. She attempted to decipher the runes, but her memory grasped at smoke.

"These runes will help guide you to your path," the seer said. "Whenever you require strength or courage, wear it. Never forget the power your rune holds."

The council's murmurs filled the hut as they exchanged whispers, trying to interpret her bindrune for themselves. However, it seemed they were no more knowledgeable than she was. Lord Barron, in particular, stared at it intensely as if committing it to memory.

The seer retrieved a different set of bowls from the ground. "Take this," she instructed, holding out two separate bowls of green liquid to each of them. "Drink all of it. But once you do, I must warn you, there is no going back. It'll do you no good to try to resist its effects."

Tristan and Rose accepted the bowls and examined their contents. "What does it do exactly?" Tristan inquired, his wary eyes fixed on the green liquid.

"It helps us to see you—the real you. It will unveil your soul, urging you to speak nothing but your truth," the seer said. "You'll feel it draw out your innermost thoughts, beliefs, and emotions. Be warned, it is powerful; not all who take it can cope with its effects."

Emmett's pale face came to the forefront of her mind, making her queasy.

Tristan peered at the green liquid again before raising the cup to his lips. He downed it, his face contorting, then handed the cup back.

Rose poured the contents into her mouth, grimacing at the bitterness. Once she had, they sat on the pillows across the fire from the seer. The intense heat of the thick flames made her undergarments damp with sweat.

As soon as she settled onto the cushion, the effects of the lotus crept in. Her mind twisted and warped, just as Zareb had warned. Rather than resist the pull, she surrendered to it, allowing the power to flow freely through the floodgates.

"Give me your hand," the seer instructed Tristan, holding her fragile hand out—it appeared he was going first.

Fearlessly, Tristan stretched out his hand. The seer took his palm, tracing the crevasses with her crooked fingers. "I see you, Tristan Montague. I hear your thoughts, hopes, and dreams. I feel your desires and cravings. I see your darkest thoughts and greatest fears... Now tell us, what drives your ambition to be the king of Cathan?"

Tristan gazed into the fire, his mouth opening and closing, trying to form words as if he were learning to speak again. "Because I believe I am what Cathan needs," Tristan responded. "I love my province. I find joy in serving and protecting it—from its enemies, even from itself. It's what I strive to do, and it's what I will always strive to do."

The king and queen's eyes swelled with pride, their hands clasped together in relief.

"I see you as a natural leader of men," the seer observed. "You've led before. You earn the trust and loyalty of your men—something that takes a true leader to obtain. I see you desperately wish to be king. You believe it is your destiny. You also harbor a lot of guilt—guilt for men lost, guilt for your younger brother almost dying in your place... Though your true guilt is reserved for what happened to your eldest brother."

Tristan's eyes hardened as they flashed at the woman in surprise. Rose waited for the seer to expand, but to her disappointment, she did not.

"That guilt has guided and driven your need for power and control," she continued. "I see you are impulsive and quick to anger. You must learn to control it or you'll drown in your own self-loathing. There's also something that has a firm hold over you... or is it someone?" The seer's eyes searched the empty air, then snapped to Rose. "A woman," she whispered. "One in this very room. I saw her in the mind of the contestant before you... You love her."

Tristan's guarded eyes flickered with fear, sweat dripping off his jaw. It was happening—exactly what Rose was afraid of.

The council leaned forward like greedy beasts honing in on their wounded prey.

Rose stared into the fire to mask her fear. This wasn't fair. They had no right to pry into their minds. She was a fool to think they wouldn't twist this to their advantage. They would exploit every weakness they could.

She took deep breaths, steadying her shaky hands, remembering Zareb's advice to keep her mind clear.

The seer continued, "I see why you are so entrapped by her. You've wanted her since you laid eyes on her as a boy. But now... now you want her more than you've ever wanted anything. Which makes you incredibly dangerous."

Tristan's body stiffened. "She has nothing to do with my worthiness to be king."

"She has everything to do with it," the seer rebutted, her gaze floating from Rose back to him. "I can feel how much you desire her. It's intoxicating to you, a poison. I see why you face such an internal struggle. You feel as though your life is being pulled in two different directions."

Tristan withdrew his hand. "That's not—" he attempted to protest, but his mouth stopped him. The lotus's influence only allowed him to utter the truth.

The seer didn't need his palm to continue. "If you don't learn to regulate your passion for her, it will consume you. It'll drive you to do unspeakable things. It's time you admit these feelings to yourself and learn how to control them, or you'll lose yourself in the process."

Sweat dripped from his brow like rain, desperate to resist. However, the lotus held firm against him. He shifted his gaze from the seer, focusing instead on the flames, gritting his teeth.

But the seer wasn't done with him. "You need to answer this, Tristan, for yourself more than anyone in this room... Are you afraid of losing her?"

His jaw clenched, reluctant to answer, but she knew the room's heat and the lotus's influence would win in the end.

"It's best not to fight it, Tristan," the seer prodded.

"Yes," he blurted out, resentful that she'd made him admit it. "I'm afraid to lose her. Is that so wrong? My ability to love will not impede my ability to rule."

"But your fear will. Why is it you're so afraid of losing her?" the seer asked, digging at him.

A long pause filled the room as he fought the herb's effects, clenching his fists. "I'm afraid because... I know I'll never find anything or anyone that compares to her. The feelings I have for her can never be replicated. She brings out the good in me. And I fear if I lose her, I'll lose that—the good. I fear I'd be a completely different man... someone I don't want to be."

The seer leaned forward. "If needed, are you willing to give her up to be the king Cathan needs?"

Tristan shook his head as his face contorted. "I—I... I don't know."

Rose sat frozen in the silence that followed as she gaped at him. She'd had no idea how much he'd been struggling.

The seer leaned away, glancing at the council, asking whether they were satisfied. The king responded with a decisive nod.

The seer redirected her misty eyes to Rose and stretched out her hand.

She fought to keep her hand steady as she extended it. The silence in the hut was so strained that the cracks and pops of the fire might as well have been lightning crackling in the sky.

The seer's gentle, weathered hand grasped hers. With delicate fingers, she outlined the lines on Rose's palm, each gesture ending with a graceful swirl or a subtle flick. Moving with such elegance, Rose was sure it was an art. She searched for a pattern, but there didn't seem to be one.

The seer's movements slowed, nearly stopping as she closed her eyes, as if she had uncovered something new.

Without warning, the seer's eyes flared back open, now glowing within a frosty blue fog Rose knew she could get lost in if she leaned too close. The sight nearly made her jump.

"I see you've come a long way since you were a child." The seer's light voice had altered, now low and raspy. Her misty eyes remained fixed, locked in a trance. "It was difficult for you, growing up. Your father was a large source of your suffering, and you feel a great responsibility to take care of your mother."

Rose shot a quick glance at her mother and Zareb as sweat trickled down her chin, dripping onto her thigh. *Please,* she pleaded internally, *please don't say anything that could give them away.*

As if the seer heard her silent plea, she switched subjects. "You'll find you have many possible matches, but only you will have the power to choose who deserves your heart. When you do, it will create a love unlike any I've witnessed. Powerful enough to destroy both of your deepest demons..." The seer's voice faded.

Rose exchanged a longing glance with Tristan, a different kind of warmth radiating from her. He returned her gaze with equal pride.

"I see something else..." The seer's gaze wandered as if she were stepping into another realm. "A fork in the road, symbolizing two distinct paths… You must make a choice. But be cautious. I foresee the road you'll choose will send ripples throughout nations far beyond the borders of Cathan… You will be a powerful leader, a star, a beacon of hope to many. They will love, serve, and follow you."

The council remained as motionless as flies in a web, but their narrowing eyes slid to Rose like they had just uncovered a new threat.

The seer's gaze shifted, focusing on something. "There is something dark that lingers in the distance. It's hard to see. I fear it may be… It's…"

The seer dropped her hand as if Rose's palm had scalded her. The woman blinked, and the foggy mist in her eyes disappeared, fear shining like she'd just woken from a dreadful nightmare.

"What? What is it?" Rose asked, confused.

The woman looked at her solemnly. *The Blood King.*

A sudden chill ran through her, turning her sweat cold. The seer's mouth hadn't moved an inch, but Rose had heard her as clear as day. It was just like how she'd spoken to the phoenix in her mind.

Who? she thought.

If the seer heard her, she ignored the question. *You're in danger here—you need to leave before he finds you.*

This time, Rose was certain the seer was speaking into her mind, but she had no time to dwell on the novelty.

What do you mean? Before who can find me? she asked. *Please, I have so many questions.*

Lord Martin stood, furiously glancing between the two. "What's going on?" he barked. His angry eyes flashed to the seer. "This isn't what was agreed upon. We asked for an interview, not this jumble of nonsense. You haven't asked the girl a single question!"

A murmur of agreement spread throughout the council. Even Lord Barron did not look satisfied.

To Rose's surprise, the seer rose from the cushion to meet Lord Martin head-on. "I was clear that I am only able to see what is given. The herbs interact uniquely with each person."

Rose stared at the seer in awe. For some reason or another, the seer was protecting her. But why? Did the seer deem her secrets worth keeping? Or maybe she saw something that needed protecting? She didn't know. But whatever the seer's reason—she would be in her everlasting debt.

"This is an outrage!" Lord Martin cried, barging towards the seer. "What are you not telling us, witch?" He reached out to seize the seer, who stood her ground.

But Tristan stepped forward, intercepting Lord Martin's path, crossing his powerful arms as he silently confronted him—daring him.

The king stood up at once. "Enough, Lord Martin!" he thundered. "Lay a hand on the seer, and I'll throw you into the dungeons myself for manipulating a succession trial!"

The veins in Lord Martin's temples bulged as his hands balled into fists, but he was wise enough to contain his fury. He sauntered back to his seat, not bothering to hide his outrage, which matched the rest of the high council.

Lord Martin's deranged gaze shifted to Rose.

A few days ago, her weaker self would have shrunk. But now? Now she'd mined her inner strength and held her head high. He had aimed, shot, and missed his opportunity to uncover her secrets.

"Tristan, Rose, you've completed your challenge," the king grumbled, his frame still shaking with fury at Lord Martin's outburst. "You are to speak to no one until we meet back in the grand hall to announce the placements. We'll follow after we've made our decision."

Her shoulders slumped with relief.

By the grace of the sky and sea gods, she had evaded their trap.

At least this time.

CHAPTER 37

Rose's mother and Zareb joined her at the far table in the grand hall as she continued to shake from the extreme temperature drop from the hut. The rest of the contestants were all already sitting at separate tables, waiting for the deliberation of the placements.

Her mother wrapped a blanket around her, rubbing her shoulders to warm her. Rose gripped it tightly, shivering in the pink dress she had slipped back on. "Well, if Lord Martin didn't already think we are hiding something, he does now. It's only a matter of time before he finds a way. Ugh, I can't wait until this is over."

Zareb placed his foot onto the bench, resting his forearm onto his propped-up thigh, leaning in. "We have more enemies than just Lord Martin. The entire council was furious; if they didn't want Rose as queen before, they definitely don't now."

She admitted publicly challenging the council on rally night might not have been the wisest decision. That night, she knew she had gained a few enemies—but she had hoped the majority, including Lord Barron, were on her side. However, it seemed that even his support was diminishing.

"Bless the gods above, the seer didn't ask any questions," her mother said in relief. "I can only imagine how *that* would've gone."

Her mother was right. It was a stroke of luck, plain and simple.

Her gaze settled on Tristan at the front table alongside the queen, Harriet, and Roman. "Do you think Tristan and I did as well as the others?"

Zareb was the one to answer. "We won't be sure until the high council makes their decision."

A few minutes later, the doors opened, revealing the king and the high council—they had decided.

The grand hall fell silent.

The king wasted no time in announcing, "It is my honor to reveal the placement for the second challenge." He opened the small parchment in his hands. "In fourth place, we have Rose with thirteen points. In fourth place, Tristan with twenty-eight points." A wave of surprised murmurs came from the court. "In third, Emmett with thirty-one points. In second place, Dawnton with forty-eight points, and in first place, we have Grant with fifty-four points!"

A loud applause filled the grand hall as Grant stood to bask in his victory, flashing a broad, self-assured grin.

Rose's gaze fell to her drink. She'd come in dead last. She should have expected as much. If she needed any more confirmation of how the council felt about her evasion of the challenge, this was it.

Nonetheless, she clapped alongside the rest, careful to keep her face free of disappointment. But she understood now she was fighting an uphill battle. How was she supposed to have any chance of winning this if the entire council was against her?

Across the room, Tristan's solemn face frowned grimly, gazing downward.

"He must be so disappointed with himself," her mother said with pity. "You should go talk to him."

She would, but something more urgent pressed on her. The phoenix had warned her she'd have to face an ancient enemy to protect the future of Vallor. And now, the seer had mentioned this Blood King. She had no recollection of reading or hearing such a name, but she couldn't help but wonder if they were interlinked somehow.

"I'll talk to him later," Rose said, shoving the ache for Tristan aside. "But I haven't told you everything that happened in the hut." She lowered her voice, fully aware Zareb was listening. "The seer... she spoke into my mind—I don't know how, but she warned me I was in danger and that I should leave."

Her mother stilled. "In danger from who?"

"She mentioned someone named the Blood King. Have either of you heard of that name?"

Both shook their heads.

Rose's shoulders sank with disappointment.

Her mother's anxious eyes searched the air. "I've been worried something like this would happen. There's been too much going on since we arrived to be a coincidence."

Rose agreed. She needed answers.

"I need to find the seer. Maybe she can tell us more about this threat." Her gaze landed on Zareb. "Can you find out where she is staying?"

Zareb was already straightening. "I'll find out what I can. Stay here," he instructed, leaving them and disappearing through the doors.

The next thing Rose knew, a pair of furious golden eyes were coming straight for her. She groaned internally; if there was someone she didn't want to deal with right now, it was Roman.

He seemed to already have his fighting gloves on as he said, "I need to speak with you."

"Now isn't a good time," she said, trying to defuse whatever fire was burning behind his eyes.

"You have a lot of nerve jolting Tristan in front of everyone. Right before the second trial? How could you do that to him?"

Tell him, she scolded herself. *Tell him the truth. Tell him you were only protecting the people you love. Tell him that you didn't want to entertain Grant.*

She opened her mouth to speak but didn't know which lame excuse would squelch the fire burning in his eyes.

Roman scoffed at her lack of defense. "Is this you still playing games?"

"Enough!" Tristan said, appearing behind his brother.

Roman spun to face Tristan. "She's using you, Tristan. Everyone can see it. Why can't you?"

Tristan's confident gaze didn't waver. "Father doesn't see it that way, and neither do I. That should be enough for you."

"You both have blinders on, and you refuse to take them off. I won't let you throw your life away for someone who doesn't deserve it. Mark my words—she'll ruin you, just like she ruined Xavier." With that, Roman stalked off.

He might as well have tied her to a stake and let the flame take her.

Rose let out an exhausted sigh, resting her elbows on the table and planting her face into her palms.

Her mother put a comforting hand on her shoulder.

"He doesn't mean that," Tristan said.

"Oh yes, he does." She lifted her head to watch him strut away. "And I wouldn't be surprised if your sister and mother are right behind him, helping him plan a way to be rid of me for good."

Tristan sat on the bench next to her, lowering his voice. "Listen, Rose. We need to talk."

She swallowed hard. "I know; I'm sorry today went... well, how it went," she said, not knowing how else to say it. "With Grant, the trial—it was my fault."

Tristan shook his head. "No, it wasn't; the council has had it in for us from the start. Either way, we won't have much time to dwell on the loss. They'll announce it soon, but my father told me the third challenge is tomorrow."

"What?" she whispered, her eyes wide. "What's the challenge?"

"He wouldn't say, only that the goal is to retrieve the sun medallion again," he explained with a bitter tone, then his face softened. "But listen, Rose, there's something else I need to tell you—"

Before he could finish, Zareb returned. He bent over, whispering into her ear, "She's staying in a room at the castle. I found out where, but we should go now. She's planning to leave soon."

The opportunity was too important to miss. "I'm sorry, I have to go," Rose said to Tristan. Before he could begin to protest, she added, "I promise I'll find you later."

Tristan's back straightened as his eyes flitted back and forth between Rose and Zareb, narrowing. "And just where are you going?

They're going to announce the third challenge soon. You need to be here."

"I'll explain everything later," she said, not wanting to miss her chance. "Please, I'll find you after. I promise."

Before Tristan could respond, she followed Zareb out with her mother close behind, leaving Tristan's fuming alone at the table.

Zareb led them through the winding maze of corridors, far away from the festivities in the grand hall. Their footsteps echoed through the empty halls as they briskly walked across the smooth, golden sun emblem set in the stone beneath them. The halls were dimly lit by flickering torches, darkened as storm clouds continued to loom through the cathedral windows, spreading dark shadows onto her pink dress. She gripped the skirt in fistfuls, lifting it off the floor to keep up with Zareb's pace.

The three reached the door in record time as Zareb spoke to the guard on duty. "We wish an audience with the seer."

"I was told to let no one enter," the guard replied.

Before Zareb could retort, Rose stepped in. Using her most convincing voice, she said, "Please, we'll only be but a moment."

The guard's gaze locked with hers, and she could have sworn a thin haze crept across his eyes. The soldier sighed. "Be quick about it." Without another word, he sidestepped to let them enter.

Zareb knocked on the door. After a long moment of silence, he knocked again. No reply.

He looked at Rose, asking what she wanted to do.

"Hello?" she said calmly, stepping towards the door. "Is anyone there?"

Still nothing.

Zareb took the initiative to try the handle. The door was unlocked, its hinges creaking as it opened wide.

"Hello?" she called out again. "It's Rose. Please, I just want to talk."

Her heart stopped beating.

The room was in utter chaos. Chairs lay overturned, and the table was toppled on its side. Once neatly stacked, books and papers were now strewn across the floor. The bedsheets and pillows were left in disarray, having been tossed about. Even the mirror on the wall was broken, sprinkling shattered glass in its wake.

"Gods in the lost city above," her mother whispered, covering her mouth in horror.

As quick as a whip, Zareb drew his sword, crossing to the opposite side of the room to see if it was clear.

"But she was just here," the soldier said, coming in behind them, his face blanched white. "No one has been in or out of this door."

"What do you think happened?" Rose asked Zareb.

Zareb checked the window. "There are no signs of blood." His eyes scoured the room again. "I don't think she's hurt, but there was definitely a struggle."

"I'll sound the alert," the soldier said, dismissing himself to tell his captain down the hall.

Rose's chest tightened, her hopes of gaining answers gone. "Who would do this?"

"I can only make assumptions," Zareb said, his eyes still darting around.

"We should leave," her mother said. "I don't like this. Any of it."

Rose couldn't help the feeling that the seer was missing because she had chosen to protect her, because someone hadn't liked that. And she would wager all the riches in Vallor that Lord Martin was involved. Punishment for withholding what the seer knew. What she might have seen. For evading their trap.

Maybe, just maybe, the seer had heard her internal plea, and because the seer had listened… she could be dead.

Rose didn't dare to think of it.

Zareb crouched to examine the candlesticks scattered across the floor. He pinched the wick, and a wisp of smoke spiraled upward. "It's still warm." He sprang back up. "She couldn't have gotten far."

Hope sparked within her. "Then there's a chance we can still find her?"

"Maybe." His eyes shone with determination. "I'll help the castle guard… but I'll take you back to your room—" She opened her mouth to protest, but he interrupted. "No. Whoever did this could still be in the castle, and I can't find them if I'm too busy worrying about you. I'll take you back to your room, and you'll stay there until I come for you. Don't let anyone enter." He handed her a sword. "Keep this with you."

She wanted to argue, but she bit her tongue. She recognized that head-strong look all too well. She'd have to do it his way if she wanted a chance to find the seer. Her mother would only be his ally in his cause. Arguing would be a waste of time.

Reluctantly, Rose accepted the sword. "Fine," she agreed, taking the hilt into her hands.

~

Rose paced in her room like a caged animal, surprised her steps hadn't worn a path into the rug. She couldn't shake the image of the seer's room. Guilt gnawed at her from within. She'd heard nothing but silence since the alarm had been sounded more than an hour ago, if the dying flames in the fireplace were to be trusted.

She bit her lip as she spun on her heel to pace back the other way. She still didn't understand how in Vallor someone managed to enter without the guard noticing. Was Lord Martin's anger so great that he'd go as far as to kill her?

A splitting scream pierced the silence.

She whipped to face the door.

It had come from the hall. She was sure of it. She'd recognize that scream anywhere.

Her mother.

Fear caged her heart as another scream came, calling out her name this time.

She didn't think as she sprang into action, snatching the sword Zareb had given her. She burst out the door, sprinting towards her mother's room, going as fast as her feet would permit.

Her mother couldn't be hurt. She wouldn't allow it. She pushed her legs faster.

As Rose rounded the corner, someone seized her. Before she could even make a sound, a hand pressed a white cloth over her mouth and nose.

"Shhh," a male voice whispered.

The pungent cloth stung her nose, the scent from an herb she knew all too well—the leaf of the Choloar plant. She struggled to escape the stranger's hold, but it was too late. She'd already inhaled too much of the toxic scent.

Her body became numb, her arms falling limply to her side. Before her legs gave out, the large figure caught her, lifting her into his arms as if she weighed no more than a feather.

All consciousness slipped away as her world faded to black...

CHAPTER 38

Rose woke up to a gentle breeze carrying a hint of mist, making her nose crinkle at the sudden spray. She attempted to open her eyes, but the blinding light beating down forced her to squeeze them shut again while the sound of crashing waves thundered in her ears.

She shifted her weight to her arms, sitting up slowly. As she did, she became acutely aware of two alarming realities. First, metal chains coiled around her wrists, scraping against the coarse, rocky surface beneath her. Second, and more horrifying, was the fact that she was perched precariously on a slim ledge against a steep cliff face.

Instincts took over as she scrambled backward, retreating as far back as the narrow edge would allow. She pressed her back against the hot rock wall behind her, the heat sinking into her dress. The ledge was so narrow that she could barely sit without her legs dangling off.

Her muscles locked up as she closed her eyes, taking a deep breath, attempting to calm herself. This had to be some horrible dream. Some nightmare.

When she dared to peek out of her eyes, she was still on the cliff.

After a prolonged moment of acceptance, she summoned the courage to look beyond the narrow ledge, expecting to see the ground miles down. But it was far worse. She saw a sea of blue below, with only a thin crest-shaped bar of sand, which would soon be gone with the high tide.

She knew exactly where she was.

Crimson Cove.

She'd come here to the beach often with Tristan and his siblings. It was beautiful in the mornings, but toward midday, they had always quickly cleared out, cautioned of its strong, unforgiving currents. Dozens of ships had met their end in this cove, wrecked in the early years of Cathan's founding and many since. So many, in fact, they claimed the waters had been turned crimson from the saturation of blood that'd poured into its seas from the sailors it'd consumed.

Rose combed through her memory, remembering the hooded figure who had grabbed her. After that, nothing. She couldn't recall a face or even a voice. Her dread escalated as she remembered her mother's scream. Had that been real? Or had that just been a way to coax her out into the open? She reassured herself that her mother wasn't defenseless—she kept a sword hidden in her room, just as Rose had. She could fight them off. She was strong.

When she looked down, Rose caught a glimpse of a shiny object hanging around her neck. Her fingers traced the large sun medallion resting on her collarbone.

Finally, clarity found her.

This was the next challenge.

Anger gripped her. Was this the high council's doing? Had they really needed to kidnap her? Couldn't they have given her a warning? Did the king know about this? She couldn't believe he did, not after everything he'd done to protect her. It had to have been the high council's scheme, no doubt spearheaded by Lord Martin himself, in hopes she'd die in this trial.

She was tempted to succumb to her panic, but if she did, it'd be that much harder to get out of this alive. No matter how much she wanted to shut down at the sight of the large body of water below her, she had to overcome her fear.

So, with a deep breath, she searched for the source of her chains. To her surprise, she discovered that she was tethered to a large, curved iron arch situated just above her, somehow joined to the cliff's rocky surface for the challenge. It was large enough that if she did fall, she'd end up hanging directly in the center of the cove.

There was no way up or down. No way but to climb. And she wasn't even sure if she could manage it with this cumbersome chain restricting her movement. How in the hell had they even gotten her on a ledge like this in the first place?

Maybe if she climbed high enough, she could build enough momentum to swing back in the opposite direction. But even with her increasing strength, she feared she wouldn't have the endurance to reach the top. It was a long shot, but she couldn't think of another option.

Why hadn't she learned to swim?

Her mind flooded with all the ways this idea could go wrong. She couldn't guarantee she could find her way back to the small ledge if she failed to reach the top. If that were to happen, she'd be dangling in the middle of the cove like a fish on a hook.

Her anger toward the council was strong enough to consider taking the risk.

Just as she began to consider executing her dreadful plan, the ledge beneath her quaked. A large crack spread through the rock between her feet, threatening to collapse.

Her fear transcended into horror.

She sprang to her feet. Having little time to react, she grasped the first holds she could find. Her hands had just found a solid grip just before the ledge gave way entirely, crumbling and falling into the sea below.

She hung there for a moment, her chest heaving. She cursed under her breath, resting her forehead against the cliffside, taking deep breaths to calm herself.

She peered back up the cliffside—well, it was decided for her now.

Summoning all her courage, she forced herself to climb. She took her time finding each hold, doing her best to keep her hands from shaking. Her outfit wasn't doing her any favors—she was still wearing the cursed pink dress and flats from the previous day.

The wind howled around her as she inched her way up. With every effort to find a new foothold, her feet continued to slip. Her useless flats gave her little to no traction, becoming a hindrance. She had no choice but to kick them off. Pressing on, she continued to climb barefoot, gradually making her way up.

She was impressed with the small progress she was making, the tiny success instilling a seed of hope.

However, that hope was short-lived. Within minutes, her arms began to waver. She fought against her shaking arms, gritting her teeth, pausing only to rest briefly.

After a few minutes, she paused again to catch her breath, panting as she surveyed her surroundings. The top was still far away—too far to reach. She'd never make it.

She studied the large, curved rod. She was almost at a point where if she let go, it might give her enough momentum to swing herself to the other side, but she couldn't be sure. She considered the idea, contemplating if it would be worth the risk.

Without warning, a large crack rumbled above her.

Her eyes shot upward—a large boulder coming straight for her.

No, no, no. Not yet.

She might not make it to the other side if she let go now. But she had no choice. There was no time to debate. The boulder picked up speed with every second she lingered.

She let go, managing to grab hold of the chain just in time as the large mass fell right where she'd been resting.

And just like that, she took to the sky, free falling into the blue abyss. She maneuvered her legs into a swinging position, trying to make herself more aerodynamic. Gravity dragged her down until, finally, she swung upward, climbing higher and higher. Her outrageous plan might just work.

Despite her hopes, the swing wasn't enough. As soon as she had reached the height of her swing, she scrambled for the rocky wall to get a handhold. But it was all in vain; her scraping fingers slipped right over the rock.

She plummeted again, losing all control as she spun around in circles.

She swung back and forth until she came to a stop, hanging helplessly by her wrists in the middle of the cove. The iron clasps dug into her skin from the weight. Grasping the chain, she tried to alleviate the strain. She peeked down at the sea of blue below her, her hopes of escaping now utterly ruined. The tide was rising and the shoreline was almost gone. Fantastic.

She had to bite down on her lip to keep it from quivering. Would they drop her into the water? Did they know she couldn't swim? She squinted up at the long chain above her, holding her fast. She was too exhausted to even consider pulling herself up.

How long she hung there, she didn't know. Twenty minutes? An hour? The rising tide below was the only proof that time was passing. The cove was full now—the thin crest of sand had all but disappeared.

Without warning, the curved iron contraption groaned, dropping her toward the water. She gripped the chain in terror, gasping. The force jolted her towards the water, but just as swiftly as it had begun, it stopped.

She winced at the sudden impact on her wrists. A sinking pit grew within her stomach. The action proved they wanted to send her into the water. She was certain they were somewhere watching her, reveling in her fear, hoping she'd die and they'd be rid of her and all of their worries.

After what seemed like ages, her arms threatened to give out. She wasn't sure how much longer she could carry on like this. She winced from the strain of her chains, her arms threatening to pop out of their sockets at any moment. Blood began to trickle down her arms from the iron clasps digging into her wrists.

She prayed to the lost city above that her mother wasn't watching.

She didn't think things could get much worse until she noticed a strange ripple in the water.

Rose's heart stopped mid-beat. Maybe it was her imagination running wild from the blood loss. She strained her eyes. Another massive ripple ran across the water. Just below the surface, a scaled creature glided through the water.

Something was in the water.

Something big.

She suddenly mined a new strength, gripping the chains again as terror took over her body. Perhaps she could try to swing herself towards the curved iron and give herself more time—

"Rose!" a voice bellowed from above, echoing through the cliffs—a voice intermingled with equal amounts of fear and fury. She knew that voice.

Relief flooded her veins as she spotted Tristan standing at the edge of the cliff. "Tristan!"

He faltered, mortified at the bloodstains marring her arms and dress. "Are you okay?"

"I'm fine," she lied, ignoring the pain.

"Dammit—hold on! You hear me? Just hold on. I'm coming, I'm coming!" Tristan called. He searched around frantically, looking for something he could use.

"Tristan, there's something in the water!"

He muttered a stream of curse words under his breath, untangling the thick rope he carried. He tied it around his waist at top speed, anchoring himself to a nearby boulder. "I'm climbing down. I'll get you out, I promise!" Without an ounce of fear, he jumped off the cliff, rappelling along the rocky cliffside at top speed.

The water was nothing but calm waves. She searched for any sign of the creature, but all she could see was an infinity of blue.

Without warning, the iron rod lowered again, sending her closer to the ocean.

She bit her lip to keep from screaming.

"Rose!" Tristan called out.

Her fear became harder to suppress as she dared to peer into the water again. "Hurry, please hurry," she begged in a whisper, hating how fragile she sounded.

So scared.

"I'm coming! Don't worry. I'm coming!" Tristan yelled as if he had heard her soft plea.

The water rippled again, revealing its secret—a massive sea beast swam beneath her, sheer-violet scales glimmering as large, translucent fins glided effortlessly through the water. Its scaly, snake-like body was speckled with sapphire blue markings, propelled by four powerful webbed feet, tearing through the water with force. Its fierce sea-green eyes lifted up at her from the depths below.

She stilled, petrified. *Please,* she begged in her mind. *Please don't hurt us.*

The beast broke eye contact but continued to circle beneath her like a predator circling its prey.

Tristan had reached the base of the iron contraption in record time. He didn't waste a moment before mounting it, putting his arms out and balancing himself as he tiptoed across the narrow contraption.

The massive hook lowered once more, inching her closer to the crashing waves, this time so low that the sea monster could easily snatch her away with a single swipe of its razor-sharp talons.

The force knocked Tristan to his knees as he gripped the iron truss. She gasped, fearing that he'd be tossed off, but Tristan held on, rising to his hands and knees, determined to reach her.

But he wouldn't.

Straight out of the blue, the beast's glorious form sprang out of the water, leaving a trail of sparkling droplets in its wake. Its bloodthirsty eyes fixated on her as its wide jaws opened, exposing a row of razor-sharp teeth.

It happened so quickly she didn't even have time to react.

In one swift movement, the beast's teeth severed her chains, and just like that, she plunged into the depths alongside the monster.

"*Rose!*" Tristan roared.

She sucked in a large breath just before she plunged into the sea.

Her body slammed against the cold water, and immediately, shock hit her. She did her best to swim, but even with her freed wrists, she flailed, the bubbles from her fall obscuring her vision.

If she hadn't been so panic-stricken, she'd be able to appreciate the beautiful sea floor. How the gentle streams of sunlight shone down from the world above, casting their rays through the water onto the glittering sand that had settled among the sunken ships littering the ocean floor.

As the bubbles cleared, she found the beast was already back in the sea with her. Its bright, sea-green eyes locked on her, frozen so still that it was as if she was staring at a floating statue.

This was it. This was how she'd die.

She waited for it to lunge or strike. Instead, the sea monster's terrifying gaze remained fixed, like a cat watching a trapped mouse.

Meanwhile, she was floundering like a fish out of water, struggling to keep herself from sinking. She dug into her memories, trying to recall if any of the books she'd read had ever mentioned a creature like it, but this was a beast she'd never come across in *any* history books. She tried to make out if the creature had any vulnerabilities. That's when her gaze fell upon something shiny strung around its neck. Her eyes widened. It was the golden sun relic, the very thing she was meant to retrieve, and that wasn't the only thing—a large iron clasp was also locked around its neck, chaining it to the bottom of the sea.

It was trapped, just like she was.

As if sensing her gaze on its collar, it glanced at it with her, its magical sea-green eyes dimming.

Before she could react, Tristan was at her side. His powerful arms quickly encircled her waist, propelling them upward, clawing for life. She tried to help, kicking her feet as hard as she could.

They broke through to the surface, coughing as they gasped for air.

"Hold on to me," Tristan said breathlessly, wrapping her arms around his neck. "I'll swim us back to shore."

"No, wait—"

The sea monster's tail whipped between them, forcing them apart, sending them back into the sea.

She somersaulted round and round, swirling in a disorienting cycle, her arms and legs flailing to regain control over her body. The sea beast bolted straight for Tristan, ready to strike. Tristan swam with all his might, but his speed was no match for the sea beast.

It swiped its claws at him, parting its jaw to swallow him whole.

No! she screamed—an internal cry.

To her utter shock, the creature listened, stopping as its head whipped to her.

Her lungs burned, screaming for air. There was no way she'd make it to the surface in time. No way to swim upward, even if she tried. She had no choice but to take in a big gulp of seawater.

She braced for the painful ordeal, but to her utter shock, her lungs didn't miss a beat.

Somehow, in some miracle, her body filtered the water, drawing air from it. She put her hand on her throat.

She could breathe underwater.

The beast was still staring at her, waiting.

I'll free you, she said in her mind. *If you promise not to hurt us, I'll free you.*

The sea creature stared at her for so long that she was sure it hadn't understood her at all. But then it changed course, coming for her instead. Tristan swam like a madman again, trying to stop the beast in its wake, but it was a waste of energy. The beast was already upon her—so close, she could reach out and touch it with a single stroke.

Up close, she could see the shimmering details of each individual scale, ranging in a perfect blend of purple, blue, and green. Its entire body was lined with a sheer, shiny protective layer while its thin, nearly see-through fins had brilliant sapphire marks.

Doing her best to steady her shaky hands, she reached for the giant iron lock secured around its neck.

The sea beast growled in warning.

She quickly retracted her arms.

It merely blinked, waiting—daring her to be brave enough.

She summoned the courage to reach back up to the iron clasp. Her fingers struggled to unlock it, slipping over the slick metal. After a few feeble attempts, she managed to pull the clasp away, and with a muffled click, the large collar fell from its neck, sinking to the ocean floor.

The sea creature lifted its snout. *Thank you,* a beautiful female voice spoke into her mind, emitting a deep purr from its chest that sent vibrations throughout the water.

Tristan had finally made his way behind the beast, pulling his dagger out, ready to strike, but the sea beast was prepared, no longer soft and gentle as it curled its mouth, snarling at him. With one whip of its tail, it knocked the blade out of his hands, sending it to the sea floor along with the clasp.

The beast's attention returned to her, looking at her expectantly. It swiveled its large head, gesturing to its scaly back—it wanted her to climb on.

She hesitated before grasping one of the large, bone-like spikes along its spine and swung her leg over the base of the creature's long neck. Rose motioned for Tristan to do the same. He shook his head, looking at her like she'd lost her mind—she could have sworn the sea beast rolled its eyes as it swam closer to him.

Rose reached out her hand, praying he'd be brave enough to take it. Tristan found the courage to reach back, gliding onto the beast behind her.

At breakneck speed, the sea creature surged upwards. Within seconds, it sprang out of the water. Its wings flung open wide, and with a few powerful flaps, it climbed into the sky, droplets slipping off its scales into the open air below.

Tristan's arm slipped around her waist, securing her tightly to him. She, however, was strangely at ease on the beast. Adrenaline pumped through her veins, giving her the confidence to loosen her hold on the spike, trusting the sea beast as it carried them higher and higher into the sky, far above the cliffs.

Any sane person would have been terrified, but she couldn't help the smile that slipped onto her lips as water dripped from her chin. She gazed at the broad horizon spread out before her. From here, she could see all the way from the western sea to the northern mountains. It was the first time she'd ever seen the vast mountain range in person. Though distant and faint, it was unmistakable.

"It's beautiful," she whispered. She could get used to flying.

The sea beast's mouth curled upward, showing off its frightening teeth. It took her a moment to realize the beast wasn't baring its teeth but showcasing a toothy grin, puffing its chest with pride as if pleased by her awe.

After their brief flight, the sea creature glided back to the cliffs. Rose peered down, spotting a small group of people waiting for them. The sea creature quickly descended, landing gracefully away from the crowd.

Tristan slid off first, not wasting a moment before returning his feet to solid ground. He reached up for Rose and she took his hand, finding her footing gracefully.

She craned her neck to look up at the beast. "Thank you. Not only for saving our lives, but for that." She pointed to the sky.

The sea beast's eyes sparkled. *And thank you for freeing me. If you ever need anything, you need only call, and I shall come,* the creature promised.

"How do I do that?"

Simply reach for the water and call me by my name—Neera, she replied. Neera looked down at the golden sun relic still hanging on her neck. *I think this is yours.* The beast's sharp talon hooked around the chain, breaking it off with one tug, and held it out to her.

Rose stepped forward and claimed the sun relic, taking the wet gold into her hands.

Goodbye, fair one, Neera said in farewell.

With that, the mystical creature spread its wings and launched itself off the cliff, disappearing from sight before swooping back up, climbing higher as it flew toward the horizon. It was no larger than a speck in the distance when the creature plunged back into the sea.

"Are you hurt?" Tristan asked, cupping Rose's cheeks as he inspected her, landing on her bloody wrists.

"A little, but nothing I won't survive."

He hugged her tightly, kissing her wet forehead. Her shivering body melted into his. "Lost city above, I thought I was going to lose you," he whispered.

She wrapped her hands around his neck in reply. "I'm okay... *We're* okay."

"I'm going to kill whoever did this," Tristan fumed, letting go. He gently retook her hands as he inspected her bloodied wrists. "Trust me, my father is livid. This will not go unpunished."

She buried her face into his chest, the exhaustion finally taking its toll as her raw wrists pulsed with pain.

Her mother was the first to reach them, sprinting towards the pair with Zareb not far behind.

Her mother was here. She was safe. Rose could have sobbed with relief.

"Thank the everlasting gods," her mother rejoiced, giving her the most suffocating hug she'd ever had. She scanned Rose from head to toe, mortified by the bloodstains on her dress. "Look at you! We need to get you to the healers, both of you."

Rose grabbed her mother's arm. "What happened? Are you okay? I heard you scream."

Her mother stared at her, perplexed. “Me?”

“Yes, I heard you scream for me last night.”

“Screaming? I never screamed.” Her mother frowned. “Is that why you left your room?”

Rose’s gaze drifted away, not responding. She had her answer, then. It hadn’t been her mother’s screams at all. It had been a setup to lure her out, and she’d stupidly fallen for it.

Zareb appeared next, astonishing her by grabbing her shoulders and pulling her into his chest. The rare sentiment was all she needed to know that he’d gone out of his mind with worry. “I’m so sorry.” His fingers dug so hard into her back that she winced. “I should’ve never let you out of my sight.”

She held him tightly back. “It’s not your fault.”

Tristan folded his arms. “My father will have something to say about the fact, I’m sure,” he said, his tone hostile.

She was stunned that he would say such a thing. She skirted around Zareb, putting herself between them. “I’m the one who ran out of my room. He told me to stay put. He’s not to blame.”

Tristan’s hard gaze didn’t waver. “Maybe,” he admitted, his eyes casting out to the small group of people. “But I think there is more than one person to blame.”

All their eyes shifted to the high council, who were attempting to reach them, but with a single bark from the king, they stayed put.

She wished they’d been allowed. Then, she could push them off the cliff herself. Or call Neera back and offer her a feast—use their bones as toothpicks.

“Rose!” King Henrik cried, pulling her into his warm embrace. Tears streamed down the creases of his face. “Oh, thank Vallor. I thought we’d lost you.”

The queen, Harriet, and Roman joined the reunion.

“Oh good lord, look at you both,” the queen said, inspecting them. “To the healers. Both of you.”

“I’ll take Rose myself,” Tristan said, daring anyone to oppose him.

“You most certainly will not,” Harriet retorted. “You’re bleeding terribly yourself,” she said, her tone resembling her mother’s.

At last, Rose noticed his sliced-open tunic, revealing three large gashes where the sea creature had swiped. Her lungs gave out. She thought the beast had missed.

"I'm fine," Tristan said, brushing them off even as he winced.

She lifted the ripped tunic to get a better look. They were worse than she'd feared. "These are deep." She reprimanded herself for not noticing sooner. "You're losing a lot of blood."

"Bring the horses!" the king commanded, retreating into the crowd.

Tristan immediately withdrew, shaking his head. "I'm not leaving her," he said, his voice raw.

"I'll be right behind you," Rose reassured him. "I promise. I'm fine."

Tristan surprised her by pressing his mouth against hers. The trembling of his lips and hands let her know she'd terrified him today. Let her know he wouldn't survive the loss of her.

She'd barely had a moment to return the kiss before he was dragged off to the nearest horse.

She planned to find her own way back, until Roman's deep voice stopped her. "Let me help you." The remnants of his earlier anger had vanished without a trace. He even offered a hand to help her onto his horse.

Good hell, did this man even have a temperature between hot and cold?

She glared at his outstretched hand. "That won't be necessary. I'll ride with Zareb." Her eyes lifted to confront his, becoming cold. "I wouldn't want you going out of your way for someone who doesn't deserve it."

She didn't even care how his face flinched as she said it. Good. She hoped it hurt.

She pressed past Roman, shoving her shoulder hard into his, not caring if everyone saw the cold exchange.

She hoped the message she'd just sent was loud and clear.

CHAPTER 39

Rose bandaged her own wrists, cleaning them in hot water and covering them with Alofa leaves to help with the pain and swelling —though they still throbbed with a dull ache.

But her discomfort was nothing compared to Tristan's.

The healers were still sewing him up when she arrived. Tristan didn't utter a single complaint as the healer worked the needle and thread, but he writhed on the bed, his hand clenched around hers. The pressure made her wrist throb, but she refused to let go. A persistent cough played on him, making her fret, but it was a good sign his body was removing the fluids.

Eventually, the challenge results were announced. Each successor had faced their own task of retrieving a sun medallion. Tristan had obtained the medallion from around Rose's neck, just as she claimed the one from the sea beast. Grant had found his amongst the shipwrecks near Crimson Cove, Dawnton had retrieved his from beneath the sea caves, and Emmett had found his on a small, rocky island a few leagues offshore.

Tristan emerged victorious in the challenge, scoring forty-four points. Rose followed with twenty-one, Grant with fourteen, Emmett with thirteen, and Dawnton finished with just eight points—barely surviving the perilous conditions of the caves during high tide.

Everyone had assumed that Tristan had rounded up the sea beast and forced it into submission. Tristan tried to clarify the misunderstanding, but a single glance from Rose silenced him. She preferred they believe the story rather than raise suspicions or questions about her ability to communicate with the beast, or the fact that she'd been able to breathe underwater. How could she explain her survival underwater for so long, aside from Tristan's bravery? She didn't truly understand it herself. And if she were accused of cheating or manipulating the challenge, she risked disqualification from the succession.

Not only did she believe it was the council who had left her stranded on the rock, but the king did as well, mercilessly interrogating each of them. But they all provided strong alibis. Each one was compelled to swear on the sacred holy relic that only the medallion was meant to hang from the iron truss for Tristan's challenge—even Lord Martin was present with the king himself at the time.

Either way, no evidence existed of their involvement, leaving them all free and clear from any consequence. Rose remained unconvinced—who was to say they didn't hire a mercenary to do their dirty work? Cowards.

Though she was quick to blame, she had to admit wrangling a sea beast seemed beyond the council's abilities, which begged the question of how the sea beast got there in the first place. Who among them could wield such power? To capture a beast of that magnitude? To chain it to the ocean floor? All this brought up an even more terrifying question.

If not them, then who?

What was more distressing was that no one had found the seer either. Then again, it'd been no one's top priority after Rose had been kidnapped, distracting them all from the pursuit.

Her mother and Zareb remained glued to her side, putting on a strong front. But she swore she could tap either one and they'd shatter to pieces on the floor.

Rose also wasn't ignorant of the fact that Roman kept glancing at her, trying to make eye contact, but she refused to meet his gaze.

The bright light that used to pour through Tristan's window diminished into a hazy glow. The sunset that evening must have been stunning as its soft pink and orange shades flooded the bedroom.

A small knock came at the door.

Rose didn't pay any attention to it until one of the healers came to the king, bowing. "It's the queen and princess of Vertmere," the healer relayed. "They wish to see Tristan."

As perplexing as their presence was for her, no one, not even Tristan, seemed as confused as she. The realization made her shift in her stance, suddenly feeling out of the loop.

The king let out a loud sigh. "Let them in."

Rose leaned toward her mother, whispering, "What are they still doing here?"

"I'm not sure," her mother whispered back, eyeing the foreign royal pair who'd just entered. "But Vertmerians have strong convictions in divinity and fate, and after today… I'm quite certain the foreigners believe Tristan has both."

Four emerald-clad guards congregated behind the Vertmerian queen, who pursed her lips in distaste as if she still detested being there. At that point, Rose thought it may just be her permanent expression. Her daughter trailed behind her, her light, brown hair neatly pinned up with a crown of leaves as she gazed at Tristan with inquisitive eyes.

"I hope we're not interrupting," the foreign queen said, her voice as sharp as a blade.

"Of course not," Queen Lenna said with a tight smile that didn't reach her eyes. She stood from Tristan's bedside. "Won't you come sit, my dear? You can have my seat."

The young princess looked to her mother, seeking her permission. Queen Isleen nodded, encouraging her. The princess gracefully settled next to him.

"I hope you're feeling better," Princess Satin said to Tristan, her voice light and airy.

Tristan maintained a neutral expression. "I am, thank you."

"That was quite the display of heroism," said the foreign queen, her eyes reflecting a rare moment of acceptance—it was the first pleasant expression Rose had seen from the woman. "I have to say, not many survive an encounter with a sea beast. Most go through their entire life without ever even seeing one. I can see why Cathan is so strong if all your men fight with such valor as you." She prompted a guard to come forward, bringing a small bottle. "We brought this soothing balm for your wound. It's made from calendula that grows near the river by our home; it aids the tissue in regrowth."

A flash of surprise flitted across Tristan's face. "Thank you. That's very generous of you." He gave a constrained smile at the unexpected gift.

Rose's mother emerged from the corner where they stood. "I'm sorry, I don't think we've been properly introduced," she said, batting her lashes with a large society smile on her face.

The foreign queen shifted to face them, finally acknowledging their presence.

"Pardon my manners," the king apologized. "This is Queen Isleen, and her daughter, Princess Satin."

Rose's mother bowed. "What a pleasure it is to meet you all." She flashed them another smile as she, Rose, and Zareb bowed politely. "I'm Evelyn, and this is my daughter, Rosalie."

Queen Isleen's eyes finally met Rose's, sizing her up and down, looking at her like a commodity instead of a human.

"It's so lovely to meet you," Satin said with a kind smile.

"Are you related to the royal family?" Queen Isleen asked.

"No," Queen Lenna answered before anyone could speak. "They're close friends."

"But they are *like* family," Harriet added from across the room, beaming at Rose with bright eyes. "Rose is like the sister I never had."

The affectionate compliment surprised Rose. She was sure Harriet was still upset with her for kissing Grant, but perhaps her almost dying had made Harriet find forgiveness faster than she'd expected. It hadn't gone unnoticed that Harriet had been distant ever since Xavier's tribunal. Perhaps Harriet had partly blamed her for his banishment. There had been so much going on that she hadn't really even had a chance to ask.

"I can't believe you tried to climb," Satin said to Rose, her brown eyes shining with admiration. "Where in Vallor did you get the strength?"

Rose gave a faint smile, warming to the girl slightly. "Survival instinct, I suppose."

"It's nothing but a miracle you both survived," Queen Isleen confessed to Tristan. "I can't imagine how you managed to wrangle the beast into letting you onto its back. It was the most magnificent thing I'd ever seen. How in Vallor did you ever do it?"

Apparently, it was a question everyone had been asking themselves as all eyes fell onto Tristan for an explanation. Tristan risked a glance at Rose as if asking what he should say. She gave him a discreet plea with her eyes, praying he wouldn't spill her secret.

"It wasn't without difficulty," he replied, not giving any more detail.

"Well, it's getting late. We should leave him to get some rest," Queen Lenna said, looking at Queen Isleen and Princess Satin. "Join us, won't you? I'm sure dinner is ready and waiting."

Queen Isleen gave a silent nod, agreeing.

Satin stood, gazing at Tristan. "I hope you get better soon," she said, bidding him farewell with a sweet smile. Then she looked to Rose. "You, too."

After they left, Rose turned to her mother and Zareb. "Go and eat. I'm going to stay with Tristan a while."

Her mother looked at her with soft eyes. "Are you sure?"

"Yes, I'm alright. You must be starving. Go."

For a moment, she thought her mother would refuse, but instead, she kissed her on the forehead and left.

Zareb hesitated. Out of everyone, he looked the worst. The bags under his eyes were proof of it. "I'll stay outside the door."

"I'm alive, Zareb. I'm safe. I'm breathing. Please eat."

Zareb hesitated a moment longer. "Fine, but I'll be back later for you."

Tristan glared at Zareb with narrow eyes as he left. Rose held off until they were alone before she went to sit on Tristan's bed, reaching for his hand. "You shouldn't blame Zareb," she said softly, not letting the glare go unnoticed.

Tristan's face darkened. "He should have never left you."

She could have told him Zareb had set out to find the seer, but then she'd have to explain why she'd sought the seer in the first place and what the seer had said during their challenge. She had no desire to delve into *that* conversation. Not right now. They'd had enough turmoil for one day.

She changed the subject. "That salve will help," she said, nodding to the calendula. "Can I put it on?"

Tristan gazed at the jar by his bedside, hesitant to trust it.

She picked it up and held it to her nose. "It's not poison, I promise."

He gave a reluctant nod, letting her unravel the bandages from his abdomen.

After a moment, he said, "Your hands are so soft... You should be a healer."

"With your family, it might just become my full-time job." She threw him a sly smile.

He let out a harsh laugh, then flinched. "Don't make me laugh."

Rose washed her hands in the basin by his bed, then poured alcohol over them before dumping the contents of the calendula into her palm. She was in the middle of spreading it onto the stitches when he ran his hands through her hair.

"I'm sorry you've been dragged into all of this," he whispered after a lengthy silence. "I'll find out who was behind it, and I'll make them pay. I swear."

She didn't reply, pretending to concentrate on rubbing in the ointment. The propped open window next to his bed allowed the fresh air to swirl around her damp hair, sweeping it back. She was tired. Tired of everything being a struggle. Tired of the council being so determined to be rid of her. Tired of trying to appease people who didn't care for her. Tired of proving herself time and time again, only to be met with prejudice.

He must have seen the doubt shining in her eyes. "They want to scare you... Don't let them." He attempted to sit up but stopped, flinching.

"Don't, or you'll rip your stitches," she warned.

Tristan sighed, admitting defeat, before he motioned for her to join him on the bed.

She hesitated, fighting the fear of his mother returning, but she slid under the sheets anyway. Careful not to hurt him, she pressed herself against him while he wrapped his arms around her. The contact made her melt, resting her head on his chest as she listened to his rhythmic heartbeat—a glorious sound. She ran her fingers along his bare chest above his bandages.

Pain slipped onto Tristan's face, not from her touch, but at the sight of the bandages on her wrists. He slipped a hand onto hers, running his thumb over her knuckles. "I wish I knew how to explain what you mean to me," he whispered. "If you could only see into my mind, hear my thoughts, feel how I feel when I'm with you. You would know without a doubt there is not a soul for me in this world but you... When I heard you'd been taken, I went out of my mind. I didn't sleep, I couldn't eat. If something had happened to you... I don't know what I would have done."

Guilt twisted her, imagining how much strain she'd put on everyone.

What disturbed her the most about the whole ordeal was knowing that a stranger had handled her unconscious body for an entire night. Her skin crawled to think of what they could've done. It scared her so much that she couldn't even speak her fears out loud.

Instead, she concentrated on his heartbeat as she said, "Thank you... for coming in after me."

Tristan's finger hooked her chin, forcing her to look up into his eyes, where she found a calm sea. "There is nowhere in Vallor you could go that I wouldn't follow. From the lost city above to the siren sea caverns below I would follow you." He ran a thumb over her bottom lip. "And you did the saving... Speaking of, I still don't understand. How were you able to speak to the sea beast?"

She didn't have an answer. "I don't know. It was just like with the phoenix. It just kind of... happened."

"I've never known anyone able to communicate with magical creatures." He gazed at her in genuine wonder, then his lips twitched upward. "Is there anything else you can do?"

A light, short laugh escaped her lips. She rested her head against his chest as she grumbled, "Not that I know of."

His hands caressed her hair, weaving through the long strands. Before she could get too comfortable, she cast a glance back at him. His fingers traced her jawline before diving into her hair, sending shivers along her skin. He lowered his lips to meet hers.

Something primal stirred in her as she stifled a sigh, arching into the kiss. She was starved—so starved of his touch. Her restraint reserves had been all but exhausted by having to shove away the constant, restless hunger for him. She wanted to consume him, to delve into the center of him and devour his soul. To discover the sounds he'd make if she just inched her hand a little lower.

He was in no shape to do *those* kind of activities, but heaven help him when he was. She'd have him singing her name in his sleep by the time she was through. He'd never be the same again.

Tristan's fingers snaked to the nape of her neck while the other pressed her into his body as hard as his wound would allow, almost fully on top of him now, mouths moving in perfect unison.

He drew back just enough to mutter against her lips, "Me and you."

She dove headfirst into the pool of his irises as if she were plunging straight into the ocean depths. She didn't care if she couldn't see the bottom. "Me and you."

His arms locked around her waist as his voice broke. "You can never scare me like that again, do you hear me? I could never live in a world you weren't in."

She smiled into his neck and kissed it. He sighed, tilting his head back to allow her better access. She grew greedy, trailing kisses along his chin, jaw, and the base of his throat, wishing she could just take him here and now.

He clenched a handful of her dress. "Rose," he groaned. "If you keep that up, I won't care if I rip my stitches."

She reined her desire in and pried her lips from his throat, forming another smile as she kissed his lips.

She held on to him for what seemed like forever, savoring his warmth. She closed her eyes, relishing the calming strokes on her back as she drifted into a peaceful sleep…

CHAPTER 40

It was hours later and well into the night when someone woke Rose, still wrapped in Tristan's arms. "I'm sorry to wake you," Zareb whispered, leaning over her. "But the queen insisted I take you back to your room."

Half asleep, she nodded, checking on Tristan, who was still out cold. His handsome face was smooth and relaxed as his chest softly rose and fell. She untangled herself from his arms, careful not to wake him. Without another word, she followed Zareb out the door.

The corridors were dark and deserted, with only a low whistle blowing through a half-closed window, letting in a cool draft that made Rose shiver.

The bags under Zareb's eyes had grown.

"When's the last time you slept?" she asked.

Zareb avoided eye contact. "The night before the third challenge."

That was nearly twenty-four hours ago. She cast him a sympathetic glance. "You should be sleeping."

Zareb's gaze fell to her wrists, still wrapped in bandages, then straight ahead again. "I can't."

"Zareb—"

"It's not that I don't want to. It's that I *can't*."

His voice was so sharp that she stopped in her tracks. It wasn't just sleeplessness reflected in his eyes. Something was eating at him—*haunting* him. If it stemmed from guilt, she needed to know.

"Why not? Please, you know you can tell me anything." She was near begging. Anything to make the sadness on his face disappear.

Zareb looked down the hall, shaking his head—shaking off a bad memory. She thought he wouldn't answer, but then he spoke in a low voice. "A group of armed men came through my village during a night like this when I was only ten. They stormed in, taking every boy they could find. I was one of them. My..." He struggled to get the words out, clearing his throat. "My mother and sister were killed because they tried to stop them from taking me. I soon learned it was my own father and a few other men in the village who had sold us for money."

She froze, horrified at the revelation. She had always wondered why he'd carried a heavy look in his eyes, why he seemed like such an old soul, but this—this was beyond her wildest imagination. "What happened after they took you?"

Zareb kept his face carefully blank, but something in his eyes grew tortured. "I was trained to be a soldier, a killer for their own purposes."

A new heartache swelled in her chest as she gazed at him sorrowfully.

"It was their own mistake to train me as well as they did," Zareb continued. "Once I was strong enough, I killed every single one of them and escaped. I went back to my village, looking for my father, wanting to kill him, too. But the bastard had already died years ago, killed by men he owed money to." He paused, his eyes faltering. "When I realized you'd been taken just like I was... I was furious with myself. I didn't want you to be robbed of your life like I was robbed of mine."

Her mouth parted as she gazed at him in a whole new light. He had no idea how much she understood, how similar they were. It explained how he'd become such a force.

Zareb's eyes finally met hers, his hand resting on the ever present sword strapped to his waist. "I hesitated to train you because it reminded me of a dark time in my life. You were so full of light, and I... I didn't want it to be smothered out. But when we overheard the council that night, it sparked a fire in me. And I'm so grateful they stoked that flame because I would've never added it to yours, I would have never witnessed that flame turn into a wildfire, and I would never have gained a friend... You know, you remind me of them—my mother and sister... of my home."

Her eyes brimmed with tears as she said softly, "Perhaps one day you could take me to see it."

Zareb's face grew into a smile.

A smile.

"I'd like that," he replied.

Her heart filled with that rare warmth as she stared at the lingering creases. It was such a handsome expression on him. It transformed him into someone completely unfamiliar to her. Pride enveloped her to know she was one of the rare people to see it.

"See?" she pointed out, a smile of her own creeping onto her lips. "I told you I'd see you smile."

Zareb looked away back down the hall. "Don't let it go to your head."

Her light-hearted laugh echoed through the corridor.

As they continued to walk, Rose's smile faded. She hadn't heard herself laugh in... she couldn't remember. She hardly recognized the sound. She supposed she hadn't had a lot to laugh about lately. She'd been so focused on getting through the challenges, she hadn't had time to think of anything else.

Her gaze dropped to her feet, her heels tapping against the stones as her dress flowed with her long strides. Coming to the castle used to ease her soul, comfort her—give her a reason to keep going. Now? Now she didn't know what to feel.

"Can I ask you something?" She tilted her head toward Zareb. "If you were me, would you want to be queen?"

She half expected him to dismiss her question, but he surprised her with candor. "You will make a great queen, Rose, and one I'll be proud to serve. But I'm sorry, I'm afraid I'm going to have to disappoint you. I know you love Tristan, it's only—I want you to have a life filled with goodness and happiness. And here..." He glanced at the castle walls surrounding them. "Here is just plagued with ambitious men and infinite struggle."

The invisible weight on her shoulders grew heavier, daring her to ask herself a question she had been avoiding.

Is this truly what I want?

She bit the inside of her cheek, shoving aside any doubt. She had never let herself think of an alternative because if she did—even for a moment—the world she'd worked so hard to build would come crashing down.

Their footsteps stopped in front of her bedroom door, the torch flames flickering in his brown eyes as they rested on her.

She put a hand on the latch. "Promise me you'll get some sleep tonight. And don't worry about me, I'll be fine. There are two guards posted just down the hall."

"Rose—"

"You can't protect me if you faint from exhaustion," she said, giving him a pointed look.

Zareb gave a defeated nod, caving. "Alright… I'll be back first thing in the morning."

"Perhaps we could train?" she said with a smile, knowing it'd rile him.

He rolled his eyes, shaking his head, not even entertaining her ridiculous notion. "Good night, Rose."

CHAPTER 41

The following evening, no matter how many deep breaths Rose took, she couldn't slow her racing heart. This was it—the moment they'd all been waiting for, the night they'd reveal the winner of the succession. The night that would determine her fate.

The throne room buzzed with murmuring voices, the air thick with a nervous energy as the court gathered, waiting for the deliberations. Whispers trailed after her wherever she went. She did her best to ignore them, focusing on trying to drink from her glass despite her aching wrists.

The sunset's rays poured through the three giant windows facing the sea, casting a crimson haze over the large room and onto the throne's gleaming sun spikes.

"It seems as though your ride on the sea beast has given you quite the reputation," her mother noted, listening to the gossip. "You'll go down in history for it, mark my words."

Rose didn't respond, her gaze fixated on the royal pair at the front of the room near the throne. Satin had strategically placed herself next to Tristan, and to Rose's annoyance, they were talking. The foreign princess didn't bother hiding her attraction to him—gawking at him with those wide brown eyes underneath her leafed crown. Her body turned towards him as she hung on his every word. Tristan remained disinterested, but still—something ugly stirred beneath her skin as she watched the girl with narrowed eyes.

Her mother followed her eyeline. "Don't worry, my dear, she's nowhere *near* your playing field."

Rose refrained from rolling her eyes. If only that were true.

At last, King Henrik and the high councilmen came to end her agony. She strained her neck to peek over the crowd to see the king's face, trying to read his expression, but he expertly masked any signs of emotion. It was equally likely to be good or bad news.

The king stood before his majestic bronzed throne. "I want to thank all of you for being patient during the deliberation and the voting. And I also want to thank each of you who have come to support this succession period."

Applause filled the hall.

"And I also want to thank each candidate for giving everything they had to this cause. But only one can be the victor. This successor showed all the traits Vallor treasures—strength, resiliency, bravery, loyalty, and all the honor that a leader can possess. It was a close vote, but the hard work is done, and the high council and I have reached a decision..." The king paused, lowering his gaze with—was it disappointment?

Rose hadn't realized that she had stopped breathing or that her heart was no longer beating. It felt like even the blood swimming in her veins stopped as she squeezed the fabric of her dress, her white knuckles standing stark against the teal fabric. She ignored everything else and focused on the words about to escape his lips.

But it was a ploy as the king's eyes snapped up with a giant smile. "*My son, Tristan Montague!*" the king bellowed as the room erupted with cheers.

It was the happiest she'd ever seen Tristan. He jumped straight up, punching his fist triumphantly into the air. Roman roared alongside him as he roughly grabbed his brother's shoulders with a victorious grin. Queen Lenna smiled wide, not even scolding Harriet for jumping up and down with her brothers. The king embraced him with open arms, clapping his hands on Tristan's back with pride.

The cheers and shouts were overwhelming, and the volume in the room only grew louder as glasses shot into the air.

Rose should have been cheering with the rest of them. She tried to make herself move, to make herself clap. But she couldn't get her body to listen as something came over her.

Her world became quiet, as if invisible ear muffs had been placed over her ears. Her ribs grew tight, restricting her shallow breaths as she bit the inside of her cheek, lowering her gaze. It took her a moment to understand what she felt—disappointment.

But not because she didn't win.

She cast her eyes on another who wasn't celebrating.

Grant was leaning against one of the giant pillars, taking a long drink from his chalice, his face artfully blank. She was sure his disappointment was far beyond hers. He'd been close—so close. If it weren't for the sea beast, he probably would've won. Despite all this, she had a feeling he knew his quest had been doomed from the start.

As though Grant felt her eyes on him, his gaze met hers. He looked at her grimly before slowly raising his glass to her, conveying his congratulations. She would be Tristan's queen after all.

"Rose?" her mother called, pulling her out of the mist and back into the world, looking at her expectantly. "Aren't you going to go congratulate Tristan?"

Rose forced her dry lips apart, mustering a smile. "Yes, yes, of course," she said, forcing herself to move. She tucked away her insecurities as she pressed through the cheering crowd.

The moment she locked eyes with Tristan, her worries melted into vapor. Her heart grew lighter, and her smile became genuine.

They'd done it.

They'd really done it.

CHAPTER 42

The next day, after their training session, Rose persuaded Zareb to race her through the forest. He was on fire today. She thought he would win, but to her ever-growing pride, she triumphantly made it back first to the castle grounds. Zareb insisted he had *allowed* her to win. She would have challenged him again just to prove him wrong, but they were both in desperate need of a bath, and her mother would scold her relentlessly if she were late for the celebration that night—a festivity honoring Tristan.

Their new successor. The fact was still settling in.

They were just reaching the stables when a messenger appeared for Zareb. She didn't pay it any thought until Zareb returned with a grave frown on his face. In her short amount of time knowing him, she'd never seen him look this nervous.

"What's wrong?"

"I've been summoned to the high council's chambers," Zareb replied, his voice strained.

Her stomach dropped ten stories. "What does it mean?"

"I don't know, but nothing good, I fear."

What in Vallor could they possibly want? He'd done nothing wrong.

She suddenly felt ill, remembering the outcome of Xavier's tribunal. "I'm coming with you."

"I don't want you there," Zareb said firmly, but the hint of fear beneath his bravado gave him away.

"I'm coming," she stated, crossing her arms.

They argued back and forth, but she wouldn't be dissuaded. She swore at Zareb up and down until he had no choice but to bring her, muttering curses under his breath that she was more stubborn than an ass on branding day.

They arrived at the council chambers in record time. She expected to see the king and his council at the high table but was stunned to find only Tristan in the king's seat, the sunlight streaming in through the windows to shine on his loosely curled blond hair. He did not look pleased.

"Of course you'd bring her along to try to save yourself," Tristan said in an icy tone. "I told you to come alone."

Rose's eyes widened in disbelief—*Tristan* was the one who had sent for Zareb?

"I tried to make her wait outside, your Highness," Zareb stated calmly, not rising to his anger.

"I insisted on coming," she said, stepping forward. "What's the meaning of this? Where's the high council?"

Tristan stood from his seat. "I thought I would be merciful and deal with this myself now I am second-in-command." His gaze went back to Zareb. "Do you know why you are here?"

Zareb nodded, his back straightening. "Yes."

"And when my father hand-selected you to be her sole protector, did you or did you not make an oath you would keep her from harm or die trying?"

"Yes, I did."

"And you were aware of the consequences if you failed?"

"Yes."

Consequences? What consequences? He didn't mean—

Rose's eyes snapped to Zareb. He'd made a life oath. *Idiot. Stupid idiot.* Her safety wasn't worth his life. He was worth a thousand of her. He had been a commander of Vallor's most powerful army. Didn't he realize how insignificant her life was compared to his? He was a fool to put her life above his own. And she was a fool for not realizing it sooner.

This wasn't happening. There had to be some misunderstanding. Tristan wasn't actually trying to blame Zareb for her kidnapping. He couldn't. She wouldn't allow it.

Rose opened her mouth to speak, but Tristan got there first. "I don't know what it's like in Semaria, but in Cathan, we take our oaths very seriously." His mouth tightened into a thin line. "You understand the events leading up to the third challenge give me grounds to take your life to satisfy your oath?"

She couldn't believe what she was hearing. "He's done nothing wrong. You can't—"

"You're right," Zareb said over her words. "I failed her."

She gaped at Zareb with outrage. No, no, she wouldn't let him die. She wouldn't let them do this. She'd fight them all. She'd—she'd—

Tristan's eyes narrowed. "And have you been training her?"

Her limbs froze. How had he found out? She was about to deny it, but Zareb said, "Yes, I have."

Tristan's eyes hardened, shifting back to hers, betrayed. "You lied to me, *again*." His voice was low and cruel—so unlike him.

She took a step forward. "I'm sorry. I should've told you the truth, but please, don't punish Zareb for that, too. I asked him to do it. He didn't want to, but I insisted he teach me to help me with the succession."

Tristan didn't bother responding as his demeaning glare shifted back to Zareb. "Is this true?"

"I thought it'd help her in the challenges," Zareb said. "She'll tell you it was her idea, but it was all mine. She's trying to protect me."

She fumed at the blatant lie.

Tristan looked over Zareb carefully. "You're a good commander, Zareb. You've helped Cathan fight and win many battles, some alongside me. You've been loyal to the crown, and I know you hold a special place in Rose's heart. It is for those reasons, and those reasons only, that I will not take your life or strip you of your title."

Her shoulders slumped in relief. But it was short-lived.

Tristan's eyes turned into an icy sea. It was a look that would serve him well when he was king. "However, I cannot allow you to stay. Since you seem so keen on training soldiers, I'm sending you with a group of men back to your homeland."

Her heart shattered into pieces. "You can't—"

"Yes, of course, your Highness." Zareb accepted his punishment with poise as he bowed. "Thank you."

She couldn't let this happen. "This is ridiculous! It wasn't his fault I was kidnapped."

Tristan remained unfazed, his face determined. "It *is* his fault. And my decision is final."

"But it's not fair!"

"Rose, please," Zareb whispered—but she wasn't having it.

She strode up to Tristan, coming face to face to the man she loved, lowering her voice. "Please, I'll do anything," she begged, pleading for any sign of mercy. "Please don't send him back there... *please*. You have the power to stop this. The council need not ever know."

To her utter devastation, Tristan's expression remained as solid as steel. "You could have *died* in that cove. Don't make this worse for him." He faced Zareb. "I'll give you until nightfall to gather your things. Consider yourself lucky I showed you mercy."

"Of course. Thank you, your Highness." Zareb bowed.

Without another word, Tristan stalked out of the room, leaving devastation in his wake. Her throat closed off. What had she done?

Anxiety crept up as she attempted to calm her thundering heart. Her eyes darted around, thinking of a plan. "I'll talk to him. I'll get him to change his mind—or I'll talk to the king. He wouldn't allow for this."

"Don't," Zareb said at once. "It'll only make things worse. If we involve him or the council, the outcome could be far more detrimental."

"But I forced you into it," she whispered. Her hands went to her temples. "This can't be happening."

Zareb gently pushed her hands away, cupping her face. "I'd do it all again if I had the choice."

Tears pricked at the backs of her eyes. "It's—it's all my fault." Her breaths shook in her chest.

"No," Zareb answered with all the reassurance in the world. "It's not your fault. He's right. I failed to protect you. *I* failed in my oath."

A tear escaped, trickling down her cheek. "But you're my best friend… I don't think I can do this without you."

Zareb tilted her chin up. "You can do all of it and more. You're strong —so strong, Rose. Stronger than me, stronger than anyone I've ever known. Guilt is a heavy burden to bear, I know. I carried it with me for a long time, so long I thought it might break me. Promise me you won't do the same."

She couldn't possibly keep a promise like that. Guilt was her constant companion. She'd carried it with her like an invisible bag sagging on her shoulders. She'd practically drowned in it.

Instead, she pretended to be strong, nodding weakly.

She'd try.

For him.

"You must promise me one more thing," Zareb continued. "Promise me that when you feel utterly alone, you'll remind yourself you need no one else. That when you look down at the two hands in front of you, you'll remember they are the only ones you need. Not mine, not Tristan's, not your mother's—*yours*. Hold yourself with them, and remind yourself that only you can give yourself the love you deserve—love far more important, pure, and true than any other human can give you. Remember that."

Another warm tear slipped down her cheek as she weakly nodded again.

"I put your sword in the grove where we practice, near the large tree we rested against. Find it, keep it safe. Don't let them take it from you."

She forced her eyes to meet his. To her utter shock, his polished brown eyes were filled with moisture.

"You are a light, Rosalie. Don't let anyone dim it or take it away." Zareb gently brushed a tear away from her cheek with his rough thumb. "I'll miss you." His deep voice cracked.

"I'll miss you, too." She wept.

She lowered her eyes, unable to keep herself from breaking out into more tears. So she stepped forward and threw her arms around his neck.

He hugged her back with fierce arms, lowering his head to rest on her shoulder as they said their final farewell.

CHAPTER 43

The crystal-teardrop chandelier hung gracefully above the room, decorated with garlands like those on the tables. Underneath it, in the center of the dance floor stood a fountain, which Rose suspected was filled with champagne, the bubbly liquid creating a perfect centerpiece. This was truly a magnificent celebration—one that she had been looking forward to.

She only wished she'd be able to enjoy it.

Her mother noticed her downfallen eyes, taking her hand and squeezing it tightly. "I'm sorry about Zareb… I know how much he meant to you. I liked him very much, too, to be honest, even if he was dreadfully serious," her mother teased, offering a small, sympathetic smile.

Rose changed the subject before tears broke out again, her eyes flickering to nearby faces who were all watching her. "Why is everyone staring?" she whispered.

Her mother gave her a knowing smile. "They're admiring their future queen—speaking of which, where's Tristan?" she asked, scouring the dance floor.

Rose saw him first, already dancing, his messy blond hair giving him away. He was wearing a striking ruby red tunic, looking as handsome as ever. His partner was dressed in a beautiful green gown, her brown hair curled in ringlets around her petite face. It took Rose a moment, but she realized it was Princess Satin.

Of course it was.

"It looks like the negotiations are going well," Rose stated dryly, plucking a shrimp off the tree-like glass tower sitting at the center of the hors d'oeuvres table.

Her mother pursed her lips. "I know he only has eyes for you, but I admit... she's becoming quite the nuisance." She eyed the foreign princess like she was an invasive insect.

Rose raised an eyebrow playfully. "You surprise me, Mum. That isn't very ladylike of you to say."

Her mother waved her comment off. "Poppycock." Her mother's eyes brightened as a mischievous smile spread onto her face. "Why, I think I see a handsome man coming your way, Rosalie."

She turned and spotted Grant coming straight for her, his green tunic matching his emerald eyes. Despite his defeat, he held himself high, inclining his neck with a small bow.

"Good evening. Evelyn. You look as radiant as ever."

"Oh, you use my love of flattery against me." Her mother blushed, smoothing her hair.

Rose fought a harsh laugh. So easily won over by compliments. But he was right. Her mother could woo many hearts if she wanted to.

Grant's green eyes zeroed in on Rose, devouring her form-fitting dress. Seeing as how the council had seen her nearly naked, her mother no longer saw a need to hide her frame. But now that she thought about it, she wondered if her mother had intentionally chosen the dark-purple dress as an intentional flaunt to Tristan. A true partner in crime.

"Would you care to dance, Rose?" Grant's voice drawled, a large grin sweeping across his face. "Your lover seems busy at the moment."

Her eyes slid to Tristan, the scene of him dancing with Satin only fueling her fire.

She took the hand he held out. "I'd be honored," she accepted with a plotting smile of her own.

Grant guided her to the dance floor, merging into a sea of couples. As they moved, she locked eyes with Tristan, then deliberately redirected her attention to Grant, knowing it'd drive him mad.

Grant led her across the shiny marble floor, drawing her in so close she could feel his crisp breath on her face. Her breath hitched, and he smirked.

"I'm glad to see you're alright. You had me at my wits' end on that fish hook."

She raised an eyebrow, nearly forgetting how half the court had almost witnessed her near death. "Careful, Grant. I might start thinking you actually care."

"I don't usually," he admitted, then a sliver of humanity shone through. "But when I saw you fall into the water… I found out how much I do care."

Her cheeks flushed at the rare sentiment.

His jewel-like eyes gleamed and he gave her a sly smile, proud he'd left her speechless. "You look stunning, by the way," he whispered into her ear. "I've always known you were beautiful under all that extra fabric, but gods, you are exquisite."

She hid her deepened blush by gifting him a sly smile of her own. "I may have alternative motives." She winked at him, knowing if Tristan was watching, the gesture would make him writhe.

Grant gave her a rakish grin. "Dressed for revenge, I see. Oh, I believe I like you on my side." He spun her around, the fabric of her dress following her movement.

Rose returned from the spin, and he pulled her even closer than before, pressing her body flush with his as he lowered his voice. "I know what happened with Zareb… I feel I should tell you—I'm partly to blame. I had kept my word to you, and intended to keep it, but after the succession announcement, Tristan came to me, going on about how he would ruin me, threatening to take my title away. No matter what I said or did, I couldn't dissuade him. He forced me into a corner, and I couldn't take the fall for it. I'm sorry I had to tell him the truth. But I didn't tell him it was Zareb. He figured that out on his own."

The repressed anger burning in her belly flared. Why did Tristan hate her training so much? What about it was so horrible? Was it really her learning how to fight?

Or was it something else entirely?

"I understand," she said, "I shouldn't have asked it of you in the first place."

Grant's stubborn head shook sharply. "Tristan had no right," he stated in the most bold yet sincere voice she'd ever heard from him.

She gazed at him with gratitude and chose to reward his kindness.

She lifted her arms to encircle his neck, drawing him closer so their bodies met, allowing him to rest his forehead gently against hers.

He molded into her touch easily, his arms enveloping her waist, taking full advantage of her rare advance.

"I wish you weren't just doing this to make him jealous," he whispered, his cocky demeanor nowhere to be found. "You play with everyone's hearts like an instrument—picking us up when it suits you, putting us back when you're done. But what's worse is we know it, and we don't care because we have no power to resist you. Because when you do pick us... we're just glad to be held by you."

Rose's eyes fluttered, slowly raising her chin, surprised to find how close his lips were to hers.

Despite her best efforts, he was sneaking up on her defenses, dismantling her walls stone by stone until she hadn't even realized there was a hole wide enough to let him slip through.

Out of the corner of her eye, she saw Tristan striding towards them.

"I was wondering how long it would take him," Grant drawled with a bored tone, his hands savoring the last few seconds he would have her like this. "Honestly, he lasted longer than I expected."

Tristan stopped beside them, not bothering to hide his irritation as he said, "May I interrupt?" It wasn't a question but a demand.

Grant looked to her for an answer, but she was too angry to speak.

"Perhaps she can come find you when she is ready," Grant replied, a self-satisfied look plastered on his face.

Tristan glowered. "I wasn't asking you."

"I thought you were dancing with Princess Satin?" she asked with a roasting glare.

"I was obligated to," Tristan said through gritted teeth.

"Well, luckily for you, you hold no such obligation to me," she responded coldly. "I'm going to get a drink."

Tristan reached out. "Rose—"

She pulled her hand back. "Don't."

She could've felt Grant's smug joy from a mile away as she retreated from them both, making her way off the dance floor.

She was nearly out of the danger zone when the music stopped, halting her exit. The court quieted almost immediately as all eyes looked to their king on the grand staircase.

"Good evening, everyone!" King Henrik's thunderous voice rang out. "Tonight, we celebrate my son, Tristan Montague, and his attained succession. We commend his heroic acts during the challenges and the sacrifices Tristan has made to be Cathan's next ruler."

The king paused, scanning the crowd until his gaze finally settled on her. She was certain she saw a glimmer of pity in his eyes, as if he were reluctant about something, but without revealing anything else, the king looked away.

"I have more good news," the king continued, more somber now despite his joyous words. "Today, we have a proposed finalization of the negotiations with Vertmere!"

The ballroom filled with cheers. During his pause for applause, the king's gaze met hers once more. A flicker of pain crossed his face as if forewarning her of what was imminent.

The gaze terrified her.

King Henrik straightened his shoulders as the claps died down. "Never since the Dividing War have any two provinces been united. And ever since I became king, I have dreamed of making Vallor whole again, to return it to its former strength, not as separately ruled provinces, but as one strong people. Today, we are one step closer to that goal." He paused hesitantly, making her throat bob. "The treaty they've proposed says that we will unite our provinces by joining both heirs to the throne through marriage to ensure our alliance will be sealed forever. Congratulations is in order for Prince Tristan of Cathan and Princess Satin of Vertmere."

Gasps of shock ran through the audience, followed by a rumbling of murmurs that spread like wildfire as claps and cheers followed, growing into a loud thunder.

But their shock was no comparison to hers.

The world stopped orbiting. Time stood still. Those around her became a blur—a cruel reminder that she was nothing but a speck in this vast universe.

No, no, no.

Rose's clasped hands fell limply to her sides as she slowly stepped back. She didn't know where to look. She didn't know what to do. She had seen the king's sympathetic eyes, and it might have very well been out of his control, but it changed nothing.

How could she have been so blind? Queen Isleen and Princess Satin weren't merely there for negotiations—they were there to secure a marriage with the next heir, waiting through these succession trials to see who would come out on top. But if that were true, why had the king led her to believe that she and Tristan could win and be together? Unless… unless the idea hadn't been brought up until after the fact. Maybe once the council realized Tristan would win, they had to find a way to ensure that Rose wouldn't be queen. And they had found one.

Rose's feet were still planted to the ground when she realized that couples had begun to dance around her, jolting her from her daze.

Out. She had to get out.

She maneuvered her way through the crowd, nearly at the doors until—

Roman appeared, dressed in a black tunic, his wide and powerful shoulders blocking her path. His golden eyes shone brighter thanks to the matching gold décor surrounding him. His face was emotionless—per usual when it came to Rose.

She had to control the impulse to slap him across the face.

Roman opened his mouth to speak, but she didn't give him the chance. She couldn't hold back the venomous question that spat out in a calm rage. "You're in charge of the negotiations with Vertmere, are you not?"

Roman had the decency not to gloat as his jaw feathered. "Yes, along with Lord Barron."

Her chin quivered as her hands balled into fists.

He looked around them as if he was searching for someone. "Where is Zareb?"

Just the mention of Zareb's name on his lips made her lose composure. "Do you have to rub that in my face, too?" she lashed out with a harsh voice, tears beginning to brim her eyes. "Isn't it bad enough you brought her here?"

Roman blinked, perplexed by her outburst. "What are you—"

She encroached upon his space, leaving nowhere for him to look but at her pain-stricken eyes. "*I* am the one who tried to protect Xavier after that night on the beach. I lied about falling on the rocks to protect *him. I* am the one who helped save Tristan's life after the first challenge. *I* saved *your* life by getting the phoenix's tears for you. *I* am the one who got us out on the sea beast. I've done everything I possibly could for you and your family, and yet still, all I get is suspicion and disapproval!"

His eyes danced between hers as the harsh lines of his frown softened, like something was finally clicking in his mind.

"You know what? It doesn't matter. You win," she dismissed with a defeated tone. With a sharp turn of her heels, she stalked off.

She could have sworn she heard him call to her.

But she didn't care.

CHAPTER 44

Rose went to the stables the next morning, doing her best not to let herself spiral into a dark place. She contained the tears that threatened to surface as she stared at the empty stall next to hers. Zareb should be here riding with her. It wasn't fair. None of this was fair. She mounted her horse, heading off for a long ride along the beach.

A dark storm was rolling in, driving the waves onto the shore with a heightened force. The wind whipped her blue dress around as she galloped along the beach, pushing the white horse to its limits, like if she just rode a little faster, she could outrun it all. It wasn't until raindrops began to pelt her face that she slowed down, first to a trot and eventually to a walk.

Rose gazed out at the stormy horizon. After leaving the celebration last night, she hadn't spoken to anyone—not even her mother, although she had heard her and Thea whispering when they thought she was asleep. Her mother had mentioned that Tristan had gone into a rage over the announcement and had refused to sign the treaty. He had even attempted to visit her, but her mother wouldn't let him in.

She didn't know if she should feel glad or sad about the fact—she almost wished she didn't feel anything.

She was so full of grief, she was empty.

She patted her horse, her cold, numb fingers brushing its coarse hair. She knew what she needed to do.

She just didn't know if she had the strength to do it.

A figure appeared in the distance; it was Tristan, riding toward her as she had requested, answering her call.

She knew he would always answer her call.

He didn't stop until his horse was beside hers. He was wearing his new shiny crown—another punch to the gut. "I looked all over for you last night, but your mother said you were already asleep by the time I was able to get away… We need to talk."

She peered up at the dark-gray clouds, poised to empty at any moment. "Yes, but not here. Come on, I'll race you." She craned her head before she took off towards the old ruins.

Though her response had caught him off guard, he recovered quickly, urging his steed to follow hers.

They raced each other like they had when they were young, when they didn't have a care in the world, when it was just them.

When nothing else mattered.

The ruins came into view. A good thing, too, because just as they arrived, the gentle rain turned into a downpour, forming large mud puddles that splashed onto the hem of her dress. They took cover in the largest open room, its walls draped with familiar green vines and tiny white flowers. Silently, they tied their horses to the arched pillars holding up the crumbling building while rain drummed on the exposed ceiling above them.

She gathered her courage as she turned to meet Tristan's gaze.

In that moment, she tried to just *be*. She tried to memorize him—how his hair lay upon his head, how his blue eyes gleamed when he smiled, the addicting smell of his fresh forest scent.

He stepped forward, and within seconds, he was holding her. She slid her arms around his neck in response, pressing him into her as hard as she could, as if to make sure he knew how much he meant to her. His arms responded with the same need, crushing her body into his as he spread his fingers wide on her back.

She leaned back to look into his eyes. They ensnared hers, dragging her down—down so far she feared she might get lost, never to be free of them. His eyes were sure to haunt her memory forever.

She bridged the distance between them, kissing him, taking what she wanted for the first time in her life, and damning the consequences. She attempted to convey all the love she had for him through it, committing the taste of his lips to memory.

She pulled back, and Tristan's lips slid up into a half smile. She stared at his mouth, memorizing the creases there.

His smile faded as he gazed at her uneasily. "You'd better stop looking at me like that, or I won't be responsible for what happens next." He was half teasing, half serious.

She snapped out of her daze. "I'm sorry."

He tucked a stray hair behind her ear. "No, *I'm* the one who is sorry," Tristan apologized without hesitation. "I don't know what came over me. I should've never treated you like that."

She put her finger over his lips as she shook her head, dismissing it. "I forgive you," she whispered, accepting his apology, her thumb brushing his lower lip.

His breaths became shallow as desire shone through his eyes. "What are you doing to me?" he whispered.

"I'm just trying to remember you like this… Mine."

His body went rigid as his eyes darkened. "No." He took an immediate step back, swatting her hand away. "Not you, too."

Her saddened eyes gave her away. "I know how much you care about me—"

"You have no idea how much I care about you, how much I think about you, how much I crave you." He cut her off with a low rough voice.

She reached to touch him again, but he took another step back.

"I don't want to say it, just as much as you don't want to hear it." She kept her voice steady. "But you and I both know you *must* sign the treaty. If you don't, everything—the succession, the war, the resources, all the men who have been lost—will have been for nothing."

"You want me to marry *her*?" he spat, repulsed. "Damn it, Rose. Do you think anyone in this world could compare to you? After drowning in your eyes? After tasting your lips? After feeling your skin under my fingertips?

You think I could even *stomach* wanting to be remotely near any woman other than you?"

He wasn't going to make this easy. As much as she selfishly reveled in his words, she had to dissuade him from thinking that way. "I don't want to think about you with someone else either," Rose admitted. "But this is bigger than you and I, Tristan. It always has been."

"We can leave," he said in distress. It was like she could see his mind reeling through his eyes. "We don't have to stay here. We can leave right now, just you and me."

Her heart wilted that he would offer such a thing. It wasn't that easy.

"Where would we go? What would we do? What of my mother? Of your family? What happens to Cathan? To all of Vallor? We can't just run away. You must stay; you are the king Cathan needs. I saw it in the challenges, and so did the high council. The only reason they were against you is because of me."

Tristan's face turned vile. "All I care about is you. None of this is worth it if I can't have you. *None of it.*"

Rose avoided getting sucked into the whirlpool of his deep-blue eyes. She'd known he loved her, but she didn't realize just how much until he looked at her like that. Until his voice cracked like a crevice forming a canyon, until his shallow breaths gasped for a lick of air, until his anger rippled like a violent storm. It was all living proof he loved her with everything he had.

But sometimes… that kind of love was more than passion.

It was dangerous.

"What will become of you?" he asked. "What will you do? You and your mother will have nothing. You'll be—" His eyes widened with realization. "You'll marry Grant," he seethed through his teeth.

She shook her head, dismissing it. "It doesn't matter who I marry. This isn't about me."

"Of course it matters!" he roared.

She simply looked at him as sorrow filled her.

"You can't do this to me." Tristan's eyes grew as wild as a forest fire. "Ever since I laid eyes on you, I knew I had to have you. I've been in love with you for fourteen years. *Fourteen years.* It's cruel to make me fall so hard only for you to rip it from my hands. I can't just unlove you. I can't forget the way your smile sends me into a frenzy. Forget how your beautiful voice seeps into my soul with every word. Forget how your mouth tastes like life itself."

Rose's vision blurred with tears. She looked out into the rain as she pressed her lips together, but she said nothing.

"Do you feel nothing for me?" he asked, softer this time. "Tell me, have I just been blind? Has this all just been one-sided? Some fantasy in my own mind?"

"No," she said at once. "I love you, Tristan. I love you more than I've ever loved anyone."

"Then why are you doing this?" he cried. "Why aren't you fighting for me? For us? Why are you giving up so easily?"

"The past couple of months have been anything but easy." She blinked furiously to keep the tears from spilling out. "Ever since I walked through those doors, I've fought tooth and nail for you. I'm just... I'm not like you. I'm not made for this court life—all the rules, all the expectations, all the judgments. The constant threats that surround us. I try not to let what people say bother me, but it hurts more than I let on, and I'm tired of it. I'm tired of trying to fit in where I'm not wanted."

Tristan took a step towards her. "Why haven't you ever mentioned this? Why didn't you say anything?"

"Because I thought I could do it. I thought I could force myself to be what you need because I love you so much, and I didn't want you not to go through with the succession because of me. I know this is who you are meant to be... I'm just not sure if it's meant for me."

Tristan took a step back, picking up on where she was going with this. "What are you saying? You don't want to marry me?"

Rose's heart wrenched in her chest. "I don't know how—"

"You don't want me because I'm going to be king?" His voice was raised, infuriated.

Her feelings of inadequacy spilled out in one sentence. "No, I don't know if I can marry you because I don't know if *I* can be queen."

He paused as a new demon rose within him. "I'll gladly give this crown back." He ripped off the golden successor's crown from his head and shoved it at her. "Take it. I don't want it without you."

She looked down at the shiny crown. It used to look so grand, but now it looked like nothing but a chain. "That's exactly why I didn't tell you. I didn't want how I felt to alter what you'd do. To get in the way of what you wanted. You wanted to be king, and you still do. The seer confirmed it. Admit it, Tristan. You want this more than anything, and rightfully so. You are exactly the kind of king Cathan needs. I can't let my own limitations set you back from being who you truly are. I *love* you for who you are. I can't imagine there isn't a girl alive out there who wouldn't fall in love with you if only they met you. You should be with someone who can rise where I have fallen short."

"Rose, how many times do I have to tell you? I want *you*. I only want you… Gods, you're all I've ever wanted," he whispered, cupping her face gently.

She fought the urge to lean into his touch. She had to tell him. He had a right to know why she'd be forced to choose someone else. He deserved to know the truth—all of it.

"Tristan, there's something I've been keeping from you. My—" She fought to keep her voice from shaking. "My mother and I have no money. We are all but destitute. That's why I had my coming out ball, why I've been adamant about entertaining Grant."

Tristan's face contorted into full-blown shock. "What?"

Her eyes met his, filled with guilt. "I'm sorry I didn't tell you. But my mother and I felt it would be better for no one to know until everything was settled."

"How can that be? Didn't your father leave you with a fortune?"

"He left nothing but debt," she corrected. "That was why we had to leave last summer. When my mother discovered our fortune was nearly gone, we rushed home to salvage the situation. But it was already gone. He was a terrible gambler. He lost everything and paid for it with his life. All we had left was what little my mother had. We used it to come here. The manor, the money, our possessions, it's all gone."

Tristan's mouth hung open. "What?!" he spat angrily, betrayed. "How did I not know this about him?"

"Because I didn't think it mattered. But now I see it matters a great deal. How do you think the council will feel when they discover my secret now, when they have another offer that is so much more enticing? The princess brings not only money, but land, livestock, soldiers, an alliance."

Tristan's eyes widened as he saw the truth in her words. But he wasn't having it. He shook his head in denial as he cursed under his breath and ran his hands through his hair. "So now you just want to give up? My father and the council disapprove, so you just accept it?" Tristan took her hand in his. "I'll find another way around this. I won't sign the contract."

She wished she didn't have to resort to this, but it looked like she had no choice.

"Yes, you will. Because if you don't, I'll leave anyway, and you'll never see me again."

He became deathly still, his simmering eyes turning into hot, blue flames.

"Even if you refuse to sign the treaty or take the crown, I won't marry you." She wished her voice had come out stronger. Wished she didn't have to break his heart like this. Wished there was another way to do this gently. But there was more to this than just politics.

Tristan paced in frustrated strides before swerving back to her. "So either way, I lose you?" he fumed, enraged. "You're just going to force my hand and give me no choice? You're going to just leave me? Again?!"

The dam in her eyes overflowed as a tear slipped out.

Thunder clapped over them with a loud rumble.

Tristan scoffed as he ran his hands through his hair again. "This has nothing to do with the treaty, does it? This is about yesterday. For sending Zareb away, for taking your sword."

Her watery eyes finally looked back at him. "I admit I was angry, but— I'm not a child anymore. If I choose to wield a sword, that should be my decision. Zareb believed I could do it. Why can't you?"

A new monster crept into his eyes. "That's *exactly* why he had to leave!" he barked. "He was filling your head with ridiculous notions. You're not made for that life. You'll be royalty."

"Ridiculous notions?" she said in disbelief. "I *enjoy* it. After all this time of feeling helpless, I feel like I can do something for myself. I'm good at it."

"I can see how it might seem like you need it. But you're just scared, and I blame myself for that. You'll feel differently once we find out who is behind all this. I promise nothing like that will happen to you again. I sent Zareb away because I care about you—because I didn't want to see you get hurt."

"Is that why?" she challenged, trying to get to the root of it. "Were you really worried about my safety? Or was it something else?"

Another loud clap of thunder rolled over them, the pounding rain falling harder, filling the air.

"That *is* the only reason," Tristan replied in a deadly sure voice.

Something inside her made her doubt, but it didn't matter now. "I can't stay here. Being here has been so much harder than I've led you to believe. I've tried to be here—to do this all for you, for my mother, but I can't do it anymore."

Tristan's hands rolled into tight fists. He paced as if trying to think of something—anything to convince her to change her mind.

A flash of devastation flickered in his eyes as he said in a low whisper, "So this is your decision?"

Rose's lip quivered as another wave of tears came to her eyes. Damn it.

"I'm so sorry," she whispered as a tear slipped out.

He clenched his jaw silently, then nodded slowly, accepting her answer this time. He turned his back on her, going to his horse.

"Wait, Tristan, please," she said, following his steps. "Please don't leave angry."

He spun sharply, pointing an accusatory finger at her. "I was ready to give up *everything* for you! It just shows that I alone was never enough for you… I was never your first choice anyway," he added in a vicious voice.

A low blow.

Her face burned red. "That's not fair."

"I'm not going to stand here and beg for you to stay." He mounted his horse roughly, then glared down at her, his harsh gaze crashing into hers. "I hope you live to regret this. I hope when you look back on this moment, you remember how *you* were the one who chose this. *You* were the one who chose to give up."

She was so shocked by his cruelty, she couldn't utter a single syllable.

He didn't give her a chance anyway. He rode away into the stormy weather, rain still pouring, leaving her to stand alone amidst the desolate ruins.

Her tears fell like the rain that fell from the heavens. Or perhaps hell.

She had known it was going to hurt. She'd known it would take a toll. But she hadn't been prepared for the crippling agony welling inside her, for her heart to feel like someone had ripped it out and squeezed it as hard as they could.

Panic consumed every organ as she gasped for air, her heart beating so fast she could scarcely suck in a breath. She looked down at her hands as she shakily wrapped them around herself. She sank back against the cold stone pillar, sliding down to the mud-soaked floor, not caring if it ruined her dress.

Her heart shattered with every thunderclap that roared through the sky—breaking her soul down more and more until she was nothing but a pile of dust ready to be blown away by the first gust of wind that came.

She curled up in the fetal position and let herself cry. Let herself feel sorry for herself. Let herself feel every wave of disappointment, anger, and grief flow out of her. She let herself wish she was a different person, the person he needed.

But most of all, she wished she'd never come back at all.

CHAPTER 45

Hours later, Rose finally picked herself off the sopping ground, the sky dimming as more dark clouds gathered. Her hands trembled, even as she forced herself onto her horse, trudging through the rain to meet her fate.

Whatever that may bring.

She was completely soaked by the time she reached the castle, but her appearance was the last thing on her mind. At least the rain would help mask the fact that she'd been crying. Gathering her courage, she entered the castle.

As she walked through the crowded corridors, the court stared with wide eyes; among them was Harriet, completely taken aback. Rose held her head high, ignoring the gawking gazes as she kept a blank expression.

She'd only been in her room for a few moments when a knock came at the door.

"Rose, it's me," her mother's voice called.

She hurried and wiped her nose, sniffling. "Come in."

Rose watched from the mirror as her mother appeared, quickly closing the door behind her. Her mother's frown showed clear disapproval, and she was likely preparing to scold her for the state she'd just let herself be seen in. That was until her mother saw her puffy eyes.

Immediately, she switched modes. "What happened?" she asked, hurrying to kneel at Rose's side as she scanned her head to toe. "Are you hurt? What's wrong?"

Rose tried to take a deep breath, but her chest gave out. "I'm—I'm sorry, Mum." Her voice shook and she gasped between sobs, somehow still having tears left. "I've just ruined everything."

"Shh," her mother comforted, cradling her head into her chest. "Calm down. Now, what's this that's got you so upset?"

"I—I told Tristan I didn't... I couldn't... marry him," she admitted through sobs.

Her mother extracted herself from her arms. "You did what?" Her eyes widened in disbelief. "Why would you do that? This isn't because of the treaty, is it? Because I've spoken to the king, he said he was backed into a corner but that he'd do everything he could to get them to change their mind."

That was just it. He wouldn't. The king was on board with the decision, or he never would have agreed. Not to hurt her. Never to hurt her. But this had been his goal all along, his dream—to unite the provinces as one. And this opportunity wasn't just for him but for all of Vallor. For a better world.

Even if it weren't the case, even if she were a good, selfless person, there was more to her decision than the welfare of Vallor.

So she said, "No. Well, maybe, but there's more."

Her mother blinked, perplexed. "Tell me."

And so she did. Rose told her everything that had happened—every word uttered, every truth unspoken. To her credit, her mother stayed silent and listened patiently without interruption. A rare occurrence indeed.

"I'm sorry, Mum. I'm so sorry," she ended, blowing her nose with the handkerchief her mother had given her. "I know how much it meant for me to marry him, but I can't for so many reasons. I do love him more than I've ever loved anyone, and I know he loves me... but sometimes, he..." Her voice tapered off. It didn't matter now. "I just wonder if it's me he truly loves or the idea of me."

Her mother looked at her sympathetically, wrapping her arms around her again. "Oh, honey." She kissed the top of her head, cradling it again. "I was afraid of this. I was afraid I asked too much of you."

"No—you've done so much for me. Given up so much for us to get here. After everything you've been through for me, you deserve a life like this."

Her mother lifted Rose's chin to meet her eyes. "Oh, my sweet summer child, you're confusing our roles. *I* am the one who is supposed to worry about what kind of life *you* will have. You don't need to worry about me. I'm as tough as bones... But I'd hoped you'd be happy here. I'm only sorry I didn't see it. I thought this is what you wanted."

"It was," Rose said truthfully. "I was happy here for a long time, but things have changed. *I've* changed."

Her mother tucked her water-streaked hair behind her ear. "We'll figure it out. If it's not Tristan, we'll find another suitor... You're sure this is what you want?"

Of course it wasn't. "No, none of this is what I want, but I feel like it has to be this way."

"I can't imagine him letting you go so easily. He'll fight for you, you know."

"I'm afraid he'll try to refuse the crown," Rose whispered. "I can't have him give it up for me."

Her mother agreed, her face growing determined. "No. We can't let that happen. For all of our sakes, he must accept the crown."

"How do we do that?"

Her mother looked out the balcony doors, rain still pouring outside as she searched the air. Rose could almost see her rearranging their plans. "I'm not sure." Her eyes returned to Rose and softened. "But you don't need to worry about that right now. We don't have to decide anything tonight. Think on it, and we'll deal with it tomorrow."

Rose nodded, her composure slowly starting to slip. She buried her face in her hands to hide the pain building back up in her chest, causing her shoulders to shake.

"Oh, sweetheart, come on." Her mother helped her stand. "Let's get you changed and into bed."

Rose let her mother help peel the wet dress from her body. Once she'd changed, her mother led her to the bed, where she crawled into the sheets without resistance. Her mother tucked her in and kissed her on the forehead, asking if she would like anything to eat or for her to stay the night, but all she wanted was to be alone. Her mother accepted her wishes and left, telling her she'd be back in the morning.

Rose thought perhaps Tristan might come to her room that night.

But luckily or unluckily, he did not.

CHAPTER 46

Rose's mother kept to her promise and left her alone until morning. As soon as the sun rose, however, she came back in full force, ordering Thea to bring breakfast, insisting she be there to watch Rose eat.

Her mother waited until she took a bite before she spoke. "I was up all night last night—" just as Rose had assumed she would be, "—and I think that if we are going to find you another suitor, we need to do it quickly. I think we should find a resolution and leave—before the situation can escalate. Do you suppose Grant would still take you?"

Rose could barely stomach the thought of agreeing to marry someone else within twenty-four hours of ending things with Tristan, but time was not on their side. Her mother was right. The sooner they could leave, the better.

For everyone's sake.

"I believe he would," she said quietly.

"Would you consider him?" her mother asked. "I know he can be a little bit of a *peacock*, but I don't think he'd treat you unkindly. You get along well enough, don't you?"

Rose would normally have laughed at the peacock comment if the situation had not been so serious. "He certainly does think very highly of himself, and he is arrogant in every way, but he's never portrayed anything different. Which, oddly, I appreciate," she admitted, playing out the scenario in her mind. "I think he'd let me be free to be who I am. But I don't know if he—or rather his family—will accept me, especially once they learn about our situation."

"He has plenty of money for the both of you. As long as they don't find out, I believe his parents will accept you." Her mother stood. Thinking. Pacing. Plotting.

"I can't keep it from him. He knows me too well, and he'll find out eventually. I can't imagine he'd treat me or you very well after that. Married or not. He's proven he can keep a secret. He wouldn't tell a soul."

Her mother gave a loud sigh, thinking. "Fine. What if you told Grant but no one else? Do you think he'd accept you?"

She thought about it for a moment. "He might… I guess there is only one way to find out."

"Then that settles it," her mother confirmed with a firm nod. "You'll speak with him, and I'll arrange to have tea with his parents to see how they'd feel about the union. In the meantime, I'll continue finding other options if things go awry. There were others at the ball that would be happy to accept you." Her mother's brows furrowed at the expression on Rose's face. "What's the matter?"

"I'm just… surprised you aren't angry with me. I was afraid you'd be disappointed in my decision."

Her mother's eyes softened. "I understand what it's like to be in the wrong marriage. I never wanted that for you. I've only ever wished for your happiness. It pains me to think I've not done a better job of making that clear."

Silence fell over them.

"Do you think he'll do it? Sign the treaty?" Rose asked, more to herself than to her mother.

Her mother tapped her nails on the wooden vanity. "I don't know. For Vallor's sake, I pray he does. I don't know if we all could bear sending our men to another war so soon."

Rose nodded, looking down at her hands.

"Now, no more sulking," her mother instructed, standing up to gather

her dress. "We have work to do. There will be plenty of time for that after you're married."

~

Rose went to look for Grant in the grand hall. Compared to the past few weeks, it was somewhat empty for breakfast. She could only assume many visitors had already left for home since the end of the succession.

He wasn't hard to find, sitting at the far left table, eating alone, his father and mother nowhere to be seen. That fact made her wonder if her mother was already making good on her plot to speak with them.

Rose approached the table with clasped hands, her long, midnight-blue dress flowing elegantly behind her.

Grant gazed upward, discovering her making her way to him. He stood up to greet her, his eyes flashing with surprise. "Rose. I didn't see you come in… You look nervous." A slight smirk grew on his lips.

Her cheeks burned—she didn't know how to do this. She wasn't smooth like him. "I'd be lying if I said I wasn't… Would you care to take a walk with me?"

Grant raised an eyebrow in surprise but nodded. "Of course. After you."

They exited the grand hall and made their way to the gardens without uttering a word. She interlocked her hands tightly to keep them from shaking—not out of fear, but because she couldn't believe this walk, this talk, wasn't with Tristan.

They had barely made it through the first arch of flowers when she blurted, "I told Tristan I wouldn't marry him." No sense in beating around the bush now.

Grant paused mid-stride, obviously not expecting those words to be the first thing to escape her lips. To his credit, he had enough tact to gaze at her with compassion. "I'm sorry. I know how hard that must've been for you. I was wondering when I saw you yesterday. I wanted to speak to you, but you seemed… preoccupied."

Her cheeks burned with heat. "You saw that?"

He shifted closer, forcing her to look straight into his bright green eyes. "Even with your wet clothes, hair soaked, and puffy eyes… I've never seen anyone so beautiful in my life."

Her heart warmed involuntarily. He was making a habit of surprising her.

"I'm to return home soon," he said, studying her reaction. "It's not a castle by any means, but it is a beautiful manor in the rolling hills—trees and farmland for miles… If you want it, it's yours," he offered softly.

Her eyes raced back to his as she parted her lips in awe, wondering if she'd heard him correctly. "You mean—"

"I want you to marry me," Grant stated with a fierce gaze.

She couldn't believe how readily he'd asked—there was no hesitation in his voice, no questioning.

Her throat bobbed. "There are things you need to know… You may not be so willing to ask me once you hear what I have to say."

Grant cocked his head. "What do you mean?"

"I'll ask you to keep this to yourself. What I'm about to tell you could ruin me forever. But the fortune you think I have… it's gone. I have no money, land, or resources to bring with me into a marriage."

Grant didn't reply straight away, didn't even let anything but a blank expression fill his face. Instead, his eyes drifted away, absorbing the information.

Rose remained silent, letting him weigh up his options, biting her lower lip. He took so long to speak that she panicked. "I understand if you can't—"

"I don't care," he stated at last.

She lifted an eyebrow. "You… you don't care?"

He closed the gap between them, looking down at her lips. "I want you, Rosalie. I never planned on it, but after spending time with you… I've grown attached. I knew I had to have you after the first time we spoke at the ball when you 'wished me all the luck in the world'… Well, it looks like I found a hoard of it."

Her body relaxed as if the mountain that had been weighing down her shoulders had finally lifted.

"But my parents are different," Grant said. "We can in no circumstance let them know. That is, until we are married, then they'll have no choice but to accept you."

She gazed at him with a new wave of surprise. "Are you sure you want to lie to them? I don't want to cause your family harm."

Grant gave her a large grin. "You'll soon find I'm their least favorite child. What's another red mark on my record?"

"You'd do that for me?" She was genuinely stunned by his grace, taking the whole situation much better than she had planned.

"I would," he confirmed without a second thought.

She gave him a small smile despite herself, her gaze falling to her hands.

He lifted her chin back up, leaning down and bringing his lips close to hers. "What do you say, Rose? Do you want to be my next red mark?"

She met his gaze, stowing Tristan from her mind as she answered. "Yes."

Light enveloped his eyes, his smile reaching ear to ear as he pressed the smile onto her lips.

She did her best not to flinch away, keeping still as he kissed her. In different circumstances, she knew she would savor his touch. Perhaps she could learn to like it—learn to love him.

His hands wrapped themselves around her waist, pulling her into his chest and deepening the kiss. After a moment, she could feel her mother's voice prodding her to encourage him. So her arms went up around his neck, trying to familiarize herself with him.

Grant pulled away, a hazy victory lying in his eyes. "I'll speak to my parents. I know they'll see the match."

She nodded, agreeing.

And that was that.

CHAPTER 47

Grant had left hours ago to speak with his parents. She had never seen him in such high spirits. It made Rose feel slightly better to know that at least someone was happy about the whole situation. Her mother had spoken to his parents at tea and considered them "quite agreeable," confident they'd accept her as their daughter-in-law.

Everything was falling into place.

Rose forced herself not to think of Tristan, trying to numb the pain in her heart, if only to save her poor swollen eyelids. She had been avoiding the grand hall for this very reason.

Her mother had mentioned that the treaty negotiations had been… strenuous. They had held the final meeting hours ago, but Rose had received no updates. It was nearing dinner when her stomach grumbled. She was no longer able to prolong the inevitable. So, equipped with the best internal armor she could muster, she went downstairs.

As she entered the grand hall, the first thing that caught her attention was the high front table, which was at full occupancy. Everyone was there—King Henrik, Queen Lenna, Roman, Harriet, Tristan. Additionally, both of Satin's parents were present—even her father, Vertmere's king, sat with his family. Satin was seated beside Tristan.

And she was wearing a large, shiny ring on her left finger.

Rose swore a rusty sword had been thrust into her chest from the pain that erupted within her, leaving her bleeding out on the floor for everyone to see. She had her answer.

Tristan had signed the treaty.

In that instant, Rose realized she'd held on to a stupid, naïve hope that he wouldn't sign it. That he wouldn't listen to her. That he really would've thrown the world into chaos just to be with her. But she knew it could never be. He had done precisely what she had forced him to do.

She tried to hide all emotion, but she was sure the betrayal was all over her face as she stared at the ring. Satin was speaking to him, looking up at him with adoring eyes.

It wasn't until Tristan's gaze collided with Rose's that she was roused from her daze as she stood in the doorway. In that moment, she swore she caught a flash of an ache slip onto his face. However, the longer his eyes lingered, the more they hardened before they shifted back to Satin.

Then he did something that made her stomach heave.

He slipped his hand into Satin's.

Satin looked down at their hands as a pink flushed her cheeks, openly receiving his gesture.

Devastation hashed its way through her heart.

Rose was so entrapped in her own body that she didn't even notice someone coming towards her to save her from herself.

"Rose," Grant said, his handsome eyes looking at her with his infamous large smile. "I'm so glad you came. You look beautiful."

She forced a strained smile like she hadn't just been trampled under a stampede of elephants.

He leaned in and placed a soft kiss on her forehead, intertwining his fingers with hers. "Come on," he said, gesturing to the far table. "Your mother and my parents are waiting for us." His eyes flickered in Tristan's direction.

It was then she recognized just what Grant was doing. He must have seen the interaction between Rose and Tristan and was throwing the gesture back. It was a calculated move on Grant's part—his challenging gaze goading Tristan with no sense of remorse.

She didn't look back to see Tristan's reaction. But she didn't have to. Grant's large smirk was all she needed to see.

She gave Grant a thankful squeeze with her hand, and he squeezed back, keeping her hand firmly in his as they approached the table.

"Mum, Dad, I don't think we've all been properly introduced." Grant gestured to Rose. "This is Rosalie. Rose, my parents. Neith and Lilly."

Rose did her best to slip a bright smile onto her trained face. They were a beautiful couple. Both had the same blond hair as Grant, his face taking after his mother's. Her smile lit up her whole face, reminding her of Grant's large grin.

"Hello, darling," Lilly said as they stood, holding her hand out to her. "It's so wonderful to formally meet you."

Neith, a large, intimidating man, even gave her a tight smile. "It's nice to finally meet the sea rider."

The sea rider?

"That's what everyone's been calling you after what happened in the third challenge," Grant whispered into her ear with a proud, informative voice.

"Don't whisper in front of others, Grant. It's rude! Please, come sit," Lilly said, gesturing for Rose to sit down. "Your mother's told us so much about you."

It was an easy conversation. Grant's parents were much more inviting than they'd been portrayed. His father was more of a serious man who didn't say much. Lilly did most of the talking, taking what Rose hoped was a shine to her.

She was reminded that Grant was the second oldest of seven children —four boys and three girls. Their family owned multiple farms and a large trading company specializing in sheep. Rose also learned they funded a large portion of Cathan's troops. His father explained the logistics to her and her mother, but much was lost on her. She forced herself to keep engaged, wanting to give her due diligence to Grant's family.

Grant kept silent, though he watched her ever so closely as she spoke with his parents, making her cheeks warm.

Once lunch was over, her mother suggested they all walk around the grounds. His parents agreed, taking their leave of the grand hall.

It was warm and sunny outdoors. The heat was welcome on her bare shoulders and arms as her blue dress flowed elegantly behind her. She and Grant walked a few paces in front of their parents, giving them a chance to have time alone.

Even with their close chaperons, Grant didn't bother to keep his distance. His hand glided smoothly into hers, bringing it to his lips and holding on to it as they walked.

Rose couldn't help but feel a freedom growing within her, reveling in the knowledge no one was watching her. No one cared now whose hand she was holding. She was free to just… be.

"I think my parents might like you more than I do," Grant said, glancing over his shoulder at them. "I knew my mother would adore you, but goodness, I'm not used to them liking my choices. I might have lied to you. You might just be the furthest thing from a red mark. It makes me uneasy. I'm nearly ready to toss you aside."

A small, sheepish grin crossed her lips as she nudged her shoulder into his. "It is nice to have a mother like me for once." Guilt hit her as soon as the words came out.

"She thinks you and I will give her beautiful grandchildren," he said with an infectious grin.

Her breath caught; the thought of having children with him hadn't even crossed her mind until now.

His smile widened at her expression. "Don't worry." He leaned down to whisper in her ear. "I intend to keep you all to myself for a *long* while."

She kept her eyes forward, brushing her hair back as heat crept into her cheeks—something that happened a lot around him.

They arrived at the base of a large tree that held a pair of swings hanging from a low, thick branch.

"Sit with me," he requested, sitting in one of the swings.

She moved to sit on the other, but his hand shot out to her waist to stop her, drawing her close to him. "No, sit *with* me," he repeated with a smirk.

Her eyes flickered back to his parents, still a good distance away and engrossed in deep conversation, oblivious to the two wandering off. Rose looked back at his challenging eyes. Two could play this game. He clearly liked to make her blush.

So naturally, she wanted him to blush instead.

Knowing it was very unladylike, she pulled her long dress up, exposing her lean legs. Then, with one fluid motion, she reached for the swing ropes and pulled herself up to sit on his lap, placing her legs on either side to face him.

Grant's hands went immediately to her hips to guide her, swallowing hard as he looked at her with dilated pupils. For once, she'd caught him off guard.

Good.

Once she was secure, her hands let go of the ropes as she placed her full weight on him, her arms snaking around his neck.

Grant recovered from the action as his green eyes sparkled like gems. "You keep surprising me, Rosalie Versalles," he whispered, his smile fading into a serious expression.

She moved to get off him, having proved her point, but his hands tightened around her thighs. "Don't you dare," he said, trapping her on his lap.

Then his lips were on hers.

It was a slow-building kiss, a deep one. She was becoming more accustomed to them now, more familiar. She shifted her position on his lap to make herself more comfortable, and she swore she heard a rumble come from his throat.

She pulled away and was met with clouded eyes staring at her lips.

"Gods, could you be more perfect?" he whispered groggily.

"Rose!" her mother yelled across the grassy grounds. "You two aren't married yet! Keep a proper distance, please," she scolded, but Rose knew her mother—underneath the scolding words, she was glowing inside.

Grant gave a harsh laugh as he stood with ease. Reluctantly, he let Rose's legs slide to the ground but he kept her close, placing his lips back on hers with another light kiss.

"I should go," Grant said, gesturing to his parents. "I have to have one more talk with my parents, but promise me you'll meet me tonight? At the beach at sundown."

She nodded, knowing exactly what he was hinting at. "I will."

He flashed his white teeth at her as he kissed her hand. "I'll see you then."

CHAPTER 48

A few hours later, Rose's mother helped her into a different dress and recruited Thea to do her hair and makeup.

"I can't believe how well this is working out," her mother said, practically singing as she set out a pair of shoes, then moving to straighten out a red dress for her to wear. "I couldn't have planned it all better myself."

Rose rubbed her lips together after Thea put on a gloss. "Do you think his parents like me?"

Her mother took the dress off the hanger. "Oh yes! I just know they adore you. So much so, in fact, his father asked me today if it would be alright if we could have the ceremony as soon as possible. You're going to be the mistress of Montague Manor, my dear."

Rose's smile lasted only a few seconds before her eyes fell to the vanity.

Her mother noticed the change. "Thea, could you give us a moment?"

Thea gave them a small bow and exited the room.

Her mother waited until she heard the door click shut. "Are you having second thoughts? Because if you are—"

"No." Rose cut her off before she could go off on a tangent. "I just—" Tears threatened to surface, but she swallowed them down. "I just wish it could've been him."

Her mother's face relaxed as she put the dress down on the bed. "I know," she said tenderly. "I fear you're about to learn one of the hardest lessons life has to offer—grieving the loss of someone who is still alive."

Rose bit the inside of her cheek as she fiddled with a makeup brush. "When's his wedding?" She looked at her mother in the reflection.

"It'll be a quick affair, held here at the castle in two weeks," her mother said.

Her head whipped toward her mother. "So soon?"

"I'm sure the king and queen are eager to secure the union, and the treaty... Tristan also asked for it to be a short engagement. I'm sorry; I would've told you sooner, only I didn't want to ruin this special night for you."

Rose strained to offer a smile. "Of course. I'm happy for him," she lied through her teeth. Practice for later. When she'd have to pretend her guts hadn't just been torn out.

Her mother looked her up and down once more, fixing a crease in her dress. "I've been waiting to see you settled for so long. I know this isn't how you or I had thought it'd turn out, but I think this is finally where I see you be happy. You look beautiful, my dear."

Rose gave her mother a gracious smile, ridding herself of unwanted thoughts.

"Now, go before he changes his mind," her mother half teased.

The sand was still warm under her feet from the day's heat. The ocean waves rushed onto the light sand in gentle waves, reflecting the orange and pink glow from the retreating sun as she walked to where she'd agreed to meet Grant. It wasn't far from her spot with Tristan. A pang stung at her heart. It wasn't the spot she would have picked, but she couldn't think of a place here that didn't already have a memory attached.

Grant looked incredibly handsome in a red tunic lined with gold accents, matching her dress almost flawlessly—a note she was sure her mother had made. When she was close enough to see his face, she found he wasn't smiling.

She offered him a small smile first, hoping it would ease his nerves. But to her dismay, his mouth stayed in a straight line. Her pace slowed.

"You look stunning," Grant said, his eyes consuming her as he held out his hand, pulling her into him.

"Thank you," she said softly, her heart pounding in nervous flutters.

Grant's hand gripped hers tight as sighed loudly. "I know you expect a proposal tonight, Rose. And I want to—you have no idea how much I want to—but my parents found out you lied about your financial situation."

Her mouth fell open in shock. "But how? Did you tell them?"

"No," he answered with a sour expression. "But I bet it'll only take you one guess to find out who did."

The only other person she'd told was—

"Tristan?" she questioned, hating how weak her voice sounded.

Grant gave her an aggravated nod.

She diverted her gaze, blinking back the moisture surging into her eyes. Her vision blurred.

"I'm so sorry. I tried to persuade them," Grant said. "You have no idea how hard I tried, but my parents won't accept the union. My father's too much of a businessman to accept you when he and my mother have bet—" he switched his word choice, "—more advantageous matches for me. You understand I can't go against them or I'll have nothing to give you."

She nodded too quickly, a tear spilling out. She wiped it away. "No, of course. I was stupid to think we could keep it from them."

His expression hardened. "Are you really trying to take the blame for this?" he asked furiously over the sea breeze. "Don't you understand what he's done? He just ruined you, Rose. Forget me. That arrogant bastard just ruined *any* chance of even a half-decent marriage because he can't stand the fact that you didn't choose him!"

Her eyes fell.

She knew exactly what it meant.

"He means to have you stay here alone forever, while he gets married and lives his life right in front of you. I always knew he was scum. I thought he'd do the right thing when it came to you, but when he flaunted that girl in front of you, I knew he'd reached a new low."

She gazed out at the sea, wishing the waves would swallow her whole. Her world was crumbling down stone by stone. She wrapped her arms around herself, taking in a deep breath of the cool breeze.

"I understand," she replied softly.

"My parents insist we leave in the morning… I've not only embarrassed them by failing the succession, but now this."

"I'm jealous." She lifted her eyes to meet his as her voice cracked. "Your home sounded so lovely."

He looked out into the ocean, then twisted sharply back. "Damn it all to hell, Rosalie. I never thought I could feel this way about anyone until you came along."

It was a great compliment coming from him.

"I'm sorry I caused trouble between you and your parents," she apologized after a slight pause. "It seems like I turned out to be another red mark after all." She tried to give him a smile, but another tear slipped out instead.

Grant cursed, stepping forward to her with a determination she'd never seen. "Listen to me," he commanded. "Do whatever you can to get out of here. The longer you stay here, the worse it'll be for you. I know how strong you are, but a place like this, with him—it will corrode you. I care too much about you to let you wither away here. Promise me you'll do everything you can to leave. *Promise me.*"

She would. For her sake as much as his.

"I promise."

He looked at her with all the care in the world as he leaned down and kissed her for the last time. Ironically, it was the first time she found herself savoring his lips.

"Take care of yourself, Rose." Grant caressed her cheek, reluctantly dropping her hand as he turned and retreated from the beach, leaving her alone yet again.

Her mother couldn't fathom it, shocked beyond belief when Rose returned from the beach in tears. She told her everything—how Tristan had betrayed her, how the secret they'd fought so hard to keep hidden was now exposed. Her tears streamed like an endless river.

"You were right, Mum," she ended, ashamed. "I should've never told Tristan."

Her mother's shoulders slumped, her eyes searching for some solution, but from her lack of words, Rose doubted she could find one. Another rare occasion indeed.

"No need to dwell on it now. We'll just have to find you another suitor," her mother said with a bite of her lip. She paced. "There are plenty more who will still accept you, I'm sure. The letters I sent out should get a reply soon. In the meantime, I'll speak to the king and queen. I'm sure they'll have something to say about this."

And that was the end of the discussion.

It was days before they heard any replies. Every single potential suitor had sent their regrets. Some said their sons had already found a match, or they claimed they couldn't make the trip. Every letter that reached them was more and more disheartening. The queen had done everything she could to remedy the situation, but it seemed as though the rumors had spread faster than any repair could happen.

Rose kept herself busy by either studying in the library, riding on the beach, or walking through the gardens—anything to keep her from the grand hall.

She woke at the crack of dawn each day to train alone, determined to keep up with her drills and footwork. The only time she felt in control was when the sword Zareb had given her was in her hands. The castle became more and more like a prison with every day that passed.

It'd been a week, and still, no suitor would agree to see her.

"This is ridiculous," her mother stated one afternoon, throwing yet another rejection letter into the fireplace. "Not a *single one* of them has agreed to even come to the castle. Even with our lack of wealth, the king and queen are willing to pay a hefty sum to any who would marry you. Even so, your beauty should've had *some* heads turn. I even sent invitations to men old enough to be your father, and still nothing. This is absurd. It's as if…" Her mother stopped.

Rose could guess what she was thinking. "It's as if Tristan is abusing his power, commanding any potential suitor to stay away to punish me?"

"Precisely," her mother huffed, collapsing onto the chair. Her frustrated expression morphed to hopelessness. "Oh, Rose, I don't know what to do. If we don't get him to back down... I'm afraid I underestimated him entirely."

"I could try to speak with him?"

Her mother's gaze flashed sharply at hers. "What could you possibly say to get him to change his mind?"

Rose rubbed at her temples. "I don't know."

"Exactly. We'll just have to try harder, that's all. We still have time to find another suitor. Perhaps we can come up with something between the two of us."

Rose wasn't holding her breath.

CHAPTER 49

Following Rose's conversation with her mother, she went to the stables, saddling her horse at lightning speed. She fought her trembling hands as she fastened the clasps, managing to stave off any and all emotion by keeping her hands busy.

It was the fastest she'd ever ridden as she let the wind carry her, wishing it could transport her to another time—hell, maybe another universe. Let it carry her high enough that she wouldn't have to feel like this. Anything but this.

When she arrived at the small clearing where she and Zareb used to spar, she dismounted her horse and tied the beast by the small stream to let it drink, patting its white mane in thanks.

She uncovered her sword from its hiding spot amongst the leaves. She wielded it like a wild storm, confronting a thick, towering oak tree that had become her new fighting companion. With vigorous strikes, she slashed at it, releasing all the pent-up anger and frustration in a fury of swings while sweat dripped from her bow.

She was so focused, she didn't hear someone coming up from behind until a twig snapped.

Not missing a beat, she whipped around and poised her sword at her attacker. Roman.

He immediately raised his hands, letting her know he had come in peace. His gaze fell to her sword, then back up to her. They stayed like that for a moment, with only her heavy breathing filling the silence.

Finally, she lowered her sword, ready for his scolding. Surely he'd come here to shame her, to be angry with her for thinking she was capable of wielding such a weapon, to lecture her on how dangerous it was.

Instead, he slowly lifted his arm, reaching for the hilt of the sword strapped to his back, drawing it while keeping his gaze fixed on her. He spread his stance, gripping the sword with both hands, waiting for her to advance.

She couldn't believe what she was witnessing. She thought maybe she'd misinterpreted his body language, but there he was, waiting for her to come closer.

So she obliged.

She sprung forward, knowing she was nowhere near a match for his brute strength. She'd have to rely on her quick feet and wit to stand a chance.

He was barely able to deflect her attack as she came forward, caught off guard by her speed and skill. She pressed closer, never letting his feet find a good stance, pushing him back toward the tree line until she found her opening.

She stuck her foot out to knock a small rock to where his foot would land, then struck a blow on the same side. Roman lost his balance as his foot landed directly on the rock, falling flat on his back.

She struck again. Roman barely blocked it in time, but the action made him lose his grip on his sword. Before he could move to retrieve it, she pointed the tip of her sword to his throat.

She'd never forget the look he gave her on that rocky forest floor. His dazzling gold eyes blazed with life, as though she held a match that had just ignited into pure flame—a flame that blazed fiercer the longer she stared. It was a look similar to one she hadn't seen from him since they were children. She couldn't pinpoint exactly what it was until it hit her—Admiration.

With a start, Rose realized her blade was still pointed at the base of his throat. Gradually, she lowered it and held her hand out.

Roman's eyes remained clamped on hers as she brought him to his feet. He brushed himself off, his eyes only leaving hers to retrieve his sword. "Where did you learn to spar like that?"

All coldness was gone from his voice. She didn't realize how much she had missed his normal, rich tone. She'd grown so used to the new icy one that she had been sure it was gone forever. But there it was—as sweet as honey.

"Zareb," she said, choosing not to lie. After all, he was already gone.

"Is that why he chose to leave?"

"Is that what Tristan told you?" she asked, appalled.

Roman's confused expression answered her question.

She gripped her sword tighter. "Tristan *forced* him to leave because of it."

His wide jaw set as his eyes cast downward. "I see," he whispered, almost to himself.

Rose scanned the forest to make sure they were alone. "How'd you find me?"

"I followed you," he confessed with a somewhat shameful look. "I saw you saddling your horse and curiosity got the better of me." His eyes shifted down to the sword in her hands. "Did Zareb give you that, too?"

"Yes. He gave it to me when Tristan took the other I had."

Roman's eyes sharpened at the mention of his brother. "May I?" he asked, holding his hand out.

She handed over the sword, ignoring the hard thump in her chest as his hand brushed hers.

He inspected it closely, balancing it with his fingers. "It's beautifully made. Perfectly sound. Rare craftsmanship. It's a wonder how he came by it."

"He told me it came from his homeland, from the mines of Semaria."

"I wouldn't hide a sword like that in the woods. If anyone found it, you'd never see it again." He handed the sword back to her.

She took it. "Please don't tell Tristan about the sword. Or any of this. If he found out…" She trailed off.

"I know."

A long silence ensued until he looked downward, clearing his throat.

"Tristan's been unfair to you... He should've never told anyone about your circumstances."

She shifted, unable to hold his gaze. "He's angry with me for making him sign the treaty," she said in a smaller voice than she wanted. "He thinks I don't love him anymore."

Another small silence followed. "Do you?"

"I always will." Her throat dried admitting it. "But we can never be. For so many reasons... some he'll never know."

"Tell me." Roman's voice was so tender it almost sounded like a plea.

She blinked in surprise. "Tell you?"

"Tell me the reasons," he clarified, searching her eyes.

Something foreign shifted within her as she managed to say, "Does it matter? It's done." Her gaze shifted away from those flaming eyes as she crouched to take a drink from the cold stream, dipping her hands into the frigid water before bringing it to her lips.

Roman bent his knees, lowering himself to the forest floor beside her. "It matters to me," he said softly.

She lifted her gaze—he was closer than she'd expected. She was immediately thrown back in time as she stared into the eyes of her old best friend, crouching in the same forest they'd spent so many summers in. The memory alone was enough to soften her heart.

"I can't be what he wants me to be. More importantly, I can't be who he needs me to be. He needs a queen. I've discovered I'm anything but." She kept her eyes on the water. "You know the other reasons... one I have you to thank for."

Roman had the decency to look guilty, his eyes falling slightly. He didn't respond for a heartbeat, as if considering his words. "I know you think it was cruel of me, but it was the best thing for everyone involved. Including you."

Rose stood, wiping her wet hands on her dress. "Forgive me if I don't thank you."

He followed, standing. "What will you do?"

She paused. "There's nothing I *can* do. Tristan has made it clear he has no intention of letting me go. So I suppose I'll have to wait and see if anyone is brave enough to go against him. But it seems unlikely, since I have so little to tempt them with."

Roman gazed at her with that unfamiliar look on his face again. "I'm sorry." He said it as though her feelings mattered.

Rose shook off the clutch in her chest, going to the horses.

"Me, too," she whispered to herself.

CHAPTER 50

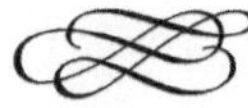

Rose's spirit withered with each day passing day. She scarcely ate or slept, the circles under her eyes becoming more obvious every time she glanced in a mirror. She couldn't remember the last time a smile had graced her lips. Every morning, she forced herself to leave her room to train or take a long ride. Once she was back, she locked herself in her room with a book for the remainder of the day.

Her mother fussed, of course, knowing she was spiraling. But there was nothing her mother could do to protect her this time. She had to come to grips with the fact that Tristan was getting married.

And she'd have to watch.

Rose didn't think it could possibly get any worse until the day before the wedding when she received a note from Princess Satin herself, requesting her presence in her sitting room.

"What could she possibly want?" her mother asked, slapping the note down onto the table with a huff.

If there was one person Rose wanted to see even less than Tristan, it was Satin.

"You don't have to go," her mother said. "She's not the future queen yet. You don't have to do anything she asks."

"But if I don't go, won't it seem impertinent?" she countered.

Her mother gave a loud sigh, not bothering to answer because she knew it was true.

So Rose accepted.

And she had a horrible feeling she'd regret it.

Rose made her way through the sunny corridors to the large sitting room. She'd been here many times, usually with her mother or Harriet. It was composed entirely of cream and blue hues, decorated with a painting of one of Cathan's famous ships, its name scribbled illegibly at the bottom. Women of the court often came here to gossip, sip tea, and enjoy crumpets.

To her surprise, Princess Satin was by herself, accompanied only by one of her handmaids. She wore a modest purple dress that accentuated her petite frame. Her light-brown hair, with its warm undertones, was neatly slicked back. Her brown eyes sparkled at the sight of her.

"Rose!" Satin exclaimed, a smile spreading across her face. "I'm so glad you could make time to see me. Come sit." She gestured to the couch opposite her.

Rose threw on the best smile she could. "Of course, thank you, your Highness." She did as instructed and lowered herself to the very edge of the cream-upholstered couch, trying not to look too stiff.

"You must be wondering why I've asked you here." Satin fanned out her dress across the fabric of the baby-blue couch. Even the way she sat was poised—the training of a princess, she supposed. "I've been learning everything I can about this place and the royal family before the wedding, and everyone I've talked to has said you're practically family."

Her words were a stab to the heart. "I could only wish."

"I hear you and Tristan are particularly close, so I thought maybe you could help me understand him."

Rose kept her expression carefully blank as she studied Satin. Did she not know of Tristan and Rose's history? The longer she thought about it, the more she realized she probably didn't, certain that everyone involved wanted to ignore the small detail.

Satin was still looking at her for an answer.

"Understand him?" Rose prodded.

"Yes. I've loved getting to know him, but I have to admit, at times, he seems quite… distant," Satin said, playing with her gloves. "I just want us to get along. I know it's an arranged marriage and all, but my parents had an arranged marriage, and they're practically soulmates." She gave a light laugh. "I'm sorry if I'm rambling; it's just that I've become quite fond of him, and I want him to be fond of me, too."

She should've never agreed to come. "Oh." She didn't know what to say. "You know, I'm not sure I'm the best one to ask. Harriet might be better; she's his sister, after all."

"Yes, I've talked to Harriet, and she was helpful, but she also told me you know him the best of anyone. Plus, Tristan talks so highly of you."

Rose felt a twist in the gut this time. "He does?"

Satin gave her a bright smile. "Of course. He adores you."

She should leave. She shouldn't be here pretending she and Satin were friends.

"Would you say he's a very… physical man?" Satin asked. Her cheeks stained to a pink color, catching Rose's expression. "I'm so sorry. That must be such an uncomfortable question for you. Of course you don't think of him like that. It's only—when I try to touch him, I swear it's like he almost… recoils. He held my hand once, but it was only once. It's the only thing he's done to let me know he sees me that way."

Oh gods. Rose quickly sought a lie. "It's probably just nerves. I'm sure he only needs to get to know you better."

Thankfully, her answer satisfied Satin enough to drop the subject.

Satin stood. "I've had the worst time deciding which dress to wear." She went to the three white dresses hanging up behind them.

The hits just kept coming.

"What do you think?" Satin asked, spinning to see Rose's reaction.

Rose couldn't bear to look at them. "They all look wonderful." She pretended to glance over them with more interest. "I think you'd look lovely in any one you choose."

Satin gave her a sheepish smile. "I knew I'd like you from the moment we met."

"You are too kind." The statement was more than honest.

"I must admit, I invited you here to ask you something else as well." Satin grabbed a light-green dress from across the room and brought it to her, looking nervously excited. "I know the wedding is tomorrow, and it's short notice, but I thought since you're like family, perhaps it might be nice if you were in the wedding as one of my maidens?"

Rose's mouth hung open. Caught off guard, she shook her head automatically. "Oh, no."

Satin sat down slowly. "What is it? Is it the dress?"

"No, of course not. The dress is beautiful. But you see, I'm *not* family. I don't have a drop of royal blood in me. It wouldn't be seen as proper. I couldn't possibly."

Satin waved a hand dismissively. "Oh, please! It'd be so lovely to have you in it."

Rose couldn't suppress the pure panic consuming her, scrambling for any reason out of it. "I'd hate to distract from your day."

"Nonsense! We'd love to have you with us. Oh, please say you will. I want tomorrow to be perfect, and I want all of Tristan's close family and friends to be there."

"Does Tristan know you're asking me this?" Rose tried to say his name normally.

Satin shook her head, not noticing anything was amiss. "I want to surprise him, and I know he'd love it."

Rose tried to say something—*anything*—to refuse, but her mind was blank. She couldn't refuse without telling Satin the real reason. If she learned the truth, Satin could possibly rethink the marriage, making Rose the reason the alliance fell apart.

"Oh, please say yes," Satin pleaded again, reaching for Rose's hand.

She cursed in her mind. Why did she have to be so nice? This would have been so much easier if she were mean and horrid. Her body took over, giving her a nod.

Satin's face broke out into a bright smile. "Oh, thank you! I know he'll be so glad to see you there. This will be the best surprise!"

Rose smiled, but she was sure it was just an awkward showcase of her teeth.

Satin stood up, passing her the light-green dress.

Rose took it with all the grace she could muster, fighting the intrusive impulse to drop it or throw it into the fire. As she went to leave, Satin stopped her.

"Can I bother you with one more question?"

Rose closed her eyes, taking a deep breath before turning to face the princess. "Of course."

Satin came closer, playing with her hair nervously as she asked in a timid voice, "Is he a kind man? I mean... do you believe he'll make a good husband?"

Rose's features softened. At that moment, she felt sympathy for Satin—marrying a total stranger and leaving behind her homeland and family was no small sacrifice. Satin had been forced into this situation, too. It was enough to soften her heart to answer her honestly.

She took a few steps toward her. "Tristan's becoming the next king of Cathan for a reason. He's everything a king should be—brave, loyal, honest. He has his weaknesses, but he's a good man. He feels so deeply." The room blurred as she thought of his handsome face. "So deeply that when he cares about you, he'll make you feel like you're the most precious thing in the world. When my father treated me like I was nothing, Tristan was one of the first men to show me how a man should treat a woman. I suppose that's why we were so close... He's the kind of man we all only wish we could marry." The last words drifted off her lips.

She snapped out of her daze as she looked back up at Satin, hoping she didn't just give herself away.

Thank her stars, Satin was still smiling, but not at her. Satin was peeking over her shoulder at someone else.

Shit.

Rose knew who it was before she even moved.

Tristan stood in the open doorway. His wistful, forlorn face told her he'd heard every word she'd said. He did a masterful job guarding his expression in Satin's presence, but she knew him—who was she kidding? She knew him better than the lines in her favorite books. Just underneath his empty, hard shell, she could see his soul breaking.

"Tristan!" Satin exclaimed, oblivious as she moved around Rose. "You aren't supposed to be here for another hour."

Tristan managed to pull himself out of his ass. "I'm sorry. I must've gotten the wrong time," he replied almost too easily. His eyes dropped to the dress in Rose's hands. "What are you two doing?"

Satin's grin grew wider. "Oh, it was supposed to be a surprise!" She groaned. "But I suppose you'd find out soon enough. Rose has agreed to be in the wedding! Isn't that wonderful?"

Tristan's eyes snapped to her guilty ones, taking a minute to realize they were serious. To his credit, he didn't miss a beat. "That is wonderful."

"Isn't it?" Satin celebrated with a gleeful bounce.

Rose saw her opportunity to leave. And by hell, she'd take it. "Well, I should go; I'm sure you have a million things to do for tomorrow."

"Oh yes, of course. Thank you so much for coming," Satin said. "We'll see you tomorrow!"

Rose gave Tristan a quick bow, looking anywhere but his eyes. She practically ran out of the room, not wanting to give either of them the opportunity to stop her.

She had successfully made it back to her room when she chucked the green dress onto the floor and let the tears pour out.

CHAPTER 51

Later that night, Rose was woken by a sudden pounding at the door. She jolted upright, immediately grabbing her concealed sword from beneath the bed and drawing it from its scabbard. She jumped as another pound shook the door frame.

"Rose!" a drunken voice yelled.

Not just any voice.

"Rose!" Tristan yelled again, pounding on the door. "I know you're in there!"

She let out a sigh of relief, relaxing her stance as she sheathed her sword and returned it to its hiding place.

He pounded at the door again.

"Rose!" he yelled. "Open the door!"

She didn't. Instead, she went over to the wooden doorframe, leaning her shoulder against it. She was almost afraid to ask, "What do you want, Tristan?"

"I'm not leaving until I-I seeee you," he said, his words slurring.

She closed her eyes, praying he'd leave, knowing she shouldn't let him in.

Tristan didn't stop. He pounded on the door even harder, making her jump against the frame.

The fool is going to wake the entire castle.

"Rose, I swear if you don't open this door, I'll knock it down. I'll do this all night if I have to," he threatened, obnoxiously loud.

She cursed, knowing he would.

Desperate to avoid being seen, she flung the door open and stepped out into the corridor, glaring at the guard down the hall who had no doubt been told to stand down by Tristan.

"Would you please be so kind as to fetch Prince Roman? I'm afraid Tristan is not in his right state of mind," she ordered the guard.

Apparently, he agreed, leaving to fetch him.

"That's not necessary," Tristan slurred after the guard, his body slouching against the wall, his eyes red and hazy.

Rose rolled her eyes as she supported his arm, dragging him through the doorway and shutting the door.

She immediately rounded on him. "Tristan! What the hell are you thinking, carrying on like that? Someone could've heard you!"

Tristan's red eyes glared at her. "Doesss it look like I care?" Without warning, he came closer, trying to close the space between them with a dangerous look in his eye.

She knew that look.

"Stop." She immediately retreated. "You're drunk. You aren't thinking clearly."

"I'm thinking clear enough," he growled more coherently as he continued to advance toward her. He cornered her, trapping her against the wall, coming so close she had to put her hand up to his chest to stop him.

"You're getting married tomorrow."

He wasn't listening. He leaned down so low she thought he'd kiss her, alcohol reeking on his breath. She resisted, but his strong arms had a firm hold around her, pulling her body into his. She pressed her palm harder into his chest to keep him at arm's length, but he wouldn't budge.

He didn't stop until he was within inches of her lips, hovering just over them.

"Gods, you are so beautiful," he said with an ache that sunk to the marrow of her bones. "Look at you; I couldn't make a more beautiful woman if I had all the power in the world."

Her heart soared, undeniably reveling in the compliment. She secretly adored him for it.

His eyes fell to her lips, openly staring at them.

"Tristan," she whispered in warning.

Saying his name undid him.

"I can't go through with this," he said, and for the first time, she saw his eyes glisten. "Look at me, Rose." He gestured to himself. "I'm lost without you."

Seeing him so broken made her own eyes water. "I know you think you need me, but you don't."

He shook his head, not accepting her answer. He grabbed her hand, forcing it underneath his unbuttoned shirt to his bare skin right over his thundering heart. She ignored how she could feel every pulse beneath her fingers.

"You feel that? It's yours; it always has been and always will be. Every beat it takes, every ounce of blood it pumps, it's all yours. Since that day in the ruins, it feels like you ripped it out, squeezing out every last drop until there's nothing left."

She forced herself to remove her hand from his chest, feeling like she was tearing off her own limb. "Tristan, you can't talk like this." Her eyes pleaded with his. "Please, you have to go."

Tristan ignored her, leaning closer instead, his cheek brushing hers. "Don't force me away… Let me stay," he whispered, his lips grazing her neck as he said the words. "Let me kiss you… let me hold you… let me know what it feels like to have your bare skin on mine… Let me taste these." He kissed the top of her breast. The touch caught her so off guard that she sucked in a sharp breath. He lifted her thin silk nightgown, exposing her upper thigh. "Let me feast on you." His teeth tugged on her earlobe as his hand moved between her legs. His thumb pressed exactly where she was aching, making her legs tremble. "Let me perform every daydream I've had of you," he crooned. His soft lips caressed her neck, down to her collarbone.

It took effort to say breathlessly, "Tristan, stop."

"Pleassse," he begged, slurring the word with a shaky breath. "I can't go through this life without you."

Rose's bottom lip quivered as she lifted her eyes to his. "I'm sorry. I want to give in to you—you have no idea how much—but I can't."

A single tear slipped out of his eye.

A chunk of her heart shredded apart at the sight.

Roman arrived just in time, bursting in without knocking. His eyes widened as he took in the scene, staring for too long at how Rose was caught between Tristan's body and the wall.

Roman's demeanor raged with a silent fury. "Get off her," he growled.

Tristan didn't respond, not moving an inch, his eyes still latched to hers, staring at her with desperation.

"Damn it, Tristan, I said get off her!" Roman repeated, coming forward to wrench him back.

To her surprise, Tristan didn't resist, stumbling backward in his drunken state, his eyes still not fully focused.

"Get out of here now!" Roman yelled, furious. "Don't you realize you are risking everything we have worked for! Leave before someone finds you here!"

Tristan glared at Roman with a rage she had never seen, his hands balling into fits. For a moment, she was frightened that Tristan would strike him, but instead, he turned his angry eyes back to her.

She'd never forget the look he gave her.

His red eyes were glossed over with a perfect mixture of agonized pain and sorrow. He glared at her, not hatefully, but with a tortured expression that resonated to the depths of her mauled soul.

The next moment, his eyes ripped from hers, forcing himself to leave.

She took a step towards his retreating figure. "I love you, Tristan."

Tristan stopped at the door, pausing for a long moment before turning around to give her one final look. "You have no idea how much I wish that was enough," he replied, the beautiful sea he held in his eyes spilling another tear.

He gave her one last look, then he was gone.

Rose opened her mouth, but no sound came out. She took one more involuntary step to the door, only to stop herself. It was a fool's errand, and she was fully aware Roman was still present.

She clamped her mouth shut, composing herself before she said, "I'm sorry you keep having to mediate… I didn't know who else to ask."

Roman didn't move, nor did he reply. Instead, he just watched her, staring at the tears streaming down her cheek.

"You must be tired," she continued. She used her sleeve to dry her tears as she sniffed. "It's late. You should get some sleep."

Still, he didn't move, staring at her with those foreign eyes again.

Her brows pinched slightly, wondering what was going through his mind.

"Will you be alright?" he asked at last. She wasn't sure if his rich voice made her feel at ease or more anxious.

"I'll be fine," she lied through her teeth.

His wide jaw tightened as he took a few small steps to her. "You don't need to do that. You don't need to pretend with me."

His words reminded her eerily of Zareb—another twist of the knife.

"You don't need to stay and pretend you care about how I feel," she said, her voice as cold as she could make it.

His mouth hardened into a thin line. "You can't keep letting him in. You keep making him feel like he has a chance."

She arched an eyebrow, scoffing. "You think I invited him here?"

"You can't tell me you didn't hope for it. Why else would he be comfortable coming to you? To touch you like that?" His face was nearly disgusted.

Rose's eyes flared as she approached him. His body stiffened as she came face to face with him. "If I wanted Tristan, he would be mine," she said with a voice so cold it didn't feel like her own. "He'd throw everything and everyone into the fire if I but asked. You know he would. The *only* reason he hasn't done that, the *only* reason your precious treaty is possible, is because of *me*. So instead of blaming me, Roman, you should be thanking me."

His face was still hard, but just underneath his cold eyes, she saw a flinch. "All I'm saying is you didn't have to open the door. You wanted to see him just as much as he wanted to see you."

She rubbed her forehead in frustration before dropping her hand. "He was banging on the door, yelling at the top of his lungs. He wouldn't stop until I opened it. I didn't want him waking up half the castle, so I let him in until you came. What was I supposed to do? Let him carry on until someone discovered him and asked questions? Until the princess found out that her future husband has no interest in her at all?"

His eyes softened slightly; he obviously hadn't thought through the scenario.

Rose let out a loud, frustrated sigh, not needing a reply. "Thank you for coming, Roman, but I think you should go."

"Rose, I—"

"Please leave."

He paused, looking like he had a great deal more he wanted to say, but she didn't care to hear it.

His jaw clenched along with his fists. He didn't say another word as he roughly swung the door open and slammed it behind him.

For what had to be the fourth night in a row, Rose cried herself to sleep, letting the tears pour, hoping they'd drown her and she'd never wake.

CHAPTER 52

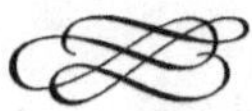

It was finally here.

The day of the wedding.

The cursed day from hell.

Rose's mother came in late that afternoon to help her get ready alongside Thea. Both of them were annoyingly overkind, tiptoeing around her like she was a chipped porcelain cup, ready to break if they so much as held it wrong. It was strange getting dressed up for a wedding that was supposed to be hers—a life that was supposed to be hers.

It felt like she was getting ready to go to a funeral instead of a wedding.

She could've only been so lucky.

Thea finished, and Rose risked looking into the mirror. Thea had left her dark-brown hair down in loose, soft curls, except for the braided crown atop her head. Her large, almond-shaped eyes were dusted with a dark brown eyeshadow. She wore the light-green dress Satin had given her, as well as a silver necklace and earrings to go with it. A traditional Vertmerian look, she had been told.

"You look stunning," Thea praised with an all-too-bright smile.

"Except for this ghastly dress," her mother critiqued, grabbing a handful of the fabric with distaste. "Just look at the color. Rose can pull off anything, but it's not going to do anyone else any favors." She waved Thea off. "Thank you, Thea. Why don't you take the rest of the day off to enjoy the celebrations?"

Thea gave them a small bow, throwing one last sympathetic gaze at Rose before closing the door behind her.

"Are you sure you want to go?" her mother asked. "Just say the word and I'll make an excuse for you."

She shook her head. "I'll be fine. I just want it over with. With any luck, no one will even notice I'm there."

Her mother gave her a skeptical look. "Well, I'm sorry, but attention will be drawn to you if you go looking like that. It's unfair how Satin will be outshined by you."

It was a ploy to make her feel better, of course, but she appreciated it nonetheless. "I must get it from my mother." She meant to smile, but it didn't come out quite right. "You look beautiful, too."

Her mother gave her a playful tap with her fan. It was a true statement —her mother was beautiful in every way. Her hazel eyes went perfectly with her dirty-blonde hair, thick with a natural wave, deepening a bit over time. Even as white strands emerged, they blended seamlessly.

A knock came on the door.

Her nerves spiked. She couldn't handle any more surprises today.

"Who in Vallor could that be?" her mother muttered as she went to the door.

It was the queen and Harriet, wearing dresses similar to Rose's.

"Hello," Queen Lenna said. It was the first time she'd seen the queen wear makeup since she'd been back. She almost looked like her old self. "May we come in?"

Her mother was the first to recover. "Oh, yes, of course."

Rose stood up immediately, bowing.

"I hope we aren't intruding, but I wanted to come give you this," Queen Lenna said, holding out a large white flower that matched the one behind Harriet's ear. "May I?"

Rose forced a nod as the queen placed the flower in the back of her braid, the perfect addition to a miserable day.

"Beautiful," the queen said, smiling.

Rose gave her the best smile she could scrounge up. It must not have been very impressive because the queen faced Harriet. "Harriet, I know you and I should already be at the ceremony, but could you take Evelyn and stall for a moment? I need to talk to Rose."

Harriet smiled, her dark curls framing her painted cheeks, bringing out her bright blue eyes. "Yes, of course. Evelyn?"

Rose's mother glanced at her for confirmation. She gave her a nod, signaling it was all right—not that she could refuse if she wanted to.

Her mother conceded. "We'll be just downstairs."

With that, the two left her and the queen alone. Queen Lenna showed herself out to the balcony, walking into the sunlight to gaze over the sea. She followed, knowing that whatever this visit was for couldn't be good.

"You know, I came here when I was about Harriet's age—young and timid," the queen said with a short ironic laugh, keeping her eyes on the horizon. "Coming here and meeting Henrik was practically love at first sight for me. There are times I still can't believe I've lived such a full life—blessed with my soulmate and four beautiful children, blessed to be queen over such a magical land. Even with my illness, I've thrived. It was a blissful time… until you and your mother came along."

There it was.

Rose's insides twisted at the hurtful sentence. Nonetheless, she kept it hidden, staying silent as she waited for the queen to go on.

"You were just as beautiful as you are now." The queen looked her up and down with a hint of a sneer. "I've always known someday I wouldn't be the only woman in my sons' lives, but I didn't expect it to happen so soon. Not when they were still children. As soon as I saw you, I knew things would change. You were young, but I knew what your mother and my husband were plotting, bringing you here every summer. And because of your mother's close friendship with my husband, he acquired a soft spot for you both." The queen paused. "You must think me cruel, and perhaps I have been, but I'm jealous of you, you see. Jealous my family adores you, that my husband loves you like a daughter, that Harriet sees you as a sister, that my sons care for you as they do."

She didn't believe a word Queen Lenna was saying. "You over-presume. Harriet can barely look at me and Tristan is the only one of your sons who cares for me."

The queen gave her an impatient look. "Dear Rose, you can't be that naïve."

She didn't believe it. Xavier's and Roman's distaste for her dribbled out of them like poison. And Harriet—she didn't even know where she stood with Harriet.

"Which is why I'm so afraid of you," the queen admitted.

Rose's eyebrows shot up in surprise. "Afraid?"

"Yes. Because I know you have the power to break my family forever."

Realization swept over her like a cold breeze. She had always assumed the queen couldn't accept her for the same reasons as everyone else in court—her social standing, her lack of nobility, or some other notion. She'd never imagined someone with so much self-confidence and power could be jealous of someone like her.

"I'm afraid things won't get better for me." The queen lowered her eyes as a twinge of pity poked Rose. "A chill has settled over the castle since you returned. I'm afraid for my son's life. I'm afraid for yours. It frightens me that our enemy still lurks in the shadows despite all our efforts. Which is why, with all the gratitude in the world, I'm glad you were wise enough to let Tristan go." Queen Lenna's eyes warmed as they settled on her, becoming soft and genuine. "I know giving him up hasn't been remotely easy for you, and I'm aware of how difficult he has made things for you. I'm sorry I didn't foresee that. I wanted to reassure you that I'll help you find someone better suited for you. I know you must think hope is bleak, especially today. But eventually, I think you'll see what I saw—that you and Tristan were never a true match... You may resent me for saying so, but it's true."

Rose did resent her for it. "Do you despise me so much you can't stand the thought of me being family?"

The queen shook her head. "On the contrary, Rose. Despite what I've told you, I like you very much."

Rose had a difficult time holding back her glare. "Is that why you prefer Satin? Because you *like* me so much?"

She was sure the queen would be upset at Rose for speaking to her in such a manner, but she didn't seem to mind. "She's a good match for him. Nowhere near as beautiful as you, that's for sure and certain, but she has the heart of a leader. She was born into royalty and knows what the life of it brings... But I didn't come to scold you. I only came to thank you."

Rose's gaze went to the sea, fire rising from her words all the same. "I didn't do it for you."

When the queen didn't respond Rose's eyes shifted to her. The queen was observing her in admiration. "I'm starting to feel foolish for not seeing what my husband has seen in you all along. You are quite the rare woman."

Rose used to pray day and night for that vote of acceptance. Now, it seemed pointless.

"Although I'm not worried about you, I *am* terribly worried about Tristan. So I've asked Roman to stay by your side today. He'll make sure Tristan won't do anything foolish."

Panic spread.

No. Anyone but him. "No," she blurted, then said slower, "I'm sorry, it's just—Do you think that's really necessary? Roman must have much better things to do today."

"Unfortunately, it is *entirely* necessary," the queen replied in a voice that let Rose know the decision wasn't up for debate.

She cursed internally. Just when she thought the day couldn't get any worse.

"On that note—we should go down, or we'll be late," the queen said, prodding her to follow.

Rose took a deep breath, unable to prolong the inevitable any longer.

She could do this. She would be fine. She would survive.

And with that affirmation, she followed the queen.

CHAPTER 53

Rose followed the queen down the mountain of stairs, finding Harriet and her mother waiting for them at the entrance of the hall. Her mother and the queen entered the double doors first, talking to each other in whispers.

Just as Rose was about to follow them, Harriet caught her arm, stopping her mid-stride.

"I'm sorry," Harriet blurted out unexpectedly.

Rose blinked, caught off guard by the guilt she lying in Harriet's icy-blue eyes.

Harriet slowly lowered her hand from Rose's arm. "I'm sorry I've been so cold and distant with you lately. It's just..." She swallowed, nervously gathering her dress with her hands. "Ever since you came back, everything's gone so terribly wrong. After Xavier's tribunal, our family hasn't been the same. My mother's health has been declining, and I'm convinced it's because of everything that's been happening. And I've tried to fix it, but no one ever bothers to ask or even listen to poor little Harriet—" She cut herself off, taking a deep breath before starting again more slowly. "All that is to say I was angry. I needed someone to blame, and I misdirected that anger at you, and I'm sorry," she ended in a whisper, her glossy eyes brimming with sincerity.

Rose's heart plummeted to her stomach; *she* was where it had all gone wrong. Half of her sympathized with Harriet's qualms and even agreed with her. Rose's return had altered everything for their family.

But to be fair, she'd had a good amount of help.

Rose took a small step forward. "I'm sorry, too, for everything."

Harriet took her hand, squeezing it. "I *really* wanted you to be my sister-in-law."

She forced herself to smile, biting her lip to keep it from quivering. "Me, too." Then she lost all composure and hugged the young princess. "Me, too," she whispered again.

They stayed like that for a moment before Rose pulled away, clearing her throat. "You should go in. Your mother will be wondering where you are."

Harriet took a deep breath, nodding. "If you need *anything,* just let me know." She offered her one more sympathetic smile before disappearing into the hall.

Rose hesitated, standing before the double doors, raising her chin with sheer determination. *You can do this,* she repeated to herself.

She squared her shoulders and entered the hall.

She had never seen such a magical room. Sunlight streamed through the grand, gold stained-glass cathedral windows, filling the room with a rainbow of soft colors. Greenery and flowers flooded the walls, ceilings, and pillars, leaving no surface uncovered. On either side of the altar, enormous bouquets overflowed from their milky-white vases. Dozens of candles flickered proudly atop gold floor-length candelabras placed throughout the room. An elegant ivory rug lined the middle aisle, leading up to the altar. Even the brass chandelier sparkled with a fresh polish.

Satin and her mother must have heavily weighed in on the décor. In a more traditional Cathan wedding, the hall would have been full of red and gold instead of greenery. The room was packed, and most guests were already seated in the wooden pews. She glanced over them lazily.

Until she saw him.

Any hope of getting through this wedding came crashing down with one blow.

Tristan was dashingly handsome, of course. His usually messy golden hair was neatly combed, not a strand out of place. He wore Cathan's traditional red and gold tunic, giving him a fairy-tale look. His skin had a golden hue thanks to the stained-glass window behind him. His face was grim, eyes staring down at the floor like he was in a trance—no doubt trying to be rid of the effects of all the alcohol he'd had last night.

As if he could sense her, he looked up.

His body froze.

His eyes drank in every detail of her, his lips parting in awe like he had just seen an angel walk into the room.

She forgot how to breathe. What in Vallor was she thinking? She couldn't do this. She couldn't sit here and watch him marry someone else. She was going to be sick. She just knew it.

Rose whirled around, the acid in her stomach threatening to make its way up her throat. She covered her mouth, closing her eyes to keep herself from vomiting. Her eyes pricked but she shoved back the tears, remembering her vow to herself not to. Her hands trembled, the stress finally taking its toll on her body. She tried to take a deep breath, but all it did was make her gasp.

She was about to make a run for it when an unexpected pair of hands grasped her shoulders.

Roman peered down, concern lacing his expression as his hand gently lifted her chin. "Hey, hey, look at me," he whispered, trying not to make a scene. "Focus."

She concentrated on his eyes, so close she could see the array of golden specks held within them. The warmth of his crisp breath washed over her face.

"Breathe," his rich voice commanded, calming her nerves. "Focus on me. Take a deep breath in through your nose... yes, just like that... and exhale slowly through your mouth."

She kept repeating the simple task, digging her nails into his forearms. Over and over, she breathed, one breath at a time, slowing her heartbeats. The deep breaths let Roman's musky cedar scent fill her lungs, helping to alleviate her nausea.

She tried to focus on something else—anything else—her gaze fell to his tunic. It matched her dress perfectly. The color went well with his tanned skin glowing like the summer rays streaming in from the window.

"You're alright," he whispered. "You're okay."

She nodded, still too afraid to open her mouth for fear vomit would come up with it.

Roman waited patiently for her panic attack to subside as her death grip on his arms relaxed.

"That's it," he said, encouraging her with a firm nod. "Keep breathing just like that."

Her heartbeats calmed—that was, until he began to lower his hands.

In an instinctual reaction, she latched on to his forearms like a leech, her body taking over. "Don't let go," she whispered, hating how pathetic she sounded. How utterly worthless she was in this state. But she couldn't help it. For some reason, his touch was the only thing that helped.

"I'm not." His calloused hand slipped into hers. "I won't."

He led her to the front of the aisle to take their places. She kept her eyes down, frightened they might run into Tristan's again, or anyone else's for that matter.

They made it to the front and up the shallow steps, taking her place beside Harriet, who offered her a weak smile.

She braced for Roman's hand to let go, expecting him to join the men on the other side, but true to his promise, he remained beside her, keeping his hand firmly in hers.

She thanked the lost city above that Roman's broad shoulders blocked her from Tristan, even if she could still see him in her periphery, staring at her.

Unconsciously, her hand squeezed Roman's tighter.

"Eyes on me," Roman whispered.

As instructed, she looked into his patient eyes—golden flames of warmth waiting for her. A strange energy swelled in her chest, the very same one she'd felt on the balcony the first time earlier that summer. One she was growing more accustomed to when he was around.

The distraction did its job until the music played.

The audience rose to their feet as the grand wooden doors softly opened, revealing Princess Satin in an exquisite floor-length wedding gown. She had opted for the classic Cathan dress, with fabric cascading in every direction, creating a long train behind her. Crafted from soft silk, the skirt gathered around the waist while the strapless design exposed her delicate shoulders. Her hair was elegantly pinned up, holding the laced veil that draped over her face. Through it, Satin was smiling brightly at Tristan.

Rose peeked to see Tristan's reaction. He watched Satin with a blank stare, making her believe he wasn't ecstatic to see her, but to her utter agony, he wasn't looking at her like she was the worst thing in the world either.

The gaze made her feel sick again. She took in another deep breath.

Roman gave her hand a firm squeeze in reassurance as Satin made her way to the front, standing side by side with Tristan.

With that, the ceremony began.

Rose had what she could only describe as an out-of-body experience—watching helplessly from the sidelines as the priest continued his speech. She didn't listen to anything he said. She didn't want to remember a single word. And was successful.

That was, until she heard the dreaded question.

The priest asked, "Do you, Princess Satin, take Prince Tristan to be your wedded husband and king, to cherish in love and friendship, in strength and in weakness, in success and in disappointment, to love him faithfully today, tomorrow, and for as long as the two of you shall live?"

Her response was immediate. "I do," Satin answered with a radiant smile.

The priest in the pointed hat turned to Tristan. "Do you, Prince Tristan, take Princess Satin to be your wedded wife and queen, to cherish in love and friendship, in strength and in weakness, in success and in disappointment, to love her faithfully today, tomorrow, and for as long as the two of you shall live?"

A painful silence hung in the air.

Tristan's hesitation made her heartbeat pound, her hand squeezing the life out of Roman's.

Tristan peered over Satin's shoulder to meet her gaze.

His blank expression cracked as his blue eyes became tortured. But as soon as she recognized the pain, it left, his eyes hardening as they shifted back to Satin.

"I do," he answered.

Rose's eyes fell—she was half relieved, half ready to die.

The priest came forward and placed the crowns upon their heads, proceeding to swear them into service for all citizens of Cathan and Vertmere. What other promises they made, she didn't know—and more importantly, she didn't give a damn.

"Ladies and gentlemen," the priest concluded with a deep bow, "may I present the future king and queen of Cathan!"

Rose glanced up just as Tristan raised Satin's veil and leaned in to kiss her gently on the lips.

Roman didn't even wince as her nails embedded themselves into his skin, nausea rolling back in full force. She closed her eyes, trying to focus on her breathing. The room suddenly felt as hot as a blazing fire.

When she reopened them, Tristan and Satin were already down the shallow steps, walking arm in arm down the aisle, on their way to the ballroom where the celebration would be held. Cheers and music filled her ears.

Her composure broke.

"Roman," she whispered in warning.

He didn't need another word. Without hesitation, he scooped her into his arms and exited out the adjacent left door. She clung to his neck, burying her face into his shoulder—hiding as she covered her mouth.

He'd barely made it to the bathroom before she violently emptied the contents of her stomach into the toilet bowl. Her body shook with every convulsion, unable to control her shaky hands. She expected Roman to step away and give her privacy, but instead, he knelt beside her, holding her hair back as she held onto the cold porcelain for dear life, throwing up again.

He softly placed a hand on her back, stroking it in soothing motions, comforting her as he waited for her to stop. A few heaves later, her body had nothing else to give, and she sat back up slowly.

Roman left her side only to fetch a towel, wetting it before he knelt back down, wiping off her face and chin with steady hands.

She couldn't keep the tears in anymore. She buried her face in her hands and cried on the cold stone floor.

Roman reached for her, pulling her firmly into his chest. His large hands cradled her head as his face contorted—as if he was in pain, too. "I'm sorry," he said, his broken voice barely above a whisper. "I'm so sorry, Roe."

Her heart warmed at the old nickname. Not once since she'd returned had he referred to her in such an intimate way. It was enough to make her fingers grip his tunic in fistfuls while he stroked her hair, letting the fabric absorb her tears.

After a good moment, her body dried out, and she extracted herself from Roman's wet shoulder. She wiped her cheeks as she sniffed. "Thank you," she whispered.

Roman's jaw clenched. "Don't *ever* thank me."

She looked up in surprise, finally meeting his eyes. Tormented ones stared back at her like he was suffering from some invisible wound.

"Do you want me to take you back to your room?"

She loosed a shaky breath, peering down at the splotches staining her dress. She couldn't go to the celebration looking like this.

She simply nodded.

Rose was about to stand, but he scooped her into his arms again. Too easily. Too smoothly. And she was too weak to resist. She found herself needing his body—it was the only comfort she could get. Like a snake coiling onto a heated rock, she wrapped her arms around his neck, burrowing her face into his shoulder so no one would see her tearstained cheeks.

Roman walked in large, brisk strides, taking the long way through the corridors to avoid the crowds.

She opened her eyes and she was in her room.

He set her gently onto the bed. "I'll get you some new clothes."

"What about the celebration?" she asked, masking her flinch.

"You don't have to go. I don't care what anyone says. I don't know why you even agreed to be in the ceremony."

She smoothed out her dress. "At least the hard part is over."

He looked like he disagreed but didn't say it aloud. He went to her closet to pull out a new dress. It was one her mother would've never chosen unless they were in mourning. The black dress had long sleeves lined with swirls and gems, with a sweetheart neckline. She hadn't worn it since her father's—since he'd died.

"Do you… do you want help?" Roman asked, his smooth voice washing over her from above.

She gazed up at him with vulnerable eyes. She should refuse his offer. She could do it, after all. It wasn't as though anything was wrong with her arms or legs, but she still said, "Yes."

Roman stepped behind her, his hands finding the laces of her dress. With deft fingers, he loosened it. The fabric slid off her shoulders and pooled at her ankles, exposing her dress slip. Averting his gaze, he picked up the soiled fabric.

Without warning, he took the green dress and tossed it into the fire.

She blinked in surprise.

"Don't think anyone will miss that," was all the explanation he offered.

When he looked back at her, he froze, his eyes latching on to the sight of her exposed skin.

His gaze engulfed her like a black hole swallowed a star, like quicksand swallowed unsuspecting prey. Like a storm swallowed a sinking ship.

Her cheeks burned hotter than the roaring fireplace.

She wrapped her arms around herself, vainly curious if he thought she was pretty. But then she reminded herself that the queen had asked him to look after her today. He was following orders—nothing more. Embarrassed for even thinking it, she brushed aside the ridiculous notion.

She stepped into the dress he held open, reaching for his shoulders to lean on. Once it was pulled up, she shifted her shoulders to him so he could tie the back.

He brushed her hair over her shoulder, his fingertips accidentally grazing her bare skin.

Her body shivered involuntarily at the touch.

His movements paused for a moment, but then he continued, tying the laces in smooth strokes.

Once he was finished, she faced the mirror. Her makeup had taken permanent damage. She sat at the vanity to fix it, grabbing a cool rag off the desk to rectify her puffy eyes. Next, she picked up a makeup brush, bringing it to her face. But as soon as she did, she couldn't do anything with it. Her shaky hands made it impossible.

She let out a frustrated sigh, tears pricking at her eyes again.

Without warning, Roman's large hand snaked around her wrist, stopping her. Gently, he lowered her hand, forcing her to put down the brush. "You look beautiful," he murmured, gazing at her reflection in the mirror.

She couldn't get over how different his voice was. Though low and rough, it was also warm and comforting.

A voice meant to rip you to shreds or carry you to the top of a high mountain.

He let go of her hand. "Come on." He gestured to the door. "I want to show you something."

Thrown by the sudden change of plans, Rose asked, "Where are we going?"

"Not the celebration," was all Roman would disclose.

She hesitated to follow, but she was eager for a distraction—any distraction.

So she left her pathetic reflection behind and followed him out.

CHAPTER 54

Rose stepped outside and the salty sea air almost instantly cured her nausea. The sun had plunged into the sea, spreading what was left of its rays across the horizon, transforming the sapphire sky and sea into a world of soft pinks, purples, and oranges. She let that fading warmth soak into her skin, embracing her like a hug—like they sky gods knew she needed it.

Roman was the first to pass through the arched wooden gate, keeping his swift pace until they had ventured deep into the garden. She silently stared at the torch-lit path, trying to recall all the names of the flowers she passed to keep her mind busy.

"You feel better?" Roman asked, speaking for the first time since they'd left her room.

She gave a small nod. "Yes, thank you."

He shot her a glare. "What did I tell you about thanking me?"

Rose was taken aback at the sharpness in his voice, not sure how to respond. So she didn't, hyper-focusing on the blooms again.

They wandered down the stone paths together in a comfortable silence, the crooked oak branches swaying overhead as they strolled. They must have been walking a long while because soon, the colorful sunset was swallowed up by the night sky, unveiling the stars and twin moons.

Tonight, the gardeners scattered *thousands* of candles throughout the paths and beds for the wedding festivities, mimicking the stars above. Even the small pond nearby had candles floating on full-grown lily pads.

She stared at the flames as Roman said, "You like lights, don't you?"

Guilty as charged.

"I love them. There's something so beautifully pure about them... How their flames dance so freely. The darker it gets, the brighter they shine. Radiating their own heat, their own special energy." She lifted her head to the sky. "The stars are much the same. In the darkness of the net that holds them, they still manage to give off their own small light for the entire galaxy to see."

Roman's mouth ghosted upward. "You'd love Eristan."

She automatically pictured the island province across the eastern seas. "Why is that?"

"At night, the shores are lined with bioluminescent plants, trees, creatures, rocks, everything." He casted his gaze out as if transporting himself there. "Any color you can think of and more. Some I can't even quite explain. When you look down into the water, the rocks shine in the dark. It feels like you are swimming through the night sky. It's one of the most beautiful places I've ever seen."

Her heaven. That was what he was describing. "It sounds wonderful."

The warmth of the candles danced in his eyes as he gazed at her. "Would you like to see them one day?"

Yes, she practically shouted into the void. *Anything to get me out of here.* But instead, she simply said, "Someday."

"Then I have no doubt you will... someday."

At last, they arrived at the heart of the garden. The oversized fountain was full of the same candlelit water lilies that drifted in the pond, floating effortlessly atop the dark pool.

Rose stopped to watch the overflow cascade to the lower levels, the simple trickle soothing her nerves.

She didn't know Roman was standing behind her until his warm breath fanned the back of her neck. Her joints locked in surprise. "I've been a fool, Roe," he whispered with remorse.

Her stomach flipped at the sound of her nickname again. She hadn't realized how much it meant to have him refer to her in such a sentimental way.

"I should've never doubted you," he ground out, clearly not used to admitting when he was wrong—a family trait.

She wasn't expecting his apology to affect her the way it did. She could almost identify it as... relief? She soaked in his words, making sure she'd heard them correctly. But there they were, as clear as day. *I should've never doubted you.*

"You seemed so sure I was the villain... What changed your mind?" She didn't turn to look at him, though she could feel his gaze burning into the back of her head.

"That night after Tristan's succession celebration, you put me in my place, and I didn't like it," Roman admitted. "You made me start to question everything. Malcolm is here for the wedding—" Malcolm? Malcolm—yes, she remembered Xavier's best friend well from his frequent visits, "—so when I ran into him last night, I asked him about Xavier. They've been traveling together, and Xavier told him the whole story. He told me about what happened that night on the beach and how Xavier admitted to using you to get out of the succession. Then you saved my life, and I'm still not sure at what cost. But when you pulled that stunt with Grant, I didn't know what to think. I thought maybe you were only using Tristan for your own advantage until... until I saw you today." He paused, shifting as the loose rock crunched under his feet. "It solidified just how grave of a mistake I made. You were never the threat I feared... You were the savior."

His words brought hot tears to her eyes. She scarcely believed them. "All I wanted was for you to believe me." She cursed her fragile voice, wishing she was in a better state to control it. "It hurt to think you thought I was capable of something like that... I was so sure that you, of all people, would see the truth."

Roman finally stepped around to face her, his jaw set tight. "I know. I should've trusted you."

Rose wouldn't meet his gaze, still staring into the fountain, not trusting herself to speak. Yes, he should have trusted her. At least he admitted it.

"Believe me when I say I *never* want to be the cause of your pain again.

I'll never question you again." His gaze seared the side of her face. "I know I don't deserve your forgiveness, but I hope someday you'll be able to forgive me, because... because I want to be friends again."

Her first impulse was to say they would never be friends again. To let him see how it felt to be rejected and deemed untrustworthy. To be scorched from the inside out. But deep down, she knew blaming him wouldn't make her feel better. It'd only prolong her pain, and she was tired of fighting. She couldn't summon the energy—too much of it had already been spent.

So instead, she weakly nodded, wiping her eyes.

His feet shuffled like he was nervous—another trait unfamiliar to him. "What if I help train you?"

Rose's wide eyes locked on his. She was positive she heard him wrong. "What?" she whispered.

"I know I can't replace Zareb," he said his name with care. "He taught you remarkably well, but I could continue where he left off. I could help finish your training."

Her jaw slackened. She'd never expected this from him, not in a million years. "You'd do that?"

He nodded slowly. "I would. If it's still something you want."

"Yes," she answered almost too quickly. "But Tristan will be furious if he finds out."

Roman scoffed. "Tristan doesn't scare me. He can't banish me like Zareb. He doesn't have that power over me, not yet."

"Still, it's a risk. He may not banish you, but there are plenty of other things he could do to make you wish you hadn't. I don't want you getting punished because of me." She couldn't handle another person suffering for her sake.

"I know the risks." He didn't look the least bit worried.

Her eyes roamed over him curiously. "Why?" she finally asked.

Roman's gaze shifted to the fountain, searching the water like he could find the answer in the soft glow. His eyes returned to hers. "You've done so well; it'd be a shame to stop now."

She studied him, contemplating his answer. It was vague, but what he was offering was too big of a temptation. "When do we start?"

"Whenever you're ready."

"Tomorrow?" she suggested, desperately needing to keep her mind on something else. *Anything* else.

The corner of his mouth twitched upward, nearly smiling but not quite. "Tomorrow it is." Dare she say he sounded *glad*.

She wanted to smile back, but her heart was far too crippled to make the muscles in her cheeks move.

"Come on." He nudged her towards the castle. "You must be exhausted."

They walked back in silence, side by side. She focused on her steps, counting them to distract her mind from wandering to—*things*. She counted them. One… two… three… six… twelve.

She counted all the way until they reached her door, the diversion fulfilling its job.

She faced Roman, about to say thank you. "You helped me today," she said instead.

Roman saw right through her façade. "Hardly… Are you going to be alright?"

The simple question jabbed her heart as her anxiety resurfaced, threatening to take over. The hour was a painful reminder that the celebration would be ending soon, meaning Tristan was about to return to his room with his new wife. She grimaced on the inside, wrapping her arms around herself.

"Of course," Rose lied through her teeth.

Roman stepped closer, towering over her. After a long agonizing silence, he said, "Tell me what you're thinking."

She hesitated, biting her lip. "How hard it'll be to sleep tonight." Her stomach threatened to retch.

His soft eyes held a depth she'd never seen. She wanted to shrink away from them, crawl, bury herself into the ground like the pathetic worm she was. But his golden eyes kept her pinned. "What can I do?" He sounded… desperate.

"You've done enough," she said, grateful. Truly. At least they were friends again. That was something to celebrate. "I'll be fine." She even summoned a small smile to convince him.

Another long pause. "Okay... good night, then." He bid her farewell with a firm nod.

"Good night," she said, doing a masterful job at keeping her voice light and airy. She hid her face from him as she went to the door, forcing herself to open and close it at a normal pace.

She immediately fell back against the door for support, trying to be as soft as possible. Tears filled her eyes as she wrapped her arms around herself, slowly sliding to the floor, burying her face in her hands.

When she could no longer hear the echo of Roman's footsteps, she let go. Her sobs came out in full force as her shoulders shook.

She undid her dress roughly, ripping it off in harsh movements. She tossed it onto the floor, not caring where it landed. Her slip was the only protection from the cool summer air, wafting in from the open balcony door. With shaky hands, she ripped out her hair pins, dropping them carelessly onto the floor.

Without warning, an intrusive image of Satin and Tristan in his bed flashed through her mind. She dug a grave for the horrifying scene, but the image seared itself into her brain like a brand. She'd barely let all of her hair down when she lurched again.

She wouldn't be able to hold it back this time.

She bolted to the bucket beside her bathtub. Her body had nothing more to give, but somehow, from the depths of hell, yellow bile poured out, leaving her feeling like her very soul had exited with it.

She set the bucket down, kneeling on the floor, gripping the smooth edge of the tub for support. Tears streamed down her cheeks. *Please, not again. Please.* She couldn't take it anymore.

The door creaked open behind her.

She cursed, scolding herself for not locking it, knowing it was her mother.

"Please go," she begged through her tears. She didn't want pity. She just wanted to grieve. "I'll be fine... please... Just leave me be."

There was silence, long enough that she thought her mother had heeded her wishes.

She lifted her heavy head.

To her utter disbelief, Roman stood in the doorway. "Do you truly want to be alone?" His face contorted as his knuckles turned white, like he was holding himself back from something.

She wiped her wet eyes timidly. How pitiful she must look to him, how weak he must think she was. She felt so foolish, so embarrassed. She tried to speak, but her sore throat was nearly swollen shut. She tried to shake her head, her eyes falling to the floor in shame. She meant to say yes, but instead, she said—

"No." Her sore throat croaked.

It was all he needed.

He swooped down, gathering her into his arms as he crushed her body against his. He cradled her head with his large hand while the other gripped her lower back, clinging to her like she was the most precious commodity in the world.

She didn't think, she just did. She slid her arms around his neck, burrowing herself into his warm shoulder for what was probably the hundredth time that day.

They stayed like that for a long time. Roman patiently let her cry again until she couldn't anymore, continually rubbing her back to calm her shaking body.

His touch somehow removed an invisible pressure off her. She found that she not only needed his touch, she *craved* it. His body was like medicine—a super tonic. The need was so strong she couldn't ignore it.

Her insides sank inward for even letting herself admit it.

Knowing the hour was late, her arms slid off to let him go, even as her body screamed in protest.

His arms held her tighter. "Don't," he whispered. His voice was so comforting, she didn't have the power to refuse. She circled her arms around him again.

Roman picked her up off the floor, wrapping her legs around his waist in a smooth motion.

The unexpected movement made her hitch before she could stop the sound from escaping her lips.

She swore she caught a wisp of triumph in his eyes, clouded with pride as they drifted to her mouth. He shook his head, snapping himself out of his daze.

Without a word, he carried her to the bed, lowering her onto the sheets smoothly, still cradling her as he lay next to her. She kept her arms locked around his neck, her fingers spreading onto the base of his neck and into his hair.

His eyes closed and emitted a loud sigh of contentment as though he was reveling in her touch. When his eyes opened again, they were covered with a haze she'd never witnessed in them before.

Her blood pulsed as he slowly leaned in closer, close enough she was sure he'd kiss her. She didn't move, by the gods, she may have even let him, but instead, he stayed hovering there—his nose brushing hers. Her mouth dried. She memorized every crevice of his lips, the perfect shade of pink, the slope they made.

His large body stiffened like he was preventing it from doing something he didn't want it to. He pulled his head back to get a proper look at her. "Do you want me to stay?"

She swore his eyes pleaded for her to say yes.

But he didn't need to ask.

"Yes." Her hands grabbed a handful of his hair again, being so bold as to bring his forehead down to rest against hers.

Roman's eyes rolled back from the small contact.

"Roman?" she whispered.

His eyes opened with barely restrained hunger as his arm tightened around her back. "Hmm?" he hummed, the deep vibrations rumbling against her chest.

"Would you take me there one day? To Eristan?" she asked softly. Timidly. As if her soul would crack if he said no.

His eyes brightened, almost as if the question amused him. "I'll take you anywhere you want to go, Roe."

And with his words, she heard the whisper of a hallowed promise. Stronger than any shout or declaration made to the sky and sea gods.

"I've missed you calling me that," she admitted in a small voice.

He drew her body closer, if it was even possible. "Me, too."

She laid her head on his chest, intertwining her long legs with his as her eyes drooped from exhaustion.

"Sleep," he commanded into her ear, then added in a whisper, "I'm not going anywhere."

He caressed her hair, relaxing her scalp as she surrendered to his touch. She thought she would stay awake for hours, but the gentle strokes of his hands and his steady heartbeat pulled her into a calm state.

And that night, she found sleep faster than she ever had before.

PART III
THE AWAKENING

CHAPTER 55

Rose woke to the song of a robin perched on her open window. Her eyes fluttered open, the sheets warmed from the morning rays strewn across her duvet. She'd almost forgotten who slept next to her until she saw Roman already awake, still dutifully beside her, not noticing she'd woken. Both hands lay lazily behind his head, cradling it in his large palms in a relaxed pose, staring at the ceiling, lost in thought.

He was the same Roman, but she still couldn't believe how much older he looked. He was now bigger than both of his brothers. His clean-shaven face was bronzed from exposure to the elements during the war. His eyes were easily her favorite thing about him—a beautiful blend of amber and gold specks that glittered in the light like the traces of gold found in the soil in Semaria. His thick, straight eyebrows gave him a far more mature appearance, looking like he could be older than her—many would probably assume so at a glance.

She had the urge to reach out and run her fingers along his jaw, but instead, she shifted her body toward him.

Roman snapped out of his trance. Unlike her, he didn't hesitate, reaching out to tuck a stray hair behind her ear. He had that look again—the look that made the foundation of her walls crack.

"How do you feel?" he whispered.

"Better." And she meant it.

He gave a satisfied nod. "Good... Your mother and Thea came in earlier this morning. I think I about gave your mother a heart attack."

Rose stilled, reprimanding herself for being so careless. "What did you tell her?"

"The truth. That nothing happened, and I was only here to help."

Relief settled in as she nodded in response, more positive than a royal flush in cards that she'd hear more about this from her mother later. She'd definitely be questioning her judgment—her sanity.

Roman propped himself onto his forearm, peering at her with uncertainty. "I had a talk with your mum... I told her I want to take you to Highland Haven."

She sat straight up. "Your family manor?"

He nodded. "In the mountains. It's not far, but far enough it'll feel like somewhere new. I have business in Caleede and it's nearby. I thought it'd make sense. You could come with me, finish your training. No one would bother us there. We wouldn't have to hide."

Rose almost couldn't believe her ears—a chance to escape had finally been offered, and in the capitol no less. "What did my mother say?"

"She agreed. She thinks it's a good idea for you to get some distance from this place."

She paused, thinking. "What about her? Will she be coming?"

"I told her she could. But she seems to think it'd be better for her to stay here."

"How long would we be gone?"

Roman shrugged. "As long as it takes to finish my business and your training."

She gazed at the sheets as she considered his offer. She'd miss her mother, but she couldn't stay. She'd go insane. If there was a chance she could escape this place, she'd take it. Even if it was only for a short time. Hell, if it weren't for her mother, she might have considered stowing away on a ship at this point.

Roman paused at her hesitancy. "But if you'd rather stay—"

"No!" She cut him off quickly.

He lifted an eyebrow.

She collected herself and added more calmly, "I want to go."

His shoulders relaxed at her answer. "Then I'll make the arrangements."

"When do we leave?"

"As soon as you want. I can be ready today—"

"Today?" She couldn't hide the excitement in her voice.

A smile almost graced Roman's lips as they tugged up slightly. "Today it is."

She wanted to smile, but she couldn't get her mouth to move.

Roman stood. "Tristan won't be happy when he learns of our plans. Luckily, he already left for his honeymoon—" she flinched at the word, "—earlier this morning, so he'll be gone a few days. He won't know we've left until it's too late. But I'd ask you not to tell anyone where we are going except your mother. I'll tell my father, but I don't want anyone else to interfere—including my mother."

"I won't... But what about Beth? Won't she miss you?"

Something shifted in his eyes. "She'll understand. I'll explain the situation."

"As long as I am not impeding anything." She didn't want to interfere with their relationship.

"You're not."

Rose nodded, accepting his answer.

He went to leave, almost reaching the door.

"Roman?"

He turned back.

"Why are you doing all of this?" she asked softly, still not sure why the change of heart.

Roman kept his face controlled as he looked down at the scar on his arm and then at her. "I owe you my life... The least I can do is make yours a little better."

She gazed at him gratefully. "Thank you."

He gave her a cross look. "What have I told you about thanking me?"

She shrugged. "It's a habit of mine when someone does something nice."

He let out a harsh sound—a laugh or scoff, she couldn't be sure. "I'll see you at noon," he said over his shoulder, heading for the door. "I'd pack warm clothes. It gets cold at night, even in the summer. But don't bother bringing too much. Harriet has a closet full that could dress a small army."

Rose almost smiled, knowing it was probably true.

~

Rose's mother came to help pack her few belongings, and for the first time in days, her heart pumped freely—it still didn't feel real.

"Well, that's the last of it," her mother said, scanning the room for anything else they'd missed. "I think you have everything you'll need."

"Are you sure you won't come?" She'd asked the question for the hundredth time.

Her mother shook her head sharply. "Oh no, I'm quite content here. I'll have much more company here than at the estate. It sounds like you two will be busy enough without worrying about me. Besides, I need to keep hunting for suitors while you are gone. I'll send word once I have any good news. There's *plenty* of time left in the season."

Rose stuffed a book into her bag. "What did Roman say to you this morning?" She would've given *anything* to be a fly on the wall for that conversation.

"Well… after the shock wore off—" her mother gave her a reprimanding stare, having already scolded her earlier, "—he told me he had an idea that might help you. I listened to what he had to say and… I agreed."

"So you think it's a good idea?"

With soft eyes, her mother swept Rose's hair over her shoulder, her thumb stroking her cheek as she said, "I think it's something you need."

"Do you think Tristan will be angry when he comes back? I don't want him taking it out on you."

Her mother's hand slid off her face, waving it, unconcerned. "You don't need to worry about me. I can handle Tristan. He needs to come to terms with the fact that, at some point, you both have to move on."

Some things were easier said than done.

Rose clasped the buckle on her bag as the dull ache in her heart sharpened. "Did I make a mistake letting him go? What if… what if I never love anyone like I loved him? What if…" Her words faltered. There was a more fearful question she couldn't bring herself to voice. The one that had been haunting her since the ruins.

What if no one else ever loved her as much as Tristan did?

Her heart crippled.

Her mother put a gentle hand on her arm. "You won't. You'll never love anyone the same way twice. But there is a greater love out there for you, Rose. You may not feel that way now, but there will be a love so strong and freeing, you won't even imagine letting it go. I feel it in my bones."

Rose looked at her mother pitifully. Who was she to sit and complain after all her mother had been through with her father? "I'm sorry you never got to have that kind of love. You deserve so much more than what he gave you."

Despite the truth of it, her mother gave her a gracious smile. "Don't worry, Rose. My life has been filled with more love than most. I have the greatest love I've ever known standing right here in front of me."

Rose's heart filled with pride. She didn't know where her mother had gained so much strength. Perhaps if she had inherited more of her mother's qualities, they wouldn't be in this position.

She gave her mother a tight hug, expressing her thanks.

Her mother pulled back, gripping her forearms. "But I'll tell you something I learned long ago. Your peace of mind is *far* more important than understanding why something happened the way it did. Don't dwell on thoughts of things that could've been."

Rose knew it. She merely nodded.

Her mother brought her back into her arms, squeezing her tight. "I love you so much, my darling girl." Her voice fluctuated with a rare softness.

"I love you, too, Mum," she replied, meaning it with all her heart.

CHAPTER 56

That afternoon, Rose and Roman departed on horseback for Highland Haven. She had strapped the sword Zareb had gifted her to her back, stealthily hidden beneath her cloak. It felt strange to be so eager to leave a place she'd once considered her home. But here she was, practically casting off on a horse with her most unexpected ally.

They followed the main road, and though the sky was overcast, a warm breeze from the south made her regret the decision to wear a long-sleeved dress and black cloak. But she knew she'd be grateful for the warmth as they headed northwest toward the mountain range.

The sound of crashing waves faded into the background until they disappeared altogether, replaced by the serene quiet of the open road. The invisible burden weighing her down for the past few weeks lifted with every mile they gained. She straightened, taking off her hood, and for the first time in weeks, she inhaled a breath untainted by the sea, replaced with fresh dirt and farmland.

Rose took in every inch of the world around her as they traveled through the rolling hills. Some fields were filled with lush, green pastures overrun by sheep and cattle, while others were utilized to grow food. The wheat fields took up the hillside, the wind grazing across the stalks in beautiful waves.

The road was well-traveled since it was the main road that led from the castle to the heart of Cathan. Countless travelers passed, most traders and barterers, while others were local farmers hauling their goods between towns. Children trailed behind the wagons, exchanging mischievous grins with Rose as they ran to stretch their legs.

Many stopped to acknowledge Roman, showing appreciation for his service when they spotted the sun crest on his cloak. It was still strange to think the young boy she'd once known had grown into the man in front of her. In truth, she didn't know him much at all. In many ways, she felt like she was traveling with a stranger. She wondered if he thought the same—keenly aware of his subtle glances sweeping over her every so often.

Despite the many friendly faces, some were not so inviting. One man, in particular, traveling with a large group of men, took notice of her, giving her an all-too-friendly grin, striding up to boldly introduce himself.

She opened her mouth to respond when Roman butted his horse between them, giving the man a dominant glare. The man scowled, about to put up a fight, but when he noticed Roman's sun crest, he lost the motivation to pursue her, retreating to his group.

A few hours later, the sky grew dark as dusk crept in. Just as she was about to suggest they set up camp, a small village came into view.

"We'll spend the night there," Roman said, speaking up for the first time in an hour. "There's a small tavern I've stayed at that should have a few rooms. It's not much, but it's safer than camping out in the open."

Rose's heart dropped, a long-lost fear taking over her body. She wished for nothing more than to brave the woods. She'd fight off a bear if she had to.

But she kept silent, not wanting to be a nuisance. A braver part of herself encouraged her to thicken her skin. After all, she couldn't cower in fear of them forever.

The lanterns had already been lit as they trotted into the small village, lighting their way to the tavern. The dusty streets were nearly barren as stragglers scattered homeward.

As she entered the tavern, she noticed two things. First was the overwhelming smell of alcohol, unwashed men, and smoke, all plaguing her nose in a nauseating blend. Second was the bar full of men who immediately took notice of their entry, each with a drink in hand, looking positively bored until she walked in. One man beamed broadly, making a point to signal to his friends, who catcalled over to them as they made their way to the bar. She ignored them, taking a few unconscious steps toward Roman.

"Would sleeping under the stars be so bad?" Rose whispered, doing an outstanding job at hiding the fear in her voice.

"Unfortunately," Roman replied, glaring at the lot of them.

They claimed the only vacant table, grateful it was tucked away by a back window.

"Wait here," he commanded.

She sat stiff as a board on the edge of the rickety wooden chair, staying alert and avoiding eye contact, particularly with the men sitting up at the bar, their gaze lingering for far too long. Her hands trembled under the table as she tried with all her might to push back the memory that threatened to surface.

A smoky room, packed with men, waiting for the—

No.

She shoved the memory back into its dark box, locking it and throwing away the key. She refused to let it rule her. Instead, she redirected her focus back to Roman, watching him speak with the bartender, a short, stubby man with a large red beard. Their exchange was brief, offering no clues as to whether they had an open room. She prayed to the gods they didn't.

Her question was answered as the man handed over two keys in exchange for three silvers and two coppers. The short man disappeared to the back, only to return with two plates of food moments later. Roman collected the plates and returned to their table, passing a group of men who threw him envious glances.

They ate in silence, Rose stuffing her face as quickly as possible, eager to retreat to her room. Roman seemed to think along the same lines, taking only a few minutes to clear the simple meal of dark meat, potatoes, and bread, which had gone stale.

Once they were done, Roman led her through the tables to the back of the tavern. They climbed the squeaky wooden stairs up to their rooms, stopping at the last one in the far corner.

"Here's your key." Roman handed her a small brass key with the number five on it. "Don't open the door for anyone but me. Keep it locked at all times. There's a bath if you need it."

It was an effort to keep her hands steady as she took it. "Where's yours?"

"I'll be in three." He pointed down the small hall. Just two doors down. "Don't hesitate to ask for anything if you need it."

"I won't."

The room was dark, lit by a solitary candle that cast heavy shadows. It was small, to be sure. The bed left much to be desired, its sheets stained and the mattress matted. She had never considered herself to be spoiled, but as she looked around at the worst room she'd ever stayed in, she realized just how privileged she'd been. She wasn't about to complain.

However, she would be putting her own blanket over the bed—just in case.

She set her bag down, removed her long black cloak, and draped it over the tattered armchair next to the bed. She slipped off her dress, leaving her in her slip, eager to wash off the dirt from the road. She maneuvered around the bed to see if the state of the bathtub was worth the risk—something moved out of the corner of her eye.

To her horror, a figure stepped out of the shadows—a young man, likely about her age, but twice her size and with pointed features. He crept toward her, leering at her with a lustful gaze.

Her eyes widened in recognition. It was the man they'd passed on the road. Acid boiled up her throat, sickened by the fact that he'd purposefully remained quiet to watch her undress.

"My, my, I knew you were beautiful, but without all that fabric, you are positively delicious." A wicked smile gleamed on his lips as he snaked toward her.

Rose swiveled for her sword, swiping it out of its scabbard. She pointed it at his chest before he could come any closer.

"I'd leave now if I were you," she warned, her arm steady and fierce.

On the inside, her bones shook with fear, but she wouldn't let him see that. Not an ounce.

He laughed at her, raising an eyebrow. "Do you know how to use that thing, sweetheart?"

"Care to find out?" She stepped forward, daring him to advance.

"Now, now, I just need a little company. With a face like that, it should only take a few minutes. I bet you'll even enjoy it," he coaxed with an evil smile.

He lunged, but she acted quicker, stepping aside as she swung at his head so he'd be forced to bend backward to avoid her blade. Just as he did, she kicked the back of his knee in. He crumbled to the ground with a loud thud.

She pressed the tip of her sword to his throat.

He held up his hands, eyes widening with a mixture of irritation and amazement.

"You disappoint me," she goaded with a cold smile. "I was hoping you'd be more of a challenge."

Just as she was about to force him to leave, the door burst open. Roman entered, his blade out and ready to wield. But he halted as soon as he saw the scene.

Roman's pupils turned darker than the bottom of the sea.

He surged forward, snatching the intruder roughly by the collar, lifting him to his feet. He dragged him to the wall and slammed him against it with full force. The man grimaced as his head collided with the hard wood.

"Feel like taking your leave now? Or shall I let the lady finish what she started?" Roman asked in such a dark voice she knew it was the war general in him speaking.

The man had the decency to look scared. He shook his head.

"Luckily for you, I've already taken more than enough lives for my lifetime. Apologize, and I'll let you leave with your life," Roman snarled.

The man glared over at Rose and said with a forced voice, "I'm sorry."

"She didn't quite hear you," Roman pressed, shoving him harder against the wall.

"I'm sorry," the man said louder, having difficulty speaking with Roman's forearm rammed against his neck.

Roman yanked him off the wall and shoved him out the door, then punched him—once, twice, nearly knocking him out cold.

The first opportunity he got, the man cupped his face and ran.

Roman took a step to pursue him—

"Let him go." Rose slid her sword back in its scabbard.

Roman fumed, sending a hostile glare in the man's direction. He clenched his jaw and fists, but nonetheless did as she instructed, slamming the door loudly.

He came face to face with her, and as quick as the anger came, it was gone. He reached for her, cupping her jaw. "Are you okay? Did he hurt you?" he asked in a panic as his eyes raked over her.

She placed her hand on his wrist, stopping his frantic movements. "I'm fine," she reassured him. "He didn't touch me."

Roman's shoulders relaxed but only minutely. "I heard a noise. I came as soon as I felt something was off. How'd he get in?"

"He was already here, hiding in the closet." She gestured to the open door. "He was waiting for me, like he knew I'd be here."

Roman glowered. "He probably paid the tavern owner a handsome amount. I should kill them both."

"Don't. We don't need to make any more enemies tonight. If you still feel like killing them in the morning, you can do it then." She turned away, if only to hide her shaking hands, as she placed her sword back by her bed.

How she loathed these stupid taverns.

"I hate to say it, but there may be more," Roman said. "I saw too many stares in your direction downstairs. I think it'd be best if I stayed—in case they decide to get drunk and act on their… impulsive thoughts."

Impulsive thoughts was a kind way to put it—more like perverted fantasies.

A wave of relief flooded her at his offer. "We can share the bed."

Roman almost grimaced. "I can take the floor."

"Don't be silly." Rose looked at the state of the floor, covered in a good layer of dust. "These wooden planks are more uncomfortable than hard dirt."

"I'll be fine," he said shortly.

A pang of wounded pride spread through her. "Did you dislike sharing a bed with me so much?"

Roman stilled. "What?"

"I'm pretty sure you've looked at spiders with kinder eyes. Was I so horrible to sleep next to?" She fought to keep her voice steady.

"No, it's just—I don't want to give you the wrong impression."

She straightened her shoulders, finally understanding. He was telling her last night was a one-time thing, that it wouldn't be happening again, that he was only trying to be kind in her moment of need.

She accepted his answer this time as color stained her cheeks. "Oh. Okay, then."

She avoided his gaze as they set up their bedding, still internally sulking from the fact he couldn't stand the thought of sleeping next to her. He chose to sleep in front of the door—the farthest place possible. He placed extra blankets down for padding.

She was so exhausted, she was sure she'd fall asleep with no trouble, but soon, the minutes dragged into hours, and still, she couldn't fall asleep, her mind refusing to turn itself off. Not with her heart still pounding from finding the stranger in her room. She tossed and turned, trying to get comfortable, but to no avail.

She let out an irritated sigh, rolling back over to face the door where Roman lay, expecting him to be long asleep from his silence.

Instead, honey eyes greeted her.

Her cheeks warmed as she quickly averted her eyes and closed them. But after a moment, she could still sense his gaze burning through her eyelids. She opened them again, finding them still locked on her.

She scooted to the edge of the bed. "I can't sleep," she whispered through the darkness.

"Neither can I."

The foreign energy she contained came full force the longer she stared at him. She knew she should turn right back over, but she couldn't pry her gaze from him. It was as though her body knew how close he was. It hungered for him, for his skin to be on hers like last night. She fought the urge to get up off the bed and lay beside him.

Roman sighed in defeat as he rubbed his eyes. The next thing she knew, he was coming over to her, revealing his white tunic and dark trousers. His face contorted as he edged toward the bed, almost like he was in pain—like it was unthinkable even to approach it. She didn't say a word as she watched him climb into the sheets, each move slow and precise, taking care not to touch her.

She scooted as far as she could to the other side, turning her back to see if it'd make him more comfortable. She closed her eyes, sure sleep would find her now. However, as more minutes passed, her crazed desire to reach out and touch him only grew, like her body sensed how close he was.

Accepting the feeling wasn't going to leave on its own, she dared to peer back at him. Roman turned at the exact moment, coming face to face with each other.

He studied her like he was taking mental notes of something. In one effortless motion, his rough hand slid into hers, watching her expression to see if the gesture was welcome.

She gripped his large palm back, daring to scoot closer, hoping he wouldn't be angry by her advance.

His simmering amber eyes boiled over. His hand let go of hers, going to her waist instead, drawing her close.

She returned the gesture, slithering her arms around his neck, entangling her body with his. She rested her head on what was becoming her favorite spot between his shoulder and neck.

Roman let out a loud, appreciative sigh, the sound mimicking what she felt on the inside.

For the first time that night, her body finally relaxed. She could have sworn she felt Roman stroking her hair, but she fell asleep so swiftly that she wasn't certain if it was just her imagination.

CHAPTER 57

Roman woke Rose early the next morning. The sun was barely peeking out over the hills, leaving a dark-red sky to fill the dusty room with its soft hue.

"It's time to go," he whispered.

Rose desperately wanted to fall back asleep and let her body wake naturally, but the smell of smoke lingering kindly reminded her they were still in the tavern. In any case, if they left now, they'd be in the mountains by late afternoon, and at the manor by nightfall. The realization helped her wake up, untangling herself from the sheets, the cool air hitting her exposed skin.

She snuck a glance at Roman, who was already up, his back facing her, acting as though nothing had happened.

So she did the same.

Downstairs, the crowd was thin, with only a handful of men having breakfast. The morning scene was a stark contrast to the rowdy night crowd. Although she wished to forgo breakfast, Roman strutted up to the counter and picked up a muffin for each of them.

The tavern owner had the decency to look nervous as Roman approached.

"The room and breakfast are free," Roman said in a threateningly low voice, refusing to pay him because of the incident last night. "And you'll give me every penny that man paid you—and the others."

Others?

Her mouth popped open in surprise.

The short man remained silent, scowling as if torn between compliance and defiance. After a moment, the tavern owner grunted and shuffled to the back, vanishing through the wooden door while muttering curses under his breath.

Not long after, he carried six large bags of coins back.

Six.

He pushed the money across the counter, not daring to get close, probably afraid Roman would make a grab for his arm. She almost thought he would; Roman's hand was already on the hilt of his sword.

Instead, he nabbed the bags and marched out.

She gave the man a reprimanding glare of her own before she followed.

Roman saddled the horses while she filled their waters by the well. They were about to mount their horses when she asked, "How many?"

He slid her a quick side glance as he did up the straps of his saddle. "Too many. I didn't wake you because I didn't want to scare you. But don't worry, they never came into the room."

An involuntary shudder ran through her. "Thank you for shielding me."

He yanked the strap of the saddle. "What have I said about thanking me?"

Rose shifted, wrapping her arms around herself as Roman's face softened slightly, realizing how harsh he sounded.

"I'm sorry, it's just—" He cut himself off. "It's my own fault I made you stay here. I thought it'd be safer. Lesson learned—no more taverns for you."

She wholeheartedly agreed.

The sky remained clear as they traveled. The roads were quieter than the previous day, with only a handful of fellow travelers passing. They stuck to the main road until they veered off, going west towards the mountains instead of continuing north to the capital.

A sprawling forest of towering trees welcomed them, becoming bigger as they journeyed closer to the mountains. A fresh, crisp aroma of pine encased her with the light breeze. Something about it felt magical; perhaps it was the way the sunlight glittered through the leaves, casting playful shadows on the green moss that covered the ground, thriving at the bases of the sturdy trees. It was full of life—pure, natural life.

The sun had fallen behind the mountains as they finally reached their destination.

Rose had to stop and stare.

The grand estate was well-hidden, with giant trees flanking both sides of the long dirt road leading to the front courtyard. The mansion was built entirely from light-gray stone, the very same stone as the rocky mountains behind it. Giant pillars held up the front porch, which had two large black lanterns, hanging on either side of the arched double doors. The base was left overrun with thick green leafy vines, thinning out as they weaved around the windows and stretched to the roof.

Not only was the manor more beautiful than she had imagined, but it was also situated beside a beautiful emerald lake, with water so clear she could see straight to the bottom.

Now she knew where they had come up with the name Highland Haven.

"It's beautiful," she whispered, not knowing how better to describe it. If she had a home like this, she would never leave.

Roman's mouth tugged to the side. "It is."

Only a single servant was there to greet them—a robust woman with a generous chest and even wider hips. Her light-auburn hair was styled in a bun, and her cheeks glowed rosy against her fair complexion. Her thin lips curved into a welcoming smile.

"Master Roman," the woman greeted with open arms, coming down the steps as Rose and Roman dismounted their horses. "It's been nearly a year since I saw you. Look how you've grown! I barely recognized you."

Roman gave her a rare genuine smile. "It's good to see you, Gretta," he said, embracing her with a bear hug.

Gretta peeked over his shoulder to Rose. "And who's this beautiful lass?" she asked curiously, openly looking her up and down.

"Rosalie Versalles," she said, "but everyone calls me Rose."

Gretta's eyes lit up. "Ah, I finally get to meet the famous Rose." She patted Roman on the shoulder as she scanned her once again. "I've heard so much about you. I feel like I know you already."

Rose slung Roman a brief side-eye. "Good things, I hope."

Gretta waved her away. "Oh, of course! Although I'm surprised to see you here with Roman and not one of his brothers. But I suppose Tristan is quite busy, just married and all," she said with a bright smile.

Rose cringed at the mention of Tristan. She tucked her hair behind her ear as Roman shifted uncomfortably.

To her credit, Gretta picked up on their body language. "Well, come in, come in! You both must be starving. We'll get you settled in, and then we'll have supper. I hope you're alright with soup for dinner. It was such short notice, I didn't have the chance to plan properly."

Inside the manor was just as beautiful. The staircase took up the majority of the entrance hall, wide enough to rival the castles. Its walls were strewn with dark wooden beams and the furniture sat in pristine condition. The open ceiling soared to the second floor, making it feel that much bigger. Despite its vacancy, the air was crisp and fresh. It was quiet. So quiet. She'd have to get used to that.

To her left, an archway led to a sitting room with an oversized fireplace and dark-green velvet couches. Above the fireplace, a woven tapestry depicting the royal family caught her eye. Her heart stung as a young Tristan stared back at her.

She didn't have long to absorb it all as Gretta guided them up the staircase. She let her fingers glide over the smooth, dark-wood railing while her shoes effortlessly skimmed the deep-plum stair runner. The halls were empty, giving Rose the impression there were few servants here besides Gretta. Maintaining an estate of this size with such limited help must have been a full-time job. But even so, not a speck of dust was in sight.

At the top of the staircase, she discovered enormous floor-to-ceiling windows that spanned the entire wall, narrow and cathedral-shaped, similar to those in the castle.

Her feet skidded to a stop, her breath stolen by the view.

The lake was at their doorstep, its waters so close that the enormous patio stairs plunged directly into the crystal-clear depths. Nearby mountain peaks surrounded the lake, offering shelter to the entire valley. In the heart of the lake sat a flat grassy island encircled by a rocky shore. The sun had left the sky, leaving behind a purple-pink glaze over the water. The stars twinkled brighter with the added elevation alongside the twin moons, no more than mere slivers in the sky that night. She soaked in every glorious detail of it.

Roman sauntered behind her, glancing over her shoulder at the view. "What do you think?"

"It's perfect," she confessed softly. "It feels like home." Her eyes widened as she realized she'd spoken the last bit aloud.

She glanced nervously at Roman, biting her cheek.

He wasn't looking at the view, but at her. A rare light formed in his eyes as the corners of his lips twitched.

"Which guest room would you like her to stay in?" Gretta asked from down the hall, still shuffling towards the rooms. "I have the west wing room made up, or I can ready another?"

"She'll have my room."

Rose's brows shot upward. "Oh no, I couldn't— I'm sure the guest room will be more than—"

Roman spoke over her. "Thank you, Gretta, that'll be all."

"Of course," Gretta said, clearly not bothered at the abrupt dismissal. In fact, she would dare say a mischievous smile rested on her face as she departed and went back downstairs.

Roman led Rose down the long hall to another staircase, which, though narrow, twisted in a circular fashion, winding to one of the towers.

Roman's room was nothing like she envisioned. It was so... *sophisticated*. The large room had three bay windows that protruded out, offering an even better view of the lake and forest from the elevated height. Dark-auburn curtains draped between the large windows, looking so soft she was tempted to run her fingers over them. The large bed had four dark-wood canopy posts holding dark-purple curtains that matched the duvet.

Across from the bed sat a wide stone fireplace with a full iron firewood rack stacked beside it.

More windows lined the right side of the room, with a large table and a telescope. Star charts and parchment remained scattered across the table as if Roman had been here yesterday. A sturdy wooden bookcase housed hardbacks on various subjects, safeguarded by glass windows to protect the precious pages held within.

Her favorite thing was the porcelain bathtub nestled in the middle of the bay windows, which would allow her to appreciate the view while she bathed. Remarkably, even after all this time, the room still carried his scent.

"I can't take this," she said.

Roman cocked an eyebrow, folding his arms. "Does my room not meet your expectations?"

"No—I mean, yes. It exceeds them, really, but—"

"Then you'll stay. Or I'll be offended."

She threw him an appreciative look, knowing he was trying to make her feel better. "If you insist."

"I do."

Rose shifted her gaze, still admiring the room.

Roman cleared his throat. "I'll leave you to get settled. I'll be just down the stairs to your right, five doors down. Don't hesitate to ask Gretta for anything you need. I'll have her move some clothes from Harriet's room into the closet for you if you need them."

"Thank you," she said, knowing it'd irk him.

He gave her a cross stare, to which she winked.

A small smile hovered on his lips but didn't fully surface. "I'll see you at dinner."

The moment he stepped out, her gaze fell on the tub that Gretta had already filled. She smiled, biting her lip as she grabbed a towel, aching to clean up before dinner.

She sniffed the bath salts, pinpointing the source of Roman's musky cedar scent. She added a generous amount to the tub, breathing in the aroma as the warm, moist air steamed her face.

Relief came as soon as she climbed in, leaning backward and bracing her back against the cold porcelain. With that, she relaxed, the bubbles so dense they covered her from shoulders to toes.

She'd almost fallen asleep when a knock came at the door.

Gretta entered with a smile, bringing more of Harriet's clothes as promised, and went straight to work, sliding them into the closet for Rose while she soaked.

"Do you manage the whole manor yourself?" she asked.

Gretta picked up another handful of dresses to hang as she said, "Oh, heavens no. But there aren't many of us. There's me, the cook, and two maids. When the royal family returns, the servants from the castle come to help until they leave again. They used to come often, but ever since the war broke out... well, not much free time."

Rose gave her a sympathetic smile. "It must get lonely."

Gretta shook her head fervently. "Oh no, I have family in the city. My mother and brother live there. It's only about a half-day's travel from here. I see them every week or so."

"That's wonderful. It's lucky they're so close."

"It is," Gretta agreed, flitting back and forth to the closet and hanging the dresses neatly. "Though, I will say that I've missed Roman and his siblings terribly. With no children of my own, I suppose they are the closest thing I've got." Gretta's eyes dimmed.

"You were close, then?" Rose wanted to know more.

Gretta nodded, a small shine returning to her eyes. "Oh, yes. It was a dream when they'd come during the summers—and even in the winter. I could tell you their favorite spots to swim, their favorite foods, and their fears. They talked about you often, especially the boys."

Rose gave her a sheepish smile, resting her arm and chin on the edge of the smooth tub. "I'd be so sad when they'd leave those weeks to come here. It was terribly boring at court without them."

"The feeling was mutual, believe me," Gretta assured her with an exasperated look. "Even Xavier, who didn't seem to care about much of anything, would perk up at the mere sound of your name. He'd try to hide it, but I knew better. Tristan spoke of literally nothing else. Then, of course, Roman always adored you, too."

Rose stared down into the heap of bubbles she'd cupped in her hands. "I suppose some things do change."

"What do you mean, child?"

Rose hesitated, wondering how much she should disclose. "Everything has changed since I left last year, Gretta… As soon as I came back into their lives, I've done nothing but ruin things for all of them. Even now, I think Roman still questions me. I feel as though he looks at me like I'm the snake hiding in the garden… Perhaps I am."

Gretta paused, draping a folded dress over her arm as she studied her. "You don't look like a snake to me. Plus, I know that boy better than almost anyone. And he most *certainly* wouldn't let a snake sleep in his bed."

Rose was thankful for the heat of the tub to mask her flushed cheeks. She changed the subject. "Thank you for the dresses," she said, grateful for the extended wardrobe.

"Of course!" Gretta hung the last set. "Right, well, I'll let you finish washing up, and I'll see you at dinner. The dining hall is just down the main stairwell. Once you've done that, take a right, and then it's the third door on the left."

With another thank you from Rose, Gretta shuffled out of the room, leaving her to get dressed.

CHAPTER 58

Rose faced the brass floor-length mirror, examining her reflection. Her olive skin glowed from the moisturizing body oil she'd put on. She could finally let her long, thick hair flow freely now they were away from court, its soft, natural waves reaching down to her chest, resting against the dark-purple dress she had selected from Harriet's closet. It was almost a perfect fit, except a tad short, the hem sitting a few inches off the floor. Although her mother would disapprove, it didn't bother Rose.

Despite the darkness that blanketed the manor, wall sconces and candelabras lit her path perfectly while she admired the paintings hung along the walls. The antique furniture was neatly arranged on the soft rugs alongside the crafted moldings. Fresh flowers filled the clear vase resting on one of the side tables, making her wonder whether Gretta had just arranged them for their arrival or if she regularly kept them filled regardless of having guests.

She'd just reached the hall leading to the dining room when voices began to carry. She recognized them as Roman and Gretta.

As she was about to step inside, she heard her name.

She halted at the crack of the double door, leaning her ear closer.

"I still can't believe I've finally met her after all this time. I used to wonder what all the fuss was about. But now I've met her, I think I'm beginning to understand…" Gretta's voice faded. "Why'd you bring her here?"

"The past few weeks have been hard for her… and a lot of it has been my fault," Roman said.

"She does seem to have a weight on her shoulders," Gretta said. "And for good reason, poor thing. I can only imagine how she must be feeling after all she went through… But she seems like a sweet lass. And my goodness—she is a pretty thing, isn't she?"

Rose unconsciously leaned her ear closer to the door.

"She's the most beautiful woman I've ever seen," Roman said, unintentionally making her heart soar. "I knew it from the first time I saw her when we were children." He paused, his voice growing more tender. "She's also kind and gentle, yet unexpectedly strong, and her mind is just as intricate… Her quick wit and love of books is the only reason I'm alive."

Her heart exploded with pride as she peered down at her feet.

"Well, that fact alone puts her in *my* good books," Gretta said. "If she loves reading, you must show her the library! It's quite an impressive collection, even compared to the castle's."

"I plan to," Roman replied.

Footsteps echoed behind her down the hall.

She quickly smoothed her hair before entering the dining room, opening the door loudly to make her presence known.

She stepped into a cozy, rectangular room with a dark-beamed wooden ceiling that hung lower than the main hall, with an iron chandelier dangling above the center of the wooden table. Four large windows lined the far wall with torches hung between them, providing a clear view of the lake. At the head of the table sat a grand stone fireplace that was already roaring, adding warmth to the chilly mountain air. She immediately took a liking to it.

"Hello," she greeted, pretending not to have heard a word. "Sorry to interrupt."

"Oh, nonsense! Come in, come in, we were just talking about you," Gretta said with a gracious smile, standing up from the table. "Roman was telling me you love to read. We have a beautiful library here. You're eating now, of course, but I've made Roman promise to show it to you soon."

Rose's gaze settled on Roman, seated at the head of the table closest to the fireplace, facing the flames. But as she entered, he quickly stood, his eyes roving over her from top to bottom, lingering on her free-flowing hair.

Just then, a young maid with short, dirty-blonde hair came in, her head down and concentrating on the soup tray in her hands. She bowed to both of them, daring to look up, and as her eyes landed on Roman, they locked. Her short frame froze.

Rose pressed her lips together to keep from smiling, taking the seat next to Roman, the girl's attraction all too obvious.

Gretta rolled her eyes, irritated at the girl's sudden stop. "Roman, Rose, this is Hazel," Gretta introduced with a small nod. "She's our new maid."

Hazel bowed again. Her brown eyes finally flickered to Rose. She looked at her, then back to Roman, then back to her again, casting a look of suspicion.

"Well, put the tray down before the soup gets cold!" Gretta scolded, motioning to the table.

Hazel jumped out of her skin, almost spilling the soup as she carefully lowered the tray, setting a bowl in front of Rose and then Roman.

"Thank you, Hazel, it looks wonderful," Roman said.

Hazel's eyes brightened. She slowly brushed the flour off her apron, staring at him as he picked up his spoon.

Another pause came over the conversation as Hazel's stare lingered on him too long.

Gretta sighed loudly. "Thank you, Hazel. That'll be all."

Hazel jumped, snapping out of her trance. "Of course." With a small bow, she fled the room.

"Don't mind her. She'll get the hang of things," Gretta said, waving her off. "Right, well, if you need anything else, just ring the bell."

The creamy orange soup was made up of a medley of vegetables. It melted into her mouth as soon as the hot liquid touched her lips, warming her from within. The pair shared a quiet meal, with only the sounds of clinking spoons and a crackling fire to break the stillness. It wasn't an uncomfortable silence; she'd just grown so accustomed to the volume of the grand hall that she'd almost forgotten how peaceful it was to eat outside of it.

After dinner, Roman gestured to the patio. "Would you care for a walk?"

Rose nodded, taking one last spoonful before wiping her mouth and setting down her napkin, eager to see the lake up close.

Roman opened the adjacent door for her, allowing the cool, crisp air to brush her skin as she stepped onto the patio. She shivered as her flats tapped across the smooth stone, stepping down the shallow set of stairs to the lower level.

The lake reflected the sparkling light of the moon and stars above, while gentle waves lapped against the rocky walls of the patio. She wandered to the stone balustrade at the edge, resting her arms on the cool, rough surface as she gazed out over the water.

Roman joined her, pointing towards the left side of the lake. "There's a hot spring that streams warm water into the lake. We'd swim closer to it in the winter when it got cold, but in the summer, we'd avoid it. It's perfect for night swims, if you like that sort of thing."

For a split second, Rose had an impulse to get in the water. But as she peeked at the stony steps lowering into its depths, fear crept in, remembering her body swirling helplessly with the sea beast.

"You're still afraid of the water?" he asked in a soft voice, not making it a question.

She wrapped her arms around herself in admission. "Ever since that day at the river, I haven't been able to force myself into the water—*willingly*, that is."

He paused for a long moment, nothing but the small waves filling the silence. "But… that was when we were children."

Her gaze lowered as she shuffled her feet.

"So during the challenge…" His voice drifted off.

"I couldn't swim. It was a miracle I didn't drown." The whole thing had been a miracle.

He looked out to the water, the wind blowing his hair into his eyes. "Would you get in if I did?"

Her eyes lifted to meet his bold ones. "What? Right now?"

"You have something better to do?" he asked, his lips tugging upward.

Fear grappled at her again, demanding she stay far away from the water, but another part of her told her she needed to learn, that it wasn't safe for her *not* to know. It was a fear she desperately wanted to overcome. So she replied with a shaky, "Okay."

Before she had a chance to reconsider, Roman removed his tunic, exposing his toned chest that caught her attention for far too long—she was no better than Hazel. He slipped off his pants, remaining only in his undergarments. He took a few bold steps down the staircase into the water before turning to look up at her expectantly.

She kicked off her shoes, removing her dress with one swoop, leaving her in her thin white slip. The night air grazed her bare skin, sending another shiver down her spine. She steeled herself and tiptoed to the top of the staircase, wrapping her arms around her body for warmth.

Her hesitant gaze lifted to meet his.

Roman's eyes locked onto her with an expression she didn't recognize, running themselves over her body, then back up to meet hers as his throat bobbed. He clenched his jaw, deliberate in his movements as he stretched out both hands.

She grasped his rough hands, letting him guide her into the water. She braced herself for the cold, and although it was cool, it wasn't as frigid as she expected, the underground spring warming the entire lake.

The water was nearly at her hips when her body locked up. She took a deep breath, trying to force her legs to move, but they refused to respond to her demands.

His hand tugged hers gently, urging her to continue.

She glared at him. "You brought me out here to kill me, didn't you?"

The question caught Roman so off guard that a harsh laugh escaped his lips. It was a breathtaking sound—one that made her heart pound as loud as a drum. "There was a fleeting moment when I thought it could be to my advantage," he said, mimicking her words. He continued to drag her down the stairs, adding, "I won't let anything happen to you... I promise."

His calm, warm voice put her fears at ease. She held her breath and forced herself into the water.

Without hesitating, he pulled her into him. Her arms and legs wrapped around him in a deadlock as her shaking body clung to him.

A small, encouraging smile formed on his lips. Energy jolted through her veins as if lightning had struck the water. It was the most enchanted thing she'd ever seen. It wasn't like the polished smile she'd seen at court. It was a genuine smile that reached his eyes. And for the first time, the smile was because of her—*for* her.

It was enough to distract her from the fact she was in the lake until Roman took them deeper. She gripped him tighter, her saucer eyes shifting to the water—like it might part and swallow her whole.

"Hey," he whispered, his dripping hand tilting her chin to look at him. "Eyes on me."

Slowly, she dragged her gaze upward.

They were close—too close—close enough that she could see the golden flecks in his amber eyes. Judging by how deep they were, she knew she could probably stand on her own, but she was too afraid to let go, especially in the dark, with only the sky and the distant lanterns from the patio for light.

Roman's arms tightened around her waist, and he nodded in approval. "You just keep those eyes on me," he rumbled, the sudden rough texture of his voice sending her heart to beat at an unimaginable rate. "We'll just get used to the water, alright?"

Rose ignored the foreign energy within herself yet again—ignored how his bare skin ignited her own. She tried to hold his gaze, but something caged deep inside her threatened to take over her limbs, urging her to move just a few inches closer…

She tore her eyes away before she embarrassed herself. It was then she noticed scars scattered across his tanned skin. She counted three large ones—on his shoulder, on his right side just beneath his ribs, and the new scar from the arrow laced with the Dragonshade which looked redder than the others. She had a hunch it'd stay that way even as it healed, the poison leaving a permanent mark on him.

"How did you get this scar?" she asked, her fingers tracing the one on his shoulder.

Roman looked down at it with her. "That was a gift from a Vertmerian soldier. We were on the battlefield when I saw one of my friends on the ground, wounded. He could barely stand when I saw the soldier he'd been fighting about to take his life. Not thinking it through, I stuck my left arm out to push him out of the way. Instead, the axe bore into my shoulder, nearly hacking my arm off. Luckily, he failed."

Rose cringed. "And this one?" Her fingers glided through the water to his right side.

"That I got during a storm at sea coming back from Eristan when the ship was breaking apart. I was trying to salvage it when I saw a large wave coming for us. I tried to warn the men, and they moved just in time, but I wasn't so lucky. The wave came over the side of the ship and slammed me into a piece of wood from the mast sticking out from the floor, if you can believe it." He said it like a wound like that couldn't have easily taken his life.

Rose's gaze went to his forearm, tracing the red scar with her fingers.

"And you know how I got that one," he said softly, looking down at it with her.

She stared at the bright-red scar. "Do you realize you got all these scars by saving other people?" She finally looked up.

Roman paused, blinking. "I suppose you're right... I never thought of it like that."

She studied him, questioning if his humbleness was authentic. "Is that how you came by your nickname by your fellow soldiers?"

His eyes became guarded as he looked out at the water. "Yes. They started calling me Drengr after the battle at Clairborn."

"What does it mean?"

He diverted his gaze, hesitant to answer. "It's the most respected name a soldier can be given. It's an old term for someone young like me who, though inexperienced with battle, is bold, recklessly courageous, and doesn't back down in a fight. Someone who has a sense of fair play and doesn't fight those weaker than him."

"If it's an honor, why do you look unhappy they call you that?"

Roman's eyes fell to the water between them. "Because it's a title I don't believe I deserve."

She couldn't stand him looking so sad. She took his jaw gently in her hand, forcing his eyes to meet hers. He didn't resist her in the slightest. "Usually, someone who says they don't deserve something is exactly the one who deserves it."

He didn't say anything, simply looking back and forth between her eyes.

"If *I* started calling you that, would you believe it then?" she asked, challenging him.

His throat bobbed as he held her gaze steadfast. "I told you—I'll never doubt you again."

"Then that's what I'll call you when you start to doubt yourself… Drengr," she said, the name rolling off her tongue.

His body shivered against hers, his arms tightening around her waist, bringing her closer.

"Now you know how I feel when you call me Roe," she joked.

His eyes flashed with surprise while hers filled with horror, realizing she'd said the words aloud.

"I just meant—I just mean…" All she did was make herself sound more ridiculous.

He put a finger up to her lips, stopping her. "I know what you meant," he whispered, looking down at his thumb as he traced her bottom lip, causing something deep within her to stir.

She was set free when he dropped his hand back into the water, but as that same hand ran along her exposed thigh to hold her again, it made the desire in her turn ravenous. She wondered how his hands would feel in more sensitive places—

Tristan's face flashed in her mind.

"I think we should go back," she whispered, her voice not coming out as strong as she wanted it to.

He nodded, but his hands pressed her closer as he began to trudge his way back to the staircase. "You did well," he praised.

"It's easy with you," she said, realizing as she spoke the words that she truly felt that way.

Roman's fingers gripped her waist one final time before lowering her onto the stairs.

She instantly regretted her decision to leave the water when the cold mountain air hit her wet skin. Her hands shook as she grabbed her dress off the ground with Roman close behind.

He held his hand out. "Come on."

When she extended her own, he grabbed it and urged her along as they ran back. Roman brought her to another set of doors leading towards the back entry.

Warmer air greeted them as soon as they stepped over the threshold. She expected him to slow down, but he sped up, running with his hand still in hers. He cocked his head back to look at her as a nostalgic grin spread on his face—playfully, he tried to trip her, sticking his foot out obviously.

A game they used to play.

She returned the smile, trying to trip him back. He avoided her foot easily, earning a deep, rich laugh at her failed attempt.

The euphoric sound made her heart flutter like a hummingbird.

"You're just as terrible at this now as you were back then," he taunted.

And with one sentence, he unleashed her competitive side, driving her to go faster.

They raced up the main stairs, praying Gretta wouldn't see them dripping water in their underwear. When they reached the top of the stairs, they continued to dash through the hall of windows, racing against each other, playing in the bright moonlight.

She thought he'd let up when they came to the stairwell leading to Roman's room, but he surprised her by chasing her up the stairs—swiping at her ankles, making her laugh breathlessly.

At the top of the stairs, he attempted to trip her once more, but she shoved his shoulder, causing him to lose his balance, though he easily steadied himself with one hand. Undeterred, he snatched her ankle and successfully tripped her this time. She landed on the soft bedroom rug with a thud.

"No!" she pleaded.

A dangerous smile slipped onto Roman's lips as he dragged her to him, his hands climbing up her legs to her thighs, landing on her waist as he pinched her sides. Even though her skin was still wet and slippery, he held her firm, making her aware of just how easily Roman could overpower her if he wanted to, but she wasn't worried.

She'd never be with him.

"Stop! Stop!" She laughed as she clawed for freedom. "Stop!" she pleaded.

She twisted her body and her hand accidentally hit him square in the mouth, sending him off her.

His hands flew up to cradle his jaw as he flinched away.

She sat up at once, covering her mouth. "Oh! I'm so sorry. Are you okay?"

"Zareb trained you well, didn't he?" he grumbled, still covering his face with his hand.

"I didn't mean to hurt you."

It was all a ploy. As soon as she reached for him, he took hold of her wrists, flipping her onto her back. He pinned her arms above her head. His beautiful pink lips dipped into a lazy smile. "It hurt a little, but not that much."

She rolled her eyes as a grin of her own formed, her chest heaving for air.

The warm glow of the fire created dancing shadows over Roman's sun-kissed skin, his eyes so seldom full of joy she had to stop to admire the flawless creases.

She hadn't laughed that hard in… she couldn't remember. It was like a medicine she desperately needed—a simple, pure moment that transported her through time to when things were easy. His body weight on hers calmed and crazed her at the same time.

Giving in to her impulse, she lifted her hand out of his grasp and slowly raised it to his sharp jaw, tracing it lightly with her fingers.

Without hesitating, Roman leaned into her hand, placing more of his body weight on her as his arms lowered into a push-up position over her.

Her back arched. Her body silently begged for more, aching for him to grind his hips against hers. To intertwine her legs with his. To dig her nails into his back and pull him closer.

She felt irresponsible for even thinking it, but her thoughts kept spiraling.

"I hope you have more fight in you by morning because that was pitiful," Roman whispered, coaxing her as his lips hovered just above hers. "That is, unless you'd rather sleep in?"

"No, I want to," she answered quickly, not wanting him to change his mind.

Roman paused, his gaze dropping to her lips, staring at them before he let go of her hands.

He cleared his throat, lifting himself off her. "Then we'd better get some sleep." He reached down to help her stand, pulling her to her feet. "We'll go at sun up before it gets too hot. Then perhaps we can cool off with a swim again." He winked.

She sighed dramatically. "I was right. You *are* trying to kill me."

He gave her a crooked grin, making her want to lay right back down on the floor with him. "It'll be worth the result. Trust me. Get some rest… I'll see you in the morning."

She nodded, tucking her wet hair behind her ear, the tips soaking the rug.

"I hope you like goose feathers," he called over his shoulder on his way out.

Once he'd left, she let out a breath. *What are you doing, Rose?* she scolded herself.

She wrapped her arms around her waist, trembling from the cold as she gazed at the empty room, feeling like somehow it had become vastly larger than it had been earlier.

She headed to the tub to rinse off the lake water before returning to the closet to select a nightgown. Though there was a plethora to choose from, many of Harriet's pajamas were short and lacy. To her pleasant surprise, most of Roman's clothes still hung in the closet, too. So, of course, she took the liberty of going through them.

One white shirt in particular stood out to her. She pulled it out and tried it on, curious to see how it'd fit. The oversized garment fell just above her knees, the fabric butter-soft against her skin. Out of instinct, she brought the collar to her nose, smelling it. His musky scent filled her lungs. She decided she'd wear it to bed, seeing as it was as good as any nightdress.

After she blew out the candles, she crawled across the soft, feathered duvet and sank into the sheets. The movement sent a waft of air up into her nose—even the bed smelled like him. She laid her head on the goose-feathered pillow, cradling it as she curled up into the sheets, closing her eyes.

As the minutes passed, she feared she wouldn't be able to fall asleep. A sickening realization swept over her that this would be the first night she had slept alone since... since the wedding. She smothered any and all thoughts of Tristan until she was sure they wouldn't be resurrected.

Instead, she thought about the day she'd just had. How, for the first time in months, she'd laughed freely. That, at last, she'd finally earned a smile from Roman—how she'd gotten into the water without returning with a traumatic experience.

She held on to those good thoughts, and for the first time in a long time, she looked forward to the days ahead.

CHAPTER 59

The next morning, Gretta came to wake Rose, setting a small tray of tea and biscuits beside her bed, readily opening the curtains. The sun wasn't even in the sky, but the soft glow behind the mountains signaled it'd soon make its appearance.

After eating a few bites, Rose got dressed, putting on black leather pants and a tight tunic for sparring. She tied her hair up and out of her face, adding a cloak to her ensemble. Once ready, she headed downstairs to find Roman, who was already waiting at the bottom of the main staircase. He looked worn, his eyes more hollow than usual, and the whites of them were slightly pink.

"Ready?" he asked, sounding normal enough to make her worries dissipate.

"Where are we going?"

"Not far; there's a spot on the west side of the lake I think will do just fine. Close enough we won't need the horses."

The woods were calm and quiet that morning, the forest creatures still sleeping before waking to survive another day. Highland Haven faded further into the distance as they trudged on. The lake gently brushed against the rocks in tiny waves, its deep-blue hue lightening as the sun pushed upward into the sky.

In front of her, Roman took lengthy, powerful strides, moving with ease as he weaved through the forest. No one would ever guess he'd grown up in a castle. She had to remind herself that he had just spent the last year with nothing but a patch of dirt to call home.

Roman stopped when they reached a clearing. It was a little smaller than the one she was used to training in with Zareb but similar. He set his canteen down along with his bag. "This is where we'll train today. We won't ever spar in the same place twice. You'll need to get used to new surroundings."

When Rose didn't respond, Roman looked over his shoulder. "You look nervous."

"I've never sparred with anyone but Warren and Zareb. I'm afraid they may have over-praised me," she said, fearing she wouldn't meet his expectations—that he'd discover he was wasting his time.

He closed the distance between them, looking straight into her eyes. "Don't ever sell yourself short."

She blinked a few times before giving him a small nod, her heart slightly warmed by his confidence.

He positioned himself in the center of the field. "I want you to do your best." He unsheathed his sword. "You'll advance first."

She drew her sword, widening her stance. For the first time, she observed him as an opponent. Roman had few weaknesses—his right arm might pose a hindrance due to the poisoned arrow wound. His shoulder injury might limit his mobility. His muscles had been built up over years of dedication and strength training—but it would make him an easier target. Unfortunately, that was where her advantages ended. She'd have to be quick and precise in her movements, try to exhaust him by making him chase her. But even so, he'd be difficult to beat.

After all, he was the general of Cathan for a reason.

Roman patiently waited for her to make the first move, swirling the sword lazily in his hand.

She leapt into action, striking with speed. This time, unlike their first encounter, he was prepared, blocking her attempts. Their movements fell into a sort of rhythm—she would advance, he would defend, and then he would advance, and she would mostly avoid. The longer they sparred, the more free-flowing their swordplay became. It evolved into an actual fight, and Rose became more confident.

Roman's strength was undeniable—he was so strong that her sword flew from her hands more than once, no matter how hard she gripped it.

She managed to keep him on his toes, though, wearing him down slowly, still holding her ground—that was, until Roman cornered her near the tree line.

Losing focus of her surroundings, her elbow hit the base of the trunk. Her arm ricocheted, making her feet stumble.

Roman seized the moment, striking to disarm her with a powerful blow. But in his lunge forward, he left his left side vulnerable.

She shifted her weight to avoid his blow, twisting herself at near-inhuman speed, stopping her blade just before it hit his neck.

He held up his hand in surrender.

A dangerous smile claimed her lips.

The taunt raised something in Roman, alright. He clenched his jaw, becoming determined. "Again," he ordered.

And so the morning went on. They sparred for so long, large beads of sweat dripped down from her brow to her chin. Round after round, Roman won, once sending her flat on her back. He demonstrated a better way to deflect a blunt blow like he'd done, instructing her to let it roll off her shoulder rather than to try to deflect.

When the sun was at its peak and their water was gone, they stopped—the shadows of the pines now facing the opposite direction.

"That was good," Roman commended, out of breath.

"You were holding back," Rose said with disappointment, a seed of doubt planted in her mind.

"Actually, Rose." He paused to catch his breath. "I wasn't."

She raised her eyebrows, not believing him.

"You're wicked fast," Roman praised, looking at her like she had performed some miracle. "Zareb was far downplaying your abilities to you. I've trained thousands of soldiers, and not one has gotten so far in such a short period. You're a natural, truly." He studied her like he was contemplating something. After a long pause he said, "I have a somewhat large favor to ask you."

Her brow quirked. "What's that?"

"I told you I have some business in Caleede, and I was wondering if you'd be willing to come with. I could use your help."

Rose straightened, surprised. Whatever it was, it beat sitting alone at the manor thinking of Tri—*things*. "What kind of business, exactly?"

"Let's just call it post-war efforts," he said, avoiding the root question. "Every ten years, the capital holds a race called the Snorri. But it's not just any race. The riders race on sleipnirs—beasts with—"

"Eight legs," she finished his sentence, remembering the magical creatures from the pages she'd read. Sleipnirs were incredibly strong, fast creatures—one of the oldest species in Vallor, if she remembered correctly. However, the horse-like beasts were notorious for being hazardous. Many men had gone to great lengths to touch one, let alone ride one. She could only imagine what it must take to train a sleipnir like that.

"Isn't it illegal to race them?" she questioned, recalling the law.

Roman squinted as he swayed his head back and forth like it was a gray area. "In theory, yes. But the man in charge of the race gets enforcers to look the other way. He claims it's how they raise money for the city's needs, but we all know it's a ploy to pay off the politicians to allow them to do so. The race generates a handsome sum of money, and even more on gambling."

"I don't understand. What's this got to do with post-war efforts?"

"Because the man in charge is named Felix Moretti. He's a powerful man with important information about a group of insurgents we've been looking for. They've been pillaging, destroying, and killing hundreds of innocent people in cities throughout Cathan."

Rose's mind went back to the night she'd overheard the council. Was that what they were discussing? Was this group of insurgents responsible for causing all the mayhem in Cathan?

Roman continued, "We've tried finding them on our own, but I don't know a soul who knows anything about them other than Moretti. I've tried meeting with him myself, but he and I have a… rough history. But he'll be at the event to watch the races. Which is where you come in."

"What can I do?" She still didn't see her part in this.

His face grew uneasy—dare she say hesitant. "He's particularly fond of… pretty women."

Rose cocked an eyebrow. "You want me to seduce him?"

"Persuade," he corrected. "He's a man who's obsessed with things he wants but can't have. I know if he saw you, he'd seek you out. You don't have to do anything except dangle yourself in front of him. Flirt with him. Get his attention. Make him want to know you. You just have to get close enough to put this—" he nicked a small bag of lotus powder from his bag, "—into his drink. Once you have, get him to tell you where the men are hiding. I know it's a lot to ask, but I wouldn't if I weren't sure you'd be safe." Roman paused, letting her think. "Before you agree, I have to warn you, it won't be pretty. The atmosphere will be quite different than you're used to, much like the tavern."

Rose chewed on the inside of her cheek, thinking about what he was asking. She did her best to suppress the same memory that threatened to surface at the tavern.

He pulled her out of her daze, asking, "What is it?"

Her eyes met his with uncertainty. "It's just… what if he doesn't like me?"

Roman barked a harsh laugh. "I tell you all this, and *that's* what you're worried about?"

She wasn't laughing.

"Trust me, that'll be the least of your worries. But if you don't want to, I complet—"

"I'll do it," she interrupted.

Roman paused. "You're sure?"

"Yes, I want to help." If she could make a difference by gathering information, she would at least try.

He nodded slowly, his expression growing determined. "Okay then, I'll make the arrangements and… get ready—because the race is in three days."

CHAPTER 60

Rose recruited Gretta to help pick a dress for the Snorri, explaining she needed something sure to be eye-catching. With a few prodding questions from Gretta, she admitted she was trying to attract a particular lord's attention.

"Well, tell me. Who is it, lass? I grew up in Caleede, I know practically every high lord there is," Gretta said, placing a hand on her hips. "Which one is it?"

"I believe it's—Moretti?"

Gretta's eyes widened. "*Felix* Moretti?" she clarified, exhaling a large puff of air. "You certainly reach for the stars, don't you?"

Rose ignored the comment. "What's he like?"

"Well, for starters, he's the richest and most influential man in the capital," Gretta stated, like it was well-known gossip. "He controls everything. Nothing goes on in the city he doesn't know about. If that wasn't enough to tempt you, he's also an incredibly handsome lad, but he's reckless to be sure. That man loves nothing more than a bag of money and status. He's yet to marry, which makes him the most eligible bachelor in Cathan. Women come from far and wide to try to catch his eye. But for some reason or another, he's denied them all. I'm afraid you'll have to go bold with this one."

Rose groaned internally. For some reason, she'd pictured Moretti as an older, plain lord with low expectations. Gaining the attention of an average man was one thing, but fighting for it against a sea of women was another beast entirely.

Gretta stepped over to the closet. "Let's see..." she mumbled, rummaging through the clothes. "Ah! Here. If you want to catch Moretti's eye, you'll want to wear this."

She looked up at the dress Gretta held.

If one could even call it that.

Rose's eyes widened in fear. "*That*? That's what you think I should wear?" Where in Vallor did someone even find a dress like that?

"Trust me, lass. This is what you need. Go on, try it on... Best you don't show Roman until you get there," Gretta added in a whisper, as if he could hear.

Rose slipped into the delicate dress made of shiny, scale-like fabric. The neckline dipped at the back to her shoulder blades, with shoulder pads that flared up and outward like small wings. Its sweetheart neckline beautifully lined her collarbone, and the scaled fabric hugged her body before gently reaching the floor. Two long slits reached her upper thighs, revealing her long, lean legs as she walked.

She faced the mirror, and although it exposed more skin than she preferred, she couldn't help but admit she felt... *new*, like the dress gave her permission to be someone different. Someone more confident. Someone she could very well like.

"You see?" Gretta grasped her shoulders and ushered her into the sunlight.

Rose sucked in a breath as the rays hit the scales. The dress burst into a sea of glittering gold, lighting up the room.

"When you enter the light, you'll shine like a goddess."

She had to admit, it was eye-catching, just as she had asked. "Okay... I guess this is the dress."

Gretta gave a satisfied smile. "You'll be the talk of the city by the time the day is over," she added with a wink. "Now to curl this lion's mane of yours." She grabbed a handful of Rose's hair.

Even as efficient as she was, Gretta spent over an hour curling it all.

She told her she didn't have to, but Gretta insisted "it completed the look." Gretta helped her put on a bit of makeup, using a golden highlighter and bronzer to accentuate her cheekbones. For her lips, she chose a light-pink shade, plumping them to look like fresh dew. Lastly, Gretta wrapped her up in a large cloak, doing it up all the way so no one would see the dress until she was at the race.

She slipped out the front doors, expecting Roman to be saddling the horses, but instead, a fancy black carriage was waiting for her.

Roman had dressed up for the occasion, too. He wore a black cloak over his leather tunic, with a V-neck and a popped collar, and trousers that matched. His hair had been left down in large, soft waves. Though he looked dashing, she didn't miss how his eyes still seemed a tad more sunken than usual.

"I thought this might be a welcomed change for today," he said, sounding just fine. He offered her a hand.

"I'd say," she agreed with a grateful smile, taking his hand as he guided her down the steps.

"Are you sure you still want to do this? Just say the word, and I'll find another way."

"No. I want to help… plus I just spent about two hours getting ready, so we are definitely going *somewhere*," she said in a sour voice, huffing.

His lips pulled into a crooked smile, sending her heart into an annoying flutter. "It's hard to see your hard work when you have a cloak on."

She winked. "That's the point. I want it to be a surprise."

He was about to turn but stopped mid-movement. His eyes narrowed. "You didn't go overboard, did you?"

"You mean, did I pick out a much-too-revealing dress? Yes, I did," she teased—well, partly.

His mouth tightened into a hard line. "Don't make me regret asking you—I already have second thoughts."

"Don't worry." She hiked up her cloak and dress to reveal a knife she had strapped to her upper thigh. "You see? I'll be fine."

He rolled his eyes. "Wonderful," he droned.

She paused, studying his eyes again before finally saying, "Are you sure you're feeling alright? You look a little pale."

"I'm fine," Roman said, brushing her off. "Now, get into the carriage before I come to my senses and change my mind."

The journey to Caleede was shorter than she had expected. Their carriage took the narrow path out of the mountains, reconnecting with the main road heading north. A plentiful number of other carriages and wagons joined them, all making their way to the city.

Excitement danced in her stomach. She'd never been to the capital. Her mother had strictly forbidden it, claiming there was too much "riffraff." Which was absurd because every other noblewoman boasted about its exquisite shopping and delicious dining. After all, it was called the gem of Cathan for a reason.

Even with her high expectations, she was unprepared for the grand city's glory.

It lay in a valley nestled between three mountains that shielded it from invaders. If that wasn't enough, an impenetrable stone wall encased the city, its borders stretching miles out of sight. As they drew nearer, she tried to estimate its height; it must've been nearly fifty feet tall. The main gate was swarming with guards and security, giving every vessel a thorough search before letting them pass. It took near an hour just to get through it all.

Once they'd made it past the gates, a wealthy city welcomed her. The roads were cleaner than any city she had ever seen, even as traders and farmers crowded the cobblestone streets, flocking to sell their goods thanks to the influx of visitors for the Snorri. Though the city was old, every building looked like it'd been well taken care of for generations.

Despite the miles of roads and sandwiched buildings, a mixture of shrubs, trees, and flowers flourished everywhere they went, with thick vines climbing buildings, both new and old. She was absolutely fascinated by the turquoise canal system that channeled the mountain runoff to the city, allowing large rowboats to easily transport goods from one side to the other. It flowed through hundreds of tunnels and bridges throughout the city, offering the perfect solution to alleviate heavy road congestion—it was genius, really.

"Do you like it?" Roman asked, noticing her eyes glued to the window.

"It's magnificent," she said. The rumors didn't do it justice. "It must cost a fortune to keep this place so clean and beautiful."

"You can thank Moretti for that," he uttered in distaste.

His tone didn't go unnoticed. "What happened between you two?"

He looked out the window. "I'm the reason a large stream of his revenue was discontinued. We found out that he may have sold a good chunk of illegal goods to our enemies during the war. I put a stop to it and tried to get him thrown into prison for it. Needless to say, he bribed his way out of serving his time. He's been rather unfond of me ever since."

The carriage veered left, moving westward toward the city's outskirts. Though it took some time to reach, she didn't mind, soaking in every beautiful speck of the city. She couldn't tear her eyes away from the busy life around her, wishing she could stay and explore the libraries, shops, and gardens they passed.

Finally, the stadium came into view, and her jaw dropped.

She quickly concluded that she had *severely* underestimated how popular the Snorri was.

A long, crooked line of carriages crept toward the building at a glacier pace, while even more trekked on foot. Hundreds upon hundreds of people gathered, crowding the front gate.

Her throat dried. She'd never seen so many bodies in her life.

When their carriage reached the front, Roman threw on his hood and exited the carriage. She followed suit as they were forced to walk the rest of the way on foot. He kept close to Rose as they fought the crowd to the main arched entrance.

After standing in another long line, they reached the front gate.

"Two tickets," Roman requested, sliding four gold coins to the gatekeeper.

The short, wide, rough-looking man who smelled strongly of body odor snatched the coins quickly. "Right. Bettin' station is down atta way, bathrooms are up atta way," the man grumbled, gesturing to the left and right. "Cause any trouble and you'll be threwn out without a refund. Bes' be in your seat when the race starts." He slid their tickets to them, along with a pamphlet.

They merged into yet another line to find their seats among the wooden bleachers. Now, up close, she grasped just how enormous the stadium was. The lofty walls loomed high above them as they shuffled like sardines to the bleachers. There had to be nearly a hundred rows to accommodate them all.

Her eyes widened when she caught sight of the racetrack. It was made up of a wide dirt path, winding and extending for *miles*, so far that she couldn't see it all from the ground. In the distance, four tall watchtowers, similar to the wooden bleachers, stood at each checkpoint to give viewers an up-close look—assuming their pockets could afford it.

It was an event unlike any she'd ever seen. Which she supposed wasn't saying much since she'd hardly seen *anything* in her short, sheltered life.

She needed to get out more.

Spectators of all ages eagerly waited for the race to start. Children no older than ten years old stood at the railings, holding up small flags with different colors and symbols she could only assume were the riders' emblems.

"Where are we supposed to find him?" she asked, squinting upward at the grand bleachers, the majority already filled.

Roman pointed to the very top balconies. "Those are for anyone important. Moretti will be sitting up there with his entourage."

She gulped, peering up at the hovering balconies as a knot of nerves bundled within her chest.

"Shall we take a look at the sleipnirs first? See where we should place our bets?" Roman teased with a smirk, gesturing to the giant covered stables.

She cringed at the mention of gambling, but nonetheless she followed, curious to see more.

The stables were crowded, primarily filled with men gathered around each stall, observing the creatures. A good number chatted at the back gate, surrounding a wide blackboard hung on the stable's wall. Numerous numbers and charts were scribbled on it, which she guessed were intended to assist them in deciding on which sleipnir to place their bets.

With her curiosity piqued, she sauntered over to the closest oversized stall.

As soon as she saw the beast, she took an involuntary step back.

It must have been over seven feet tall. She knew they would be big, but nothing like this. Not only did their height overwhelm her, but also their muscled bodies, each one of their eight legs rippling with them. This sleipnir, in particular, was white, with midnight-blue hair that matched its large eyes.

She gaped at the sleipnir in wonder, knowing full well that a beast like that could kick the door open with one leg, free itself, and flatten every single one of them.

She tore her eyes from the beast, walking down to see the others, all a variety of colors, she discovered. One was red with bright-orange hair, one dark-green with white hair, another purple with a black mane. Some of them bore markings, while others were solid-colored.

There was one sleipnir in particular that only a handful of men bothered to look at. It was pure black, with hair to match. Even its eyes were black as coal—without a doubt, the most intimidating of the bunch. She wondered why no one was betting on such obvious winning potential.

Roman snatched her from the crowd, pulling her between two of the stalls. "There he is," he whispered, gesturing to one of the gentlemen looking at the black sleipnir.

Felix Moretti was younger than she imagined, likely in his mid-thirties. He had a lean and muscular figure, not as big as Roman or Zareb, but he certainly looked like he could hold his own. His tousled dark-brown hair fell just above his shoulders, framing sharp facial features that boasted a thick, short, well-groomed beard with smooth, light golden-brown skin. Despite his dark traits, he had dazzling light-blue eyes.

It was no wonder women came from far and wide to try to catch his eye.

"He can't see me with you or else he'll suspect something's off," Roman whispered, tugging at his hood to cover his face. "But I promise I'll never be far. You'll never leave my sight. If you need help or anything goes wrong, don't hesitate to call out." He handed her the small pouch of powder.

Rose nicked it, stuffing it into her dress. She reached for her cloak, untying it before letting it slip down off her shoulders, revealing her golden dress. She smoothed her curls, stealing a glance at Roman as she handed him her cloak.

His eyes bulged out of their sockets. "Rose," he growled, grabbing her arm before she could leave. "What the hell is that?"

She glared at him, irritated at his clear disapproval. "A dress?"

"You in a normal dress would've been enough." His eyes ran up and down her again. "This… this will draw attention."

"Isn't that the point?"

His jaw tightened. "If the bastard touches you—"

"You won't do anything. Don't let your temper give us away. I can take care of myself—you know I can. He won't do anything I can't handle."

Roman glared at her so hard and long, she thought he might just drag her back to the manor.

"This was your idea."

"Don't remind me," he said through gritted teeth, finally letting go of her arm. "Just… be careful."

She gave him a firm nod. "Wish me luck."

Before Roman could stop her, she escaped, slithering back into the crowd, strutting towards Moretti, who was still in the same spot talking to the four men who surrounded him.

Moretti had no idea what was coming for him.

CHAPTER 61

The stares Rose attracted as she walked through the stables made her self-conscious. Perhaps Roman had been right to second-guess her choice. But it was too late to back out now. She tucked away the insecurity and held her chin high, pretending to admire the beasts.

Out of the corner of her eye, she caught one of Moretti's friends openly staring at her with approving eyes. As she neared, he leaned toward Moretti, whispering something in his ear.

Moretti's gaze flickered to her, then back to his friend, and then snapped back to her.

Rose did her best to pretend she didn't see any of it, her eyes lingering on the black beast. But then, ever so strategically, she met his bright blue eyes.

She kept her face uninterested, letting her eyes roam over him, assessing his worth. Then, without offering anything else, her eyes abandoned his and she continued to walk, fully aware his were still locked on her.

"Excuse me, miss," a deep voice called behind her.

The faintest smile of victory pulled at her lips. She slipped it off before she spun around.

"May I be so bold as to ask for your help?" Moretti asked, flashing her a razor smile.

"What help would I be, exactly?" she asked, keeping her voice smooth and lush.

"Help settle a debate between me and my colleagues," he explained, tilting his head to the four men behind him.

Rose took a few lazy steps forward, folding her arms. "And what debate is that?"

"I was hoping you could tell me what I ought to do about this sleipnir." He cast his gaze up to the giant dark beast. "He's turned out to be quite the handful. Trampled his rider to death this morning, I'm afraid." He spoke so casually it was as though it was nothing more than an inconvenience. "Which puts quite the damper on this fine race people have paid good money to see. We're debating whether to let another rider race him or to take our loss and kill the beast. You see, they're afraid he's too wild to tame."

Kill it? Her eyes flashed. "What do *you* say?"

"I'd like him to live to see another day," Moretti confessed, showing mercy. "Sleipnirs are quite the investment, you see—finding them, training them, breeding them. But my friends—" he glanced over his shoulder at them, "—aren't convinced a rider will take him due to his history. I find my hands are tied if that's the case." His gaze came back to her. "I am curious to hear what you, as an unbiased third party, would have to say on the matter."

She shifted her eyes to the beast, ignoring the four men's leering stares as she stalked past them up to the sleipnir's stall for a better look, determined to keep her face devoid of the fear that was clamoring inside.

She looked up into the beast's dark, coal eyes, staring back at her, expecting to see a wild, untamed fire, but she found nothing but a puff of smoke. Her attention turned to the sleipnir's powerful body, marked by scars strewn across its abdomen.

"These scars. What are they from?" she asked.

Moretti tilted his head, his interest piqued by the question. "They're from the riders training them, of course."

"With?"

"A sharp rod." He didn't hide the fact, nor look ashamed.

She hid her disgust. "It's no wonder he trampled him," she said, her voice hardened, forgetting she was supposed to be witty and charming.

The sleipnir blinked as it shifted its snout towards her, its ears twitching.

Moretti raised an eyebrow. "It is custom. Every sleipnir is trained this way."

"Just because it's the way things are, doesn't mean it's what should be."

Truer words were never spoken, a soft foreign voice spoke in her mind.

Her eyes whipped to the sleipnir, doing her best to hide her shock as she said, *Can you hear me?* She spoke to it in her mind like the sea beast and the phoenix.

Yes, he answered, his voice surprisingly warm and gentle. His mind brushed against hers, letting her know he would not hurt her if she did the same.

I'm Rose, she introduced herself. *I come as a friend. I won't hurt you.*

I know you won't, he replied. *Your heart is far too kind.*

They are debating whether or not to keep you, she explained. *They insist you take another rider or they'll kill you.*

I don't want any of them riding me again, the sleipnir seethed in disdain. *I'd rather die. If you were me, you'd say the same.*

Her eyes softened with empathy. She reached to touch his thick, soft, silky hair, gently placing her palm on his cheek. Moretti took a quick, nervous step forward, but his face relaxed in awe, watching her interact with the sleipnir.

I understand how you feel, she said. Her father had taught her the same way that rod had taught the sleipnir—violence for obedience.

It was then she got the stupidest idea she'd ever had in her entire life. *Would you let me ride you?*

She could feel the surprise within the sleipnir's mind. *If it's you, I will. But only you.*

She faced Moretti. "I think you should let him race."

Moretti stepped closer. "I agree, but it still doesn't solve the problem that no one dares ride him."

"I will." She sounded bolder than she felt.

The four men burst into laughter. However, Moretti didn't laugh with them.

"You wish to be his rider?" he probed, intrigued.

She held his gaze. "That's what I said."

"You recall the part where I told you he just killed a man this morning," Moretti reminded her, pointing out the obvious.

"He won't hurt me."

"Have you ever seen a race? What happens to the riders?"

"No," she admitted. But she lifted her chin, keeping her head high. "But I'm an excellent horse rider and a fast learner."

Moretti's lips curled into a sly smile. "I admire your courage, truly. But fast learner or not, it's too dangerous. I can't allow someone with such a pretty face to die unnecessarily."

"Me being a rider would generate more money than you've ever made before," she pointed out, trying to appeal to his greed.

"As true as that is, your death would also put a damper on things."

It was clear she'd have to try a different approach. "Perhaps I could make you a deal. You like making bets. Let me race. If I win, I keep the sleipnir."

His eyes quirked. "And if you lose?"

"I'll do whatever you want," she said with a cautious gaze.

Moretti's handsome face morphed into a dangerous smirk.

She had him now.

He assessed her with admiration. "Alright. If you lose—" he brushed her cheek with his knuckles, "—you come home with me."

"Deal," she agreed. "But don't get your hopes up. I may not look like much, but I'm full of surprises."

He gave a heartless laugh. It was clear he liked the game. "What's your name, sweetheart?"

"Draya. Draya Santres," she lied, spitting out the first name that came into her head.

"My name is Felix, Felix Moretti. Now, let's get you saddled up."

No saddles, the sleipnir said. He must have felt her mortification because he added, *Trust me.*

"Thank you, but I'll ride bareback," she said, pretending to have all the confidence in the world.

Moretti's brows raised, questioning her judgment yet again, but for some reason, he let her put herself in danger. "I hope you know what you're doing, Ms. Santres." His voice was laced with warning.

"Oh, don't worry… I'm an excellent rider," she drawled with a smirk, knowing the insinuation would drive him wild.

Moretti's lips slipped into a serpentine smile, his colleagues practically drooling behind him. "As you wish," he agreed with a light nod. "I'll go tell the supervisors the good news. The race starts in fifteen minutes." He leaned in closer again, lowering his voice to a whisper. "I'd wish you good luck, but I'd be lying to both of us," he confessed huskily into her ear, pulling back to look her dead in the eye before leaving.

Panic attacked her as she watched him strut away. Shit. What had she just agreed to?

I won't let anything happen to you, the sleipnir's calming voice rang through her mind.

She gazed up at the terrifying beast. *I'm putting my trust in you. I know nothing of these races.*

We'll win, he willed in confidence.

Rose wished she was so sure. She peered down at her dress, now more than ever regretting her outfit choice. Her legs would be rubbed raw. She needed to find different clothing.

Stay in that, the sleipnir recommended. *It's light, and it's better your legs are bare. They'll hold better to my body.*

Rose couldn't hide her skepticism. *How can that be?*

Come closer and feel, the sleipnir invited.

She opened up the gate, feeling remarkably small next to the giant beast. Her bare hands glided over its soft hair, although they weren't *gliding* at all. As soon as she tried, her hand refused to move. It was as if the fibers of its hair somehow became magnetic.

Incredible, she said, astounded. *Why don't the other racers do this?*

We won't let them touch us bare. This alone will give us an advantage, the sleipnir boasted with pride.

She peered at the other sleipnir handlers and riders, each of whom wore gloves.

"Rose," a harsh voice called.

She whirled, finding Roman's hooded figure staring at her back. "What the hell are you doing?" His eyes flickered anxiously to the sleipnir.

She looked around before pulling him into the stall.

He stiffened, eyeing the sleipnir with hesitation, but the creature was the least of their worries.

"It's okay, he won't hurt us. Listen, I've agreed to be a rider."

Roman's honed body became deathly still as his eyes darkened into a shade deeper than the beast beside her. "Tell me you're joking."

"You're going to have to trust me. I know what I'm doing."

Lies, and he knew it.

In slow, dangerous movements, he stalked toward her, herding her into the corner of the stall. He lifted his hands on either side of her head as he leaned in, leaving her breaths uneven. "I thought the plan was to get Moretti's attention. Not a death wish."

"That's exactly what I'm doing. This will get his attention far more than any amount of flirting. We made a deal: if I lose—which is highly likely—I'll have to go home with him."

Roman's mouth twisted into a snarl. "I don't want you *sleeping* with him," he hissed.

"I wasn't planning on it," she shot back.

"I'm not letting you. You'll get yourself killed. These riders have been training for this for years. *Years*. Do you know what they're like? They're cold, ruthless brutes, all of them. They won't think twice before knocking you off your sleipnir. You have absolutely no idea what you're walking into."

"I won't get hurt. I have a plan. Somehow, I can speak to the sleipnir like I spoke to the phoenix. I'll be fine."

He gawked at her like she'd grown two heads. "This whole thing was a mistake. We're going back. Right now." He turned to leave.

Rose held her ground, grabbing his arm and spinning him back to face her. She cupped his face, drawing him so close he had to brace against the wall again to avoid colliding with her. "Remember when you told me you'd never doubt me again?" she coaxed, realizing she was trying to use what little charm she had on him. "I need you to do that for me right now."

His eyes faltered, but his jaw clenched in frustration. "I couldn't live with myself if something happened to you," he confessed in a whisper, so vulnerable her heart soared at the sentiment. He was worried about her, for her safety.

Fool. She was a simpering fool to let such a tiny gesture have so much power.

"Nothing will happen to me," she promised. "Trust me."

His conflicted eyes fought an internal battle as a mixture of emotions ran across his face. "Damn you." He caved, letting out a loud breath. "What can I do?"

She leaned in closer to his lips. Roman's muscles tensed under her hands. "Help me get on," she blurted before she did anything stupid, nodding to the sleipnir.

Roman surrendered, defeated. His large hands slid down, gripping her thighs, hoisting her legs around his solid waist. His golden eyes clouded with what she could only hope was desire.

He pressed his forehead against hers and said in a fierce whisper, "You better fucking come back to me. You hear me? I thought I lost you once... Don't you dare make me live through that again." His cheek brushed against hers, pressing his lips against her neck just under her ear.

The light kiss ignited her body into pure flame, creating a burning desire the likes she'd never felt. Not with Tristan, not with Xavier—

Not with anyone.

The next moment, Roman hoisted her up onto the beast. She slipped onto the sleipnir's back easier than she expected, securing herself by tightening her legs around him while her hands reached for his long black mane for support. As she settled, she sensed people staring, watching in awe as whispers filled the stalls.

She paid no attention to them as she gazed down at Roman, who anchored her. He looked as if he was thinking about ripping her back off the sleipnir. But he tore his eyes over to the gate, opening it and stretching it out wide.

His stare was still searing into her back as she rode out.

She had no idea what she was about to face.

CHAPTER 62

Despite Rose's lack of experience, riding a sleipnir felt intuitive, similar to riding a horse in a sense—but far more frightening. She had to make a constant conscious effort not to be swayed back and forth by the sleipnir's movements. Make no mistake, her core muscles would be aching in the morning, but she knew that falling off could lead to being trampled—not exactly the way she'd prefer to go.

Murmurs of surprise rumbled throughout the stadium as she arrived at the starting line. The bleachers were filled to the brim, leaving her in awe at the thousands upon thousands of faces staring down at them. She tried not to look, not wanting to add any more anxiety to her head space.

She kept her eyes on the wide dirt track, observing the terrain. It looked flat for the most part, but consequently, she couldn't even see the majority of it from the ground. And though it was sunny, the weather was about to take a turn, stormy gray clouds encroaching the skyline.

It's a bit more complex of a track this year, the sleipnir said. *Mostly flat with a few hills, trees, a jump, and a mud pit. There's also a wide river crossing, which will be our biggest battle.*

A heavy weight of fear settled in her gut. *How do you get through water?*

It's quite straightforward, really. You just need enough speed to propel you through the stream. Our legs do the rest. Most riders will get off and swim alongside us, but you'll stay on my back, seeing as you're not a swimmer.

How do you know that?

I can sense your fear of water, the sleipnir revealed. *Strange for your kind.*

She suppressed an eye roll. *What else do I need to know?*

The jumps. They come faster than you think. When they do, stay light. Open your chest and shoulders. Keep your weight in your heels and legs. Whatever you do, don't fall off, or you'll die.

Dually noted.

The sleipnir seemed amused. *Don't worry. You're a natural, I can tell. Even now, I can feel you are at ease.*

Much thanks to you, Rose said in truth.

"You lost, princess?" a rough voice called, interrupting her internal dialogue and drawing her attention to the rider at the adjacent gate.

He was a large, beefy man with sleeve tattoos covering both arms and exposed shoulders. He had long, auburn hair and a bushy beard to match. The sleipnir he rode was blood red with a white mane, sitting an inch taller than hers, and it had twice the number of scars on its abdomen. His dark eyes fixated on her, scanning her body with a lustful grin. Her skin crawled.

She refused to look him in the eye.

He didn't like being ignored.

"Are you here to wave the flag for us?" the man asked, taunting her as he put his elbow on his massive thigh, leaning over the gate. "Or perhaps to put that pretty mouth to good use," he joked with a wink as the other riders laughed.

She clenched her teeth in disgust but stayed silent, refusing to give him the satisfaction of a reaction. Despite her efforts, the man kept gawking.

"You mute, princess?" he asked loudly.

"Sometimes they're the best kind," another rider joked, earning yet another eruption of laughter.

"Why don't you come over here and I'll let you ride more than just this sleipnir?" the bearded man encouraged with a venomous smile, patting his lap.

She nearly threw up in her mouth. She was about to lose her patience—

"Go suck your own cock, Halmar. We all know you're the only one who has," Moretti shouted as he came into view, strutting across the starting line.

The other riders "Ooohed," laughing as Moretti came over directly to Rose and her sleipnir. He gazed up at her from the ground. "Don't worry about him. He's only worried he'll lose all the money he just bet on himself," he said, glancing over at Halmar with a mocking laugh.

Halmar wasn't amused but said nothing, swiping his reins into his hands as he looked away.

Moretti lowered his voice, speaking directly to her, a humorous glint lingering in those bright blue eyes. "I'm giving you one last chance to forfeit and come home with me now. Any second thoughts?"

"Not one," Rose assured him, flashing him a tight, flirtatious smile, pretending to be confident.

Halmar fumed at the smile she gave Moretti, cursing under his breath.

Moretti returned the gesture with a lopsided smirk that would make any maiden swoon. "May I give you something, then?" he asked, holding something small in his hands.

She hesitated before stretching her hand out.

Moretti took her hand and slid a ring onto her middle finger—a dainty gold band with a small black oval gem.

Her mouth hung open, hating how the gesture made her defenses crack—she supposed she was a little like her mother.

"For good luck," he said, squeezing her palm gently before letting go.

She lifted her hand, inspecting it. "Thank you," she said, taken aback by how much she liked it. "It's beautiful."

"Just like you," Moretti praised, taking a few steps backward, then adding with another grin, "Try not to die out there."

She didn't know what to say, still unsure of the stranger. With one last glance, Moretti strode off back to the stands, all the riders straightening in their saddles as he passed.

She watched him depart with a new curiosity. Her eyes fell back down to the ring on her hand.

He likes you, the sleipnir said. *A lot.*

How do you know? she asked.

That ring symbolizes intention and protection, the sleipnir said, with a light scoff. *As if he stands a chance.*

She was shocked at the idea of Moretti already having such thoughts. *He only met me minutes ago. He couldn't care less if I live or die.*

On the contrary. He cares very much, the sleipnir stated as if he knew it for a fact. *That was a calculated display of support. He wants people to know he is rooting for you.*

She contemplated the idea. *Only because we're making him a lot of money.*

That, too, the sleipnir agreed, *but it doesn't make the former any less true.*

Rose's gaze went to the stand, searching for Roman, but he was nowhere to be found. Slowly, she touched her neck, her fingertips brushing the spot still burning from his kiss. Her heartbeat quickened as she replayed the scene in her mind.

How does Roman feel about me? she asked.

I won't tell you, the sleipnir replied.

Why not? You didn't seem to have a problem telling me about Moretti.

Because it's a question you need to ask him yourself. Felix doesn't matter to you. Roman does, the sleipnir stated as if all knowing. *You like him. I could tell by the flutter of your heartbeats when he touched you.*

No, she denied. *I can't like him.*

Why not?

It's complicated, was all she would disclose. Her heart wrenched as Tristan's handsome face flashed across her mind.

Pushing it away, she took a large, cleansing breath and straightened her back. She had more worrisome things to consider.

Like the small fact that she might die.

The trumpets sounded, signaling the race was about to begin. "Welcome, citizens of Vallor… to the sixty-seventh Snorri race!" The announcer's voice rang through an enchanted bullhorn.

Cheers of excitement erupted from the crowd as the racers waved and cheered with them, including Halmar, who roared beside her.

"Each contestant will compete for the title of Snorri Champion. There is only one lap this year, starting and finishing right here at the white line. The rules are simple… there are no rules," the announcer said slyly.

Another wave of cheers erupted, more barbaric. Bloodthirsty.

She supressed a shiver.

"The goal is to survive and cross the finish line first. Will it be the two-time champion, Tridar Higgins?"

The man on the brown sleipnir thrust his fist into the air.

"Or will it be our last-minute entry, Draya Santres?"

An even louder roar came from the audience. She lifted her hand to the crowd, forcing a smile.

"Moretti seems to know something we don't, apparently," he muttered, then raised his voice again. "Without further ado, let the race begin! Riders, approach your marks."

The riders and their sleipnirs entered their pens, stopping at the closed, covered gate. Her nerves reached their capacity as her hands squeezed the sleipnir's hair in a death grip.

Don't be afraid, the sleipnir reassured her. *Trust your instincts. We'll get through this.*

The world around her drowned out and her mind went quiet as she concentrated on remembering how to breathe. If her sleipnir could manage to race as fast as her heartbeat, they'd win in a sinch.

"Riders ready," the announcer boomed. "On your mark… get set… *go!*"

The gates flew open, and all hell broke loose.

Rose's sleipnir went from a standstill one second into a full gallop the next, thrusting them forward from the pen. He sprinted at such an intense speed, it was hard to keep her eyes open, the wind thrashing her dress. Her fellow riders were blurs, all crowded together in a clump, making it impossible to step even a foot out of line—or more than one rider would pay the price.

She focused on keeping her body light and low, thankful for the friction between her skin and the sleipnir. The cheers from the crowd drowned out, leaving the starting line far behind them—just how far she didn't know. She didn't dare look.

Despite their weight advantage, they fell progressively behind, hanging back near the end of the pack. She wondered if perhaps the sleipnir had slowed down for her sake.

It is safer to stay back, the sleipnir explained, his nostrils taking in deep, controlled breaths. *It gets dangerous if you stay close. The other riders will attempt to throw you off if you do. It's better to stay behind, but not too far, or you'll never recover the lost time.*

Within moments, the first obstacle appeared—a towering, steep hill inclining abruptly with a vast crevasse between the raceway, stretching somewhere between fifty to a hundred feet, if she had to guess. She didn't know what she'd expected when she heard the word "jump," but it wasn't this. She attempted to take a breath, but the wind stole it before it could reach her lips.

Five riders were close by—two in front, and three not far behind. To her dismay, one of the riders ahead was Halmar, who kept throwing glances at the rider next to him, mounted on a tan sleipnir with brown hair. They looked at each other like bulls stuck together in a pen. She internally thanked her sleipnir for its wise decision to hang back.

As they neared the jump, her sleipnir accelerated. She raised herself higher, her legs holding on to the sleipnir's body with all her might as they climbed, scaling the jump at top speed. Her vision blurred, eyes watering from the rushing wind. She couldn't risk letting go to wipe her eyes. It was a miracle she could see Halmar ahead.

Without warning, Halmar veered his sleipnir straight into the rider beside him.

What happened next was a blur.

The hooves of the tan sleipnir somehow became tangled, forcing the rider to leap off, risking being trampled rather than crushed by the fall. The action sent his sleipnir right down the hill—headed straight for her.

Get down! her sleipnir commanded.

Rose crouched as low as possible, her chest flush with its back—fortunate because, despite her quick reflexes, the airborne sleipnir's hoof flew inches from her head as it spiraled backward. Slowing down wasn't an option; they were too close to the edge to lose momentum. She did her best to reset her position for the jump.

Her sleipnir drove its hooves into the ground. With a mighty shove from its eight legs, it sprang into the sky. She kept her chest open, just as he had instructed, and for a few fleeting seconds, it felt as if they were flying, gravity holding no bounds.

Then, just like that, they were falling back to the ground.

The free fall caught her stomach. Her eyes squinted for the other side—the edge was too far. Perhaps they had miscalculated. Or maybe Halmar's intervention had done its work.

Her life flashed before her eyes.

But her sleipnir had calculated its projection skillfully—stretching its legs forward just enough to reach the edge. Its hooves struck the track with a resounding thud, dislodging a clump of rocks and dirt that tumbled into the ravine below.

Rose had braced for the landing, but her chest still smacked against the sleipnir's neck, the collision knocking the wind out of her. She gasped for air, but by some miracle, she hadn't broken a rib, and what's more, she'd managed to stay on the sleipnir.

That was very good, the sleipnir praised. *That fall was an intentional move. We'll have to be careful—he insists on staying close to us no matter what I do.*

Of course he does, she spat spitefully, glaring up ahead at Halmar, who didn't look happy they had made it over the ravine.

They were amid the riders now, the leaders of the pack still going strong. Rose's beast increased his speed on the long, flat terrain stretches, but he remained wary of the aggressive riders.

Shortly after, they reached the tree line, smack into the middle of the track, and the designated path vanished.

It's our next obstacle, the sleipnir explained. *We'll have to weave through the trees. Keep yourself low and watch for branches. You'll need to pay close attention or you'll lose a limb—or worse, your head.*

Rose grimaced, tightening her grip on the sleipnir as she tucked her knees against his torso. The riders ahead disappeared into the trees one by one until it was their turn.

Trees and branches were a blur. No matter which way she ducked or swerved, the branches followed. She swore the branches themselves were... *moving.* Even the roots beneath them seemed to stir. It could have been just a trick of the eye. But as they continued, it become undeniable.

She had heard of places like this—places that still possessed their own magic, even in Cathan, where it had all but disappeared. This forest apparently, was one of them.

Her heart lodged within her throat. The sleipnir had failed to mention the forest was *alive*. It was hard enough to avoid branches when they were still, let alone *attacking* them.

Her sleipnir had slowed down considerably, jumping and dodging the different levels of limbs and roots coming at them. She was forced to crouch, lean, and dodge much quicker than she could keep up with, almost earning a fatal blow from a branch she didn't see until it was nearly too late. The outcome left a deep gash on her shoulder, tearing both her dress and skin.

Terror gripped her as she winced, clutching her shoulder. She couldn't do this. They were coming at her too fast.

Trust yourself, the sleipnir coached, sensing her fear. *Listen to your instincts, your body—they'll tell you what to do.*

Rose scrounged up every scrap of courage she had and narrowed her eyes into pure will. The sleipnir was right. She had come too far to give up now. She let go of the control and listened to the trees—every leaf flutter, every branch groan, the air in between. She let her body take over, letting it act on its own.

After she got the hang of it, she did well.

Extremely well.

It was eerie how accurately she moved. She sensed everything, from the buzzing insects darting to the other riders around her. It felt so familiar that she almost believed she was living out a scene from a past life.

Her sleipnir increased its speed as she discovered her rhythm, overtaking the riders who had been ahead.

They were just about to emerge from the woods when a massive fallen tree trunk blocked their path. At the same time, a large branch swung down, ready to smash them flat.

She quickly ducked as her sleipnir jumped through the narrow opening like an airborne arrow, barely escaping before the branch and tree trunk colided with a loud crunch. A blink later, they had shot out the other side victorious.

Her body slumped against the sleipnir, by the grace of the sky and sea gods she was still in one piece.

Back on the open track, her sleipnir sped up, pushing to cover as much distance as possible before reaching the river.

After she got the hand of it, riding felt… exhilarating, really—like they were untouchable.

But her confidence disappeared as the sound of the river reached her ears.

As they rounded the bend, a jolt of danger shot through her senses.

She hadn't the slightest idea where the instinct came from, but it was strong—so strong that it took over her body. She leaned sharply to the right as her hand flung itself into the air, snatching an arrow meant for her head.

She only had a moment to process what she'd done, staring in awe at the arrow. She turned back to see Halmar had somehow managed to acquire a bow and arrow. He shot her a furious glare, angry that he had missed his target.

Where did he get those? she asked, clenching her jaw.

Probably paid someone to hide them in the woods, the sleipnir huffed.

Halmar nocked another arrow, posing to strike again.

Not this time, prick.

Without thinking, she tossed the arrow up to aim it, caught it again, and instinctively hurled it back at him. She didn't expect it to reach him, but to her amazement, it struck him just where she intended. His shoulder jerked back, the unexpected force almost knocking him off his sleipnir. The shock made him drop the bow with a grunt.

Rose was certain he'd be forced to slow, but hell-bent, he yanked the arrow from his shoulder, tossing it aside like it was nothing. His livid expression turned malicious, the action only intensifying his resolve to kill her. At least now, he'd have to figure out a different way.

She redirected her focus to the track ahead. The river was visible now, its white-capped waves rushing with the speed of rapids and spanning double the width of the ravine.

Doubt bubbled up again.

Remember what I told you, the sleipnir reminded her. *Trust your instincts.*

Rose forced her body to relax, brushing the insecurities aside. She focused on the cool breeze on her skin, the hint of mist, and the sleipnir's powerful muscles shifting beneath her. She held her breath as they met the water, closing her eyes to brace herself, waiting to sink into the water's depths.

But it never came.

Because somehow, to her complete and utter shock—the sleipnir was running on water.

At first, she was sure it was her imagination, her mind coping with the fear. But as the moments passed, reality sunk in, and the sleipnir's hooves kept defying gravity as they galloped.

She couldn't contain the smile that burst on her lips, which exploded into vibrant laughter. She let go of the sleipnir's mane and raised her arms up and out, tilting her head back to the sky like she was flying.

Her sleipnir practically smirked in triumph as it charged ahead with renewed vigor. The other riders watched them pass in pure bewilderment as they sped through the water.

They reached the dirt track again and went back to full speed. The river had been their saving grace, putting them at the head of the pack. She counted only two riders in front of them.

Which meant they were in third place.

The two riders in front gaped back at her, their astonished faces revealing they had witnessed the miracle. At least they had the decency to look worried.

Rose and her sleipnir charged for them like a lioness hunting for its prey.

Both riders exchanged determined glances, nodding to one another.

She sensed eels under the rocks.

They'll try to kill us, the sleipnir said. *I sense their fear.*

What do we do?

Pray it takes Halmar a long time to get through the river. Or we'll have attackers on both sides. You did well with the arrow.

Let's hope our luck doesn't run out, she said, trying not to let the anomaly go to her head.

They were gaining ground, catching up to the two sleipnirs with every passing second.

The two riders drew together until they were side by side, exchanging something. What it was, she couldn't say. She saw nothing in their hands, yet they let go of their reins. They spread apart again, riding neck and neck. Her suspicion only grew as they slowed.

Something's wrong, she warned. *We should slow down.*

The sleipnir listened, slowing its pace. Rose peeked behind her, seeing if anyone was following them. To her disappointment, Halmar was exiting the river despite his shoulder wound.

She cursed in her mind. *Halmar is nearly out of the river, and he looks vengeful.*

How far? the sleipnir asked.

Not far enough with these two slowing us down, she replied, wondering if it was their intention—no doubt to scare her into retreating back with the others, letting them finish her off.

Her mind reeled. Her eyes searched for something—anything—to give her a hint of what they were plotting. A flicker of a glare caught her eye. She squinted, looking closer to ensure her eyes weren't playing tricks on her. Another glare glinted in the dim sunlight, soft and subtle, but it was there.

They were going to clothesline them.

They're holding a rope between them, she warned.

I can't see anything. Are you sure?

Yes, she confirmed confidently.

They were getting close—too close. They would have to act, and quickly. Rose put on a brave mask, taking the risk.

Faster, she urged. *When I say get down, lower your head as far as you can.*

I will, the sleipnir replied, trusting her with its life.

She readied herself, adrenaline pulsing within her. If it hit them, it would string the sleipnir first, and she'd be crushed or trampled. Neither of which she would survive. If she didn't time this exactly right, they'd both be dead.

She held her breath as she watched the invisible rope inch closer, the glare approaching them.

NOW!

The sleipnir immediately ducked its head as she threw herself backward, pressing her back flush with the sleipnir's. The rope hovered just above her, whizzing by, but not before she managed to seize it with her hands, twisting her body as she sat back up. She held on, knowing her next move might throw her off the sleipnir.

She clutched the creature with her thighs and, with all her strength, yanked on the rope.

The sudden force wrenched the riders forward off their sleipnirs, sending both crashing to the ground, vanishing under their pounding hooves.

Rose flinched away.

Her sleipnir skipped with glee. *You did it!*

Rose glanced back to see if Halmar was still following. To her dismay, the distraction had allowed him to catch up, effortlessly leaping over the wreckage they'd left behind. He ignored the fallen riders, his gaze fixed solely on Rose.

Faster, she urged. *Halmar is close.*

I can't, the sleipnir said. *We're almost at the mud pits. If we hit with full speed, I could break a leg.*

Rose's attention moved further down the track. The sky was completely gray now, cracking with thunder. The good news was the finish line was coming up sooner than she thought. They just had to get through the mud pits and they'd be home free.

The hopeful thought they'd glide over the mud pits like the water was shattered as her sleipnir sunk knee-high in the muck. It was far deeper than she'd anticipated, the sleipnir struggling to lift its legs.

I'm stuck! the sleipnir grunted in frustration.

She glanced back to see Halmar plunge into the mud pits, closing in on them. She had to do something.

Light rain began to fall as she dismounted the sleipnir, her flats sinking into the cool mud as she kicked them off. The lightened weight helped, but it wasn't enough. Rose pushed with all her might to free him, but her feet kept slipping. She was so preoccupied, she almost didn't hear the footsteps running up—

A hand grabbed a fistful of her hair, yanking her backward into the mud.

Rose! her sleipnir called out.

The rain turned into a downpour as she rolled, becoming coated in a wet, muddy mess. She tried to get up, but Halmar reached her before she could. He knelt above her, putting his hand on her breasts, pressing her into the mud. His grotesque face twisted into a sick smirk as he squeezed them, forcing her deeper into the muck. He was going to suffocate her.

She clawed at the mud, desperate to escape, until she remembered the knife hidden under her dress. Not wasting a moment, she drew it and struck the hilt of the dagger against the side of his skull.

Halmar recoiled. Taking her opportunity, she stood, but as she did, Halmar grabbed her ankle, grunting loudly, still on his hands and knees. His grip tightened with such intensity that she swore she felt something snap. She wanted to cry out, but she wouldn't give him the satisfaction.

With an irritated grunt, she swung the knife at his throat. He dodged her strike, but the distraction, combined with the slick mud, allowed her ankle to slip free.

Without sparing a moment, she sprinted back through the rain, ignoring the sharp pain in her ankle. Her sleipnir stood by, having managed to free its hoof from the mud. He crouched low, allowing her to mount swiftly.

Together, they raced away out of the mud pit.

Without warning, other riders caught up. One passed them... then another... then one more.

We're on the home stretch, the sleipnir said with determination. *Now we fly.*

Now we fly, Rose repeated.

He bolted into a gallop at top speed. She pressed her body close to his back, trying to remain light, ignoring the pain shooting from her ankle. He projected them forward with such speed, she was forced to hunch her back, grasping his mane with every bit of strength she had as rain droplets pelleted her skin.

They passed the third rider… then the second… and still they flew, accelerating so fast, she was certain the sleipnir's hooves were barely scraping the ground.

As they neared the finish line, the chants and screams from the sidelines filled her ears.

The white ribbon was only feet away when she and her sleipnir caught up with the last rider, racing head to head. Her sleipnir's speed remained steady as they soared through the air, overtaking the final rider and crossing the finish line first.

A roar of adoration exploded from the crowd.

She couldn't believe it—*they'd won!*

CHAPTER 63

A victorious grin spread across her face.

Don't look so surprised, the sleipnir said as he slowed, panting from using his lungs to capacity. *I told you we'd win.*

You were incredible, she praised, smiling down at him as she wrapped her arms around his thick neck.

No, you were. I knew you could do it.

"There you have it folks! For the first time in history, a rookie has won the Snorri!" the announcer proclaimed.

Another wave of cheers filled the stands, sounding like a war cry.

Rose scanned the crowd for Roman but couldn't see him. However, through the rain, she caught sight of a black-hooded figure near the gate, leaning his shoulder against it, clapping slowly. A flicker of recognition formed as she strained to see his face, but she couldn't see who it was under the hood.

She was about to go to him when Moretti appeared. "Are you hurt?" he asked.

She had almost forgotten why she was here in the first place. "I'll live," she answered with a tight smile. Her eyes shifted back to see if the hooded man was still there, but he'd vanished.

"Come here, let me help you." Moretti gestured, reaching for her.

She took his hand, wincing as her foot hit the ground.

"Not hurt, huh?" he said.

"Only my ankle."

He lifted an eyebrow, gazing at her shoulder wound caked with mud.

She had almost forgotten. "It's only a scratch."

He moved to pick her up, but she stopped him. "You don't have to do that." She peered down at her filthy dress.

He scooped her up anyway. "I don't give a damn about my clothes, you beautiful angel." He brought her face to face with him. "You are the most incredible woman I've ever met."

You've succeeded, the sleipnir stated. *He's smitten. Already, he's thinking of how to get you to marry him.*

She wasn't sure of how she felt about the fact. A stranger like him looking at her in such an intimate way made her uneasy. They'd known each other for less than a few hours. Yet here he was, looking at her like he'd known her for years.

"We'll get you to the medic tent," Moretti reassured her. He took a few steps then stopped, realizing the sleipnir was following them. He gaped at the beast, amazed.

We won, don't you understand? You're free, she said.

I'm not leaving you, the sleipnir said. *Where you go, I go now. I owe you my life.*

Don't you want to go back to your family? Your own kind? She was shocked he'd give up his freedom.

His head hung. *I have no family, and I've grown fond of you,* he admitted.

Tears pricked the backs of her eyes. *What do they call you?* she asked, ashamed she'd not asked before.

Onyx, he said with a proud puff of his chest.

Her heart warmed as she looked back at Moretti. "Onyx is with me now," she said, claiming him proudly. "After all, I did win our bet," she added with a sly smile.

Moretti smirked in response. He began walking again, carrying her easily in his arms. "You know, I've been thinking about that, and I can't help but feel a bit cheated. How was I supposed to know you were superhuman? I need more time with you." His face was so close, his forehead almost pressed against hers.

Rose threw on a flirtatious smirk. "I suppose I could make it happen. But it'll cost you."

Moretti's handsome face broke out into a heart-stopping smile. "Then it's settled. You'll come with me after I get you looked at."

He took her to the medical tent, letting the healers tend to her shoulder and foot. Fortunately, her ankle injury ended up being no more than a sprain.

She learned from Moretti that Halmar had gotten stuck in the mud after she'd escaped, stepped on by another rider's sleipnir. Luckily for their sakes, neither he nor the other two riders with the rope had been killed. Moretti couldn't stop praising how she had handled it all—raving about how she'd managed to see the clear rope.

Not long after, Moretti was called away to handle business for the race. He left, promising he wouldn't be long.

She lay there lost in thought, still amazed that she'd managed it. A sense of pride grew within her. She'd never done anything like that.

Without warning, a hooded figure slipped into the tent.

Roman whipped off his hood. "Are you alright?" he asked, coming straight to her, lifting her chin as he scanned her frantically.

"I'm fine," she said to soothe his worry. "Really."

Roman gnashed his teeth. "Damn you. I nearly died ten times having to watch that."

Her heart lifted from the worry in his voice. "I wasn't sure if you were."

"You never left my sight."

"What did you think of it?" she couldn't help but ask.

He reprimanded her with a glare. "I thought of how idiotic and reckless you are."

Rose's gaze fell from his chiding tone.

"But I also thought you were the most glorious thing I'd ever seen." He slipped his hand into hers.

A jolt of energy traveled up her arm from the simple touch. She peered down timidly at their intertwined fingers.

He leaned down, his musky scent washing over her. "You could've won over anyone with that performance."

An involuntary shiver ran up her spine. "I did win someone over… I've agreed to go back with Moretti." She watched for Roman's reaction.

He kept his expression carefully blank. "Good. It'll be easier to catch him off guard." His eyes lowered to her hand, noticing the ring on her finger. His face remained indifferent, though the muscles in his jaw ticked.

"I'll be back as soon as I can," she said, not knowing why her heart cringed as he looked at the ring.

"Just—be careful. He may seem friendly and easygoing, but the company he keeps is not."

"I will."

She went to let go of his hand, but he held it firm. Her breaths quickened as she swallowed hard.

"You really were incredible out there." His raw voice lowered to a whisper as his eyes locked on to hers. "I don't think I'll ever not be in awe of you, Roe."

Her eyelids fluttered. She tried to open her mouth to say something, but no sound came out.

Roman's voice went back to normal. "Today reminded me you can take care of yourself… Do what you have to do."

Before she could form a sentence, he let go of her hand, threw on his hood, and left the tent.

She stared at the door flap for a long moment before her gaze fell to her wrapped ankle. *Do what you need to do?* What did he mean? Did he not care anymore if she threw herself at Moretti? Or did he trust her enough to decide for herself?

She supposed she'd find out.

CHAPTER 64

Rose convinced Moretti that she'd come to the Snorri alone and was spending the summer with an aunt living on the outskirts of the city. Her fictitious aunt had forbidden her to come, but she had slipped away, eager to see what all the fuss was about. If Moretti had any questions about her story, he didn't ask, appearing to accept the tale.

Moretti never left her side on the journey back into the heart of the city. She was relieved to hear the mention of food, not having eaten a single bite since breakfast. His colleagues accompanied them in the carriage, all of whom were highly intrigued to know more about her.

Moretti remained quiet, listening intently to her responses to the endless questions thrown at her. She told them as little as possible, sticking to half-truths. His gaze frequently shifted to the window, perhaps looking to see if Onyx was still trailing them, drawing attention as they traveled through the streets.

Rose wrapped her arms around herself, still caked in mud in what had to be the nicest carriage she'd ever stepped foot in. With every movement, the drying mud flaked off her dress, leaving the black carpeted floor a dusty mess. Moretti didn't mind her unruliness in the slightest—so much so that he'd kept his hand on her knee the entire way.

"You can wash up when we get there," Moretti assured her, noticing her tugging at her dress. "I have a large assortment of dresses; you can choose and keep any one that suits you."

"Do you bribe every maiden you meet with a dress?" she asked, half serious.

His friends snorted at her question, acting as though the notion was ridiculous.

"You'd be the first—well, aside from my sister and mum," Moretti added, thinking about it more.

Rose raised a brow. "I don't believe you."

"Believe what you wish, goddess, but it's true."

"Goddess?" She laughed at the nickname.

"That's what they're calling you," Moretti said with a smooth grin. "You're practically royalty around here now."

"And rightly so," Talon spoke up, his dark hair hanging in front of his eyes. "I've never seen anything like it. It was bloody incredible. How'd you learn to ride like that?"

Rose's lips slipped up into a coy smile. "Instinct, I suppose," she claimed vaguely.

Talon's eyes gleamed. "Perhaps you could teach me a thing or two." He leaned closer with a handsome smile.

"Perhaps *I* ought to teach you a thing or two about manners," Moretti said, resting his elbows on his knees and leaning forward toward his friend in warning.

Talon backed off, slumping back into his seat with a scowl.

After what seemed like an eternity, the carriage pulled up at their destination. Rose peeked out the window, expecting to see his estate. Instead, she saw an enormous tavern.

Blood drained from her face.

Moretti exited first. "Coming, goddess?" He winked with a smile, holding out his hand.

She scrambled for an excuse, fighting her trembling hands. "I can't—"

"Don't let the riffraff scare you," he said, defusing her refusal.

She resigned, taking his hand and suppressing the lump threatening to rise in her throat.

"Onyx can stay out here with the horses. He'll be well taken care of until you return. I promise."

She threw a questioning glance at Onyx.

Go. I'm in no danger, Onyx prodded her. *I'll be close by; if you need me, just call.*

Onyx's reassurance was the only thing that got her through the double door.

It was the grandest tavern she'd ever seen—nothing like the monstrosity she'd stayed at with Roman. The three-story building had tall ceilings, new furniture, and sleek, polished wooden finishes. The wall behind the hand-carved bar displayed more bottles of wine than she'd ever known existed. Even the glass coasters were embossed with a large roaring lion that read *The Lion's Den* at the bottom. Men and women crowded around the bar, all holding drinks.

As soon as they'd walked through the doors, cheers greeted them, but they weren't for Moretti.

"The goddess has arrived!" a man in the crowd roared, lifting his mug into the air in celebration.

The volume boomed as others cheered alongside him. Rose shoved aside her fear and let a proud grin slip onto her lips, playfully bowing.

"Round's on me!" Moretti declared at the bar, and everyone cheered again.

Once their attention was redirected to their drinks, Moretti gave her a lopsided grin. "Come on." He put his hand on the small of her back.

Rose took it one step further, sliding her hand into his. If it was for her own reassurance or just playing the part, she wasn't sure.

Moretti welcomed her advance without a thought, tugging her closer.

He ushered her to an adjacent dining room. The wooden tables were placed on the outskirts, leaving a gap for the stage in the center. Two opposite staircases led to the upper balconies above them with doors lining both sides, leading into what she could only assume were bedrooms, some couples already going up to claim them.

Her eyes got hung up on the stage, fighting the impulse to flee as her hands began to tremble.

"There is a room upstairs you can wash up in," Moretti said, gesturing upstairs and handing her a brass key.

Rose forced her gaze to the balcony above them as dread crept its way into her soul. She hid the fear, but he'd already caught the hesitancy.

"You'll be safe," he clarified with confidence. "No one would be so foolish as to try something with you."

"Except maybe me," Talon retorted, wiggling his eyebrows behind them. His friends laughed.

It was supposed to be a joke, but it only made her shift in stance.

Moretti gave Talon a dark look that made him recoil. "Say that again."

"Oh, come on, it was a bloody joke." Talon groaned.

Moretti shoved him away, returning his attention to Rose. "Go on, no one will try anything."

She pulled it together. "Too bad. I like a good fight," she teased, even mustering a playful wink.

Moretti's mouth broke out into a broad grin. "You think that's a joke, but I've seen men kill for women much less worthy than you. Now go on, I'll wait for you."

She took her time going up the stairs, careful not to put too much weight on her ankle. With shaky hands, she grasped the key and entered the spacious suite, locking the door tightly behind her. She scanned the room, checking under the bed and the closet for any unwanted visitors.

When it was clear that she was alone, she exhaled softly, allowing herself to gaze into the mirror. She was a mess. She took off her golden dress and found a new one in the closet before she began scrubbing her body in the wide porcelain basin. Carefully, she placed the small pouch of powder on the large wooden vanity, her focus shifting to it as she shook out her wet hair, wondering how in Vallor she'd manage to slip it into Moretti's drink without him noticing—there were too many eyes.

An idea popped into her mind. She debated it, contemplating if the risk was worth the reward. She settled on leaving it as a backup plan.

She tucked the small pouch away again in her breast, adjusted her new lavender dress, and went downstairs to find Moretti.

He sat in the middle of the table, lazily sitting in a plush chair, with an empty seat next to him reserved for her. He must have sent his friends away because they were no where in sight.

Thanks to her ankle, she'd only taken a few pathetic steps toward him when a stranger appeared.

She had to fight the impulse to jump out of her skin.

"Hello, goddess," the large man said, blocking her path. "I feel quite fortunate to meet the winner of the Snorri. That was quite the show you put on."

Rose strained to give him a smile, not liking how his gaze lingered. "Thank you." She tried to sidestep past him, but he blocked her again.

"My name is Lorance Ilian. Perhaps you've heard of me?" He wore an expensive tunic with a family crest, parading that he was some wealthy lord in this enormous city. His long hair trailed past his brown eyes to his chest. He couldn't have been a year older than Zareb.

Rose remained indifferent. "Sorry, no."

He took a step closer. Rose's fingers curled into fists. "It's no matter. Why don't you come sit with me so we can get better acquainted?" he asked with a leery smile that made her skin crawl.

"No, thanks."

His face flickered with annoyance. "Excuse me?" Apparently, being told no was a new concept to him.

She stole a glance at Moretti, wondering if he'd come to rescue her. He was already watching them, wholly aware of what was going on. He merely observed, waiting to see what she'd do.

Lorance gripped her arm, redirecting her attention to him.

Out of instinct, her hand moved to the blade strapped to her thigh, raising it up to his throat. "Don't touch me," she seethed venomously. "I've never killed a man, but I wouldn't mind the practice."

She could have sworn she saw Moretti smirking like a predator out of the corner of her eye.

A group of men wearing the same family crest as Lorance circled the pair. Some of them even drew their swords like she was a real threat.

"Enough!" Moretti bellowed over them as he stood. "Let her go, Lorance, and tell your men to stand down. Or I'll let her put that blade to good use. I wouldn't mind seeing my greatest competition eliminated."

Lorance gifted Rose a defeated scowl before striding away with his "jolly" band of men. She steadily lowered her arm and hid her shaky hands, stowing her knife back in its hiding spot.

Curse these bloody taverns.

Moretti was waiting by the window with a drink in his hand. The storm that had poured at the Snorri now splattered over the glass in fierce droplets, filling the crowded room with the pattering.

"You hold your own. I'll give you that. Fuck, that might have been the most attractive thing I've ever seen." His bright blue eyes flashed back to her. "You're a walking magnet, aren't you, Santres?" The mention of her fake name reminded her she was supposed to be pretending to be someone else. "You must hear that all the time."

She gave him a humble smile. "I've been told once or twice."

His mouth slipped into a large grin, letting her know he liked her fire. He pulled out a chair for her, all the while looking down at the oval black ring she was wearing. She knew he'd like that she kept it on.

"So, are all these men friends of yours, or do they work for you?" she asked.

"Both," he answered. "Though the latter is what keeps them around."

She gazed at him with empathy. "You really believe that, don't you?"

"Yes. If you'd had an upbringing like mine, you'd say the same."

Her father had believed the same thing. "I'm sorry, but that's just too sad to believe."

Moretti's eye twitched with curiosity. "What is it you'd have me believe, Draya Santres?"

"I'd like to believe true wealth comes from something that cannot be bought."

"Such as?"

She picked up her glass from the table. "Such as love, family, friendship. From the looks of it, you could use better ones." She took a sip.

Moretti's eyebrow lifted. "Is that so?"

"Yes. You should be able to trust friends with anything."

"I trust them enough."

"But not around me."

"Oh, not a chance in hell, goddess—I don't even trust *myself* around you."

Blood rose to the surface of her cheeks. Her stomach rumbled not a moment later, reminding her of how hungry she was.

He gestured to the food spread on the table. "Come on, let's eat before that stomach of yours shakes down my fine establishment."

Dinner was exquisite, with no expense spared. Every dish had the finest luxuries available. Her plate was lined with gold, as was the silverware and the cup. Even the chair cushion was filled with goose feathers. The food was almost too beautiful to eat, and once she tasted it, it melted like butter in her mouth.

Time and time again, she waited for a chance to slip the powder into his drink, but the public setting made it impossible.

She needed to stay guarded around Moretti, and she was. But against her better judgment, she felt an unexpected sense of ease with him. Their conversations were effortless, and even his casual movements around her seemed as instinctive as breathing.

Once they were done eating, the servers came too quickly to take their plates—and, more importantly, their glasses. She cursed.

It was time to enact plan B.

She strategically shivered, putting her arms around herself as she rubbed her upper arm.

"Are you cold?" he asked, picking up the hint.

"A little," Rose admitted.

"Well, we can't have that." He got to his feet, stretching his hand to her.

She took it, letting him lead her upstairs, back to the suite she had used to change. Once they entered, Moretti went over to the fireplace, his back facing her as he worked on lighting the fire.

With him distracted, she took her chance. She took out the small pouch of the lotus powder and emptied its contents into her mouth, tucking it into her cheek to delay its dissolving, then stuffed the small pouch back into her dress.

She gazed down at him and the embers he'd brought to life.

"Moretti?" she said above him in a smooth voice.

He stood to face her, unaware of the danger lurking past her lips.

Without warning, she slid her hands behind his neck, urging his lips down to meet hers.

And meet they did.

Within seconds, he brought her closer. To her pleasant surprise, he was an excellent kisser—better than Grant. His hand went up to her jaw, cupping it sweetly, lifting it to kiss her deeper.

Her tongue slid along his bottom lip, asking for entrance. His soft groan vibrated on her lips as he submissively granted it. Her tongue slid into his mouth as he opened up. They kissed for a long moment, Rose wanting to ensure he'd gotten enough of the powder's effects.

She knew it was working as it began to make its way through her, overpowering her senses just as it had during the second challenge. She braced herself for it, letting it run its course instead of fighting the sensation.

He pulled away first, looking like he'd been swept away to heaven itself. His hot breath spread over her face.

"I'm sorry," she apologized at once. "I just—"

His lips silenced her apology, kissing her again, coaxing out her desire unconsciously. "I want to ravish you until you can't stand properly," Moretti murmured, unaware his sudden urge for honesty was the powder's effects working. "But I don't want you to think that's all I want. As much as I want to keep kissing you—" his eyes flickered to her lips then back up into her eyes, "—to take advantage of you in every single way, I'm not going to. Because I want more from you. I've never felt this way about anyone, and let me assure you I've had my pick of the litter. Women from all over Cathan have come to see me, each of them willing to hand over their bodies and souls to me. I've never wanted anyone. None. Until the moment I saw you walking by today." He put his forehead against hers. "After the race, after I saw you gallop across the water like it was nothing and the smile that grew on your lips when you did... Gods." He swallowed hard. "It was at that moment I knew I was looking at an angel—and I just knew I had to have you."

Her breaths grew uneven. She hadn't expected him to be so genuine, but then again, she had just drugged him. "You saw that?" Of course, he had. The whole bloody arena had seen it.

"You think I'd send you into that race alone? I watched over you throughout the entire track. I had men posted at each point, thinking you'd need my help. But you didn't."

She hadn't been expecting that either. She hadn't been expecting any of it—well, perhaps the lusting part, but to care for her genuinely so quickly was astounding. She knew it to be true from the lotus.

Her heart cracked. She felt terrible for using him all of a sudden. She'd wanted him to be someone she disliked—someone she wouldn't care about hurting. But now... now she could feel the powder make her face the truth.

"Say something," he whispered, searching her eyes.

"I... I don't want to hurt you." She attempted to pull back but held firm.

"Hey," Moretti whispered, still so close their noses were brushing. "You can't kiss me like that and get shy now."

She let a small smile escape her lips. "I like that about you—how you make conversation easy."

He returned the smile. "Good. Because I want to know more about you." He moved to sit on the large bed.

A knot formed in her chest. She didn't want to answer questions about herself. She was supposed to be doing the questioning.

She sat down next to him anyway.

He wasn't having that—he pulled her onto his lap as if it was the most natural thing in the world to do. She leaned into him, smelling his expensive cologne as she did. "What if we take turns?" she suggested, thinking on her feet. "I ask something, then you."

"Seems fair enough," he said with a smile. "I'll go first. Why'd you enter the race?"

"You were going to kill Onyx if I didn't," she stated, hiding the truth with another. "He and I... have a special connection."

"I can't believe I'm jealous of a sleipnir."

She rolled her eyes. "I've heard you have a somewhat controversial reputation. Why is that?"

"Because I grew up with nothing. I wasn't given a cent like so many others here. Much of what you see in Caleede is generational wealth.

What I have now, I had to fight for. It wasn't given to me. I had to take it. Many people disagree on how I did that."

"Is that why you deny so many women? You think they'll only choose you for your money?"

Moretti smirked. "Partly. What's your family like?"

"I live with my mum. My dad died, and I have no siblings."

He wouldn't accept such a vague answer. "Come on, you have to give me more than that."

She gnawed on the inside of her cheek, digging deeper, weaving her way through the effects of the powder. "My mother is what some might call overprotective of me. In my eyes, she's a fighter because she had to be. She endured my father when he didn't deserve it... He wasn't kind."

A twinge of sadness graced his handsome face. "You and I have that in common."

"How is it you make your money?"

"Investments, trading, shipments, some rare black market items," he blurted, looking surprised as he told her the last bit. "What's a girl like you doing not married yet?"

She wanted to lie, but the powder wouldn't let her. She chose her words carefully. "Because my mother and I have no money. Another gift from my father. I was going to get married, but... I ended things. I've been looking to find a suitor ever since, but the man I was in love with is powerful. He made sure no one would want to come within ten feet of me."

"Why would he do that?"

"Because I hurt him terribly," she stated, her heart aching to think of Tristan. She cleared her throat. "Were you involved in the war?"

"No, but I played a small part, shipping weapons and supplies to the troops."

At last, she was getting somewhere. "Were there any other provinces you sold supplies to during the time?" she probed, digging for more.

His eyes narrowed, fighting the effects. But he had no idea what was happening, so he had to respond. "Uh, yes. A few others."

"Who?"

His brows grew together, suspicion lacing those blue orbs. "I sold them to a band of men willing to pay a lot of money for some supplies and information."

"What kind of information?" she pressed.

He stood up off the bed, his eyes darkening. "Information about something they were looking for. Why do you ask?"

She stood, too. "Because I'm trying to find them. Do you know where they are?"

"Yes," he said through gritted teeth, admitting it. "But what would a girl like you be doing looking for men like that?"

"They're hurting people, and I want them to stop. Don't you?"

"I don't much care for what doesn't concern me."

"Can you tell me where they're hiding?"

"Even if I wanted to, I couldn't tell you. If those men even *thought* I betrayed them, I'd be a dead man."

She stared at him in awe. "You're scared of them."

"You'd be a fool not to be. They've killed thousands of people. I made a deal with them to protect Caleede. They promised they wouldn't touch me or the city if I gave them what they wanted."

"What was it they wanted?"

He clenched his teeth. "I… I can't tell you. I'm bound not to."

His refusal to answer caught her off guard. She didn't know anyone able to resist the lotus's effects. How was that even possible? Unless… unless it was magic. She didn't have time to dwell on it as he continued.

"You can't just go off looking for these men on your own. It's not safe." His eyes narrowed. "What the hell are you doing? Is this the only reason you came here?"

"No," she replied, surprising herself. She fought the clawing words coming out. "I… I was curious to see what you were like."

He stepped forward boldly, closing the gap between their bodies, peering down at her with his dazzling blue eyes. "And have you liked what you've seen?" he asked in a dangerous whisper.

Her heart pounded into her rib cage. "I like you more than I thought I would… Do you like me?" she couldn't help but ask.

Stupid.

His eyes grew softer, his voice submissive. "Yes," he answered. He slid his hands around her, pulling her closer. "Even though a million red flags are going off in my head. You can understand why I'm having a hard time trusting you."

A wise decision. "Perhaps you shouldn't."

"Oh, I know I shouldn't," he agreed, interlacing his fingers with her hair. "But I've always been a risk taker, and I believe you are worth the risk." His eyes flickered down to her lips, begging for them. She didn't have to move as Felix's lips molded with hers, opening and closing in controlled motions—he really did kiss well.

He panted for air as he said, "I need to know more."

"More about what?"

"You." His hands cupped her jaw. "This man you loved, do you still love him?"

She meant to say no, but instead, she said, "Yes, but he's married to another."

"So who was the hooded man who visited you in the tent? Is he someone you have feelings for?"

So he'd been watching.

"Yes." She ignored how her pulse quickened at the confession.

"So I have competition. Of course I do. How could I not, with a girl like you?" The fact clearly only made him more determined. "How much do you like him?"

The powder's effects tugged on her, but she simply said, "A lot."

The fact darkened his eyes. "That won't do."

Her brow twitched. "What?"

"I couldn't possibly share you… and what's more is I know you feel something for me, too." His ragged voice came closer, enough to feel his warm breath on her skin. "You wouldn't have kissed me if you didn't."

Rose's heart sank, knowing where this would lead but not wanting to hurt him. She pulled away. "It's getting late. I should go. My aunt will wonder where I am."

"Don't be scared of me," he pleaded, pulling her back into him.

"I'm not," she replied with a sure voice. "It's only back home they'll worry about me. I should go before it gets late."

"You're more than welcome to come home with me." Moretti stroked her cheek with his thumb. "Forever, if that's what you wish."

Her mouth parted, hanging open, dumbfounded, knowing he was completely serious. "You barely know me. How are you so sure you'd want me to stay?"

He remained close, hovering over her lips. "Because I've heard your voice, tasted your lips, and looked into those eyes. I know what I want. And I take what I want."

She swallowed hard. "I can't stay."

"I want you to stay, but I don't want to scare you. So please give me something to hold on to. Promise me you'll come back." Begging seemed foreign to him. "I can't just let you disappear."

She paused, allowing herself to think if she'd like to stay, to learn more about him and his life in the city. It was clear he didn't care she had no money. He had enough of his own. And perhaps here would be better for her, far from the castle, from Tristan. She and her mother would be well taken care of.

"I'll come back," she said, surprising herself.

"When?"

"Soon."

His eyes were pained as he lowered his lips to hers again—slowly, this time, sweetly, like he had all the time in the world with her.

"I'll be waiting," he whispered against her lips.

CHAPTER 65

Moretti let Rose take one of his cloaks as she left. Although he insisted on joining her, she managed to persuade him that it wasn't necessary, not wanting him to discover where she was staying. After they had shared a few lengthy kisses, he reluctantly agreed to let her depart alone.

She rode Onyx back to Highland Haven. The ride was swift and effortless. Despite the heavy rain, it felt like a breeze after the intense race they had just won. Thick clouds shrouded the sky above, making the roads dark. She typically despised traveling in rainy conditions, but Onyx alleviated all her fears, his eight legs propelling them swiftly through the downpour.

They were both soaked to the bone when they reached the large estate. She showed Onyx the stables, making sure he was comfortable and dry before going back inside.

Rose quietly opened and closed the door, removing her soaked cloak and wringing her wet hair out. She headed for the stairs, her sore muscles yearning for a soothing salted bath.

Roman sat on the stairs, crouched over with his elbows on his knees, watching her.

She jumped out of her skin. "Roman!" she exclaimed, clutching her chest. "You scared me."

He looked worse than he had this morning. His eyes were slightly more sunken and hollow, his eyelids an alarming shade of purple, and he was hunched like he was in pain.

She studied him, concerned. "Are you okay? You look ill."

"I'm fine," he dismissed, standing. His large, muscular body stiffened. "How'd it go?"

She threw him a guilty glance, foreshadowing the bad news. "Not good. He couldn't tell me where they were, even with the powder. I think he's bound by some sort of... magic. I've never heard of anyone able to resist its effects. The only thing I could get out of him was that he was helping them look for something."

Roman's eyes grew even darker, his hands balling into fits. "Damn it."

"Why are you so bent on finding these men? Who are they?"

After a moment of acceptance, he ground out, "They're the same group of men who destroyed Corrin. The exact group of men who were *really* responsible for starting the war. Who burned and slaughtered an entire city. And that's not the only one. They've continued to ravage and burn countless others, taking supplies and leaving a trail of bodies behind them. It's happening again, and I want to find out why."

And she had failed. Failed these people.

Pain stung her—but she wouldn't accept defeat. Not yet. "I told him I'd return," she explained, thinking of how they could get more information. "If I spent more time with him, I could gain his trust—"

"The hell you will," Roman lashed out. "It'd be fruitless. He'll never be able to tell you anything if he's bound, even if he wants to. Besides, I should've never asked you to get involved."

"I'm sorry. I know you're angry I didn't get what you wanted, but—"

"You think I give a damn about that?"

She didn't understand where his anger was coming from, if not from her failure. "Then why are you so angry with me?"

"Because I can see it on your face," he snarled, looking pointedly at the new dress she wore. "You let him touch you."

Her eyes sparked with fire. "You told me to do what I had to do. I did this *for* you."

His eyes were still dark, but his face relaxed. "You're right. I'm sorry." He rubbed his face with a loud exhale, pausing before he added, "Thank you for trying." His voice was softer, but he still looked like he wanted to punch the wall.

Without another word, he retreated up the stairs to his room.

Rose glared at his back so fiercely she was surprised it didn't set him on fire. She turned away, fuming.

After everything she'd been through today, after everything she'd done, he was going to blame *her* for doing exactly what he'd asked? For putting herself in danger yet again, only to be treated like she had been back at the castle?

Her blood boiled. She whipped around, ready to round on him, but he was already out of sight. She took a few steps, tempted to follow him, but she stopped herself. Her limp reminded her she'd never catch up.

Instead, she turned towards the kitchens for a cold rag to put on her ankle.

Early the next morning, Rose found herself at the lake's edge, standing on the stone staircase that led into the crystal-clear water. Though the sun had yet to rise, a gorgeous blend of deep-pink and orange painted the fluffy white clouds. As a result, a soft mixture of pink and purple hues cast over the peaceful forest as birds flew atop the still trees, gliding through the calm, colorful sky.

She wrapped her arms around herself, still clutching the letter from her mother that had arrived that morning. It was short and sweet, and her mother hadn't uttered a single word about suitable matches, which told her the situation at the castle was still fragile.

Her mother must be at her wit's end.

The very idea of going back made her shudder. She couldn't just stay there, hoping for a suitor to rescue her while Tristan paraded his new wife around. Reality forced her to think of a life outside its walls.

And Moretti might be her ticket out.

Rose acknowledged he could be a good match for her. He had already accepted her circumstances. He understood the struggle of starting from nothing and building a life for himself, which was appealing to her. Although she knew little about him and he might very well be crooked and self-serving, he was capable of looking after her. The effects of the powder confirmed that everything he'd portrayed was true. Not to mention, her mother would find him more than agreeable.

So why not him?

She cast her gaze on the small island in the middle of the lake, eager to see the view from the grassy, rocky plateau. She must've felt courageous from her success at the Snorri because she peeled off her dress, glaring at the water like an opponent to be conquered.

She went down the steps, the cool water soothing the swelling on her ankle. The dull fear of the water threatened to take over her limbs as she continued, but she pressed on, not wanting to be controlled by it any longer. With the water now reaching her hips, she hesitated at the end of the steps.

"Going for a morning swim without me?" a deep voice questioned.

Roman stood at the top of the staircase, already stripped of his clothes. The sight caused a rush of heat to flood her face as she ran her eyes over his body, his tan skin even more perfect in the magenta-filled sky. He'd left his hair down, hanging into his eyes, still sunken and baggy.

"I want to see it." She nodded out to the small island.

"You were just going to swim out there on your own? With your ankle like that?"

"You don't think I can?"

"On the contrary. I think you can do anything," he said with all the confidence in the world, stepping down the stairs into the water. "But I'm coming all the same."

Rose faced the pink water. "Are you sure you want to?" she asked hotly.

He grew impatient. "Just let me come with you... *please*."

Her gaze landed back on him, his gorgeous golden eyes softening her anger. She nodded, surprising herself by agreeing.

He waded into the water past her, pushing off from the last step and creating ripples that danced across the mirrored surface. She forced herself into the water after him, treading water on her own.

"You're getting brave," he said, praising her.

"Or reckless," she mumbled, questioning her choices as of late.

Despite her glum tone, he gave her a gorgeous smile that nearly made her go under. "Or that."

She rolled her eyes, splashing him.

Together, they swam to the island, her strokes becoming bold and fluid, confident enough to dunk her head and see the large fish scavenging the rocky bottom.

Her muscles screamed at her in the best way as they reached the rocky shore, her chest heaving for air. It made her feel slightly better to see Roman breathing just as hard. He reached down to help her up, and together, they climbed to the top of the small grassy plateau.

She stopped to catch her breath, but the view took it right away.

It was so peaceful. So beautiful. Amid its rocky terrain, purple and blue wildflowers thrived—enough for her to pick a handful and still leave plenty wild. Trees swayed in the morning breeze, sending a comforting wave from afar as the mountain peaks towered overhead.

The longer she stayed here, the more it felt like home. And that terrified her. Because this wasn't her home, and it never would be. It was only temporary, just as everything in her life seemed to be. She wouldn't let herself hope. She was too bruised, too broken to deserve something this pure. She'd have to accept it.

Rose walked over to the edge, soaking every detail in. She was so transfixed on the scenery she didn't realize Roman was standing right behind her.

"Was it worth the swim?"

An involuntary shiver coursed through her as if his graveled tone had come alive and grazed her skin.

"It's my new favorite place in the world," she whispered. She looked over her shoulder at him—at the only thing that could make this view better.

His handsome face dripped, water running off his smooth cheeks, his soaked hair bringing out his natural wave just below his ears. She desperately wanted to give in to the impulse to reach out to him, to take his face into her hands and find out what he tasted like. She found herself imagining it—craving it.

As if he knew what she was thinking, he said, "You know, I've seen my fair share of Vallor. I've been to the shores of Eristan, seen Ostlyn's sacred temples, explored the vast forests of Vertmere, climbed the snowy mountains of Artistan, but none of those compare to the scene I am looking at right now."

His eyes were on her.

Her and her alone.

Unconsciously, she licked her lips and pressed them together, trying not to read too far into his words—convinced that the hope fluttering in her chest was only her heart grappling for something that didn't exist. "Wasn't it hard? To come back home after all that?"

"More than you imagine." He cast his gaze out. "It was like returning to a vaguely familiar place. Everything looked the same, only... everything was different. When I came back, I desperately wanted it to ease my soul. I craved the peace it used to bring. But no matter how much I willed it, it couldn't ease the pain I'd just endured. It couldn't erase all the terrible things I'd seen and done. The lives I'd taken. Coming home was merely a painful reminder of all the things well out of my reach." His gaze returned to hers, his eyes searing themselves into her soul.

Her breath caught in her throat. His words... they could very well have been her own. He'd hidden his pain so well that it had made her forget that he'd just come back from war. "You know, you saved thousands more than you took."

He shook his head as if the fact changed nothing for him. "The castle must feel much the same to you," he acknowledged, changing the subject. "Now that you've had time and distance... do you know what you'll do? When you'll go back?"

She knew the answer, already coming to terms with it. "I'll suffocate if I go back. I'll do what I must. I'll find a suitor away from the castle and marry him."

Roman's mouth grew into a hard line. "You say it like you already have someone in mind."

She lowered her gaze. "Maybe."

"Moretti?"

She didn't respond, looking out into the distance, neither confirming nor denying it.

A fire ignited in his eyes as his fists clenched. "That prick is as slippery as a snake. You have no idea what he's truly like, what he's done."

"That may be true, but I know he'd take care of me. And despite his selfish nature, I know he doesn't give a damn about my situation. Which is more than I can say for anyone at court."

His eyebrows raised. "You actually talked about being together? You can't be serious. You barely know him."

She shrugged. "I know him differently than you."

The statement only fueled his anger as he scoffed. "You're being ridiculous. He gives you *one* afternoon of attention, *one* taste of his money, and you're going to let it seduce you? Come on, Rose, you're better than that."

She fumed at his blatant arrogance, his words stinging her like she'd just barged into a forest of stinging nettle. Now he was going to insult her by saying she was only after money? The nerve.

She faced him, coming so close he had nowhere to look but straight into her eyes. "Tell me, do you see a better match lining up for me? To willingly take me when I have nothing? To go against Tristan? If you know anyone who's up for the challenge, please—I'm all ears."

He scowled as he immediately opened his mouth, but no sound came out. He couldn't respond because she was right. She was a doomed cause, ruined in the court's eyes. Even he couldn't deny it.

Rose lifted her chin, her point proven. "Judge me all you want, Roman, but I'm not going back to court to wither away."

Without another word, she left, braving the water and swimming back towards the manor herself.

CHAPTER 66

After their swim, Roman would barely so much as look at Rose. When they did have to speak, he made it a point to keep his sentences short and direct. She hadn't even gone back to see Moretti, and his grudge against her still wouldn't budge.

The following days ran together as they settled into a routine of sorts. They would rise before dawn, have a light breakfast, train until it became too hot, eat lunch, swim for an hour, and then have dinner. She'd end each day by reading and going to bed early, only to wake up and do it again the next day.

Roman never trained her in the same place twice. He began teaching her more than the sword, introducing how to use a small knife in a fight, then archery to keep opponents at a distance. Once, he took her east of the lake to loose rocky terrain, where she struggled greatly. Another time, he took her to a swampy area next to the river, turning them into mud pies. The result was a good scolding from Gretta as they trailed the mud through the hallway.

Onyx enjoyed his new freedom by taking her for long evening rides and exploring the woods. With each passing day, she improved as a rider under Onyx's guidance. Before long, they'd become so accustomed to each other that they didn't need to speak to know what the other was thinking.

It was all like a dream she didn't know existed. As time passed, she became stronger—more comfortable in her own skin, finding an inner peace she'd never had.

Although she was thriving at Highland Haven, the same could not be said for Roman.

Every morning, she'd go downstairs and find the bags under his eyes larger than the day before, the usual golden glow of his eyes dulling. She wasn't sure exactly what his ailment was, but what really worried her was the thought that the Dragonshade hadn't entirely left his system.

She summoned the courage to mention it one morning, suggesting he rest instead of train. He nearly bit her head off, responding with a short, snappy, "I'm fine."

She didn't dare bring it up again.

One afternoon, Roman had to go to the capital for business and said he'd be back later. She offered to join him, but he refused, saying he wanted to go alone. He returned later that day, and whatever his mysterious "business" was, it must have gone terribly because he returned in an even fouler mood than when he'd left.

She wondered how long this could continue until one morning, Roman wasn't there to greet her.

She found Gretta in the kitchens, covered in a mess of flour, kneading dough. "Have you seen Roman?"

"Oh, he's not feeling well this morning," Gretta explained with a tight smile that didn't reach her eyes. "He told me not to worry, though; he just needs a bit of rest."

"Is there something I can do?"

"Oh no, dear, you go on and enjoy the day. I'm sure he'll feel better if he just gets some rest."

"Oh, okay… Thank you, Gretta."

Rose debated going for a ride with Onyx, but instead, she spent the day in the library—something she'd been doing a lot in her free time, which seemed to be often these days.

Gretta wasn't lying when she'd said the manor's library was impressive. There were so many books, Rose was sure it'd take her lifetime to get through them all. Some of them were even written in languages she didn't recognize. The worn, faded covers and fragile pages signified they contained something ancient. The perfectly dusted two-story room was filled with dark bookshelves as tall as the ceiling, making good use of the rolling ladders that helped her navigate the mountains of pages.

The library had books containing the histories of Cathan, magical creatures, rare plants within its lands, and more. She frequently found herself studying the other provinces, desperate to know more about the magical world she lived in.

She hadn't realized how long she'd been reading until the light shining from the paned windows faded, the sun retreating to the mountains, casting a dark purple-pink haze.

She had just begun to gather the books scattered on the table when Gretta burst into the library, carrying a steaming cup of broth in her hands.

Rose frowned, placing a book back onto the shelves. "Gretta? What is it?"

Gretta was practically in tears. "It's Roman. He's gone from bad to worse within a matter of hours. I've insisted on calling for the healer, but he refuses. He says he's already been to one. He's asking for you."

Rose put the stack of books down. He'd seen a healer? When had he—

That day he went into the city—it hadn't been for business at all. He'd gone to see a healer, and by the looks of it, they'd had no cure for his ailment. Why had he not come to her sooner? Did he dislike her so much he'd refuse her help? She, who had saved his life from the Dragonshade? Hadn't she earned his trust?

"Take me to him," Rose said at once.

Together, they rushed through the darkening corridors, candles lighting their way through the silent halls, the stillness unsettling her even more.

"He wasn't able to get out of bed this morning," Gretta explained, struggling to keep up with her long strides. "I've been doing all I can, but nothing I do seems to help."

Rose placed a hand on her shoulder. "It's alright, Gretta. I'm sure he'll be fine." She could only hope. Pray. Curse him and his stupid pride.

Gretta opened the door to his room, where Rose found him weakly sprawled on the bed. The room was modest compared to hers, having a large bed with a solitary window on the opposite wall. But she hardly had time to dwell on details.

He was worse than she'd feared. His amber eyes had dimmed to a dull brown—their life was all but faded, so sickly they'd sunk into their sockets, leaving a deep dark-purple ring around them. The pigment of his skin had faded into a ghostly pale shade and a wheeze escaped his lips with every breath.

It was as though he was dying before her eyes.

Pure panic sieged her from within.

"He says he's exhausted, but he won't sleep," Gretta expounded with a distressed sob. "And he keeps complaining his lungs hurt, but nothing's wrong with them."

Rose studied him with desperate eyes. Although she knew a great deal about healing, she was no expert. The fear that the Dragonshade was still in his system resurfaced. He needed someone more experienced. She didn't have time to experiment.

Rose turned to Gretta. "I don't care what he wants. Call for a healer."

"No," Roman wheezed.

Her and Gretta's heads snapped to him. The order was supposed to be firm, but in his weakened state, his voice was barely a whisper.

"Gretta… leave us," he whispered.

Rose glared down at him, wondering how he could be so stubborn. "Roman, you need help."

He shook his head slowly. "No… Gretta, just… go."

Rose looked at Gretta, ignoring him. "Go then and send for a healer. *Now.*"

Gretta didn't need to be told again, leaving at full speed.

Rose grabbed the sheets, lifting them to examine his body, ensuring she wasn't missing anything. "You stubborn ass," she muttered, putting them back down, trying to hide the worry in her voice. "You survived Dragonshade, but you want to die now?" She put her hand on his forehead to check for a fever—he was ice cold.

He leaned into her palm and he closed his eyes as if he craved it—as if he needed it to survive. "Lay... Come... lay with me," he rasped. His clammy hand reached for hers. "Please."

Rose stood shocked by the vulnerability shining through him. He acted as though he was powerless before her, looked at her as though if she let go of his hand, if she denied him, he'd die right there and then.

Something deep within her dragged her into the bed.

Roman didn't waste a moment before he crushed her into his cold chest. One hand slid up into her hair, cradling her head, while the other dug into her back, pressing her so fiercely into him it felt as though he was gripping for his life.

She stiffened against him, stunned by his sudden desperation. But after a moment, she wrapped her arms around his neck, instincts kicking in as she combed her fingers through his hair, attempting to soothe him.

He rested the bridge of his nose against her hair and took his first deep breath since she'd entered the room—smelling her, she realized, breathing her in like she was the only oxygen left in the room.

The knowledge set her soul ablaze.

He moved down to her neck, his lips lightly brushing her skin as he spoke. "I... I need you to stay."

It was at that moment she realized she had an enormous weakness for him.

"I'll stay as long as you want me to," she whispered.

They laid there, simply savoring the feeling of each other's weight as she did her best not to let her mind wander to places it shouldn't. Guilt sunk in as she realized how much she had missed sleeping beside him, how she had missed having him selfishly like this.

She reprimanded herself; she ought to seek a remedy or diagnosis for his condition—some kind of cure—rather than take advantage of him in his weakened state. But somehow... a stronger inner instinct told her to stay just as he'd asked.

She lifted her chin to look at him, only to find him asleep. *Asleep.* Relief flooded her. It was a small mercy.

Half an hour passed and Gretta returned, about to speak until she saw them.

"He's asleep," Gretta whispered through the darkness, awestruck, looking back and forth at the pair. "How'd you get him to sleep?"

"I have no idea," Rose whispered back. "One minute, he asked me to come to lay next to him, and the next, he was out cold."

"You angel of a girl." Gretta sighed in relief, slumping into the chair beside the bed before she fell over, fanning herself furiously. "I've tried everything, *everything*, to get him to sleep. To make matters worse, the healer said he wouldn't be available until tomorrow afternoon…" She paused her fanning, straining her ears. "Listen to that… even his wheezing has stopped… It's a miracle," she said, continuing to fan herself again.

Rose stared at her with concern, unaware of his insomnia. "How long has he not been sleeping?"

"Ever since you arrived," Gretta admitted. "Though I didn't know that until a few days after. He asked me not to say anything, so I didn't. The first night I caught him in the library, I didn't think much of it. But after I found him more than once, I knew something was going on. It wasn't just a fluke. It was every night."

Her eyes widened. "He hasn't slept in *seventeen days*? What in Vallor does he do?"

Gretta shrugged. "Who knows. Sometimes he's in the library or on the patio, other times the kitchen… I've caught him staring up the staircase to his bedroom quite a few times."

Rose's heart quickened. "You mean the room I'm sleeping in?"

Gretta nodded. "You should've seen the way he looked at those stairs. Looked as though he'd seen the stairway to heaven." She laughed lightly. "Sometimes I thought he'd do it—go up them. He even took a few steps once, but every time, he turned and left… I think he missed you."

Rose blinked, bewildered. "*That's* your explanation for why he's so sick? You think he *misses* me? That's madness. It couldn't be. We're together every day."

"I don't know." Gretta bit her lip. "I've never seen anything like it. I've cured my fair share of ailments, but this… this is different. Nothing seems to be wrong with him. I thought perhaps it was a phase, maybe some sort of post-traumatic stress from everything he's been through. But somehow, he just kept getting worse and worse. Until now. It's almost like it's some sort of… magic."

But Rose held no power and possessed no magical abilities. There was no possible way she could be the reason for his being so ill… could she?

"I swear I didn't do this." She was worried Gretta would think this was all her doing. "If I did, it wasn't intentional."

Gretta looked at her, flabbergasted. "Goodness, the thought hadn't even crossed my mind, child. I know you'd never do anything to hurt him."

A wave of relief came over Rose. "I'm sorry, I've just had a lot of…" She changed her phrase. "People have a hard time trusting me."

"And some people still believe the world is flat," Gretta replied with a twinkle in her eye. "Best not to dwell on what others believe. What's more important is what you believe of yourself."

Rose gave her a small smile, comforted by the familiar words.

"Well." Gretta cleared her throat, getting up. "I'll leave and let you both sleep before my blabbering wakes him. Is there anything I can get you? A change of clothes or an extra blanket?"

Rose shook her head. "No, I don't want to risk waking him. I'll be fine," she said, giving Gretta a thankful nod.

"Bless you. Just ring for me if you need anything. Good night, lass." Gretta dismissed herself, closing the door softly.

Rose looked back at Roman, who was still out cold, feeling foolish for how she counted his breaths. For how she watched to make sure his chest was still rising and falling. For the urge to want more.

Her eyes fell away, and she chastised herself for letting her imagination wander. He only wanted her here to keep an eye on him, nothing more.

But… if what Gretta said was true? No—she wouldn't let herself go there. She'd been disappointed one too many times. Fate would never be so kind.

So instead, she learned to be content with this moment. Even if it was like this, even if he regretted inviting her into bed tomorrow, she would cherish being by his side.

She allowed herself to rest her forehead against his, and slowly, sleep found her.

CHAPTER 67

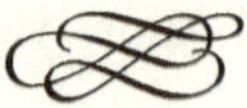

Roman slept throughout the night and into the following day.

Rose refused to leave his side, wanting to keep a close eye on him. Over time, his skin regained its natural tanned hue, his eye sockets no longer dark and hollow, and even the purple bags under his eyes had disappeared. His breaths and body temperature had normalized. She couldn't believe it. He had been on the brink of death, and now he seemed to be recovering simply by... *sleeping*.

Gretta came to check on them throughout the day, thrilled to find him on the mend. She brought Rose a book to entertain herself as she lay beside him. Even as her hunger gnawed, she wouldn't move.

Night came again. The cool moonlight streamed through the window, offering little light, creating dark shadows. She thought he'd sleep through the night again until he began to stir.

Roman slowly opened his eyes, taking a moment to become conscious of his surroundings. Relief came as her favorite pair of eyes were revealed to be back to their perfect golden state.

"Rose?" he muttered, sounding more like himself.

"It's me," she said, scooting closer. "How do you feel?"

"Better." He looked around the room. "How long have I been asleep?"

"Since last night." She did her best to hide the flood of emotion threatening to burst, but her composure broke with just one brush of his gaze. Her hand gripped his collar firmly, bringing him closer. "You can't scare me like that," she whispered, wanting it to come out harsher than it did.

To her surprise, he gave her a lazy smile.

Gods, has he always been this handsome?

He drew her in as one strong hand cradled the nape of her neck. "I didn't expect you to care so much."

She didn't find it funny. "Of course I care."

His eyes searched hers as if trying to decipher what those words meant until he let out a dry cough. "Is there water?"

"Oh—yes. I'll get it." She got out of bed, seeking the glass in the darkness. Spotting the tray with the pitcher by the window, she poured the water into the glass.

It wasn't until she felt Roman's breath on her shoulder that she realized he'd gotten up to follow her.

He placed his hands smoothly on her hips.

A soft tremor shook her knees, causing her to almost drop the glass. She masked all of this and faced him, fighting to keep her hands steady as she held it out.

He drank it in a few large gulps. Once it was empty, he set it down and said, "I want to take you somewhere."

Her eyes widened. "What? Now? It's the middle of the night. You need rest."

"I've rested enough. I'll be fine as long as you're with me… Trust me," he added, brushing her cheek with his knuckles.

His touch caused a wild desire to rise within her, forced to fight the burning need for his body against hers. She gazed at him hesitantly but found herself nodding.

He took her hand, intertwining his fingers with hers. A flutter ran up her arm from the innocent touch, pushing her limits.

After putting on their cloaks, Roman led her through the darkened hallways, the torches out for the night, leaving only moonlight and stars to guide them. She was nearly blind in the darkness, but Roman led her with memory.

He took her out to the patio, the night air warmer than the previous nights, summer coming into full swing. They walked to the edge against the stone railing, looking out over the lake and the silhouette of the mountains. Only the faint sound of crickets carried in the stillness of the night.

Rose inhaled a deep, fresh breath, stretching her stiff muscles from lying in bed for nearly twenty-four hours. She lifted her hand to the back of her neck, massaging it while rolling out the muscles. From the corner of her eye, she noticed Roman staring.

She lowered her hand as she met his gaze.

His eyes were filled with a force she'd never seen in them—it was as if he'd seen something he'd waited his whole life for. "Can you call for Onyx?"

She gave him a questioning look but did as he requested.

Onyx? she called out in her mind.

After a moment of silence, she heard him.

I'm coming, was all his sleepy voice said, faint from the distance.

"Where are we going?" she asked.

"Somewhere I think you'll like," Roman alluded mysteriously. "It's quite a journey from here, but with Onyx, it won't take too long."

A few moments later, Onyx came trotting through the night toward them, blending with the darkness so well she could hear him before she could see him.

Roman helped her onto the sleipnir, swinging himself up behind her and reaching around her to lead him.

The simple gesture woke something deep inside her, clawing to escape. She couldn't help her body from leaning backward into his chest this time, strategically placing her hands on his thighs for balance.

His chin hovered over her left shoulder, lips millimeters from her ear. "Ready?" his graveled voice rumbled.

She nodded, her throat too dry to find her voice.

And so, together, they rode through the night, the dense darkness making it difficult to see much of anything. Luckily, the two moons and stars shone brightly as they traveled through the trees.

Roman hadn't been exaggerating the distance. Even with Onyx sprinting nonstop, it still took a few hours to get there, Highland

Haven left far behind them as they drove deep into the mountain range.

She couldn't have cared less about the time as long as she got to keep the excuse of touching him.

At last, Roman told Onyx to slow down.

Rose examined the towering rocky mountainside beside them. For a moment, nothing seemed noteworthy until she noticed a large curved opening at the mountain's base—a cave. The dark void looked even more menacing in the shadows.

"Where are we?" she asked, peering at the black pit with hesitation.

"The Infinity Pools," he answered as the moonlight shadowed half his face. "People come from all over Vallor to see them… I can't take you to the shores of Eristan yet, but this will do for now."

He held out his hand to help her down, but her eyes were still fixated on the cave.

"I won't let anything happen to you," he reassured her, sensing her fear. "I promise."

She knew he wouldn't. And that was the only reason she stretched out her shaky hand, gripping his firm one.

The cave didn't become any less intimidating as it swallowed them. With each step into the darkness, they left the moonlight and Onyx behind. Echoing drips filled the cave while their footsteps crunched over the loose rock beneath them. She moved closer to Roman, taking hesitant steps as her hold on his hand tightened.

Then she saw them.

In the pitch dark, soft sea-green lights illuminated the cave, scattered across the rounded walls and floor. She gaped in astonishment at the glowing rocks, all different shapes and sizes.

She rested her hand on her collarbone, her eyes drifting toward Roman, who was already watching her. He tugged her hand, encouraging her to take a closer look.

Rose obliged, approaching the wall with slow steps, her eyes fixed on the stones. She raised her hand and lightly traced the glowing rocks with her finger. Smooth and cool to the touch, they radiated a soft, comforting glow like sea-green emeralds.

Roman approached her from behind, pressing his chest against her back, while his fingers traced the same rock.

The simple gesture brought her entire body to attention.

"It's similar to the kind of light Eristan's landscape has," he said next to her ear. "Most things in Eristan need sunlight to glow at night, but these rocks possess their own natural properties… It's quite the mystery."

Rose could scarcely concentrate on what he was saying. His rich voice stroked her very soul, making her body react in a way she wished it wouldn't.

Or maybe she did.

"Beautiful," she whispered, the only word she could think of, but even that didn't do them justice.

"Wait until you see the pools." He retook her hand, leading her further into the cave.

There her body went again. *Stupid fluttering organs.*

The rocks lit their way, stretching the full length of the tunnel. She stared at them as they passed, captivated by their subtle glow.

After strolling for a few minutes among the glowing rocks, they came upon the end of the tunnel, entering a vast chamber filled with seemingly endless pools of water, separated by slender rock walls, with a large pool at the center. The interconnected pools appeared to go on forever. She didn't know where the room began or ended as the water reflected the shimmering rocks above.

She gasped, bringing a hand to her lips, parting in awe as she walked towards the sparkling water.

It was as though she was standing amongst the stars.

"You see how the name Infinity Pool came about." Roman shifted his gaze out into the infinite reflection. "They say these waters bring out truth. That once you enter, you'll leave your old self right here and come out new. They're also said to hold rare healing powers."

"This… this is incredible." That much was an understatement.

Roman nodded in agreement. "It really is."

Without warning, he peeled his shirt off, tossing it aside, exposing his upper body to the glowing light. She tried to swallow, but a lump prevented it. He stripped the rest of his clothing off, except for his undergarments, taking the initiative to enter the clear water, his movements slow and cautious.

She followed suit, taking off her dress, and dropping it next to Roman's clothes, leaving on her slip. Without hesitation, she tiptoed into the water—cool, but not as cold as she braced herself for.

"You're not afraid anymore," he praised, noting her confidence.

"No... Thanks to you," she admitted, walking until the water was at her waist. The smooth stones massaged her feet with every step, her movements sending ripples through the sparkling water.

"You're exceeding at everything, honestly," he acknowledged. "Soon, you won't need me at all."

"You'll be glad of that." Her voice came out colder than she'd meant it to.

She felt his eyes on her, but she couldn't meet them, keeping her gaze on her hands gliding effortlessly over the water.

"What?" he questioned.

She figured if he was going to be angry with her, she might as well know why. "You've barely so much as looked at me since the Snorri. It's been weeks, and you're still angry with me."

Roman's face faltered. He didn't respond—perhaps because she was right.

"You just shut me out that night." She rounded on him, her raised voice echoing off the cave walls. "After everything I did with Moretti, after I risked my life for you again."

He scowled at the mention of his name. "I don't want to talk about him."

"Well, too bad," Rose shot back. "I don't deserve to be punished for trying to help you."

His throat strained to control his voice. "I'm not trying to punish you."

"Aren't you? Because it sure as hell feels that way."

He wouldn't meet her gaze, his hands clenching into tight fists under the water.

She sensed him withdrawing. So she walked through the pool, the water swirling with her movements as she faced him.

"Look at me," she begged. "It's not fair of you to hold it against me."

Roman's bitterness burst through as he snatched her wrist, dragging her into him. Her hand shot to his chest to steady herself, the abrupt movement making a small splash that resonated through the cave, sending harsh ripples through the calm water.

His eyes pierced down into hers just as she'd demanded. "I'll tell you what's not *fair*," he growled in a low, raw voice. "It's not fair how the prick got a *real* smile from you. It's not fair how he came into your life for all of two seconds, and you're considering *marrying* him. It's not fair that you sometimes still wear the bloody ring he gave you." He drew her closer, his fingers still wrapped around her wrist in a death grip. His voice lowered into a harsh whisper. "It's not fair how he has the ability to take you without consequence. While I'm stuck here, having to pretend I'm fine when I can't even so much as fucking *breathe* without you." He stopped himself, pausing as his eyes flickered between hers. "It's not fair to know he'd be better for you. If you want to be with him—"

"I don't," she interjected, stopping his rant.

Roman was about to open his mouth to continue when he realized what she'd said, snapping it shut. His eyes latched on to hers as he searched hers vigorously, as if discerning whether he'd heard her right or it was just a figment of his imagination. "You… you don't?" he questioned softly.

Did he really not see?

"Why do you think I've waited so long to go back?"

He faltered as his dripping hand reached up slowly to cup her face, his thumb stroking her cheek. He swallowed hard, looking down at her lips before shifting his gaze back to her eyes, studying her as if he were trying to commit every detail of her face to memory.

Her breaths became ragged as her eyes skimmed his face, gliding up from his collarbone over his jaw and nose to finally meet his gaze.

She waited—so patiently waited for him to do what her body was begging him to.

Millimeter by millimeter, he lowered his lips to hers, hovering for a long moment as if he meant to tease her.

Then, ever so slowly, he closed the remaining distance.

And just like that, her world cracked open.

Lightning coursed through her body, electrifying every vein. He tasted like nothing she'd ever known had existed. Superior to any drug she had ever known. Better than any dream she had ever imagined.

They took their time exploring every part of each other in the slow, smoldering kiss, like molten lava flowing downriver. Burning them both alive. They let the flames scorch them, knowing they'd never be the same, knowing that they'd have to bear scars forever. It was worth every mark.

A forceful burst of energy came from deep within her—this time, it bubbled up and exploded, taking over her limbs. Her hands lifted to the back of his neck, sliding into his hair. Water streaked down her arm as she grabbed a handful of it gently.

Roman still hovered close, breathless. "You have no idea the kind of power you hold over me, Roe."

She became utterly still, holding her breath.

Hoping.

Praying.

Begging the gods that he'd say the words she'd been yearning for.

"I've tried to fight it," he said through gritted teeth, full of self-resentment. "Gods know I've tried to fight it. To keep my distance. But the more I try, the more I'm consumed by you. You creep into my thoughts—thoughts that come uninvited, unwanted, but still they come. Sometimes in drips, other times in waves so powerful I can scarcely breathe."

Her gaze danced between the pair of golden stars as she waited for him to continue.

"I knew I was in trouble the first night I returned home," he confessed, casting his gaze out onto the water as if he were transporting himself back to that moment. "I recognized you on that balcony instantly. You'd gotten even more beautiful—which I didn't even know was humanly possible. I tried to ignore the annoying attraction, especially after learning you were still in love with Tristan. I knew I'd never stand a chance with you. Then I learned of what happened with Xavier... and I was angry. I tried my best to hate you. But when you saved my life after the first challenge, I thought maybe, just maybe, you might care for me, too. I had to remind myself you were still taken. So I forced myself to suppress my feelings for you."

She hung on every word, not breathing as her joints locked.

"Then, after the third challenge, despite everything, I was falling for you. My heart wrenched right out of my chest when I saw you fall into the sea." He made it sound like it was one of his worst memories. "I was seconds away from coming in after you—hell, I was ready to throw the entire succession over. But you saved me from exposing myself when you burst out of the water on the sea beast. Then it all came to a head that day in the woods where we sparred for the first time. When you laid me flat on my back, holding your sword to my neck." He gave a short scoff mixed with a laugh before his face settled back into its grave expression. "It was that precise moment I knew I'd held off my feelings as long as I could. I was in love with you. But it didn't matter. The fact changed nothing. If anything, it made me angry with myself for being so weak. I tried to love Beth, but I couldn't. Not with you around. So I convinced myself you were the problem. I tried to blame you for everything bad that was happening. I thought by blaming you, by hating you, I could move past it. I tried desperately to live the lie I told myself..." He swallowed hard, pausing. "But then I realized you weren't happy either. Not only that, but it was slowly killing you. And he saw it." Roman clenched his fists. "The bloody bastard *saw* it. You were hanging by the thinnest thread, and he did *nothing* to help you. Nothing to stop it. So when the council proposed the idea for the treaty... I agreed out of selfishness."

Rose's heart stopped.

"It was for you I agreed to include the arranged marriage," he admitted. "You were right. I did it because of you, but not because I didn't want you to be queen... I did it so you wouldn't have to be."

She couldn't even find words, her mind attempting to piece it all together.

"I was ready to let you go with Grant," he continued. "I thought if it was what you wanted, that'd be enough for me, but he ruined that for you, too."

Her mind raced. "All this time," she whispered, looking at him with wide eyes, "I thought you hated me."

"Hate you? No... No, I could never hate you. I suppose that's the irony, isn't it? Love. Hate... such a fine line."

Her heart threatened to beat out of her chest, her gaze sinking from his to the water.

He hadn't done any of it because he despised her—he'd done it because he loved her.

The realization made something deep within her come alive.

Roman shifted in the water. "I understand how twisted this is," he admitted with tormented eyes, "to want you like this. After everything I've done, after everything I've put you through. I know I have no right to want you..." His eyes ran over her. "Or to wonder where you are or what you're doing at any given time. Or to want to know what consumes your thoughts in that beautiful mind of yours. Or to hear your soothing voice that sets my soul at ease. Or to let my eyes linger on your face for far more than an appropriate amount of time. Or to crave your touch..." He caressed her cheek with his fingers. "Or to be hungry for your lips every time they say my name," he rasped as he ran his thumb over her lower lip —making it tremble.

There was no trace of the scowl or icy eyes she'd become accustomed to whenever he looked in her direction. It was a whole new Roman in front of her, a side of him she'd never imagined could be directed at her.

"What about Tristan?" she questioned, whispering his name, wondering what his plan was to tell his brother.

Their future king.

"I know," Roman acknowledged. His gaze fell, pausing, but then met hers again with determination. "But no matter how betrayed he may feel, he's married."

"Is that what we're telling ourselves?"

"At some point, you have to stop thinking about his happiness and start thinking about yours."

Still, a cloud loomed over her. "He'll never forgive us," she said, knowing it to be true.

His mouth tightened. "He'll forgive you... but he'll reserve his true hatred for me. I can only hope that one day, he will see it as a mercy. That you are protected and taken care of."

She hesitated, torn, even though her body screamed for her to accept him. "I still love him," she whispered pathetically, hating that she had to tell him. Knowing full well it might ruin everything.

"I know," he said, the fact clearly angering him, but he controlled his voice. "Tristan, you loved before me. I know that. But I'm not noble. I'm not going to deny myself the one thing I've ever wanted because Tristan desires something he can't have. And if I'm being entirely honest, I don't care. I'm not the good brother. I'm the selfish one, and I'll continue to be when it comes to you."

Rose couldn't find the words to say. So instead, she stayed silent, staring at him in awe. What he offered was so much more than anything she expected to ever receive. And for some reason, that made her feel guilty, because there were still things she'd kept hidden.

She finally collected her thoughts. "There are still things you don't know about me. I don't know if I can reciprocate all of what you offer."

He shook his head almost instantly. "That couldn't be further from the truth."

"It's true," she replied sharply, then she added more softly, "My heart has been shattered into tiny pieces, scattered so far and wide, I'm not sure if I'll ever find them all again. And not just by him—" she didn't want to say Tristan's name again, "—but by others, too."

Roman's gaze grew gorgeously tender. "That's just it." He slowly tucked her hair behind her ear. "I can only hope one day you'll have enough faith to tell me about each one of those beautiful scars you wear. But I do know that whatever is left of your heart—cracks, pieces, shreds, or whatever you like to call them—it's still the best heart I've ever known. I'll gladly accept every broken piece you're willing to give."

Rose gazed up at him, tears fogging her vision. She'd never heard such endearing words spoken in her life.

She lifted her hand to cradle his sharp jaw as water dripped down them. "You deserve more," she admitted. It was more than true.

He barked a harsh laugh. "The hell I do." When her lips didn't lift, his fell back into a thin line before he grimly added, "You do not know me as well as you think you do, Rosalie Versalles. You are so much more than I deserve."

Water trickled through the caves as she whispered, "I have absolutely nothing to give you."

"You honestly think I give a damn?"

Her mouth twitched upward at that, and she stroked his cheek with her thumb in appreciation.

"But I'm selfish," he said. "I want you to pick me because you want me, not because you have to survive... Which is why I bet a hefty sum on you in the Snorri."

Her heart stopped mid-beat. "You did what?" Her voice was barely audible.

"One hundred thousand golden medallions, to be exact."

She stopped breathing altogether, unable to comprehend what he'd just said, blankly staring into his eyes to make sure it wasn't a joke.

"The winnings alone make you the wealthiest woman in Cathan, maybe in all of Vallor," he admitted. "Not to mention the bags of money from the tavern. It's all yours. You can choose to marry or not marry anyone you wish to. I'm sorry I didn't tell you sooner. It was selfish, I just... I wanted more time with you."

Rose couldn't speak, couldn't breathe, couldn't move. She could only stare up into his eyes, spellbound.

"I know you've never truly had a home of your own," he continued, his voice growing nervous, looking down at her hands. He reached out to take them into his. "I should've let you pick, but when I saw it, I couldn't help but think of you. It's a large estate south of here. Rolling hills for miles, plenty of land and water. It's on a beautiful orchard, night skies so clear the stars look like shining diamonds..." His words faltered, his face concerned by her expression.

Her eyes were overflowing with silent tears. She couldn't help it. No one had ever given her a gift like this. Nothing could compare to what he had done for her.

He'd just given her her life back, her agency, her freedom.

And yet, at the same time, he had completely and utterly captured her heart.

A tear slipped through her defenses as she boldly brought her lips up to his, trying to convey all the love and gratitude words never could.

His lips molded to hers as if they were made solely for each other.

She pulled back with shallow breaths and opened her mouth to say thank you, but no sound came out. So she closed it again as she took in a deep breath. Her heart beat so loud she was sure he could feel it pounding against his chest.

"You don't have to say anything," he whispered, each word gently brushing her bottom lip, making her desire for him only grow. "I'll give you time. I'll wait… Hell, I'd wait until the end of time for you, Roe."

She let out a harsh laugh, choking back a sob, tears freely flowing out of her eyes now. "I don't need time." She gazed up at him. "The only time I need more of is with you."

His chin trembled as he took her wet palm and brought it to his lips, then pressed it against his cheek. His other hand slid up into her hair, bringing her to meet his lips.

She kissed him back with an unsatisfied hunger as her nails sank into his back, dragging them across his wet skin, forcing him to come closer.

His lips traveled down her jawline, leaving a trail of tender kisses in his wake as he took his time to explore. He moved to her neck, nipping and caressing it, going further down to her collarbone.

Her lips parted, letting out the sigh she'd been containing. She arched her neck as the ends of her long hair fell into the water.

This had to be what heaven felt like.

His movements became ravenous at her sigh. His mouth retreated home to hers, this time more greedy, forcing her lips apart as his tongue slipped in.

She responded with the same urgency. She couldn't fight her body any longer as she ground her hips against his, earning a deep-throated growl.

The foreign energy was taking over her limbs again, but this time, she leaned into it, bending backward as she pulled Roman down with her, slowly sinking through the water. Her hair seeped deeper, flowing effortlessly around her.

She withdrew her lips. "Do you trust me?" she asked, almost as if the voice was not her own.

His breathlessness matched hers. "Always," he stated between breaths.

She captured his lips again, pulling him gently backward, deeper, until they were fully submerged underneath the crystal-clear water, the rocks glowing alongside them, showering them with their light even underwater.

She took a chance and inhaled through her nose. As she'd suspected, she could breathe underwater, just as with the sea beast. She kept her lips on Roman's, giving air to him through her mouth. She could feel his surprise under her fingers as his muscles tensed, but his desire overruled any sense of survival. They sank lower to the floor with every passing moment.

His hand slid to her chest, cupping one of her breasts. Her back arched, moaning into his mouth as she bit his bottom lip, begging for more.

He smiled against her lips.

A tease.

She smiled back despite herself, pushing him deeper. His smile remained, trying to grab her arm, but she swam away playfully, then turned back and stretched out her hand, cocking her head, ushering him to explore more of the water's depths with her.

He took it, and together, they swam along the rocky bottom side by side.

The fear that had bound her like a chain had at long last set her free. The quiet blanket of the water over her ears calmed her. Being submerged felt like second nature. In fact, the longer she was, the bolder she felt, the more at… *home* she felt. It was strange. So strange to think she could've ever feared it.

She brought Roman to her lips every once in a while to give him more air. It was an excuse, really. He could easily resurface if he wanted, but she looked for any reason to repeat the action, always leaving her lips on his for much longer than necessary.

He knew it. And it didn't stop him from kissing her back just as hungrily.

Finally, after what seemed like hours, they resurfaced, still hand in hand.

His chest heaved between breaths as he spoke. "That was…. incredible… How can you do that?"

"I don't know. I discovered it when I was underwater with the sea beast. I thought maybe it was just a fluke until now."

His eyes glittered with amazement as he placed another soft kiss on her lips. He'd quickly become addicted.

All too soon, his lips released hers. His breaths were still far too harsh, still lacking energy from lack of sleep. She wanted to stay here with him forever, but he was in no state to keep swimming. "We should go back."

He gave a loud, resigning sigh. "Come on, then," he said, kissing her temple.

CHAPTER 68

After dressing, Rose and Roman exited through the cave to where Onyx grazed, waiting for them.

I see you finally found out what everyone else could see with their bare eyes, Onyx said, looking at their intertwined hands.

She rolled her eyes but nonetheless gave him a sheepish grin.

The ride back felt quicker than the journey there, perhaps because they were now running downhill rather than up, Onyx flying through the night with ease. Roman kept her close, one arm draped around her while the other gripped Onyx's mane. She pressed herself up against his chest as much as she possibly could.

Every once in a while, he would kiss her wherever he pleased. Once on the cheek, another on her neck, and another just under her ear. Each grazed kiss was lazy and slow—his fingers tracing her inner thigh all the while.

She did her best not to fall off Onyx with every touch.

It was still dark when they arrived back at Highland Haven, but the sky had begun turning into a lighter blue than before, telling her that the sun would rise in a few hours.

They did their best to be quiet as they entered the manor, and from the silent halls, it seemed everyone was still sound asleep.

Roman didn't stop until they reached the stairwell up to his bedroom. "Thank you for coming with me," he said, tucking her hair behind her ear and placing another kiss on her forehead—like he was leaving.

She panicked. "You're not coming up?"

He raised an eyebrow. "Do you want me to?"

She tried not to sound desperate as she quickly said, "Yes." She couldn't imagine ever being parted from him again.

He looked hesitant, like he was restraining himself. "Are you sure? Because… I'll never have the self-control to leave."

Oh, foolish boy.

Rose gripped his hand, finding herself in the middle of a warm, golden desert. "I hate to break it to you, but you're never sleeping in a separate bed again."

A ridiculously handsome smile grew on his lips. "Never."

He refused to let go of her hand while climbing up the winding staircase. The room was cool and dark without the candles or the fire, but moonlight shone bright enough through the windows to light their way.

Roman was striding to the closet to find a change of clothes when he suddenly stopped, his gaze lingering on a piece of clothing hanging on the chair beside the bed.

She stilled. It was his shirt she had stolen to wear to sleep.

He went to pick it up, smelling it. His head snapped to her. "Have you been sleeping in my clothes?"

She didn't say anything, thankful for the shadows as her cheeks flushed crimson. She tucked her hair behind her ear, peering over at him.

He slowly stalked toward her, shirt in hand. "You're telling me I've been awake downstairs, all alone, with nothing but your face seared to the back of my eyeballs while you've been up here, in my bedroom, wearing my clothes and sleeping in my bed?"

"And soaking in your tub," she reminded him.

He looked like he'd been deprived of life itself. "You wicked creature."

"I'm not apologizing. You insisted."

Roman raised his brows before giving her a crooked smile that had her seeing stars. "Come here."

A simple command, really—a small phrase.

Which was what made it so dangerous.

Her body conceded, not stopping until she was close enough to feel his rich breath on her face.

Golden flames seared her as his hands went to the hem of her dress. The air vanished, stolen from her lungs as he pulled it off over her head, leaving her in only her underwear.

Her heart was pounding with such force she was sure it'd break through her ribcage. He hadn't even touched her, and already, her body ached for his.

He took the shirt and put it on her, its hem falling just above her upper thigh. "It's yours now," he murmured softly. "Just like me." His voice was so raw, she closed her eyes to savor it.

His hands slid ever so smoothly down to her thighs, picking them up and hitching them around his waist, leaning his forehead against hers. With all the grace he possessed, he placed his lips onto hers, kissing her slowly, lazily, yet intently.

She held on to his broad shoulders, kissing him back with the same desire.

Roman broke the kiss, placing her gently on the bed.

She scooted backward at once, sliding across the silky sheets. He followed, prowling on his hands and knees over her.

His lips grazed her neck, rolling his warm tongue over her olive skin while he ground his hips against hers. She bit her lip to hold back a moan, arching her back. Roman's hands slithered just beneath her breast. She arched more, permitting him to touch her.

He ran his thumb over her hard nipple.

Rose couldn't hold it back any longer as she let a soft moan escape her lips. Unconsciously, grinding her hips harder against his, feeling his hard length between her legs through the thin fabric.

The knowledge he wanted her set her world on fire.

Roman growled at her moan, lightly biting her neck in response, scraping his teeth against her skin.

She couldn't get enough. He could be in her skin and it wouldn't be close enough. She intertwined her legs with his, widening them for him as he thrust against her more roughly this time.

She gasped.

She wanted him.

All of him.

But in the same moment, Roman's arms began to tremble, weakened from exhaustion. He fought it, but he had to pull back.

He sat up, letting out an irritated grunt as his gaze fell, breathing hard.

Selfish. How had she not noticed sooner?

She propped herself up on her elbow. "Are you okay? You're shaking."

"I'm fine," he replied, his chest still heaving as he tried to breathe.

She went to pull the covers back. "You need sleep."

His hand shot out, pulling her straight back into him, so close his lips brushed against hers. His eyes plunged into hers, straight into the vast depths of her soul. "I'll sleep, but only because I'm going to need every ounce of strength I have when I destroy you," his husky voice rasped. "And trust me, I'll be taking a very… *very* long time with you. I'll make every second count."

Rose's eyes fluttered closed, focusing on his voice as he continued.

"I'll ravage you until you're so overcome with pleasure, you won't be able to control any sound or move you make," he rumbled against her throat, his lips moving up slowly to just under her jaw. Her eyes rolled back as his hand slid up her leg. "I'll worship every inch of you. I'll take these and give them the individual attention they deserve." He reached for her breasts, cupping them in his hands. "Then I'll taste you." His hand spread between her legs. A small, muffled gasp escaped her lips. "Oh gods, to taste you." He teased her with his fingers, careful never to touch the throbbing ache that lay just between them. "I'll feast on you until you reach your edge, and then I'll push you over it. Again and again. I'll have you so addicted to pleasure you'll never want to leave this bed."

Rose bit her lower lip, liquid pooling in her underwear. She struggled for breath, gulping it in, her eyes fluttering open to see the golden gates of heaven staring back at her, inches from hers in a clouded, lustful haze.

Her hands skimmed up his bare chest to the nape of his neck, bringing him down with her on the pillow.

Without wasting a moment, he lifted her leg over his hip as he lay beside her, crushing her chest into his. She fought the hitch as he placed a slow-burning kiss on the base of her throat.

His drooping eyes demanded sleep. "I love you, Rosalie Versalles," he declared in a soft whisper.

"And I love you, Roman Montague," she whispered back.

CHAPTER 69

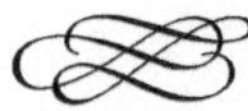

Rose was the first to rise that day, expecting to see sunlight pouring over the bed. Instead, rain tapped against the glass, providing a comforting white noise. She almost thought last night was just a dream until she felt Roman's arm draped lazily across her waist, relaxed and content. Her stomach fluttered at the sight.

She ran fingers through his golden-brown hair, then down his chest, drawing lazy circles on his skin, savoring the feeling of him under her fingertips.

She forced herself up, untangling herself from him and stretching her arms. She was about to get up when Roman's hand grabbed hers.

"Where do you think you're going?" he asked, a handsome smile already formed on his lips.

It was such a welcomed sight that she couldn't help but smile back. "I'm starving," she whined, struggling to tug him towards the door.

"So am I," he said with a wicked grin.

His strong arms easily dragged her back onto the bed before he placed a long, slow kiss on her lips. He pulled back just far enough to say, "Good morning."

"More like good afternoon," Rose corrected, looking outside. "We must've slept through most of the day."

"Well, what do you expect when you keep me up all night," he teased with a playful wink. "What do you want to do today?"

"What do you mean?"

"I want you to pick. Whatever you want to do, we'll do."

She looked out the window at the rain. "Could we just... skip training and stay in?"

Roman leaned forward, placing a chaste kiss on her forehead. "If that's what you want."

"It is. And food."

He laughed—actually *laughed*. The beautiful sound made her silly little lovesick heart flutter, making her want to eat him, too.

"Come on, then, let's feed you before you starve." He surprised her by lifting her and tossing her over his shoulder, earning a startled squeal.

They found Gretta helping in the kitchens, overjoyed to see Roman awake and well. She whipped up sandwiches for them and visited with them as they ate. Gretta's smile widened when she noticed their hands clasped together, clearly aware that they had shared the same bedroom the night before.

Hazel, on the other hand, looked devastated, her usually bright face solemn as she helped Gretta with the dishes. Rose tried to offer her a warm smile but received nothing but a cold-cutting glare.

Once they finished eating, Rose requested to visit the library. She sifted through the large, glorious room, finding more books to add to her "to read" pile. Roman recommended some and dissuaded others as they browsed through novels and short stories alike.

He read a few chapters aloud while she leaned back against his chest, gazing at the pages alongside him. His deep voice soothed her to her core, vibrating against her spine. The sentiment made her close her eyes and tip her head back onto his shoulder, memorizing the sound. She was confident she could listen to him read forever, discovering one of her new favorite activities to do together.

She was obsessed with how he made it a point to subtly touch her occasionally—a brush of his hand, a light kiss on the head, holding her from behind. Anything to remind her he was thinking of her at all times.

It made her completely mad and content all at once.

After finishing in the library, they pillaged a few sweets from the kitchens and returned to his room.

Rose gazed out the large, protruding windows, watching raindrops plop into the lake. Thunder grumbled in the sky as misty gray clouds covered the mountain peaks, obscuring all but their bases.

Looking out, she couldn't help but think of her mother. She missed her terribly, wanting to tell her everything that had happened last night, curious to know if she thought she was making the right choice or if she was completely mad.

With a twinge of sorrow, her mind wandered to Tristan, wondering if he'd found his own happiness.

Roman approached her from behind, breaking her trance. He wrapped his arms around her, kissing her neck while resting his chin on her shoulder. "What are you thinking about?" he asked softly.

"I'm thinking of the castle. Of my mum and…" Her voice drifted off.

"Tristan," Roman finished for her, his voice not angry but still not pleased.

Her chest tightened as she turned around to face him. She forced herself to meet his gaze, expecting his eyes to be cruel. It was worse—they looked hurt.

"I'm sorry, I—"

"You have nothing to be sorry for. You were clear about how you still feel about him."

She took his face into her hands, unable to stand the soul-crushing look he was giving her. "You must understand, Roman. Look at me," she ordered, making sure he was listening to what she was about to say. "It's true I love him, but I'm no longer *in* love with him. I can't be… not after you."

He nodded weakly, still not looking sure.

"You believe me, don't you?"

Roman gazed at her softly, tucking her hair behind her ear. "Of course I do."

"It's just… I'm scared to go back. To see your family, to see him. That's all."

"We don't have to go back until you're ready."

"When is that? When are we going to tell them? *What* are we going to tell them? We can't hide here forever." She was already imagining Tristan's rage—his family's disappointment in them both.

"We don't need to worry about it right now. We'll figure it out when the time comes. Let's just enjoy the time we have together like this." He took her hand in his. "Can I ask you something?"

"Anything."

"What exactly was the deal you made with the phoenix to save me?"

A nervousness crept up, taking hold of her limbs, as she thought about the terrible day she'd almost lost him.

"He asked for my help," she replied, thinking back on the words that haunted her mind. "He asked me to sing to help it be reborn, to heal it… I think, in a way, he knew I needed to be healed, too."

"So you can speak to all magical creatures?"

She nodded. "Thus far at least."

He thought for a moment. "And the seer in the second challenge… Could you speak to her, too? You two looked like you were having some sort of… internal dialogue going on."

"Yes, she spoke to me." It was strange to be admitting it all out loud. "She warned me there would be another war, one the likes we'd never seen, and I'd be at the heart of it. I was afraid I'd be the cause of this war unless I let Tristan go… just adding to the long list of reasons why I had to end things."

Roman's eyes widened. "Have you told anyone else this?"

"No one. Who would believe me?"

"You're telling me you've had to carry this burden all alone this entire time?"

She didn't know why, but tears pricked her eyes, perhaps because she was relieved to finally share the burden. "Yes."

Roman's eyes grew bitter. "And I sat there and accused you."

"Don't blame yourself. You didn't know."

"I should've," he seethed with self-resentment. "I should've known something wasn't right. You were only protecting everyone else like you always had. I was such a fool."

"It's no one's fault. I chose not to tell anyone." Her skin grew cold as she thought about what else the seer had said. "She also spoke of someone she saw in my future, someone she seemed terrified of. She called him the Blood King."

Roman frowned. "The Blood King?"

She nodded. "Does that mean anything to you?"

"No... no, it doesn't."

Her shoulders sank. Despite thorough research in the library over the past few weeks, she hadn't been able to find a single book that mentioned the Blood King. And it appeared that no one else knew the answer either.

Silence reigned until he reached for her, noticing her distress. "You don't need to be afraid. Nothing will happen to you. Not while I'm around." He wrapped his arms around her. "We'll find out more. I'll help you."

Rose's heart swelled three sizes as she tightly hugged him back. She shivered, burrowing into his arms, seeking warmth from the cold air the storm had brought.

Roman motioned toward the fireplace. "Come sit." He took her hand, guiding her to the warmth of the flames. After picking up a blanket and some cushions from the bench, he settled in front of the fire.

She joined him on the floor, nestling herself between his thighs, leaning her back against his chest. A blanket of warmth surrounded her on both sides, from Roman and the fire, sprawling across her skin. She relaxed at once.

A comfortable silence floated as he rested his chin on her shoulder. She melted, pressing the bridge of her nose against his neck, releasing a contented sigh as her body sunk into his.

"Roman," she said softly.

"Hmmm?" he hummed.

"Why couldn't you sleep? You were withering away. I swear you almost died, and now, suddenly, you seem fine..." She gazed up at him. "How is that?"

He stilled, not replying straightaway, taking his time to think. "I think it's because of you."

Her stomach plummeted. "What do you mean?"

"I haven't been able to sleep alone since the night we spent together after the tavern," he confessed, his voice raw and unsteady. "I didn't sleep much that night because of the unexpected visitors. But over the next few nights, I knew something wasn't right."

Rose turned to him, the heat of the fire moving to her back, seeping through her dress.

"I couldn't get you out of my mind," he continued, looking away. "It felt like my entire body was underwater, like a relentless pressure was surrounding me, squeezing the air out of my lungs. I couldn't take a single breath without feeling like there was a knife lodged in my windpipe. I'd close my eyes, and all I could see was you. All I could *think* about was you. And I'm not talking about a small crush." He paused, cupping her face. "I ached for you… Gods, how I ached for you." He winced as if remembering the painful experience. He slipped his hand into her hair. "The pressure would disappear around you. You were the only cure for my madness. I had to fight my body every minute of every hour not to go find you. I'd even find myself staring up at the staircase in the middle of the night, debating if I could just… slip in next to you, if only to sleep for a few hours. But I didn't want to scare you away."

Her heart tore in half. "Why didn't you tell me?"

He shifted his gaze like he was trying to guard himself. "I thought I could handle it, that it'd pass with time. I was ashamed of being weak. I *hate* feeling weak. I'm not accustomed to it. And more so because I wanted it to be your own decision whether or not you wanted me."

She reprimanded herself for being so oblivious to his pain. "I'm so sorry. I had no idea." Her fingers stroked his jaw, but he still wouldn't meet her gaze.

"I've never been needy, and it's hard for me… I've never needed anyone like I need you."

Her heart swooned as she scooted closer to him. "Be needy with me. Be *greedy* with me." She placed herself onto his lap, straddling him as she combed her hands through his hair. "Because you'll never have to be without me again."

His arms snaked around her waist, pulling her closer. His perfect golden eyes clouded with tenderness. "You understand you are my entire world, don't you?"

She swallowed hard, her heart pounding. "I'm beginning to."

Roman took her chin, making her look at him. His gaze dropped to her lips as he traced his thumb along her bottom lip. The simple touch made her skin burn alongside the fire's flames. She ached for him. She ached for him more than she had ever ached for anyone in her life.

And what thrilled her more was that she knew he ached for her, too.

She lost her composure when his thumb stroked her lip again. She parted her mouth and took it in, enveloping it down to his lower knuckle. She flicked it with her tongue, then, ever so slowly, she allowed it to slip from her mouth, catching on her bottom lip as it dropped out.

She dared to lift her eyes.

His demeanor had changed from content to lustful in an instant. His hooded eyes fixated on hers with such an intensity that she was both excited and somewhat frightened at the same time. With a firm grip, his large hand encircled the base of her throat, drawing her lips to his.

His mouth tasted like divine life itself—a sweet, addicting taste she'd never be satisfied with. She sucked his lower lip, taking it in between her teeth, tugging at it.

Roman responded by taking her hips into his hands and grinding her against him.

She let a small moan slip into his mouth.

Roman pried his lips away, going straight for her neck, his teeth scraping her skin.

She let out another moan as she arched her neck, asking for more. Always more.

His lips traveled down her neck to her collarbone, moving until the fabric of her dress stopped his path. He pulled back, his hands going for the back laces of her dress. She turned, giving him better access. When he finished, he reached for the hem, lifting it off and throwing it to the side. The heat from the fireplace beat hotter on her bare skin.

She grabbed for his shirt in response, exposing his chest, needing to feel his skin against hers. She took it a step further, going to her chest band, unwrapping it, and exposing her breasts to the cool air.

Roman's gaze slowly shifted downward, swallowing hard. It was as though he'd seen a feast and he was starving.

Her cheeks burned as he devoured her with his eyes.

"If we keep going… I'll lose all control," he breathed in warning, giving her one last chance to back out. "I touch you again, and I won't be able to let you off that bed, even if you beg me to." He wanted to make sure she understood.

She held his gaze, fearless. "I understand." Like she'd ever want him to stop.

As if she'd just released him from a leash, his self-control snapped as he dragged her roughly back into him. His lips crashed onto hers with a new sense of desire as his calloused hand went up to her chest, rolling his thumb over her nipple.

She whimpered, gasping at the absolute pleasure taking over.

His mouth grew into a triumphant smile against her lips.

Two could play that game.

Her hand went down to the waistband of his pants, her fingertips playing with the fabric before slipping her hand in. Her fingers had barely brushed the tip of him when a moan rumbled deep within his throat.

She'd found a new goal: make him make that sound over and over again.

He laid her down on the blanket as she reached for him, aching for his body weight to be on hers.

"You are mine," he claimed with a rasp, trailing feathered kisses along her stomach. "Rosalie Versalles… you are mine… and I'm never… letting you go," he muttered between kisses, trailing higher and higher.

She squirmed under him, her breaths shallow and weak.

His lips reached her breast, just the place she was hoping for. But he didn't give in to her desire so easily, teasing her as he kissed everywhere but the tip.

She let out a small, irritated whine.

His eyes flicked up to hers, a smile playing on his lips.

She glared at his cruelty. "Please," she begged, hating how weak she sounded.

He returned to kiss her lips before pulling back to hover over her. "Please, what?"

"Take them."

He returned his lips to her chest, offering a few more kisses before finally taking the peak into his mouth.

She gasped, her back arching off the floor, her body writhing beneath his as he lavished her with all the attention she craved. He switched sides, refusing to neglect the other—just as he'd promised.

Her moans grew uncontrollable. She needed more. She gripped his hovering hips and ushered them closer, grinding her pelvis against him as her legs fell open.

He hissed at the sudden thrust, feeling his hard cock pressing against her as she moaned louder.

Desperate for more, he pushed himself off her, wasting no time before he tugged her underwear down. He slid them off her legs and added them to the growing pile of clothing next to them.

He stilled as his eyes worshiped her, licking his lips in a way that sent her into a different dimension.

She reached for his pants, eager to see all of him. He allowed it, not objecting as she unbuckled his belt and slid it off. Next, her fingers undid his trousers, pulling the them down as he helped her free them from his legs.

She sat back, examining him with greedy eyes.

He was a perfect specimen, his muscles even more prominent in the shadows, rain hammering against the window behind him.

She couldn't contain herself any longer. She leaned forward.

"No," he denied with an unmerciful smile. "I'm not finished with you yet."

She laid back, giving him an impatient grunt.

His lips tugged upward into a crooked grin.

He moved down toward her legs, his warm lips brushing her inner thigh lightly, leaving trails of kisses and bites, rising dangerously close to the ache between her legs.

She thought she'd reached her wit's end. She put her hands above her head to restrain them, grabbing a handful of the blanket, muffling a moan.

He lifted his eyes to meet hers, and without warning, he slid a finger inside her.

She practically cried out, biting her lip as her back arched again. He hooked his finger, gliding against her ribbed wall. She rocked herself against him shamelessly.

His free hand went back up to play with her breast again. She writhed in pleasure, aching to reach her peak.

As if he knew, he withdrew.

She moaned in protest, her eyes opening to meet his again.

He lifted the finger to his mouth to taste her, his eyes never leaving hers as he licked it clean.

More liquid trickled between her legs.

"Roman," she breathed, hating how desperate she sounded. "I need you."

"And to the gods, I need you," he groaned. His gaze shifted between her legs, then back to her. "But I haven't even had the main course yet." A wicked smile swept in like the wind as he gripped her thighs, dragging her towards him.

She held her breath, the area between her legs throbbing for what he was about to do.

He gently bent her knees so she was displayed like a feast. His eyes became feral as he let out a low moaning sound before kissing the sensitive skin at her core.

She'd never forget the first stroke of his tongue.

Her body reacted immediately. Every muscle tensed from the pleasure as she gasped.

"Roman," she moaned, grabbing a fistful of his soft hair as he had his way with her, his tongue flicking and sucking as he pleased, his deep moans vibrating her most sensitive parts.

Her back lifted again as he shoved his tongue inside her.

His free hands slid up to her chest, reaching for her heaving breasts, playing with them lazily.

She whimpered, the pleasure inside her threatening to burst. "Ro... Roman," she warned, about to reach her peak.

He didn't move, moaning into her.

The vibration of his lips sent her over.

She cried out. Loudly. So loudly. Luckily, the rain would drown out her cry from being heard from downstairs. She clutched his hair in fistfuls as her hips bucked, shaking uncontrollably, her climax shattering through her in beautiful waves.

As she came back down, she waited for him to release her, but instead, he continued, his hands pinning her thighs so she would stay just where she was.

He pushed her over the edge again.

True to his promise, she couldn't control any sound or movement she made. Crazed noises erupted from her—sounds she didn't even recognize, movements purely pleasure-driven as her body took on a whole new experience.

She was left in a puddle of pleasure on the floor when he finally released her. She didn't know how it was possible, but the throbbing between her legs remained.

She was still not satisfied. She still hadn't had enough.

She looked up into his conquering eyes as he brought his lips back to hers.

"Gods, you're perfection," he murmured against her lips. "If I knew how good you tasted, I would've done that a lot sooner."

She kissed him back, her body still weak.

He began to move back down her body, but she sat up.

"No. It's my turn." Taking control, she pulled him down onto his back on the blanket beside her. He let her pin him to the floor, switching positions as she straddled him.

She ran her hands down his scarred chest, her lips following them down, past his belly button and lower.

Her hand got there first, wrapping gently around him, stroking his silky, swollen skin with gentleness.

Roman took a sharp breath as his jaw clenched, every muscle engaging beneath hers.

Her lips went to where her hand was, kissing the tip as she stroked him, getting a sample of the sweet, sticky liquid already leaking there. She moved her tongue downward, licking him from top to bottom, ever so slowly teasing him.

"Good gods," he uttered hoarsely, drenched in desire.

Without warning, she took all of him into her mouth.

He bucked, hissing. "Fuck," he swore under his breath, his eyes rolling to the back of his skull.

She smirked in pride around him, taking him in smooth, slow strokes, allowing herself time to grow accustomed to every inch, flicking the edge of him with her tongue.

He moaned as she took him deeper, attempting to reach for her, but she swatted his hand away, wanting him to know how it felt.

"Look at me," he commanded with such a low, pleasured voice, she obliged.

Her eyes flickered up to meet his, her mouth still around him.

Somehow, the small gesture was his breaking point.

He let out what she could only describe as a feral growl before he pushed her back gently but firmly, forcing her off him. "Come here," he breathed.

Her two favorite words from him, she decided.

He swept her up off the floor, wrapping her arms and legs around his waist and carrying her over to the bed as he kissed her hungrily.

He practically threw her onto the sheets, his golden eyes lost in desire as he towered over her. "I'm taking you," he warned. "I'm taking all of you—your body and soul. And I'm never giving it back," he swore to her as he nudged her legs apart.

She let out a small whimper, feeling him at her entrance.

"You are mine." His lips went to her neck again, biting it gently. "Say it," he demanded.

"I'm yours," she stated breathlessly.

His eyes softened. "Say it again."

A plea.

"I'm yours," she said, swallowing hard, then in a softer, submissive whisper, "I'm yours," she repeated, her hand going up to cup the side of his face, willingly giving herself over to him.

His fingers softly but firmly wrapped around her jaw, turning her face away from his as he leaned closer, bringing his lips next to her ear. "And I am yours," he whispered to her soul.

He entered her with one smooth motion.

She sucked in a sharp breath while Roman let out an uncontrolled sound she'd never heard in her twenty-four years.

"You've got to be fucking joking," he said, his voice laced with a powerful ache.

An immediate sense of pride filled her to know it felt better than he imagined.

His motions started slow and gentle, taking his time to familiarize himself with every inch of her. His hips rocked in slow, beautiful thrusts, letting her become accustomed to him.

She arched her back again. This time, his arm slid under her, securing her close, while the other held him up.

"I'm yours," he murmured against her lips, between fervent kisses. "Gods, I'm all but yours."

He drove himself deeper, his hips moving faster with each thrust. She raked at his back with her fingertips, clinging to him for support. Her chest grazed his as she swayed with him. Their kisses grew ravenous as they devoured each other, their tongues dancing together.

Her climax climbed again, coming back in full force. She pulled back, opening her eyes, wanting to see him. She found her favorite golden eyes waiting for her, taking her captive.

"Don't stop," she begged against his lips. "Please… whatever you do… don't stop."

Her lips went to the base of his throat, nipping at it while simultaneously swirling her tongue over his skin—a magical spot, she realized, as he let out a deep-throated groan while his eyes rolled back.

"Just look at you," he drawled with uncontrollable moans, his eyes raking over her. "I… I can't…"

Words failed as they were both shoved off the cliff they were hanging on.

Roman roared as he went with her this time, his strong arm crushing her into his chest as she dug her fingernails into his shoulders, crying out. His arms shook with pleasure as he poured himself into her, his thrusts wild and uncontrollable.

She couldn't breathe. She couldn't think. All she could see was him. All she could feel was him. He was her, and she was him.

One being.

One heart.

It was the precise moment she knew she could never live without him again.

Once he had poured every ounce of himself into her, he gently released her back onto the bed, his hands brushing the hair out of her face, stroking it. "I love you," he whispered breathlessly, his chest heaving as he rested his forehead against hers. "Gods, you'll never know how much I love you, Roe."

"I love you, too," she murmured between ragged breaths.

She meant it with every fiber of her being.

They laid beside each other for a long while, not worried about such a small thing as time. Roman cradled her against his chest as he stroked her hair, attempting to catch their breath.

"Can I ask you something else?" he said after a moment, his question mixed with hesitation.

She looked up at him, signaling he could.

"At the Infinity Pool, you mentioned feeling broken, that it wasn't only Tristan who hurt you… What did you mean by that?"

She stopped tracing her fingers over his chest, growing still.

He noticed the hesitation. "You don't have to tell me."

"I want to. It's only… I haven't told anyone, ever. I… I'm afraid you might look at me differently."

"Nothing you could say or do would persuade me of that."

"You might not be so sure after what I tell you." She sat up, wrapping the butter-soft sheets around her body.

He sat up with her as she looked away, trying to hide her pained expression. He took hold of her face, making her look at him. His gaze held her as firm as the mountains surrounding them.

"Don't you dare hide from me. There is *nothing* you could say that would make me love you any less."

She looked down to her hands, playing with her fingers.

Roman slipped his hand into hers, holding it in reassurance.

"It was my father," she admitted, forcing herself to speak of him. "He was… unkind to me." She averted her eyes to the dying fire, entering the darkness she'd tried so hard to expel. "Cruel would be a more accurate word," she corrected herself. "I know my mother had to bear burdens from him I never knew, but the way he treated me, in particular, was... different. Ever since I could remember, he looked at me with such disdain. Like... like he never really wanted me. He put on a mask in public so no one would suspect a thing, but behind closed doors, he could barely stand to look at me. And when he did, it was to punish me for the smallest things. He even hit me, but not often. Bruises left too much evidence. I tried to stay out of his way. It was the main reason I couldn't wait to go to the castle every summer—just to escape him... That was, until he heard me singing in the gardens one day. He realized I had a rare talent. He started taking me to festivals, events, markets, all of them. People paid handsomely to hear me sing. As I grew older, he noticed how men looked at me..." Her words faltered.

Roman's eyes darkened, his grip tightening around her hand, but he said nothing, patiently waiting for her to continue.

"When I turned sixteen, he started taking me to more mature places—taverns, pubs, ale houses, take your pick," she continued. "He used me to distract them while he pickpocketed and stole, perhaps cheated in a game or two. You see, he lost a great deal of money to bad investments one year. Trade and crops were sparse due to the harsh winter. To help our financial situation, he got involved in the black market, making deals with bad men. He foolishly thought he could win back all the money he'd lost, but he only got himself more and more in debt. He got in trouble with powerful men he owed a great deal of money to. Which is why we had to leave that summer to salvage the situation."

She paused, swallowing as she looked down at her hands.

"He got desperate. He took me to the local tavern one night without my mother's knowledge and made me wear a thin, revealing dress. It wasn't especially unusual; I wore similar clothes when I sang. But that night, he took me to a different tavern, one we'd never been to before. When we arrived, I noticed the atmosphere was... different. The room was packed to the brim with men and only men. Closed to the public. Little did I know it was an auction... for me." She dropped her eyes, terrified to hold his gaze. "The instant I realized what he was about to do, I tried to escape, but I was no match. He dragged me onto the stage, put chains on me like I was a slave. The bidding started high—so astronomically high. I was shocked. He'd have more than enough money to pay off his debts. After he sold me, he'd be a free man."

She paused again, tears threatening to surface as she forced herself into the memory.

"I'll never forget the man who bought me. He was a mountain of a man, larger than I'd ever seen. He wore a dark hooded cloak so I couldn't see his face, but his movements were so precise, so… unnatural. His voice was low, smooth, foreign. He bought me for more than triple the previous bid. No one could argue. None of them had that kind of money, but he did. They made him prove it. He walked forward from the back of the pub and threw the mounds of gold on the table. You should have seen the look on my father's face. It was the most terrifying feeling… I found out just how much I was worth that day."

Roman's lips lifted into a snarl. His eyes filled with hatred. "That bastard sold you?"

She dared to look at him, ashamed. "He did."

His eyes were full of questions, but he remained silent, waiting patiently for her to continue in her own time.

"Not long after, the man took me by the arm and dragged me out the back of the tavern. I tried to get away, but a full-force punch from me did absolutely nothing to him and nearly broke my hand. I was doomed. He threw me in a large carriage. I was sure he was taking me to a room with a bed made just for me." Tears finally slipped out of the corner of her eye.

Roman balled his hands into white fists, thoroughly enraged.

"But instead, when we finally stopped, I looked out of the carriage window, and I saw my home." She exhaled, relief filling her just as it had then. "I couldn't believe it. He was setting me free. He'd just paid a fortune, and he chose to let me go. I remember him still wearing the hood as he got out of the carriage, holding out his hand to help me down." She looked down at her hand, recalling the ghost-like jolt of lightning that ran up her arm. "I stepped out and told him I couldn't repay him. And do you know what he said? 'Work on that punch. That'll be payment enough.'" She let out a harsh, tearful laugh despite herself, though the smile quickly faded.

"He made me promise I'd learn how to fight for myself. He said it'd be the only way I'd always be safe. I vowed that I'd repay him by keeping that promise."

"You definitely have." His face was more relieved than she'd ever seen it. "Did you ever find out who he was?"

She shook her head. "No, I never saw his face. And I never saw or heard from him again."

"What happened when your father found out you'd been returned?"

"I don't know. He was found dead in the alleyway the next day." She kept her voice void of emotion, ashamed to feel glad about the fact. "We don't know by who or why, but I'd take a good guess it was someone who wanted the fortune he had just received because the money was also gone. Maybe it was his debtors finally reclaiming what was theirs. We never knew for sure."

Roman paused, processing it all. "What did your mother think of it all?"

"She wanted to keep it a secret, save our reputation. She thought that perhaps I could redeem us by finding a suitor. So we covered it up, pretended he'd died a good man. We told no one what he was truly like or what he'd done. She carries a large guilt for what happened that night. It's why she's so protective over me now. Why she thought the palace would be safer for me. Why getting married to Tristan was the perfect solution... until everything happened."

His brows grew together. "Why would any of this make me think differently of you?"

She looked up into his eyes, whispering, "Because *I'm* ashamed—ashamed I lied to you and your family about our situation. That you were right about me all along—I was using you all."

He shook his head. "I wasn't right at all. You loved Tristan. It was real. I know that now."

"Yes, I loved him... but these past few weeks have helped me realize something." She paused, looking across the room, back into the fire. "That even with everything that stood in our way of being together, we were two different people meant for different things. The fact doesn't mean it wasn't any less real or wasn't true. Or that he won't always hold a place in my heart, because he will… but he wasn't able to see me for who I truly am." She paused, daring to look back at him.

He wasn't looking at her, his eyes cast out. He had that soul-crushing look on his face again, the one that sent her into a spiral of guilt.

She scooted towards him, taking his strong face into her hands, forcing him to face her head-on.

His crestfallen eyes shifted, surrendering to her.

"You not only see me—you see right *through* me. You let me be who I am, and you love me for it. You challenge me. You put me first without hesitation." She ran her fingers up into his hair. "You saw my sword, and instead of taking it, you fought with me… You don't mind my fire."

He lowered his forehead to rest on hers. "I not only don't mind it, I crave it," he murmured as he brushed her hair back over her shoulder. "I would never smother it. I just want to be near it, if only to be kept alive by its warmth."

Her eyes softened as she looked back and forth between his.

He pushed her gently back onto the bed, looming over her as he hovered. "I'll never let anything like that happen to you again."

Being wholly accepted by him made her ache for him all over again, her gaze fluttering from his eyes down to his lips.

He recognized the flare of desire as his own became hooded, hunger creeping back into them. He leaned down and kissed her with a renewed craving, slowly forcing her mouth open, letting his lips mold to hers.

And just like that, she knew she'd finally found home.

CHAPTER 70

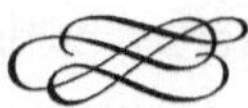

As cliché as it sounded, the next few days were something out of a romance novel. Rose and Roman were inseparable, spending every waking moment together. Each night was the same, sleeping intertwined. An ever-constant thirst for him lived within her, and he was just as crazed —which, in turn, led to them making love whenever they got the chance. The simplest of touches turned within an instant. A brush of a hand. A peck on the cheek. A lingering stare.

Dangerous games.

One afternoon, their usual training session in the woods took an unexpected turn, evolving into a different kind of session. She'd never been so happy to be pinned to the ground.

Best lesson yet, in her opinion.

Gretta was ecstatic about the blossoming relationship, beaming every time she saw them. She learned to leave food at the door in the mornings when they missed breakfast, knowing better than to enter. Her spirits were so lifted that she'd hardly scolded them as they trailed lake water through the halls, barely making it back to the bedroom before they claimed each other.

Two weeks later, Roman decided to go hunt. Despite Rose pointing out the ominous dark-gray clouds overhead, it didn't deter him as he muttered a complaint, something along the lines of not having fresh meat.

She was leaning in to kiss him goodbye when he grabbed her arm. "You think you're not coming with me?" He brushed her nose with his, his lips slipping into a crooked smile as he handed her a bow and arrow. "Come on, we'll see if I've taught you anything."

Which was how they ended up roaming the woods that day. Onyx took them farther north than usual. Rose didn't mind in the slightest as Roman stroked the inside of her thigh every so often from behind, just to make sure the ache for him never left.

The usual turquoise lake morphed into a deep indigo from the dark clouds blanketing the sky. Highland Haven appeared only as big as a single gold coin as they ventured forth deeper into the mountains.

Once they'd gone far enough to satisfy Roman, they left Onyx by a small creek to drink while they continued on foot. They decided to split up to cover more ground, agreeing to meet back at the creek in an hour.

It was embarrassing how she missed him from the moment he left. It had to have only been a few minutes, and she already wanted to go back and find him.

She pressed on, brushing the ever-present need for him aside.

The forest was quiet, the trees still—the calm before the storm. A distant rumble of thunder from the west echoed off the mountains as she kept alert, looking for any signs of tracks or scat like Roman had told her to. To her pleasant surprise, she found a peculiar set of tracks that was reasonably fresh but unfamiliar.

She bent down, running her fingers along its edges. The soil was soft and moist between her fingers. She'd never seen a track quite like this. It looked like a deer's, but it was too large—much too large. Perhaps a moose?

She followed the trail. Its leg span was farther apart, much like Onyx's. Its prints wound through the trees, and she took a mental note of random nibbles on the leaves and branches along the way.

The tracks led her to a large clearing. She continued cautiously, careful to keep her feet light.

A rustling sound came from up ahead.

She strained her ears. More rustling.

Slowly, she readied her bow, stepping out of the tree line. She stealthily cocked her arm, ready to strike.

She froze at what she saw.

In the clearing stood a pearl-colored creature, looking almost radiant against the natural hues of the forest. It resembled a deer, only much larger. Its antlers were intricately beautiful, graced with soft blooms, reminding her of plum branches blooming in early spring.

She recognized the creature from illustrations in her books.

A snawfus.

Based on what she'd read—which was but a mere few paragraphs—it was supposed to be extinct. Said to hold depths of untold power. Arguably, the most powerful magical creature in the realm. Throughout history, many humans had sought to kill them and harness the creatures' power for themselves. Even esteemed leaders from the past had done so, gaining their power and strength from the blood of the snawfus. It was regarded as a tremendous honor. Undoubtedly why they went extinct.

But apparently, that fact didn't hold true.

Rose took another step to get a better look, emerging out of the woods while keeping her arrow aimed at its heart, unsure of its nature. She must not have been paying enough attention to her foot placement because a twig snapped loudly beneath her.

The creature's head whipped toward her.

Her arms strained, holding her ground as its light-gray eyes bored into her soul. She held her breath, adrenaline pounding through her veins.

If she wanted to, she could let go of the arrow. She was confident enough in her skills to know she wouldn't miss. It wouldn't have time to escape.

But what she saw in the snawfus's eyes was nothing like she'd ever seen. It looked so innocent, so pure. No aggression or fear could be found in them, even as she kept the deadly weapon pointed at its heart. The fact made her heart soften, and she decided to put her faith in the magical creature.

Ever so slowly, she lowered her bow, placing it on the ground at her feet, sure to never take her eyes off the snawfus.

The creature's misty eyes widened. Its body shifted toward her slowly, coming closer.

She almost wondered if she'd made a mistake by dropping her weapon. There was no way she could outrun it. It'd catch up to her with a few strides of its long legs. If it wanted, it could easily trample her to death. She could do nothing but hold her ground and pray it wouldn't hurt her.

Its eyes never left hers as it neared, locking her in a trance.

It didn't stop until it was face to face with her.

You didn't kill me, the whimsical, feminine voice said in her mind.

Rose jumped, though she supposed she should've expected it. This was now the fourth magical creature to speak to her.

No, she replied.

Why? I sense you know what I am. The power I possess. Don't you want it for yourself? the snawfus asked.

No. I have no need of it, she responded in all candor.

The snawfus looked at her with brighter eyes. *Then you are a rarer creature than I—one with a pure heart. Especially rare for a siren, but then again, I've never met a half-breed.*

Her blood ran cold. *What did you just say?*

The snawfus blinked, realizing she didn't know. *My dear, you are a siren.*

A siren? The monsters that almost destroyed Vallor?

Rose stepped back, shaking her head in denial. *That's impossible.*

You have a shield covering you, the snawfus observed. *Powerful blood magic placed on you as a baby.*

She shook her head with more vigor. *No. No, that can't be. Both of my parents are human.*

If you don't believe me, answer me this. Aside from your obvious abilities to talk to another magical creature and your almost inhuman beauty, do you find men drawn to you? Can you sing so well that it entrances anyone who hears? Do you have enhanced physical capabilities? Are you able to manipulate water? Even breathe in it?

Rose widened her eyes in realization. Her breaths became shallow, her mind racing.

Did she, at long last, have the answers to her questions? With the sea beast, the phoenix, Onyx, and now the snawfus.

Could she speak to them because she was one of them?

She looked back up at the snawfus in awe.

The snawfus gazed back knowingly. *You are the one—the one I've been looking for. I've been searching centuries for you. You are the first human or siren who has not tried to take my power for yourself—the first who has come with a pure heart. Fate has brought you to me, Rosalie. To fulfill your destiny.*

What destiny is that? Rose was almost afraid to hear the answer.

To defeat the Blood King, of course, the snawfus said.

There was that name again.

A frost-biting burn spread through her veins to her heart, stopping it mid-beat. *Who is he?*

A dark, powerful entity born centuries ago. He must be destroyed, or every human and creature that roam these lands will be nothing but ash. A whisper of a memory. He's creating an army so strong and vast, no human will be able to stop it.

But what can I do? Rose asked, resentful of how everyone seemed to know the answers but her. *I'm no one.*

That is precisely why you are the one.

She grew frustrated. *You're speaking in riddles.*

A sudden loud snap in the forest trees made the snawfus's ears twitch, alerting it to something nearby.

We're short on time. I can't tell you everything. You must seek the answers out for yourself. Start with your mother. She'll tell you what you need to know. Next, finish your quest and find the men you were searching for. You'll meet your destiny with them. However, there's one thing I can do to help. I'm going to give you the most precious thing I can to help you defeat him.

What's that?

Me, it said simply.

Her brow furrowed, not understanding.

The snawfus lowered its large head, resting its forehead against hers. *I willingly give myself over. I live on in you.*

The last thing Rose remembered was a flash of blinding white light as she crumpled to the forest floor.

The next thing Rose knew, she was waking up in Roman's bedroom, her head pounding with a headache as she came to.

"Rose?" a worried voice said. She knew that voice as well as her own. "Rose? Dammit, Rose, can you hear me?" Roman's panic-stricken voice rang out, jerking her body—bringing her back to the world.

But she wasn't the same.

Something foreign stirred deep within her consciousness, breathing the same air, moving in the same body, thinking the same thoughts—interwoven with every fiber, every vein, every strand of hair.

She'd felt the dormant creature before. Only she didn't know it then. But now... now the deep magical force quaked with power. She was forced to embrace the hibernated presence that was now undeniably... *alive.*

She knew exactly what it was.

It was her siren.

Herself.

She felt Roman's fear. *Felt* it. Like the emotion was her own.

The sensation made her recoil at once, feeling as though she was touching something she shouldn't.

Her eyes fluttered open. The world around her was clearer than she remembered, sharpened to lethal perfection. She peered up to find Roman's astonished eyes, anxiousness pouring from them.

"Roman?" she mumbled.

His shoulders relaxed as he looked up to the heavens. "Thank the gods." He pressed a firm kiss to her forehead.

"What happened?" she asked, searching her memories. "How'd I get here? Did you see the snawfus?"

"What snawfus? Is that what did this to you?"

"Did what to me?"

His hesitant eyes shifted hesitantly to the mirror. "See for yourself."

She got off the bed and went to stand in front of the mirror.

She inhaled sharply.

Her muscles froze at the sight of the striking stranger staring back at her. She'd never thought of herself as vain, but she was a great deal more attractive than she could've ever imagined herself being.

The most drastic change was her hair—the once cool-brown color was now a thick, pearl mane. It matched the snawfus's fur precisely. If it was a coincidence, she didn't know, though the change had left her lashes and brows dark.

Her eyes were the most striking thing, though—practically bewitching. A light sea-green color filled them, radiating the magic within. But upon closer inspection, she discovered the tiniest bit of gold dust in them, like sand on a beach. They were intended to be a weapon, to lure anyone who so much as glanced in her direction.

Her olive-tanned skin was clear, not a blemish in sight, and the scars on her neck and wrists were now gone. Her lips were still the same large pink ones, glowing with a newly hydrated plumpness.

There was no denying it.

Her beauty was ethereal.

She spun back to Roman, who was still staring at her. "What happened?" she asked, touching her cheek in disbelief.

"I could ask you the same thing. I was walking downstream when I saw a flash of white light. I came as soon as I could to find you passed out on the ground, looking like… like this." He gestured to all of her.

She searched her memories again, trying to remember any detail of what had happened after the snawfus touched her. But all she had seen was a flash of bright white light, and then… nothing.

She faced the mirror again in disbelief. "Do you not like it?" she asked in a concerned voice, the pride of her siren slipping from her lips.

Before he even spoke, she knew the answer. She could feel his desire seep from him like a thick fog. It was powerful—his want for her. His need. How he worshiped her.

It *fueled* her.

A prickly shiver shot up her spine.

"Of course I do. It's still you, isn't it?" he stated, as though it was the most obvious thing in the world.

Her eyes fell. "Partly."

His face contorted. "What do you mean? What the hell happened out there?"

Even though she was terrified he might run like hell, she told him everything that had happened in the forest, right down to the last detail, leaving nothing out.

"So you see... I'm a siren, Roman," she whispered, ending her story.

His eyes flooded with understanding. "It all makes sense now. The way you could tell the arrow was laced with Dragonshade poison, how you could see the invisible rope in the Snorri. How you could train and move so quickly. How you escaped the sea beast. How you were able to run on the water with Onyx. How you can breathe underwater. Talk to the phoenix. Why I was in physical pain without you next to me—all of it."

She clamped her hands together. "I believe so," she whispered.

He tore his gaze from her to the window as he folded his arms, brooding as he thought.

She left him to absorb the information as she faced the mirror again, trying to familiarize herself with the face staring back at her.

A cold drip sunk deep into her bones as she looked at Roman through the mirror's reflection, still peering out the window.

What if nothing he felt for her was real? What if it was her siren's powers luring him to her? And what if it wasn't just Roman? What if Tristan, Grant, Moretti—all of them had fallen victim to her unknown siren powers?

A new fear planted itself inside her.

What if... what if every love in her life had been fabricated?

The thought cracked each rib inward, causing the debris to stab her heart.

It was a long while before either spoke.

Roman finally looked back at her, observing her in the reflection. "What is it?"

She hesitated, stowing away her fear. "I've only read bits and pieces about sirens. Their beauty is their most deadly weapon. A trap to lure others in. They're able to feel and manipulate emotions, which makes it easy for them to control those around them—to use them." Her eyes fell to her hands cautiously, as if they'd do something against her will. "Their superior physicalities allow them to live for hundreds of years. Consequently, they have been hunted down by humans for generations, out of fear that if they outnumbered them, they'd rule them just like they had in history. So they killed them off. It's said they were almost annihilated—just like every other magical creature. There's hardly any left in Vallor." She paused, her eyes meeting his. "What if I'm exactly what the high council thought? What if they had a right to fear me? What if somehow they knew that I was this monster?"

Roman planted his feet in a wide, determined stance. "You aren't a monster and never will be."

She wished she could share his certainty.

He came to her, bringing his hand to her chin, lifting it so she'd have to look into the eyes she held so dear. "You are the *furthest* thing from a monster."

She braced herself as his ache for her was magnified through the simple touch.

"Gods, look at those eyes. You can't look into those eyes and not see an angel."

It was strange to feel his mind, how much he wanted her. The knowledge amplified her desire for him, too.

She leaned towards him, her mind subconsciously reaching out, digging its claws into his, burring them into his soul. Bringing him closer. To devour him, to take—

She backed up, suppressing the feral beast from ripping out of her skin.

She didn't have to feel his pain to know it. It was written all over his face.

"I'm sorry," she apologized, stepping back again. "I just don't want to hurt you."

His determination only grew with her confession. "You're not going to hurt me." He took a step forward.

She took another step back. "You shouldn't be so sure," she snapped, but then she softened at his hurt face. "I just need to know how this is possible. I need to know more. I need to speak to my mother."

They both knew what that would mean.

They'd have to return to the castle.

Roman looked out the window again, rubbing his jaw as he let out a large breath. "If we go back, there's a good chance you'll be seen. I don't know exactly how they'll react, but I can guess it won't be good. You could be putting yourself in danger. You were already a target before; now, you might as well have a red beacon over your head."

"She could come here?" she threw out the idea.

Roman thought. "We could do that, but I know my brother. As soon as he realized she was leaving, he'd know she was coming to you. He'd follow her. And I don't want him showing up unexpectedly."

She searched her mind, thinking of other options, but nothing else seemed possible. "It's too important. We'll have to take the risk. At least it'll only be him and not the entire court."

Roman sighed, caving. "Fine. We'll send for her to come."

"But there's something I have to do first. And you're not going to like it."

Roman's eyes darkened as soon as she told him.

CHAPTER 71

"Rose, don't," Roman pleaded, following her outside as she called for Onyx in her mind, but she sensed he was already coming to her. "It's too dangerous. Think about what you're doing. To hell with the castle. You're walking into an entire city. A very dangerous one at that. What if you're discovered? What if Moretti hands you over for money—or worse? It could be like the tavern all over again."

She ignored him.

He grabbed her arm, spinning her to face him. "Look at me. It's not worth it."

"No one will be watching for me like at the castle." She pulled her arm out of his grip. "The crowd will be to my advantage. Besides, I'm a siren. I don't know exactly what that means, but I do know I possess powers. I know I can persuade him to tell me where these men are. The snawfus said finding them would help lead me to my destiny, and this is the only lead I have. I have to try."

"This is madness."

"Maybe," she admitted, watching Onyx approach them warily. "But if I can prevent more lives from being lost, I must. I have to know more. I'm tired of being in the dark. It's time I get answers."

Roman gave a frustrated grunt. "I'm not going to be able to talk you out of this, am I?"

"Nope."

"Fine," he said in submission, "but I'm coming with, and we aren't taking Onyx. He'll draw too much attention. I'll stay far away. You won't even know I'm there—but I'm coming."

She didn't try to argue.

The winds lashed Rose's cloak, while heavy rain loomed within the dark, cloud-covered sky. She did her best to keep her hood from flying off in the wind, keeping her face hidden from the few who walked the city streets. They hardly noticed her, preoccupied with securing their belongings against the impending storm.

While riding through the streets, she caught sight of a flyer fluttering in the wind. Her gaze fixed on the piece of parchment nailed to the wooden post as her eyes widened.

It was a missing person poster with a sketch of herself, though her name was listed as Draya Santres. A sizable reward was promised to anyone who could provide information. To her shock, this wasn't the only one. Posters were plastered across almost every window, lamp post, and door, with some even fluttering through the streets, scraping against the cobblestones.

"You sure made an impression on Moretti, didn't you?" Roman drawled beside her. "What the hell happened between you two anyway?"

Her guilty eyes met his. "We kissed… more than once… maybe a lot."

His eyes bulged out of his sockets, an ugly aura expelling from him in a powerful wave. "What?" he hissed.

"I couldn't get a chance to put it in his drink, so I put it in my mouth and got him to take it that way." She paused, as Roman still glared. "I was helping, remember?"

His glower didn't falter. "I don't like this. The whole city will be looking for you, thanks to these damn flyers."

On the contrary, the storm may just work in their favor. "This is the perfect time. The streets are practically empty. I'm not wasting the chance. I may not get another one."

She steered her steed forward, navigating through the streets to the front gates of Moretti's estate without any complications, Roman doing as promised and hanging back. Although she couldn't see him, she knew he was well within eye range.

The guards came to attention as she approached, careful to keep her face hidden under her large hood.

"I'm here to see Moretti," she stated, keeping her voice silky and smooth.

The guard on the right was the first to speak. "Who asks?"

"Draya."

They recognized the name in an instant, their backs straightening.

"He's not at home at the moment, Ms. Santres. He has business in town," the other guard said. "But upon your return, we were ordered to tell you to wait here, or we can take you to him."

"Then take me to him," she ordered.

With a nod, the guard led her through the city, northward down the cobblestoned street. The trip was quick since there was no heavy traffic. Even the canals, always full of boats, flowed peacefully empty beneath them.

To her pleasant surprise, he led her straight to the Central Library, said to be one of the most beautiful libraries in all of Vallor.

And that it was.

A shallow multi-level staircase led up to the moody building. It looked nothing like what she had imagined, its black exterior lined with a golden trim and gutters that framed the edges and doors. The most impressive thing had to be the enormous glass dome sitting directly on top of the massive building, providing a beautiful skylight for those within.

The interior proved to be just as elegant. She couldn't help but crane her neck to gaze at the gigantic domed glass ceiling that hovered overhead, the tinted ceiling so tall she swore the top entered the clouds.

Her shoes tapped across the black-and-white-checkered floor as she followed the guard across the lobby, her gaze drawn to the line of black wooden bookshelves, each bearing a single brass letter, keeping the books in an orderly alphabetical fashion. The colorful spines of the hardbacks popped out strikingly against the dark wood.

She didn't have long to admire the lobby as the guard led her directly up the black spiral staircase, down the hall, and to the right, stopping at a double door.

He knocked in a precise pattern.

"Come in," a sharp, familiar voice called.

The guard entered as she waited just outside. "I have someone to see you."

"Not now," Moretti retorted, irritated.

"It's someone you'll want to see," the guard pressed.

"Whoever it is can wait. Can't you see I'm in the middle of something?"

Rose took a deep breath as she walked into the room, keeping her face hidden.

Moretti was in a meeting, surrounded by men, sitting at a large rectangular table cluttered by parchment and maps.

Their quills halted the moment she walked in. A wall of windows behind them offered a sweeping view of the city, though the gloomy weather prevented the sunlight from brightening the room, forcing them to light the candles on the table.

"I can come back another time," she said in a smooth voice that didn't sound like her own.

Moretti's head flew up sharply from the parchment in front of him, his dazzling blue eyes sparkling at the sight of her.

"Gentlemen, could you give us a moment," Moretti said, his tone letting them know it wasn't a question.

One by one, they shuffled out, each of them trying to peer under her hood, but she kept her face hidden. Once they were alone, she returned her attention back to Moretti. He hadn't moved from the head of the table.

"I was afraid I'd never see you again," he said, looking at her with unadulterated relief. "When I didn't hear from you, I thought something might have happened to you."

"I know. I'm sorry," she said, walking around the table toward him. "But I'm here now."

He looked her over. "You don't sound pleased to be."

"I am... I'm just nervous." Which was true.

"It's hard to tell with that hood on," he teased, tilting his head to the side to get a better look.

She took a mental breath as she pulled the hood back, revealing her face.

He took a step backward as his eyes widened in awe, examining her from head to toe. It took him a long moment to recover from the shock. She could see his internal wheels turning, trying to piece together what he was seeing.

"How?" he whispered, his eyes still drinking her in.

"It's a long story," she said simply, clasping her hands together.

"You're... you're a siren?" He looked her over again, both amazed and intrigued.

She took a small step toward him. "Yes. But you don't need to be scared of me."

His eyes never left hers as he came closer. His aura was different than Roman's—more smooth and refined. "I'm not *scared* of you. It's just—you were beautiful then, but now... now you're the most glorious creature I've ever seen." Moretti leaned unconsciously closer to her lips.

Her siren reveled in his praise. "Thank you."

Moretti's mouth spread into a wide grin. "You have no idea how powerful or beautiful you actually are, do you? You act as though you couldn't hurt a fly. Damn you." He tucked her silky white hair behind her ear. "The fact only makes you even more attractive."

She gave a dangerous smile despite herself—her siren's doing.

His eyes shifted to her lips. He swore. "Look at that smile... and that *smell*." He drew a deep breath as his eyes glazed over. "It's addicting."

Her siren craved more praise, yearned for it—to be complimented, desired, and adored.

She stopped it before it escalated. "I came because I need your help."

He snapped out of his daze slightly. "Help?"

"I need to find those men," she stated, not beating around the bush. "I can't leave without an answer this time."

He straightened as his expression hardened. "That's the only reason you came back, isn't it?"

Rose's eyes shifted with guilt. "It's important."

"I told you I couldn't tell you, even if I wanted to," he said, his voice cold yet hurt at the same time.

"I think you could if you let me in," she said, intertwining her hand with his. "Please, I have no idea what's happening to me, what it all means. These men could give me answers. Answers I need. Answers that could save thousands of lives."

She struggled to locate the magic she knew had to be lingering somewhere inside of her, fumbling for it like she'd lost something small hidden in the shadows. It took her a moment to find the source, wrangling it into something useful. Her siren, in kind, prodded her to let it take over.

Cautiously, she let the magic fill her. She dragged him down into her sea-green eyes, her siren reaching out to his subconscious, comforting him—easing him into a false sense of security. The walls protecting his mind cracked as her siren's claws snaked their way around his mind, gripping it.

"Where are they?" she asked.

He swallowed, beads of sweat forming at his temples as he struggled to answer. "I..." he tried to say. "I can't tell you."

"Yes, you can," she encouraged, hovering closer to his lips, squeezing her grip tighter.

He struggled against her pull, the magic embedded within him fortifying his thoughts. But her siren persisted, squeezing the answer out of him—another large crack formed in the wall.

She despised the feeling of invading his mind, but she was desperate.

She won the battle as the last of the barricaded wall crumbled and he let out a painful sigh. "Last I heard, they had made camp just outside of Carnthe, close to the northeastern border, but that was some weeks ago."

Her heart leapt. Finally, something they could use. "How many of them are there?"

"Not many. I'd say no more than twenty."

She raised an eyebrow in surprise. How could that be? How could so few do so much damage? Overrun cities? Kill all those innocent people?

"What were they looking for?" she asked, wanting to know more.

He struggled a great deal more with this one, his face twisting in pain. "They were... looking... looking for a girl."

That certainly wasn't something she would have ever guessed. "A girl? What girl?"

Moretti swallowed hard, still wrestling for words as his face flinched. "A girl named Rosalie Versalles."

A chill swept through her—even her siren quivered.

"Did they ever find her?" she asked, her voice deathly still.

"Yes." He struggled for breath as if she were holding him by the throat. "She's at the castle."

Shock hit her like she'd just been dunked into icy water. "How'd they find her?"

"Because I told them," he answered, at least having the decency not to look proud of the fact. "It was the piece of information I leveraged to save the city. I know Prince Tristan well. He often came in place of the king for meetings during the war. He was the one who told me about her. Just the way he spoke about her—I could tell she meant a great deal to him. He told me her name was Rosalie Versalles. I thought nothing of it until the men asked if I knew anything about her. So I told them."

She processed the information with a pause. "What did they want with her?"

"They didn't say, and I didn't ask."

She believed him.

They knew. Whoever these men were, they *knew* her. But how? And why were they looking for her? And if they already knew she was at the castle, why had they not shown themselves? Were they connected to what happened to her in the third trial?

Her mind raced. The castle wasn't safe. Her mother wasn't safe. No one was safe. She had to go back. She had to warn them.

She released her siren's grip. "Thank you."

Moretti blinked as she retreated from his mind, giving him back to himself. He gasped in a small breath. He read her fearful expression. "You know this woman?"

She didn't answer, her mind working overtime.

"Draya?"

"My name is not Draya," she admitted. "It's Rosalie Versalles."

His eyes widen with fear. "Tell me you're lying."

She blinked at him in response.

His mouth fell open. "*You're* Rosalie? Tristan was the previous suitor you mentioned before? You're the throne seeker?"

Apparently, court gossip had spread to the capital. She shouldn't have been surprised. "It's not my favorite title, but yes."

Moretti stepped forward, grabbing her lightly by the shoulders. "Does anyone know you're here?"

"No, no one... besides my companion." She shouldn't have told him that bit.

"Who?"

She hesitated, but she felt like she owed it to him to be honest. "Prince Roman."

His face hardened into ice. "Was he the man in the tent?" Moretti clenched his fists.

She nodded weakly.

His lips curled up into a snarl. "Damn you. Why didn't you tell me the truth?"

"Why should I have? I didn't know you. I had no idea what you were like," she said, defending herself.

"This was your plan all along, wasn't it? The Snorri, the conversation we had at the tavern. You had no interest in me. You just wanted to use me."

Her eyes lowered with guilt. "I'm sorry. I had no idea that you would be—"

"Be what? A human being?"

"Kind," she corrected, looking back up.

He sneered at her, betrayed. "A trait I reserved only for you. But now I see I was mistaken."

"I'm sorry." It surprised her how much she cared. "I didn't mean to hurt you."

"Just use me."

She took a few steps back, bumping into a chair. "I'm sorry. I'll go."

Moretti stopped her by grabbing her arm. "I need to know—was any of it real? And damn it, tell me the truth. I deserve that, at least."

"Yes. Everything I told you about my feelings was true." The powder had confirmed her statement, even if he didn't know that. "But then after that… things changed."

He took her answer with a grain of salt. "You can't go back to the castle. If those men are searching for you, you need to run like hell."

She wouldn't cower away. "No. I have to warn them. My mother is there."

"Send for her. Take her with you. I'll help you. Come with me. I'll hide both of you."

She studied his face. Then she said with a softer voice, "Sounds like you don't hate me so much after all."

Moretti's expression remained hard as he came closer, even as he said, "Of course I don't hate you. I want to despise you, but this is my fault; if I knew it was you—gods, if I only knew—I would've never told them."

"Sorry" wouldn't help her now. She was wasting time. "I have to go."

She turned, making her way quickly to the door.

Moretti followed close behind. "I'm telling you now, don't go back. You won't survive."

She didn't stop as she said, "I'll be fine. I know how to take care of myself."

Thunder clapped overhead as Moretti snatched her arm again just before she reached the door.

"You have no idea what you're up against," Moretti said, pleading for her to see reason. "These men fight like nothing I've ever seen. I can't even tell you what they look like. They wear black hoods and masks—they could be anyone. Even coming to the city like this was a risk."

"I have to try." She couldn't just sit back and do nothing.

He gripped her arm tighter. "I can't let you."

"Let me go, Moretti," she warned, sensing his desperation.

"I'm not letting you get yourself killed."

"I survived the Snorri—I can survive this."

Her siren recognized his greedy desire to keep her there, to force her to stay with him. He thought for a long moment while he searched her eyes. Finally, he gave a loud, exhausted sigh. "If you come to your senses and change your mind, my offer still stands." He released her arm.

His disappointment became hers. The feeling was so strong that she wanted to reach out and comfort him, but she knew it would only make his pain worse. Instead, she gave him a small smile. "Thank you. I won't forget this."

Moretti drew close. For a split second, she was worried he'd try to kiss her, but his lips veered to press themselves to her cheek.

"I only pray you're here to remember me," he whispered in farewell.

Roman and Rose didn't speak until they arrived back at Highland Haven, too worried about being seen or overheard to stop and discuss what she'd discovered. Once they reached the estate's front steps, she recounted everything Moretti had revealed as the sky threatened to pour rain.

"I should go kill the snake," Roman said with a vengeful scowl.

Moretti was the least of their worries. "We have bigger problems; we have to go back, Roman. What about your family? The people at court? What if they've infiltrated the castle under their very noses because of me? It's all my fault."

He shook his head sharply. "No. We stick with the original plan and send for your mother to come here. It's not safe. For anyone. If it's you they want, the best thing to do is stay away."

She couldn't just sit here and do nothing. "What if something's already happened to her?"

"Your mother is strong, just like you. She'll be fine. If they wanted to hurt her, they would've done it already."

Rose had been so involved in their discussion that she hadn't noticed Gretta exit the manor until she heard shouting.

"Roman!... Roman!" Gretta called from the front door, shuffling out as fast as she could, holding something in her hand. "It's a letter from the castle... it's your mother. Her illness has taken a turn for the worst."

The hits just kept coming.

Roman snatched the parchment from Gretta, reading his father's scribbles. After he finished, he lowered the letter, letting it fall to his side as his gaze drifted. "It looks like I have to return after all." His eyes returned to her. "But I still think you should stay."

Not a chance in hell. "I'm coming with you."

"We just got done discussing how dangerous it will be," he said with a stern look.

"I'm coming," she repeated, refusing to be left behind. "Besides, I don't want you withering away without me."

He looked like he wanted to disagree, but instead he sighed, looking down at her with a defeated expression. He squeezed her hand, leaning down to gently kiss her forehead. She could feel his desire for her grow as he breathed in her scent. But he contained himself. "Then we leave as soon as possible. Send for Onyx… If we ride him, we can be there before nightfall."

PART IV
THE RECKONING

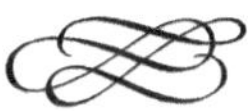

CHAPTER 72

Onyx made a short trip of it, galloping so fast, he practically hovered just above the dirt road. Even with Roman's added weight, his mighty hooves drove them forward in haste. The storm still loomed overhead, the winds powerful gusts creating rolling waves across the cornstalks, the dark dulling their golden husks.

It was dusk by the time they approached the castle.

Rose masked her face, pulling up a cloth and resting it on the bridge of her nose, leaving only her eyes visible. *Thank you, Onyx.* She stroked his neck. *You can go down to the stables to drink and rest. You'll like it there. Hugh is known to spoil the horses.*

Call for me if you need me, Onyx replied with a hint of unease. *I don't get a good feeling about this place.*

His words only added to her nerves.

Rose followed close behind Roman, wishing to hold his hand, but she fought the temptation, keeping her arms pinned against her sides. If someone saw them, she didn't want to escalate the situation.

Today was about Roman's mother.

Their queen.

Roman's quick strides led them to the royal bedchambers. The corridors were oddly deserted at this hour, hinting that news of the queen's condition had already spread.

Roman knocked on the door.

After a moment, the king answered, sorrow oozing out of the room like a dark mist. His usually refined posture had diminished into a sluggish stance. "Roman." His tired eyes shone with pure relief. "How did you get here so quickly?"

"It's a long story for another time," Roman replied. "Is Tristan here?"

"Not right now. He and Satin stepped out for a moment. It's just us." King Henrik's eyes shifted to her behind Roman curiously, peering under her hood.

Her hands shook as she lifted her hood and bowed. "Your Majesty."

The king's puffy eyes widened as he stilled. He stared, taking in the evolved version of her.

His lengthy silence allowed doubt to creep in. She'd been stewing over this moment the entire ride, terrified she'd lose his favor, recognize her for the monster she was.

But instead, he stepped forward, embracing her.

She had always known he had a soft spot for her. But now, with his arms around her, she could feel his pure love for her burst out of him, hitting her hard and fast. It was enough to bring her to tears as she clung to him.

The king pulled back. "Come in," he urged after he'd recovered. "We have much to discuss."

Queen Lenna's chamber was dark, lit by a few flickering candles and a roaring fire. The décor brought back memories of Highland Haven. Dark cabinets and books lined the walls, bordering the fireplace. Next to the window sat a simple hand-carved vanity. A brass mirror carved with the sun emblem hung just above it. Rose caught a glimpse of her reflection and nearly jumped—it would take some getting used to.

The queen rested in the center of a large canopy bed. Her usually neatly styled hair lay matted against the pillows, her sharp eyes now weak and frail. She'd lost weight, causing her pale cheekbones to protrude more harshly. Each small breath that escaped her chapped lips was accompanied by a wheeze.

Roman's shock coursed through her, a helplessness that he tried to bury as he took in the state of his mother withering away.

She slipped her hand into his.

He didn't hesitate to grip it back. His guilt amplified at the touch, washing over her like a tidal wave.

Rose blamed herself for keeping him from his responsibilities. He should've been here. He'd missed what little precious time he could have had with his mother because of her.

She lowered her head in shame.

"Mum," Roman said, his voice rough and raw. "It's me, Roman."

The queen gave him a weak smile, holding her fragile hand out to him. "I may be dying, but I think I can recognize my own son when I see him."

He barked a harsh laugh, but the smile left quicker than a lightning strike. "How are you? Truly?"

The queen waved her hand. "Nothing I haven't experienced before." She suddenly sat up with a start, coughing. It sounded more like a wheezing gasp, coming from somewhere deep within her lungs.

Roman was at her side instantly, rubbing her back as she coughed into her handkerchief. Rose caught a glimpse of the crimson-red color that blotched the white cloth. Her hope the queen could overcome this episode dwindled.

Roman helped his mother lay back down.

Once the queen had recovered, she finally noticed Rose, her eyes widening in surprise. "Rose, is that you?" the queen whispered, studying her from head to toe.

Roman looked up at Rose, stretching his arm toward her. "Yes… it's a long story. But Rose is—"

"A siren," the queen supplied in a light, raspy voice. Her gaze dropped to their intertwined hands, and she raised her eyebrows at them. "Are you two…?"

"Yes," Roman replied without hesitation, his chest puffing out with pride. "She's mine."

Rose's heart swelled while her siren's ego threatened to burst at the seams.

She looked back at the king and queen, ready for the horror that was sure to be spread across their faces, for the disappointment, anger, and disapproval. Just as it had when she was with Tristan.

But instead, the queen smiled.

Smiled.

"This is the best news," the queen whispered, surprising Rose further by reaching out her hand.

Rose hesitated. Not because she didn't want to, but because she didn't know if she was prepared for the suffocating rush of sadness that was sure to follow.

But she couldn't refuse the hand she'd waited for so long to be stretched out.

She took it. Without warning, a memory of the queen's flashed through her mind. The queen was in the fields during the peak of summer, watching Rose and her children playing together, laughing and chasing one another, running through the blooms.

Just as quickly as the vision came, it left.

Rose looked into the queen's shaky eyes as if she knew she could see the memory, too.

"I always knew you'd be a part of our family," the queen said. "It was only a matter of time."

"So did I," the king said, beaming.

Rose blinked, flabbergasted.

This had to be a dream.

Roman looked just as confused. "You're not angry?"

"Of course not," the queen replied. "Why do you think I had you watch over her during the wedding? You think I didn't know why you took her to Highland Haven?" The queen looked to her with knowing eyes. "I told you I'd help you find a suitor, and I did."

Rose's mouth parted in awe. She… she had planned it. All of it.

The queen didn't mind her being family, after all. The simple fact made her eyes blink furiously.

"But perhaps we need to keep this good news to ourselves for now," the king said. They needed no explanation. "Did you learn anything more from Moretti?"

Roman nodded. "They were camped outside Carnthe last we heard. It's definitely the same group moving across Cathan. And there's more." Roman looked at Rose. "We found out they've been looking for Rose. We don't know why, but there's a good chance they may have already infiltrated the castle."

The king only nodded with a solemn expression, the news not alarming him like she thought it would. "So it's confirmed. I'm afraid I've had my suspicions for quite some time. I just prayed to the gods I was wrong."

Rose didn't understand. "Why raid the cities? What are they after?"

Roman and the king exchanged a discreet glance.

She looked between them. Did they know something she didn't?

"We still don't know for certain," the king answered. But she could feel the shift in their auras, secrecy hiding beneath. The king's gaze returned to her, and he changed the subject. "I am afraid I must admit that I have known you were a siren since you were born."

Rose's arms slackened to her sides. She looked to the queen, but even she couldn't meet her gaze. They both knew.

"You knew this whole time?" Roman said, recovering first, outraged. "Why didn't you ever say anything? Why didn't you warn us?"

"Evelyn and I were protecting her the best way we knew how," the king explained. "We knew the same men who killed her father would come for her, too. So we agreed to keep it a secret." His eyes shifted to her. "Not to keep you in the dark but for survival. I put you in the succession to help your chances, but even these ancient walls are no longer the safe haven I once believed... Your mother should be the one to explain the rest. That is not my tale to tell."

Rose blinked a few times at the revelation, having countless questions, but she didn't even know what question would begin to cover all the things she wanted to know.

"What's to be done?" Roman asked, his eyes on high alert from the news. "How do we find out who they are?"

"I'd tell you if I knew," the king said grimly. "I've already done everything in my power to ensure the castle is secure. But somehow, they continue to evade our defenses." He turned to Rose. "I'm afraid you would've been safer to stay away."

Roman wouldn't accept that answer. "There must be more we can do."

The queen sat up again, cradling her ribs as she coughed into her handkerchief, gasping for another breath—more crimson blotting the snow-white cloth.

"I'm afraid we'll have to finish this conversation another time," the king said, kissing his wife's hand and rubbing it.

After the queen had recovered from her fit, she looked at Rose expectantly. "Rose... I'm sorry, but do you mind leaving us for a moment? We need a word with our son... alone," she said between shallow breaths.

"Of course," she agreed before Roman could refuse.

Roman gazed at her hesitantly, not liking the idea of her leaving. "Stay close, and keep your sword with you."

"I won't go far," she promised.

Roman placed a chaste kiss on her forehead and let her go, but not before he looked down at her lips, making her blood pump faster.

She gave one last small bow to the queen before she left the room, giving the family a moment of privacy.

She threw her hood back on and began the trek to find her mother.

An invisible pressure dissipated as she gained distance from the queen's room. She didn't realize how draining it would be to take on everyone's emotions, sucking the energy right out of her body. She'd have to be more careful in the future.

She kept her head down in case anyone else came down the hall. Luckily, most of the court had already finished dinner and returned to their rooms, leaving the corridors clear.

She was about to round a corner when a voice came from behind her.

"Rose?"

She nearly tripped.

She knew that voice all too well.

CHAPTER 73

Rose's siren came to attention as she stood paralyzed by fear, hope, anxiety, dread—she couldn't tell which one took hold. She tried to force herself to move, but her siren refused to do as she commanded.

The deliberate, careful steps behind her came closer as the familiar gaze burned into her back. She closed her eyes, bracing herself for whatever was about to happen.

He was right behind her now.

"Rose?" Tristan's voice was all too tender.

She wasn't breathing when she turned to face him.

A good thing, because she was swept straight to sea as an ocean greeted her, as hauntingly deep and vast as she remembered. She used to dream about being bathed in that color after being frozen for so long. She did her best to stay afloat, even as her siren threatened to capsize her ship.

Rose wrapped her arms around herself. "Hello, Tristan." Her voice was barely above a whisper.

"You're back." His eyes screamed with pure relief. Without asking for permission, his hand slowly reached for her hood, his energy flooding her the closer he got—a beautiful aura of colors.

"I wouldn't," she warned.

He ignored her, slowly lifting the black hood.

His pure shock plunged through her as soon as the fabric fell, his eyes devouring every centimeter exposed.

She praised the gods Satin wasn't here to see the starstruck look.

Tristan didn't speak, letting his gaze linger for far too long. Finally, he said, "How?"

"I don't know… I'm still trying to figure that out."

He lifted his hand, brushing his thumb over her cheek. The moment his fingertips touched her bare skin, she was hit with an array of emotions —strong enough that she cringed. The pain of her absence, how lonely he was, how distant he was from everyone.

His hand dropped, his expression becoming guarded, almost as if remembering how angry he was at her. "Where've you been?"

She hesitated to answer. "Highland Haven."

His frame stiffened. "Of course. I should've known."

She shifted uncomfortably. "Where's Satin?"

"She's resting," Tristan replied, looking over his shoulder quickly as if he could see her.

An awkward silence fell.

"How are you?" she blurted before she could stop herself.

His eyes became darker than the bottom of the ocean floor. "Don't do that. Don't ask how I am. I might do something stupid like open up to you."

Rose opened her mouth, but nothing came out, so she closed it again, not sure what to say.

"Don't do that either," he said with a dark tone.

She blinked. "Do what?"

"Look at me like that. Like you still care about what happens to me."

Her eyes softened. "Of course I care." She almost reached out but stopped herself.

Tristan's jaw clenched. His eyes fell to the ground, hands running through his messy blond hair. "Fine. You want to know how I am? I'll tell you." Tristan surrendered, casting his gaze down the corridor. "I walk these halls that have grown haunted in your absence and pretend the ghost of you doesn't linger here. But it does. It's everywhere. I can't escape it. Every part of this castle holds a memory of you. Every day, I go on pretending there isn't a gaping hole in my chest that you used to fill. I told you, you have my heart. And I have to accept the fact it'll never be returned. It's yours by design. You helped shape it, after all. At times, I had the smallest hope I'd be able to move on from you… until I looked into the mirror at night and realized how empty I am. When I see you in my dreams at night, I pray it becomes my reality. Whenever anyone even speaks your name, I slip a mask on so I don't fall apart at the seams. I shove away the gnawing emptiness when I see the gardens or the beach. All that is to say I've been nothing but a shell of a person. So you want to know how I'm doing?" Tristan's eyes finally met hers. "It's been a fucking living hell."

Tears pricked at the backs of her eyes as they fell to the floor. She couldn't hold his mournful gaze any longer, blocking out the excruciating pain rupturing through his heart. "I… I'm so sorry," she said, her eyes still set on the floor. "I never meant to cause you so much pain."

Tristan lifted her chin, forcing her to look at him like it was her punishment to see him like this. "I know," he replied, his aura still aching for her nonetheless.

Silence fell over them as they looked into each other's eyes.

"Perhaps we just need more time," she whispered into the quiet hall.

He arched a skeptical eyebrow. "Do you really believe that time-heals-all bullshit?"

She nearly laughed, realizing how ridiculous it sounded. "No. I suppose not. But that's what I keep telling myself."

The way he held her face, the way they stood looking into each other's eyes, had her hoping that maybe—just maybe—they'd heal.

Tristan cleared his throat, his eyes flickering to his mother's door. "I should go."

She nodded, stepping away. "Oh—yes. Yes, of course."

Tristan passed her so close that a wave of his fresh forest scent wrapped itself around her.

He paused as he placed his hand on the latch, facing her again. "I'll see you later?"

It was supposed to be casual, but his eyes harbored the worry she'd disappear again.

"See you later," she said, reassuring him she wasn't going anywhere.

A ghost of a smile spread across his lips before he opened the door.

She let out the breath she'd been holding, throwing on her hood again as she left the hall to look for her mother.

Because, by Vallor, she had some serious explaining to do.

CHAPTER 74

Rose found her mother hidden away in her room.

As usual, it was immaculate. Each book, every piece of furniture, and even her hair brushes were meticulously arranged in a straight line on her desk. The familiar scent of her potent magnolia perfume lingered in the air, mixed with the taste of rain from the cracked window.

She stood at the edge of her mother's canopy bed, glaring at her mother, who fell on the pressed sheets, still taking in her transformation.

"Goodness, you look just like him—how did this happen? How did you lift the blood spell? Did someone try to hurt you?" her mother asked all at once.

Rose narrowed her eyes. "No, no one hurt me, but *I* get to ask the questions right now. You said I look like him—him *who?*"

She was terrified of the answer, but she needed to know, even if it turned her world upside down.

No more lies, no more half-truths, no more secrets.

She could recall only a handful of moments when her mother was this apprehensive. This would be another to add to the list.

"Your father, Rose. Your *real* father."

Rose didn't think she'd heard her right. "My *real* father?"

Her mother didn't shrink away, holding her gaze as she let her absorb the news.

"What do you mean, real father?" Rose asked again, becoming more assertive. "If Rathe wasn't my father," she said, speaking his name for the first time in a year, "then who is?"

Her mother's lips grew into a sad yet bright smile. "The most wonderful man I've ever known. His name was Thren Devereaux... and he was a siren."

Rose's jaw slackened. "You mean..."

Her mother nodded slowly, patting the spot beside her on the bed.

Rose didn't move. "How could you keep that from me?" Her heart stung, full of betrayal. "How could you let me believe that monster was my father?"

"Because I was trying to protect you."

Rose scoffed. "From what?"

"From the same men who killed Thren."

Rose's brows grew together, silently pleading for her to elaborate.

Her mother cast her gaze to a distant memory. "I met your father when I was young. Younger than you. He was the most beautiful man I'd ever seen." She smiled like a lovesick girl. Rose nearly toppled over at the sight. "And as luck would have it, I was out in society and looking for a suitor. I was quite the popular item, if you can believe it." Rose had no trouble imagining that. "I went to the lakeside estate with my family for a celebration and that's when I met him. I fell for him at first sight. Who wouldn't? He was incredibly handsome, quick-witted, and could make me laugh like no one else. I didn't know what a siren was back then, but I quickly learned. We spent a blissful summer together. By the end, he said he was in love with me and wanted to get married. I said yes, but my family disapproved, convinced it was only his magic luring me to him—'a deadly infatuation,' my father said. When I told them I'd marry him with or without their blessing, my family disowned me." Her gaze fell.

That couldn't be right.

Rose folded her arms. "You told me they died before I was born."

"To my knowledge, they are still very much alive and well. As far as I know, they're still living in Catalena, happy and as wealthy as can be. I tried to reconcile with them a few times—I thought time would help—but they had no interest in contact."

A vengeful fire sparked within Rose at her mother's crestfallen expression. She should punish her extended family for such a crime.

"Turns out your father drew more attention than we'd bargained for. He made enemies, and long story short, we had to go into hiding—to be safe, because we had more than ourselves to think of." Her mother rested a hand on her stomach with a small smile. "You see, it was never Henrik and I that were old friends. It was Thren and Henrik," her mother explained. "Henrik had just become king when we learned I was pregnant. He helped us settle into a small town in Carnthe, where we thought we'd be safe. As time passed, we were lulled into a false sense of security. The men found us, somehow discovering I was pregnant, and wanted the child, wanted you. Your father distracted them while I ran… They killed him because he refused to give me up." Her mother's eyes sparkled with tears. "Luckily, before he died, we found a seer who could help protect you. We had her place a protection spell over you while you were still inside me—to suppress your siren and make you appear human."

Rose didn't blink, afraid she'd miss something if she did.

"I wanted to die that day," her mother admitted with sorrow. "I can't explain the utter agony I experienced those weeks after. I thought about ending my life every day, but I had to pick myself up off the floor. I still had you. My best chance was to get remarried quickly. I was in a village market one day when I met Rathe. Even though I had no money or a family, he didn't care. He had more than enough for us. He seemed like a dream catch. He fell in love with me quickly. Soon after, we were married, long before he found out I was pregnant. I made him believe you were his and we were content for a time, at least as much as I could be without Thren."

Her mother smoothed her hair back. "But when you came two months early, a fully grown baby, he started questioning me. I stuck to my story, insisting you were his child. I thought he accepted it… until I realized he didn't want to hold you, or play with you, or do anything of the sort. My heart ached that he disliked you for no fault of your own."

Her mother sniffled and grabbed a folded handkerchief from the side table, dabbing her eyes. "I believe he knew you were not his child and resented you for it—a constant reminder of how I'd deceived him. But I had to stay. I was too afraid for your safety to go off on our own. I tried to shield you as best I could. My hope was for you to marry well, to find a man who would love you the way your father would've." Her mother cast her gaze at the stone walls surrounding them. "That's when I thought of the castle. What better protection for you than inside these walls? I reached out to Henrik, telling him what happened to Thren, and I asked if I could bring you here each summer to see if any of his sons might consider marrying you... You know what happened after that."

Rose plopped down on the bed before she fainted, absorbing the history her mother had just revealed. The men looking for her were the same men that had killed her father—her real father. After all these years, they hadn't given up looking for her.

"They're coming for me," she whispered, piecing it together. "They know I'm here."

"I believe so," her mother replied solemnly. "That's why I agreed to your training—why I joined you. Why I've been so adamant about finding you a suitor. But Tristan's made it impossible. I'd say we could try to make it on our own, but without the protection of the castle or wealth, we'd be sitting ducks."

Protection they might not have, but money, they did.

"I have news on that front."

Her mother straightened with eager eyes. "Well, don't make me wait! Tell me."

"I may have ridden a sleipnir, raced in the Snorri, won, and now I'm the wealthiest woman in Cathan," Rose proclaimed, proud of it all, really.

Her mother's eyes widened in horror, putting a hand to her heart. "You did *what*?"

"I raced in the Snorri. It's a race between—"

"I know what the Snorri is," her mother snapped, waving her handkerchief. "But why in Vallor would you risk it? Do you realize how lucky you are to be alive?"

"It's a long story, but it was important and... quite thrilling." Rose grinned despite herself.

Her mother rolled her eyes. "Indeed," she huffed. "You're your father's daughter, all right."

Rose built her courage before saying, "There's more."

Her mother raised an eyebrow. "More?"

"Roman and I...well, we—before I came into my full siren—we..." She searched for the words, looking down to fiddle with her dress.

Turned out her expression was all her mother needed.

"You mean..." A hand flew to her mother's mouth. "Oh, Rose. That poor boy."

A punch to the gut, if there ever was one.

"Am I that horrible?" she asked with a sharpness.

"Of course not, just—give me a moment," her mother snapped, pausing. "Has he proposed?" She eyed Rose's empty hand, which she hid behind her back.

"No, we've just begun seeing each other that way."

Her mother couldn't fathom it. "I don't understand. I thought you and Roman didn't get along. What changed?"

Rose reflected thoughtfully for a moment. "Everything. I thought he'd never understand me, but he does, Mum." Her heart ached just thinking of him. "He sees what I am and lets me be just that... His love comes with no expectations."

"Exactly how close have you two become?" Her mother tilted her head, attempting to look her in the eye.

Rose's cheeks burned as she looked away. "As close as you can get."

Her mother's brows raised. "That didn't take long, but I suppose I should've known after I found him in your bedroom after the wedding. You were just so broken. I didn't know what to do." She paused. "Has he gotten sick yet?"

Rose's eyes shot to meet her mother's. "How'd you know about that?"

"I experienced something similar." Her mother went to her desk and opened the drawer, rummaging through its contents. "It's something that happens when your siren desires them, draws them in. It's powerful magic, to be sure. It can make him unable to survive without you if it's strong enough. It's quite a painful way to die."

Rose's heart faltered for a few beats. "You mean he really could've died?"

"Yes. And you'll need to be careful if you're—" her mother paused, looking for the word, "—*intimate* with him in your full siren. As a human, he may never be able to move on from you… Ah!" Her mother found what she was looking for, holding up a small golden band. Her mother brought it to her, placing it into her palm. "Take this ring, give it to him. It'll help him remain unaffected by your siren when you're apart."

Rose looked down at the thick golden band with runes inscribed on it. "How do you have this?"

Her mother held up her hand, showing the ring she never took off. "Because I had to wear one, too. Your father had it made for me by the same seer who cast the protection spell over you. We had two made, knowing this day might come. He'll need to wear it always."

Rose inspected the ring. She had always believed it to be a cherished family heirloom. "Why hasn't this happened to Tristan or anyone else?"

"I don't know for certain; the magic affects everyone differently. It's not your choice. It's your siren's—your magic. For some reason, it desires Roman above anyone else."

Rose needed a moment to process. She stood from the bed and went to the window, gazing out. That night on the balcony, when she first laid eyes on Roman, she'd felt something stir within her—that unfamiliar energy… Could it have been her magic?

"How do I know if he truly loves me?" Rose asked almost rhetorically into the night sky, now free of storm clouds. "How do I know his love isn't just my siren luring him in? Forcing him to stay?" She faced her mother. "How did you know it was love and not infatuation?"

Her mother rose from the bed. "I didn't. Perhaps I never will. But it didn't make our love any less real to me."

Rose looked back to the window, wishing she could be so sure.

Her mother joined her. "I know you must have more questions, but it's getting late, and we need to decide what we're going to do. I say we take the risk and leave. Go into hiding. We have the resources now, and we aren't defenseless."

"What about the queen? I can't ask Roman to leave her now." She had already kept him away too long.

Her mother bit her lip, tapping her foot. "You're right. We'll wait until the queen is at peace… I fear it won't take long," she said, her voice saddened. "Then the three of us will go back to Highland Haven until we figure out what to do next."

Rose slowly nodded, agreeing.

Her mother took her hand, looking her in the eye. "Whatever you do, don't tell Tristan about Roman. He's had enough trouble getting accustomed to his marriage as it is, and I don't want him interfering again."

She didn't have to tell her that.

Her mother gave a firm nod. "Right. Now let's go… Roman must be going stir-crazy without you," she muttered from experience.

CHAPTER 75

The king, Tristan, Roman, and Harriet surrounded the queen's bed while Rose and her mother sat in the armchairs by the fireplace. Although Queen Lenna was asleep, her breaths remained a chore. Rose's siren felt the strain within the queen's heart, its weak beats diminishing each hour.

It ate her alive to know there was nothing she or any healer could do. This was a condition born from the body, beyond the reach of any known tonic. And if she had learned anything from her thorough studies, magic could only cure magic.

Sitting and taking on the emotions in the room was excruciating, especially from the king. As if she needed powers to know he was dying inside, too. The mere way he peered down at his wife's sleeping body said it all. The twinkle in his eye had been replaced with a relentless ache. Rose couldn't shut it out, no matter how hard she tried.

A form of torture for the monster she was.

Harriet kept stealing side glances at her, either in awe of her transformation or perhaps out of suspicion. Her dark hair fell like a curtain hiding her face, her usual spark overshadowed by her mother's condition.

And Harriet wasn't the only one who kept an eye on her.

Tristan's gaze continued to sweep over her, only they were not quick, nervous glances like Harriet's. They stayed on her for minutes at a time, once for so long that Roman let a piercing glare slip through. Tristan was oblivious, too focused on Rose to notice.

Unlike the others, Roman averted his gaze. She knew it was for no other reason than being afraid he'd give himself away. He was forced to ignore the aching bond tying them together like an invisible rope, knowing if either tried to sever it, it would be as painful as losing a limb. Rose tried hard to follow his lead, but she was failing miserably, her eyes raking over him every so often.

Finally, Roman's restraint broke as his golden eyes met hers.

Her siren stirred at the contact, wanting to get up and go to him. To wrap her arms around him and lay her head on his shoulder. To comfort him while she played with his hair.

Instead, she forced herself to remain seated. Her siren's complaints ate at her patience.

All too soon, his eyes abandoned hers.

"Have you heard no word from him?" Roman asked, breaking the room's silence. "He should be here."

They all knew who he was talking about—Xavier.

The king dipped his head with grave eyes. "Not a word. I've sent three letters and two messengers to Amernth days ago, and still nothing."

"That shouldn't surprise anyone in this room," Tristan retorted coldly, crouched over in his seat. "He's never cared about this family."

Harriet's eyes narrowed. "How could you say that? You know it's not true."

"Then why has he not responded to our letters? Why isn't he here?" Tristan asked.

"It's not like he ever thought he'd be permitted to return," Harriet snipped.

Tristan met Harriet's stubbornness head on. "He doesn't *want* to return. Even now, when clemency has been declared for the sake of our mother, he's *still* choosing not to come home."

"Why should he? You drove him out! Both of you did," Harriet said, glancing between him and their father. Her icy-blue eyes cut to Rose.

"*She's* the only reason he was banished in the first place. But you don't mind—you get to be king after all."

The jab made Rose's eyes fall to the floor.

Tristan stood fuming, ready to retaliate alongside Roman, who prepared to rise to Rose's defense, but the king saved him from exposing himself.

"Enough!" King Henrik bellowed.

Harriet jumped at her father's rare yell.

"Have you all forgotten your sense of propriety?" the king rebuked in a dark tone, still holding his wife's hand. "Your mother is dying, and all you can do is bicker amongst yourselves and blame those around you."

Harriet's eyes fell to the bed in shame, unable to hold his chiding gaze.

Rose's gaze retreated to the dancing flames as she traced her fingers lightly over her collarbone. Harriet was right. It was her fault. At least a good part of it. Maybe more than she cared to admit. Her chest tightened as she dropped her hand.

"It's getting late," Harriet said after a moment, still sulking from the retribution of her father. Her gaze fell to her mother. "We should get some sleep… It may be the last night for a while."

Rose looked at Roman, already dreading not sleeping next to him.

Tristan shifted to her and her mother. "I can escort you both back if you'd like?"

Roman sent another subtle glare at his brother.

Her mother saved the day. "Oh no, I couldn't keep you any longer from Satin." She faced his younger brother instead. "But Roman, would you be so kind as to escort us?"

"Of course," Roman accepted in a controlled tone, doing a magnificent job of looking indifferent.

They all stood to go out but the king, who sat down on the edge of the bed.

"Aren't you going to sleep?" Rose asked softly.

He shook his heavy head, refusing to take his eyes off his queen. "No, not me. I'll sleep here with my wife."

Another ripple of heartache sliced through her.

"Come on," Roman whispered over her shoulder. "Let's give them time alone."

Rose did her best to block his crippling pain as she followed Roman out, escaping the overpowering fog of saddness behind her.

She only had a fleeting moment of relief before a new energy slammed her. A blanched, thin-looking Satin stood staring at her in the middle of the corridor.

Rose fought not to gape too long. The happy, wide-eyed, innocent girl was gone without a trace, replaced with a tired, hard-shelled woman whose aura held nothing but contempt. The sharp expression reminded her of Satin's mother.

Satin didn't bother hiding her disgust as she inspected Rose, her eyes running over her in revulsion. "You're back," Satin whispered. Her eyes held Tristan accountable. "You didn't tell me she was back."

"I didn't know. She just got here a few hours ago," Tristan stated as his eyes clashed with hers.

Rose stepped forward. "He didn't know. I just arrived. I came for the queen." She regretted trying to make the situation better when Satin's scowl deepened.

"No one bothered to tell me you're a *siren*," Satin spat the word. Her eyes ran over her again, like she'd just put the last puzzle piece together. She turned to Tristan. "And you're just going to let her come back? Do you remember what her kind did to my family? To my province? They nearly annihilated my people."

Tristan's voice hardened. "She's no danger to anyone here."

But Tristan's defense of her only fueled Satin's anger.

"I won't allow for it." Satin whipped to the others for support. "She's manipulating all of you. Especially *you*." Her gaze ended on Tristan.

"She's not manipulating anyone." Roman's voice lost all warmth as he folded his arms. "And this is her home just as much as yours."

Tristan went to Satin's side. "What are you doing up so late? You should be resting," he said in a lower voice, but she waved him off.

"Tristan's right," Harriet said, joining them as she rubbed Satin's back. "The stress isn't good for the baby."

Rose's heart fell straight through the floor.

Baby?

Harriet hadn't realized her mistake until it was too late. Her mouth parted in horror as her guilt-ridden eyes flung to Rose.

Rose's hand went to her stomach in instinct. "You're pregnant?" Her voice was barely above a whisper.

Satin lifted her chin as if in entitled victory. "Yes."

And just like that, Rose found herself thrown right back onto the floor the night of the wedding. This couldn't be happening. This was a cruel joke—a sick prank. It had to be. They'd barely been wed for a month.

Her wounded eyes sought refuge from the storm, looking to Tristan for confirmation.

Tristan glared at Harriet before guilt pulled his eyes to the floor, staring at it as his jaw locked until he found the courage to lift his eyes to meet Rose's.

It was all the confirmation she needed.

A bubbling underground river of jealousy threatened to burst from the depths of Vallor, but she reined it in, aware everyone's eyes were on her.

"Congratulations," Rose finally managed to get out, blinking furiously, her voice nowhere near as strong as she intended it to be.

"I don't want nor need your congratulations," Satin replied.

Tristan grabbed Satin's arm, spinning her away from Rose. "Satin," he scolded in a harsh whisper.

Her mother stepped forward, placing a reassuring hand on Rose's back. "You have it, nonetheless. I'm sorry, but you'll have to excuse us. I'm just exhausted, and Roman was about to escort us to our chambers. Good to see you, Princess Satin," she finished with a strained smile that faded quickly, leaving no room for a reply.

Her mother guided her down the corridor, with Roman at their heels.

Rose tossed her hood back on, not having the strength to look at Tristan again as she followed her mother.

She should have anticipated this. It was inevitable. This was what the treaty was for—to mix royal blood with royal blood. To intertwine the fates of their provinces forever.

But to happen so soon?

To have a child bonded Satin and Tristan in a sacred way Rose would never have with him.

Her siren lashed out in a fury, screeching an internal cry as her world quaked with rage. But she bottled the fury. Contained the scream that clawed to escape her lips.

She concentrated on her steps to keep her mind from dwelling on things it shouldn't.

They arrived at her mother's chambers first. Just as they reached the door, Rose asked in a low, dangerous voice, "Did you know?"

Her mother's expression fell. She nodded in admittance. "Yes. I knew."

Rose's nails dug into her palms. "And you didn't think to warn me? Is there anything else you haven't told me? Any more secrets?" she asked icily.

Her mother's lips tightened into a thin line. "I was going to tell you, but I'd only just told you about your father. I wanted to give you a little time to breathe before another bomb was thrown at you. I'm so sorry."

Rose knew she was. Her siren could feel guilt streaming out of her mother like a waterfall. It made her feel worse for trying to blame her.

She didn't want to say something she'd regret, so she settled on, "Good night, Mum," then dismissed herself without waiting for a reply.

With her mind in a far-off place, muscle memory took over, leading her to her own room. Roman followed, feeling him staring at her back as she strode through the halls.

"Are you alright?" he asked softly.

She forced herself to nod as exhaustion finally hit her, drained by the emotions that forced themselves on her. "I'm fine."

He cursed. "What can I do?"

"Nothing. I'm okay."

With a few large strides, he caught up with her, taking her hand and rotating her to face him. "I'm sorry. It's my fault you had to come back."

Of course he'd look to blame himself for nothing he'd done.

"You don't need to be sorry. I chose to come," she reminded him, still not regretting her decision. "It just… caught me off guard, is all."

More like knocked her right on her ass.

Tears threatened to rise.

She didn't want to cry about it in front of him.

"I need a minute," she said before she broke. "I'm going to go check on Onyx."

She hooked a right, turning toward the stables instead of continuing straight.

He continued to follow, his voice careful as he said, "I don't want you going off on your own."

"I have my sword."

"Are you sure—"

"Please, Roman, I'm just asking for a minute," Rose snapped, letting him know it wasn't up for debate.

Before she could feel guilty for his hurt expression, she left.

He didn't try to stop her this time.

It was as if Onyx had already known Rose would enter the stables with a tearstained face. He pressed his forehead against hers without uttering a word, his mind brushing against hers in a soft caress. She wrapped her arms around his large nose as she wept.

After she felt like she'd shed enough tears, she composed herself and dried her eyes with her cloak.

In an attempt to keep her hands busy, she fetched him food and water. Next, she took the initiative to retrieve the bristle brush and swept it over his large body, grateful for the solitude of such a simple task.

She was in the middle of brushing his back when he asked, *Are you angry at your mother for keeping your true lineage from you?*

Her strokes slowed as she considered the question. "I should be," she answered aloud. "I *want* to be. But now I've come into my full siren, I've discovered it makes me a powerful empath. And I could... *feel* everything she felt, everything she had to go through alone. She was barely nineteen when she had me. She fought for me in a way her parents never fought for her. No matter how mad I want to be, it's hard to be because... I understand her. How could I be so certain I wouldn't do the same thing for my daughter if I were in her shoes?"

Onyx gave her a knowing look. *Still, it hurts all the same.*

"Of course." She stared at the brush as she grazed it across Onyx's scarred abdomen. "You know, I can't help but wonder if... if I'd known... maybe I would've chosen to do things differently." Her words faltered as she thought of what the royal family was like before she had disrupted their world. How close they had been. How much happier they all were.

But if she had caused their divide, perhaps she could help mend it.

And she could start with where it all began.

"How fast do you think you could get me to Amernth?" she asked out of the blue.

We could be there in three days if we left now, Onyx replied.

She chewed her lip. Maybe—just maybe—it was enough time to reach Xavier.

She didn't let herself wonder if she was seeking another escape from this place. Perhaps it was a fool's errand, but she had to try.

"Do you even think we'd be able to find him?" Rose asked.

"I'm afraid that won't be necessary," a deep voice said from behind her.

Rose halted the brush mid-stroke, her fingers clenching around the handle with white knuckles, knowing that voice like the back of her hand she was staring at.

She let the brush slip off Onyx, forcing herself to turn to look toward the open gate of the stable.

"Xavier," she whispered.

He took one look at her and swore. "You've got to be fucking joking."

CHAPTER 76

Xavier scanned her painfully slow, absorbing every inch of her.

His reaction reminded her just how rare a creature she was.

The way his eyes gently held hers… it was like a moment frozen in time to when they'd first met. When her silly little girlish heart raced, and her skinny knees buckled.

"You're back," Rose breathed.

He sauntered toward her with slow, measured strides, not stopping until he was a breath away. Gently, he raised his hand, tracing her cheek with his fingers. "You're real," he crooned.

She held her breath, her eyes fluttering up into his.

He'd changed since she last saw him. His dark hair was trimmed now, resting just below his ears. The fitted black tunic clinging to the muscles he'd built during his absence, his face clean-shaven and shadowed by the stable lantern.

His sober, icy-blue eyes penetrated her defenses. "What happened to you? Are you a si—?"

"Yes." She was too tired to go into detail. "It was a surprise to me, too."

"But how? Your father—"

"Wasn't my father." Her sea-green flashed. "My real father was killed before I was born."

Xavier's face twisted in confusion. "Why didn't you tell us?"

"Don't go feeling too left out. I only just found out myself," she retorted cooly.

He took in the information with a slight pause, accepting her answer even though a thousand more questions lingered just beyond his lips.

She changed the subject. "What were you doing in Amernth?"

"I was with Malcolm," he said, referring to his best friend. "He and I have been traveling together."

Her mind cut back to the moment she thought she spotted him hidden among the trees. "And you've been there this entire time? You never came back?"

Xavier's brow quirked with questioning eyes. "How could I? I was banished."

Her eyes penetrated his, searching them. She couldn't be sure if he was lying, but her siren senses couldn't detect a whiff of deceit coming from him. It was enough to satisfy her, so she let go of the subject.

For now.

Rose shrugged, playing it off. "Nothing. I just wondered where you'd been spending your newfound freedom."

Xavier glanced over her shoulder to Onyx. "How in Vallor did you come by a sleipnir? And how'd you tame it enough to ride?" He sounded both impressed and intrigued.

Me? Tamed? I think not. Tell him I'm just as dangerous as ever, Onyx said, puffing his chest.

A smile spread across her face, earning her an annoyed glare from Xavier, who didn't understand what was so amusing.

"He says I didn't tame him. He lets me ride him because he chooses to," she summarized.

Xavier's widened eyes flitted back and forth between them. "You can speak to him?"

"I can—part of my siren's abilities, I think."

"May I?" He gestured to Onyx.

Rose arched an eyebrow. A bold request. Nonetheless, she stepped aside.

He stepped forward to Onyx, stretching a steady hand out to touch him, but just before Xavier's hand reached him, Onyx jerked his head. Xavier quickly withdrew.

Onyx let out what she knew to be a chuckle. *Humans are so skittish,* Onyx said, amused.

She rolled her eyes. "He's only teasing. He won't do it again," she emphasized pointedly at Onyx.

Xavier didn't look so sure, but to his credit, he reached out again.

This time, Onyx allowed it.

Xavier's rigid body relaxed as he admired the beast. "So he stays with you? Willingly?"

"Yes. For some reason or another, he thinks he owes me for saving his life."

That's because I do, Onyx said, *and I suppose I've grown fond of your two-legged awkwardness.*

She smiled again.

"How'd you manage that?" Xavier asked. The curiosity in his gaze brought back memories of when he got a telescope for his twelfth birthday. It warmed her to see a glimpse of his old self.

"It's a long story," she replied.

He observed her again, his eyes stopping on the handcrafted sword on her back. "Where'd you get the sword?"

She glanced over her shoulder at the hilt. "Zareb gave it to me."

His eyes sparked with intrigue. "The soldier from Semaria? Why would he do that?"

"He trained me with it. We grew to be close friends, he and I." Her voice was strained—the sting of Zareb's absence still fresh.

Xavier didn't say anything for a moment, his eyes remaining on the sword, then they met hers. "You any good?" A slight tug raised the corner of his lips.

She blinked, staring at the smile. She fumbled for words, surprised by his playfulness. "Test me, and you might just find out."

Xavier's mouth widened to a full smile. "Always the smart-ass."

She stared in shock. She hadn't seen that enchanted sight in *years*. Her heart pulsed; she was relieved to see he remembered how to use the muscles.

"It's good to see you smile," she said softly, lifting her gaze from his lips to his eyes.

"To tell you the honest truth, I thought I forgot how..." He glanced to the open stable doors. "Were you really going to charge into the night to find me?"

She shifted her weight to lean against the wooden pen. "I was considering it, for your mother's sake."

He frowned. "You doubted I'd come?"

"We were beginning to wonder... You do have a habit of running," she added, her voice harboring bitterness.

Xavier's mouth tightened into a thin line. "I've made my fair share of mistakes, but I wouldn't miss the opportunity to say goodbye to her. Even if it does mean I have to share the same air as my brother."

It wasn't hard to discern the malice in his tone. This was getting ridiculous. "Don't you think this feud has gone on long enough? I don't know what happened between you two, but—"

"That's right. You don't," he said, his voice as cold as winter snow.

Rose dropped the subject. Her eyes shifted away, pressing her lips together to avoid snapping back. He respected her not wanting to elaborate on how she was a siren, so she would respect his boundaries, too.

He cleared his throat, folding his arms tightly across his chest as he shifted uncomfortably. An icy steel wall formed in his eyes. "By the way, I never got to say congratulations."

Her head tilted, confused. "Congratulations?"

"On the wedding," he said, obviously. "I couldn't make it, of course—being exiled and all. Not that I would have come anyway."

Her mind ran in circles, trying to decipher what he meant. "What?"

His icy eyes grew irritated. "Tristan." He spat his name through his teeth. "I'm not a fool. I do know what an invitation looks like."

Rose paused.

He didn't know?

Xavier's expression became hard as she gawked at him. "Why are you looking at me like that?"

She opened her mouth only to close it again. "No one... no one told you?"

"Told me what?" he asked.

She blinked as the realization set in. He really had no idea. "Xavier... Tristan and I never got married."

A tense silence followed. Now it was his turn to stare. Nothing but the sound of shuffling hooves and popping torches filled the air.

His iceberg eyes melted into a river. He slowly unfolded his arms. "What?" he whispered.

Her throat bobbed. "We didn't get married," she repeated.

"You didn't... you didn't marry him?" His voice was raw. Hesitant.

She shook her head.

Xavier's expression flipped like a coin. He drew closer, shadows dancing across his sharp cheekbones. "Who did he marry?"

She couldn't hold his gaze. "The Vertmerian princess, Satin... She's with child." Her voice cracked, having to say it aloud.

"Why didn't *you* marry him?" he asked, monitoring her reaction carefully.

The question stung sharper than it should have. "Does it matter?"

He took another step closer. "It matters a great deal."

She gazed back up into his eyes. The look he was giving her... it was like the information had... *changed* something for him. "There were a lot of reasons I ended things."

"*You* ended it?" he clarified.

She nodded again.

His lips parted as his face inched to hers, holding her gaze with a new tenderness. "I didn't know. If I did... Gods, I'm sorry, I should've been there." He reached out to her—

She knew that look.

She swiped his hand away, stepping back. Her young heart screeched in rebellion, sensing his hurt before it spread onto his face.

But she was hurt, too.

"You're right," she said with as cold a voice as she could muster. "You should have. But you didn't want to be."

His face twitched with regret. "I know, and I hate myself for what I did to you."

She kept him pinned under her scrutinizing gaze. "And like an idiot, I forgave you. Almost immediately, I forgave you. I hate how you made me believe it was my fault you lost the crown, but now I find it's exactly what you wanted all along."

Xavier's eyes faltered as if he couldn't stand her disappointment.

"Why?" she demanded, raising her voice even as it cracked. "Why couldn't you love me back? What about me was so repulsive to you?"

The question broke him. Like a bolt of lightning, he trapped her with his body against the wooden post, forcing her inches away from his face.

"Damn it, Rose, don't you get it? I *do* love you," he declared onto her lips, sliding his hand into her hair and gripping a handful. "Just as the ocean reaches for the shore, I've reached for you. Even though I try to retreat, I just come rushing back to you in a relentless, vicious cycle. One that's so mesmerizing I couldn't stop it even if I wanted to. Even with the thousands of miles between us, you haunt my dreams, plaguing my mind—every breath, every thought. I love you more than you can possibly imagine. I've known I loved you from the moment I laid eyes on you."

For some reason, his confession only made her more angry.

"Then why?" Rose asked, her sharp voice cutting through the air with a vengeance. "Why didn't you say anything when I told you I was in love with you? Why did you tell me it was a childish notion, that I was too young to know what love was? Why did you make me believe I was an idiot for even thinking it?"

"Because Tristan was in love with you, too!" Xavier yelled.

Her anger halted its rampage as her face softened.

He let out a loud breath and dropped his hands to his side. "Before you told me how you felt, Tristan came to me a week earlier and told me he was in love with you. If you had heard the way he talked about you..." Xavier's voice drifted off. "I knew I could never cross that line with you. It would've crushed him. I was a fool to think he valued our family bond above anything else. We agreed neither of us would have you. But then, you two became close. And you became... *fond*—" he said the word through gritted teeth, "—of him, too. So I let him keep you, despite our agreement, for your sake. For a long time, I was nothing but an empty shell. I thought after you left, maybe—just maybe—I could finally learn to live without you. But you never left. Not my mind anyway. Not for a second. Not even to sleep. Then I got sent to Corrin with my brothers, and I saw all those people burned—children, babies."

He paused as his eyes hardened. "I was angry. Angry at myself, at Tristan, at my father. Angry that no one would be held responsible. I was determined to find the men who killed them. We got a tip they came from a city just over the border with Vertmere, so we went to the king, who claimed it was merely an insurgent group acting on their own accord, not for the crown. But we'd heard rumors he'd been receiving a portion of these raids. He denied it, of course, and we had no proof. I successfully kept my mouth shut during the meeting, but as we were leaving, the Vertmerian king said not to worry. It was just a few minuscule lives, and it wouldn't be worth losing more over… When he said those words, everything I'd managed to keep bottled up exploded. I lunged at him. I never intended to kill him. But despite my intentions, it led to the start of a war. I've felt the weight of that impulsive decision ever since."

Xavier paused, shifting. "I derailed after that. I drank far too much and tried to shut out the world as best I could. I wanted to retreat into a dark hole and never come out. When you came back… I wanted to tell you everything. But you were already in love with Tristan. And I sure as hell couldn't stay and pretend not to notice how you looked at him the way you used to look at me."

Rose bit the inside of her cheek, almost sorry she'd made him re-live the tale.

She felt the pent-up rage and sorrow building within him like a dam near its breaking point, filled by all he'd lost. And she feared that stagnant water was eroding him. One more nick and it'd burst. It was no wonder he'd shut everyone out.

"You should've told me how you really felt," she said. "You should've let me make that choice for myself."

"I know," he said, eyeing her lips with desperation. "Believe me, I know." He brushed her pearl-white hair back, caressing her cheek with his thumb. "But I thought I was doing what was best for you."

Things could have been so different. If he would've just told her…

Her heart iced over.

"You're a coward," she said with wet eyes.

Remorse hit as soon as the words escaped her lips, but she couldn't help it.

She'd spent years loving him.

Years.

Xavier's eyes hardened, but he didn't retreat. "I understand you're angry. Trust me, no one is more angry than I am." His eyes dipped to her lips again, then back to her eyes. "But I promise you, I'll never do that again." He leaned down, attempting to close the space between them.

Her guard sprang up.

"Xavier—"

"I love you," he whispered as his forehead met hers. "I love the way you crinkle your nose when you laugh, the way your large eyes grow even bigger when you apologize. The way you melt like putty when someone plays with your hair. The way your laugh lights up an entire room. The way your voice brings out emotions I didn't even know I could feel." His voice was so tender, it shifted the very ground on which she stood, too lost in an icy storm to regain her footing.

Xavier lowered his lips closer to hers.

Her hand shot to his chest, trying to stop him. "No, Xavier, wait—"

He didn't listen, crushing his lips on hers.

His euphoria under her fingertips was indescribable, so powerful it was hard to tell if it was his happiness or her own. He kissed her as if he'd been starved of air, been deprived of every delectable thing. His hand cupped her jaw, tilting her head up, deepening the kiss, his lips consuming hers.

A pull of emotions ripped her in two—half nauseous with guilt, half desperate to explore him. Her siren rose underneath her skin, poised to slither into his mind—she fled the mist before she lost herself.

She ripped herself off him.

He looked as if his body and soul had existed apart in two different realms that had finally collided.

Xavier swore in a drunken whisper on her lips. "You're telling me that's what I've been missing?" He brushed her hair back, his eyes begging for more. He leaned to kiss her again.

"I shouldn't have let you do that." Rose tried to gain distance, but he kept her pinned.

"Why not?" he breathed, his lips nearly on hers again.

Her siren urged her to let him, ready to taste his fresh, cool breath again.

She beat it down until it relinquished control.

"Because I'm in love with someone else," she revealed quickly, breaking the news.

"I don't care," he declared, as if the fact was no more than an insignificant nuisance. "I'm not letting you slip through my fingers again. Whoever it is will have to fight me for you."

She hung her head down with guilt.

"Who?" he demanded.

She bit her lip, not knowing how to tell him. "You don't want to know."

Xavier gripped her jaw, forcing her to look at him. "Who?" he growled.

She forced her lips apart. "Roman," she whispered.

He finally released her, taking two involuntary steps back. Not a single word left his lips as his mind processed the name she'd just uttered. He just stared at her, his face growing more vile by the second.

"That has to be a sick joke," he managed to get out with a scowl.

"He was there for me, Xavier," she said, pushing herself off the stable post she'd been pinned against. "When you left, when we said our goodbyes—it was the closure I needed to move on. I let you go, thinking you never intended to return. I was at my lowest after Tristan's wedding, and Roman stepped in. He helped me. When no one else was there, he was." Just talking about him made her miss him terribly.

Xavier's jaw locked, the fire in his eyes dimming fast. "I see." His gaze faltered to the ground, searching it.

A ferocious pain attacked her heart as her throat tightened; she was unable to swallow, to even breathe. It was excruciating—like poison surging its way into every vein. Savage and harrowing.

Not her pain.

His pain.

She gazed at him pitifully. "I couldn't wait for a ghost forever."

Xavier nodded slowly, not meeting her eyes. "He's the best of all of us… He deserves someone like you."

His pain did not yield. She couldn't bear it.

"I tried to tell you," she whispered lamely.

The mask she'd managed to melt hardened back into ice, sealing itself back into place just as fast as it had slipped off. "I should go," he said, dangerously low, "be with my mother… How bad is she?"

Rose let the subject go, ignoring the muted ache that pulsed at her heart. "It's not good," she said, not bothering to sugarcoat it. He wouldn't want that. "But she'll be thrilled to see you."

Xavier peered at the castle through the open doors in hesitation. His pause was so long she wondered if he was reconsidering.

"I could walk with you?" she offered.

She was sure he'd refuse, but to her surprise, he nodded.

She did her best to smother both their emotions as she said, "Come on, I'll take you to her."

CHAPTER 77

Rose and Xavier climbed the stairs to the queen's chambers in silence. She was grateful for her hood acting as a barrier to ease the tension. But no amount of barriers would be powerful enough to block the heartache that continued to leak from him.

Judging from the gleaming floor and the fluffed rugs beneath her feet, the servants had already made their rounds. They'd polished the candelabras and replaced the torches to brighten their way as they trekked up the main stairwell. They hadn't seen a soul besides the guards. She was sure because of the hour, they were the only ones still awake, until Rose heard a pair of voices.

Harriet and Roman waited outside their mother's door under the arched sun-etched keystone. Harriet had her arms crossed, glaring at Roman, whose back was turned to them.

"We have to find him." Harriet's voice carried. "He wouldn't choose not to come. He should be here by now. What if something's happened to him? She is our best chance to convince him to come home. Let her go find him."

"Do you know how dangerous that would be for her? Besides, we don't even know if he's still in Amernth. It's too far," Roman argued.

The siblings' conversation came to an abrupt halt at the sound of their approaching footsteps. Harriet saw them first, peering over Roman's shoulder as her youthful eyes lit up with joy. Rose could've felt Harriet's excitement from across the castle.

"Xavier!" Harriet exclaimed, sprinting down the hallway to him.

Xavier's face shifted into a handsome grin, holding out his arms as Harriet crashed into him.

Rose was hardly paying attention, her sea-green eyes fixed on Roman, who'd whirled around. Her eyes softened as a river of guilt tore at her for her kiss with Xavier.

Roman's golden eyes warmed at the sight of her, her siren immediately sensing how hard it was not to copy his sister and run to her. Instead, his gaze passed over her to his brother. His warmth dimmed. Nevertheless, he welcomed Xavier, enveloping him in a hug before clapping his shoulder. "Took you long enough."

"How is she?" Xavier asked, glancing at the door with hesitancy.

"Terrible." Tristan's voice came from behind them. "But what would you care?"

Rose spun, finding Tristan and Satin coming toward them. She stiffened as Xavier's lips curled into a scowl.

"Last time you were here, you nearly killed Rose," Tristan said as he strutted toward them. "But then again, you never cared much for her life, did you? Or Mother's, it would seem."

A violent force raged just beneath Xavier's skin.

Anticipating his action, she placed her hand on Xavier's forearm before he could take a step. "Don't," she whispered.

Roman's eyes flickered down to her hand on Xavier's arm. A burst of emotion came from him, but it was gone so fast she couldn't determine what it was—the contact of her hand on Xavier overpowering her senses.

"Stop it," Harriet said, glaring at Tristan. "He's only just returned."

Thankfully, Xavier heeded Rose's advice, clenching his fists instead. With a calm voice, he said, "It's okay, Harriet. Tristan knows all about the value of lives, don't you, Tristan?"

Tristan was about to retort, but Rose intervened. "This isn't the time or place. Your mother needs you all right now. This is about her."

"Speaking of mothers, why don't you go find your own?" Satin said, seeming particularly unwell herself. "This is a private family matter, and you're *not* family."

Rage simmered inside her. Her siren took over her limbs before she could stop it. She prowled toward the girl with lethal, smooth movements, like a cat approaching a mouse. "Perhaps I soon will be. Then we could be sisters," she said with a dangerously sweet voice.

Roman's energy lit up beside her. He smashed his lips together to keep them from curling up into a smile. Tristan's gaze, however, went straight to Xavier's with a burning hatred.

To Satin's credit, she didn't back down. "None of them would be foolish enough to marry you."

An awkward silence filled the corridor.

"Maybe you're right," Rose acknowledged humbly, "but I'm not worried about that at the moment. I'm staying. If the king asks me to leave, I'll do so. But you do not get to tell me what to do. Not yet." She faced Xavier. "Come on." She made for the door.

Xavier's icy eyes narrowed at Satin. "It's nice to meet you," he drawled sarcastically. He turned to Tristan. "She's perfect for you," he muttered, his eyes raking him up and down before he followed Rose.

She knocked on the door, waiting until she heard the king's voice within. "Come in."

Rose entered. The queen's frail body rested on the bed with her eyes closed, rasps filling the humid air. The bloodstained handkerchief was still clutched in her hand. Rose's heart cracked at the sight.

The king sat in the chair beside her bed, grasping his wife's free hand. His weary eyes darted to Rose as she crept in. He straightened in surprise, expecting the maids.

"Rose," the king said, his eyes easing. "What is it?"

The queen's eyes fluttered at the sound of her name. "Rose? Is that you?"

She gave the queen a small smile. "Yes, and I've brought someone who wants to see you."

She stepped aside to reveal Xavier.

"Hello, Mum," Xavier said.

Queen Lenna's eyes widened. Her soul lit up with pure singing joy—so strong it felt like a hot ray of sunlight beating down on her after a long storm. She savored it, welcoming it amidst the overwhelming sadness.

Xavier knelt on the opposite side of the bed from his father, taking her hand and bringing it to his lips.

"Xavier," the queen said with happy tears, admiring her firstborn as she cupped his face. "You're really here."

His eyes glistened, his voice low and rough. "I'm here." Xavier glanced briefly at his father.

The king gave him a firm nod. "Thank you for coming."

Xavier's voice turned abrasive. "I didn't do it for you."

One by one, the family filed in, gathering around their mother's bedside. Rose shifted, feeling like she was prying on an intimate moment. As much as she loathed to say it, maybe Satin had been right. Perhaps it wasn't her place to be here.

"Would you like me to step out?" Rose asked the king.

As soon as she said the words, Roman's face strained.

"Stay," the king requested, his eyes grazing the queen's. "Perhaps you could help tend to her? I've asked the other healers to give us some time alone."

Rose nodded at once, glad to be useful. "Of course."

Satin's fury was evident, not only in her aura but in her narrowed eyes. She leaned in to whisper something to Tristan, who shot Satin a glare, whispering something sharp back before leaving her to move closer to his mother's bed.

Whatever he'd said, Satin looked like she had been slapped in the face.

Rose tried not to let her siren be too smug about the fact.

Rose opened the balcony to let the fresh air in, making sure the queen had a view of the sea and gardens. The moons were at their peak in the midnight sky, radiating their bright light alongside the stars. She did her best to make the queen as comfortable as possible—changing rags, adjusting pillows, stoking the fire, and preparing an herbal tea to ease the pain. But as busy as she kept her hands, she felt useless. She desperately wished she could offer something else—anything to heal her.

Staying in that sorrowful room was tormenting. She was ashamed for wanting to escape, if only to take a break from the flurry of emotions that drained her energy. But she couldn't leave. Not when Roman needed her. Even if she couldn't comfort him the way she wanted to.

At one point during the long night, the queen placed her hand on Satin's stomach, peering up with regret, knowing a grandchild was on the way that she'd never meet.

Queen Lenna's pain was so great that Rose flinched away.

No one left the queen's side that night. Tristan and Xavier didn't exchange a single word, but they didn't fight either, which was in and of itself a miracle. The conversation even allowed for a few good laughs, the beautiful sound filling Rose's heart with warmth.

With each passing hour, the queen's breaths grew weaker. Although her spirits were lifted, her fits became less manageable. She coughed more often, wheezing terribly after every fit.

Dawn cast a soft pink glow through the open doors as Rose's eyes threatened to droop, the lack of sleep and heavy emotions taking their toll on her body. The warmth from the fire she stood by only added to her drowsiness.

"Rose?" the queen's brittle voice called. Rose lifted her heavy eyes from the fire to the bed. "Come here." The queen stretched out her hand.

Rose hesitated before obeying, bracing for the inevitable pain that was sure to follow. She made her way past Harriet sitting on a bench at the foot of the bed. The king was still at her bedside, while Roman and Xavier sat in chairs on either side. Tristan and Satin watched her from the daybed against the wall as Rose approached the bed.

She reached for the queen's hand as a wall of grief slammed into her.

"Rose... you've given me... a great many gifts... some I could've never dreamed of having without you. Thank you..." The Queen rasped between words. "From the bottom of my heart, thank you. And I'm... so... so sorry." Queen Lenna squeezed her hand. "I'm sorry I couldn't see that you were... never what kept my family apart... You were what was holding us all together."

The heartfelt apology poured out of Queen Lenna with genuine regret. Immediate tears filled Rose's eyes.

"You beautiful girl," the queen continued, stroking her hand. "I have one more favor to ask of you… I know you're not fond of singing… but you have such a beautiful voice… I'd love to hear it… one last time."

A suffocating silence filled the room. The request wasn't as burdensome as used to be. The phoenix had proven it wasn't tainted. Not the way she had once believed. It was a light, rather than a haunting shadow, a gift rather than a curse. As Rose looked down into the eyes of a dying woman, how could she refuse?

"I haven't sung in some time," Rose cautioned softly.

A weak smile formed on the queen's lips. "I have a feeling it's just as beautiful as I remember."

Rose forced a tense smile, refraining from eye contact with the others, afraid that it would paralyze her into silence. Taking a deep breath, she clasped her hands together, and a soft, melodic voice flowed from her lips.

Frost clings to battered leaves
and petals' velvet depths wane.
Gazed upon in rose-distorted glass
Frozen in time, it stands still.
Until summer comes.
When summer comes, you'll be
near shores of high-rising tides,
feasting in grand halls under pale moonlight.
When summer comes, you'll be
Dancing in a sea of orange hues
And playing in pearl granules.
When summer comes.
Frigid cold steals back happiness.
How can one season feel so endless?
Though you can't skip a bitter winter,
Summer will never miss its turn,
Returned to rose-distorted glass
Until summer comes.
When summer comes, you'll be
Looking up into icy blue skies,
or burning up next to amber flames.

When summer comes, you'll be
Drowning in ocean depths,
Wishing you could stay.
When summer comes.
Forced to find strength in softness,
It finds itself blooming in disaster.
The cursed beauty will no longer be used,
the rose-colored glass shatters.
At last, summer is here to stay.
When summer comes, you'll be
near the shores of high-rising tides,
feasting in grand halls under pale moonlight.
When summer comes, you'll be
Dancing in a sea of orange hues
And playing in pearl granules.
When summer comes
When summer comes
When summer comes

Rose's last note faded as the queen's hand went limp in hers, and her aura faded until it was nonexistent.

Queen Lenna was gone.

The last thread that'd been holding everyone together broke—slicing their souls into a thousand pieces.

The king's anguish was indescribable, suffocating Rose's bleeding heart from every angle. His broad shoulders trembled uncontrollably as he sobbed. With his eyes squeezed shut, he grasped his beloved's hand, kissing it before bringing it to his forehead.

It was what Rose imagined it would be like to lose Roman.

She shrunk from it, taking a step back. It was unbearable, as though a part of him was dying alongside her—she supposed it was. Tears of empathy streamed from her eyes, absorbing everyone's grief; she had no idea how to turn it off.

She wanted to escape—flee from it. But she wouldn't leave Roman, not now.

Roman's face twisted in pain as silent tears ran down his cheeks, leaning his forehead into his palms. His aura hit her in a different way than the others. Magnified. Excruciating.

She couldn't stand the distance any longer.

Rose knelt before him, wrapping her arms around his strong shoulders, trying to absorb his pain. He clung to her without a moment's hesitation, his hands gripping her dress. He burrowed his face in the curve of her neck, his tears soaking her shoulder.

"I'm sorry," she whispered so low only he could hear. "I'm so, so sorry."

He gripped her tighter. "Thank you," he whispered. "Thank you for doing that for her."

Rose didn't look to see if Tristan was watching; right now, she really didn't care.

Xavier helped serve as a distraction. "We should tell the servants," he announced softly. "They'll take her and prepare her for the ceremony."

"Not yet," the king said through tears. "I need one last moment with my wife—alone."

His tortured tone was so piercing, they all respected his wishes.

Harriet left first, barely able to hold back her sobs. Xavier followed close behind, his icy eyes void of all emotion. Tristan and Satin followed after, then Roman.

Rose was the last one out, reaching to close the door. Just as she was about to close it, a loud sob erupted from the king, who lay beside Queen Lenna on the bed, cradling her for the last time.

A tear escaped Rose's defenses as she watched him through the narrowing gap, gently closing the door. She held on until she heard it click, quickly wiping her tears before anyone saw.

They gathered outside the door, waiting for the king to say his goodbyes.

Harriet broke the silence, turning to Xavier. "What the hell took you so long?" she asked, sniffing.

All eyes looked to Xavier, curious to hear his answer.

Xavier only said, "I've been busy in Amernth." His eyes flitted to Roman.

"Did you find anything?" Roman asked.

Rose straightened, looking between them, unaware they'd been corresponding with one another.

"Nothing," Xavier said with irritation, leaning against the wall as he crossed his arms. "These men are about as elusive as a puff of smoke. Did you learn anything more from Moretti?"

Rose's gaze returned to Roman in awe. They *had* been writing.

"A little," Roman answered. "Thanks to Rose, we learned they were last seen camped just outside of Carnthe. And there's more." His gaze shifted hesitantly to Rose. "We still don't know why, but they're looking for Rose. And they know she's here."

Xavier straightened from his sluggish position against the wall. "What? Are you sure?"

"I believe so," Roman said grimly.

Tristan's outraged eyes flared, furious for being kept out of the loop. "How long have you known this?"

"We just barely found out," Roman replied. "Moretti said they were looking for her."

Tristan raised a skeptical eyebrow. "And we're going to trust him? Moretti is nothing but a self-serving prick."

"He was telling the truth… Don't ask me how I know," Rose said, too exhausted to explain.

Xavier's eyes snapped to Rose. "Why didn't you say anything?"

She opened her mouth to speak, but Roman got there first. "Perhaps she wasn't sure if you'd stick around long enough for it to matter."

Rose intervened before they could fight. "I didn't tell you because it wasn't important at that moment."

"Not important?!" Xavier exclaimed, pivoting to fume at Roman. "How could you let her come back? If they're here, she needs to leave. Now. Before they discover she's returned. It may already be too late."

"The safest place is here," Tristan disagreed. "If they already know she's here, going somewhere else isn't going to help. They'll only follow her."

She chewed her lip. The snawfus had told her these men would help her find her destiny. Maybe Tristan was right. She needed to stay to find out more, not run away.

"If they're here, then perhaps here is exactly where I ought to be," Rose said, agreeing with Tristan. "This could be the opportunity I've been waiting for. Maybe it's time I move to offense, show myself, draw them out. Maybe then we'd stand a chance."

Tristan nodded. "And we'd be ready this time."

Satin scoffed, shaking her head in silent disapproval.

"We aren't prepared for this," Xavier said, vexed. "I've seen what they can do. We have no idea of their numbers, weapons, or what they even want from you. You need to know an enemy to fight them." He looked at Roman. "Help me out here."

Roman was silent, looking down, lost in thought.

Xavier's face twisted into an aggravated scowl. "You can't seriously be considering this ridiculous plan."

Roman let out a defeated sigh. "As much as I hate to admit it… I agree with Rose. If they wanted to kill her, they would have already. We'll have to confront them eventually; here would be just as good of a place as any. At least here we have an advantage."

"And just how are you supposed to *draw* them out?" Harriet asked. "It's obvious they want to stay hidden."

"Not necessarily," Roman said. "They had to be the ones in the woods that day. The ones who kidnapped Rose and put her in the cove. They are here. We just need to create another opportunity for them."

An opportunity.

She had an idea.

"We could hold a ball," she said as she searched her mind. "It would be the perfect place for exposure without raising suspicion. I could reveal myself as a siren and get the court's attention—the news would spread like wildfire. It may just draw them out."

Tristan nodded, his eyes growing brighter at the idea. "We could say it's a celebration to honor our mother; no one would think twice about it."

"And what if these men decide to take out their rage on the people of this court?" Satin spoke up, glaring. "I'm not willing to protect a siren who's just using our grief for her own benefit."

"Satin, stop it," Tristan said with an impatient snap. "She isn't going to hurt anyone."

Satin scowled back with malice. "You're making a mistake. This will bring hell upon us all, I promise you."

Without another word, Satin left them, stomping down the hallway.

Tristan sighed in frustration, letting her go.

"He's taking a long time," Harriet said, gazing at the door with puffy eyes. "Do whatever you have to do… I just want this all to stop." Without another word, Harriet opened the door and returned to her mother's room.

Xavier didn't miss a beat after Harriet closed the door. "You realize once the court discovers what you are, the council will turn on you. They've given us space for my mother's sake, but as soon as they find out about you, they'll lock you up, sell you, maybe even kill you."

She winced out of reflex.

Roman squared his shoulders as his beautiful honey eyes held hers. "I'll stand by you, whatever you decide."

She paused, considering the risks. "I have to try," she concluded. "It's our best chance."

"I'm telling you, this is a mistake," Xavier warned. "I have half a mind to drag you out of here before this all blows up."

"Feel free to run any time it's convenient for you," Tristan seethed.

Xavier ignored him, keeping his gaze on Rose. "I'm not leaving you again."

"Then don't say things like that," she rebutted. "If you want to help, you're going to have to stay to do that."

Xavier looked at Roman, to his last hope. "Are you going to try to talk any sense into her?"

Roman paused to think, rubbing the side of his face. "No. I trust her. I'll talk to our father. If he agrees, we'll hold the ball… tonight."

CHAPTER 78

It didn't take much to convince the king of their plan.

Whether it was the loss of his wife or the growing urgency to uncover who the insurgents were, King Henrik was prepared to take the risk if Rose was.

They implemented every possible precaution. The king commanded double the guards to ensure the castle would be secured twice over. Once the ball commenced, no one would be allowed to enter or leave the grounds. Every attendee would be accounted for, leaving no stone unturned.

They did all this if only to reassure Rose's mother, who despised the idea—taking Xavier's side. They argued back and forth, but Rose emerged victorious with the king's added reassurance that nothing would happen to Rose under his protection. As for the funeral preparations, the king ordered the passing ceremony to be the following night, allowing the servants enough time to prepare.

High emotions shadowed Rose at every turn, the ache in each member of the royal family draining her reserves. It was as if the god of death hovered over her shoulder, sapping the happiness out of her. At times, it became so unbearable that it forced her to flee the room entirely. She was afraid she'd be driven to madness if it stayed like this for much longer.

After having brunch with her mother and taking a long, well-needed nap, Rose stepped out onto her balcony, savoring the moment of solitude.

She tilted her head back and closed her eyes. The sound of the sea waves quieted her mind as she soaked in the beating sunlight.

She dropped her gaze down to the sword strapped to her hips. She brushed her fingers along the intricate design of roses and vines. It made her think of Zareb. She missed him terribly. She wondered where he was now, if he'd found safety in Semaria. He'd given his life to serve Cathan, and with one trespass, one mistake, he'd lost it all. All because he chose to help her.

Her heart hardened. She wished she could write to him, if only to ease her mind.

A knock came at the door, and before she could even answer, they let themselves in.

Rose didn't need to look to recognize who those footsteps belonged to, sensing it in the dangerous way he shifted his weight—the commanding strides of a general. Only when Roman was standing beside her did she lift her eyes to meet his.

A weight lifted off both of them at the same time. The ache of his absence faded, but she could still sense the haunting sadness even as relief filled his eyes.

A smile slipped onto her lips to cheer him up. His mouth tugged upward in response as he leaned down to claim her smile, parting her lips with his. She opened without resistance, her hands gliding up his chest to encircle his neck.

"Damn, this ring does nothing," he rumbled against her lips. "I couldn't think of anything else."

"You were gone a lot longer than a few hours," she said pointedly.

"I know. I'm sorry." His lips pressed into a thin line. "But there's something I want to show you. Something you need to see." He took her hand and urged her to follow him.

His face was all too somber, so she agreed without question.

With her hood up, Roman led her to the castle's lower levels she'd seldom been to. The winding staircase led down… down, passing the dungeons that had held Xavier earlier that summer—a lifetime ago.

Still, they descended as the air turned cooler. Damp. Ancient.

Rose hadn't even known the castle extended this far down.

At last, they reached the end of the staircase leading to a stretched hallway. At the end stood a weathered wooden door, beckoning them into a shadowy tunnel. Roman grasped the large torch next to the hole before entering.

A twinge of claustrophobia crept in as they pressed on. While the tunnel could easily accommodate five grown men, its curved ceilings felt uncomfortably low. Rose fought the urge to turn back, forcing one foot in front of the other, unconsciously squeezing Roman's hand tighter.

Roman gently pressed her hand to his chest, pulling her closer. He kissed her knuckles, spreading a tingling sensation up her arm.

"Where are we going?" she asked, not knowing exactly why she whispered the question.

"The oldest structure within the castle, and maybe even Vallor itself… the royal tombs," Roman answered.

Rose crouched to avoid a long spiderweb hanging from the ceiling. "And why would we be doing that?"

He gazed down at her. "Because the past may just help us understand the future."

Rose wasn't sure how long they'd been walking, until she noticed roots hanging between the stones above, indicating they were no longer beneath the castle. "Where are we exactly?"

"An underground tunnel that leads to the old ruins underneath the original castle," Roman explained.

When they finally came to the end of the tunnel, Roman took the initiative by opening another large, creaky door. Its hinges squeaked in a high pitch as it swung open.

They entered a vast, oval-shaped chamber constructed from light-gray limestone. It was well lit compared to the dreary tunnel they'd just trudged through, with torches placed every ten feet or so along the walls. The flames emitted a subtle white flame, different from the torch Roman was carrying.

She gawked at the flame. Magic. Those flames were kindled by ancient magic. Eternal flames that would never go out.

Numerous tombs surrounded her, filling every inch of the curved walls. Four arched hallways stretched between them, branching out in every direction toward what she presumed were even more tombs. Cathan's sun symbol was carved on the archways and each tomb.

At the center stood a life-sized statue of a stout older man with an exceptionally long beard and sunken eyes. He, too, bore Cathan's sun symbol around his neck.

"This is where they buried the kings and queens of old. Back when Cathan was first settled," Roman said as he approached the statue in the center of the room. "This is the first king, Argarion Atticus."

The founder of Cathan. An eerie breeze grazed her skin. "Will your parents be placed to rest here?"

He shook his head. "No, they prefer to have a boat ceremony… Something about not wanting to spend eternity in a hole," he added with a saddened smile.

Her thumb stroked the back of his hand. "I'm sorry." The pathetic phrase spewed out of her on repeat.

"To be honest, it hasn't hit me yet." Roman looked away down the halls. "There's been so much going on, I haven't been able to stop and think about it."

"She loved you, you know. I know how proud she was of you… How you led the war for us."

"Being good at killing isn't what she was proud of… The only reason I have for her to be proud is standing right in front of me." He kissed her temple. "I do regret she won't get to see us married… or meet our children." His gaze dropped to her stomach as he gently brushed it with his thumbs.

Her cheeks flushed with the heat of eternal flames. The thought of carrying his child aroused her more than she'd care to admit.

She took those thoughts and buried them deeper than this tomb. Now was not the time for that.

But one day… she'd allow herself to dream.

"If we aren't here for your mother, what are we doing?" she asked, surveying the chilling chambers.

His eyes conveyed a hidden burden. "What I'm about to show you is an ancient secret that's been kept since the founding of Cathan. You cannot tell a soul what you're about to see. You must promise."

Rose's curiosity was piqued. "I promise."

He switched his torch for one of the eternal flames, stretching out his free hand again. "This way." He gestured to one of the hallways.

She accepted his hand, clutching it like she was being led into a dragon's lair, secretly cringing on the inside that there were still more tunnels to be explored.

A small smile played on his lips. "You're looking at me like the first time I made you swim at Highland Haven. I'm not trying to kill you."

She shrugged. "It's always a possibility."

"You and I both know it's quite the opposite."

Rose gave him a dangerous smile. "I suppose it's a good thing I like you, then," she mused. She glanced down at his lips, gaining a sudden hunger for them. But if they started, she'd never stop, and she refused to be down here any longer than necessary.

Roman let out a harsh laugh that echoed off the walls. "An incredibly good thing," he concurred, pressing a kiss to her temple.

They trudged through one passage after another, their footsteps carrying down the silent tunnels. Turn after turn, she followed him. She counted one...two... seven... twelve.

These passages weren't just a maze—it was a labyrinth.

She prayed Roman knew where he was going because she was lost. Each turn looked the same as the one before. No doubt the purpose of it all.

She frowned as they reached a dead end.

Without hesitation, Roman approached the stone wall. His fingertips glided over the dusty grooves, searching for something. He stopped on a singular stone, blowing the dust away, uncovering a small sun symbol in the upper corner. Ever so gently, he pressed the stone inward.

The wall shifted, triggering a chain reaction that shook the ground. Rose steadied herself as the wall slid to the side. Dust settled to reveal an ancient wooden door covered with runes, so old it had to have been created long before the castle was built.

Roman retrieved a key tucked away in his pocket, holding it out so she could see Cathan's emblem on its head. With it, he unlocked the door, producing over a dozen clicks ricocheting into the ground beneath their feet.

Before he opened the door, he glanced at the bronze key in his hand. "Do you know why Cathan's symbol is the sun?"

Rose paused, not knowing why it was pertinent, but she still responded. "The sun signifies life itself. It sustains us by bringing energy, power, and light to our world."

"It does… but there is a little more to it than that."

He pushed the door open to a black abyss. She braced herself as a chilling breeze swept over her face. A shiver ran down her spine as she realized she'd be expected to enter the void.

She buried her instincts to flee as Roman held his hand out, leading her down to what felt like the very core of Vallor.

"Do you remember the story of the first king, Argarion?"

Her mind flashed back to the statue they'd just seen. "Yes, of course. Argarion was the king who split Vallor into seven provinces. Every child in Cathan knows. We celebrate it every year on the solstice."

"He also defeated the greatest enemy that mankind ever faced."

Rose nodded, remembering from their history lessons. "The leader of the revolution—he was the one who tried to conquer Vallor for himself. But Argarion proclaimed he was never to be mentioned in any book, wishing for his name to be forgotten, that a man that evil did not deserve to be remembered in history."

Roman nodded. "And how was he defeated?"

She shrugged. "No one knows exactly, only that he was rendered powerless by Argarion and killed for his crimes."

"I thought so, too… until what I read today."

Rose skidded to a stop. "What could you have possibly read that could make you question centuries-old history?"

Roman turned back to her as he reached into his cloak, pulling out an old, worn leather book. "Because I read Argarion's journal."

She stared at the tattered book, its worn edges secured with a leather strap. "Where did you get that?"

"The same place I got this." He held up the key he'd used. "My father gave me this key with a locked chest the night we returned to the castle. I found the book in the chest and started skimming it. I didn't know how much meaning it held until I realized what it was."

Her eyes widened with intrigue. "What does it say?"

"A lot. But most importantly, Argarion explains how he fought against an ancient enemy. He still refused to use his name; however, he does refer to him by a nickname—the Blood King."

Rose's chest seized.

It couldn't be.

"Do you think..."

"That it's the same Blood King the seer and the snawfus foretold of? It's entirely possible," Roman responded gravely.

Her heart plummeted through the dust-filled air. "How could that be? Argarion killed him thousands of years ago."

Roman shook his head, holding up the journal. "Not according to this. He destroyed his powers, yes, but the Blood King escaped. Argarion spent the rest of his life trying to find him but never succeeded. Everyone else presumed he was dead, but Argarion was the only one who knew the truth."

Her mind scrambled to put the pieces together. "But if he's still alive, that would make him thousands of years old. How could he live that long? Unless he was..." Rose's voice trailed off again as the realization set in.

"A siren," Roman finished. "Argarion even confirmed it in an entry."

The eternal flame in his hands flickered, casting a dark shadow across his face. She swore the tunnel itself was closing in on them, attempting to swallow them whole.

She started to walk again. "But even for a siren, that's an incredibly long life," she pointed out.

"He must have figured out a way to survive all these years."

"So you're telling me I'm supposed to defeat the most powerful siren of all time?" she whispered into the shadows.

Anxiousness crept into his eyes. "It's a theory."

She bit her bottom lip as she fiddled with her fingers. She was going to be sick.

"Luckily for us, Argarion wrote about how he destroyed the Blood King's powers," Roman said.

Her eyes whipped to his. At last. Hope. "How?"

"Argarion stole a powerful talisman that belonged to the Blood King," he explained. "A personal item always in his possession said to contain unlimited power. It was made of a rare sunstone that fell from the sky centuries ago, shaped like the same sun symbol that fills Cathan's walls. Which leads us to why I've brought you here."

The end of the tunnel opened into a small, dark room. The faint rushing that reached her ears intensified into a roar—an underground river, she realized—a swift and forceful one at that.

A strong presence came over her. A wave of… *energy*. Powerful and ancient.

Not a moment later, a deep buzzing noise filled her ears, drowning out the roaring water. Rose's vision sharpened even as she entered the dark.

Roman locked his eyes on hers, startled.

Her brows pinched. "What is it?"

"Your eyes are glowing," Roman said, staring at them in awe.

Her fingertips brushed the soft skin under her eye. Another heightened ability to add to the list. She didn't have time to dwell on it as her gaze settled on the source of the humming: a small, shiny object perched on a rocky pedestal at the room's center, matching the talisman Roman had just described.

A snake-like feeling slithered in her veins, threatening to take over her limbs—

She recoiled from the power, taking a step back.

"Is that the talisman?" she whispered as if it could hear her.

Roman seemed unaffected by its aura. "Yes," he said, then looked at her, noticing her hesitation. "What's wrong?"

"Can't you hear that?"

"Hear what? The river?"

"No, that humming sound."

He shook his head.

Rose's gaze returned to the talisman, resting innocently on the gray stone pedestal. Its intricate golden chain held a glorious sun-shaped red stone. She initially thought it was a solid color, but upon closer inspection, she discovered flecks of yellow, orange, and red shimmering within.

She heard it… *calling* to her, whispering, urging her to come closer, to touch it—to wear it. It drew her siren in like a moth to a flame.

It scared the living hell out of her.

She wrapped her arms tightly around herself, preventing them from doing something they shouldn't. "I feel like it's… like it's alive somehow," she whispered.

"You can *feel* it?" Roman asked in surprise.

"Yes. Whatever it is, it's powerful, dangerous, and incredibly dark."

Roman took a few steps towards the talisman, unaware of the danger it held within its ruby depths.

"I think I've connected the dots." He turned back to face her. "When my father sent me and my brothers to Corrin, I lied to you. It wasn't just to train troops. It was to protect this, though I didn't know it at the time. Not long after you left last year, my father told us about an important object that had long been hidden. Said it was vital to Vallor's survival. I didn't know what it was or why it was so important. Only that it needed to be protected at all costs. When my father discovered a group of men were looking for it, he made a decoy—a fake replica. He ordered my brothers and I to take it to Corrin to see if it would draw this mysterious enemy out of the shadows, and it did. As soon as we left the city unprotected, they came. They burned it to the ground, only to find the fake talisman."

Goose bumps raised on her skin. And not from the cold. "The same men looking for *me*?"

"We can't know for certain," he replied, "but I'd bet my life on it. It's all too much of a coincidence, and I don't think they are men. I think they may be sirens, too."

"So all this time, you think the Blood King has been searching for the talisman? To be reunited with it?"

Roman nodded slowly. "And for some reason… you."

Rose suddenly felt small. "What do we do?"

"I'm not sure. But at least we finally have an idea of who this enemy is and what he wants. We just need to find out more."

It was all so much to take in, but she finally had answers.

So why did it only give her a thousand more questions?

"Perhaps we could use it?" Roman said, studying the talisman. "If the Blood King's after it, perhaps it holds the power we need to defeat him?"

No, a mystic voice said firmly in her mind, alarming her—the feminine voice sounded like the snawfus. *Don't even touch it,* it warned.

Why? she spoke back into the void in her mind. *Why? Please, can you hear me?*

But there was no reply.

"No," she said after a long moment, heeding the warning. "Whatever it is... something is telling me not to go anywhere near it. Are you sure it's safe down here?"

He nodded firmly. "Yes. There's nowhere in Vallor safer than these tomb walls. Only royalty and the high councilmen know of its existence. And now you. But I'll see to it there are more guards on duty, just in case."

The tension left her body. She was glad to be reassured. She glanced at the talisman one final time, the magical object calling to her siren once more.

She shut it out.

"Come on, it's getting late. We'll need to be ready for tonight," she said, anxious to be above ground again.

After all, they still had a ball to attend.

CHAPTER 79

As the sun dipped below the horizon, twilight wrapped the world in a warm glow, casting a tangerine blanket over Rose's room as she got ready for the ball.

She'd opted for a dress made of a light sea-green, form-fitting fabric. The elegant trumpet gown hugged her hips, cascading down to the floor. It went perfectly with the golden mask Thea had designed, interwoven with a green ribbon around its edges.

Thea had achieved the wet hair look Rose had requested by applying some sort of unique mixture to her wild mane, infusing it with a deliciously fragrant jasmine scent. She let her wavy pearl-white hair flow freely beyond her shoulders, forgoing the usual court updo. She looked like she'd returned straight from a swim.

It was perfect.

Looking into the floor-length mirror still took her by surprise. The lethal beauty she now possessed was like a honed weapon, poised to strike any unsuspecting bystander.

Definitely not the worst fate imaginable.

Her gaze lowered to the mask in her hands. An idea came.

She had Thea fetch her some shimmery gold paint, similar to what she wore for her coming out ball. She stuck her fingers into the cool, thick liquid and went to work, drawing the bindrune symbol on her chest, just as the seer had during the second succession trial.

The seer *had* said that it would give her strength.

And tonight, she was determined to harness whatever strength she could find.

Rose stood atop the magnificent marble staircase in the same spot as she had earlier that summer, her siren eyes peering through her golden mask at the dancing couples below.

The girl who had stood here before... was gone. Forever. Pain gripped her heart to know she wouldn't be coming back.

But that was a death to mourn another day.

Taking a deep breath, Rose stepped down the smooth marble stairs, keeping her head held high. With each step, heads turned. Whispers circulated. Jaws dropped. Their eyes fixated on the shimmering symbol on her chest. Her shaky knees threatened to buckle, but she pushed through the insecurity. She scoured the crowd, keeping an eye out for anything suspicious.

The court stopped dancing altogether as the music faded into silence. She had captured the entire room's attention. Good.

She was halfway down the staircase when she stopped, taking another steady breath.

Her hands lifted to untie the ribbon securing her mask, sliding it off her face inch by inch. She lifted her chin, flashing her sea-green eyes upward to the crowd.

Gasps of shock spread like wildfire. A mixture of emotions slammed her from all directions—some curious and eager, others blazing with hostility.

Before, she would have cowered under the scrutinizing eyes, but not tonight.

Tonight, she had to fake confidence until she bled it.

With that thought, Rose let a menacing smile ensnare her lips as she straightened her back and shoulders. She continued descending the stairs until she was walking among them.

The crowd parted like the Meridian Sea as she strutted through them, scanning each person as if judging to see if any of them could meet her high standards.

And there was one that surpassed them all.

Roman stood in the middle of the parted sea, just as besotted as the rest. His soft lips parted in awe as his gold eyes fell prey to hers. His thick brown hair spilled in natural waves, hovering above the golden shoulder pads of his tunic.

Those dangerous muscles shifted to face her.

Her feet faltered as her world went quiet, her vision fogging from the steam boiling within her.

She fell into him like the rain fell into the sea. Stretched for him like the trees stretched for the sun. Burned for him like a wildfire devoured a dry forest.

She was still standing there as he stalked to her, his strides solid. Bold. Unafraid.

He held his arm out to her.

Without hesitation, she took it.

And with one graceful motion, he whisked her across the dance floor, and got lost in a realm entirely their own.

CHAPTER 80

An hour later, Rose stood next to her mother, Roman, and Xavier, all huddled together while couples swirled around them on the open dance floor. Tristan and Satin were among them, doing a remarkable job of pretending to be a cheerful couple for the court, even though Rose was acutely aware of his frequent glances in her direction.

Her gaze drifted to the balcony, where every pillar had a guard surveying the crowd, anticipating something—anything. But no such threat had appeared. Still, she remained vigilant, scanning faces for any hint that something was amiss.

Roman and the others followed suit. Even the king, despite appearing as if he'd been dragged through hell, remained on the throne above the sidelines, overseeing the celebration.

"I don't like this," Roman said next to her, disgruntled, glaring at the lingering stares. "Every single man in this room is looking at you like you're the next course."

Rose knew it, no matter how much she tried to ignore it. She could feel the room's curiosity for her, the stares reminding her of the men at the tavern. She shifted uncomfortably in her stance.

"I could say I told you so, but it seems so repetitive," Xavier said on the other side of Roman, taking a long drink of wine.

"I can't hide under a cloak forever," she said, which was true enough.

"I could've used a few more days of it," her mother muttered next to her.

She knew Roman and Xavier would agree.

Harriet was on the dance floor, swaying with an attractive young man, exchanging soft whispers and playful smiles. Rose recognized him but couldn't remember his name. He belonged to a House of even lower status than Rose. Harriet was absolutely out of his reach. But it appeared Harriet paid no mind to that, drawing him closer. Perhaps Harriet had a secret beau after all.

As the night wore on, Rose attempted to pretend she was enjoying herself, but the sheer number of emotions swarming threatened her sanity. A migraine quickly set in, making her realize that crowds were her worst nightmare.

Roman noticed her distress, intertwining his pinky discretely with hers.

With his touch, she was able to focus on him. The overwhelming emotions in the room faded into the background like white noise. Her stiff shoulders relaxed. She stepped closer to him.

"Are you alright?" he asked.

"I'm fine, just... don't let go," she whispered.

He leaned down to her ear. "Never," he whispered, risking a discreet kiss on the neck just under her ear—the very spot where he kissed her at the Snorri.

Out of nowhere, Xavier straightened, mumbling something about needing another drink. He'd seen. Rose was about to open her mouth to protest, but Xavier was already on his way over to the tables.

"Would you like to—" Roman was cut off as a beautiful blonde appeared.

Rose immediately let go of Roman's hand.

"You're back!" Beth said, her blue eyes bright, solely set on Roman. "I was starting to get worried. I'm ever so sorry to hear about your mother."

"Thank you," Roman replied, his eyes softening. "Would you like to dance?"

It took Rose every speck of self-mastery to keep her siren contained.

By some miracle, she retained her composure, keeping her face clear of any negative emotion as she stomached the interaction.

Beth's face brightened at once. "Of course."

Roman glanced at Rose, asking for permission.

She did her best to push her insecurities aside, giving him a small smile. What could one dance hurt?

"You don't mind, do you, Rose?" Beth asked, her looking her up and down with a disapproving glare as if to ask why her permission was needed.

"Oh, of course not." She forced a wider smile.

With that, Roman grasped Beth's hand and guided her onto the dance floor. Rose folded her arms and sulked.

"She deserves a conversation, Rose," her mother said, looking at the pair sympathetically. "Her soul is about to be crushed."

At last, it clicked. Rose's eyes grew with realization as she looked back at the couple. Beth was still under the impression Roman had come back for her. Guilt crept in. She was selfish. Greedy and selfish. Any and all friendship she'd had with Beth was now completely ruined. She had never intended to steal him from her. He'd just... snuck up on her.

Before long, her mother was also whisked away by a dance partner, leaving Rose alone on the sidelines.

She tried not to be irritated by Beth's besotted gaze as she ripped her gaze from them, craving a distraction. She was about to get a drink when she realized her mistake. Countless eyes were fixed upon her—leering, eager, longing to dance with the siren.

She was about to run for it when a familiar feminine voice stopped her. "Leaving so soon?"

Rose took a mental breath before she turned to face Satin, giving her a bright smile. It was an effort to make her muscles move. "Just going to get a drink. Would you like one?"

"No, thank you," Satin replied sourly. "I don't need anything from you."

Rose nodded and began to turn away. She intended to ignore the dig, but then her siren—or perhaps another darker aspect of herself—overpowered her. She moved closer to Satin and spoke in a low voice. "I understand why you're angry with me. I get it. Truly. But this continued hostility towards me is starting to get old."

Satin stepped towards her, lowering her voice so only she could hear. "Tell me," Satin said, her voice so cold it could have given her frostbite. "Have you ever fallen instantly for someone you thought was the one? Be so blind as to marry him, feeling like the luckiest girl in the world, only to find out he's in love with another woman? The same woman you thought was a friend? To have to find out on your wedding night, making love to one another when he cries out her name?" An angry tear spilled out of her soft brown eyes.

Rose was so stunned she couldn't reply.

No. No, he wouldn't. Tristan wouldn't think of her when they... when they...

She was going to be sick.

"You should've told me," Satin said, betrayed. "You shouldn't have led me to believe there was nothing between you two. Looking back, I know I should have seen it myself. Why else would he feel obliged to save you in the third challenge? All of you took my naivety for gullibility, and now I have to endure a loveless marriage with a child I'm not even sure he wants."

Oh, Rose, what have you done?

"I'm sorry. I should've told you," she admitted. "But he'll love your child. He's wanted nothing more than to be a father."

Satin glared at her with intolerant eyes. "You can offer me no such false reassurances."

"We don't need to be enemies, Satin," Rose said, looking for any sign of a white flag. "I know we have our differences. I'm not asking to be your best friend, but can we put it aside and at least be civil?"

Satin eyed her for a long moment, giving her hope she was at least considering her words. But then her soft face turned unsavory as a sneer slipped through. "We could be the last two people in Vallor and I'd still choose to die alone than be civil with you."

Rose recoiled at the raw animosity. Deep down, she felt pity for what Satin had gone through. Just as she had made Tristan marry Satin, she'd made Satin marry him. Holding on to such deep resentment would be a heavy burden—with a child, no less. So she did her best not to hold it against her, but that didn't mean she'd stick around to let Satin demean her.

Rose was about to leave when another voice intervened.

"Satin," Tristan said, cutting in. His expression was stern, making it clear he'd heard. "You've been up and about a lot this evening. Perhaps we should sit down."

Satin folded her arms. "I've had enough. I'm going to bed."

"I could come with you," Tristan offered, stepping towards her.

But Satin pulled back. "No. I don't want to be anywhere near you—*either* of you." With that, she strode away, clutching her stomach with tenderness.

Rose waited until Satin was well out of earshot before she spoke. "Tell me it's not true," she whispered. "Tell me you didn't call out my name on your wedding night."

Tristan's eyes darted to hers as surprise filled them. His silence and crestfallen expression gave her all the answers she needed.

Her siren gloated on the inside. The fact made her mouth go rancid, repressing the disgusting feeling.

"No wonder she hates me so much," she muttered to herself.

"I was drunk out of my mind," Tristan admitted. "I should never have slept with her, but she wanted it so badly. And I felt guilty I even agreed to marry her at all… I often wonder what our marriage would be like now if I had just managed to keep your name off my lips."

Rose didn't know what else to say except, "I'm sorry."

He shook his head at once. "You don't need to apologize… but you could dance with me." He stuck an arm out, his dazzling blue eyes shining at her.

She would've refused him if it weren't for the men lurking to catch her alone. And to her annoyance, Roman was still occupied with Beth, both in a heated conversation now. Her siren's blood boiled at how Beth held his face in her hands. Rose fought the urge to go and take a handful of Beth's hair and—

She faced Tristan, shoving down the horrible thoughts. "Alright." She took his hand, letting him lead her to the middle of the room.

He twirled her playfully before pulling her into his arms as a small smile played on his lips. That smile was a stab to her heart.

A reminder of what could have been.

"I haven't had a chance to thank you," Tristan said, "for what you did for my mother, I know she didn't make your life easy. And to sing like that… it was an incredible gift."

She gave him a small, gracious smile. "Of course."

Silence fell over them for a few bars before Tristan leaned in closer. "You look incredible," he said, his voice tender. "It reminds me of how you looked the night we camped on the beach." His lips lifted into a reminiscent grin. "Do you remember?"

A smile slipped out despite herself. "You mean when you set up the tent too close to the shore and it nearly took us both out to sea? I was scared out of my mind, but for some reason I could only laugh when we got back inside. I'm sure we looked like drowned rats scurrying back to a hovel."

Tristan let out a harsh laugh. "And then I walked you back to your room… It was the first time I kissed you." His eyes lowered to her lips.

Without warning, she was flooded with a vision of the memory.

She was standing as close as they were now. Her heart beating out of her rib cage as she stood in the dark corridor with water dripping off her dress onto the stone floor, waiting for him to close the gap. He slipped his hand into hers, lowering his lips, and worshiped hers for the first time.

She was thrust back into the present just as her siren began to rise to the surface, urging her to close the space between them like they had then. To feel his skin on hers. Let him take her back to his roo—

She immediately slammed an invisible wall down, fleeing from the lust.

Tristan, however, picked up on the subtle change, knowing her all too well. "You still feel something for me," he whispered as he searched her face. "I can see it in your eyes."

"Stop it," she snapped, not liking the insinuation.

His eyes hardened. "What, I'm the only one who can't look at you like that? You think Xavier looks at you any differently?"

She returned his glare with full force. "He isn't married. You are."

"And whose fault is that?" he retorted, coming closer, his ocean-blue eyes attempting to drag her back out to sea.

Rose dropped her arms, her heart grinding into dust as she said, "Mine... completely and utterly mine."

Before he could say another word, she fled, retreating so quickly that she barely heard him call out her name. She avoided eye contact with the onlookers as she weaved through the couples.

But as she did, she was struck by a surge of energy so consuming her feet skidded to a stop. It was the most powerful aura she'd ever encountered.

And she'd felt it before.

CHAPTER 81

Rose spun to the source of the energy, following its trail.

A hooded figure loomed overhead on the balcony, concealed like a monster in the shadows. Two guards lay sprawled at his feet, arrows embedded in their chests, as he, like a predator, prowled to the railing. His arm was cocked, ready to send an arrow through her heart.

This was it.

She stayed exactly where she was, ready for him. *Come on. Take the shot,* she urged.

But at the last second, the hooded figure's aim shifted. Panic seized every organ as he pointed his arrow at his true target. Her eyes followed his aim.

Utter dread consumed her soul.

"*Roman!*" she screamed.

Even with her inhuman speed, she didn't have time to stop what would happen next.

Roman's head whipped toward her scream. But her cry had only distracted him. The arrow was already airborne.

No. Not again. To the everlasting gods, please—please!

In a twist of fate, the king was making rounds and was close enough to break free from his circle of guards. He reached out, yanking Roman back—just as the arrow pierced the king's heart.

"*No!*" Rose cried, reaching out.

Chaos ensued.

Screams and shouts of alarm spread through the crowd like a tornado. Bodies ran in every direction to reach cover. The guards sprang to action, fortifying the room. But she was hardly paying attention as she ran against the current, trying to reach the king crumpled on the floor.

Roman was already on his hands and knees beside his father. His golden eyes lifted up to hers. "Help him," he begged.

A pool of blood was already oozing from the king's chest and mouth, gurgling as he struggled to cough it out.

Rose knelt down, scrambling to tilt him to the side to keep him from choking, but more blood just kept replacing what pooled on the floor. She pressed her palm around his gushing wound, blood staining her hands. But it was a fool's errand. It was too much. There was nothing she could do to stop it now.

So instead, her bloodied hands reached for his. She was immediately hit with his internal panic. "It's okay," she whispered as tears filled her eyes. "It's okay. You're not alone. It's okay."

King Henrik's wide, fearful eyes relaxed at her voice as she squeezed his hand. He knew what she meant.

She kissed his hand. "It's okay," she repeated. "Go. Be with Lenna. It's okay. You can let go. Don't be afraid."

The king's eyes twinkled for the last time as he gulped another pool of blood and—

His grip went limp.

Her swimming gaze lifted to Roman standing overhead.

He took a staggered step back. Despair threatened to consume him, but as soon as her siren detected it, his eyes hardened, spinning into a dark rage. "*Barricade the doors!*" he bellowed, prowling in a fury. He drew his sword with a quick whip. "*No one leaves! No one!*"

She pulled the arrow out of the king's chest, carefully wiping it clean with her dress before she inspected it. There was a faint glint of red on the tip, confirming her guess. *Dragonshade.*

Rose looked up to where the hooded man had stood, but of course, there was no trace of him or the energy she had felt.

She sank back onto the floor.

Her plan had failed.

After the shock wore off, the court members were all escorted to either the grand hall or their rooms. Rose assisted the healers before they took the king away, then washed the blood from her hands, though blotches still stained her dress.

Another one to burn.

The only ones left in the ballroom were Tristan, Harriet, Roman, and Xavier, along with Rose and her mother. Across from them stood the twelve high council members.

All of them listened to the report from the head guard.

"What do you mean you didn't find him?" Roman growled with a death stare.

To his credit, the soldier stood with confidence. "We've accounted for everyone, General. There isn't a soul missing or added."

Roman cursed, folding his arms.

How could that be? How could they have missed someone with a bow and arrow in hand looking like that? People couldn't just disappear into thin air. If what the guard said was true, then they'd have to assume—

It was someone within the court.

"What do you want to do, Tristan?" Lord Barron asked.

All eyes fell on Tristan, whose face was paler than fresh snow. He didn't move. His eyes didn't even flicker, staring into space. It finally hit her—with their father gone, the succession was in motion.

Tristan was their new king.

Silence filled the hall, each high council member looking at Tristan expectantly. But Tristan was lost in another world.

"Tristan," Rose prodded softly.

Tristan finally snapped out of it as his glossy eyes lifted to meet hers, threatening to overflow. A wave of his internal fear crashed into her—pure, justified fear. He didn't let a soul see it but her.

Within a blink, the fear was gone, and Tristan straightened. His jaw tightened as determination took over his expression. "The enemy must be someone among us. We'll need to interrogate each court member."

"We could start with her," Lord Martin sneered, his beady eyes set solely on Rose, probably resenting that she was allowed to return at all.

There it was—the suspicion. But who could blame them? Their mistrust of her had just been validated a thousand times over. Their king was dead. The court was in danger. And it was all because of her—a lying siren.

She had planned to prove her innocence to the council by finding the true culprit. But now, with empty hands and the king gone… she was on the chopping block. Her fear escalated—fear that none of them could accept her, that they'd only see her as nothing but a threat.

A throne seeker.

She tried to read them, but their emotions were so muddied she couldn't decipher whether the council intended to hold her responsible.

Roman's mouth curled into a snarl. "Are you suggesting she was in two places at once? She couldn't have—"

"I wasn't talking to you," Lord Martin silenced him, returning his attention to Tristan. "She's a siren. We have no idea what she's capable of or what powers she possesses. All we know is that none of this happened until she returned."

Roman and Xavier discreetly drew closer to her, their hands gripping the hilts of their swords. Her mother came closer, too, preparing for a fight.

Rose's eyes flickered to Tristan, wondering if he'd defend her, too. But to her surprise, his eyes were already intently on her. Observing her. Waiting. Giving her an opportunity to speak for herself.

Understanding, she straightened her posture and took a step forward. "I know you've heard stories of my kind—stories of terror and slaughter, tales of the destruction of land and theft of lives. Some of you have even experienced the consequences of these actions firsthand, and I grieve with you.

But I am just as estranged from my kind as you are. They are not me, and it's neither fair nor just of you to hold their past transgressions against me. Just as it would be unfair of me to hold you accountable for the near extinction of my kind... I've known most of you nearly all my life. I've sat and eaten beside you and even looked up to some of you." Her eyes rested on Lord Barron, his handsome eyes watching her closely. "Ever since the moment I returned, I've fought for your approval. At one point, I dearly wished for it. But you had already decided my fate before the succession had begun."

She paused, the room silent. "I used to wonder why such powerful men like yourselves would be so intentionally belligerent towards someone like me—a common girl with no title, power, or political sway. A girl who was only trying to secure a future for her family after being sold as a slave, auctioned to the highest bidder by a man I called my father. But now I see it's because you're afraid—afraid of change, afraid of what the future holds for your province, and rightly so. As I stated in the succession, if we are to survive the storm brewing, we must set aside our fears and prejudices and all give our full support to our king." Her eyes flickered to Tristan. "So Cathan can remain strong as we face this new enemy... Together."

The room was quiet. The very breaths she took sounded too loud. She studied each of their faces, ending on Tristan. A discreet hint of satisfaction shone in his eyes.

Lord Barron broke the silence. "King Henrik was one of the greatest in Cathan's history. He created peace within our lands, helped crops flourish, reduced poverty, and created a new way of trade that supplied wealth and livelihood to many who had none. When war broke out, he sent his sons—his most precious possession—to aid. And he took care of those who served him, including every one of us... Is there any among you who would argue that?"

Silence.

Lord Barron continued, "He saw something in Rose, and I believe in his judgment. She may be the thing we need as we enter a new era. We all know of the dangers that approach. If we are to stand a chance at facing these foes, we need to look beyond our own resources. We all saw how she sprang out of the water like a sea god, cured a poison that had long been forgotten. Imagine what else she could help us do?"

Most of them rumbled in agreement, but others didn't look so convinced. Not surprisingly, Lord Martin was one of them.

"She's done nothing but try to rip this castle apart! Don't let her persuade you with her beauty and fancy words," Lord Martin drawled, seething. He pointed his grubby finger at her. "This woman has earned her title as the throne seeker for a reason. She could be using her powers right now to deceive us. Do you all think it's a coincidence she's reached for the most powerful men in Cathan? They had no idea of the trap laid out for them, enticing them to act against their nature. Just as the night Xavier was banished from our lands." His gaze went to Xavier. "I'm surprised you bothered to return, given the circumstances. Did you forget how she stole your life from you? Your succession?"

Xavier's eyes iced over. "Let me make this very clear," he said in a voice that could have most assuredly made him king. "She did nothing but what I wanted her to. *I* manipulated *her*. She is innocent in my failed succession. I chose my fate. My father may have lifted my banishment for my mother's sake, but the only reason I've chosen to remain in this hellhole is because of her."

"Look how he defends her! After everything she's taken from him," Lord Martin exclaimed. "She may not be queen, but look where she is standing. Look who is standing beside her. Do not be fooled by her perceived lack of ambition. She has positioned herself exactly where she wants to be."

She balled her fists, hating how Lord Martin had struck a chord within her. Because deep at her rotten core, her siren *was* attracted to power. It was in her nature, embedded in her very design, no matter how much she wished it wasn't.

She remained calm. "I'm here only because I care about Vallor's future. This is my home, and I will serve my province however I can."

Another round of mumbles rippled around the room.

Tristan finally intervened. "Rose had nothing to do with the attack; there are plenty of witnesses, including myself, to attest to that. So unless someone has actual evidence against her, I suggest we find the real murderer."

None opposed it as Lord Martin fumed in silence.

Tristan cleared his throat. "Right then. Captain," he called to the guard, giving his orders on how to proceed with the interrogations.

Rose released a large breath as the tension eased from her body. She locked eyes with Lord Barron, offering him a sincere bow of the head in gratitude for his continued faith in her.

His handsome eyes crinkled with a smile. He inclined his head back as if to say he was in her service.

To her surprise, he and several other high councilmen came to speak with her, intrigued to see her transformation firsthand. Even Lord Orrin and those councilmen who had opposed her during the succession participated in the conversation—all except for Lord Martin, who stormed out, taking his livid aura with him.

It would seem Rose had earned her place back in court.

For now.

When she finally escaped the conversation, she found Tristan standing at the foot of the staircase, studying her. She drifted over to join him at the base of the stairs.

"What you just did—" he gazed over at the huddled council before swinging his gaze back to her, "—is exactly why I wanted you by my side. I don't care what your insecurities were... You would've made an incredible queen."

Her heartbeats increased at the praise.

He came closer, lowering his voice. "I'm sorry I never knew about your father," he whispered into her ear, his aura full of mixed emotions she couldn't pinpoint. "Gods, if I had... I'd have never let you go back. I'll forever be amazed by you." His lips brushed her cheek as he said the words. "Always."

Rose kept her body carefully still. "Is that why you had me speak?"

"I knew you'd win them over better than I could," he admitted. "With them on your side, you'll be safer... and despite all that, I suppose I did it for selfish reasons, too. You've always been the one person who believed I could do this. My biggest supporter… I guess I just wanted you here with me to see it."

She looked at him softly. "I'm glad I could be. Truly. I just wish it was under different circumstances."

Tristan couldn't even force a smile, pain leaking from his frayed edges. He cleared his throat. "I should go help with the affairs." He gave her a curt nod, leaving her to return to the council.

Rose watched him as he joined the three councilmen huddled under the south balcony. Her siren couldn't help but admire him in his element. He'd finally done it. He would finally fulfill the role he'd fought so hard for.

Xavier appeared by her side, snapping her out of her daze. "Attention suits him, doesn't it?" He masked his expression, but his aura exposed his agitation over her lingering gaze.

"He was born a leader… just like his older brother," she said.

Xavier's eyes clamped onto hers. His anger dissipated as he asked, "Would you have been my queen?"

"What do you think? My teenage heart was half out of its mind in love with you," she replied before thinking.

Xavier's jaw locked. His eyes fell to the floor, then he nodded as if accepting his fate. "I hate that word… *was.*"

She softened with empathy. "Can you do me a favor? Just promise me when the next girl comes along that shatters your world, you won't let her slip through your fingers."

Xavier's icy eyes sliced through her like a winter storm. "You shattered my world when I was only ten. The pieces have long since been lost and will never be put back together… Not so long as you exist in it."

Her jaw slackened, caught off guard. She had no clue what to say. But before she could utter a word, he left.

Despite the growing distance, pain poured from his retreating figure in such powerful waves it paralyzed her.

After a moment of recovery, Rose let out an exhausted breath, running her fingers roughly through her hair. What a mess tonight was turning out to be.

She turned to find warm, golden sands waiting for her—a scorching desert she happily welcomed, until she saw the hard expression Roman wore. He approached her with controlled steps.

His voice was short and crisp as he said, "I'm going to help the head guard with the interrogations."

"I'll come with you," she said, knowing her siren would be able to pick up things they couldn't.

"No. Stay with your mother."

Her heart fell. "But I could help—"

"Please, Rose. Just do as I ask," Roman snapped with a glare.

The quicksand she was teetering on swallowed her whole. She was so surprised by the hostility in his eyes, she did as commanded. "Okay."

Without so much as a backward glance, he left.

It felt like he had just shoved her from the astronomy tower, leaving her to fall until her body and soul splattered on the cobblestones.

She deserved it.

A taste of her own medicine.

Her lungs refused to function as her eyes watered. She tried to steady her trembling breaths, grateful for the dim glow of the ballroom candles to cast a shadow over her face. She shifted her weight, her feet aching to be freed of these ridiculous heels.

Without another word, she left.

She didn't care if someone lurked in the corridors with an arrow aimed at her heart.

In fact, she quite hoped for it.

CHAPTER 82

Rose fled the ballroom on the hunt for untainted air, the sound of her heels clicking on the stone echoing through the barren corridors. Each step made her feet protest, but she pushed through the pain. It was trivial compared to the throbbing ache in her chest.

She was forced to succumb to the fact that her siren was becoming more uncontrollable. There was darkness within her—pure, undeniable darkness. And to her horror, it was growing stronger by the hour, taking hold of her thoughts, her words, her feelings. If she had looked at Tristan for even a split second longer… what she might've done…

She'd expected her siren to have power over others—what she hadn't expected was for that same power to extend to herself.

She made her way toward the corridor that led to the torch-lit terrace, not paying attention to where her feet took her.

Her quick steps nearly caused her to stumble into a couple in the middle of a passionate kiss. She skidded to a stop, going to turn back the other way until she recognized who the man was.

Xavier.

He was with a woman she didn't know—a pretty girl with auburn hair who was glued to him like they had been stuck for a while, evident in her tousled hair and ragged breaths. Something ate at Rose from within, feeling like a piranha had been set loose in her stomach.

As soon as Xavier saw her, he wrenched himself from the woman.

Still stupidly gawking at the pair, Rose said, "Oh—um. Sorry, excuse me." They were the only words she could manage before she fled.

She rounded the corner sharply, practically running in the other direction. The image of Xavier kissing that woman was still seared into her brain like a hot flame.

She'd only made it down a single corridor when quick footsteps came from behind.

She whipped around, about to pull out the knife strapped to her thigh—

Xavier shoved her arm down, stopping her. "Rose." His bloodshot eyes looked concerned. *Concerned*. "What are you doing out here alone?"

Her nose stung with the stench of alcohol. "Have you been drinking?" she questioned in irritation.

"Not nearly enough," he murmured. A thick scowl crossed his brow until he noticed her distress. "You shouldn't be out here alone. What's happened?"

"Nothing." She tried to bypass him, but he stuck out his arm, grabbing her.

"Don't do that." His sharp eyes looked directly into hers. "Don't bottle up your feelings like you always do. You've gone through hell these past couple of days, and you have every right to feel how you feel."

She despised how he knew her so well. Through his touch, she could feel his compassion multiply, his worry and his relentless desire to bring her closer. To touch her. To kiss her, to do more than kiss—

The simple fact made her siren want to touch him, too.

Rose smothered her uncontrolled thoughts again, guilty for even thinking it as she freed herself from his grip. "I can't open up to you."

"Why the hell not?"

"Because I can't lie to you!" She pushed him away. "And I don't want anyone to see me like this."

"Like what? A human being with feelings?"

"That's just it. I'm *not* human! I'm not like you, any of you. I'm a monster—a manipulative, selfish monster who does nothing but hurt people around her—people I claim to love, but if I really loved any of you, I'd leave. Perhaps your mother was right, Beth, Satin, all of them. I should just leave. I should leave and never come back. Let you continue with—*that girl*." She jabbed down the hall.

Xavier grabbed her by the shoulders, forcing her to face him. "You know damn well that every fiber of my being wishes it was you. Aren't you glad I'm kissing her instead of coming to find you?"

Rose sucked in a sharp breath at the sudden confession.

"Get leaving out of your head right fucking now," Xavier said. "It won't help—I know. Don't listen to them. Any of them. They don't know you."

He didn't understand. It wasn't *them* she was upset with.

She was upset with herself.

"I hate hurting all of you," she said weakly. "You forget I can feel everything. I can feel how much you want me. I can feel how much I hurt Tristan. I can feel how much I disappoint Roman when I so much as look at either of you. I have no idea how I'm supposed to shut those feelings off. And more importantly, how not to let them affect my own."

Xavier's jaw clenched, his eyes softening. "That must be difficult."

She folded her arms, grimacing. "Don't try to be understanding. It only makes me feel worse."

"What would you rather me do? Hate you?"

"Yes!" she exclamied. "Be angry at me, hate me. All of you."

"I'm not going to make it that easy for you. And I doubt my brothers will either."

Her siren grew prideful of the fact. And she loathed it—*loathed* that sick, slimy thing inside her.

"I love Roman," she said flat out. "Doesn't that make you want to hate me? How am I supposed to live with the fact I've ruined your life and now Tristan's? What if Roman's next? What if I mess it up or let him down just like I have with both of you?"

"You're taking too much credit, just like always. You think this is all your fault, but it's mine." His voice broke as his jaw trembled, letting a shred of humanity show through. "It's my fault I didn't stay, it's my fault you had to go through this, it's my fault that my parents are dead. It's all my fault." His eyes drifted upward to the heavens. "I'm sorry... Gods, I'm so sorry."

The apology wasn't for her.

He lowered his head, attempting to hide his icy eyes melting into a puddle.

Her heart broke for him, for what he'd lost. She reached for his hand, taking it in hers, trying to absorb his sorrow.

His hand almost clenched back around hers, but he pulled it back as though it'd burned him. "Stop," he said, his eyes harboring self-loathing. "That may be a simple gesture to you, but your innocent touch sparks a blazing fire in me, rising so high I'm convinced the heavens can feel its warmth." His face flinched like he was in pain. "Damn it, Rose! Can't you see how hard it is for me to be this close to you and not devour every morsel of you? How hard it's been to hear how much I've put you through?"

A pain stabbed her heart. "I didn't mean to make you feel guilty—"

"But I do!" Xavier exclaimed, throwing his hands up. "All I feel is guilt when I look at you. Fuck, just *look* at you. As if you weren't enough temptation before. You're a walking magnet, and I've tried to fight the pull, but I can't. I fucking can't. And I feel so guilty about it, Rose. Because even though you told me you're in love with my brother, this whole time, all I've been able to think about is how I can get you back to my room and ravage you like I've done so many times in my dreams. I feel guilty because I'll *never* be sorry for kissing you when I did." He cupped her face with his hands, forcing her to face him as he lowered his voice to a husky whisper. "Because now I don't have to imagine what your lips feel like. Now, when I'm alone at night, I'll be able to replay that kiss over and over again, all the while gripping the sheets as I cry out your name."

She blinked furiously, swallowing hard, trying to tame her siren's celebratory pride.

She reached up to take his wrists, lowering them from her face. "Xavier I... I can't go there."

His jaw feathered. "I know. That's why I can't have you touch me like that. I know I'd get to the point I wouldn't care who you love. I'd be selfish and take you anyway... Gods, I'd take you so many times."

Her heart slammed so hard against her ribcage, she was sure it would be bruised.

"Quit looking at me like that," he said harshly.

Rose quickly averted her eyes to blink back the tears blurring them.

"Gods, don't stop looking at me," he whispered weakly.

His voice was so tender, she looked up.

Her siren clawed vigorously, desperate to break to the surface. To reach out and comfort him again. To allow him to take her back to his room and—

She shut it down.

"I'm going back to my room," she said, more to herself than to Xavier. "Don't follow me. Go back to the girl. She's probably still waiting for you… I know I did," she couldn't help but add.

A roar of pain came from him. "Rose." He tried to close the space between them, but she swiveled too quickly.

She dashed back to her room, nearly breaking her heels. She ripped them off in the middle of the hallway, setting off in a sprint before tears escaped. Or maybe just to escape herself.

She wanted nothing more than to leave this place and never come back. She had made up her mind.

She was leaving.

Tonight.

CHAPTER 83

Rose barged into her room, quickly shutting and locking the door. She tossed her shoes onto the floor, changed out of her blood-stained dress and chucked it into the fire, slipping into a new one. Her tears spilled over.

Her siren yearned to take control, to transform her into someone stronger, someone who wasn't so weak.

She went to the mirror. She wanted proof that even a trace of the girl she'd once been was still hidden within her. But she couldn't find her.

There really was another death to mourn.

Rose glared at the bindrune painted on her chest, symbolizing her supposed strength. It felt like a cruel joke.

Her long, polished nails dug into her palms. None of them deserved this, none of them. *She* didn't deserve this. Another wave of outraged tears leaked from her sea-green eyes.

Before she could talk herself out of it, she grabbed a bag and shoved everything and anything in it.

Her mind raced as it formulated a plan. She'd go to her mother, consult with her, and they'd leave together. They'd go to the home she now owned, thanks to Roman. They could live out their days in the country, having as normal a life as possible. She had more than enough money for them to be comfortable. It was the only way to save Roman from herself.

A loud knock on the door startled her.

"Rose, it's me." Roman's voice carried through the hall.

She closed her eyes with a silent curse. With all her strength, she contained her siren's demand to open the door. She continued to gather her things, quickening her pace.

Another knock. "Please let me in."

She ignored his pleas, hoping he'd assume she wasn't there.

Silence.

The door latch jiggled. "Rose, I know you're in there," he said louder.

She kept silent, praying he'd leave, still quietly scrambling for her things.

"Rose!" he yelled this time.

Silence again.

She waited, straining her ears. It was quiet. Not a sound. She sighed in relief, he had gone.

The door burst open.

Roman barged in with his sword drawn, prepared for a fight.

He found no such threat. Instead, his eyes fell to the bag and the belongings in her hands.

His eyes became darker than a moonless sky.

He flung the door shut loudly behind him and slammed his sword back into its sheath.

Without a word, he stalked toward her, taking slow, calculated steps, eyes deadlocked onto her so vigorously, she thought he might lash out. But his movements remained controlled even as his hands balled into white fists.

Rose backed away, not in fear, but because she knew the proximity would weaken her willpower. Still, he came closer, not stopping until her back hit the wall.

He pinned her against it, hands on either side of her head, pushing her back onto the cold stone. His enraged eyes gouged themselves into hers.

"You're not leaving me." His voice was low. Dangerous. Possessive. "Not now. Not ever."

She didn't understand. "How did you know I was—"

"After I was done being an ass, I turned back to apologize, and I saw you leave the ballroom. I followed you into the corridor and overheard your conversation with Xavier. I thought you didn't mean it, but were you actually going to go through with it? You were really going to leave me?"

A crash of his anguish filled her at the mere thought, the agony that would surely be his if she left him.

He grew impatient. "Answer me. Would you have even told me if you left?"

Rose took a steadying breath. "Not if I thought it was what was best for you."

He slammed his fist against the wall, making her flinch. "Damn what you think is best for me!" he shouted.

She had never seen him look so desperate.

So scared.

She didn't even know he could be scared.

"I don't care what you believe. I'm not my brothers. I will never put myself in a position to lose you." He came closer. "Do you honestly think I wouldn't come after you?"

She couldn't find her voice as—just a few millimeters and her lips would collide with his.

"Why can't you talk to me like that?" Roman asked.

She blinked, her eyes lifting from his lips. "What?"

"With Xavier. Why can you be honest about your feelings with him but not me?"

"He just caught me when I was having a moment. Besides… you were busy with Beth tonight anyway," she couldn't help but add, her voice bitter with jealousy.

His eyes narrowed. "I owed Beth an explanation. I made her promises I didn't keep and I was trying to fix it. Nothing more."

"Do you still have feelings for her?" she asked, hating herself for being so insecure.

Roman scoffed. "If you even *think* I could prefer her over you, you know *nothing* of how I feel about you. Can you say the same?"

She paused at the question, her brows drawing together.

"I heard Xavier admit he kissed you," he seethed. "Is that true?"

She opened and closed her mouth stupidly. She wouldn't lie to him. "It happened while I was in the stables."

Roman's face darkened, his palms forming into fists again.

"He didn't know," she said quickly before his thoughts could spiral. "He thought I'd married Tristan, but when I explained I hadn't, he kissed me before I could tell him about you."

Roman pushed himself off the wall, his hands aggressively rubbing the back of his neck. "And you let him? Now that he's back, do you wish for him instead?"

"Of course not!" she said at once.

"Let's get this out in the open right now." His hard eyes barreled straight into hers. "We'd be fools to ignore the fact you've had a history with both of my brothers. A long history. You've loved them both, and I knew that going into this. I'm not holding it against you. But I told you, I'm selfish. I want you to be with me because you chose to be… and you need to tell me right here, right now, if you think you made the wrong choice."

Rose gaped in disbelief.

She came in so close she should've felt his breath on her face, but she didn't—because he *wasn't* breathing.

She cradled his jaw in her hands. "It's you, Roman," she whispered, stroking his cheek with her thumb. "Without a doubt in my mind, it's you. I know because when I'm with you, I'm torn in the best way possible. I feel as though one half of me is burning, filled with a crazed desire to constantly be near you, to consume you until there is no more you and I, only us. The other half is perfectly calm, so safe and perfectly content I'm confident no one else could make me feel both simultaneously. There is no one in Vallor I'd rather visit Eristan with. No one's voice I'd rather hear read to me. No one else I'd swim along that cave with." She gave him a faint, reminiscent smile. "No one else I'd rather spend my life with."

At last, he breathed. The fire in his eyes receded into unadulterated relief.

He intertwined his calloused fingers with her soft ones. It felt as though a hot iron had been pressed into her palms. It was different with him, her siren's desire. It wanted him more than any other human she'd laid eyes on.

His golden eyes slipped down to her lips, and the subtle gesture nearly broke her willpower. Her siren clawed for freedom, clawed like it never had before, tearing her skin apart as it tried to shed her restraint—

His lips had just brushed hers when she put a hand on his chest, stopping him as she ducked under his arms, escaping his grasp.

Roman turned with her. "What is it? Talk to me," he practically begged.

She stepped back. "I… I just need time to understand more before I… before I…"

"Before what?"

"Before I lose control!" Her siren flared with impatience. "My siren, it… likes you. No, it worships you. If I touch you… if we do what we did at Highland Haven… I fear in this form I will take not only your body but your very soul."

It was meant to be a warning.

But her words only fueled the fire blazing in his eyes.

"I'm sorry to tell you that ship sailed long ago. Gone. Lost forever. You already own my body, my soul, my very existence." He took a step toward her.

She stepped away. "But don't you see? I don't want to *own* you. I just want to love you. And what good is love if it is not freely given?"

His brows pinched. "What does that mean?"

"What if you've only been in love with my siren this whole time?" she said, voicing her fear. "What if you loving me has nothing to do with me or who I am, but the power that I possess, tricking you to make you think you love me? What if I'm ruining your life, just like Xavier and Tristan?"

Roman let out a frustrated grunt. He flexed his hand out wide, like he was trying to prevent himself from throttling her. "Have you not heard a word I've ever said to you? I'm in love with you, Rosalie Versalles. *You*. I loved you before you were a siren. I love you now, and I always will."

She wished that was all the reassurance she needed. "The spell only suppressed my siren. I've always been one. I see that now. At times, I could even feel it within me. I just didn't know what it was." She paused, trying to get through to him. "Doesn't it matter to you? That my siren could be messing with your mind, your thoughts, your feelings? I could be doing it right now and you'd have no idea. Aren't you worried that you're in love with a monster?"

He shook his head in denial. "I couldn't give a damn what it is you are. I know what you're doing. Don't you dare try to push me away."

"I'm not trying to push you away." She pulled at the roots of her hair in frustration.

"Then how could you even think of leaving me?!" he shouted, attempting to touch her.

She pushed him in the chest, forcing him to stay away. It barely set him back a step.

His eyes flared. "Is that supposed to be you not pushing me away?" he growled.

"I want to protect you!" she cried. "I'll always protect you, even if it's from myself… I'm dangerous, Roman," she ended in a near whisper.

Roman gazed at her as though the statement was obvious. "Of course you're dangerous."

Her heart stopped in apprehension.

He let out a loud, frustrated sigh, coming closer again.

She allowed it this time.

He stroked her cheek. "Look at you. And I'm not talking just about your beauty, which is… undeniably out of this world." His throat bobbed, struggling not to devour her. "But just look at all you've done. You've saved lives because of your beautiful, quick-witted mind. You've trained faster than any soldier I've ever seen. Hell, you rode a sleipnir for the first time in your life and won the most deadly race in history."

Her siren's chest puffed itself in pride, secretly loving the praise.

"But what's even more dangerous than all that… is resting here." He pointed to her chest. "This heart would save someone's life when they didn't deserve it." His fingertips brushed the bare skin over her heart, just above the fabric of her dress. "This heart that would give up its own wants and happiness for strangers. The kind of heart that can spark loyalty and friendships that cannot be bought. To have a heart like that is a power I'm convinced no one else has, and *that* makes you the most dangerous creature to walk this world."

Her heart pained from the ache of being so full. She opened her mouth to speak, but the love pouring from him choked any words.

His hand slipped up to support the nape of her neck as the other lifted her chin to meet his eyes. "What did I tell you at Highland Haven?" he whispered, resting his forehead against hers. "I am yours," he breathed.

Her heart throbbed. "And you are mine," she whispered back.

The invisible rope that bound her broke. Her siren eyes sucked Roman in like a moth to a flame. His controlled eyes relaxed, becoming hazed—drunk-like. Her firm hands gripped the seam of his open tunic, pulling him towards the bed.

He didn't resist in the slightest.

She lowered herself backward onto the bed, her pearl hair spilling around her as she kept her gaze fixed on him.

Roman prowled over her, lowering himself to close the aching gap between them.

The moment their lips touched, she relaxed, taking her first free breath that day. It was all she needed for her worries to sink out of sight. For the noise to drown out. To be so calm yet so utterly alive at the same time. Leaving Roman wouldn't solve anything.

He was her saving grace.

He lifted his lips from hers and encircled her waist with his arm. Hovering over her, he murmured, "Can you feel how badly I want you?"

She could. It roared in her ears like a humming vibration within her—and it was only getting stronger.

"Why don't you show me?" she challenged softly against his lips, looking up at him.

He didn't deny her. His mouth returned, kissing her slow and deep, relishing her taste. His hips ground into her.

She arched, digging her nails into his back.

Roman lifted himself to remove his shirt, revealing his light-pink scars against his tan skin. She sat up, bringing her lips to his scars, kissing them as though she could heal them, starting with the one on his shoulder. Roman let out a contented sigh.

The physical connection between them was unlike any drug she'd ever known—so utterly intoxicating, yet so medicinal. She didn't just want him —she *needed* him. Like this. With her and only her.

She didn't know how she hadn't seen it sooner.

She moved her lips from his shoulder to the scar on his waist, caressing it with her lips, swirling her tongue against his perfectly imperfect skin as his rough hands stroked her hair.

Her lips trailed lower until she hit the belt of his trousers. "Take them off," she ordered.

He did as commanded, stepping back off the bed and undoing his belt. It was empowering to have the general of the world's largest army at her feet, ready to obey her every command, her every whim.

He reached for his trousers, pulling them off and exposing himself to the cool air.

Her mouth watered as soon as she saw him, his swollen skin waiting for her to take it.

She edged closer to the bed, kneeling down on the floor as if she were praying to him. Worshiping him.

Which was precisely her intention.

She gazed back up at him.

He peered down at her, his eyes aching with anticipation. Chest heaving. Patiently waiting.

In one movement, she took him into her mouth.

Roman swore. His hand shot to the bed frame for support, gasping a sharp breath as his muscles contracted.

Hearing the coarse sound that escaped his throat made the ache between her legs throb.

She took her time to play with him, sucking and nipping as she pleased. Her hands cupped below, supporting him as she devoured every juice that leaked from him. She focused on the tip at a faster pace, stroking him all the while with her hands.

He let out a deep-throated moan. "Rose… I won't be able to last if you keep that up."

She released him with a pop. "Then I guess it's a good thing we have all night to do it over again." She smirked.

Roman let out an unbridled moan as he grabbed her off the floor and tossed her on the bed.

She grappled for her dress, stripping it from her body, and did the same with her band and underwear. Roman watched patiently as she peeled off each layer of clothing.

His eyes worshiped her exposed skin, exploring her like a map, committing it to core memory, before they finally returned home to hers. "Good gods, Rosalie," he said, his voice coarse. "Could you be any more perfect?"

Her eyes grew with the realization that this was the first time he had seen all of her since she'd come into her full siren. His praise fueled her, resulting in another throb between her legs.

His mouth captured hers unchecked this time, his strong hands slipping to the base of her jaw, lifting it to gain better entrance. He kissed her as if he could consume her whole.

She eased herself back onto the bed, dragging him to the center of the mattress. Roman followed, taking both of her wrists in his hands, pinning them above her head, then looked down at the beautiful mounds displayed for him, ready for him to take.

And take them he did.

He started with the right side, taking her into his mouth with a masterful tug.

She let out a loud moan, arching her back in appreciation. She gripped the headboard, grinding herself against him, aching for him to take her. "Roman."

He hissed at the rocking motion as his mouth came back to capture hers. "Say it again," he said. "Say my name again."

"Roman," she moaned, begging for him.

As if he couldn't bear not being inside her any longer, he lifted himself, nudging her legs apart. He hovered at her entrance before he paused, swearing. The golden flecks in his eyes burned like embers as they flickered back up to hers. "You're soaked," he murmured.

She replied by taking his hips in her hands and pushing him into her with one smooth glide.

"Fuck," he swore, letting out a surprised hiss. One of his hands shot to the headboard for balance, gripping it like a lifeline.

She smirked, empowered she could pleasure him so easily.

A crooked smile played on his lips. "Is this how we're playing?" He stroked her breast as his hips rocked in smooth movements.

She let out a reckless moan as she squirmed.

"Gods, I could hear that sound every day for the rest of my life and still crave it," Roman rasped.

She dug her fingers into his back as he moved with her. "You can be rough," she said breathlessly. "I'm not made of glass."

Roman's pupils widened as his muscles stilled under hers, tension etched in his clenched jaw. "Release me and I will ravage you," he warned.

Her ache multiplied. "Consider yourself released."

She soon realized how much he'd been holding back.

He took a handful of her hair, crushed his lips onto hers, the kiss so savage she could scarcely suck in a breath. He rammed his body against hers, leaving no space between them.

Gods, he was perfect.

He withdrew, taking hold of her waist, lifting her onto his lap. He pinned her against the oversized wooden headboard. She grabbed it for support as he lifted her legs, wrapping them around his waist while he knelt before her on the bed.

He entered her again, releasing a deep, appreciative moan. He rocked her against the wooden board with each thrust, pounding the stone wall with a rhythmic thud.

His lips attacked her neck, his teeth scraping and biting her skin. She sighed with pleasure as she tilted her head back, willingly opening her throat to him.

She wasn't ready for the raw pleasure seizing her. Each perfect thrust was angled to send her most sensitive parts into a frenzy. She ached for him to return with every motion as he swayed against her.

His rough hands tightened around her hips, and his movements and sounds became more unhinged. She knew he was peaking, and the fact made her close, too.

Without warning, a loud crack erupted behind her.

She released the headboard and clung to him as the thick wood fell uselessly to the floor.

He paid no attention to it—his grip tightening around her so they didn't miss a beat.

"You are everything to me," he whispered in full surrender, sending a jolt of lightning through her veins. "Everything."

Her siren stirred.

No, not stirred—*writhed.*

A deep surge of power swelled within her, rising abruptly to the surface. It unfurled over every inch of her body, beginning in her chest and rushing to her limbs and fingers. The air in her chest turned into fire, burning through her in the best way possible.

Her siren shrieked for liberation, wrenching against the chains she'd kept shackled. A crack formed in the invisible wall. It was moments from escaping—

With all her strength, she shoved Roman away, retreating until her back was against the cracked headboard.

With her eyes shut, she swallowed hard, working to regain her composure. Taking a deep breath, she prayed the feral creature inside her would subside.

"What's wrong? Did I hurt you? Gods, I'm so sorry," Roman said with harsh breaths. He reached for her, but she recoiled from him.

Her siren screamed in rebellion. Rejecting him was like asking her heart to stop beating. "No, I'm fine—just don't touch me," she said, still not feeling like herself.

She might as well have slapped him.

He stopped in his tracks, gazing helplessly as rejection emanated from him.

She ran her shaking hands through her hair, trying to calm her racing heart.

"You're scared of me." He looked as if his heart was cracking in two.

"Of course not," she shot back, almost annoyed he was blaming himself. "I could never be afraid of you."

His eyes faltered. "What is it? Did you… was it not enjoyable?" he asked, his hesitant voice terrified of the answer.

She sunk into remorse, knowing how it must look to him. "You felt incredible, Roman," she whispered.

It was the biggest understatement of the century.

Roman's shoulders sunk in relief. "Then what's wrong?"

"I don't know what's happening to me," she said, looking down at her own hands as though they were foreign objects attached to her. "My siren… it's trying to take over."

Roman's eyes softened, coming closer to her.

She tensed.

He became determined, taking her hand anyway, pulling her toward him, pressing her body into his. "Don't shut me out. Talk to me." His deep voice caressed her very soul.

Her heart swelled from his pure intent, knowing all he wanted to do was make her feel safe.

"My siren… I told you it wants you more than anyone." Her eyes flickered up to his.

"I couldn't be more glad of the fact."

"No, I mean… it wants to *claim* you. I've tried suppressing it, but it's becoming harder to control. Ever since that day in the woods with the snawfus, it's been getting stronger. With you like this… when you touch me like that… I've never felt so powerful in my life."

Roman gathered her into his arms. "I'm not afraid," he assured.

She shook her head in doubt, dismissing his answer.

"Hey, look at me." He lifted her chin as her eyes met beautiful embers. "Even though I admit you consume every inch of me, I welcome it. I'm not scared of the fact that when you walk into the room, the rest of my world fades and all I see is you… I was *lost* until I found you." His calloused fingers traced along her jaw, his eyes tracking the trail of his touch.

She eased into his palm, still buzzing from the energy. "I'm not as brave as you," she whispered.

Roman's lips spread into a crooked smile that put her world at a standstill. "Bullshit. You're the most fearless person I know."

She wished she could share his faith.

"Come here," he murmured, intertwining his hand with hers.

She hesitated.

"Come here," he demanded firmly again.

She gave in to her favorite command, wrapping her arms around him, pressing his bare skin onto hers as the ache in her soul subsided.

Roman took it a step further by swinging her leg over him so she was straddling his lap. She felt him beneath her, still hard. She sucked in a breath, her body reminding her they both still ached to be released.

Her power resurfaced almost immediately.

She attempted to pull back, but Roman's grip kept her thighs pinned. "Don't," he whispered against the base of her throat. "Don't you dare pull away from me."

She swallowed hard. "Roman, I… I don't know what will happen if I let go."

Roman gazed up at her with all the confidence in the world as he snaked his arm around her waist, leaving a blistering trail along her skin. "Just let go." He kissed her throat as he spoke against it. "Let fucking go."

So she did.

She entwined her fingers in his hair and brought his lips back to hers. His hands tightened around her hips in response, sliding her back onto him.

She let out a uncontrollable moan at his return.

Her siren rose abruptly, only this time—she didn't try to stop it.

For the first time, she let her siren break free.

Her true form manifested. Power coursed through every vein and down into him, locking them together, making them one. Out of the corner of her eye, she caught sight of a new dim sea-green glow coming from her vanity mirror. She sucked in a breath as she realized the glow was coming from her own eyes. Her olive skin gleamed with a subtle golden sheen, as though she had just emerged from the rain, while her sea-green eyes glowed like a light beneath the water. Her pupils dilated to an inhumanly large width.

She looked down at Roman, to see if he was frightened.

But he wasn't.

Instead, his eyes held her like she was his starlit sky, his galaxy, his entire universe.

She could feel him perfectly now, actually *feel* him—inside his body, his soul, his very essence. All she smelled was him. All she felt was him. Every heartbeat. Every breath that entered his lungs. Every muscle that shifted in a smooth sequence against hers. He writhed in pleasure, absolute euphoria coursing through his veins. She could feel his determination to keep her, never to let her escape him.

Her siren gripped every one of those tethers binding them, taking hold of his muscles, his brain, his bones, all entirely at her mercy. She could ask him to do anything in the world, and he'd do it without a second thought. If she told him to burn all of Vallor for her, he'd do it.

It was a terrifying yet utterly exhilarating feeling.

She took control, pushing him flat onto his back. He was helpless to fight against her as she trailed kisses over his chest, rocking her hips against him.

His hands death-gripped the sheets, holding on for dear life. His jaw dropped in a silent cry as his eyes squeezed shut.

"Dammit, Rose," he barked. "How the fuck do you feel this good? I… I can't… I fucking can't."

Her siren's pride grew tenfold, loving that she could make him experience such pleasure.

Before Roman could burst through his skin, he sat up, casting her onto her back.

His body was on top of hers in a heartbeat, and he sheathed himself into her again, harder this time. Wild. Uncontrolled.

Her nails dug hard into his back, making his strong frame shake. He let out a feral moan. A territorial instinct stirred within her at the sound.

"You are mine," she murmured, her voice a beautiful blend of melody and possession as she leaned in to whisper in his ear. "Completely and utterly *mine*."

Roman could barely speak, his body so overcome with pleasure he had to fight for the words to reply. "I am yours," he got out in willing surrender. "Gods, I am forever yours."

Never had his voice been so raw, so unhinged, so crazed that it sent humming vibrations straight to her chest.

She pushed him off her as she rose up on the bed, wanting to be on top again. Roman sat up with her—she let him.

Her lips collided with his, devouring his lips like they were all that was left in the world. She let out another moan, rocking her hips harder into his as she ground into him with eagerness, pleasure building.

His movements became frantic as he gasped for the air she was stealing. He was reaching his climax, every muscle in his body engaged against hers.

She moved her lips down to his neck, just below his jaw, caressing and nipping at the sweet spot there, lightly grazing her teeth against his smooth skin.

His eyes harbored flames he could no longer tame.

He grabbed her waist, anchoring her against him as his eyes rolled back into his skull.

He forcefully fell back onto the bed as he came, jerking so violently he thrust her upward.

His roar was so fierce, she was sure the whole castle heard.

Rose was so overwhelmed by his pleasure that she found hers, crying out as she held on to him, shock waves shattering her body.

Her arms trembled as she lowered herself over him, digging her fingers into the bed and tearing at the sheets. Her pace quickened as she pulsed around him, squeezing him with every wave.

Their climax lasted a long minute before her thrusts slowed.

She collapsed onto his chest, both of them heaving for air.

Roman draped a possessive arm around her, pressing a kiss to her forehead, his body still shaking with pleasure. "I am yours," he professed.

"And you are mine," she whispered.

He kissed her, his strong jaw feathering with each motion as his hand went up into her hair, massaging her scalp. "Anywhere you go, I go," he murmured. "I don't know how I could live without you."

"You won't have to. Ever," she promised, kissing him again.

A soothing silence fell as they caught their breaths, clinging to each other as though they might be torn apart at any moment.

"I know I said I wasn't made of glass... but I don't think the same could be said for the bed," she teased, gazing at the broken headboard with a siren's smile.

Roman's mouth stretched into a broad, knowing grin. "That wasn't me."

She looked over at the headboard, not realizing her own grip had forced it to break. Her eyes glided to the sheets, seeing her fingernails had somehow clawed ten large rips into the mattress. Her guilt-filled eyes found Roman's.

Roman let out a deep laugh, unfazed. Gods his laugh. "Don't worry, I'll get them to replace it in the morning," he said, running his fingers through her sweaty hair

"No. There's no need," she replied with a suggestive smile, leaning her lips closer to his. "I'll just break it again."

Roman's eyes blazed with desire. He swallowed hard. "Gods, I can't believe I'm saying this, but I need you again—I'm not satisfied." He dragged his gaze down to her lips and then back up to her eyes. "And from the fire in your eyes, I don't think you are either."

His hand slipped between her legs, gliding over her slick skin. She shivered at the aching touch.

"No," she admitted, biting her bottom lip. "And I think we should keep going until both of us are satisfied." Her hands slid behind his neck, pulling him down to her. "Don't you agree?"

Roman took her thigh, dragging her towards him until she was pressed into him once again. "I completely agree," he murmured.

They rolled back over and found each other again… and again. She couldn't believe their stamina. She knew it defied what was considered "normal" to continue like this. She was unable to fathom any explanation besides her siren's power and the hold it had on them.

At one point, Rose believed they were done, but as soon as they entered the tub to wash the sweat off, they reached for each other again.

She never wanted this feeling to leave—the feeling of how much he needed her and how much she needed him. Physically, emotionally, all of it.

Eventually, they both collapsed from exhaustion, their bodies demanding sleep. But only a few hours later, she stirred awake, glancing over at him sleeping beside her. Her stomach fluttered. He laid there so vulnerably, so trusting.

She leaned over and placed what she intended to be a light, innocent kiss on his lips, but to her surprise, her movement woke him.

He kissed her back, still groggy.

She pulled back, guilty for waking him, but Roman's hand found her thigh, dragging it over his hips while he wrapped his arms around her.

His kisses began slow and deliberate but soon turned hungry as he positioned himself on top of her. Their bare skin pressed together as they played with each other lazily—nipping, stroking, teasing, until he entered her.

He only lasted a few minutes before he reached his breaking point. She smirked with pride when he finished—that was, until he smirked back, turning her over to return the favor, feasting on her like he'd been starved for weeks, his tongue lavishing her most sensitive parts.

Her cry was so loud, Roman had to cover her mouth with his hand as she finished, trying not to wake anyone.

Then, lazily, they caressed each other until they found sleep again.

She'd never been more content.

CHAPTER 84

Rose woke up late the following morning to find Roman was already gone from the bed.

She sat up, allowing the cool morning breeze to wrap around her bare skin. A distressing ache filled her at the empty space next to her, but her worry was all for nothing.

Roman's broad figure stood on the large open balcony, gazing out at the ocean. His back faced her as he basked in the morning sunlight, wearing only dark trousers that left his upper body bare. His hair was a tousled mess from her fingers' relentless strokes.

Wrapping the sheets around herself, Rose followed him onto the balcony. She slid her arms around his warm, firm torso from behind.

He took her hands in his own, kissing her palms before guiding her in front of him into the sun's embrace. His strong arms wrapped around her as he pressed her back against his chest.

His aroma of cedar blended with the crisp sea air, easing her soul into a relaxed state she could only fall into around him.

He melted into her as he rested his head on her shoulder, kissing her neck in the exact spot that made her weak in the knees. Her eyes fluttered at the feathered touch, resting her head against his chest.

They stayed like that as the light breeze washed over them, gazing out over the distant ocean waves.

Through their contact, Rose felt a mixture of emotions. Part of him brimmed with pure joy—reserved for her—while another held a terrible sorrow, growing stronger the longer he held her.

"What time is the passing ceremony?" she asked, not forgetting what today would mean.

What he had lost.

Roman hesitated, placing a feathered kiss on her shoulder. "At sundown," he said softly against her skin.

She turned in his arms to look at him. "You know I'll always be here for you."

He pressed his lips higher on her neck. "You better be," he whispered, brushing her hair back over her shoulder to place another feathered kiss below her ear.

A comfortable silence fell.

"I've been thinking… and I hate to admit it, but Xavier's right," Roman said. "We were fools to think we could take them on without knowing more."

Rose silently agreed. After last night… suddenly leaving didn't seem so outlandish.

"He had a clear shot at me last night, Roman," she whispered. "A clear shot, and he chose you. What if that arrow after the first challenge was never meant for Tristan, but for you? I can't have you or anyone else getting hurt because of me." She couldn't lose him. She'd die from it.

Roman seemed to be thinking along the same lines. "We'll take your mother and go back to Highland Haven. And I hate to say it, but we may need to pay Moretti another visit. Maybe there is more he could tell us."

A pit formed in her stomach, but he was right. It was the only lead they had. At least if they went back to Caleede, she could sift through the libraries there. Perhaps there was a hidden book there that could shed more light on this Blood King.

"We'll leave tonight after the passing ceremony."

He shook his head. "No—we should leave now. It's too dangerous to stay any longer. With my father gone, we're more vulnerable than ever."

"We'll stay until it's over." Before Roman could protest, she took his face into her hands. "You need to say goodbye. For Harriet's sake. For your parents'. They deserve that. What could a few more hours hurt?"

He gave a loud resigning sigh. "Fine, but the moment it is over, we are leaving—the very moment," he stated with a pointed look. "And don't breathe a word of it to anyone but your mother."

"And Xavier," Rose added with a hesitant voice.

Roman's eyes raced to hers, his body becoming rigid. "What?"

"What does Xavier's future hold after tonight? Eternal exile? He needs a sense of purpose again. He's lost. Alone." Rational or not, she knew it was primarily her fault—or more, her siren's. "He has just as much right to find these men as we do. If we leave, the court will be safe, but we'll be more vulnerable than ever. There are only three of us against these men. He could help… and there are few I trust more than him."

Roman gritted his teeth as his jaw feathered, resentment leaking from him. But another more logical part of him must have seen reason, because he said, "And Xavier, then."

At that moment, she realized just how desperate they truly were.

CHAPTER 85

Though the invitation to join their cause almost sent Xavier's jaw to the floor, he accepted. It was hard to tell who felt more relieved when Rose announced their departure that night—her mother or Xavier. They all agreed to retreat to Highland Haven until they could gather more information.

Roman hadn't left Rose's side since last night. She didn't need her siren to know how incredibly anxious he was—glancing over his shoulder as they walked through corridors and as they ate. It made her even more nervous than she already was.

The sun dipped into the sea, marking the beginning of the passing ceremony. Typically, the ceremony itself was a momentous affair. However, Tristan had instructed that only a few should be invited. The council agreed that, given recent events, it should remain intimate.

The pathway leading to the beach was marked by tall oversized torches, traditional sun emblems hanging just below them, with beautiful flowers winding between the posts. It was customary for the party to walk down the path together to commemorate and honor their memory one last time.

Tristan and Satin were at the forefront of the small group, with guards positioned on either side. Rose was surprised to see Satin's hand clasped in his, the simplicity of the gesture warming her heart. Although Satin fought hard to portray indifference, it was obvious that she still cared deeply for Tristan. Satin's sympathetic glances at his solemn figure had Rose fostering hope that maybe they could resolve their differences after all.

A short distance behind, Xavier and Harriet followed. A special pain bled from their youngest sister, tears welling in her eyes as she clung to Xavier's arm, resting her head on his shoulder. In contrast, Xavier's face revealed no emotion; his presence was so muted that Rose could barely sense it. It came as no surprise that he tried to numb the pain. He had trained himself to block out his feelings. This was his way of coping, how he could stand it.

To their right stood Roman, Rose, and her mother. She would have preferred not to walk in the front, but it was customary for the family to lead the way. Roman needed her beside him, not just for support but also for his sanity, a fact he often reminded her of. She cherished the way he subtly stroked her hand with his thumb as if reassuring himself that she was still there. Still real.

She was becoming accustomed to the stares, but tonight, Roman had insisted she wear her cloak and hood, trying to minimize the attention. In her opinion, it was quite useless, but it gave him a sense of ease, so she wore it, walking with bare feet that molded into the sand.

The small group made their way to the sea, where towering torches lit the grand boat waiting for them on the shore, carrying the bodies of King Henrik and Queen Lenna.

Rose successfully maintained her composure until her gaze fell upon the king and queen. Seeing their hands intertwined together, lying side by side on the boat… something about the gesture brought up nearly unmanageable grief. Tears welled in her eyes as she clutched Roman's hand tighter.

The priest came forward and recited the ancient farewell. His words barely reached her ears as she stared at the couple who laid so peacefully together atop the kindling, the lavender blooms and greenery gently releasing their fragrance into the air, carried by the sea breeze.

Twilight had settled in when Tristan took the priest's place, standing precisely in front of the large boat.

To Rose's annoyance, her siren came immediately to attention.

"To say we lost the best king Cathan has ever had would be an understatement." His face remained sober amidst his raging aura. "But his legacy will stand the test of time, not only in the pages of history but in our hearts. When you look out over the peaceful fields of Cathan, I hope you remember King Henrik and the life he ensured for every person here. What I admired most about my father was that he didn't just tell me how to be a man; he lived it. Even on the worst day, he lived what he believed." Tristan paused, his jaw tightening as pain flickered in his eyes. "But what has to be the most inspirational was the love he had for my mother."

Tristan craned his head to glance at the beached boat behind him.

"She was his whole world. Whenever she had difficult days, he'd drop everything to be with her, no matter how important his other tasks. Even late at night, he would head to the kitchen, prepare soup, and spoon-feed her himself. He hated dancing, but he was out on the dance floor at every chance because he knew she loved it. When he'd leave for duties, she went with him. They had their own language. They could have a conversation without having to utter a single word, which was infuriating beyond belief." He let out a harsh, sharp laugh, then scanned the crowd, shifting to... Rose.

His gaze trapped hers like a viper catches its prey, swift and unsuspecting, suffocating her.

"My father once told me the only reason he was able to be the king he was, was because of the queen he had." Tristan's voice finally cracked, his ocean-blue eyes searing into hers as if he was speaking solely to her. "She was his reason. His light. The good in him. He knew it, and he held on to it. And I truly believe having her by his side made all the difference in the kind of king he became."

Tristan finally set Rose free as he took hold of a torch and lifted it high above his head. "I promise from this day forward, I will do my best to be a devout king to Cathan like my father was," he stated, louder now. "I will do my best to honor him by leading Cathan into a new era."

He held up the torch in the air firmly. "*In strength!*" Tristan yelled at the top of his lungs.

"We can endure!" the large group chanted back, Roman's voice loud beside her.

"*In truth!*"

"We find purpose!"

"*With loyalty!*"

"We serve!"

"*With honor!*"

"We live, fight, and die!"

"*In love,* we surrender!" Tristan added with a roar into the ocean's waves. He made his way to the boat, lowered the torch, and set it ablaze.

A hot wave blanketed Rose as the sparks crackled and flew into the starry night sky. Several men, including Roman and Xavier, stepped forward. With all their strength, they pushed the boat into the dark water.

Rose's mother wept beside her, tears brimming in her eyes as she grieved the passing of her dearest friends. In truth, Rose supposed they had been her only family.

She rested her head on her mother's shoulder, holding her arm with a renewed gratitude for still having her here with her.

Her mother cleared her throat. "I regret that you never experienced that, Rose," she said with a shaky voice. "You never got to see how much your parents loved each other, too. I'm sorry he can't be here; he would have known how to help you. I wish I had asked him more about his… nature. He made it all look so easy."

"You did everything you could for me."

Her mother gave a weak smile, patting her hand.

Rose tossed her gaze out to Roman, a wave of his grief blowing in with the wind.

"Go on, quit fussing over me," her mother said as she wiped her eyes. "I'll wait here with the others."

Rose kissed her on the cheek and set out into the cold water.

She stepped into the sea without hesitation—it was her second home now, and it welcomed her with its waves.

She stopped by Roman's side, watching the burning boat grow brighter in the dark waters as it drifted further out to sea.

"I understand now why they would rather have it happen this way," she said, thinking out loud. "This way, it doesn't seem so permanent, does it? Now, it just feels like they're setting off to sail on their next adventure together. Only this time, there's no return."

"Yes," Roman whispered, his voice raw. "I think it's exactly how they wanted it."

A short pause fell over them.

"In a way, it's a blessing they got to leave together," she whispered over the gentle waves. "I know this may be selfish of me to say, but if you died and I had to watch you go on that adventure without me… I don't think I could bear to let you leave the shore." Her voice broke at the mere thought. She bit her quivering lip.

He shook his head, bringing his dripping hands to her chin, forcing her to look up into his eyes. "I'd be right there along with you. I know I would. I have no idea how your mother survived it all these years."

Rose looked back at her mother. A newfound appreciation blossomed within her. "Because she had me," she whispered in realization. "She endured all that pain, all of that suffering, for me. I want to be angry at her for keeping the truth from me, but how can I, after all she's done?" She looked back into Roman's eyes. "If we had a child, you'd stay and fight for them, too, wouldn't you?"

Roman's eyes flinched in pain. "It would be extremely difficult, but yes. I'd try to bear it."

"Me, too." Tears filled her eyes again as she looked out at the boat, now distant, the flames engulfing every inch of it.

"What's wrong?" Roman asked her as a tear slipped out.

She took a deep breath, containing the thoughts threatening to run wild. "I hate knowing I'll have to watch both you and my mother go on your own adventures eventually." She dared to meet his honey eyes. "You realize I'll live much longer than either of you. Even if you last to an old age—which I'll make sure of—everyone will eventually leave me—you, my mother, Zareb, Tristan, Xavier, Harriet… Everyone I hold dear will be long gone. I don't think I could go on."

"It's a good thing you chose someone younger than you," he joked, a smile tugging at the corner of his lips.

Rose let out a short laugh, nodding as she looked down, wiping away a tear.

Roman leaned in close, and with Tristan present, she stiffened, thinking he might forget and kiss her anyway. Instead, he said, "You don't need to worry about that right now. I'll stay with you every second my weak human body allows," he vowed. Then, lowering his voice to a whisper, he added, "I am yours."

Rose choked back a sob. "And you are mine," she whispered.

The waves relentlessly crashed against their knees, but she ignored the chill. Roman, on the other hand, shivered.

She nudged him. "Come on."

The small party had already departed, trekking their way back to the distant castle, leaving only Xavier, Tristan, Harriet, and Rose's mother behind. Satin had left with the others, her maid helping lead her back up to the castle.

A weighted silence fell over them as they took a moment to recognize this was all that was left of their family.

"What happens now?" Harriet asked her brothers bluntly. Her eyes were puffy as her dark, curled hair flowed with the breeze. "Will you finally set your differences aside? Or is this where everyone parts ways?"

No one spoke as guilt wrenched a gaping hole in Rose's heart. They all knew the answer.

Harriet's desperation for hope sent her gaze to Xavier, holding him accountable. "Are you going back to Amernth?"

"No," Xavier said. Harriet's relieved expression only lasted a moment as he added, "But I'm not staying either."

Glaciers collided as Harriet's eyes met her brother's. "Xavier—"

"Good, because this is no longer your home," Tristan interrupted. "I allowed you to remain for our parents' sake, but your banishment is reinstated… Leaving shouldn't be hard," he added with malice. "It's what you're used to."

Harriet's eyes widened in outrage.

Xavier took a few threatening steps toward his brother. "You're right. I have no desire to stay. With you as our king, we're all doomed. Give your reign a few months, and Cathan will be nothing but another set of ruins."

Tristan turned hostile as he moved closer, narrowing the gap between them. "And whose fault is that, *brother*?" Tristan provoked, his repressed anger finally spilling over. "*You* were supposed to be the one in my place. *You* were supposed to be king. But you opted out like a coward, leaving me to pick up what you so carelessly abandoned, sending everyone's lives into chaos, but most especially mine. I didn't ask for you to give up the crown. My life would be entirely different if you hadn't destroyed everything. All of this could have been prevented if you hadn't gone after Rose and just stayed! All of this is your fault—all of it!"

Rose stepped forward to intervene, but Roman stuck an arm out to stop her. "They need to do this," he whispered.

Her anxious eyes went back to them. This wouldn't end well.

"You're right, Tristan," Xavier said with an antagonizing nod. "I should've never considered your feelings. I should've taken everything for myself, never let you have the throne, and I sure as hell never in a thousand lifetimes should have let you have *her*!" he shouted, pointing to Rose. "I willingly gave her to you, and you *still* managed to make a mess of things. Thank the gods Roman was here to help her escape you. Even though, given the chance, I would've saved her, too. But you, filthy coward, made sure I was out of the picture, fearing she'd pick me over you." He advanced towards Tristan, his breath fogging Tristan's face. "So tell me… how does it feel to know after all that, she *still* picked another brother?"

The air left her lungs.

Shit.

It was a mere second before Tristan's fist flew through the air.

Xavier was ready for him, evading the punch and quickly countering with a strike of his own. His fist connected with Tristan's jaw with such force, Tristan staggered backward.

Tristan spat out the blood oozing from his mouth. His feral eyes lifted as he drew his sword in a single fluid motion.

Xavier followed suit, unsheathing his own sword.

Years of hatred all came out in one explosive storm.

Each held nothing back as they fought, their swords clashing together, hit after hit, swing after swing. Tristan kept coming for Xavier, lashing with all his might. Xavier stood firm, parrying his brother's blows. Both were evenly matched, channeling their pain and anger into every strike.

At last, Tristan found an opening and went straight for Xavier's head—

Rose took an involuntary step forward.

Xavier found his footing, twisting away. As Tristan exposed his arm, Xavier struck, landing a blow on his shoulder. A deep gash opened, spilling blood onto Tristan's cloak. Snarling, Tristan retaliated, swinging back with fury.

Xavier barely had time to retreat, leaning away to dodge his blade, but it still didn't stop it from slicing into his chest. Xavier cringed for a heartbeat.

But that was enough time to allow Tristan to advance. Despite his wounded arm, he shoved Xavier to the ground. A fearsome glare darkened his gaze.

"Stop!" Harriet cried, tears streaming down her cheeks. "Stop it, please!"

Xavier sprang back to his feet, clutching his bloodied chest. He grunted as he swung, fueled by fresh rage. He advanced, pushing Tristan backward toward the sea.

They were going to kill each other.

Rose turned to Roman in desperation. "If you don't do something, I will."

Roman clenched his teeth, knowing he'd have to intervene. He unsheathed his sword and positioned himself between them. In two quick moves, he'd knocked Xavier to the ground and deflected Tristan's strike, making him to tumble into the sand next to Xavier.

"Enough!" Roman bellowed in a voice that reminded Rose of his father.

Tristan and Xavier glared up at their youngest brother from the ground, collecting their ragged breaths.

Tristan was the first to stand up, but instead of lunging for Xavier, he stormed straight for Rose.

Driven by pure protective instinct, Roman maneuvered his way in front of her. But the action only escalated Tristan's rage.

With a powerful shove, Tristan almost knocked Roman into the sand.

"Tristan, stop!" Harriet begged.

"Tell me it's not true," Tristan seethed, glaring at Roman.

Roman didn't deny it, guilt lying just behind his eyes. "Now isn't the time, Tristan."

Tristan snatched Roman's collar, bringing him face to face. "You've been in love with her this whole time, haven't you?" Tristan shouted. "Admit it! I always thought it was just an innocent crush, but now I see you were just biding your time, waiting for the right moment to take her for yourself. You forced me to get married, feeding me all this bullshit that it was for the good of Vallor. The marriage contract was for no one's benefit but your bloody own!"

Tristan's fist collided with the side of Roman's face.

Roman took the hit, his head snapping to the side. Ever so slowly, he turned his head back to Tristan. "I'm letting that go for the simple fact I understand your anger. But I hope you got it out of your system because it won't be happening again."

Tristan's malicious glare shifted to Rose, his jaw quivering with rage. Utter betrayal strewed in his deep-blue eyes. She sensed the brewing of an angry hurricane. And she was looking into the eye of the storm.

Before she could find words, Tristan stalked away.

"Tristan, wait." Rose tried to follow, taking a few shaky steps in the sand. "Wait!"

Roman grabbed her arm. "Let him go."

She had no choice but to watch his retreating silhouette with pained eyes. "I should've told him… He shouldn't have had to find out like that."

Roman glared at Xavier, still on the sand, clutching his chest. "Yeah, thanks for that."

Rose took a calming breath and turned to Xavier. "Are you alright?" She reached for his torn tunic to get a closer look at the wound.

"I'm fine," Xavier snapped, swatting her hand away as he stood.

She masked the flinch of hurt.

Roman, however, came at Xavier, aggressively swinging his sword at him. Xavier's eyes widened as he attempted to block his blow, but just like Tristan's, his sword fell uselessly onto the sand.

Roman pointed his sword at his throat. "She's trying to help you," Roman fumed, infuriated. "All she's ever done is try to help you. What have you done to help *her*? What have you done to help any of us? You bloody *left*. You left me to finish a war you started. You left Tristan to pick up your crown while you rode off, washing your hands of this place. Blame Tristan all you want, hate him if you wish, but just know who you really hate is yourself. Take my advice and stop feeling sorry for yourself. Take control of your life before it takes you." Roman dropped his voice. "And if you ever try to kiss her again, I'll break your jaw just to make sure you never can."

Rose gazed at Roman, astounded, not sure if she should be thankful or scared.

Roman sheathed his sword and reached for her hand. Her mother stood closely behind, prepared to follow them back to the castle.

Harriet stopped them. "You're leaving, too, aren't you? Take me with you," she pleaded as she hung on to Roman's arm. "Please. I'll die here. Don't leave me with him."

Roman's regret shone through as he put a hand on her shoulder. "Where we're going is too dangerous."

Harriet's eyes narrowed. "What of Evelyn? How is it *she's* able to come along but I am to be left behind?"

"She has a point," Rose's mother agreed.

Rose shot a glare at her mother. *Not helping.* "It's too dangerous for her to stay," she told Harriet. "Men are looking for me, powerful men. I can't allow them to take my mother to get to me. And she's had her own training. She's not defenseless."

Harriet looked between her brothers. "So that's it, then?" she cried. "You're both going to choose her over me again?"

"You know that's not true," Xavier said as his jaw clenched.

"Isn't it?" Harriet argued. "If it wasn't for her, you'd have no reason to leave."

"I have every reason to leave," Xavier pointed out.

Harriet's eyes brimmed with tears as she turned to Rose. "Please. *Please* take me with you. He'll make me marry someone I don't love, and I'll be sentenced to a life I don't want."

Rose recognized the feeling radiating off Harriet. "You love someone already, don't you? You want to run away and be with him."

Harriet's eyes widened in disbelief. "How do you know?"

"Because I could feel you when you danced with him last night," she said.

Xavier and Roman immediately came to attention.

"Who?" Xavier demanded.

Harriet lifted her chin despite his scolding eyes. "Conrad Ledgum."

"The Ledgums?" Roman raised an eyebrow. "They're barely considered a part of the court."

Harriet folded her arms stubbornly. "Which is precisely why I didn't tell anyone. I knew you'd all look at me like that."

"Tristan will never allow you to be with him, and neither would our parents," Xavier said. "And quite frankly, neither would I. You're barely sixteen."

"Like I said, that's why I didn't tell you," Harriet said with a snap.

Guilt festered in her. Harriet, who had been one of her closest friends growing up, who'd always defended her among her peers at court up until this summer, had been brushed aside as of late. And now, with her parents gone… it didn't seem fair.

"Is there no way she can come with us?" Rose whispered to Roman.

Roman shook his head. "If these men are truly sirens, there is no guarantee I can protect her. Hell, I don't even know if we can protect ourselves. She'll be far safer here."

She couldn't help but agree.

Harriet guessed their answer. Her voice trembled as she asked, "When are you leaving?"

"Now," Roman answered. "Before anyone realizes we've gone."

"Fine," Harriet replied, a tear slipping down her cheek. "I guess this is goodbye, then." Harriet moved to leave, but Xavier grabbed her arm.

"I'll come back for you," he promised. "When the time is right, I swear I'll return for you."

"I just lost Mom and Dad," Harriet whispered, her lower lip shaking.

"And now I'm losing you both, too. Just… just do me a favor and leave." Harriet yanked her arm back and turned on her heels, striding towards the castle through the night.

The four looked after her with despair. Silence loomed over them, save for the ocean waves rising with the tide.

"We should try to smooth things over with her," Xavier said to Roman with a solemn expression. "Who knows when the next time we see her will be."

Rose agreed with Xavier. "We'll meet you both at the stables in an hour."

Roman hesitated, about to argue, but Rose shot him a pleading look.

"It's Harriet," she whispered, her eyes flickering between his.

Roman caved, knowing she was right. "Fine," he said. "But go straight to the room and don't come out until I've come for you."

"We'll be ready," she promised. She glanced at Xavier's bleeding chest. "And be sure Xavier gets that looked at before we leave."

CHAPTER 86

Once Rose and her mother returned to their rooms, they grabbed their bags without delay and filled them with last-minute essentials. They did as instructed and stayed in her mother's room until Roman came for them. But as the minutes went on, Rose became anxious. He was late—more than late. He should've been here by now.

Her mother gave an exasperated sigh as she put a hand on her hip, tapping her foot. "Where are they?"

"Do you think something's happened?" Rose asked as she paced.

No sooner had she spoken, a knock came.

Without hesitating, she went to open the door, but it wasn't Roman or Xavier.

To her utter shock, it was Satin, and she was in tears.

"Satin? What is it?" Rose asked with concern, looking down the hall to see if she was alone. "What's happened?"

"It's Tristan," Satin said in a frail voice, wiping her eyes. "He's out of control. I-I've tried to help, but he refuses to listen to me, no matter how hard I try. You have no idea how much I hate to ask it, but… he'll listen to you."

"Wait, slow down. What do you mean out of control?" Rose asked.

"He's been drinking and breaking things and yelling nonsense ever since he came back from the beach," Satin explained, sniffling. "I'm afraid he's going to hurt himself or do something rash. Please, people will start to notice if he keeps carrying on. I don't know what else to do."

Rose cursed, knowing full well it wouldn't be the first time he drank his way to rock bottom. She looked to her mother to see what she thought, but her mother shook her head skeptically. It was a bad idea. No, a horrible one.

"I'm the last person he wants to see right now," Rose said.

"You and I both know that's not true," Satin said with desperate eyes. "I know he may not love me, but *I* love *him*. I hate it, but I do, and he's hurting right now, and I know you're the only one he'll listen to... Please," she begged a final time.

At last, since the first time she'd arrived back, Rose caught a glimpse of the girl she'd known before the wedding—the kind, sweet girl she'd befriended. Perhaps this was finally a way they could part as friends.

Rose let out a defeated sigh. "Give me a moment."

Satin nodded gratefully as she shut the door. She grabbed her cloak, throwing it on.

"Rose, you can't be serious," her mother chided. "If Roman finds out you are—"

"He'll understand." She threw up her hood.

"Rose, I don't—"

"He's lost, Mum. I could feel it at the beach. He's about to come undone, and I can't help the feeling that I put him in that position. Everyone tells me this isn't my fault, but it is. It really is. He is the king of Cathan because I made him be. That burden is now his because of *me*. He told me he didn't want this, that he'd rather leave this all behind, but I didn't. I made him stay. He is forced to live this way because of *me*."

"You're just making excuses because you want a chance to say goodbye," her mother said, calling her bluff.

Rose's eyes fell as she opened her mouth to deny it, but instead she said, "I need to help him if I can."

Her mother released an agitated puff. "Fine, but I'm coming with you. And we have to be back before anyone knows we've gone." Her mother grabbed her own cloak. "Or Roman will kill us *both*," she added with a grumble.

~

Satin guided them along the lengthy corridor to Tristan's room. As soon as they approached the door, a loud commotion rang from within, the echoes of the raucous plaging the empty halls.

"He's just inside," Satin said with drooped eyes. "I'm going back to my room. I'm exhausted… and quite frankly, I'm about to puke my guts out."

Rose gave her a sympathetic look. "Go. I'll speak with him."

Satin gave her a firm nod. She'd only taken a few steps when she spun back. "Do you still love him?"

Rose was startled by the abrupt question, but she responded, "I love Roman."

"That's not what I asked."

Rose hesitated, choosing her words carefully. "I care about him. I care about all of them."

Satin nodded. Her hushed voice carried through the corridor as she said, "I believe you… I'm sorry."

Without another word, she was gone.

Rose and her mother exchanged glances. "What in Vallor was that?" her mother asked, astounded.

"I don't know… It's been a long day for everyone," Rose said, glancing at the door as she second-guessed her decision.

Her mother raised both hands in surrender. "You were the one who wanted to come."

Rose rolled her eyes, glad of her support. "I won't be long," she promised. She stepped forward through the door, not bothering to knock.

Utter chaos greeted her.

CHAPTER 87

It was as though a tornado had blasted its way through Tristan's room. The bed lay in disarray, its fabric torn and exposing scattered goose feathers. The wooden bookcase had tipped sideways, slumping against the corner wall. Books were strewn across the floor, fallen open, and the normally well-organized round table was overturned with parchment scattered everywhere. The fireplace flickered as the sole source of light, all the candles either knocked over or snuffed out.

Tristan hardly noticed Rose's arrival as he grabbed a chair and hurled it against the stone wall with a fierce grunt. He didn't stop at that; he just kept smashing it into the ground over and over.

"Tristan!" she called. "Tristan, stop, stop!" She rushed over to him, putting a hand on his shoulder, stopping him before he hurt himself.

Tristan dropped the chair, his chest heaving. Tears of anger filled his eyes as pain roared deep inside him. He dragged his hands through his hair, yanking it as he sobbed. He staggered backward and collapsed onto the bed's edge, scattering a puff of feathers into the air.

Tears welled in Rose's eyes as she felt his aura crashing into her like a tidal wave. His soul was a bottomless pit of darkness—empty and devoid of hope. And he was sinking deeper. Fast.

She knelt between his legs so he'd have to look her in the eye. She gently took his face in her hands, tilting his jaw to meet her gaze, ignoring the smell of alcohol on his breath. "Tristan, it's me," she murmured, brushing a tear from his cheek. "Hey, hey, it's me. It's just me."

His sparkling ocean eyes crashed into hers like a fierce storm. However, after a moment, the sea settled, as if he finally understood who he was looking at. When a fresh tear slipped out, she wiped his cheek again.

"They're gone," he whispered with despair.

Her eyes pricked again, her heart crippling with his. "Yes... they're gone."

He took a shaky breath, pulling his face away from her hands. His expression turned heart-wrenching as he squeezed his eyes shut and lowered his head into his hands. His shoulders shook from his shaky breathing. "How am I supposed to do this?" he whispered into his hands.

Rose grasped his wrists and pulled them away from his face. She lifted his chin, making him look at her. "Look at me, Tristan," she demanded. "You can do this. If anyone in Vallor can do this, it's you. You are good, and it's hard for good men to be king. You were born for this."

He pulled his face from her grasp again. "I'm not good," Tristan admitted with self-loathing. "That's why I lost you."

She froze, taken aback. "That's not true."

"You know, a small, foolish part of me still had hope," he said, his cheeks tearstained. "Hope that you'd tell me you couldn't live without me. That you'd come back and miss me just as much as I missed you. Instead, I find out you weren't missing me at all." His eyes looked up to hers, but she couldn't meet them. "How long have you been in love with him?"

She gathered the courage to face the deep-blue abyss that matched the sea. "How do you know I love him?"

He glared at her through hardened eyes. "I know you. You look at him like he's the entire starlit sky... and you love stars."

She sucked in her cheek and bit it. "I only realized it a few weeks ago."

"Have you been with him all this time?"

She nodded weakly. "After the wedding... he saw how broken I was. He wanted to help me, give me space to heal."

Tristan's mouth twisted. "He helped, alright... helped himself to you."

He rose to his feet, pacing through the wreckage of his room while running his fingers through his disheveled hair.

Rose knew what he was trying to do. "Don't blame him. He didn't steal me from you."

"But that's precisely what he did, isn't it? In hindsight, he knew exactly what he was doing. Pretending he was helping. Setting it all up perfectly. It's all just so convenient." He kicked the broken chair.

His aggression didn't faze her. "You don't get to play the innocent card in all this, Tristan. You did your fair share of making sure I could find no one else. You and I both know you were being cruel to dissuade other suitors."

"*I* was being cruel?" he exclaimed. "Is that what you think? I was *protecting* you! I didn't want you to have to marry solely for the fact you needed it to survive. I wanted you to have the opportunity to find someone you loved."

"You think Grant couldn't love me?" she challenged.

"I *know* he didn't love you! If he did, he would've married you whether or not you had money. But what did he do as soon as he learned you were destitute? He left!" He shot a pointed hand toward the door. "You think I'd entrust you to someone like that?"

"His *parents* were the reason he had to leave. He would have nothing without their approval."

He jerked his hand back and pointed at himself, poking himself aggressively in the chest. "I would've given all the money and good standing in the world for you!" Tristan yelled. "No matter what people said."

"What about Xavier?" She tried not to rise to his anger. "What's your excuse for him?"

Tristan's eyes darkened like a crazed animal's. "You mean my so-called brother who cut your neck open? Who used you? Do you forget it was me who found you bleeding out into the sea? Who held your unconscious body, praying to the gods you weren't dead? He'd have only hurt you. All he does is hurt you, over and over, and I couldn't let him do that again."

"That wasn't your decision to make!"

"I'm sorry!" he yelled in dire desperation, stepping forward. "I'm sorry if how I went about it was wrong, but I was trying to protect you."

Rose's glare softened. In his own twisted way, what he had done was out of self-preservation, just like thorns on a rose—they protected themselves not out of malicious intent but to make sure they endured. She knew because that's how she had survived her father. And Tristan... Tristan was going down the same path.

"I understand you have your thorns," she said, almost to herself. "That's why I can forgive you. And if I can forgive you for all you've done, don't you think you can forgive Roman and I?"

Tristan cringed. "Please," he pleaded. "Anyone but my brothers."

She shook her head slowly. "It's too late for that."

Tristan's face twisted in pain as he stepped towards her again, determined. "Tell me you don't love me."

She hadn't been expecting that. Her mouth stumbled to respond. She wanted to reply no, but for some reason, she couldn't.

Her siren refused.

His eyes came within inches, barging into hers. "Tell me honestly. Is there any part of you that still loves me? Don't bother trying to lie. I'll know if you are."

Damn him for knowing her so well. She wasn't a good liar. She never had been.

She tried to avoid the question. "Tristan, it doesn't matter—"

"*Answer me!*" he shouted.

"Of course a part of me will always love you!" she cried, tears spilling over her lower lids. She hated him for making her say it—loathing herself for feeling that way in the first place. "But you watched me cry inconsolably over something you had done and you didn't even notice. You didn't even *flinch*. You were so caught up in your own needs that you neglected mine because you were scared of the answers."

His desperation took over. "I'm sorry." He lowered his voice. "You're right. I should've asked. But I care. I care so much I can scarcely breathe. I'm sorry I sent Zareb away. It was wrong of me. I see that now. I shouldn't have taken your sword. I did so many things wrong. But please, Rose, please don't do this to me. Don't be with *him*."

She stood firm. "I can't change the fact I love him, and I wouldn't want to… And more importantly, you have a family to look after. You need to find a way to forget about me."

Tristan choked back tears, pacing again. "How am I supposed to do that, Rosalie?" he yelled, his hands balling into fists. "How?!"

"It's just my siren making it harder for you to let go," she said, not knowing if it was true or false. "You wouldn't be acting this way if it wasn't."

He gave a heartless laugh, withdrawing from her. He went to the bottle of alcohol on the nightstand and took a swig.

Without warning, he threw the bottle across the room, shattering the glass.

She jumped at the crash.

"*Why?*" Tristan screamed. "Why couldn't you love me how I loved you? You should have cared! Your heart should have bled out the way mine did. Your body should've ached like mine did when you left! You have no idea what it feels like to see the love of your life entirely and utterly fine without you!"

Her vision blurred at the confession. Tristan calling her the love of his life hit harder than she wanted it to. But he talked about pain like she didn't have any.

She had lost him, too.

He took a small step closer. "I'll tell you why. Because you never truly loved me… and that…" His voice drifted off, defeated. "That will be the end of me."

Her blood boiled.

How *dare* he?

"I never *loved* you?" she echoed in a dangerously calm tone. "Do you know how it felt to see you get married before my eyes? To feel so sick my entire insides were exiting my body? Do you even know what that did to me?"

"You told me you wouldn't have been with me either way! You wanted me to be king!" He pointed an accusatory finger at her.

"I wanted you to be king because I knew *you* wanted to be king." She jabbed her finger back at him. "And don't stand there and pretend you didn't."

"*I wanted you!*" he bellowed. He dove his hand behind her head, taking a fistful of her hair as he drew her in close, lowering his voice. "When are you going to get it through that fucking beautiful head of yours?" His frustrated expression was almost annoyed. "It's *always* been you. If I had a choice between you and a million things I've ever wanted, I would choose *you*."

She knew it was true.

But the time was gone and passed.

"There are things I should've done differently," she admitted, "but this has turned into a blood sport, Tristan… We keep hurting each other, and I'm done with it."

He let go of her, his face contorting with anger. "Then why are you here? Why even come?"

"Because your *wife* was worried about you," she snapped.

He shook his head. "I don't think so."

Rose's eyes fluttered, not expecting his tone to be so soft.

He closed the space between them. "You came because deep down, you still feel something for me." His lips moved to hover over her neck, brushing them lightly against her skin. "You came because, despite everything your lips are saying, your eyes tell me otherwise. You want me to have you, like I promised." His arms snaked around her waist. "You want me to take you on that bed and worship you so exquisitely, you'll forget anyone else in the world exists."

Tristan's words terrified her as her siren screamed in victory—celebrating.

A wave of his desire streamed its way into her veins. The most powerful man in Cathan lusting after her not only empowered her—it *fueled* her.

Her siren's claws sharpened, ready to take his soul.

Rose fought it back, throwing every chain she could at it. It wasn't right. It wasn't right to desire someone so clearly wrong for her. Not when she had someone for whom she cared more than anyone else. It was greedy.

At that moment, Rose knew her siren would be her worst enemy.

For eternity.

Tristan saw the internal conflict in her hesitation. He lowered his lips, hovering over hers. "Admit it," he demanded.

She shoved her siren's lust aside.

With all her strength, she shoved Tristan so hard he fell back onto the floor—but not before he managed to grab her hand, dragging her down with him. They toppled down in an entangled mess.

She hadn't even recovered from the fall when he climbed on top of her, pinning her hands above her head, his chest pressing down against hers.

"Stop fighting it," he begged.

He ground his hips into hers.

A surprised gasp escaped before she could stop it.

His lips came crashing down to claim the sound.

His euphoria under her fingertips was indescribable—so powerful she had no idea if it was her or him. Her siren was clawing for its life. For its survival.

She didn't know if she could stop it.

Rose found the willpower to cock her fist, punching him in the face, making him fall off of her.

She gave him the best detesting glare she could. "Don't *ever* do that again," she said with a scowl.

She pushed herself off the floor, making her way to the door.

In a flash, he was behind her, grabbing her arm and spinning her around. He wasted no time locking the door before shoving her against the wall.

"I'm done asking nicely," he growled.

His lips captured hers again, his tongue invading her mouth. His hungry lips devoured hers as if he was trying to suck her siren up and out of her.

She shoved him again, but he anticipated her resistance this time. His chest crushed against hers harder, trapping her to the wall as his fierce hands ran themselves down over her hips, across her back, exploring her body.

She could fight back harder. It might not be as easy as fighting off the man at the tavern, but she knew she could escape if she willed it. She wasn't powerless, but her siren paralyzed her limbs.

It craved him. Thirsted for him. Begged for him.

"Kiss me back," his ragged voice demanded.

Rose made a pathetic attempt to escape his hold, giving him a fighting glare. "Go to hell."

He ignored her, kissing her harder, prying her mouth open again. Her lips were sure to be swollen later from him.

His hips thrust themselves into hers.

She bit back her physical reaction as best as she could, but her body exposed her as a soft moan escaped her lips.

Shit.

His desire exploded—surging upward like a sunken ship resurfacing from the depths of the sea. His hand forced its way up her dress, wasting no time. He went straight between her legs.

Another gasp escaped her.

Rose kept praying he'd come to his senses. This wasn't him. He wouldn't do this. He'd stop. He'd see how wrong this was. He wouldn't dare hurt her like this. He wouldn't do this to Satin.

She bit his bottom lip hard enough to draw blood, but the gesture only fueled him.

He moaned into her mouth. His fingers found their way under her slip, gliding over her bare slick skin. He swore breathlessly at the moisture waiting for him as pride gathered within his dangerous gaze.

She swallowed hard, ashamed.

"I knew it," he rumbled through his ragged breaths, relieved as he leaned his forehead down to hers. "I fucking knew it."

"Tristan, don't," she begged. "Please don't."

"I promise you'll enjoy it," he breathed, trailing kisses along her collarbone. "You'll beg for more by the time I'm done. I promise I'll cherish you. I'll worship you like I have my whole life. I love you. I've *always* loved you, and I'll never stop loving you."

He kissed her again.

Push him! she commanded her limbs, but her siren restrained them with its vice grip. It craved all the victims it could get.

And he was such a powerful one.

"Kiss me back, dammit," he commanded. "That's an order from your king."

She gave him a defiant glare as she shook her head, not ready to give in to him. Not ready to admit defeat.

Tristan's hand rocked against her in a way that set her body squirming.

She couldn't fight her body any longer. Another small moan escaped her beautiful lips.

His eyes practically rolled out of his head at the sound.

Without another word, he withdrew, grabbing her by her wrists and dragging her to the torn-apart bed. He threw her onto it, feathers flying from the force. She didn't resist—not as much as she should have.

"Tristan, no," she begged, shaking her head.

She tried to crawl to the other side, clutching at the sheets as more feathers scattered into the air, but Tristan grabbed her ankles, dragging her back to him.

"I'm not letting you escape me again," he breathed, his voice like a wild animal. His self-control was gone, vanished without a trace. "I'll chain you to this bed if I have to."

Rose looked up at him with pleading eyes. "Please don't do this, Tristan. You are better than this, please. It will kill him."

"You should've thought about that before coming here," he stated without remorse. "He can come pry you from my cold, dead fingers before I let him take you back."

It was like he was possessed—all sense of reason gone.

His lips were on hers again, this time more demanding, more feral. His hand skimmed across her throat down to her chest as he slipped into her dress, cupping her bare breast.

Her body arched as she moaned into his mouth.

He sat up and tore his shirt off, exposing his carved chest. Gods, he truly was beautiful.

"Take off your dress," he ordered.

Rose shook her head, glaring at him, fighting off both him and her siren. "Not in a million years."

Tristan pinned her down with his powerful thighs, his chest heaving above hers. "Do it, or I'll rip it off your body."

She knew he would.

She couldn't let this happen.

She refused to.

He sighed, getting off the bed to grab his sword.

She took the opportunity to escape the bed, but he still blocked her path to the door.

He faced her with his sword in hand just as her feet hit the stone floor.

"I'm not letting you leave this room," he warned with perilous eyes. "So I suggest you get back on that bed before I make you."

"No." She grabbed one of the books scattered on the floor and chucked it at him.

With ease, he dodged it, continuing his steps.

She picked up another, hurling it at him again. He dodged that one, too, unfazed by her failed attempts, holding the sword lazily at his side.

Rose raised her hand to throw another at him, but he caught her wrist with his free hand. "I wouldn't," he warned, his eyes taunting her mercilessly.

She dropped the book.

He grabbed her dress roughly by the skirt as his sword went down to the hem. With lethal precision, he sliced upward.

Rose flinched as her dress dropped uselessly at her feet, exposing her thin slip.

"Tristan, please," she pleaded with him a final time, knowing she was about to lose this internal battle. "I don't want this."

"I'm sorry, Rose," he breathed between her lips, his deep, lustful voice speaking to her very core. "I just don't believe you anymore."

He was just about to claim her when the door burst open.

To her utter relief and shame, it was Roman.

It took Roman only moments to piece together what was happening. His eyes darted throughout the wrecked room, bulging out of their sockets at the sight of her shredded dress on the floor.

Then he saw the sword in Tristan's hand.

The pit of hell itself formed in Roman's pupils, ready to swallow Tristan into oblivion.

Roman paused as his savage eyes went to Rose first. "Did he hurt you?" he asked in a frighteningly calm tone.

Tristan scoffed, rolling his eyes.

She shook her head. "No."

"Did he touch you?"

Rose hesitated, shooting Tristan a fearful side glance.

"Did. He. Touch. You?" Roman hounded, louder this time.

She gulped, afraid to answer.

"Yes, I did," Tristan replied for her, unapologetic as his hand tightened on the hilt of his sword. "And she liked it."

Rose didn't know how Tristan could be both so brave and foolish.

Roman's murderous gaze sliced to Tristan, then returned to Rose. He prowled towards her, his hands shaking with barely contained rage. "Do you want him?"

She still wasn't breathing, living on borrowed breath. "What?"

"Do you *want* him?" he asked again, his merciless gaze bearing down into hers. "Do you want him like you want me?"

She knew the answer immediately. "No."

"Do you need him like you need me?"

"No."

"Do you love him like you love me?"

She finally understood what he was doing. With every answer, another wound opened in Tristan's chest, cracking his fragile frame.

"No," she whispered.

"Do you want to fuck him like you want to fuck me?" he growled.

Rose looked Roman dead in the eye. "No."

Roman nodded, satisfied. He turned to Tristan, sizing up his brother. "You hear that? She doesn't want it. She doesn't want *you*. Get it through your fucking head."

Tristan's face remained fierce. He cocked his head smugly. "Her body tells me otherwise. Perhaps she's just too scared to tell you the truth."

Roman scoffed, taking another formidable step toward him. "Is that why you had to tear the clothes right off her back?" he asked, nodding to her dress crumpled on the floor. He lowered his voice as a terrifying smile took hold of his handsome face. "Funny, when I bed her, she practically tears the dress off herself because she can't get it off fast enough."

Tristan charged at Roman without a moment's hesitation.

Roman veered to the right as Tristan lunged, dodging his attack.

Child's play.

Roman drew his sword from its sheath.

"Don't!" Rose pleaded with them both.

But this was past negotiation now.

In all their training, she'd never seen Roman fight with such bloodthirst, his barbaric eyes looking like he could kill. Like a fool, his gentle nature the past few weeks had made her overlook that he was the general of the largest army in Vallor for a reason.

It shouldn't have thrilled her siren the way it did.

Strike after strike, Roman backed Tristan into a corner, stepping over the debris of the room. Tristan was far too drunk to fight properly. That, coupled with the fresh injury on his shoulder, made him no match for Roman—a fact that Roman took full advantage of. Within moments, Roman had knocked Tristan's sword out of his hands, leaving him defenseless. Even then, he didn't stop, lifting his sword to strike a fatal blow.

"Roman!" she yelled.

Roman's sword stopped just as it reached Tristan's neck, the blade piercing through the top layer of skin, drawing blood.

A calculated move.

Roman glared down at his brother like he was nothing more than a disgusting cockroach. "We're leaving." Roman's cold-blooded voice chilled the air. "If you even *think* about trying to stop us or hunt us down, I promise I'll finish what we started here." He crouched to Tristan's level, his sword still at his throat. "And if you ever—" he dug the blade deeper into Tristan's neck, making him wince, "—*ever* touch her like that again without her full permission, blood or not—king or not—I swear to the gods above and below, I will kill you."

Rose never would've believed the words came from his lips if she hadn't witnessed it herself. Roman had a dark side after all. For some reason, it made her feel better—like it leveled the playing field.

Tristan's eyes filled with a loathing she'd never seen in him, not even for Xavier.

A new rivalry born before her very eyes.

Roman forced Tristan to his feet and dragged him to the one good chair by the knocked-over table. He began tying him to it with the rope used to hold back the curtains.

"What are you doing?" Rose asked.

"I'm tying him up so we have time to get out of here." Roman grunted.

"There's no need for that. He wouldn't stop—"

"Wouldn't he?"

Rose gazed at Tristan.

Tristan was immediately outraged. "The hell you're leaving!"

Roman's glare shifted back to her with a knowing look.

"You're not taking her anywhere. Are you both out of your minds?" Tristan looked back and forth between the two of them. "The safest place for her is here! And you know that, you selfish bastard. You just don't want to stay because you know if you stay long enough, she'll come to her senses and leave you. She'll see you manipulated her."

Roman punched him in the face.

Rose flinched.

Tristan's mouth dripped blood again, likely from the same blow Xavier gave him only hours earlier.

"This is treason!" Tristan shouted at Roman.

Roman didn't care.

"Rose, please," Tristan begged. "Please don't do this."

She diverted her eyes as she wrapped her arms around herself.

"Don't look at her," Roman growled, grabbing Tristan's jaw and snapping his face back to his. "Look at me. *I'm* doing this. Not her."

Tristan jerked his chin from Roman's grip, ignoring him. He looked at Rose again with desperate eyes. "Rose. Don't leave again, please. We can—"

Roman had had enough. He placed a gag roughly over Tristan's mouth, tying it with aggressive tugs. "Let's go," he grumbled. He grabbed his sword off the floor, marching for the door.

Rose hesitated, looking back at Tristan's pitiful frame. His eye was already swelling from Roman's strike, the blood trickling from the corner of his mouth. His eyes still pleaded with her, though they were full of betrayal. He tried to say something, but the gag reduced his words to incoherent mumbles.

Roman moved to where she was standing and gently but firmly took her shoulders, twisting her to face him. "We need to go now. If anyone finds him before we leave, we'll be sitting ducks."

Rose nodded weakly.

Roman removed his cloak and set it over her shoulders, covering all that was left of her slip and throwing the hood over her head. With a nod, she followed. When she reached the door, she looked back at Tristan one last time.

She wished she hadn't.

Tristan's betrayed eyes gouged hers, ripping her soul to shreds. She felt every dark part of him—his unworthiness, his love, his pain, the endless pit of darkness he was falling into. The storm that had been brewing had morphed into a terrifying tsunami.

"I'm so sorry," she whispered, looking at him through blurred vision.

She could still hear his muffled cries through the gag as she closed the door.

Roman had her things waiting for her outside the door. She grabbed her sword and bag. The corridors were blissfully empty, suggesting that most of the court had remained in the grand hall for the passing ceremony celebration. Roman helped her into a new dress, covering her exposed body with his cloak as she put it on as quickly as she could, eager to put as much distance as possible between herself and this place.

Roman was silent as they moved through the halls. He wouldn't even look at her. His powerful strides urged her to almost run to keep pace as they headed to the stables where they had all agreed to meet.

"Roman," she whispered so softly, she was surprised he heard it.

His eyes met hers for the first time since they'd left Tristan's room.

"It was a mistake to leave him like that," she said, risking angering him.

"You think I wanted that?" He rounded on her. "To part ways with my brother like that? But you just couldn't help yourself, could you?"

"I'm sorry. I should've never gone in there," she admitted with regret.

"No, you shouldn't have," he agreed harshly. "So why did you?"

"Satin came to the room," she explained. "She was so upset. She told me she was worried about Tristan and didn't know who else to turn to. I couldn't tell her no."

Roman stopped dead in his tracks. "What?"

She nodded. "I know, it was a surprise she'd confide in me, but—"

"No. Satin came to my room and told me the exact same thing."

Rose's brows grew together. "What? You mean it wasn't my mother who came for you?"

"No, why would she?" Roman asked, his fury waning slightly.

She stilled. "She wasn't there when you came to the door?"

"No, I never saw her."

"Then… where is she?" A tremor coursed its way through her.

Roman scanned the corridor—as if someone was watching.

Rose's hand went to grip the hilt of her sword. "I don't like this. Something doesn't feel right."

"No," Roman agreed. "It doesn't… Maybe she's with Xavier."

"And if she's not?"

"Then we'll find her. Come on." He made her walk ahead as he glanced over his shoulder before following.

A fierce storm loomed on the horizon, unleashing a cold wind that made even the mightiest trees bend to its will. She tightened her grip on her cloak as her siren eyes scanned the darkness for any sign of her mother.

Amid the wind, Xavier was standing at the double door frame, waiting for them in the shelter of the stables. But her mother was nowhere in sight.

Rose's panic escalated.

"Took you long enough," Xavier complained as they entered the stables. With one look at Rose and Roman, Xavier knew something was wrong. "What's the matter?"

"Have you seen my mother?" she asked, still hoping she'd pop out of the shadows.

Xavier shook his head. "No, I haven't seen her since the beach. I thought she was with you?"

Rose gazed at Roman with horrified eyes.

"Don't go there," Roman said. "We'll find her."

"You mean she's missing?" Xavier fumed. "What the hell could've possibly happened in an hour?"

Without warning, horns blared into the wind, alerting everyone inside and outside of the castle—a sign of intruders.

Roman cursed under his breath. "How'd he get out so fast?"

Xavier's eyes whipped back to them. "What the hell happened back there?"

"I may have gagged Tristan and tied him to a chair…" Roman said, not sounding like he regretted it but still acknowledging it wasn't the smartest move.

Xavier opened his mouth to say something but paused briefly before shrugging, as if it was understandable. "I've had the same urge."

"Not helping!" Rose snapped. "What are we going to do? How are we supposed to find my mother now that the whole castle is on alert?"

"We should leave," Xavier said, sizing up which horses to take. "If we don't, we'll never make it. We'll never get this chance again."

"Get Rose out of here," Roman instructed. "I'll go back for Evelyn."

"No," she said. "I'm not leaving without you."

"We can't all fit on Onyx," Roman pointed out. "You two can get a head start, and I'll be right behind you as soon as I find her."

"And if you're caught?" Rose asked. "Tristan will throw you in the dungeons as soon as he finds you."

Xavier agreed. "She's right. You don't stand a chance."

Roman glanced over his shoulder at the gates. "At least I'll know you are safe. He'll never let you leave if we're found."

"He won't let you either," she bit back.

"I'll stay," Xavier volunteered.

She shook her head. "No, I'm the only one he won't hurt. I'll go back."

"He won't let you leave his sight," Roman argued. "And he'll finish what he started tonight. I'm sure of it."

Xavier narrowed his eyes, picking up on his tone. "What did he do?"

Roman ground his teeth, his jaw feathering. "He tried to force her to fuck him, that's what." His hands clenched back into white fist just having to say it.

"He did *what*?" Xavier exploded, his eyes sparking with outrage.

"We're running out of time!" Rose reminded them. "The question is, what do we do?"

Silence fell over them. Xavier, still reeling over the news, paced.

"I suppose we stick together," Roman concluded.

Rose looked to Xavier for confirmation.

He gave a loud, defeated sigh, unsheathing his sword. "Let's go, then, so we can get the hell out of here before they realize we're gone."

Xavier moved to exit the stables, but before he could even take a step, a group of soldiers entered.

They were outnumbered.

CHAPTER 88

Following a thorough search and the confiscation of their weapons, Rose, Roman, and Xavier were led to the dungeons in silence. The guard escorting Rose kept her at arm's length, deliberately avoiding eye contact, likely warned to be wary of her siren powers. Only flickering torches lit the dark, damp cells where they were each imprisoned, with Rose positioned directly across from the two brothers.

To her utter relief, her mother was waiting for them in a cell of her own. She'd never been so happy to see someone behind bars.

"Rose!" her mother exclaimed, her entire frame relaxing. "Thank the gods."

Rose grasped her hands through the adjacent bars. "Mum! What happened? Why are you here?"

Her mother glared at the retreating guards. "After you went to see Tristan, I heard you shouting. I tried to open the door, but it was locked. I went to find Roman for help, but the guards took me on the way. They threw me in here and told me the castle was on lockdown but wouldn't tell me a thing more." She let out a frustrated puff. "What happened after I left?"

Rose looked uneasily at Roman. He wouldn't meet her gaze.

"You were right," she said, ashamed. "I should've never gone to see him."

Distant voices drifted from the gates while keys clanked, echoing through the dungeon, then footsteps.

A black-eyed Tristan came into view. His split lip, courtesy of Roman, was curled into a hostile snarl. Though he seemed sober now, his sunken eyes looked almost hollow, bordering on sickly, exuding a new darkened aura.

Rose had never seen him appear so unlike himself—so estranged. Her gut twisted, making her queasy. She'd seen that look before—in her father.

Two high councilmen entered after him. To her dismay, the first was Lord Martin. His beady eyes never left hers as he followed his king, his gaze sweeping her up and down. A small, disturbing smile overtook his lips.

A flicker of hope emerged when she saw the second was Lord Barron, but his mouth was pressed into a tight frown, appearing just as happy as his companions.

A shadow of doubt wormed its way inside her.

"You almost fooled me," Tristan spat, his tone so frigid and remote she wouldn't have recognized it if she weren't watching his lips move. "Where is it?"

The four exchanged blank stares. A distant leak from the ceiling dripped into a nearby chamber pot.

Xavier spoke first. "Where is *what?*"

"Don't play games with me!" Tristan bellowed. *"Where is it?!"*

Rose jumped, taking a step back.

"What are you talking about?" Roman asked coldly through the bars. "Where is *what?*"

"The talisman!" Tristan roared.

Dread filled the marrow of her bones. The talisman? It was gone? She'd seen it with her own eyes not twenty-four hours ago. It was safely locked in the tomb... wasn't it?

The confusion on Xavier's and Roman's faces mirrored her own.

"You lost it?!" Xavier exclaimed, clutching the bars of his cell. "You've been king for what, a day, and you've already lost it?"

"I didn't *lose* anything. It was stolen," Tristan spat. His soulless eyes rested on Roman. "We have witnesses who have testified on the holy relic that they saw Roman go down to the tombs after the passing ceremony. The talisman was there before he went in, and now it's missing."

All eyes fell on Roman.

Roman's expression was unyielding. "That's a lie. I never touched it."

Lord Barron spoke up, his handsome face still grave. "I saw you enter the tombs after the ceremony with my very eyes. This is not a stupid piece of jewelry; it has been the key to Cathan's prosperity and peace, which we've preserved for hundreds of years. It is everything keeping Vallor together."

There was no way it was true. He couldn't have. There had been no time… unless—was this why Roman had been late? Had he gone against her wishes and tried to retrieve the talisman for safekeeping?

Lord Barron was the only high councilman she had always trusted and respected. What reason would he have to lie? Rose probed Lord Barron's mind to see if she could feel anything, but to her utter astonishment, she felt… nothing. Nothing but a black hole. She frowned.

"Do you have any idea what they're talking about?" Xavier said in a lowered voice to Roman.

"No," Roman assured him, standing firm in the flicker of the torches' shadows. "I promise on the ancient books of Vallor, I didn't touch it."

Tristan scoffed. He turned away from his brothers, focusing on Rose instead. He approached the bars of her cell, his interrogating eyes narrowing as he spoke in a low, dangerous whisper. "Did you have anything to do with this? Were you just the distraction while Roman stole the talisman?" His voice was intended to be harsh and detached, but his eyes betrayed a flicker of fear.

Rose's arms slackened, shocked he could believe such a blatant lie. "No. It wasn't us who stole it. I swear."

"Listen to me, Tristan," Roman interrupted, making Tristan's eyes snap to him. "Take me and Xavier, fine, but let Rose and Evelyn go. She isn't safe here. If someone *has* stolen the talisman, she could be in danger."

A wicked scowl claimed Tristan's lips. He lifted a familiar bronze key—

the one the guard had confiscated while Roman was being searched. "You stole this key and used it to take the talisman, didn't you?"

Roman straightened, knowing where this was headed. "Father gave me that key the night I returned to the castle. He wanted me to have it."

Tristan lowered the key, clenching it. "Why in Vallor would he do that? This key is supposed to be handed down to the next king of Cathan. You want me to believe our father would break ancient tradition and let *you* in on Cathan's darkest secret? To what purpose?"

"I don't know, I didn't get the chance to ask. But I promise you, I. Didn't. Take. It." Roman emphasized each word.

Tristan's predatory gaze moved to his next victim. "It turns out you, Xavier, have been charged with treason as of this afternoon." He delivered the news in such a casual tone, he might as well have been discussing the weather. "I've been told by Lord Martin that we have witnesses who say you were seen in the woods on the day of the first succession trial. Father knew, as well, and chose not to act on it. No doubt to protect you."

Rose's stomach felt like it had been gutted, leaking out onto the filthy straw floor. That day. That awful day when Roman almost died. The day she swore she saw those eyes. Eyes that both froze and thawed her heart. Had it been Xavier? Had he lied to her?

No. It couldn't be. He wouldn't.

Rose threw an anxious look to Xavier for confirmation.

To his credit, Xavier remained calm. "Or perhaps he knew it was a lie," he replied flatly.

Lord Martin stuck up his nose. "Are you calling my spies liars?"

"Of course I am, because it's not true," Xavier replied with a deathly even tone. "I was banned from the borders. Call upon Malcolm. I was with him."

"You were with him the entire time?" Tristan pressed.

Xavier's face twitched as he admitted, "No."

"It was you who tried to kill me that day, wasn't it?" Tristan accused, betrayal shining in his eyes. "Dragonshade is a poison sourced from the northern borders of Artistan, which the dragons of old used for their hatching grounds, not far from Amernth. That is where you were all this time, were you not?"

Xavier's eyes sharpened like crystallized icicles. "Yes, I was in the north, but that doesn't mean I did it."

"Then what's your excuse for being in the woods?" Tristan pressed.

"I don't have one. I was never there," Xavier hissed between his teeth.

Rose's eyes darted between Xavier and Roman. They weren't going to win this. There was too much stacked against them and no proof of their innocence. Her heart raced, leaving her lightheaded.

Lord Barron grew impatient. He stalked to Roman's cell to confront him directly, his dark robes gathering straw as he said, "If you admit fault, we will be merciful in your sentence. Just tell us where it is, and I promise you, you'll be much better off."

"I'm telling you, I don't have it," Roman repeated. "Get the lotus powder. I'll prove my innocence."

"Unfortunately, that is a rare commodity to come by in Cathan. It was supplied by the seer, who has yet to be found. Besides, the Lotus powder is too unreliable in this situation, especially when its effects can be manipulated by magic," Lord Martin said, glaring at Rose. He turned to Tristan. "Perhaps we're going about this the wrong way. There may be a bigger game at play."

Tristan stiffened. "What do you mean?"

"I only wonder if Roman and Xavier are mere pawns in a much bigger game," Lord Martin insinuated, gazing at Rose. "And she's the master."

Tristan's eyes flickered her way. For the first time since he stepped foot in the dungeons, his raging eyes morphed into a state of panic.

The tide in the room shifted—the true reason for all this.

They didn't want Roman and Xavier.

They wanted *her*.

Lord Martin whipped back to Rose, pointing at her accusingly. "You've been power-hungry ever since you arrived here. You and your pernicious mother clawing for any position at court, using your charm on our king to allow you to visit every summer. You kept your powers strategically hidden, patient for a few years until you smelled blood in the water when you heard rumors that Xavier's succession was in jeopardy. You dethroned Xavier, forcing him from his position to satisfy your own agenda. Then, under your influence, you had him attempt to kill Tristan to throw the succession in your favor. Then, after that failed, you swayed yourself into Tristan's and Grant's affection, keeping your options open to the two most likely candidates to win. Then, when Tristan won, you were thwarted by a foreign queen. But that didn't stop you..."

Lord Martin's gaze switched to Roman as he continued. "You moved on to the next brother, the general of Vallor's largest army. Once you learned of the queen's health, you rushed back with your siren fully intact, bringing him and Xavier back to help you gain control over this court. You persuaded Roman to tell you about the talisman and then tried to bed Tristan as a distraction as Roman stole the talisman for you!"

Rose's mother was the one to bite back. "She has done none of what you say. You have no idea who took the talisman. And so you all don't look like fools for letting it be taken under your noses, you look to blame Rose—who has done *nothing* but help not just the royal family but all of Cathan. But what would you know of that, Lord Martin? While you sit and hide in the protection of this castle. Well, danger has finally crept its way into these walls. There is no more hiding." Her mother looked to Tristan. "Your father saw it, and he'd have never allowed for this, let alone blame an innocent girl for the high council's negligence."

Lord Martin's mouth curled, the insult striking a chord with him. "She is not a *girl*. She is a siren. Nor do I trust the whore who birthed it."

Tristan slammed his fist against the bars. "*Enough!*" he bellowed. "We came to find the talisman. There is no evidence of Rose's involvement. It is mere speculation on your part, Lord Martin, and I do *not* condone the continued self-serving accusation."

Rose's lungs finally accepted air back into her lungs. It gave her a sliver of solace to know Tristan still cared enough to protect her.

However, that comfort vanished when Tristan's harsh gaze returned to Roman. "But we *do* have concrete proof that Roman had access to the talisman and that Xavier committed treason during the first challenge. Since the lotus powder is out of the question, our options are limited..." His eyes searched the air as he thought. "It looks like we'll have to deal with this the hard way." Tristan gestured to the guards. "Take them to the cliffs."

An avalanche slammed Rose to the floor. She knew what happened to those accused on the rocky seaside. He couldn't be serious. He would never. They were his brothers. His *blood.*

But as Tristan said earlier that summer—blood doesn't make a brother.

Panic overrode her as the guards came to seize Roman and Xavier.

"Tristan, no, wait," she pleaded, gripping the cell's cold, slick bars. "Please wait! You have to believe me. We're telling the truth."

Tristan's powerful eyes capsized her hopes with one cannon blast. "Restrain Rose and Evelyn and escort them back to their chambers," Tristan said to the guards waiting just outside the iron gate. "They don't need to see what happens next." He returned to her cell, lowering his voice. "I'll keep guards posted outside your door. You're welcome to stay in my room if it makes you feel safer."

The bloody snake.

"To keep me safe or to keep me in your bed?" she whispered, her siren switching sides as its claws poised, ready to slash him to bits now Roman's life was threatened.

Tristan had no intention of answering her question. He strutted for the iron doors with Lord Barron and Lord Martin following dutifully behind him.

Rose's frame shook with fear. She couldn't let him do this. He wouldn't. He was bluffing.

"Tristan, if you do this, I'll never forgive you," she called after him in warning. "There will be no redemption for you."

Disregarding her warning, Tristan strode out of the dungeons, taking his dark aura with him.

The guards arrived to open her cell, swiftly placing chains around her wrists, but before they could lead her anywhere, she spun around, breaking free from the guard's hold. She went straight for Roman, taking his face in her hands, the bulky shackles on her wrists clanking.

"What do I do?" she whispered, her voice trembling.

"Leave," Roman commanded. She knew his voice was meant to be strong, but it came out hoarse. "Get out of here. Go with your mother and don't look back. Take Onyx and go to Moretti. He'll help hide you. He's the only one who knows about these men."

Rose shook her head in denial. She wouldn't accept this. She couldn't. Her siren's rage wouldn't allow it.

"No. I won't run. I'll fight them off. I'll kill every last one if I have to."

She meant it. She'd kill them all and deal with the consequences later.

"No," he said at once. "Even with your abilities, they'll kill you before you reach the gates. Even Tristan will not be able to save you."

Rose's eyes pricked as the guards came closer, preparing to drag him to his fate.

She flung her arms around his neck, slamming her body into his. She clutched his tunic in fistfuls, inhaling a greedy amount of the musky scent of cedar that had become her personal drug. She had just found him. She was supposed to have years with him. He was supposed to take her to Eristan. He'd promised.

"I love you… Gods, Roe, I love you," Roman murmured into her ear.

She squeezed her eyes shut, not just to keep the tears back, but to memorize the fluctuation of his voice, letting the rough groves engrave her heart.

"In whatever realm or life is next for me, I will wait for you, and I will find you."

She pulled away just enough to look him in the eye. Gods, those beautiful honey-golden eyes she'd let herself be glazed in. The desert she'd been scorched by. The flames in which she had been consumed.

Her eyes were swimming. She wasn't strong enough for this. She wouldn't survive. He was her air supply. She would suffocate without him. She'd go mad. She'd…

"I won't let you go on that adventure without me."

"Yes, you will," Roman stated. "Dammit, you will. Just…" His voice weakened as he strained to speak. "Just remember me, please."

He said it as though it was a real possibility that this was the end.

The guards grew impatient as they tried to tug Roman to the door, but Rose wouldn't budge, pressing her lips to Roman's, running her hands through his hair.

"I am yours," she whispered, hoping he gathered what she meant—that she was sorry for going to Tristan's room, sorry she wasn't able to make it right.

She was sorry.

So, so sorry.

He leaned his forehead down to hers, nothing but pure love radiating through him. "And you are mine," he whispered back.

Without warning, he was ripped from her arms. His eyes stayed locked on to hers until he was forced through the iron doors.

Rose faced Xavier, whose eyes were heavily fortified by a thick wall of ice. She walked right up to that high wall as she placed a hand on his chest, and watched it melt under her fingertips. Past it, she could feel his fear, his anger, his regret all at once.

"Rose," Xavier whispered, defeated.

Rose wrapped her arms around him, feeling the spike in his blood pressure. "You should've never come back," she whispered.

"No, I should have never left. I should have told you the truth about how I felt about you. I should've let you in. I should've protected you. You were right—I was a coward. There were so many things I wish I would've done... I love you, smart-ass, and I always will."

Rose's eyes shifted between his. She parted her mouth to say something, but no sound escaped. It felt as though an invisible hand wrapped itself around her throat, stopping her.

He kissed her softly on the forehead, pouring the last of his soul into hers. The guards were at his side within moments.

"Get out while you still can," Xavier said, repeating Roman's words. "Now."

Before Rose could get another word out, he was gone.

The rest of the guards closed in around Rose and Evelyn, herding them toward the door.

"What are we going to do?" her mother whispered, eyeing the guards anxiously.

"I'm not running," Rose stated before her mother could dissuade her. "I don't care how dangerous it is. I won't leave them."

To Rose's utter surprise, a strong wave of willpower poured out of her mother's resilient hazel eyes. "I know," her mother agreed. "We have to save them, but how?"

"I think I have an idea," Rose said.

"No more talking," the guard ordered, grabbing her roughly by the arm.

The guards hauled them from the dungeons back to the main corridor. However, unlike Roman and Xavier, who had been led away by two guards, they were escorted by five.

Apparently, Tristan wanted to be absolutely certain she made it back to her quarters.

As they walked silently, Rose tried to make eye contact with the guards, but they avoided her gaze as if knowing if they looked into her eyes she could reach into their minds like she had with Moretti. Her siren smirked inwardly. She had to admit, she was flattered by their effort.

Her mother threw her an uneasy glance, questioning her with her eyes as if to say, *Now what do we do?*

Carefully, Rose scanned each guard for her sword. She found it attached to the guard five steps ahead on her right, hooked onto his belt. She strained her ears for the jingle of keys. Her heightened senses led her gaze to the guard on her left. The keys dangled from his hip, secured under his red cloak.

She prayed to the lost city above that this would work.

She opened her mouth and sang.

Starry skies casts illusions of hope,
soft winds press against white sails.
Salty air fills a sailor's tired lungs,
a helm rests under steady palms.
Little do they know, the danger lurking below.

Rose could feel the men's auras begin to soften, some more quickly than others. The guard leading them swerved back to her.

"No singing," he scolded, his eyes meeting hers.

A mistake.

Her sea-green eyes swallowed him whole.

The first sign is a change in the wind,
Dark clouds summoned to bring chaos in.

Your guides are gone, and so is the light.
Waves grow fiercer, but none grow wiser,
for my voice alone reaches your ears.
You believe this song
will drag you to the sea,
but it is the silence
that will drive you to insanity.
You'll long for my eyes, but all you'll find
is a bottomless pit of your own demise.
Oh, the silence will drown you,
it'll drown you.
You better run, it'll drown you.
Created from tears of forced love,
the lustful and weak are drawn to the call.
Between angelic notes and dulcet tunes,
are the echoes of grief and pain
darkened souls yearn for.
You believe this song
will drag you to the sea,
but it is the silence
that will drive you to insanity.
You'll long for my eyes, but all you'll find
is a bottomless pit of your own demise.
Oh, the silence will drown you,
it'll drown you.
You better run, it'll drown you.
Oh, my silence,
my silence will drown you.
Oh, you'd better run, I'll drown you.

That was all it took. One song, and her beguiling voice enthralled them, creating just enough of a distraction to get close enough to the guard with the keys.

She lunged for his sword.

The guard had little time to react as Rose swiped his weapon. She sliced the belt loop holding the set of keys attached to his waist. She threw the keys to her mother, who caught them and quickly began to unlock the clasps while Rose kept the guards at bay with bound hands, buying her more time. Finally, her mother was set free.

Her mother got her hands on a fallen sword, and together, they went to work, disarming the soldiers one by one as quickly as possible.

A few moments later, she and her mother managed to wrangle the five soldiers up and tie them together, gagging and stuffing them into the nearest room they could find before someone discovered them. They quickly closed the doors behind them, remaining in the room for now until they could find their bearings.

Her mother was bent over, breathing harshly, while Rose was unfazed.

"Well, you've gotten much better," her mother huffed.

Rose swung her sword lazily in a circle, showing off. "You should have trained with me and Zareb."

Her mother brushed back a strand of hair that had come loose. "Yes, well, I don't have the speed or youth of a siren on my side."

Rose stalked up to the guard sitting on the floor who had her sword attached to his belt. Her siren took over as she crouched to his level. His eyes gripped on to her like he was hanging from a ledge she had shoved him out on.

"Hello," she said, a predatory smile playing on her lips as her fingers slid down the buttons of his tunic. "You don't mind if I take back my sword, do you?"

The guard gulped, shaking his head. His human heart pounded so closely to the surface, Rose was certain she could easily reach into his chest and grab it. His temples beaded with sweat as she glided her fingers strategically over to the rose-engraved hilt, wrapping her fingers around it, and extracting it from its scabbard.

She leaned forward to whisper, "Thank you," then rewarded him with a kiss on the cheek. She stood and faced her mother. "Come on, we need to hurry. They'll reach the cliffs soon."

Without another word, they left the room and ran down the corridor, ignoring the muffled cries of the tied-up, groaning men behind them.

CHAPTER 89

Rose and her mother had nowhere to hide once they reached the courtyard, allowing the guards to spot them almost immediately. Horns blared above them as they sprinted as quickly as her mother's legs could carry her. With the cover of darkness and the storm's wind, they managed to reach the outskirts of the castle.

Onyx! Rose shouted desperately into their bond. *I need you!*

He was present in her mind in an instant, sensing her urgency. *Where are you?*

The south entrance, she said, sharing her location with a mental image.

In just seconds, his massive, muscular frame appeared, racing as fast as possible through the darkness. She thanked the gods that his color matched the night as arrows flew at him, not that they could have hit him anyway—they were out of range now.

"Come, get on!" she ordered her mother over the wind, helping her onto the beast.

Despite her fear of riding, her mother didn't hesitate, mounting the beast with Rose's help. She didn't need her siren to sense her mother's anxiety as her body stiffened.

"Onyx won't let you fall," Rose reassured her as she sat in front. "Just grip with your bare legs and hold on to me."

Her mother barely nodded, shakily wrapping her arms around Rose's waist.

To the cliffs, she said, guiding Onyx.

A thunderous rumble clapped overhead. From the far corner of her eye, the royal guard scrambled to chase them, but Onyx, with his mighty eight legs, had already put a good distance between them.

Within a few minutes, the small party appeared. All twelve councilmen, along with a plentiful number of guards, were present. Tristan stood a short distance away from Roman and Xavier, who were standing near the cliff's edge. The torches barely shed any light as the wind thrashed, threatening to extinguish the flames.

The sight made Rose urge Onyx to go faster, repressing her siren's bloodthirst to slaughter them all.

As if her mother had read her mind, she said, "Don't overplay your cards, Rosalie. I don't know what you're planning, but there are too many to fight. Trust me, you don't want to be responsible for their deaths," she warned, speaking over the rushing wind.

Rose tightened her grip on Onyx's mane. She had to handle this with care. If she didn't... she didn't want to think about it.

The execution proceedings halted as Onyx's powerful body burst onto the scene. The council members and nearby guards quickly parted the way, steering clear of Onyx's formidable hooves, which stomped into the heart of the gathering. Only Tristan kept his feet planted, fixing a glare at her. He didn't look surprised.

Rose's gaze darted between Roman and Xavier, both bound and standing just a few feet from the cliff's edge, where the jagged rocks below waited to greet them. Their mouths were both silenced by a gag.

As soon as she saw Roman, her heart exited her chest, rolling off the cliffside.

Half of Roman's handsome face had been marred with black and blue bruises in their short time apart. The white of his right eye was blood red, and his bottom lip was swollen and split. He fought not to flinch as he put weight on his left leg. She checked Xavier, too, who, thank the gods, looked unharmed.

Her eyes blazed with a wicked fire. They had *beaten* him. They had beaten him until he could barely stand, undoubtedly pressuring him to reveal where the talisman was.

Despite all this, Roman remained fierce, looking at her like he was going to kill and kiss her at the same time.

Her rage boiled like hell's fury. Rose knew what she had to do. Even if it killed her, she would do it.

For Roman.

Five guards lifted their bows and aimed at her heart, but she ignored them. Her eyes honed in on Tristan, who was watching her, waiting for her reaction. His face was savagely cold, devoid of any and all remorse.

Her voice was as sharp as a needle. "Tell them to lower their weapons."

"I told you to stay out of this," Tristan said.

Rose's feet hit the ground, stalking toward him. The guards surrounding Tristan blocked her path, but she paid them no attention as she stopped in front of them.

"I need to speak with you." She crushed her arms to her sides to prevent her sword from swinging.

"There is nothing you can do or say that will alter what is about to happen," Lord Martin interjected snidely.

She didn't even spare a look in his direction.

"Let her through," Tristan ordered.

The guards parted for her, lowering their arrows.

Rose approached him with care, keeping her siren's rage under control. She attempted to reason with him one final time. "You're making a mistake. Roman didn't take the talisman. We need to be finding who truly did."

Tristan budge. "You think I want this? He stole the key and the talisman to make me look like a fool. Both of them tried to kill me, and still, you defend them." His eyes turned dark. "Well, now they both will see that choices have consequences."

Tristan began to turn away, but she grabbed his arm, forcing him to face her.

The guards strained their bows at her again.

"I'll let you have me," Rose said in haste.

Tristan's eyes finally lit from within, like she'd dangled a piece of meat in front of a starved animal.

She took her opportunity, stepping closer. "I'll let you have every single part of me. I won't fight you. I'll kiss you back. I'll give you all of me. Just let them go."

Tristan didn't waste the opportunity. He closed the gap between their bodies. "Give me your word," he demanded.

A crack of thunder rumbled through the air. Louder. Closer.

She could feel Roman's fury a few feet behind Tristan as he violently shook his head. He and Xavier lunged forward, but the guards restrained them.

"I promise I won't leave," she whispered, ignoring the ugly parasite eating at her insides.

"Prove it," Tristan demanded, his eyes flickering down at her lips.

She knew what he wanted.

Rose closed her eyes, shutting out Roman and Xavier's screaming waves of rage as she lifted her lips to meet his. She even slid her hand into his hair for good measure. Acid burned up her throat.

As hard as she tried to throw up a wall, she couldn't shut Roman out. His soul-crushing presence in her mind was far too powerful. Painful. Crippling. It was as if each of her ribs had broken one by one and caved inward, puncturing her lungs.

She pulled away. Tristan's eyes had become possessive, lustful, and powerful. "Again," he demanded.

Rose had never hated herself more.

She brought her lips back up to his again. This time, his lips devoured her mouth. His hands snaked around her waist and up into her hair.

Roman's pain amplified.

After Tristan was satisfied, his hand slid down into hers. *Mine,* he proclaimed.

"Stand down," Tristan ordered the guards with the bow and arrows.

Oxygen was finally allowed back into her lungs.

"No!" Lord Martin cried out. "She's playing with you! They are guilty. Don't let this *siren* seduce you."

"I'm the king." Tristan's dark voice overpowered Lord Martin's by miles. "And I say stand down." He turned to his brothers. "For Rose's sake, I'll allow you to live. Instead of being killed, you'll both be stripped of your titles and banished from Cathan. If you ever set foot in this province again, or if I even hear so much of a whisper of your return, I will not hesitate to put you both back on this ledge."

Enraged murmurs flooded the high council, opposing in an uproar.

"You cannot let this go unpunished," Lord Barron said, taking a small step forward.

Rose's heart faltered. Out of all the high councilmen, she'd hoped he would be the one who would claim mercy.

"The talisman is still missing," Lord Barron continued. "We cannot let them go. We'll never see it again."

"They'll be escorted out of Cathan. We'll make sure they have nothing in their possession. I'm not claiming their innocence. I'm merely changing their sentence, which, as you all know, is well within my rights as king. It's decided." Tristan turned to address the guards. "Take them to the border." Without another word, Tristan began to lead her back to the castle, her hand still in his.

She looked at Roman one last time before being torn from him forever. She considered begging Tristan to let her say goodbye, but if she went to him… she didn't know if she could go through with it.

So, instead, Rose's glistening eyes met Roman's bloody ones. She nearly choked as she committed him to memory, as if she hadn't already. She cursed the darkness, wishing she could see the golden spark in his eyes. To heal him.

But above all, she wished she could rip out her own heart and lay it at his feet. To let him know that even though she would be sharing a bed with Tristan, her heart would still belong to Roman. Let it serve as evidence of his name etched on her heart. Forever marked.

There would not be a day, a minute, a second that she wouldn't think of him.

Roman shook his head in denial. He lunged for her again, but his injured leg collapsed beneath him. He tried to say something, but his gag made it no more than muffled protests.

Tristan dragged her along as Roman thrashed like a caged animal.

Three more guards had to join the other two just to restrain him. One of them sucker punched him in the gut, forcing him to his knees. She bit back a sob.

Don't fight it. Let me go, she pleaded.

A sudden movement caught her eye.

Lord Barron marched up to a soldier and snatched the bow and arrow from his hands. Without hesitation, he drew back his arm and aimed the arrow straight at his target.

"*Roman!*" she screamed into the wind.

Her warning came too late. The arrow traveled with such a fierce ferocity that he wouldn't be able to escape its path.

But the arrow never reached him. Another body flew out in front of it, blocking its way and it hit—

Rose's mother.

"*No!*" she screamed, escaping Tristan's grasp and immediately running to her mother's side.

Lord Barron nocked another arrow, ready to shoot another.

"Seize him!" Tristan shouted the order, withdrawing his sword.

The guards rushed to restrain Lord Barron.

Rose was hardly paying attention. She flung herself down beside her mother, sprawled on the ground. It had hit her shoulder. She gently pulled her mother's head into her lap, cradling her as she examined the wound. She pulled the arrow out immediately, pressing her hand down to stop the bleeding. But something wasn't right. She was bleeding badly, even for an arrow wound. Her mother was already gasping for air, shaking. Her body grew hot as her pupils dilated.

Rose gazed at the arrow lying next to her with fear. Gripping it with her bloodied hands, almost too slippery to grip, she wiped it with her cloak, recognizing the poison on its tip.

Dragonshade.

Her heart hardened into stone. Her eyes shot up, searching for Lord Barron, but he was nowhere to be found.

Behind her, Roman struggled. "Rose!" he shouted, freeing himself from the gag. "He's getting away!"

At last, she saw Lord Barron's fleeing figure heading towards the woods.

This was her chance. She couldn't lose him. There was too much at stake.

Rose looked hesitantly down at her mother.

"Go," her mother insisted. "I'll be fine."

She didn't have much time. She had to make a choice.

"Keep pressure on this. I'll come back for you," she promised.

Her mother waved her off. "Yes, yes, I know. They won't let me die. Now go. *Go!*"

Rose stood with the arrow still in hand and sprinted like the wind.

"No! Rose, don't!" Tristan yelled after her. "Don't put yourself in danger!"

She ignored the calls behind her, sprinting with inhuman speed. Leaving the party behind, she bolted for the woods where Lord Barron had vanished. Onyx was already on his way, galloping beside her until she managed to mount him mid-run, adrenaline pumping overtime.

Because, by the sky and sea gods, she was going to kill the bastard.

CHAPTER 90

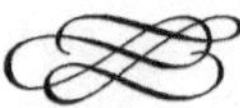

Onyx flew at incredible speed. Rose was convinced they would reach Lord Barron within a mere minute. However, to her shock, he was nowhere in sight when they broke the tree line.

Where'd he go? Onyx asked, jerking his head in irritation. *We can't be far behind.*

Rose peered down to find Lord Barron's footprints, but she did not see nor hear him over the howling wind. How could that be?

Her siren eyes focused in the darkness, aiding her to see better. Finally, she spotted his silhouette in the distance—he wasn't alone. Another hooded and masked figure on horseback reached down to take something from Lord Barron. She caught a glint of a red ruby.

The talisman.

As soon as the masked man had it in his possession, he took off, disappearing from sight. She had no idea which direction he had gone.

Lord Barron, however, continued on foot in the opposite direction. He was moving fast—too fast.

Realization dawned as her eyes widened.

Lord Barron was a siren.

Her grip tightened. *There!* she directed Onyx, guiding him to the left through the trees.

They were gaining on him. Even with Lord Barron's impressive speed, he was no match for Onyx. The magnificent beast drove his eight hooves into the ground with incredible force, driving them forward.

When they were close enough, she let her siren's instincts take over. She lifted the blood-crusted arrow in her hand, and just like in the Snorri, she hurled it, snapping her wrist to send the arrow soaring.

The arrow struck his shoulder, knocking him to the ground in a small forest clearing.

With his fall, she caught up to him.

Rose jumped down from Onyx and drew her sword, pointing the blade downward at him to pin him to the forest floor, prepared to end him.

Lord Barron turned, leaves sticking to his robes. He grasped the arrow lodged in his back, tearing it out with a grunt.

"You have good aim for such a young siren," Lord Barron praised. "I can see what's so special about you." He eyed her with a lustful smile.

She almost puked.

"How are you a siren?" she asked, keeping the blade at his throat.

He didn't look the least bit afraid. "I was born that way," Lord Barron said vaguely.

"You don't look like a siren."

He smirked. "Why? Because I'm not as pretty as you?"

She placed the edge of her blade against his throat.

He shifted back a bit, putting his hands up. "You don't want to do that," Lord Barron warned.

Rose took a lethal step toward him. "Give me one good reason I shouldn't." She glared as she pressed her sword a little harder against his throat.

A wicked smile played on his lips. "Because I am not Lord Barron."

Like a ripple in the water, Lord Barron's body began to shift. His skin altered, his face melted, and he grew larger and taller.

Rose was so caught off guard, she stumbled backward. Thankfully, she managed to keep a grip on her sword as her mind attempted to keep up with what was playing out before her eyes.

She barely believed it. She was no longer looking at the middle-aged high council member but a mountain of a man.

A true siren.

He was ethereal, the most perfect creature she'd ever seen. His sandy-golden hair framed a pair of bright, vivid-violet eyes that gleamed like her own. His clothes were tattered, barely clinging to him, as rippling muscles broke through the fabric, revealing his fair skin.

He took advantage of her surprise as he stood up, now towering over her. "Do you prefer this, love?" the siren asked with a gorgeous, transcendent smile.

A chill ran down her spine; his voice flowed like a gentle stream.

Rose glared at him, but her siren was dripping with undeniable attraction, curious to finally meet another of their kind. She squashed the irrational sensation, unable to forget what he'd just done. Her mother could very well be dead because of him, reminding her she didn't have much time.

She was about to answer when she realized she didn't need to—he'd read her emotions.

"You don't need to lie to me," he said, stalking her like a dangerous predator. "You forget I'm not like them. I can feel it. You're attracted to me."

"Then you can also feel I'm going to kill you," she said through clenched teeth.

He laughed, a beautiful, dark, cocky sound. "By the gods, you really are beautiful, even by a siren's standards. You can kiss me if you want." He stepped closer, filling her lungs with the scent of fresh pine. "I'll kiss back," he taunted, mocking her.

"Stay away from me," she hissed, not lowering her sword for a second.

"Why don't we go somewhere private?" he continued, his violet eyes shining like stars in the heavens, drawing her in. "Then we won't be interrupted by your three human boyfriends who are sure to try to come save you. But then again, it might be good. I'll get to kill them, too."

Rose's face darkened, her grip on her sword tightening. She caught him off guard with a swift kick to the shoulder, knocking him to the ground as she exploited the arrow wound. She wanted nothing more than to end him, but she had too many unanswered questions and she didn't know how quickly the Dragonshade would take her mother's life; time was not on her side.

Thunder cracked through the heavens, clouds threatening to rain as the siren lifted a suggestive eyebrow. "You know, if you wanted me on my back, you could've just asked."

Onyx sank his hooves into the dirt, threatening to charge him, but Rose held up her hand, telling him to stay put. "Who are you? What do you want?"

"I can't tell you..." He breathed hard. "I'm bound not to."

She delved into his mind to see if he was telling the truth, but just as before, there was nothing. It was like he was void of any aura or emotion —a black wall of darkness, a blank space. Nothing.

"You can't see into my mind." His flawless, sloped, masculine lips spread into a smirk. "But if you come with me, I'll teach you. If you're lucky, I may just let you enter... willingly."

Rose's eyes narrowed, hating how he had information she so desperately needed. "You killed the king. You tried to kill Roman. I'm not going anywhere, and neither are you. You'll never leave these woods again."

"If you think you can beat me, think again. You may have had your human pets teaching you how to fight, but going up against a well-trained siren is well out of your reach," he declared as his ethereal face hardened. "I can assure you, you will lose."

"I don't know about that." Rose peered at his wound. "That arrowhead is laced with Dragonshade. It may just weaken you enough to let me beat you. If it doesn't kill you first."

His enchanted laugh blew with the same wind that tossed his sandy hair. "You think I'd bring a poison I didn't have the cure to?" He retrieved a vial from his robes.

He'd had the cure this whole time.

"It was *you*," she realized. "*You* were the one I saw in the trees during the first challenge and on the balcony. *You* were the one who tried to kill Roman."

"Guilty." He shrugged, indifferent. "I dressed up as one of your precious boyfriends in case anyone saw me hiding in the trees. And I would've killed him if you hadn't interfered."

"Why? Why would you want to kill him?"

He hesitated as though he was sorting through his words carefully. "For you," he said as if it was obvious. "I tried my best to protect you, to get you on the throne, but these humans were too scared of you. If you stay now—protected by the king or not—they *will* turn on you, just as they have on every siren in history. You're meant for so much more than this pathetic human life," he spat. "I tried to make you see that when I chained you to the cliffs and wrangled the sea beast. After the third challenge, I thought you'd see you were different, but you were blind to what was right in front of you. You have no idea who you truly are or where you come from. Come with me. I can show you, teach you, tell you everything you want to know."

Instincts told her his words were true. But even with all that he had to offer, she was against him. Not after all he had done. What he had tried to do.

She lifted her chin. "I don't want you or anything you have to offer."

The cunning corners of his mouth lifted. The handsome action alone was enough to make her defenses cave. "I was hoping we could do this the easy way, but…" He looked over her shoulder, and the creases of his grin deepened. "It looks like I'll have to persuade you."

Rose glanced behind her.

Roman rode at breakneck speed on horseback. His mangled body clung on despite his grimaces with each jolt. Her siren sensed his turmoil from afar, the stifling panic that would ensue if he lost her.

The siren's smirk spread wide. "Finally, I can get this over with." He brought the small vial to his lips. "It's been awful doing it the stealthy way." He tipped it back.

Rose lunged for it, but he shifted his shoulder to avoid her blow. He grabbed her wrist and brought her into his chest.

A ravishing smile played on his lips. "We don't need to play games. You've already won me. If you want me to come closer, I'll willingly do so." His velvety violet eyes roamed her as his sweet breath intoxicated her. He lifted his hand to stroke her pearl hair. "Gods, my siren adores you. It's been an absolute nightmare trying to keep it at bay." He leaned forward, about to place his lips on hers.

Rose shoved him back, slashing her sword at him. He dodged her attack with ease and lunged for the arrow on the ground. With his arm raised, he prepared to throw the arrow at Roman, who kept coming closer.

She took advantage of the distraction and shoved her elbow into the wound on his back.

The siren emitted an involuntary grunt as the arrow slipped from his grip to the forest floor. He lashed back around, drawing his sword, and swung. She pivoted, focusing on her footwork as their blades clashed.

Despite her best efforts, his blows were strong—too strong.

And what was worse was she could tell he wasn't even trying his hardest.

Despite her speed and agility, he pushed her back. Every strike she blocked forced her to retreat further. She was so focused on him, she overlooked the large fallen tree behind her.

She tripped, landing on the forest floor. Zareb would have reprimanded her for making such a foolish error.

He could have ended her right there and then, but for some reason, he seized the fallen tree instead, hoisting its weight like it was nothing more than a feather, about to set it on top of her so she couldn't escape.

Onyx reared his head into him, knocking the siren back with such force that he flew a few feet into the air and back into the dirt. The siren rolled once and then halted his momentum by digging into the dirt with his hands. He glared up at the beast, his violet eyes glowing with irritation.

Rose was on her feet in an instant, lunging for the arrow.

But the siren was too quick. He knocked her back with one blow of his arm, forcing her onto her hands and knees.

The next moment, Roman was there. With lightning speed, he slashed at the siren with his sword. Striking with all his strength, Roman managed to stand his ground against the siren despite his injuries, his rage providing the fuel his spent body needed.

Her siren beamed with pride, but Rose had no time to dwell on his heroics.

With the siren preoccupied, she searched for the arrow among the dense bushes. At last, she spotted it—and luckily, she also found the half-empty vial. She quickly grabbed them both.

She spun back around just in time to see the siren knock Roman's sword out of his hands, swinging at him with such remarkable speed and power she was sure he could chop a tree down with one blow.

Roman avoided his sword, but each swipe came closer and closer to slicing him open.

He was going to die.

Rose's siren surfaced like a volcano erupting from the depths of Vallor, her power swelling within, taking over her limbs. She refused to lose him —not when her mother had just risked everything to save him.

She charged at the siren, stepping between them, blocking the siren's sword with her own with a loud crack.

The siren faltered backward in surprise.

Rose advanced, her muscles now somehow stronger than his. How that was possible, she didn't know. But she channeled every ounce of the power flowing through her body, swinging her sword again and again as she steered the siren away from Roman.

At last, one of her strikes landed with enough force to momentarily weaken his arm.

She seized her opportunity, and with her hand that held the arrow, she plunged it into his exposed chest. Before he could react, she shoved her sword through his heart for good measure.

The siren faltered, stumbling back as he looked down at his chest. His eyes widened as blood dribbled down his torn clothing. His starry violet eyes flashed back to her, their beautiful color dimming with each passing moment.

He fell forward, but not before he grabbed her arm, dragging her to the forest floor with him, bringing them both to their knees.

"Listen to me," he begged, his raw voice taking her aback with its pure sound. "I was sent to kill Tristan and Roman… and anyone else you love… to lure you out. He… he wants to isolate you so… so you'll leave…" He struggled to take a breath. "Keep your ability to talk to creatures hidden; do not tell anyone else. Do you hear me? Not a soul..." He gasped. "Protect your mind at all costs... Save us all."

He leaned forward and kissed her.

She was hit with a surge of power as he unlocked his guarded mind to her. A vision blinded her—memories. It was him among the trees, on the balcony, kidnapping the seer, cradling Rose's unconscious body, the kiss he'd stolen the night Rose went missing before the third challenge, how he lured the sea beast into a snare—he revealed it all to her.

The vision shifted. She found herself in a dimly lit room resembling an underground library, where stone shelves were intertwined with trees, roots, and flowing streams. Yet, large windows revealed only an expanse of blue sky. She had never seen anything like it.

As quickly as the visions came, they left as the siren's lips fell from hers. His violet eyes dimmed and rolled back. He landed on the forest floor with a heavy thud.

Rose scrambled backward like she was afraid he might come back to life.

Breathless, she stared at his lifeless form in a mix of terror and astonishment. Something didn't feel right. His tone... what he'd just revealed...

She raised her fingers to her lips, his magic still tingling there. Through his touch, she felt as if he... as if he had *cared* for her, cared about what would happen to her after he was gone. The bastard had just admitted to trying to kill everyone she loved.

So why couldn't she help the terrifying feeling she'd just made a grave mistake?

Within seconds, Roman was at her side, crushing her into his arms. "Are you alright?" He clasped her face with his hands, searching for wounds.

She nodded... then shook her head as she grappled for him, burrowing her face into his shirt as she dragged him closer.

His chest heaved from his heavy breaths. "What the hell happened? Who is he? Where is Lord Barron?"

"That *was* Lord Barron... Or at least pretending to be. He was a siren, Roman. He was in plain sight this whole time."

His brows scrunched together. "How?"

"He was a shapeshifter." She lifted her head off of him, looking at the siren's lifeless body. "I saw it with my own eyes."

"You can do that?" His eyes widened.

"No, at least I don't think so."

He couldn't speak to me like you either, Onyx added, looking at the body with curious eyes as he sniffed him.

"Onyx couldn't speak to him... Sirens must have different abilities," she said as the realization set in.

Roman cautiously approached the body as he looked it over from head to toe. He lifted his arms and checked his pockets, searching down to his shoes.

He swore. "No talisman. I bet my money he was the one who stole it and hid it."

She wiped her hair from her brow. "He gave the talisman to someone else, who took off with it. He wasn't working alone."

"Then there could be more." His eyes scoured the woods around them.

She remained fixated on the lifeless body, the siren's final words echoing in her mind. She couldn't shake the feeling that, in some way, he had been trying to help her.

Her eyes searched his handsome face, still trying to make sense of it all. It was then that she noticed an unfamiliar mark on his right forearm. Her eyes narrowed as she bent down for a closer look, tilting his heavy, limp arm. A large red scar ran the full length of his forearm, tracing the path of his veins... a bindrune—a beautiful dark mark.

"Come on," Roman said, taking her by the shoulders and guiding her from the siren to her feet. "We should go."

Rose wanted to go after the man with the talisman, but she had no idea what direction he'd taken. They could try, but her mother—

Her eyes flickered with horror. "My mother."

"She's fine. She's with Xavier. But... she's not good," Roman said as his bloody eye twitched with guilt.

Rose grabbed the small vial from her pocket like a lifeline. "We have this. This may just be enough to save her."

Roman's shoulders slumped in pure relief. "Thanks the gods. We'd better hurry, or Tristan will—"

The devil himself cut him off.

"Tristan will what?" Tristan dismounted his horse and unsheathed his sword. He glanced at the siren, then at Rose, his eyes widening at the sight of blood smeared across her hands. "Are you hurt?"

"I'm fine." She brushed herself off like she could wipe away the blood. "It was him, Tristan. Everything. Lord Barron wasn't Lord Barron. He was a siren. He must have been pretending to be him for who knows how long. He stole the talisman and gave it to someone else he was working with. He's riding on horseback, but if you hurry, you could catch him. Cut him off before he can leave the woods."

Tristan's face contorted with disbelief, his eyes going back to the siren's body. "No. No, that's not possible. Lord Barron was father's most trusted councilman."

"It's true, Tristan," Roman said. "Look at the clothes he wore, the sword he bears—the high council's sun emblem. The siren was a shapeshifter and he wasn't working alone."

Tristan stared down at the body in shock.

"Now, do you see?" Roman asked. "She isn't safe here."

"She's not going anywhere. If all this is true, she needs to be under constant surveillance," Tristan said.

"Look at her!" Roman exclaimed, gesturing to Rose's bloody hands and cloak. "This happened right under our noses. She's not safe here. She never has been."

"I promise you it won't happen again," Tristan said, seeking her trust.

Roman had had enough. He took a threatening step toward Tristan.

Rose stepped between them before Roman could kill him. "I'm leaving, Tristan. Whether you allow for it or not, I am leaving. I'm not asking for your permission. I'm not negotiating."

Tristan's ocean-colored eyes swirled as he leaned in closer. "You promised you wouldn't leave."

She withstood his waves. "We didn't take the talisman, Tristan. The proof is lying here on the forest floor. And deep down, you know it wasn't us. He may still be in the woods. There's still time if you take your men now and search. I would do it myself, but my mother needs me." She swallowed hard as she gazed into the eyes of her fiercest protector—the man she'd once loved. In many ways, she still did. That's why she declared, "But you and I… we are done, Tristan. For good." Without waiting for a reply, she climbed onto Onyx.

"Rose, wait!" Tristan pleaded, his voice breaking.

She ignored his desperate plea, his pain pulsing through her, prickling her veins as Roman followed suit, climbing onto Onyx.

"Rose, please," Tristan begged again.

She nudged Onyx. His hooves went from standing to a gallop in a matter of seconds.

"Rose, don't," Tristan called behind her. He took a step towards Onyx's retreating figure. "Rose… *Rose!*"

The storm drowned out his cries as another clap of thunder roared overhead, this time so close it shook the ground.

Onyx sped back to the cliffs to retrieve her mother and Xavier.

"Is he following us?" she dared ask, too scared to look back.

Roman shifted, glancing over his shoulder. "No."

She exhaled in relief, but soon an ache took hold in her heart.

She could have sworn she heard a ghost of a cry carry with the wind.

CHAPTER 91

The violent wind battered them as Rose and Roman made their way back to the cliffs. Dark clouds blanketed the sky, obscuring the stars and moon, as lightning flashed haphazardly over the ocean. A raindrop splashed against Rose's cheek, followed by more pattering around them.

The high council members and the guards were nowhere in sight, likely having fled to the castle for their own safety. Cowards. Fortunately for them, she didn't have time to care.

Xavier and her mother remained huddled near the cliff's edge. Xavier was cradling her mother against his chest. His head snapped up at the sound of Onyx's hooves.

"Thank the lost city above," Xavier said, looking to the sky in reverence.

Rose jumped off Onyx. "Is she still alive?"

"Yes, but barely."

Rose took her first full breath that night.

She drew the vial from her cloak and knelt beside her mother's unconscious form, next to Xavier, who was still supporting her head.

She put the vial up to her mother's lips and poured the contents down her throat, her hands shaking all the while. This would fix her. It had to fix her. She wouldn't let herself think of an alternative.

"You're going to be okay," Rose willed, stroking her mother's sandy hair, wet from the rain. "Get her on Onyx," she said to Roman and Xavier. "We need to find cover so I can treat her wound properly."

Xavier moved to pick her up, but Roman blocked him, taking it upon himself. "I've got her," he said, lifting Rose's mother into his arms, even though his legs and arms shook from the strain as the rain poured around them.

Rose was about to follow, but something shifted in the darkness.

Her arms went limp.

She almost didn't believe her eyes. More than fifty soldiers emerged from the tree line, racing towards them on horses. She didn't want to look at who was leading them.

Tristan.

The storm brewing underneath his skin had finally exploded into a dark typhoon. He had no intention of letting her go.

Tristan… No.

Xavier cursed beside her.

"I knew the bastard couldn't do it," Roman growled.

"What do we do?" Xavier asked. "We can't fight them all."

Rose's mind scrambled for something—*anything*—to get them out of this mess. Without force would be preferable. She didn't want any more bloodshed. Violence would be her last resort.

She scoured their surroundings in the dark, seeking any form of escape. As her she turned to the giant waves, her eyes lowered to the water beyond the jagged rocks, reminding her of the third succession challenge—

She had an idea.

Knowing it might be a fool's errand, she approached the cliff's edge, looking down to the rocky shore beneath her feet.

"Rose, what are you doing?" Roman yelled over the wind, taking a nervous step toward her, her mother's unconscious body still in his arms.

Rose shut her eyes, concentrating on the crashing sound of the waves below. The vast open space caused the wind to whip her bloodstained cloak aside.

She extended out her hand, searching the power she knew lay hidden within her. Delving into the depths of her mind, she uncovered a bubbling, vibrant pool of magic, calling upon it.

A powerful jet of water defied gravity as it surged from the ocean's depths into the air, splashing up to meet the palm of her hand. The smooth, cold water felt like a shock of energy.

A bolt of lightning struck nearby, followed by a deafening crack of thunder.

Neera, she called to the sea beast through the void. *Neera, if you can hear me, I need you. I need your help.*

After a brief pause, she opened her eyes, daring to look back into the tumultuous sea. Seconds ticked by and… nothing. Nothing but enormous waves crashing into the rocks below.

Rose's heart faltered, letting the large stream of water fall back into the sea.

It hadn't worked.

"Rose!" Roman called to her again.

She whirled back. Tristan and his men were practically upon them.

She fought to stay calm as raindrops slid from her hair down to her brow. If Tristan captured them again… there would be no winning scenario. Roman was in no condition to fight again. Even with her magical abilities, she didn't know how to use them, at least not enough to wield them as a weapon.

But she had to try. She had to do *something*. She attempted to bundle and wound the magic within her, wield it as she—

A loud, trembling rumble erupted from below.

Rose whirled, but there was nothing but dark ocean waves.

A deafening screech pierced the sky.

Tristan and his men skidded to a stop, their heads snapping upward at the terrorizing sound.

Lighting flashed again as the sea beast's silhouette appeared in the sky.

Rose's heart leapt.

Neera had answered her call.

The large creature's elongated, scaly form slithered through the air as enormous water droplets fell from her body with the rain. Her slender wings unfurled wide, maneuvering with deadly accuracy. She screeched again, diving to the ground toward Tristan and the soldiers.

The soldiers scattered. Some fled to the castle, abandoning their posts, while others sprinted back to the woods for cover.

The beast circled back around, landing just in front of Rose.

Neera took a drawing breath through her nostrils, and in one deadly motion, she bared her teeth and opened her mouth to unleash a powerful current of water from the depths of her belly. The tidal wave washed the fleeing soldiers back into the woods, the forceful stream drowning out their screams and shouts.

Neera finished her spray as her large head snaked back to look at Rose. Her sapphire eyes sparkled at her happily.

You came, Rose said with relief.

Neera gave her a frightening smile. *I told you I would.*

Rose gave her the most appreciative look she could muster, but gratitude would have to wait. *We need to get out of here. Can you help us?*

Neera nodded, understanding. *Get on,* she said, lowering her large neck to the ground.

"Get on," she relayed the order to Roman and Xavier.

The two exchanged hesitant side glances, but to their credit, they did as she commanded, Roman still cradling her mother in his arms as they all mounted Neera.

Onyx shook his large mane, spraying a flurry of droplets, his coal eyes stubbornly resistant. *There is no way I'm letting that carry me with those claws. They eat things like me,* Onyx said, backing up.

I won't eat you, Neera said, practically rolling her eyes.

See? Rose said to Onyx. *She promises not to eat you.*

At least not today, Neera added with a cheeky tone.

Not a moment too soon, Neera leapt into the air. Rose clung on to a spike, careful not to let it impale her. She glanced back, checking that Roman was still keeping her mother safe on his lap. Xavier looked like he was going to be sick.

Neera dipped down and swept Onyx carefully into her grasp with her large, webbed talons. Her wings worked overtime to get them higher and higher into the sky.

The soldiers below reformed, launching arrows at them. Rose ducked behind Neera's large spike to avoid their path.

Neera roared, sending another stream of water from her mouth, driving the soldiers back into the muddy ground.

Rose dared to peek down.

Almost immediately, she found Tristan's distant figure glaring up at her.

Despite the distance, she felt his overwhelming betrayal, his complete devastation, his feral rage—it all collapsed around him like a dying star, forming a black hole powerful enough to warp time and space, swallowing all light, attempting to pull her into the void with it.

A raw, soul-piercing cry of agony erupted from his mouth, a sound that would haunt her peace forever.

She winced, unable to bear his pain, clinging to Neera's large spike as they soared upward into the sky.

Where to? Neera asked.

To Highland Haven, Rose answered.

CHAPTER 92

Relief washed over Rose as the grand estate appeared, sheltered by the dark mountains. Neera's excitement flooded through her fingertips at the sight of the crystal lake, not to mention Onyx's relief to be back on solid ground.

They landed at the manor swiftly. The sudden arrival of the small group nearly gave Gretta a heart attack, especially since Rose's mother was still unconscious in Roman's arms with Neera lingering in the background. Nonetheless, Gretta overcame her shock and ushered them inside, helping Rose prepare a spot for her mother.

Although the circumstances were hurried, Gretta's aura shone bright at the sight of Xavier, even if she couldn't fully show it. Rose couldn't help but gravitate towards Gretta's happiness. It was more than a welcome feeling, seeing how her own sorrows, along with Roman's and Xavier's, were enough to drive her to insanity.

They disinfected her mother's shoulder and helped her into a fresh dress. Rose tried to tend to Roman next, but he brushed her off, acting as though he deserved to endure his pain for a little longer.

She did her best not to melt into a puddle of tears when her mother finally woke. Rose threw her arms around her in pure relief. It had worked. The antidote had saved her life.

Darkness still filled the sky by the time she made her way out to the patio for a breath of fresh air. The bright stars were twinkling above, offering a pure, innocent comfort. From here, she could even see the giant ripples of water in the lake from Neera's exploration.

Rose brushed her matted hair back. Gretta had insisted she bathe, but she was so exhausted, she had hardly been able to summon the energy.

As she gazed at the night sky, tears began to form in her eyes. She attempted to hold them back, but it was futile. The silent tears overflowed, streaming down her cheeks, Tristan's screams haunting her. He had done so many things to deserve this fate, and yet she knew her siren had driven him to darkness. *She* had driven him to darkness.

She sniffed. Her heart ached so much she wished to be rid of it altogether. If only to be free of the weight pressing harder and harder into her chest.

Rose barely noticed Xavier coming up behind her.

"I'm so sorry," Xavier spoke softly, his eyes full of despair. "I should have taken that arrow."

She sniffed again, dabbing her eyes with her sleeve. "No, my mother knew what she was doing. She understands better than anyone what it's like to lose the love of your life. She was trying to save me from the same fate..."

She hadn't realized what her words would mean for him until Xavier clenched his jaw.

His eyes faltered, doing an outstanding job of hiding his bruised heart. "Just be glad you have no regrets, Rose. You've always been there for her, always. You'll never have to wish you chose something different, wish you'd done more."

She knew he was speaking from a place of regret for his own mother.

Her gaze went to Roman, who sat on the stone steps leading into the water, staring out into the night, soaking his swollen ankle from sprinting in his condition. His bloodied eye had become so swollen it was almost sealed shut. Stubborn git. She could have healed it by now.

Her attention shifted back to Xavier as he said through his teeth, "I'm their older brother. I'm supposed to protect them, even *Tristan*." He spat his name. "Roman was right. I should've done better by them. I should have never made Tristan take the burden of the crown."

Rose pressed her lips together as a tear slipped out. "A burden you and I both share."

Xavier paused. "You should know it was Tristan that beat Roman."

Her eyes snapped to him in disbelief. "Tell me that's not true," she whispered.

Xavier nodded, his eyes cast down. His aura was so conflicted she didn't know if he was more angry or sad about the fact. "I've never seen him like that, Rose. The look in his eye... it was like he wasn't even himself. He nearly killed Roman with his bare hands." Xavier's icy eyes flashed to her. "He won't stop until he finds you. We can't stay here long. It'll be the first place he looks."

Her heavy eyes faltered. "I know."

A brief pause fell, the sound of the small waves from the lake filling the silence. Rose tried to take a deep breath, but her heart and lungs contracted.

Xavier hesitated before his arms wrapped around her.

She returned the gesture, taking another deep breath, and this time, her body didn't miss a beat. She dug her fingers into his cloak. "Thank you for staying... for being willing to make more mistakes," she whispered. She pulled back to look at him.

Xavier leaned in closer, his eyes falling to her lips for a short breath. But then he clenched his jaw, changing course, giving her a restrained kiss on the temple.

Her shoulders relaxed in relief.

He gazed at her a little too tenderly as he brushed her crusted hair from her face. "I told you, smart-ass. I'm not leaving you again... not until you command me to."

She could only muster a weak smile in response. A part of her knew he wished she could offer him more but she couldn't.

With that, he gave her hand a small squeeze and returned to the manor to find Gretta, leaving Rose and Roman alone on the patio.

She turned her attention to Roman, who was already walking out of the lake, his frame shaking with every step as excess water ran down his muscular legs. She walked to meet him halfway.

She was about to speak when she saw tears of blood leaking out of his swollen eye.

He looked like he'd just escaped from hell.

"It should've been me," he grieved, his deep voice breaking. "My father and Evelyn... it was supposed to be me."

Her eyes filled with tears again as she shook her head. "Don't do that." Rose took his face into her hands. "They loved you. They'd do anything for you."

Roman shook his head in self-loathing. "It's different with Evelyn. I always knew my mother wouldn't stay with us long, and my father would've been in agony if he had to live without her, but Evelyn... she's like you—such a force... You'd never think it was even possible for someone like her to be capable of dying."

Rose wrapped her arms around him, finding her favorite spot in the crook of his neck as their hearts bled together. "None of this is your fault... It's mine. He was never after me," she whispered. "He was after all of you—the people I love... I should've never been so selfish to stay, to think I could handle it."

Roman pulled back just enough to look into her eyes. "We were all fooled. The siren must've killed Lord Barron long ago and took his place," he theorized. "I only wonder how long he had been pretending... how long he'd been waiting."

A realization set in. "He must have pretended to be Satin to lure you and me out to distract everyone while he stole the talisman."

Roman nodded in agreement. "And pretend to be me when he did so I'd be blamed."

"He said he was bound... I think he was working for someone—someone who didn't want me to know why he was truly there."

Both of them knew who that someone might be.

Roman thought, looking out at the water as his golden eyes mulled it over.

A wave of pain ran over him, but this time, it was a different kind of pain, more cutting.

"What is it?" Rose asked, her eyes searching his.

Roman shook his head, dismissing it. "It's not a conversation for tonight. This night is about Evelyn."

"Tell me," she insisted.

Roman gave a loud sigh, shifting his swollen eye. "What happened in that room with Tristan…"

"It should've never happened," she said.

Roman nodded generously before his honey eyes met hers. "I just need to know. How much of what happened was your siren… and how much of it was you?"

She knew what he was asking. He wanted to know if she had gone to that room because she, *Rose*, still wanted Tristan, siren aside. To see if she had gone to that room because she still wasn't ready to let him go.

Her mouth dried as she tried to swallow. "Roman, I swear on the gods above and below I didn't want it." Another tear ran down her face as her eyes fell to her feet in shame. "But my siren… it wanted me to, and it makes me sick to have that darkness be a part of me."

Roman didn't so much as breathe.

Her hands shook as she looked back up at him with hesitant eyes. "If you don't want me… if you can't do this, I underst—"

Roman cut her off, grabbing her arm, drawing her in with a sharp movement. "Don't," he breathed as he leaned down to press his forehead to hers. "Don't you dare even think losing you is something I could survive."

Tears poured out onto her cheeks. She hated being like this. She hated herself—that sick, wet, slimy thing living in her.

She choked back a sob as his gaze gently held hers. "You don't need to be jealous of anyone, ever."

He wiped her tears with his calloused fingers. "I'm not jealous. I'm territorial. If I were jealous, it would mean I want something I don't have… and I have you, Roe. I know it. I can feel it. Every time our eyes meet, I see the same fireworks in your eyes that are in mine. I feel your body relax into a state that happens only when I'm around. I see the smile that is reserved for me, and only me, and I know there is no one else you'd give that to."

She sniffed as more tears poured out.

He caught a tear with his lips as he wrapped his arm around her waist. "I know men are going to want you. I knew it going into this. Hell, I knew it before you were a siren. I know I will always have to continue to fight for you. The challenge doesn't sway me. I fight for what I want. And I want you... To the gods, I'll always want you."

Rose let out a shaky breath of relief. Her voice cracked as she declared, "I love you more than anything in this world. More than the starlit sky, more than the books I read, more than I've ever loved anyone... I am yours."

Roman's eyes filled with moisture as a bloody tear spilled out. "And you are mine," he whispered back, lightly pressing his lips against hers.

She kissed him back, then moved to the bruises on his face. Her lips lingered softly over each mark before she returned to his lips again, kissing him tenderly, trying not to hurt the swollen cut on his lower lip.

"The next move is yours, Rose," Roman murmured. "What do you want to do?"

Her gaze shifted to the sky, looking to the burning stars floating in the heavens above them. "We go into hiding and do what the snawfus told me to," she proclaimed, still searching the stars. "I'm going to learn everything I can, and then we're going to find these men... I fear the game is barely afoot."

ACKNOWLEDGMENTS

Coming to the end of writing this book was something I could have only dreamed of a few short years ago. What started as an outlet grew into a passion that I knew I wanted to share with others. I'm tremendously grateful for the opportunity to have this book in your hands today.

First, my husband and beautiful girls, you bring so much meaning to my life that I can scarcely think of what it would be like without you. You are my inspiration and joy. I love you more than words can say.

To my mom, who sat and listened to me read my silly story when it was only a rough draft, thank you for believing in me and my dreams.

To all the editors and talented artists who helped bring this vision to life, I thank you for being willing to help me at the beginning of my writing journey. I am forever grateful. The world needs more of you in it.

And lastly, to all my readers: your support, kindness, and encouragement mean the world to me. Thank you from the bottom of my heart for taking the leap and going on this adventure with me. I'm so grateful to each and every one of you.

ABOUT THE AUTHOR

Jamie June is an emerging author who loves romance and fantasy. She lives in Utah and obtained her bachelor's degree from Utah State University. When she's not reading or writing, she enjoys the outdoors and spending time with her family. The Throne Seeker is her debut novel and book one in the Vallorian series.

For more news and updates, visit her website, join the mailing list, or follow her on social media.
www.jamie-june.com

www.ingramcontent.com/pod-product-compliance
Lightning Source LLC
Chambersburg PA
CBHW021928110726
47901CB00003B/756

9798998546211